CRIMINAL SEDUCTION

DARIAN NORTH

A SIGNET BOOK

SIGNET
Published by the Penguin Group
Penguin Books USA Inc., 375 Hudson Street,
New York, New York 10014, U.S.A.
Penguin Books Ltd, 27 Wrights Lane,
London W8 5TZ, England
Penguin Books Australia Ltd, Ringwood,
Victoria, Australia
Penguin Books Canada Ltd, 10 Alcorn Avenue,
Toronto, Ontario, Canada M4V 3B2
Penguin Books (N.Z.) Ltd, 182-190 Wairau Road,
Auckland 10, New Zealand

Penguin Books Ltd, Registered Offices:
Harmondsworth, Middlesex, England

Published by Signet,
an imprint of Dutton Signet,
a division of Penguin Books USA Inc.
Previously published in a Dutton edition.

First Signet Printing, July, 1994
10 9 8 7 6 5 4 3

PUBLISHER'S NOTE
This is a work of fiction. Names, characters, places, and incidents either are the product of the author's imagination or are used fictitiously, and any resemblance to actual
persons, living or dead, events, or locales is entirely coincidental.

to
Michael Bradley

Some rise by sin and some by virtue fall.
                                        —Shakespeare

The need to go astray, to be destroyed, is an extremely private, distant, passionate, turbulent truth.
                                        —Georges Bataille

Looking back he saw that he had always been waiting for her. Waiting to be enfolded. To be swallowed by the darkness in her eyes.

She brought the fevered fall, the burning rush that scoured away all that he had been and left him tasting ash. But he knew now, looking back, that he had wanted it.

That he had always been waiting.

1

Time passes slowly in the Flint Hills of Kansas. It is a lonely country. A rolling sea of grass atop a mountain range so ancient that the mighty peaks have been worn down to hills. It is ranch country. Unsuited to the plow. Subject to blizzards, duststorms, tornadoes, drought, fist-sized hail, violent wind, and frequent flooding in the lowlands near the rivers.

Sometimes when Owen Byrne rode out across the hills on horseback, he felt that he was riding back into history, and that if he kept going he would come upon settlers, buffalo, and bands of Osage Indians, then dinosaurs, and finally the glaciers and volcanoes that had shaped the land in the beginning. Sometimes he stopped his horse and listened for the past, certain that it was there, whispering all around him. And sometimes he sat on the ground, with his horse and dogs all watching him expectantly, and he tried to imagine everything that had ever happened on that one spot. Every wandering insect and sprouting seed. Every drop of blood spilled in birth or death.

But not today. Not for months. Worry had cured him of idle daydreams.

Beneath him, the filly covered the ground quickly with her smooth lope. He tried to shut out everything but the metronomic thud of her hooves and the bite of the wind against his face, the pleasure of her strong, graceful stride carrying him toward the horizon, but there was no escape. The persistent buzz of anxiety continued. He tried to summon blind optimism, telling himself that things would work out ... somehow. *Somehow.* The word sounded so flat to him.

An airplane passed high overhead, and he reined in the filly to stare up at it. Sunlight glinted off the silver skin. From such a distance, the plane seemed more bird than machine. A giant soaring bird bound for some exotic destination. He had never flown, and it had occurred to him that he might never fly. That his life was set and what there was now in his thirty-second year was all there would ever be.

Poised there, a tall man on a rangy buckskin in the midst of a rolling emptiness, Owen Byrne himself could have been a vision from the past. With his long canvas trail coat and his scarred chaps and his battered black western hat, he seemed the elemental lone rider. A part of the horse and the land and the dream of an earlier time. But Owen was neither dream nor vision. He was just a man doing his daily work.

The filly tossed her head nervously and drifted into a sideways cakewalk. She was only green broke, and her tolerance for standing quietly was limited. "Easy," he whispered, gathering her firmly and forcing her to hold still a moment before he cued her back into the slow lope she favored. As he rode he scanned the ground for more dead calves.

He had found another aborted fetus just that morning, putting the number to thirty since Thanksgiving. His initial hope that only a small percentage of the herd was infected had given way to resignation.

"It's a new virus from South America that's similar to Bangs," the vet had reported. "Spread by sexual contact. Nothing much happens to the bulls, but every infected cow will lose her calf before term."

Since the sole product of the ranch was calves, that had been devastating news. Owen had barely absorbed it when the vet went on, explaining that the bulls would be fine with quarantine and a course of antibiotics, but the virus rendered cows sterile. They would never breed back. The Byrne Shamrock Ranch not only would have a reduced calf crop to send to market, but also would lose a significant number of good angus mother cows. And because mature cows were not worth very much by the pound, whatever price the packing house paid wouldn't come close to the cost of replacing those cows in the herd.

Just that morning he had shipped off the first group of affected cows. The truck came for them and he took over the loading, pouring all his anguish and despair into physical exertion. Not only was the financial loss devastating, the animals going to slaughter were mama cows that he had fed and cared for and known for years. Mama cows in their prime.

But the culling had to begin. They couldn't afford to feed barren cows through the rest of the winter. Hell, the way things were going he didn't know if they could afford to feed their productive cows. He reminded himself of the year that thieves had gotten away with a semi-load of cattle on Christmas Eve. They had managed to survive that loss. Somehow they would manage this one. *Somehow.* There was that word again.

The filly lunged over the crest of a hill, and the sprawling pens, the old settlers' cabin, and the winter-bare skeleton of the huge pear tree came into view. His mother had wanted the tree cut down after his brother's funeral, but Owen had talked her out of it. Not just because trees were scarce in this part of the country but because Terry had loved the tree and had carefully built the network of pens and chutes so it would be protected.

To Owen this was his brother's true monument, not the ornate granite slab at the Cyril cemetery. This was Terry's grand creation, engineered so that working the cattle—branding, dehorning, castrating, and vaccinating—was faster and easier than with the old ways. Now that Owen did most of the work alone the setup was invaluable. Without it he could not have managed, and so he thought of the working area as Terry's legacy to him.

Thoughts of his brother's death made him feel that he was nearing a vast darkness that he dared not venture into, so he quickly cleared his mind by allowing the filly to run. She stretched out eagerly and the pups trailing alongside could barely keep up.

Ahead in the pens were the ranch's bulls. Owen always separated them from the herd for several months to insure that no cows would be bred to calve in the middle of the following winter, jeopardizing the survival of the babies and in some cases the survival of the mamas too. Of course this year, with the virus, the separation was even more critical.

He was almost to the cabin when the filly suddenly snorted and shied sideways. He might have forced her onward but the pups echoed her distress. Then he caught it too, the faint but unmistakable tang of blood on the air.

He dismounted and tied the filly on the far side of the cabin. Then he went around to where the bulls were shoving and snorting, fighting for places at the feed troughs and blocking his sightlines with a wall of muscular bodies. They were always hungry when they were penned. Ravenously hungry. And almost as ravenously horny. He had often wondered what a social scientist would make of bull behavior.

The animals avoided each other while they were turned out with the herd, even though there might be no cows to service for days or even weeks at a time. Yet during their sojourn in the pen they aroused each other's sexual appetites constantly and rode each other in a descending order of power and size. His brother had always called it the pecker order.

"Say there, boys," he said, carefully looking them over for injuries. "Who's bleeding here?"

They extended wide wet noses toward him and snuffled loudly, trying to catch the scent of cubes or grain. He climbed partway up the fence and the muscled mass shifted restlessly. From the higher vantage point he could look across the broad backs of the larger animals in front and see the younger, smaller animals who had been pushed to the rear. And he could see that they were stepping around an animal on the ground.

"Great," he told them aloud, knowing immediately that the downed bull had to be the new one his father had just bought.

Owen got a sack of pressed feed cubes from the cabin and filled a trough at the opposite end of the series of pens. Predictably, the bulls stampeded toward the food, bellowing and butting each other for first position. He closed a gate to keep them from returning, then went to the prostrate animal.

The little bull was a beauty, even lying in a pool of blood and manure with a glassy stare to his eyes. Owen squatted beside him and heard a faint rasp of breath from the blood-crusted nostrils. He stroked the animal's neck, whispering "easy fella, easy," but the animal did not even stir at his touch. A deep weariness settled into Owen's bones.

His father had come in last night from the auction, bragging about what a great buy he'd made and about how he'd talked someone into trailering his purchase straight on out to the pens for him. Owen had been so incredulous over his father spending money they couldn't spare on a bull they didn't need that he hadn't asked any particulars about the animal. Like his age. Never once imagining that his father had turned a very young animal in with the big bulls. But Clancy Byrne, who had been steadily discarding what common sense he'd ever possessed, had done exactly that. He had thrown a little guy in with the big fellas, and the little guy had been ridden and knocked down and butted and run over all night long.

Owen went back to his horse and pulled the rifle from his saddle scabbard, then climbed into the pen again and walked across the hardpacked ground. A line of cirrus clouds drifted across the brown hills in the distance. The bulls finished devouring the feed and stared at him through the fence. The pups moved impatiently back and forth, hoping for a signal to chase.

He turned and sighted in one smooth motion. The rifle cracked. The animal on the ground jerked once. The pups took off. The hole between the glassy eyes leaked blood. Then he finished feeding the bulls and left.

He rode hard and carelessly afterward, till the wind brought stinging tears to his eyes and he had to slow down to see. He was overcome with rage. It consumed him so completely that he was afraid of it. He dismounted and led the filly, willing himself back to normal. There was no accounting for the extreme depth of his anger. His father had certainly done worse things over the years. He himself had been forced to do worse things.

He breathed deeply as he walked, pushing the rage down with each breath, forcing the demon back into its box. When it was gone he felt drained. Weary of his own moods and of something greater. Some vague, unnameable thing that was coming at him from all directions.

He was swinging back into the saddle again when he thought he heard ringing. He held the filly in and leaned forward slightly to listen. No, he hadn't imagined the sound. Someone was ringing the big bell at the house. The somber clanging floated on the wake of the wind, now clear and deep, now barely distinguishable. Finally he made out the pattern. It was not the frantic clangor of an emergency but just a call to come in. He shifted in the saddle, worried about checking the fence repairs in the creek washout, but intensely curious about the summons.

He gathered the filly, turning her toward the barn and the house and the bell. The fence check could wait a little longer. If necessary he could do it after dark with his truck spotlight.

By the time he rode in, took care of the filly and put her into her stall, the winter sun was descending in the sky. He stepped out of the shadowy old barn and headed down to the house. There were no visitors or strange vehicles in sight, and he could see no explanation for the bell call. The house lay mutely below him, a narrow rectangle of handcut native limestone that had withstood a century of Flint Hills storms. It nestled in the cleavage between hills with the front facing east toward the distant road and the back facing west toward the barns and pens. Both ends were solid walls so that no door or window opened directly into the ferocious north-south gusts.

Near the back door was the bell, a heavy brass ship's bell that the original settlers had brought. It was suspended between two tall steel pipes with a long pull rope to one side. They seldom used it anymore now that the pickup trucks were equipped with CB radios.

His boots crunched over dry grass and crusted snow as he passed the abandoned windmill's skeleton, the bunkhouse where he lived, and the tall hogwire fence of the vegetable garden. At the back door of the house he cleaned his boots on the metal scraper, then went into the enclosed porch.

As soon as he was inside, he stripped off his spurs and jammed his gloves into his coat pocket. Then he shed the long canvas duster, the heavy wool overshirt and the zippered shotgun chaps, hanging them on pegs that lined the wall. Lastly, he took off his hat, automatically raking his fingers through his hair to erase the mark of the hatband. He never wore a hat indoors, unlike his father. To Owen a hat was just a part of his working uniform, useful only for covering his head and shielding his eyes from glare.

Freed of the cowboy trappings, he was transformed from a historic vision to a contemporary man. A man with the dark brown hair and the intensely blue eyes that were common on his father's Irish side of the family, and the self-contained, thoughtful nature that had so long characterized his mother's people.

"I'm in!" he called as he went from the porch into the kitchen. Heat from the antiquated furnace hit him in a wave, and he heard the whirring of the sewing machine from the front room.

He crossed the kitchen, leaned through the doorway to the living room and saw his older sister hunched over the old black Singer. "Ellen!" he called above the machine's clattering whine.

She took her foot off the pedal and looked up from under her awning of bangs. Her harshly frosted hair hung in disarray and there were dark crescents beneath her eyes. She was thirty-five but looked far older.

"You just missed a call from Mike," she said with annoyance. "Her dad's on a binge and he took off to drink in his truck. She's afraid he'll pass out somewhere and freeze to death tonight."

Owen was surprised that his sister would call him in early to help the Wheelers. She despised old man Wheeler, and the task was one that could be accomplished after supper with the pickup's searchlights. But all he said was, "Okay. I'll find him."

He stepped back into the kitchen to pour himself some coffee. Ellen followed and he held up the pot. "Want some?"

She signaled no with a wave of her hand. Her nails were bitten to the quick. He remembered when her hair was shiny and her hands were groomed and her face had no deeply etched lines.

"What's wrong?" she asked, peering at him closely.

He stared into his cup. "I found another aborted calf. And there was trouble with the bulls."

"What happened?"

"The new bull Clancy bought got ridden almost to death."

"Is he crippled?"

"He's dead. I had to shoot him."

"Shit!" She slammed her fist on the kitchen table. "We should just tell Daddy to go lose the whole damn place in a poker game. It would be faster and less aggravating."

There was the sound of a car outside on the gravel drive, and then Meggie burst through the door. At twenty-six Meggie was the youngest of the Byrnes. She worked three days a week at a K Mart and would have to do so for years before she paid off the loan on the car she drove. But the car was important to her, and to Ellen. Without it they were stranded whenever the men were gone with both the trucks.

"Hey, everybody," Meggie said, struggling through the door with two full grocery bags. The wind had pulled wisps of her dark red hair loose, and it was sticking straight out.

Owen hurried over to take the bags from her.

"You know that fancy high-dollar bull Daddy bought at auction last night?" Ellen said before Meggie had finished unbuttoning her coat. "He's dead."

"No!"

"Yup." Ellen sounded almost smug. "Gang-banged right

in the pen. I'm telling you both. We're all gonna be in the poorhouse soon and this ranch will belong to somebody else."

Meggie looked from Ellen to Owen. "Does Daddy know yet?"

Owen shook his head. "I haven't run across him yet today."

"I know where he is," Ellen said. "When I was talking to Mike, she said she saw him at the bank this morning. He was on his way to an estate sale to look at some hunting dogs."

"She saw him at the bank?" Owen asked.

Ellen nodded. "In line at the window and talking about *buying hunting dogs.*" She emphasized each word.

Meggie chewed the corner of her lip and looked at Owen. There was a strained moment of silence. Then Meggie said, "Well, I guess it is his money."

"Yeah," Ellen said sourly, "and it's his ranch too. But I'd say we've all earned a say in things. Owen especially. He's worked his ass off to keep this place going."

"Wellll . . ." Meggie smoothed her hands over her hair and gave an airy shrug. "If Daddy does buy a bunch of dogs, we'll sure have a lot of fresh bull meat to feed 'em, won't we."

"Jeeze!" Ellen rolled her eyes and stalked from the room.

Owen finished her coffee, thinking about Mike Wheeler and where her father might have gone.

"Oh . . . Owen . . ." Ellen returned to the kitchen to hand him a torn envelope. "Sorry. I forgot to tell you why I rang you in. You got a long-distance call from New York. The woman said it was about your stories and you should call her back today."

Meggie frowned. "You need to tell people not to be calling here with messages like that, Owen. What if Daddy answered the phone and it was some Yankee asking you to call New York?"

"Daddy never answers the phone, Meg." Ellen said. "He always waits for one of us to get it. And besides, he's gonna have to find out what Owen's doing sooner or later."

"We agreed . . ." Meggie said, speaking slowly and enunciating to give her words more weight, "after Daddy's last time in the hospital . . . that we weren't gonna upset him.

And you know how he'd react to this writing business and all this calling back and forth to New York City."

"It's not like Owen is doing something criminal," Ellen declared. "And I'm sick and tired of protecting Daddy from things. What has he ever protected any of us from?"

"Oh, sure . . . that's the way you show your gratitude . . . come on back here to sponge off Daddy after you lose your husband and don't have a place to live and—"

"That's enough." Owen pushed roughly away from the table and out of his chair.

"What?" Meggie asked indignantly. "I'm just trying to remind you guys about Daddy's health. Geeminy, I'd think that "

"Enough!" Owen gripped his forehead with his hands and pressed against his closed eyes with the heels of his palms until he saw strange, disconnected shapes. When he looked up again both of his sisters were staring at him. They had the nervous, almost fearful aspect that interaction with their father brought on, and Owen hated being the cause of it, but he could not summon up one of his usual conciliatory gestures.

"I'm going to make my call," he told them impatiently.

Both women nodded and went into the living room. He knew they would listen. Privacy had never been a priority in the household, and there was only the one phone hanging on the wall beside the stove. He considered driving to the pay phone at the Cyril drugstore, but that was thirty minutes away. He stared down at the name and number on the scrap of envelope. Bernadette Goodson. His literary agent. Seeing her name in Ellen's scrawl sent a charge through him. Bernie Goodson's customary means of communication was by letter; a phone call had to mean news.

He took a deep breath, lifted the receiver and dialed. The connection was slow. Finally, an assistant answered. Then Bernie came on the line.

"Owen! How are you! How is life in Kansas?" Bernie was born on an island where they spoke the king's English, and a trace of her childhood accent remained. He liked the distinctive sound of her voice and her unfamiliar phrasings.

"Just the usual," he said.

"Hope I didn't take you away from anything crucial."

"No."

"Good. Well I had a long conversation about your new

manuscript this morning, and I wanted to talk to you about it right away. Remember the editor who recommended me to you? The one who liked your other things so well?"

"The one with the appropriate name?"

Bernie laughed. "Yes. Arlene Blunt."

"Sure. I remember her. I have her rejection letters pinned up on my wall."

"Now, Owen, editors don't get to buy everything they want. I've explained that to you."

"Yes. You've explained that." Owen's chest was as tight as if he'd just come in from running. He didn't dare invest any hope in this call ... but nonetheless, he felt a rising buoyancy.

"Well, Arlene got back to me this morning on your new manuscript. And she was very impressed. She thinks you're extraordinarily gifted.

"She hasn't been able to interest the higher-ups in it but she's still trying. The problem with this book is essentially the same as with your others. First off—even though everything is so interwoven that it seems like a novel—it *is* a collection of stories. That's a tough sell right there. Second—your writing is so dark. Suicides and women trapped on farms and your vision of the countryside dying ... It's all so overwhelmingly grim. So raw. I mean, even your animals are ... well ... too animalistic. People want animals to be cuddly and nice, or at least benign."

The hope rushed out of him in a sigh. This manuscript had been rejected just like the others and would join them on his closet shelf.

Bernie paused as though expecting Owen to speak. When he didn't she went on. "Of course I'll continue to send the manuscript around to other houses, but we have to be realistic ... Arlene was our best hope because she already has such a positive attitude toward your work. It's tough out there for a new writer. The market is bad and publishers have their eye on the bottom line. They're afraid of risk. They don't want to take a chance on anything that's too disturbing or too different from what's selling well."

"So maybe I should learn to write television comedy scripts," he said.

She laughed. "Nobody wants you to go quite that far. But, the reason I'm calling is to encourage you to try a different direction with your next work. Maybe if you could leave out the animals. And what about doing a novel instead of stories?"

He leaned his shoulder against the wall with its fading pattern of dancing roosters.

"Arlene suggested that maybe you should be a little more aware of what's selling. Not that anyone wants you to change your writing voice, but . . ."

"I know what the bestsellers are, Bernie. I may live in the middle of nowhere, but I do get to the library and the bookstore occasionally." Owen looked up at the stained ceiling. "I won't ever be published, will I?"

"Owen! I've never heard you sound so pessimistic. You're sure to sell something eventually, and once you do there'll be a market for your fiction. With talent like yours, you just need to keep going until you get that one break."

"Right," he said.

She laughed gently; then there was a rustling as though she were changing position at her desk. He assumed she worked at a desk. He'd always imagined her with graying hair and glasses sitting behind a big oak desk like a librarian.

"I'm afraid I have to cut this short. Arlene Blunt and I have a shared crisis going. Nothing to do with your book," she added quickly. "It's rather sad. One of my longtime authors had a contract to do a true crime for DeMille with Arlene editing, and the poor man had a heart attack yesterday and can't do the job."

"True crime?"

"Nonfiction. You know . . . *The Onion Field, Savage Grace, In Cold Blood.* High-quality murder. The deep epic stuff. DeMille likes American tragedy . . . sensational but meaningful."

"I've read *The Onion Field* and *Savage Grace,*" Owen said. "They were fascinating."

"Yes. True crime can be terrific." Bernie sighed. "My poor author is out of the picture completely, but DeMille still wants the book done, and fast, so Arlene and I are scrambling for a replacement. So far every writer we've contacted is either committed to a project or can't possibly go to work in the time frame involved."

Owen's pulse roared in his ears and the hand gripping the receiver turned clammy and damp. He swallowed hard.

"What about me, Bernie?"

"What?"

"What about me doing this crime book?"

"But it's not fiction and it's not anything you know about."

"Bernie . . ." He marshalled his argument, desperate to make every word count. "A lot of what I write is straight out of my life, so in a sense I've already written some nonfiction."

She was silent.

"I can do it, Bernie. Truman Capote was a fiction writer when he wrote *In Cold Blood,* wasn't he?"

"Well, I have always said that your writing is so profound I have to eat potato chips with it to stay balanced. DeMille would like that. But you have no experience with courtrooms or the legal process."

"My approach will be fresh, then. And I'll do a better job of explaining things to readers because I will have just learned it myself.

"Think about it, Bernie . . . Murder isn't so far from what I've been writing. Trying to understand the human circumstances that lead to murder is very close to what I've already done. I could never sit down and write a spy thriller or something romantic, but *this* . . . a book about the ultimate dark act . . . I think I could really do this, Bernie."

"Ummmm."

The hunger inside Owen swelled, threatening to consume him. This was his. It was meant to be his. Somehow he had to convince her.

"I can do it, Bernie. I have to do it. Things are bad here and we could lose the ranch. I probably wouldn't have the nerve to ask for this if it weren't for needing the money. But I do. And I am. And I'm begging for the chance."

She was quiet a moment. "The trial is here in New York, Owen. Not in Manhattan but upstate a bit. How would you manage that? Last year, when I suggested that you come here and meet Arlene, you gave me a long lecture about how impossible it is for ranchers to leave the ranch."

"I'll figure out something," he said, having no idea what, but too determined to let anything stand in his way.

"And how will you afford to come here and stay through the trial if you're having financial difficulties?"

"Don't worry about me, Bernie. I'll take the bus and I'll bring my sleeping bag and I'll live on fast food."

She laughed ruefully. "Have you ever been out of those hills of yours?"

"Yes." Luckily she didn't ask how far out.

"Good Lord, I'm not sure what to think at this point. Let me speak to Arlene and get back to you. It's really her decision. Who knows? As desperate as we are for a writer and as fond as she is of your work—she may just go for it."

"Try to convince her, Bernie. You won't regret it. I promise."

"Ummm. Well, I'll try to get back to you today."

"Fine."

"And Owen. I really am on your side, you know. I just don't want to see you jump into something that you can't handle."

He hung up the receiver and stared at nothing. Some moments passed before he realized that Meggie and Ellen were crowded into the doorway watching him. Their eyes were wide.

"What's going on?" they asked in unison.

Owen found Michelle Wheeler's father passed out in his truck beneath the line of cottonwoods that marked the creek running between Wheeler Ranch and Byrne Shamrock Ranch. He hefted his inert neighbor with a fireman's carry and loaded him into the passenger side of his own pickup. Sandy Wheeler would be safe in bed tonight instead of freezing to death, but he would be a bear in the morning, especially after he learned that a Byrne had been the one to bring him home. Sandy Wheeler and Clancy Byrne had hated each other for fifteen years.

Bouncing over open land, Owen took the shortest route to the Wheeler house. As he drove he considered how ironic it was that his writing might be the key to saving the Byrne ranch. His father was of the belief that intellectual pursuits were pure garbage and that any man who spent a lot of time with books was reduced in masculinity. A Western now and then was okay but anything else was suspect. "Too much butt-sittin' and brain-churnin' turns a man queer" was one of Clancy Byrne's homilies.

Clancy didn't know a thing about Owen's writing or about the manuscripts in the closet. Meggie had decided that this shocking development might be fatal, so she'd insisted that they keep it a secret. Which suited Owen fine. He didn't rel-

ish living with constant ridicule from his father, or the gloat-
ing that Clancy would have done over each failure.

And failure was all Owen had to show so far. One failure
after another. Though he had managed to attract the attention
of an editor and had secured the referral to Bernadette
Goodson Literary Agency, still not one word of his had been
published.

But now, after all the rejections and the secrets, now he
might have a real chance. He could write his way into print
with this. He knew he could. If they would just allow him
to try.

Owen rounded the curve that gave him a view of the
Wheeler buildings, and his anxiety over what was being decided in New York was immediately replaced by the realization that Michelle was waiting there and he had to tell her
everything. He had to make her understand what this meant
to him.

The Wheeler buildings were similar to his own home, except that here everything had a more advanced air of decay.
As if it had already been abandoned. And in a sense it had.
Mrs. Wheeler had left one night when her youngest was
still in diapers. And each of the eight Wheeler children had
left as soon as they came of age. Now the ranch was home
to Sandy Wheeler and his brother, Uncle Kaye, both in their
sixties, Gram Wheeler, the aged family matriarch, and
Michelle, who had come home to take care of them all after
seven years in Kansas City. They survived because the
ranch was debt-free, because Grandpa Wheeler had been in-
sured when he died, and because, so far, luck had been with
them.

As soon as Owen neared the house, Mike came hurrying
out. Relief showed on her face when she saw her father in the
truck. Mike was twenty-seven, with straight honey-brown
hair, clear eyes and the calm, steady air of someone with no
uncertainties. It was often hard for Owen to connect the Mike
he knew in the daytime to the one he made love with at night.

"Where'd you find him?" she asked.

"The creek."

She shook her head. "The drinking is getting worse, but he
won't listen to anyone about it. Today when Gram tried to
talk to him he just took off. We were worried sick. And Uncle Kaye's gone with the other truck, so I didn't have a way
to go find him."

Owen looked toward Uncle Kaye's bunkhouse. The man had slept alone out there since his teens, helping his older brother and turning more and more eccentric with the years. Sometimes Owen feared that he too might become the dotty old guy in the bunkhouse, and he had to assure himself of how different his situation was from Kaye's. Owen ran the Byrne ranch. He slept out in the bunkhouse by choice. In the future he and Mike would marry, have children, and live in a house of their own.

"Where is Uncle Kaye?" he asked.

With an exasperated sigh, Mike rolled her eyes. "Beats me."

Owen hefted Sandy into the fireman's carry again, and Mike held doors open on a path to Sandy's bedroom. Together they stripped off his boots and jeans and tucked him beneath a quilt.

"What's going on?" Gram Wheeler called from her room.

"Owen found Daddy. We're putting him to bed."

"Is he snockered?" the old woman demanded.

"Yes."

"Has Kaye come home yet?"

"No, Gram."

"I aim to give that boy a piece of my mind!"

"Yes, Gram. I'm leaving now for a while. Owen's driving me to get Daddy's truck."

Mike was talkative on the ride out to the creek. She rambled on about the chicks she would order in spring from the hatchery and the garden seed she had sent for and all the canning she would do later if the garden came on strong.

Owen remembered Mike Wheeler as a teenager. She had hated everything about country life and dreamed of escaping it just as her older brothers and sisters had before her. The day after her high school graduation she left for Kansas City and Owen had not been surprised. What surprised him was when she suddenly returned to the ranch two years ago and embraced country living with single-minded fervor. Whatever had happened to her in the city had remade her completely from the younger Mike he'd known.

"Mike . . ." Owen said, breaking into her monologue as he pulled up beside her father's truck. "I need to talk to you."

Her face went very still. "What about?"

He hesitated, wondering how to begin. "I might have a chance at a job."

"What?" she asked, more confused than questioning.

He told her a simplified version of it all, then admitted, "I'd have to go to New York and stay till the trial was over."

"Go to New York? New York City?"

He nodded.

"You can't do that, Owen! You don't want to do that! Believe me, please!" She grabbed hold of his arm as if she might be able to keep him there simply by holding on. "People like you and me were not meant for cities. We don't belong there!"

"It's just for a few weeks, Mike. Maybe a month. I can handle anything for that long."

"You don't know. You don't have any idea." She released his arm to bury her face in her hands. "Oh, Owen . . . there are so many ways to get hurt in a place like that. You're too trusting . . . too . . ."

"Michelle, Michelle . . ." He pulled her gently to him. "I'll be fine. I'm just going to do a job. I promise I won't hang out with any drug lords, jewel thieves or paid assassins."

His teasing had no effect. She huddled in his arms for several minutes with her fingers clutching the front of his coat; then she pulled away.

"Who will take care of the ranch?" she asked.

"We're working on that."

"With your dad's health problems he can't do it. And you don't have the money to hire the kind of help you'd need." Her voice strengthened as she thought of all the reasons why he could not possibly go. "There's no one available even if you could afford it. The only people left in this county are either old or they've got their sights set on something easier and better-paying than ranch work. And you don't have enough time to send south for a wetback."

He let her wind down before he said, "Meggie has someone she thinks will do it."

"She does?" Mike asked weakly.

"Rusty Campbell. His family ranches up near Junction City. He's the youngest of four brothers, and all of them have settled at home so Meggie thinks he'll come down and stay just for the chance to get away and be his own boss awhile. I'll either pay him when I can or give him his pick of some calves."

"That sounds pretty fishy to me, Owen. I'll bet that guy is really coming just because of Meggie."

"Maybe so, but there's nothing wrong with that."

"Sure . . . Before you know it, Meggie will be wanting to get married."

Owen frowned at her.

"It's your turn to marry next, Owen!"

"But Mike, we can't get married. Right? Your father won't hear of me moving into your house and you don't want to live with me in my bunkhouse. And—"

"It's not that I'd mind living in your bunkhouse," she insisted. "I just can't stay there and then have to go to the main house to wash or cook or whatever. That's your sisters' territory."

"You know . . ." he offered tentatively, "if this works out I could have a career started . . . with an income separate from the ranch. Maybe enough that we could build a house of our own."

The idea brightened her instantly.

"Where would we build?" she asked.

"Knowing your dad it would have to be Byrne land."

She stared out the window. "When do you have to go?"

"The trial starts next week. If they decide they want me, I'll be leaving immediately."

She studied his face a moment as though wanting to say something; then she turned abruptly and slid out. Owen watched until she had pulled Sandy's truck around and was headed safely toward her home.

As soon as Owen walked in, Meggie pushed him toward the phone with the news that Bernadette Goodson had called again and wanted Owen to call her office right away. Meggie's eyes were shining and she had her fingers crossed for luck.

Owen dialed. Meggie sat down in a kitchen chair, waiting expectantly. Ellen came from the living room to lean in the doorway. He tried to ignore them, but they contributed to his nervousness.

"Finally," Bernie said, when she heard his voice. "I was afraid I'd have to leave without giving you the news."

Owen held his breath.

"Arlene likes the idea. DeMille is not convinced you can pull it off, but they're receptive. The deal is that you start attending the trial and within two weeks submit a detailed proposal. If the proposal suits them, you've got the contract.

"Now here are the odd bits . . . Since this is rather an unorthodox situation, Arlene and I managed to convince the publisher to give you two thousand up front . . . right now . . . as expense money. If you do the book for them, that will be considered part of your advance. If your proposal isn't accepted, the two thousand will be written off and you won't be required to pay it back. Arlene wants you to forget the bus and use some of that to buy a plane ticket and be in New York as soon as possible so she can meet with you and you can start your research. Can you do that?"

A great wild joy filled Owen and he wanted to shout to Bernie and to his sisters and to anyone else in hearing distance, but he held it all in, held himself very tightly so that nothing was disturbed. So that nothing could disappear before he had hold of it. "I can do that," he said calmly.

He turned toward his sisters and nodded to let them know. Meggie held her arms up in the classic victory pose and mouthed a silent *yes!* Ellen grinned.

"I have some other good news for you," Bernie said. "I've found an apartment you can use. Free. The people are in California for three months and couldn't sublet it without losing their lease. How does that sound?"

"It sounds great. But are you sure? I mean, I never expected you to go to so much trouble."

"Stop. I want this to work for you, Owen."

"I know. Thanks. I'll do a good job, Bernie. You won't be sorry."

"I just hope *you* won't be sorry." A voice shouted at Bernie in the background, and Owen heard a faint jingling sound along with her muffled reply. "It's crazy here," she said apologetically. "Now, I express-mailed you a package of clippings and background material on this case. That way you'll be able to go over the stuff on the plane and be knowledgeable when you meet with Arlene. It's the Serian murder, you know. The one they call the Black Widow murder. It might not be big news in Kansas, but it's a very hot item here in New York. Very sensational."

"Okay."

"This isn't a sure thing, Owen. You do understand that, don't you? You could do all this traveling and disrupt your life and have them turn down your proposal."

"I understand," he said, but a whole new set of possibilities lay suddenly before him and nothing else mattered.

2

The weather was clear for Owen Byrne's flight to New York, and he had a window seat. He offered his seat to the boy who shared the row with him, thinking that a child should be the one to have the view, but the boy said he never bothered looking out anymore because it was always the same boring stuff.

Owen could not understand such an attitude. Especially from a child. The boy went back to his electronic game. Owen regarded him for a moment, then leaned close to the small window, touching his forehead against the Plexiglas so he could see in all directions. He watched the uniformed crews perform the flurry of ground activities attending departure. He watched a rabbit dart across the runway as they taxied into takeoff position, and then he watched the ground fall away when they surged up into the bright afternoon air.

A fearful wonder filled him. He had not just left his home, the Flint Hills, the state of Kansas—he was no longer connected to the earth at all. And he felt almost as though he was entering another dimension. A separate reality.

Suddenly he was beset by memories of Terry. His brother had loved airplanes and had saved for years to pay for private pilot lessons at the airstrip near Strong City. He remembered Terry flying over the ranch in a small red-and-white plane, dipping low and then accelerating into a climb so that the buzz of the engine roared through the house. Swelling with pride and love, Owen ran out into the yard and stared up at the flashing white belly of that plane as it climbed away into the sky. That was his brother up there. His brother who could do anything.

Soon after, Terry had stopped flying. Owen never knew why.

Now, peering out at the farm ground far below, a giant patchwork quilt stitched together by the thin straight lines of graveled roads, Owen thought about how much his brother had hungered for this view, and he wondered what it was that Terry had found up here. Had it been just the novelty that attracted him? Had it been the thrill of control and possible danger? Or had it been complete freedom from the land that Terry had sought? The questions would never be answered. Owen could only guess at what dreams or terrors had driven his brother. And he wished, as he had wished so many times before, that he had been closer in age to his brother. That he had been his brother's friend rather than just a tag-along kid. Because he was certain that if he had been Terry's friend his brother would still be alive.

There was a soft pinging sound and the seatbelt sign went off. Quickly, Owen shook off the disturbing memories. The trip was having an odd effect on him, stirring up thoughts he usually avoided. He stood to retrieve Bernie's package from the overhead storage bin. He had been anxious to open it but had not had a chance yet, since it had arrived at the Cyril post office just in time for him to pick it up on the way to the airport.

He laid the package on the empty seat between him and the boy while he searched for his reading glasses and the steno pad and pen he'd packed. The padded brown envelope was manuscript size and covered with URGENT and OVERNIGHT EXPRESS stickers. A wave of doubt swept through him, leaving uneasiness in its wake. Had he jumped into something he couldn't handle?

He opened the stapled end of the envelope and tilted it, spilling out a stack of news clippings and copies of clippings and magazine tearsheets onto the seat. Headlines jumped at him.

SERIAN FIRE ACCIDENT OR SUICIDE?
ARTIST JINXED BY HAUNTED HOUSE
SERIAN DEAD BEFORE FIRE   POLICE QUESTION WIDOW
FIRE COVERUP FOR BRUTAL AXE MURDER?
SEX ORGY BEFORE INFERNO   SHE WATCHED HIM BURN
FAMOUS ARTIST FORESAW DEATH   MYSTERY WIFE DEFIES COPS
WITNESS DISAPPEARS   PRIEST SOUGHT AS WIDOW'S LOVER
BLACK WIDOW USED VOODOO FIRE RITUALS
HOUSEKEEPER CLAIMS WIDOW SEDUCED HUSBAND'S FRIENDS

He read. One article pulled him into another, compelling him onward, and he was nearly through the stack before he realized he hadn't taken any notes. He pulled off his wire-rimmed glasses and leaned his head back. In spite of the lurid headlines and innuendo, there was indeed great tragedy in this story.

Owen could picture Bram Serian, the artist, leaving his impoverished rural background as a young man, carrying nothing with him to New York but his talent and determination.

He felt a kinship with Serian. How well he understood the restless yearning, the fever, the need, that had driven that young man. Serian could be his other half. A more determined, more ruthlessly ambitious version of himself. Although there was nothing to indicate that Serian had been ruthless in forsaking his home. Indeed, there were few facts about the man's early life at all. Even in the various obituaries Serian's pre-fame history was vague and contradictory, almost as though his true birth was his arrival in New York. Or even later. The date of his first successful gallery show.

Serian's meteoric explosion into the art world of the seventies had to have been stunning. His work was suddenly in demand. New York society fawned over him. Women flocked to his bed.

Most young men would have been quickly seduced by it all, but not Bram Serian. This big rugged man, described by one writer as a cross between the outlaw Butch Cassidy and the biblical Moses, kept his rough ways, shunned the media and remained separate, holding on to an independent certitude that made him admirable to some and infuriating to others.

Owen wished he could have known Bram Serian. He felt the loss strongly, as if Serian was a distant relative he'd never met but was nonetheless connected to. How could such a vital, gifted man die so uselessly and horribly at only forty-six years of age?

Of course there was no answer to that so Owen considered what he did know. Aside from the peaks and valleys of the artist's career there were two other major topics in the articles. The first was Serian's home, Arcadia.

When Serian first arrived in New York, he lived and worked in a loft in Manhattan. After he became successful, he kept the loft and continued to spend time there, but bought a farm upstate for his primary home. He converted the huge barn on the property to a fully equipped studio that could accommodate all of his various sculpting, painting and woodworking projects. This studio was the object of much interest, but no one except his working assistant was ever allowed inside.

Once the studio was complete, Serian began renovating the ramshackle frame house. The work blossomed into a complex project, and Serian announced to friends that the house itself would be an ongoing work of art. Years passed. Serian devoted most of his time and resources to the house, living in the finished portions while he continued to build outlying wings. Friends were drafted as laborers, and visiting artists were encouraged to contribute touches. The result was Arcadia, the legendary unfinished masterpiece that one critic hailed as the century's major art-building and another critic described as Bram Scrian's "personal haunted manse."

Then of course there was Scrian's wife. The "Black Widow" of the tabloid headlines and the subject of much printed speculation in the seven months since his death. Serian had been thirty-three, a year older than Owen, when he married. People had been shocked by his choice of a wife. Apparently the bride was a complete unknown to his friends and associates, and she was to remain unknown.

She was aloof, reclusive, and mysterious, a combination that spawned much rumor among Serian's imaginative crowd. There were hints that she was the secret daughter of a high-ranking American and a woman of old-line Vietnamese blood, that she'd been a spy during the war and was either in danger or possibly dangerous, that her escape to the States had been dramatic and violent. Some said she had saved Serian's life in Vietnam and that he'd married her out of obligation. Within these gleefully printed bits of gossip was a framework of basic facts. Lenore Serian was Amerasian, the daughter of an Asian mother and an Anglo-American soldier, and she had come to the States with nothing.

From what Owen had read the marriage didn't change Bram Serian's life at all. It sounded as though Serian worked on his house, produced his art and lived in the same manner after his marriage as he had before. He continued to divide his time between Manhattan and Arcadia, and he continued to shun the media, never once giving an interview, refusing to be photographed, and completely blacklisting any acquaintances who even mentioned his name to the press.

Toward the end of the eighties, Serian's career slid into oblivion. He fell into ridicule and then relative obscurity, yet he continued to attract a loyal band of followers. Then, six months before his death, talk began about Serian staging a comeback, and finally a gallery show was announced that would supposedly effect this comeback. The show was scheduled for September.

Serian invited guests to Arcadia for an August weekend of working on the house and partying. Everyone had a good time until late Saturday night, which had actually become Sunday morning.

At 4:25 A.M. on the morning of Sunday, August the seventh, Serian's housekeeper called in a report that the studio was on fire. Volunteer firefighters fought the blaze but the studio was destroyed. As feared, Bram Serian's body was discovered in the smoldering ruins. The authorities considered it an accident initially, but the autopsy revealed that Serian's skull had been smashed before the fire started, possibly with an axe.

Lenore Serian was charged with her husband's murder. The media went into a feeding frenzy, and suddenly everyone who had ever known the Serians wanted to contribute information about Lenore. All the speculation about her past was printed. Serian's longtime art dealer accused Lenore of being jealous of the artist's career. His followers attacked her as being everything from simply rude to a complete psychopath.

There was an interview with a local teenager who claimed to have seen her conducting burning rituals and sacrifices in the woods surrounding Arcadia. And there was an alleged lover who disappeared before the police could question him. The lover was at first identified as a Catholic priest, but that was later amended to a Catholic brother, which was closer to a monk than a priest.

As if all that wasn't enough, the Serian housekeeper sold stories to numerous tabloid publications and a television show, claiming that Lenore treated her husband with frigid cruelty while seducing his friends into weird sexual rites out in the woods. According to the housekeeper, Lenore had a strange, almost supernatural hold over her husband, but with the dawning of a new start in his career, he was trying to break free of her.

This was the heart of the motive according to police. Lenore killed her husband to keep from being dispossessed—banished from Serian's life and the home she had so obsessively clung to for thirteen years. According to unnamed sources, there was evidence that the murder was not an impulsive, hot-blooded act but something Lenore had planned, stalking her husband and waiting for the right moment.

Owen thumbed through what was left of the material and saw the front cover of a tabloid publication. Except for the masthead and a line proclaiming BLACK WIDOW ARRIVES FOR ARRAIGNMENT the entire front page was given over to the photograph of a woman. She'd been caught getting out of a car, with her dress hiked up and her long stockinged legs extended. Though the grainy black-and-white picture was heavily shadowed, her startled, feral expression was clear. Owen studied her. She was very striking, very exotic. But there was something fierce and provocative in that elegantly contoured face. Something that made every charge against her believable.

Loudly, the boy next to Owen insisted, "I don't want just a glass. They gave me the whole can last time," and Owen looked over to see a flight attendant serving drinks from the aisle. The boy had on headphones connected to a portable CD player and could not hear the level of his own voice.

With a forced smile, the flight attendant handed him the can, then turned to Owen. "Would you care for a beverage, sir?"

Owen hesitated.

The boy shouted, "It's free, ya know," as though he had pegged Owen for a novice.

The flight attendant gritted her teeth. Owen told her any soda would do, and, with a frown, she slapped a whole can down on his tray and moved on. Her rudeness surprised him.

The boy turned to Owen and grinned as if to congratulate him on learning so quickly. He opened his mouth to speak, and Owen reached across to pull the headphones free and avoid more shouting.

"You've gotta get everything you can," the boy counseled, taking a sip of his soda.

"Who told you that?" Owen asked.

The boy shrugged. "Nobody. I'm smart enough to see how things work by myself."

Owen studied the boy. "Do you fly often?"

"Whenever my dad decides to see me. Sometimes it's often." He held up the CD player. "Sometimes I get stuff instead."

When the plane began to descend into New York airspace, Owen again pressed close to the window. He had expected the entire eastern portion of the United States to be paved and filled with tall buildings but instead he saw farm ground below. In Kansas the small percentage of hilly land was used as pasture, but here the farmers had cultivated their hills, following them around and around so that their patchwork was made of curves and circles. And the uncultivated land was not pasture at all but a velvety dark green that appeared to be native forest.

The plane banked and he saw water. The ocean? Was that the ocean below? The only person available was the boy, and he could not bring himself to expose his ignorance to the jaded ten-year-old, so the question went unasked. And then they were on the ground and he was caught up in the furor of deplaning. He handed down belongings from the overhead bins for people and carried a stroller off the plane for a woman with a baby.

He took his luggage outside into a pleasant day. It was at least fifty degrees, and there wasn't even the suggestion of a breeze. Not like February in the Flint Hills at all. When he climbed into the cab, he rolled his window partway down and inhaled New York air as the cabdriver chanted softly in a foreign language.

They exited the airport grounds and drove through a stretch of sand and tall grass that he guessed was a coastal marsh. The air had a rich, salty feculence that he knew instinctively was the smell of marshland, and he smiled to himself at the newness, the strangeness of it all.

The highway curved along the coast. They crossed old-fashioned drawbridges with waterways snaking back and forth underneath. He saw wide canals lined with big houses and private docks and a bobbing flotilla of luxury boats. Then the canals and marsh gave way to a view of endless water on one side of the highway and solid land on the other. Neighborhoods appeared on the land side with lines of old two-story brick houses. He'd never seen so much brick. And big trees. Huge old trees nodding over the streets. Stretches of park. Glimpses of children playing. On the strip of shore-line between the highway and the wide open water there were joggers and walkers and bike riders.

Then they rounded a curve, and the open water narrowed to a bottleneck between jutting points of land. High above it, spanning the white-capped water, was a gloriously long, delicate bridge. The Brooklyn Bridge maybe? But no, a highway sign identified it as the Verrazano Narrows bridge linking Brooklyn to Staten Island. Such an awesome sight and yet he had never even heard of it.

They passed beneath the base of the bridge and the highway curved again and the narrows widened into New York Harbor. And he stared out at the sun-spangled glare, stared at the boats and ferries and barges and huge, huge ships and the honest-to-God Statue of Liberty and more bridges, and then he saw Manhattan. It rose from the water like a mirage shimmering in the afternoon light, a true Emerald City, part science fiction, part cathedral, a stunning, ethereal vision. And he felt like a man who had looked across a crowded room and suddenly seen the most beautiful woman in the world.

By the time he arrived at Bernadette Goodson's, he was numb from sensory overload. He stood on the sidewalk holding his big suitcase in one hand and his carryon in the other, both of them Ellen's because no one else in his family owned luggage, and he stared up and down the street. The entire population of Cyril could have been housed in that one block.

The street was quiet compared to the broad commercial avenues they'd taken to get there, and it looked to be primarily residential except for the brass plaque that read BERNADETTE GOODSON LITERARY AGENCY. The buildings were four and five stories and constructed of brown or gray stone. Great slabs of stone that had been smoothed and shaped and sometimes ornately carved. He wondered over the common walls between the houses and the way the front steps extended right to the sidewalk so that there were no yards at all. He wondered what it would be like to be so surrounded by people. And he wondered how the trees could grow so large and luxurious in their squares of unpaved earth.

He studied Bernie's building. It was brown with a waist-high decorative iron fence separating it from the sidewalk. The steps were broad and flanked by carved lions, and there was an inset of stained glass above the heavy wooden door. It was an imposing door. An imposing building.

Just then the door opened and a young man in red suspenders leaned out and smiled. "Are you Owen Byrne?" he asked.

"Yes."

The man laughed and called back over his shoulder, "It's him!" Then he hurried down the stairs, opened the little black iron gate and extended his hand. "I'm Alex," he said. "Bernie's assistant." The hand he held out was pale and smooth compared to Owen's. "Let me have one of those," he insisted, and Owen handed him the carryon.

As they were going up the stairs, Alex smiled again. "The receptionist works in that front bay window there ... and she came back and told us there was some nutcase in cowboy clothes who'd been staring in at her for ten minutes."

"I didn't even see her," Owen said, with some measure of embarrassment.

"Nobody can see in through those curtains, but she thought you had the evil eye." Alex laughed. "Anyway, Bernie guessed it might be you."

They stopped for introductions just inside the door where a solidly built woman sat at a computer. She shook hands self-consciously and said hello in a musical accent, before answering the large, many-buttoned telephone. Owen had never had a woman shake his hand. And he'd never touched a black person before. He felt clumsy and inadequate.

Alex led him through a series of rooms which opened directly into one another, all with dark burnished wood and high ceilings. "This is an old brownstone mansion," he said. "Bernie has the first floor and the rest of it is divided into apartments."

They entered a room with large windows and french doors facing out onto a tiny ivy-laced courtyard. The woman who stood up to greet him had a heart-shaped face, an engaging smile framed by dimples, and masses of thin bracelets tinkling on her arms. She was also black like the receptionist, though it struck Owen how inept a description that was. Her skin was a luminous brown and only her short, perfectly shaped hair was black.

He nodded to her, expecting an introduction from Alex, but instead she came around and reached for his hand. Another handshake from a woman. He wasn't sure how firm to make it. But she didn't stop with the hand contact. She pulled him into a semihug with her free arm and lightly kissed his cheek.

"I knew I would get you to New York someday," she said and her voice jolted him.

"Bernie? You're Bernie?"

She laughed. "And you're Owen. We finally meet."

He stood there feeling incredibly stupid and hoping he hadn't inadvertently said something to offend her during their years of communication. He had never guessed she was black.

"Are you suffering culture shock?" she asked as Alex took Owen's heavy sheepskin coat and hung it on a bentwood halltree.

"Yes, ma'am," he admitted. "There's a lot to take in."

She smiled her wonderful, dimpled smile. "Although I've always been taken with your country charm, the 'ma'am' has to go. It makes me feel old and queenmotherish."

He grinned, feeling awkward but pleased.

"The trial doesn't start for three days so you have a bit of time to see some sights and orient yourself. I've had something come up here, and I can't show you to your apartment; however, it's quite easy to find. I thought you might want to go there and unpack; then I'll pick you up and take you to dinner about seven."

Owen nodded.

"Alex will give you the keys and the directions. It's in the East Village, an area you will either love or hate." She moved around her large desk to a wall of shelves. Her bracelets tinkled softly and her elaborate earrings swayed. He guessed her to be early thirties, close to his sister Ellen's age, and he marveled at a world where a young attractive black woman could be such a success. It wouldn't happen around Cyril. There the combination of female and black would be too heavy a burden.

"I've collected more news articles for you and a number of books I thought might prove helpful. True crime, police procedure, and what-have-you. It's quite a large bundle. I hope you can manage it all."

"Oh, no problem. Thank you."

"Where's your typewriter?" she asked, suddenly scrutinizing his luggage. "You did bring your typewriter, didn't you?"

"No ... I ..."

"No matter." She waved a long tapered hand. "We've recently switched to computers so I have a typewriter stashed in the closet that you're welcome to use. Unless you were planning to rent a computer?"

"No. A typewriter is fine."

The receptionist's voice came through the telephone intercom. "Bernie ... it's LaFehr on line two."

Bernie leaned close to her space-age phone, held down a button and said, "I'll take it." She then turned to Owen. "I think we're all set," she said. "I'll give you to Alex now and I'll see you at seven."

Before Owen could reply, she was picking up the phone receiver to take her call.

Alex carried the typewriter and the box of books as they went down the front steps together. "I came here from Indiana," Alex admitted. "Not from the real sticks like you, but from a pretty small town. I remember how overwhelmed I was the first few weeks. But don't worry ... you'll adjust."

"Did you have women like Bernie in Indiana?" Owen asked.

Alex chuckled. "I can tell you're in for some real eye-opening experiences here," he said. "This city is full of interesting people."

They walked to the corner because Alex said it was easier to hail a cab on the busy avenues. While Alex searched the passing traffic for available cabs, Owen watched the human traffic streaming around him on the wide sidewalk. So many striking people. Every skin shade. Every hair color. Every body type. All striding confidently down this city street like they owned the world.

"Owen!" Alex called from the curb where he was holding open the door to a yellow cab. He helped Owen load his things; then, as Owen was sliding into the backseat, Alex handed him a slip of paper with the apartment address, grinned knowingly and said, "You're not in Kansas anymore."

His cab sped downtown and pulled up to an old six-story apartment building. Owen stared. The "East Village" had sounded glamorous, but the reality was something different. There was none of the gentility that characterized Bernie's neighborhood. Here a scattering of scraggly trees struggled to offer greenery, and everything was covered with a film of grime.

All manner of people filled the sidewalks and spilled out onto the streets, and he was startled to see a man sleeping on a piece of cardboard right in the doorway of the building. He unloaded his suitcase, carryon, typewriter and box of books onto the sidewalk and the cab sped away. An old woman pushing a wheelchair full of bug-eyed chihuahua dogs detoured around his belongings, muttering as she passed, "God oughtta clean up all this trash."

"Sorry, ma'am," Owen said, moving things out of her way.

"You won't get me," she replied. "My babies are killers."

He watched her push the load of shivering chihuahuas away, and he couldn't help but smile. There was a weird kinetic energy here, an exhilarating, vital energy that was unlike anything he had experienced.

Unable to carry everything at once, he left his suitcase at the bottom of the steps while he took the typewriter, books and carryon up to the door. Carefully, he piled them to the side so that someone exiting the door wouldn't trip over them.

"Excuse me," he said to the man on the cardboard. "Are you all right?"

"Gotta get my sleep!" the man shouted; then he opened one eye, hefted himself up on an elbow to scrutinize Owen and said, "You got a dollar?"

Owen apologized for disturbing him, fished a dollar from his wallet, then went back down for his suitcase. Only it wasn't there. He looked up and down the street. People passed by as before but his suitcase had vanished.

At the top of the stairs, the man was sitting up, cackling with wild laughter.

"So you've already lost your virginity," Bernie said when he told her about the suitcase.

She had come for him at seven, and he hadn't known about the buzzer he could press that would unlock the front

door so when she rang the bell he'd run down all five flights
of stairs to let her in.

"And how do you like the apartment?" she asked as they
walked to the restaurant.

Staying in a New York City apartment had sounded impressive to him, especially after Alex called it a studio and
Bernie referred to it as a *pied-à-terre*, but the place had
turned out to be nothing more than a room and bath in a
dingy building with a broken elevator. It was basically just
a square, smaller than his bunkhouse in Kansas, with a tiny
kitchen in one corner, a sleeping platform in another corner,
a couch and chair that focused on the room's single window, a closet-sized bathroom and an even smaller closet.

"The apartment is just what I need," he said gratefully.
"And the price is right."

"Yes." She grinned. "And climbing all those stairs will
keep you fit while you're here."

"True. So where are we headed to eat? Am I dressed
okay? These are all the clothes I own now."

The dimples showed again. "My dear, you could wear
your cowboy chaps over a ball gown and still be acceptable
in the East Village."

She took him to Sixth Street, where, for a block, there was
nothing but Indian-Pakistani restaurants. They were all
packed together, one after another, tiny little places all serving the same kind of food.

"My daughter thinks they have one large kitchen in the
back that cooks for all of them," Bernie said, laughing as she
led him into a long narrow room that would have been
cavelike, except that it was filled with tiny colored lights
and mirrors, and festooned with every manner of tinsel and
crepe paper decoration. "This is Rose of India," Bernie announced. "My absolute favorite. If we get lucky someone
will have a birthday. That's a real show in here."

She ordered for both of them and the food began to arrive
immediately. Triangle pastries filled with potatoes and veg-
etables. Spiced chick peas in puffy bread. Banana fritters. A
wafer-thin crisp bread laced with black pepper. She talked as
they ate, asking him about his trip and suggesting where he
might shop for inexpensive clothing to replace his stolen
items. Then she became quiet. Pensive.

"Alex seems like a good assistant," Owen said, stretching
to fill the silence.

"Oh yes, he's quite competent. Ready to agent on his own I'd say . . . except that he has such domestic troubles I doubt that he'll get himself together any time soon."

"Oh," Owen said, immediately uncomfortable at the mention of anything labeled "domestic troubles."

Bernie sighed. "He has one of those stormy, on-again, off-again relationships. Very tempestuous. And destructive if you ask me. But then we've all fallen into one of those at some time or another, haven't we," she said, smiling ruefully.

Owen concentrated on the arrival of the tandoori chicken. No, he hadn't fallen into one of those relationships. The fact was that he'd had only one real girlfriend before Mike. A girl in his freshman year of college. There had been other females along the way but none that had been important or lasting.

"So," Bernie said, "you're still single, right?"

He nodded.

"How about a significant other?"

"A what?"

"A girlfriend, a companion, whatever."

He hesitated. These sorts of conversations were about as pleasant to him as dental work, but he felt obliged to Bernie and didn't want to offend her.

"I have someone I'm close to," he said. "A neighbor. Mike Wheeler."

"Ah . . . Mike, huh? I wouldn't have guessed."

He shrugged. "Her name is actually Michelle. But her family favors nicknames."

Bernie covered her face with her hand and laughed so hard her shoulders shook.

"What? What did I say that was so funny?"

She shook her head. "I wish my daughter was in town. She'd like you."

"Where is she?"

"She's got classes. At Boston University."

"You're not old enough to have a daughter in college."

"Oh, yes I am. I'm forty-something years old. Married for three of those years and divorced for twenty, and the mother of a beautiful twenty-year-old daughter."

"No."

She leaned toward him across the table, dimples flashing playfully and silver bracelets jingling. "Yes." Then she took a deep breath, grinned and shook her head. "Moving right along into business ... You're to be at your editor's office at ten tomorrow morning. The agreement over the expense money will be there for you to sign, and then she'll go over what DeMille wants and how to go about the proposal."

He put down his fork, unable to continue eating.

"Don't be nervous. Arlene wants to help you."

He nodded.

"Any questions?"

"Probably. But I can't think of a thing."

"Call me any time. Alex too. He instructed me to offer you whatever help he can give, and he wrote you up a little writer's survival guide." Bernie held out several densely typed sheets of paper. "Tips for using the bus and subway. Addresses of good bookstores. Locations of branch libraries and instructions for use of the central research library. Where to buy cheap typing paper." She laughed. "I told him he might have an undiscovered talent for writing tourist guides."

Owen accepted the sheets. "Tell him thank you," he said. "I appreciate everything and ..."

"I know. I just hope it all works out. I still have my reservations about you taking this on."

Owen shrugged and tried for a grin. "The worst I can do is fail."

That night Owen lay in the unfamiliar room listening to street noises when he was used to hearing only the wind. He wished that he had Mike in the bed with him, just as he'd had the night before.

She had come to the bunkhouse after midnight. He'd been sitting in front of the potbellied stove, staring into the flames, elated and restless, filled with disquietude. Thinking about leaving. Excited about leaving. But worried about leaving. Would Rusty Campbell take good care of the ranch? Who would keep Meggie and Ellen from fighting? Who would chauffeur Clancy around on the days when his leg was bothering him? And what about Mike? Who would she call when she needed help?

Suddenly he heard the knock at his door and he opened it to find Mike, smiling hesitantly, carrying a box of warm cookies and wearing her best dress beneath her down parka.

He had been hoping she would come, but he knew how hard it was sometimes for her to slip away.

"Surprise. I brought you cookies for the trip tomorrow."

"Thanks," he said. Her face was shadowed in the lantern light, but he could tell she was nervous.

"You look nice," he told her as he hung up her coat. "I haven't seen you dressed up for months."

She turned away from him and hugged herself as though cold. "Can you stoke the fire up?"

"Sure."

He squatted in front of the old stove to stir the coals and add wood. Then he rose and turned. She was naked. Standing there with her dress at her feet and her arms crossed over her breasts like a reluctant Viking goddess.

"I just love surprises," he said and she grinned shyly.

In nearly two years of intimacy, Mike had always insisted on being hidden beneath the covers before she undressed, and the new bravery was a surprise.

"I'll do anything you want me to," she announced in a determined tone.

He moved closer and caressed the line of her shoulders. "Anything?" he teased. "What's this, a going-away present?"

"I'm serious, Owen. Anything you want. Just tell me and I'll do it."

"Mike . . ." He cocked his head and tried to force her to meet his eyes, but she threw herself against him in a fierce hug, burying her face in his chest.

"I want to get married," she said. "I don't want to wait anymore."

"Okay." He stroked her fine, soft hair. "How are we going to work out the living arrangements?"

"I don't know. I don't care. I just want to get married in the morning before you leave for New York."

Owen rested his chin on top of her head. "Mike . . ."

"I mean it. I have my good dress and my birth certificate, and I want to stay here with you until morning so we can drive someplace and get married."

"Mike, that's not possible. For one thing we don't have a marriage license and that's not something you get instantly."

A tremor of silent sobbing shook her body, and he gathered her tightly, wanting to protect her and ease the pain but uncertain as to how.

"I wish you could come with me," he said.

She pulled back and looked up at him, incredulity showing through her tears. "To New York? There's no way I'd go to New York."

Her statement bothered him but he kept silent.

She frowned. "You wouldn't go either if you didn't have to, would you?"

"I wouldn't pass up a chance to go, if that's what you're asking. I've always wanted to see New York. The same way I've wanted to see San Francisco and Los Angeles and Paris and Rome and a whole lot of other places."

"You're letting that imagination of yours get carried away, Owen. You've got all those faraway places pictured as wonderful when the truth is that they're dirty and crowded, and full of foreigners and lowlifes. Believe me, when I left Kansas City, all I could think was good riddance!"

The wood popped in the stove and a gust of wind rattled the window. Owen stared at his suitcase beside the door. He knew how much she feared his going.

She sighed. "We both need to get some sleep, I guess."

"Yes," he agreed. "We do."

"Does that mean you don't want to make love to me?" she asked with a timid but coy smile.

He lifted her, stumbled, and ended up falling with her onto the bed. Laughing, she scrambled under the covers, and everything was back to the familiar.

He slipped beneath the quilts with her and roamed the contours of her body with his hands. He pressed his erection against her thighs and belly. She was more aggressive than usual, touching his penis and then guiding him to her blindly with her eyes tightly closed. He entered her slowly, carefully, watching her for any sign of displeasure, wishing as he always did that he could be certain she was enjoying the act.

He wanted to prolong it, but she knew just where to touch him and just how to move so that his control dissolved and he couldn't keep from climaxing. When it was over, she curled into his arms and he asked, as always, "Was it okay? Did you come?" and as always she said, "Yes. Of course." But he never quite believed her.

"I love you," he said. "I'll call you every night."

"Don't you dare! That would cost a fortune. Don't call me at all. Just send letters. You're a writer . . . so write."

"I'll miss hearing your voice though."

She pressed her cheek against his chest. "I'm going to sleep here all night," she said defiantly. "I don't care what anybody says. And tomorrow morning I'll pack your suitcase and—"

"I've already packed."

"Oh. Well . . . Then I'll go home in the morning and fix you a cooler of food to take. Potato salad and coleslaw and—"

"Mike . . . Mike . . . There will be food on the plane and I think they have food in New York too."

"Not anything good, I bet. Not like you get here at home."

"No," he'd agreed. "It won't be like home."

Owen had said that primarily to please her, never imagining that he would spend his first evening eating strange and wonderful food in an outlandish little restaurant, while discussing "relationships" with a charming, intelligent, dark-skinned woman.

It wasn't like home. That was certainly true.

The next morning he went for his meeting at DeMille & Sons Publishing. Arlene Blunt, the senior editor who held so much power over his work, turned out to be a tiny woman who could have passed for a teenager. She had a corona of curly brown hair that sprang from her head like coiled wire, and pale cosmetic-free skin. One of her ears had three pierced earrings and the other had two. Her handshake was firm.

She took him on a brief walking tour of her floor, explaining that this was editorial and that DeMille had other floors in the building for sales and art and the business side of things. Then she took him to her office and, without any preliminaries, she said, "Your proposal has got to be very, very good or you can kiss this whole idea good-bye. Have you ever written a proposal before?"

He hadn't.

Thus began a crash course in proposal writing. She led him through the mechanics of it and then explained that he needed to produce two sample chapters and an overview of the book, written so that the most skeptical of her bosses would salivate over the commercial potential. After the lesson was over, she leaned back in her chair and rolled a pencil back and forth in her hands.

"How do you see this case so far?" she asked.

Owen gathered his thoughts for a moment. He knew the question was a test so he put aside his natural reticence.

"Bram Serian took in this woman, a war refugee, and tried to undo the damage of her past," he said, "but it was impossible. She had been through too much, and their relationship was doomed from the start.

"He struggled with her for thirteen years, fighting against her problems, even while his career was foundering and his own foundations were shaky. And then he realized he could no longer continue the marriage."

Owen paused to think again.

"Maybe she was dragging him down and contributing to the destruction of his career. Maybe he became interested in someone else. Maybe he simply wanted to be free of her. Whatever . . . he started to talk about divorce.

"To Lenore Serian . . . a volatile, disturbed woman whose entire life revolved around her husband and her home . . . the idea of divorce must have been terrifying. She had no friends. No relatives. No other existence beyond the boundaries of Arcadia.

"Killing him was probably an act of desperation for her. Almost an act of self-defense. She was trying to fight back and hold on to the only home and the only world she had left."

"Ummmm." Arlene absently combed the pencil through her hair, making it stick out at even wilder angles. "I like it. I like it a lot. You'll have to modify as the trial unfolds, but it's a respectable beginning." She sat forward in her chair and grinned. "You could actually be good at this, Byrne."

He returned her smile, feeling intense relief.

She shook his hand again, then walked him to the elevator. When he stepped out of the building onto the busy sidewalk, it suddenly struck him that he was a country boy in the middle of a monster city, that he had just signed on the dotted line of a publishing agreement, and that he didn't know what the hell he was doing. But he felt as lighthearted as an eighteen-year-old again.

3

Owen did not use his three days for sightseeing. He pored over the books Bernie had collected for him, dissecting them in a determined effort to learn what made a true crime story work. And he immersed himself in the Serian material, reading and rereading the news clippings and magazine articles until he knew whole portions by heart. The few indulgences he allowed himself were small. He made a visit to St. Patrick's Cathedral in his mother's memory. He took walks through the teeming East Village. He went inside bookstores. He tried Chinese and Polish and Arabic food in cheap restaurants. And, of necessity, he replenished his wardrobe.

After buying the clothes, he went back to the apartment and put on a new shirt. Then he opened the closet door to look in the mirror, something he seldom did at home because there were no mirrors in the bunkhouse and because he was usually unconcerned with his appearance anyway. But when confronted with his reflection, he forgot the shirt and was drawn into staring at the face he saw.

In his mind he carried a picture of himself as greatly resembling his father, but seeing his image reflected in this stranger's mirror, in this strange city and at this strange turning of his life, he could find no traces of Clancy Byrne. Even the dark brown hair and the blue eyes no longer mattered now that his father's hair and eyes had paled with age.

He couldn't find his dead brother in that face either. Or any other Byrne. Somehow the face had finally become his own.

On Tuesday morning Owen set out for the opening day of the Serian murder trial. Anticipation and fear rode with him in equal measures.

Armed with maps and train schedules and advice from Alex, he rode a bus uptown to Forty-second Street. He was

headed for Grand Central Station, a familiar name from his
childhood, when his mother had shouted, "This ain't Grand
Central Station!" every time the children ran through her living room. He expected to find a bustling, overblown train
depot with no more character than the airline terminals he'd
encountered on arrival, but upon first sighting it he stopped
midstride to stare, oblivious of the foot traffic streaming
around him on the sidewalk. The brash beaux arts exterior
was so massive and timeless that it called to mind pictures
of the Parthenon in Athens or the Coliseum in Rome.

He pulled himself back to the purpose of his trip and entered the building, joining the flow of people pouring into
the doors at the southwest corner. He was carried along
through various drab corridors, then into a soaring grand
concourse that astonished him as much as the exterior had.
High above the huge open space were breathtaking vaulted
ceilings that held constellations from the night sky. He tilted
his head back and gawked shamelessly. And it struck him
that this was a dreamer's monument. This building was more
than the sum of architecture, money and politics. It was a
tribute to civilization. A reverent vision. A miracle.

It made him want to build. And he wondered if Bram
Serian had felt something similar when he started Arcadia.

After buying a ticket for a northbound train, he went in
search of his boarding gate. On the way he saw a bakery and
joined the line to buy a fresh bagel with cream cheese and
a large cup of coffee to take along.

Because it was time for the morning commute, most trav-
elers were rushing into Manhattan rather than out and he had
an entire section of a car to himself. He settled into a spot
with room to stretch out his legs and he pulled his breakfast
from the bag. The pleasure he felt was so simple that it
seemed almost childish. A ride on a real train. The smell of
good coffee. A comfortable seat. He smiled to himself as he
unwrapped the bagel.

The doors closed and the train inched slowly through the
dark bowels beneath Grand Central. On and on the darkness
continued and he stared out into it, occasionally catching a
glimpse of shadowy movement. He wondered if there were
people in the tunnels or if it was simply a trick of the darkness. Then suddenly the train burst out into sunlight and
picked up speed, swaying gently in a soothing racketing
rhythm.

He tried to visualize the path of travel, remembering that Alex had told him to picture New York State as funnel-shaped, with Manhattan down at the tip of the skinniest part. They were headed up the neck of the funnel along the Hudson River.

Aided by maps and a talkative conductor, he identified Harlem as they raced through it, then watched as they traveled deep into the layers of high-powered commuter suburbs, across the outlying band of wealthy estates and horse farms, and finally into the countryside. Bram Serian's countryside. A land of rolling hills and dense woodlands broken by the occasional dairy farm or apple orchard. Alex had described it as lush and picturesque, but on this February day fog hung in the air, patches of snow clung to the hillsides and melted between tumbled boulders, and bare-limbed trees pierced the mist like gnarled witches' fingers.

Anxious about missing his stop, Owen gathered his carryon, which was now functioning as a briefcase, and was waiting at the door when the conductor announced Stoatsberg.

At the tiny Victorian train station, he asked the lone occupant for directions to the courthouse. The man sucked his teeth, looked Owen over and said, "Going up to the trial, huh? If you ask me, the whole thing's a waste of our tax dollars. That woman's guilty as sin and it's a crime that we citizens have to foot the bill so some fast-talking attorney can try to weasel her out of being punished."

Owen was taken aback by the man's surliness. "I'll bet that woman has paid a lot of taxes herself through the years," he pointed out.

The fellow glared at him, then jerked his head in a general direction. "Just go straight up that way and you'll run into it."

Turning up his collar, Owen stepped out onto the quiet street. It was several degrees colder in Stoatsberg than in Manhattan. The sidewalk was deep in gritty slush, and the only sound was the rush of dank water down the gutters. He passed a deserted lumberyard and a shuttered bar, then was surrounded by old, haphazardly tended houses fronting on cracked sidewalks with postage-stamp yards full of car parts and snow-covered toys. There was no stirring of life, human or otherwise.

Block after block was the same, and he thought about how

winter was often unflattering to small towns. In Cyril freezing weather drove people inside and reduced the color spectrum to dingy grays and whites, spare blacks and browns. But here the temperature wasn't all that low, and the bleakness was so pervasive he doubted a change of season would help. It was hard to believe that an artist had chosen to live near such a place.

Nearer the somber, dome-crowned courthouse, the walkways had been salted and cleared. Curbside parking was full and people hurried across courthouse square, either to one of the low brick office buildings that flanked the open space or toward the wide granite steps of the courthouse. An elaborately equipped van with television logos on the doors was parked to one side.

He went up the steps and into the courthouse. The lobby was a study in marble. Brown marble floors, gray marble moldings and lintels, white marble columns. Massive, solid, timeless, but with the requisite clutter of vending machines and cheap plastic signs. A portable security station blocked access to the wide central staircase and the small afterthought of an elevator. He joined the line of people turning out their pockets and opening bags and cases for inspection.

The officer who pawed through Owen's carryon had a bored expression. "You got a tape recorder in here," she said, without looking up at his face.

"Yes. I'm researching a book and . . ."

"I don't care what you're doin', pal. No tape recorders or cameras go past me. You people think you can come up here and get away with anything, don't you?"

"I'm sorry. I didn't know . . ."

She jerked her thumb to the right. "Tell it to the sergeant."

The sergeant wasn't interested either. He took the recorder and wrote Owen a receipt without acknowledging his presence. The incident answered one of Owen's questions about trials. Taping was not allowed.

Number 6, Judge Martin J. Pulaski's courtroom, wasn't hard to find. It was the one with the big crowd. Three court officers stood guard, arms folded and faces stern, as they watched the growing mass of humanity. An arrangement of velveteen ropes and bright chromium poles had been set up to keep order, but there was confusion nonetheless. Owen found what appeared to be the end of the line. The woman in front of him made eye contact. She had cotton candy hair

and an ample bosom beneath a sweater festooned with dancing teddy bears.

"Is this the line for the Serian trial?" Owen asked.

"You got it," she assured him; then, gesturing to a sign on
the wall she said, "Better take off your coat."

He read the hand-lettered sign—NO FOOD. NO DRINKS. NO
PETS. NO SMOKING, CHEWING OR SPITTING. REMOVE ALL COATS
AND HATS BEFORE ENTERING—shrugged out of his coat and
thanked her.

"I'm waitin' for my sister," she said. "If she doesn't make
it soon, I guess I'm stuck with tryin' to save her a seat inside."

He forced a polite smile.

"Don't you just hate it that we're so far back? We'll probably have to sit in the rafters. There's some gals I know right
up on the front of the line ... see that bunch where they're
all crocheting? But there's no way I'd ask them for cuts.
They're all pretty full of themselves. Anyway, we'll know to
come earlier tomorrow, right?"

"Right." He pulled a notebook out and began recording
whatever came to mind, hoping to appear so absorbed and
busy that she would be discouraged.

Instead it excited her. "Are you from the papers?"

"No."

"What's all that for then?" She edged closer in an effort
to read his notes.

He closed the cover. "It's research," he said, trying to
keep it vague.

"No kidding! What are you, a writer or something?"

"Something."

"I'm Phyllis. What's your name?"

"Owen Byrne."

She puckered her face in thought a moment, then said,
"Never heard of you. I'm not surprised you're here though.
She's the kind who'll make a good story."

"She?"

Phyllis frowned and rolled her eyes. "You know ..." she
lowered her voice, "the Black Widow ... Lenore Serian."
She glanced around suspiciously, then lowered her voice another notch. "My son Tommy is a witness. He did a lot of
work over at that place and he saw her burning things and
doing spells."

"Doing spells?"

"Witches' spells and voodoo stuff. Whatever it's called where she comes from."

Owen tried to keep his expression neutral.

"You should interview my son. The things he could tell you . . ." Her features suddenly lifted with delight. "Look! There's Spencer Brown. I knew all along he'd be the one that tried this. That old bag-a-wind district attorney is scared to death of going up against a big-shot defense lawyer so he put Spencer in instead."

Spencer Brown, first assistant in the district attorney's office, crossed the floor with a confident, easy stride. He was in his thirties, sandy-haired, with the body of a linebacker and the face of an altar boy.

"Go gettum, Spence!" someone called, and Brown gave a victory salute before disappearing through the double doors into the courtroom.

The crowd cheered.

Following in Brown's wake was a stocky, dark-haired man nervously pushing a metal cart laden with boxes. DISTRICT ATTORNEY'S OFFICE was stenciled on the end.

"That must be Dapolito," Phyllis said. "He's not really one of ours. Heard somebody say he grew up in Brooklyn."

Up and down the line people complained to one another about the press being allowed to go in ahead of the spectators, but the grumbling was halfhearted. Their attention was riveted on the hallway. Waiting for more players to come on stage.

An impeccably dressed young black man appeared, pushing a two-wheeled luggage rack with huge leather litigation cases strapped aboard. One of the court officers held the door open for him.

"He's got to be on her side," Phyllis said. "Our D.A.'s office doesn't have any persons of color working for them."

"I noticed it was pretty colorless up here," Owen said, but his quiet sarcasm sailed right by her. It was hard for him to believe that he had traveled so far and was so close to Manhattan only to find himself in a sad little town full of attitudes as narrow as those he'd grown up with.

Several minutes passed. Tension hummed along the line. Then around the corner came a stoop-shouldered, slightly rumpled fellow with thinning hair and a mild, genial expression. "That's Rossner!" someone whispered, and Owen did a double take. This was Charles Rossner? The barracuda defense attorney?

Rossner's arrival created a flurry of whispers and then a hush. Lenore Serian had to be next. The spectators' faces gleamed with predatory excitement.

It was fast when it happened. She came around the corner, flanked by two tough-looking men who propelled her through the crowd. Her dark hair was twisted up tightly at the back of her head, and she wore a plain tan dress. In the newspaper photograph, she had projected an icy menace, a hardened woman-of-the-world aura, but there was none of that now. Her face was softer and much younger than it had appeared in newsprint. There was no obvious makeup. No jewelry. No sexy clothes. No sultry, angry glare. Lenore Serian was not at all the snarling villainess that the crowd had waited so hungrily for.

She passed by Owen, so close for a moment that he could have reached out and touched her, and the reality of her struck him with the force of a blow. Lenore Serian was not just a personality manufactured to entertain the public or a character invented for his book. She was a real human being. Just as real as he was. A flesh-and-blood person who was either a ruthless monster or an innocent woman undergoing a terrible ordeal. Either reality was chilling.

Then she was gone, swallowed by the heavy doors to courtroom 6. There was a collective release of breath and an exchange of knowing glances up and down the line. Lenore Serian's guilt hung there, implicitly agreed upon by wordless strangers.

"She'll get what she deserves up here," Phyllis announced smugly. "No city bleeding hearts on our juries."

He wanted to escape from Phyllis, but he was stuck unless he gave up his place in the line.

The doors were flung open, and an officer barked, "Enter in an orderly manner, please!" The ensuing stampede carried him forward and into a churchlike wooden pew beside Phyllis. An officer ordered their row to scoot closer together, and he reluctantly complied as Phyllis moaned about not being able to save her sister a place.

Fortunately, the excitement of his first time in a courtroom enabled him to quickly block Phyllis out. This was it. A temple of the justice system. Somehow it managed to be both more and less than he had envisioned.

There were impressive brass chandeliers, but half the glass globes were missing. The matching wall sconces were draped with electric chords from haphazardly rigged microphones and portable heaters. And the gracefully arched windows flanking one side of the room had been stapled over with heat-conserving plastic. It was the sort of work his father would have engineered, saying belligerently, "It gets the job done, don't it?"

Yet in spite of the recent desecrations the room's dignity survived. It had been crafted for the ages—a solemn blend of rosewood, walnut, and marble with the hand-hewn detailing that was no longer seen in public buildings. The flag stands had been cast of heavily ornamented brass with eagles poised on top, and the letters for IN GOD WE TRUST had been sculpted in bronze. There were three huge magisterial portraits on the walls, their oils darkened with history.

The room was heavy with the past. It floated in the air with the dust and the faint scent of aging wood. He envisioned the builders. Even in its most shining moment this out-of-the-way courthouse had never been as grand as St. Patrick's or as mighty as Grand Central, but he could feel the men who had planned and sweated over it, who had lovingly carved the wood and marble, working for something greater than a weekly paycheck. Even in a traditional setting like Cyril, that wouldn't happen today. If a courtroom was needed, they would order a prefab kit and slap it together with screws and caulking. And on opening day it would already be falling apart.

"Isn't this exciting!" Phyllis wiggled beside him to illustrate her state of mind. "I've never been to a murder trial!"

Phyllis. He felt sorry for her, but that didn't make her any more palatable. With a small noncommittal shrug he angled away from her and flipped open his notebook to make a rough sketch of the room.

He ignored the people swarming about and studied the layout. His eye was drawn first to the judicial bench, the highest spot in the courtroom. It towered center front, tall and solid and commanding, both altar and throne. Several steps down from the bench, against the right wall, stretched the jury box, two mute lines of chairs enclosed by a railing. Between the jury box and the bench was the lonely witness stand. He could well imagine how intimidating that position could be.

On the middle level, huddled at the base of the bench, were two small desks. Owen guessed them to be for the court clerk and the judge's law secretary. Then there was the court reporter's station in front of but several steps below the witness stand. And finally, on the level of the main floor were the opposing tables for defense and prosecution. Defense on the left. Prosecution on the right, closest to the jury.

The barrier separating all this from the spectators' section was a wooden railing, a substantial affair of heavy, classically turned balusters with a handrail rubbed smooth and dark from the touch of human hands. Behind this barrier were the pews where he was sitting. They filled the remaining two-thirds of the room, line upon line, with a center aisle leading from the gate in the railing to the double doors in back.

Though he had seen the arrangement before on film and in photographs, he had never appreciated the true impact of a courtroom. There was an awesome power to it even while the room was at rest.

Contrary to what he had imagined would happen, Judge Martin Pulaski was already seated. He appeared to be reading law books. Every few minutes he raised his eyes to glare at particularly noisy spectators. As trial time approached, he closed his books and leaned forward to speak to his law secretary.

Owen studied Pulaski. Without the formidable bench and the black robe, the judge would have been an unimposing man in his sixties, with a fine-boned, almost feminine face. His graying hair and mustache were clipped in a blunt military style, and he had glasses with heavy black frames.

All of the participants were present except the jury. The court reporter was putting paper in his machine. The court clerk was hunched over, writing in a large ledgerlike book. And the law secretary was standing at the bench, listening attentively to the judge. All were brown-haired, earnest-looking men in their thirties.

Owen was tall enough that he could see everything fairly well. Even the floor-level lawyers' tables. He could see straight ahead to where Brown and Dapolito were seated at the prosecution table. They were faced toward the bench. One broad back and one narrow back. Brown appeared casual, leaning back in his chair with his elbows cocked and his fingers laced behind his neck, but Dapolito was a study

in nerves, darting glances around the room as he rummaged
through the stack of folders beside him.

To the left Owen could see the defense's territory. The
front pew had been roped off and was occupied by Lenore
Serian's daunting escorts and the young black man with the
litigation cases. A narrow table pushed up to the railing in
front of them held stacks of folders and boxes labeled EVI-
DENCE. The defense table itself was occupied by Lenore and
her attorney. Rossner was turned toward her, speaking, but
she stared straight ahead, shoulders square, head high. Her
face was hidden from Owen by the angle.

"Some dress, huh?" Phyllis said loudly. "Looks like a potato sack to me."

Owen took a deep breath and continued with his sketching
and notes.

"It's pretty hard to believe that someone with money
would wear that for going to court," said a woman seated on
his other side. She had leaned around him to agree with
Phyllis.

Owen suggested to the women that they might want to sit
together and was relieved when they liked the idea. He rose
and let the second woman slide into his place next to Phyllis. Their effusive gratitude brought a little twinge of guilt,
but it quickly faded.

Six court officers had taken up positions around the room.
"Quiet in the court!" one of them announced in a booming
voice.

The court clerk stood. "People of the State of New York
against Lenore Serian. Are the people ready?"

"Yes, the people are ready!" Brown and Dapolito responded forcefully.

"Is the defense ready?"

"Yes, we are." Rossner's reply was relaxed but respectful.

"Shall we bring in the jury and begin these proceedings,"
asked the judge in a gruff, almost challenging manner, "or
are there problems we must contend with first?"

"Ready for the jury, your honor," all three attorneys answered in unison.

"Good. I'd like to hear both opening statements today."
The judge motioned to a court officer standing near the
empty jury box. "Bring them in, please."

Brown and Dapolito stood. Lenore and Rossner stood. She
appeared out of place in the front of the room, surrounded

by age-darkened wood and attorneys in charcoal or navy. She looked too slender, too different, too powerless standing amongst them in her plain tan dress. And it struck Owen that this was a ritual of men. The black-robed judge, the clerk and secretary and reporter, the dark-suited attorneys and assistants—all were men. And she seemed very alone standing up there.

"Jury entering," called an officer as he opened a door in the far right corner of the room.

The twelve jurors and four alternates filed in hesitantly, took their seats and focused on the judge as though afraid to look anywhere else. They were a mix of young and old, male and female, all with the solid bearing of the hard-working middle class. There were no Asians or hispanics or blacks in the group, but if Phyllis's attitudes were representative of the community, then the two Mediterranean types and the red-headed woman probably counted as minorities. It was just like Cyril, Kansas. And not so long ago he probably wouldn't even have noticed.

"Good morning, ladies and gentlemen."

The jury murmured a response, like a class to a teacher.

The judge surveyed the courtroom for several silent moments, cleared his throat loudly, then swiveled toward the jurybox. He rested his forearms on the bench, clasped his hands together and softened into paternal benevolence as he beheld the assembled jurors.

"We come together in this courtroom today to embark on a very serious undertaking . . . Justice. You, the members of the jury, are here to perform a duty which is sacred to our nation. The duty of the jurist. This duty lies at the heart of our justice system and it is people like you who keep that system vital."

Pulaski cleared his throat again and thrust his chin forward. His gaze never wavered from the sixteen rapt faces before him.

"Beginning today you will be asked to weigh the case against Lenore Serian. But before you set about such a serious task you must first understand that this woman, Lenore Serian, is innocent. I want you to look at her right now and say to yourselves—this woman is innocent. It is the burden of the prosecution to prove otherwise . . . to prove to you that she is guilty as charged and to prove that to you beyond a reasonable doubt."

The judge shifted his attention to Prosecutors Brown and Dapolito, and his expression turned to heavy-browed scrutiny.

"You will now hear Mr. Brown's opening statement. Opening statements are not part of the evidence and are not to be accepted as such. They are simply promises . . . previews of what each side hopes to show you. Your reaction to whatever Mr. Brown says must be, 'Prove it.' "

Silence hung in the courtroom.

Brown leaned over to whisper to Dapolito. His body language conveyed annoyance at the judge's speech.

"Mr. Brown," the judge said sharply, "shall we begin?"

Every eye in the room focused on Spencer Brown. He stood. The cocky insolence of his posture made Owen think of a high school football captain, and Owen wondered how the judge could remain neutral to the personalities in his court.

There was a brief period of fumbling as the podium against the wall was dragged out and positioned, and the microphone was tested. Finally, Spencer Brown, first assistant district attorney, tapped the microphone, settled his notes into place and scanned the room.

"Mr. Brown," the judge said impatiently, "I believe you have our attention." It occurred to Owen that maybe the judge wasn't so neutral after all.

"Thank you, your honor," Brown replied. "Ladies and gentlemen . . . six months ago, on August seventh . . . a life was taken—the life of Bram Serian, husband, neighbor, community member and well-known artist. His death was mourned around the world, and the shock of that death was so great that at first no one stopped to question whether it was accidental or not. Everyone assumed that this terrible tragedy had to be accidental.

"An old wooden building suddenly going up in flames is a regrettably common occurrence in our rural area. Only later did an autopsy provide us with the horrible revelation that Bram Serian's skull was deeply fractured and that Bram Serian was already dead when that fatal match was struck. Only then, ladies and gentlemen, did the ugly truth surface. Bram Serian was murdered. And the person with the *motive*, the *means*, and the *opportunity* to carry out that crime is seated right here in this courtroom today . . . Lenore Serian."

As Brown said the defendant's name, he swung around to point an accusing finger at her, directing every juror to stare. Owen thought he saw the woman flinch, but then she squared her shoulders and raised her chin defiantly.

Spencer Brown turned back toward the jury, puffed up with confidence and righteous indignation. "Lenore Serian cold-bloodedly planned the murder of her husband, waited for the perfect opportunity and then carried out her plan. No one witness can come forward and prove her guilt, and no one piece of evidence can prove it, but we can piece together a puzzle that reveals Lenore Serian absolutely and conclusively as the murderer of her husband."

From there Brown launched into an overview of the Serian marriage. He talked about how they were together for thirteen years and how they had a comfortable life, owning not only the big house but also a loft in the SoHo area of New York City. As Brown settled in at the podium, his words took on a singsong quality that was almost lulling.

"Witnesses will testify that Bram Serian was older than his wife. She was a Vietnamese War refugee and penniless when Bram Serian took her into his home and into his heart. Bram Serian was the kind of man who put his money where his mouth was. He felt a deep obligation to help people who had been hurt by the war, and that was what led him to this woman in the first place. But Lenore Serian was not satisfied by this great man's love and generosity. She was not satisfied by her husband's continued patience and understanding and loyalty through the years.

"Bram Serian's artwork had become very valuable and earned him a place in society and the benefits of a high income and leisure time. Most wives would have been happy with this, but testimony will show that Lenore Serian was not happy. She wanted her husband all to herself. She was insanely jealous. She even resented her husband's meetings with his long-time art dealer. She refused to go out in public with him or attend his art shows or any of the other functions where his presence was in such demand, and she tried to manipulate him and prevent his attending these important functions. She wanted to keep him secluded with her on their estate, and though she allowed him to have guests frequently, she never joined in the entertaining of those guests. She never relaxed and had fun. She hovered about, watching her husband like a hawk, and she made everyone around her feel uncomfortable and unwelcome."

Brown drew a deep breath and paused to look at the defendant. Owen wondered what she was thinking.

"The truth is, ladies and gentlemen, that Bram Serian was faced with the temptations that many famous men face. He was besieged by beautiful women wherever he went, and perhaps some of his wife's bizarre jealousy was caused by this. But that does not excuse Lenore Serian's actions.

"It is also true that Lenore Serian had not had an easy life, and by all indications she was incapable of the kind of relationship a good marriage demands. Witnesses will tell us that she was incapable of love. Incapable even of friendship! But this does not excuse her from her actions. She was and is a mature, sane individual who completely understands the difference between right and wrong."

Owen paused in his note taking to watch Brown again. He was repeating his thoughts. Covering and recovering the same ground. Talking about Serian's relationship with his wife and then hammering on the subject of an impending divorce. As he strayed from the exact wording of his prepared scripts, he embroidered on his sentences and twisted them this way and that in confusing convolutions.

Suddenly Brown shifted position, looked down at his notes and boomed out, "What did this mean to Lenore Serian? It meant that she was losing her hold over her husband. And that she stood to lose everything! Everything!

"There were vicious fights within the hearing of Natalie Raven, the housekeeper. Lenore Serian was overheard screaming, 'I won't let you do it!'

"It was in this frame of mind that the accused rode into town with Natalie Raven and went by herself to the hardware store and, as the store owner will testify, bought a glass oil lamp and two jars of lamp oil for her husband's studio.

"Bram Serian had converted an old barn on his property into his art studio. This studio was his private place and no one was ever allowed inside.

"The Serians' housekeeper of four years will testify that Bram Serian did his own cleaning and furnishing of that studio and would never have requested that she or Lenore purchase something for it. Furthermore he was always worried about possible damage to his paintings and had in the past refused candles for the studio because he said the small amount of smoke could ruin a painting.

"We will hear evidence that Serian was afraid of fire and worried about the flammable nature of some of his work materials. He had quit smoking in the year before his death, partly as a health measure and partly because he was concerned even about a lit cigarette around his work. When he was building the studio, he rejected the idea of a wood-burning stove and went to great lengths to install an electric stove with the appearance of a fire in it but no real flames at all."

Brown threw out his arms. "Is this a man who would suddenly want an oil lamp for his studio!"

The prosecutor paused to let his contemptuous disbelief sink in.

"But Lenore Serian liked fire. We will hear evidence that this woman was fascinated by fire. That she was constantly burning things and lighting the fireplaces and kept candles going in the house day and night."

He shuffled his notes.

"Now to the events directly leading up to this heinous crime. On the day before the murder, Bram Serian invited twenty-two people up from Manhattan to enjoy a weekend in the country. He was known for his hospitality, and many people in the art world had been his guests over the years. In addition to having fun, Serian expected his guests to contribute labor to his famous house.

"The group worked until mid-afternoon, after which there was swimming in a pond and a general good time. They had a cookout for dinner and finished up about eight o'clock; then some went out to try night fishing and some settled in to drink beer and listen to music. Serian was in good spirits. Everyone was talking about his scheduled art show. As the evening wore on, the crowd gathered together outside in lighthearted camaraderie.

"Lenore Serian had not joined in the festivities or engaged in even the most rudimentary polite conversations with any of the guests. She kept herself on the fringes, and the only time her voice was heard all night was when she was shouting at her husband.

"Serian announced to his guests that he was going to bed and suggested that others do the same since it was after two in the morning. There were guest rooms on the main floor, and there was a dormitorylike arrangement for guests in the basement. The housekeeper's room was on the second floor and she had already gone to bed.

"At two-forty-five A.M., a loud argument took place between Lenore and Bram Serian out in the yard near the door to his studio, and this argument awakened the housekeeper. The housekeeper looked out her window and observed the end of this argument, then watched Bram Serian unlock his studio, enter it and shut the door. She assumed he was spending the night there as this was a common habit of his.

"Within the next hour Bram Serian's skull was bashed in. He had been drinking and was very tired . . . most likely sound asleep when the fatal blow was struck. It doesn't take much strength to strike a fatal blow downward against a human skull. Gravity is on the side of the attacker, and even a small person could swing a heavy object downward. An axe head was found on the floor near the body, and an axe would have made the perfect weapon. One downward swing would have disabled or killed the victim.

"Then, in a diabolical plot to make the murder appear accidental, Bram Serian was doused with lamp oil. The glass lamp that Lenore Serian had purchased just weeks before was smashed next to him. And the fire was lit. The killer struck a flame and Bram was engulfed in fire. The beauty of this plan, from the killer's point of view, was that it didn't matter if Bram was dead or alive when the fire started because either way the killer believed it would be accepted as an accident.

"The swiftness and intensity of the fire must have surprised the murderer into making a few mistakes then. The key was left in the door. Several paintings were carried out of the building but then abandoned in the trees.

"At four-fifteen the housekeeper awakened again. She looked out the window and saw flames coming out of the studio. Lenore Serian was standing in the yard, watching the fire spread. The housekeeper leaned out her window and shouted at Lenore, and only then did Lenore Serian scream 'fire' and call for help.

"It was the housekeeper, Natalie Raven, who phoned the fire department, and it was the housekeeper who woke the guests and organized them into a bucket brigade. It was the housekeeper who searched the house and grounds in the hope that Bram Serian was not inside that burning building.

What did Lenore Serian do? She stood on the sidelines watching.

"A witness will testify that the studio door was open, when Bram Serian never left the door open and unlocked. We will hear testimony that a single key was in the lock on the door, when Bram kept his keys on a large ring.

"The killer left that door open. The killer used a copied key and then forgot to remove it from the door. The killer moved those paintings out to save them from the fire. The evidence will show that that is the only reasonable explanation. And the evidence will also show that the only person with the *means*, the *motive*, and the *opportunity* to enter that studio and brutally bludgeon Bram Serian to death, pour kerosene over him and strike a match was Lenore Serian, a woman who wanted to control her husband and keep her home at any cost.

"Thank you."

Spencer Brown turned and strode to his seat with the righteous air of a crusader.

As soon as he sat down, the room erupted into noise and motion. Radio reporters hurried out of the room to call their stations.

"Quiet!" an officer shouted.

The judge faced the jury. "Thank you for your attention during this long session, ladies and gentlemen. Once we have progressed past the opening addresses, you will not be expected to sit so long without a break." He cleared his throat, and his mouth curved into a tightly controlled smile. "We will now dismiss for lunch. Should you have any questions about your lunch plans, you may ask the court officer who accompanies you into the jury room."

He cleared his throat again and assumed an air of Lincolnesque sternness. "You must not discuss this case," he admonished them, detailing the rules, and ending with a reminder that they were not to read about the case or listen to news reports on television. Owen thought about how hard it would be to sit in that jury box all day and keep from discussing it with family and friends every evening.

The crowd was ordered to remain seated while the jurors left the room. As soon as the two silent lines of people were ushered out, everyone jumped up.

"Clear the courtroom, please. Clear the courtroom!"

He held back to give Phyllis and her newfound friend a

head start. The room emptied fast. When he finally stepped out of the pew, he was among the last to leave. He pulled the door open wide and stepped back so the person directly behind him could exit first. "Thank you," she said, pausing so that they ended up walking side by side.

"On assignment?" she asked.

He looked around. "Are you talking to me?"

"Yes. I asked if you were on assignment here."

She had a bright, fresh face, fluffy dark blond hair and well-defined breasts beneath a fitted jacket. New York seemed to be full of attractive women.

"I'm not sure I understand the question."

"Sorry." She smiled. "I'm so nosy. I was behind you at security this morning, and I heard you say you were researching a book."

Her smile was a hundred-watt dazzler filled with perfect white teeth, and though he couldn't possibly know her, she seemed vaguely familiar.

"Have we crossed paths before somewhere?" he asked.

She stopped at the head of the stairs, flashed another smile and drew herself into a professional pose. "This is Holly Danielson at the Black Widow trial."

The line meant nothing to him, and his expression must have revealed that because the professional pose disintegrated. "You know . . ."—she gave a tiny shrug—"Metro Eye at Five. Or as we sometimes say, Jive at Five."

"A television reporter?"

"Maybe I look different off-camera, huh?"

"Actually, I'm not from New York . . . and even if I was . . . I don't usually watch television news. But . . ." he added quickly, "I did flip through the channels last night so I probably have caught a glimpse of you."

"Oh . . ." She recovered her smile. "I'm here to cover the trial. What about you? Are you working on contract or freelance or what?"

"A little of each," he admitted, starting down the wide stairway to the quiet of the lunchtime courthouse lobby.

"That sounds very mysterious," she said, falling into step beside him again.

Her probing made him smile. "There's no mystery, just uncertainty."

"But you are a writer?"

"Marginally."

"Specializing in trials?"

"Hardly. This one is my first."

"Don't worry. You'll pick it up fast. After I'd done two, I felt like I could practice law."

"Do you report on other things besides trials?"

"Sure. Anything I can get. But this Serian thing is a big break for me. Lots of exposure."

As they passed through security, he considered what would make a person want to stand in front of a television camera and talk to an invisible audience. He couldn't imagine it himself.

"So . . . you might possibly be doing a book? Right? Mr. . . . ?"

"Byrne. Owen Byrne."

Her eyes widened. "That's an Irish name! I thought you looked Irish."

"I do?"

"Sure. You've got the hair and the eyes. I never saw so many great blue eyes as when I was in Ireland. Just like yours."

He stopped and glanced around self-consciously. "Excuse me . . . but I really have to go."

"Ahhhh . . . I embarrassed you, didn't I? I guess I'm too used to being around other reporters. We kid each other all the time."

Owen was flattered by her attention but extremely uncomfortable. He shifted his bag to the other hand. "I'll look for you on television tonight," he said as he turned and headed toward the door.

"Wait, where are you going?"

"To find some lunch."

"Follow me, then. I'll introduce you to some news types."

"Thanks anyway, but I think I'll just—"

"I'm doing you a favor," she insisted. "If you want to pick up trial talk and make some good contacts, this is the way. Believe me."

On the walk to Main Street, Owen heard all about Holly Danielson. How she was from Southern California. And how she had been a communications major in college and worked at a small station in Los Angeles before finally landing the New York job. And how she had had her teeth fixed by the same dentist who did the movie stars. And how she never had been elected cheerleader in high school but that didn't matter anymore.

She asked about his background and he admitted to being raised in the Midwest, before diverting her attention back to her own history. Luckily, she was easy to divert. He didn't relax, though, until they arrived at the coffee shop and he was saved from further questioning.

The place had red leatherette booths and a curving, chrome-edged lunch counter that could have been airlifted straight out of a small town in his home state. The lunch rush was in full swing, and the room was jammed with people, most of whom Holly seemed to know. She led him through the noise and the drifting layers of cigarette smoke to a table near the back and introduced him to Ray from the *News* and Sharon from a news-radio station and Marilyn who wrote a column for a paper whose name Owen didn't catch. Holly slid into the booth and an extra chair was dragged up for Owen. The center of the table was occupied by three overflowing ashtrays.

"You're a writer, huh?" Ray asked. He was round and soft with a wattle beneath his chin that moved when he spoke.

"I'm working on it," Owen admitted.

"You book jockeys get all the breaks. All the glory and the big bucks. One of these days I'm going to write a book. As soon as I get a little extra time."

Owen nodded.

Ray lit a cigarette with Marilyn's lighter and gave a knowing smirk. "You think I'm an asshole, right?"

Owen hunkered down in his seat and wondered how to respond, but then Ray chuckled and added, " 'Cause you know I'll never sell a book without a good agent, right?"

Owen hesitated, but before he could answer the group moved right into a discussion of the trial as though their only real interest was the murder. That was fine with Owen. He relaxed and enjoyed the rapidfire exchange.

"We found out that Rossner not only hired a jury psychologist, he had a professional polling outfit do a survey of some kind."

"You're kidding!"

"Rossner is such a scheming sleazebag."

"That's why she hired him, dear."

"Do you think all that made any difference in the jury selection?"

"Nah. Not in the long run."

"What do you mean? Of course it made a difference. The psychologist was telling him which jurors to go with. That had to alter the pattern of selection."

"Sure. But I don't think *anyone* can really predict who's going to be a friendly juror and who isn't. Even the old rules about liberals and blacks being better for the defense aren't true anymore. Hell, there aren't any rules today."

"Speaking of blacks, do you think Rossner is hurting himself by bringing a black assistant into this courtroom?"

"Good question."

"It could'a been worse," Marilyn said. "He could of brought a black woman."

Everyone laughed at the comment from Marilyn, whose own complexion was the color of coffee with cream. Owen wondered if she was considered black. He had seen so many shades of skin in the past few days that he was becoming confused about where the lines were drawn between categories.

The food arrived but did not slow them down.

"He's grandstanding, I tell you. Probably found a black guy just to get attention. Probably hopes it will cause trouble."

"I don't think so. I think Jacowitz has been with him for awhile."

"Never mind that, what about Brown's opening? What did you think?"

"It was technically good. But the guy's kind of a drone, isn't he."

"Such a shame. You'd think a hunk like that would be able to put some oompf in his delivery."

Ray rolled his eyes and the women laughed.

"The big question is whether Brown put all his cards on the table or whether he's saving surprises for later."

"I'll lay you odds that's what Rossner will do. He'll say just enough to get his opening points across, but as sneaky as he is . . . you can bet he'll keep something hidden up his sleeve."

"Okay . . . Okay . . . Let's talk motive here. I believe she murdered her husband. She did it. No question in my mind. And she planned it all in advance, thinking she could use the oil lamp to make it look accidental and using the party as a kind of camouflage. She was crafty and cold-blooded and completely in control. I agree totally with the prosecution on all that. But, I don't see the possessiveness motive. I think it was strictly money."

"No! It can't be just money."

"Why? Money is one of the top three motives for any crime, isn't it?"

"Sure. And she married him for his money . . . and his name and position and all. I mean she had to have, didn't she? She was a refugee with nothing so naturally she latched on to him as her golden goose."

"Okay, but what did she gain by killing him? The goose is no longer alive to crank out the golden eggs. All but a few of his new paintings burned in the fire. There's no life insurance and there's no cash or bonds or stocks or anything. And the famous house is unfinished, probably unsalable and reportedly in debt. So how could the motive be money? Possessiveness makes complete sense."

"Wasn't there fire insurance?"

"If she can collect on that—which she won't if they prove she set the fire."

"So maybe there's money stashed somewhere that no one knows about."

"Yeah. Down on those islands where the drug dealers hide their money."

"Or maybe things just went wrong? Maybe she thought she could get all the paintings out before the barn burned. Maybe she thought there would be no questions from the fire insurance company. Who knows . . . maybe she thought hubby had life insurance."

"But you were just saying how crafty she was. If she was so crafty she wouldn't have made all those mistakes."

"Oh hell, I don't know. But she could have left him any time, divorced him with a generous settlement after all those years of marriage. Why take the risk of murder? I like the possessiveness angle."

"Which makes it into a crime of passion, right?"

"Passion? I doubt it. That woman has the coldest eyes I've ever seen. I don't think she has feelings at all. Not passion. Not love. Not even like. Just look at the turnout today. Not one friend or family member to support her."

"Really?"

"That's what the court officers said."

Owen was completely engrossed in the dialogue when,

without any signal that he could see, they all stood. According to the wall clock they had been at the table together exactly thirty-seven minutes. He followed them to the cash register, where they methodically divided the tab. Then Sharon and Marilyn hurried away to find phones, leaving Ray, Holly and Owen to walk back to the courthouse together.

The fog had lifted, and the afternoon sky was a wash of weak sunlight. He followed Holly out of the restaurant with bits of their conversation rebounding in his thoughts. The part about Lenore Serian's eyes bothered him. They were not cold eyes. If anything they were too intense. Too hot.

"Have you got all this legal palaver figured out, Byrne?" Ray asked. He was walking on one side of Owen and Holly was on the other.

"Not yet," Owen admitted.

"Go ahead," Ray said expansively. "There's no meter running. Hit me with a question. Ask me anything."

Owen asked about the hearings that had been held before the trial and got a nonstop lecture on how the pretrial hearings were used to establish the ground rules for the jury trial and how the hearings dealt with things like suppression of evidence and illegally obtained statements, and how all the hearings were named after the original cases that had set the precedents and how damn long they could take and how boring they were. Ray didn't stop until they were in sight of the courthouse. He lit a cigarette. "If you want to know more you can check with the judge's clerk and find out about getting a list of the particular hearings they held for this trial."

"I've got all the notes on the pretrial," Holly told Owen quietly. "I'll make copies."

Ray glanced at her with raised eyebrows. "The pretrial phase is like watching batting practice. There's no jury, no crowd and no drama . . . It's just the judge and the lawyers all trying to out-jargon each other with the most incredible legal diarrhea. Only the dedicated go. Like our Holly here. And she usually doesn't share her notes."

"He's not a reporter," Holly protested.

"This is true." Ray turned to Owen as though confiding a secret. "Other reporters share information. But not Holly. You're lucky you're not a reporter."

"Ray!"

"What? I'm just telling the guy how lucky he is." Ray

drew in a last lungful of smoke and then flicked the cigarette into the gutter. "What are you frowning at?" he demanded of Owen. "You don't like hearing you're lucky?"

"No . . . no. I don't like seeing people throw trash around."

"What?" Ray looked down with a pained expression. "Jesus Christ! What d'ya think they invented street sweepers for?"

"You don't throw trash around at home, do you?" Owen asked.

"Hell yes! What d'ya think they invented wives and mothers for?" Ray slapped his thigh and erupted into braying laughter.

Holly reached over and touched Owen's sleeve in a plea for him to let it drop.

"Okay, okay," Ray said. "Let's see . . . where was I? Oh, yeah . . . I was just getting to jury selection." He shook another cigarette out and held it between his fingers. "Jury selection is a little more fun. They start out with a pool of prospective jurors."

"A huge pool for the Serian trial," Holly added. "They were being cautious because of all the publicity. They were afraid they would have to excuse large numbers for being prejudiced by what they'd already heard."

Ray lit up before continuing. "First, they whittle the group down with generalities. Problems or obligations that would make it a hardship to serve on a jury. Personal connections to principles in the case. And so forth. Then they pick a random panel of twelve, put them in the jury box, and let the lawyers zero in on individuals. It's called *Voir Dire,* which means 'truth telling' in French. And I hear that Rossner and Brown turned it into a pretty good show."

"I have it all, Owen." Holly skirted a puddle of melting slush to protect her suede pumps. "Bio sheets on the jurors too. You're welcome to copy it."

"My, my, Holly . . . aren't we generous."

"He's not any kind of competition."

"How do you know? He could be a tabloid spy or an undercover stringer for the Brits or—"

"Oh, shut up, Ray."

Ray shut up.

"I don't want to impose on anybody," Owen said half-heartedly. The truth was that he very much wanted to see Holly's notes.

"You are not imposing," Holly insisted. "Ray's just running his mouth off. If you do use the material, it will be for a book, months from now, so there is no conflict." She glared at Ray and he tucked his chin down into his coat like a turtle seeking escape.

Holly's hair shone with golden glints in the sunlight, and her cheeks were flushed with the cold. She had a generic, apple-pie prettiness that reminded Owen of old movies and fifties' beauty contestants.

"So why were you sitting in the peanut gallery?" Holly asked him. "Why aren't you in the press section?"

"I'm not a member of the press," Owen said.

"What do you mean? You're a writer. You qualify. I'll give you the number to call to get a press pass. And in the meantime, you can sit with me. I'll get you in on my tech pass."

"You might as well," Ray said. "There's room and you're entitled." Owen could tell that Ray's sudden solicitousness was designed to please Holly.

"Great. Thank you. Will the crowd be as large after lunch as it was this morning?"

"Definitely." Holly grinned. "And it's a good thing I invited you to sit with me because you're too late to get into the spectators' pews."

"You mean I wouldn't get my same seat back?"

"No. People have to wait in line and fight their way in all over again. Only the media has places saved for them."

"Then, thanks again."

"Any time." Holly smiled and Ray feebly followed suit.

As they went up the courthouse steps, Holly reached around Owen to poke Ray. "I can't wait to hear Rossner's spiel, can you? Mister Slick himself. I feel like I'm about to see Gunther Gabel-Williams tame lions."

"Or Michael Milken sell junk bonds," Ray snorted. He fished in his pocket for another cigarette. "See you inside, kiddies. I need more poison before I go in."

Owen held one of the oversized doors open for Holly. "Rossner can't have anything too surprising to say, can he? Aren't all the facts common knowledge at this point?"

"Just wait," she assured him. "He'll twist things around

so much that by the time he's finished you won't know black from white or up from down."

"I doubt that he can sway me too much. Brown's accusations were all very logical and believable."

"We'll see," she said, "we'll see."

"Ladies and gentlemen of the jury, I'm Charlie Rossner, defense counsel for Lenore Serian." Rossner stood to the side of the podium, one elbow resting on it. Brown had been formal, self-righteous, authoritative. Rossner was casual—the gentlemanly neighbor over for a chat.

"I've come up to your proud, historical county courthouse to fight for justice, just as all of you good citizens on the jury are fighting for justice. But I've got to tell you right now"—Rossner scratched his earlobe and looked at the jury with a puzzled expression—"I'm wondering why we're all here." He turned toward Lenore, and the puzzlement mingled with sympathy and a touch of incredulity. "This woman shouldn't be in a courtroom defending her life against a murder charge. What murder? The evidence will show that nobody is certain there's even been a murder.

"Bram Serian died and there was a terrible fire. Yes. But the evidence will show that Bram Serian was drunk when he went out to his studio that night, stumbling, falling-down drunk. And though he had been trying to quit smoking, he could not break the habit."

Rossner paused to let this sink in.

"Stumbling drunk and smoking at three A.M. in an old wooden building full of flammable materials and a breakable oil lamp! This is not the prescription for a carefully planned murder, it's the prescription for a tragic accident."

The attorney settled at the podium again, relaxed and genial. He hitched up his trousers and looked from one juror to the next with a we're-all-in-this-together expression.

"Let's face it . . . Lenore and Bram Serian did not have a storybook marriage. But few couples do. If we could all see behind our neighbors' bedroom doors, how many perfect marriages would we find? Not many, I'm afraid. The difference here is that the Serians are public figures so the warts in their marriage get magnified and held up to the light."

Rossner punctuated this by lifting both hands in the air. Owen was impressed. Rossner projected the image of the down-to-earth, ethical, idealistic lawyer he had read about and admired when he was young.

"Lenore may have been a bad hostess and she may have nagged her husband some and she may have gotten a little jealous now and then. Those are not criminal acts. Bram Serian had his faults too. Like all talented people he had a lot of quirks and he wasn't always easy to live with.

"But the fact is that the Serians had managed to make a life together for thirteen years and the evidence will show that neither of them intended to break up that relationship they'd struggled to build. Regardless of what happened in their chaotic lives, this couple held together. They had something that bound them, and neither wanted a life without the other. They were a devoted couple. A solid couple.

"As to this business about the oil lamp . . . we'll hear how common those lamps are and how many wives buy them for their husbands and how many people use them out in workshops and tool sheds. That oil lamp was intended for exactly what most folks use it for—a light for a stormy night when the power goes out. And the evidence will show that Bram Serian's studio was already so full of flammable material that an accidental fire could have been started at any time without the addition of an oil lamp.

"If she was planning something diabolical, she could have used what he had on hand without drawing attention to herself. Being an artist's wife, she knew he'd have paint thinner and all manner of dangerous chemicals out there.

"And then, once we've wound our way through all that nonsense, we'll hear about the night of the fire. We'll hear about how many people were up wandering around near the studio before the fire started. Other people with as much opportunity to set a fire, if indeed there was a fire set by a hand other than Bram Serian's.

"We'll hear about accidents that happen to people who smoke and drink beyond the limits of common sense. And finally we'll hear from a doctor who will tell us that Lenore Serian's hands and arms were severely burned while trying to fight her way into that fire and save her husband . . . a heroic rescue attempt that not one other person tried. Not the devoted housekeeper. Not one of Bram Serian's twenty-two guests. Not the trained firefighters who responded so courageously to this emergency.

"And we'll hear that the reason she didn't raise an

alarm ... the reason she stood in that yard like a stone watching the fire destroy her life while everyone else yelled and carried on ... the reason was that Lenore was beaten and exhausted and in a state of shock."

He drew himself up, eyes blazing with the injustice of the situation.

"We'll hear, ladies and gentlemen, that Lenore is innocent ... as much a victim of this tragedy as her beloved husband, and that there is no blame to assign here. I say to you that the evidence does not support a crime at all. That, indeed, the only crime committed is the crime of charging Lenore Serian and bringing her before this court."

Rossner sat down. The courtroom was absolutely quiet.

Owen glanced sideways at Holly, and she grinned at him with a knowing "I told you so" expression.

Later that night, after Owen had commuted back to the city and typed up his notes, he went down to a corner pay phone to call home. Ellen answered.

"You really shouldn't call," she warned him. "You don't have the money for long distance."

"I have to know what's going on, Ellen."

"Well ... I guess I can talk. Daddy's asleep in his chair, and Meggie's out visiting Rusty at the bunkhouse."

"Is Rusty working out? Is he doing a good job?"

"He's doing exactly what you told him to and he does everything pretty much like you do it." She snorted sarcastically. "But you'd think we had John Wayne visiting. Meggie and Daddy act like the guy hung the moon. Daddy even let him win at dominoes."

"Has he found any more aborted calves?"

"No. The vet says we may have come to the end of it." She hesitated. "Rusty's been talking up artificial breeding. Telling Daddy about how you don't have the headache of keeping bulls and you don't have to worry about venereal diseases spreading when you pop the old frozen sperm to the cows."

"Clancy isn't listening to Rusty, is he?"

"Yeah, he is. He sat down with Rusty after supper to look at an A.I. catalog. They were writing down semen prices on certain bulls and all kinds of stuff."

"That's crazy. Artificial insemination isn't cost-effective when you're raising calves to go to the feedlot."

"Well ... that's the other thing. Rusty's been talking up the benefits of switching to a registered operation. He says it's the perfect time to do it since so many cows have to be replaced anyway."

Owen was too dumbfounded to respond.

"Daddy hasn't said yes or anything," Ellen assured him. "But he hasn't said no either."

"I can't believe it. A few years ago, when he had the money for a change and I mentioned the possibility of a registered herd, he went through the roof."

"I know," Ellen agreed.

"How does Rusty Campbell suggest that we pay for purebred mama cows and an A.I. program?"

"That hasn't come up yet."

"You or Meggie should explain to him that we're broke before he puts any more ideas into Clancy's head."

Ellen then launched into a bitter monologue, saying that she couldn't explain anything to Rusty because Meggie monopolized him completely, saying that nothing was the same with Owen gone, saying that she wasn't going to keep on cooking and cleaning for people who treated her like a cur dog.

Owen tried to soothe her. When he had calmed her down, he asked about Michelle Wheeler.

"Haven't seen or heard from her," Ellen said.

"Would you give her a call ... make sure everything's okay ... please?"

"I'll try," Ellen said. "Gotta go. Daddy's awake."

The line went dead in his ear. He hung up and stood there on the noisy avenue for several minutes, staring at nothing. When he returned to his building and started up the stairs, he walked slowly, carrying a weight of guilt and worry with him.

4

On Wednesday, day two of the trial, Owen entered the court-house with somewhat more confidence and went quickly up the crowded stairs into the crush surrounding courtroom 6. The line of spectators shifted impatiently behind the velvet ropes. Reporters stood in clusters, checking notebooks and bolting down the last of their takeout coffees before going inside.

At the double doors, he flashed his brand-new press ID and was waved through, past the front of the spectators' line and the crocheting women. He saw Phyllis and ducked his head as he sailed past her through the double doors. Inside there was a librarylike atmosphere of hushed activity. The press section was sparsely occupied, but all the major play-ers were in place, the judge and his minions, the defense and the prosecution, and most of the court officers.

He saw Holly up front and hesitated, wondering whether to say hello or to quietly slip into a rear seat, but she caught sight of him and motioned him forward.

"Sit here," she instructed, sliding over so he could have the aisle position. He stowed his bag under the pew and looked around. It was a spectacular seat. Directly ahead of him were Brown and Dapolito. To his right was an unob-structed view of the jury box. To his left was the defense ta-ble.

He was close enough to see details. The damp half-circles under the arms of Spencer Brown's suit jacket and the thin-ning spot on the crown of Charlie Rossner's head. The lac-quered combs that held Lenore Serian's hair and the slender line of her shoulders beneath the bulky sweater. If only she would turn around. He stared at her back, willing her to turn around. Or at least to turn toward Rossner so he could see part of her face.

"Checking out the star attraction?" Holly asked.

"Trying to."

"She's not so hot. I can't understand all this hype about her being a sex goddess."

Dapolito scratched his neck furiously, Brown hummed the air force anthem under his breath, and Rossner read a stream of papers being passed to him by his assistant.

Owen leaned toward Holly to whisper, "This is strange being up here so close to them all. Like we're intruding."

"You'll get used to it."

"We could actually speak to them from here."

"Don't. Judge Pulaski wouldn't like it."

He glanced back at the reporters filing into the rows behind him. "I should sit farther back. I have no right be up here."

"Forget it," Holly said. "You're with me and this is my spot. The only reason we didn't sit here after lunch yesterday was because that snotty French magazine crew took over the entire row for the afternoon."

"Are the seats assigned?"

"No. But the regulars all have our territories staked out." She turned her head to include a woman sitting on her other side. "Right, Pat? We all have our territories, don't we?"

"Just like hyenas." The woman chuckled and leaned across Holly to extend a hand studded with silver and turquoise. "I'm Pat Melville," she said. "Patricia Velez Melville. You must be the writer Holly was telling me about this morning."

"Owen Byrne," he said, returning her firm handshake and thinking that shaking hands with women was beginning to seem normal.

"Pat is a reporter for the regional paper and a stringer for Associated Press." Holly winked at him. "She's a fountain of information on this area if you need any questions answered."

"So you're a local?" he asked.

Pat laughed. "Depends on who you ask. I've lived here nine years. Buried my husband in the cemetery here. But I'm still referred to as that Mexican woman from Arizona."

From somewhere in the room a loud disembodied voice asked, "Would you describe Lenore's sweater as rust or russet?"

"Russet always reminds me of potatoes," someone answered.

"Keep it down, people!" warned a court officer.

"Did you hear whether the judge ruled yet on the Nellicliffs' testimony?" Pat whispered.

"He hasn't reached a decision yet," Holly replied.

"But aren't they testifying today?"

"Supposedly."

A man behind Pat tapped her shoulder, and she turned for a whispered conference with him. Holly leaned away from Pat and bent her head close to Owen's. "So, are you doing a book on this or not?"

"It's not my decision," he admitted. "I have to put together a proposal that the publisher likes."

"Wow, big pressure, huh?"

"Yes."

"But you're having fun too, aren't you?" Holly grinned. "I mean murder is so hard to resist."

A bang echoed from the back corner of the room. Heads swiveled to look, and he automatically followed them. A pair of sound technicians were wrestling with some fallen wires and trying to position a camera. Television was not allowed, but there was to be a brief period of filming later for a documentary on the New York justice system. He watched for a moment, then turned back around. Everyone in the front was riveted to the diversion. The judge had lifted his eyes from a sheaf of papers and was regarding the activity with a ruminant frown. Court officers, court clerk and court reporter were all transfixed. Dapolito and Brown stared over their shoulders. Rossner had shifted his chair around. And Lenore . . . Slowly, Lenore Serian turned.

Her gaze brushed right past him. So near that he could have caught her attention with the slightest movement. He held very still. Watching her as he would have watched some rare creature glimpsed in the wild. And he saw that she was neither the fierce siren of the newspaper photograph nor the vulnerable child-woman of yesterday. She was strong and poised and possessed of an austere elegance.

Suddenly the doors were thrown open to spectators, and Lenore snapped back around to face the front. He resumed breathing. Court was called to order, and the jury was ushered in by twos. They were more relaxed today, scanning the room as they took their seats. A few stole curious glances at the accused before giving their attention to the judge's morning comments.

"Juror number seven looks hung over," Holly whispered.

Before Owen could count seats and find number seven, Pat leaned in with, "I found out number three does oil paintings of people's pets."

"No!" Holly flipped through her notebook. "I thought three was the one with the beauty shop in her garage."

Pat shook her head. "You're confusing her with ten. Remember in *Voir Dire* . . ."

Owen listened and scribbled notes, amazed at how much more he understood today than yesterday. He could follow the conversation as the two women skipped from individual jurors to a point of jury selection to the judge's ruling that the prosecution would not be allowed to question the rescue squad witnesses about previous rescue visits to the Serians.

For Owen, the criminal process had assumed the geometric symmetry of a board game. It started with the crime, then jumped by turns to the grand jury, the arraignment, the pretrial hearings, the jury selection, the opening statements, the trial body, the closing arguments, the jury deliberations, and finally the verdict. It was a two-team game—the prosecution against the defense—and though it was the accused who stood to win or lose, she didn't appear to have much of a part in the play.

Owen flipped to a clean page in his notebook. Holly had offered to share actual transcripts of the trial with him, but he wanted to take notes regardless. He wanted his own impressions on paper and he didn't want to rely too heavily on Holly's generosity.

The court clerk stood and cleared his throat forcefully. "The people call Reggie Howland."

Witnesses were not allowed in the courtroom except while testifying, so a guard had to lean out the door and motion for the witness to enter. Howland, an angular man with a prominent Adam's apple, moved self-consciously down the aisle, through the gate in the wooden railing and up to the witness stand. He put his right hand on a worn Bible held out by the court clerk, and he raised his left hand in the air.

"Do you swear totellthewholetruthandnothingbutthetruth-sohelpyouGod." The clerk's words ran together so that they lacked both inflection and meaning.

"I do," Howland said, his ears turning a bright red.

"Please be seated."

Howland sat down in the witness box, and the court clerk

returned to his desk, opened his ledger and said, "In a loud and clear voice, please state your full name and address for the record, and please spell your last name." Both the clerk and the court reporter recorded the information as the witness recited it.

Spencer Brown bounded from his seat, suit straining across his broad shoulders as though he'd suddenly expanded.

"Good morning, Mr. Howland." Brown smiled. "Could you tell us what your occupation is and what other activities you engage in?"

"I'm a farmer and a volunteer fireman."

"How long have you been a farmer?"

"Round fifteen years."

"And how long have you been a volunteer firefighter?"

"Round four years."

"During that four years as a firefighter, have you had any special training relating to your firefighting duties?"

"Sure. We're always having meetings and training sessions with experts from all over."

"Has this training included instruction in use of the phone?"

"Some. You gotta know what to ask callers and how to calm them down and get information. That sorta thing."

"So you are experienced and well trained at taking information from people who call in to you?"

"That's part of the job."

"And what is the procedure for recording an emergency call. Do you make notes or is there a formal written procedure?"

"We have a log right by the phone. We fill in the name and address and directions to the place, and then there's a section for notes. Anything special about the directions or about what the people say like maybe if there's injuries or if the fire's spreadin' or whatever."

Dapolito handed Brown a rectangular ledger, and Brown held it up. There was an exchange in which the judge spoke to both Brown and Rossner about the ledger. After it was deemed a proper piece of evidence, it was logged in and given an identification number by the court clerk.

"Now, Mr. Howland, were you on duty the morning of August seventh?"

"Sure was. I was the one answered the phone when the Serian call came."

"Would you find that call in the log please?"

"Here it is right here."

"Would you take this red pencil and circle it please."

"You want me to circle everything or just the first bit or what, cause I don't wanna write on stuff I shouldn't."

"How about just bracketing the call."

"Huh?"

"Just make a mark where the entry begins and another mark where it ends."

"Got'cha. There. Done."

"Would you please read what you have marked within those brackets."

"Ahh ... Four-twenty-five A.M. Serian farm. Highway thirteen, five miles south of Gruber's feed store. Art studio. Possible death. House in danger. Woman reporting—Natalie Raven."

"When did you make that entry in the log?"

"I made it as I was talking to the woman."

"As she was speaking to you on the telephone?"

"Oh, maybe I finished putting a few words down after I hung up, but mainly it was while she was talking."

"Subsequent to your writing this down, what did you do?"

"Afterward, you mean?"

"Yes."

"I got the alert out to all the guys and called the rescue squad and got the truck rolling."

"So time is of the essence when you get an emergency call such as this."

"Sure."

"Are you generally able to record every word an emergency caller says?"

"No. Fraid not. Some people get pretty long-winded when they're upset."

"Was there anything the Serian caller said that you didn't have the opportunity to write down?"

"Sure. Miz Raven ... the caller ... she was screamin' and shoutin' all kinds of stuff."

"Do you recollect what she was screaming and shouting that you were not able to enter into the log?"

"Not all of it. But there were things that stuck with me. She broke down right after she gave me the directions ..."

crying for us to hurry ... saying 'She's burning it. Burning it all. I know he's dead.' Those kind of things stick in a guy's mind."

"Those were her exact words? 'She's burning it. Burning it all. I know he's dead.' "

"That's what she said all right."

"Did you act on those words in any way?"

"Sorry, I don't follow you."

"Did you take any special action because of what she said."

"I called the rescue squad because of her yelling about someone being dead, if that's what you mean."

"Thank you, Mr. Howland." Brown turned and went back to the prosecution table.

Howland rose.

Rossner rose.

The judge, who had been bent over a legal pad taking notes, pushed his glasses higher on his nose and inclined his head toward the witness. "Mr. Howland, if you would please remain seated, I believe defense counsel has some questions for you."

"Oh ... sure. Sure." With ears reddening again, Howland dropped back down into the chair and blinked hard.

Charles Rossner hesitated a moment as though lost in thought. He stood halfway between the defense table and the witness, his pants rumpled and his tie hanging slightly crooked, staring at the plastic-covered windows behind the jury. Then he rubbed his chin and turned toward the witness with a smile.

"Hello, Mr. Howland. I'm Charlie Rossner. How are you?"

"Ah ... fine. I'm fine, thanks."

"How long did you say you've been a volunteer fireman?"

"About four years."

"That's commendable. It's hard work, isn't it?"

"Oh, sure. Real hard sometimes."

"And would you say it's very high-pressure work?"

"The most high-pressure thing I ever did, for sure."

"High-pressure at the scene of a fire?"

"You bet."

"But it starts even before that, doesn't it? The minute you answer an emergency call there's pressure, isn't there?"

"Sure. The call's real important. You have to get the right

information and if the fire's out in the country you have to make sure the directions to the place are clear."

"How much of your training actually focused on taking phone calls?"

"Well, we heard a speaker and got some handouts about what to ask callers."

"Was there any simulated phone work? Where you took practice calls?"

"No."

"Were you given a specific phone procedure to use?"

"Not really."

"Have you taken many calls during your four years?"

Howland hesitated. "There's other guys who cover the phone more than me."

"Oh? So you're not usually the person who answers the phone for emergencies like the Serian call?"

"You could put it that way, but that doesn't mean I can't handle it."

Rossner paused, screwed his face into a puzzled, thoughtful expression and scratched his head.

"Let's back up. Have you answered many emergency calls in your four years?"

"A few."

"How would you describe those calls?"

"What d'ya mean?"

"Are the calls similar in any way?"

"Every fire's a different story."

"Are the calls calm and rational?"

"Sometimes. If it's a brush fire or an abandoned shed or something."

"How about when it's a home or a barn? Are those calm?"

"No."

"Is it fair to say that those calls are hysterical? Hard to understand?"

"They can be."

"Like the Serian call."

"Yeah. Like the Serian call."

"Are the callers generally frightened?"

"Yeah."

"Distraught . . . upset?"

"Usually."

"And these people who call in . . . these frightened, distraught callers . . . Do they speak clearly?"

"Mostly not."

"Do they always make sense?"

"No."

"Even for someone with experience . . . can it be hard to understand them?"

"Sure."

"For instance, when you wrote down the caller's name in the log, what did you write?"

"Natalie Raven."

Rossner smiled sympathetically. "Why don't you open the log and refresh your memory, Mr. Howland. What did you write first? The part that was blacked out and corrected later." Howland's entire face flushed scarlet. "I wrote Nellie Raymond and later somebody fixed it with the right name. There's nothin' wrong with that."

"When you were on the phone with the caller, you thought she gave her name as Nellie Raymond?"

"Yes."

"Because you couldn't understand the woman saying 'Natalie Raven,' right?"

"Right. She was talking fast and crying. But I did my job. I sent the truck where it was supposed to go."

"And because of that the Serian house was saved."

"I guess you could say that."

"And that's what's important, isn't it? Not what's said on the phone?"

"You got that right."

"You can't afford to waste a lot of valuable time listening to hysterical callers, can you?"

"No. You've got to get the outfit mobilized."

"So you don't have time to worry over whether you hear Nellie Raymond instead of Natalie Raven?"

"Right."

"Or whether the caller says he or she . . . two words that can sound alike?"

"Right."

"So the caller could have said, 'He's burning it. Burning it up. I know he's dead'?"

Howland glanced apologetically at Spencer Brown. "Yeah, I guess so."

"And you don't have time to consider what you've heard or whether you've heard something correctly, do you?"

"No."

"Okay, now after you put out the alarm what did you do?"

"I grabbed my gear and hopped a truck to go fight the fire."

"And were you the first to arrive?"

"No. Ted Waterhouse lives over that way, and he got there before us."

"Did you tell him or any of the other firefighters about the phone call?"

"No."

"You didn't discuss the call with anyone? Say you were concerned about the meaning of it?"

"No."

"So at that time whatever you thought you heard didn't sound all that ominous or suspicious?"

"Guess I didn't think about it too much then."

"You didn't think it sounded suspicious?"

"Guess not."

"When did you begin to think about it?"

"After the sheriff started asking me questions."

"How many months after the fire would that have been, Mr. Howland?"

"Oh, two maybe."

"You weren't sure of what you heard and you didn't think it sounded suspicious until two months after the fire, when the sheriff started asking questions?"

"I guess that's right."

"Thank you, Mr. Howland."

The prosecution's second witness was called. Again there were the routine preliminaries; then Brown approached the witness. Ted Waterhouse looked enough like Spencer Brown to be his younger brother.

"Good morning, Mr. Waterhouse."

"Morning, Spence."

"Would you tell us what your occupation is."

"I fix appliances . . . washers, dryers, refrigerators . . . I do it all. Even fixed that rowing machine of yours, didn't I?" He grinned proudly. "And I'm also a volunteer firefighter."

"How long have you been in the appliance repair business?"

"Since I got outta high school. Five years this June."

"And how long have you been a firefighter?"

"A year or so. Kind of felt like my name . . . Waterhouse

. . . fit the job description." He grinned and looked out over the spectators for a response to his joke.

There were chuckles throughout the courtroom. Brown's mouth stretched into a tight, mechanical smile.

"Did you respond to the Serian fire?"

"I did. I live on out that way, you know, and when I got the call I wasn't but five minutes from there."

"Had you had occasion to visit the Serian premises at any time prior to the fire call?"

"I had. I fixed the freezer some time back. And just two weeks before the fire Natalie called me out to fix the washer."

"So you were familiar with the Serian place. You knew what it looked like under normal circumstances."

"That's right."

"Were you the first respondent on the scene at the fire?"

"That's right."

"Tell us, please, what you observed upon your arrival."

"Well, I pulled into the yard and the first thing I saw was the fire. Only half of the barn, or studio I guess, was burning when I got there."

Dapolito produced a poster-sized diagram of the studio, and they went through the process of entering it into evidence. Then it was placed on an easel, and Brown asked the witness, "Which portion of the studio did you observe to be burning?"

Waterhouse indicated the end of the studio where Serian had had his living area and where the position of the body was marked with a line drawing.

"Could you see into the interior of this burning building at all?" Brown asked.

"Yes. The door was wide open and I looked in there and that whole end was a wall of flame. I knew that if somebody was in there they were past the point of needing rescue."

"So you were able to see into the interior because the door to Bram Serian's art studio was standing wide open?"

"Yes."

"What else did you observe upon your arrival?"

"I saw this whole line of people trying to do a bucket brigade, and I saw Mrs. Serian standing over near the trees."

"And did you observe what Mrs. Serian was doing?"

"She was just watching."

"When you arrived on the scene with your gear and your uniform, did she run over to you and did she—"

"Objection!" Rossner called. "Leading the witness."

"Sustained," the judge shot back immediately. "Rephrase, Mr. Brown."

With an air of tolerant annoyance, Brown asked the witness whether he had had his official firefighting paraphernalia.

"Sure. I had on my hat and coat and boots and I was carrying gear."

"So you were immediately identifiable as the first official figure who had arrived on the scene?"

"Yes."

"What was the reaction when you made yourself known to the people on the scene?"

"Some of them started shouting things like 'Thank God,' or 'Do something.' Miz Raven came running and screaming and crying, trying to drag me up to the fire. Telling me to go inside the building and rescue Bram Serian."

"And what did Mrs. Serian do?"

"Nothing. She just kept watching, real calm like."

"What occurred next?"

"I heard other trucks pulling in, and I ran out to let the fellas know what was happening."

Brown thanked the witness and sat down; then Rossner rose and ambled from the table with his hands in his pockets and an affable smile on his face. "Morning, Mr. Waterhouse. I'm Charlie Rossner."

Waterhouse leaned back and crossed his arms. "I know who you are," he said.

"Good. Good. Because I know who you are too, you're the best repairman in town aren't you?"

"That's what they say." Waterhouse shrugged and let his arms relax.

"You fixed Mr. Brown's rowing machine and you fixed the Serians' freezer, right?"

"That's right."

"And the Serians were so happy with the job you did on the freezer that they called you back to fix the washer, right?"

"Right."

Rossner smiled. "I guess famous artists have their appliances break down just like the rest of us."

"That's right." Waterhouse grinned and several members of the jury chuckled.

"When was this that you went out to work on the washer?"

"The week before the fire."

"One week before?"

"Give or take a day. I'd have to look it up to say exactly."

"That's fine. So what was wrong with Bram Serian's washing machine?"

"Outtake was clogged and it couldn't drain right on the spin cycle."

"Could you explain that for us."

Brown nonchalantly raised his arm. "Your honor . . . this line of questioning is going nowhere. Mr. Rossner is fishing."

Pulaski eyed Rossner.

"I assure you, your honor, we may be fishing in the washing machine, but we know what we're after and it is relevant."

"Overruled," Pulaski snapped. "But don't play with the court, Mr. Rossner."

Rossner inclined his head to the judge, then turned his attention back to the witness. "Continue . . . please . . ." he urged.

"There's a hose about this big around," Waterhouse used his thumb and index finger to form a circle, "that goes from the bottom of the washer tub to the pump. When the washer drains, the water has to go through that. But there was something caught in the hose so the water couldn't drain as fast as it should."

"Okay. I see what you're saying. So you had to get down in there and take out whatever was clogging up the hose."

"Right."

"What was it?"

Waterhouse looked perplexed and glanced over at Brown as though for advice.

"What was it, Mr. Waterhouse?" Rossner repeated.

"Let's see . . . I get so many of those . . ." He frowned in thought, but something about his expression made Owen suspect that the witness was stalling and that his memory was sharp. Finally he said, "A lighter. That's it. A cigarette lighter."

"Could you describe it for us."

"Well, it was real nice. Silver. With carvings. Like a fancy belt buckle. And the initial S right in the middle."

"How do you think that lighter got into the washer hose?"

"That's easy. Happens all the time. People leave stuff in their pockets and the clothes get thrown in the washer and there you go."

"What did you do with the lighter."

"I gave it to Natalie."

"Natalie Raven, the housekeeper?"

"I guess. I mean I didn't know then that she was the housekeeper but that's who I gave it to."

"What did you think her position was in the household?"

This time Brown's objection was sustained. Rossner appeared thoughtful for a second, then casually launched his questioning in a slightly different form.

"Did Natalie Raven tell you that she was something other than a housekeeper?"

Waterhouse squirmed uncomfortably. "No . . . not exactly."

"What *exactly* did she tell you?"

"It wasn't so much what she told me as how she acted."

"And how did she act?"

Brown's objection had a whining undertone that Owen found annoying, but the objection was sustained.

Rossner paused again, then dropped the line of questioning to return to the original thread. "Did Natalie Raven say anything when you gave the lighter to her?"

Waterhouse hesitated and glanced at Brown again. Brown shielded his eyes with his hand as though hiding.

"What did Natalie Raven do when you handed her the lighter?" Rossner repeated.

"She cursed and said Bram had started smoking again."

"Can you recall exactly how she said it . . . cursing and all?"

Waterhouse looked up at the judge as though for permission and the judge nodded. "She said, 'That goddamned sneaky Serian has started smoking again,' or something pretty close to that."

"That goddamned sneaky Serian has started smoking again?"

Waterhouse looked down at his hands. "Yes."

"Okay . . ." Rossner paused for several beats. "Moving on to the night of the fire . . ."

Rossner took the witness through the night of the fire again without revealing anything new; then the judge called for lunch recess.

Owen went to lunch with Holly and Pat Melville. At Pat's insistence they went to a Chinese restaurant, where the food tasted like the canned variety that Ellen sometimes served at home. He ate the daily special and listened as Pat Melville supplied local perspectives.

"Bram Serian always fit in well around here," Pat said. "Not that he made any close friends ... It wasn't like that. He was community property. The area celebrity. And everyone loved him because he minded his own business and dressed like a country boy and spoke the right lingo at the feed store. But Lenore"—Pat shook her head—"Lenore was always disliked. Her origins were suspect and her relationship with Serian was suspect, and everyone thought she was cold and arrogant."

"How much were they actually in residence at Arcadia?" Owen asked.

"From what I hear, Serian was in and out," Pat explained. "But Lenore stayed here all the time."

"Did she have any friends locally?"

"No. Not one. And you rarely saw her come to town with him. I've heard that she didn't drive so that could explain some of it. But people who had contact with her say that she was just plain spooky and that she liked hiding out there."

"I find that hard to believe," Holly said. "A woman needs friends or relatives around. Especially when she's stuck out in the country and her husband is away a lot. She must have had someone to keep her company."

"You think maybe Ted the repairman fixed more than washers out there?" Pat asked sarcastically.

"Well, it's possible, isn't it?" Holly said. "Everyone says she screwed her husband's friends ... why not local guys too?"

"Maybe," Pat agreed. "But why haven't any guys come forward to claim the conquest? Now that Serian's dead you'd think at least one of these secret lovers would step forward and brag."

Holly shrugged. "Who knows what their reasons might be for keeping silent. And even if they did step forward Rossner might find a way to block their testimony. Look at the Nellicliffs . . . they've got information to add but he's trying to stop them from being heard."

On the way back to the courthouse, it struck Owen that he had learned very little from the testimony thus far and that the entire procedure was inefficient and in many ways absurd—the hours of questioning to establish facts as seemingly insignificant as grains of sand on a beach, followed by the endless energy spent at speculation and gossip.

Yet it was also compelling. And he did not want to miss a moment of it.

After lunch the judge finally ruled on the Nellicliff testimony. His decision was announced before the jury entered so that the jury had no idea what was going on or that there had been a dispute over the upcoming testimony.

Earl and Ida Nellicliff were retired nurses who ran a volunteer medic and ambulance service. They were among the many who converged on Arcadia that August morning, and presumably they had their own grains of sand to add to the prosecution's case. However, the testimony that Spencer Brown was most interested in getting into the record was the couple's accounts of previous emergency calls to the Serian house. Rumor had it that these accounts were extremely damaging to Lenore Serian.

The courtroom was completely silent as the judge gave his ruling and read a statement explaining it. The Nellicliffs would not be permitted to describe previous visits. They had no probative value, the judge said, citing several legal cases.

Rossner had won.

The jury was called in and Brown went through the motions with the Nellicliffs, but their testimony had little significance. Both of them had concentrated their efforts on treating the minor injuries sustained by firefighters and guests during the chaos, and neither had had contact with Lenore Serian.

Rossner had no cross at all for either witness.

Court was adjourned for the day at 4:45, and Holly raced out to call her producer on the pay phone. Owen ignored the court officer who was trying to clear the room and lingered in the press section with the stragglers who were comparing notes and drawing out the process of gathering up their possessions. He was waiting for Lenore Serian to forsake her chair and turn around.

"Come on, people, out!" the officer ordered and Owen slowly picked up his bag and rose.

Just then the two bodyguards moved up close beside Lenore and she stood. She turned toward him. And Owen could have sworn she looked straight at him though she told him later that she hadn't. The large ruddy-faced man draped a voluminous black hooded cape around her shoulders, and the small, dark haired man grabbed her elbow and then they were off. Moving together.

Owen fell into step behind them. The smaller man glanced back with his sharp, hawk's eyes, warning Owen to keep his distance with one swift, threatening glare. His name was Joe Volpe, which meant "fox" in Italian. His big ham-handed, ruddy-faced partner was Frank Riley. They were retired New York City cops who worked together to provide services so specialized and exclusive that their agency had an unlisted phone number. Owen had learned all this from Holly and Pat at lunch.

"That Brown is sweating," he heard Riley say. "We should buy the man better deodorant."

One side of Volpe's mouth angled upward in amusement.

When they reached the double doors leading to the corridor, Lenore hesitated. Then she pulled the cape's hood up and nodded. Volpe opened the door. Shouts struck them like a blast of heat.

"Come on, Lenore!" "Just a brief statement." "Is it true that you've consulted another lawyer besides Rossner?"

A court officer stepped in. "Move it outside, people!" he shouted, and the little knot of persistent reporters stampeded for the stairs.

Volpe and Riley hurried Lenore to the elevator. They faced forward as the doors slid shut, and Owen saw that Lenore held the hood together so that only her eyes showed. A chill ran through him. She looked like an angel of death shrouded in her black folds.

5

Owen followed Lenore Serian out of the courthouse and saw the descending mass of reporters and photographers swallow her as soon as she left the relative safety of the building. Then he stayed to watch the television reporters videotape their pieces for the evening news.

Positions were staked out. Two technical crews set up inside the lobby and the rest scattered out in the cold, on the steps and down on the square so that the courthouse loomed in the background. He wandered from crew to crew, watching and listening. There was a flurry of hair combing and a flash of mirrors as makeup and collars and jewelry were attended to. One of the women outside had insisted on removing her coat and was trying hard not to shiver as she spoke into the microphone. One of the men was arguing with his crew about whether to walk across the street and tape in front of the hotel that Lenore and her defense team had retreated into.

Eventually each of them accomplished their business, finishing with the standard phrase: "This is Holly Danielson reporting from . . . , this is Amy Chang reporting from . . . , this is Gil Flores . . . , this is Leland Wilson . . ." All of them reporting from the Black Widow murder trial. But each of the reports had a different slant or emphasis, and Owen realized that viewers would have varying perceptions of the trial depending on which channel they turned their televisions to that night.

After taping her spot, Holly tried persuading him to have dinner with her group, but he said no, that he was anxious to get back to the apartment and type out his notes while everything was fresh. There was more to his refusal though. Things he couldn't say to Holly. That he was worried sick over how to produce the proposal that was expected of him. That he was afraid of failure. And more. He was bothered by the speed and ease with which he was slipping into place here. It felt somehow wrong. As though he was betraying his other life. His real life.

When he reached the East Village, shortly after eight, he resisted the tantalizing aromas of exotic foods and sought out a rundown diner where he could get hamburger steak, canned peas and instant mashed potatoes drowned in gravy, a meal so like his sister Ellen's cooking that he could close his eyes and pretend he was home. Only the hamburger tasted wrong. It was better than they ate at home because the beef in their freezer came from range animals that had been injured beyond help, shot and hauled to a local butcher. His family never tasted the choice grainfed steer meat that was raised for the American public to consume.

The dinner did not help his mood. He headed back toward his building but could not make himself go up. He walked, circling blocks and retracing his steps, until finally he changed some bills and dialed Michelle Wheeler from a corner pay phone.

"Owen! You're not supposed to be calling. It's too expensive."

"I miss you, Mike. I wanted to hear your voice."

"Hmmm . . . should I be suspicious? Are you feeling guilty over something?"

"No. I just miss you."

"I miss you too. It seems so strange having you gone."

"You must be alone in the house. You're not whispering or pretending I'm the chicken feed salesman."

She laughed. "You're right. Nobody is home except me. Daddy took Gram into Emporia for a sale at the K Mart. I don't know why she can't buy her clothes from catalogs the way I do."

"Maybe she wants an excuse to leave the ranch once in a while."

"No. She was born and raised on this place. She'd die without it."

"Apparently not in the amount of time it takes her to go to K Mart and back."

"Whoa, what's this I'm hearing? Are you turning into a New York smartmouth already?"

Owen laughed. "Could be. It's a dangerous place for that."

"Umm, well, just so you don't catch it. And don't say that

word *dangerous*. I'm already worried enough about you. Do you see a lot of . . . you know . . . black people and drug addicts and queers and all that?"

"Mike . . ." He sighed and considered what he could say to her. "Things aren't like you think they are. People aren't like you think they are. I wish . . ." But how could he possibly make her understand that most of what they'd been taught and conditioned to think was wrong. Just plain wrong.

He'd always suspected it was wrong. No, stronger than that. He'd always believed it was wrong. But now he knew it first-hand and he had real people's faces in his mind to prove it.

A mechanical voice cut in to ask for more money, and Owen fed the last of his coins into the slot.

"I wish you were here," he said.

"Not me! But I wish you were home."

"It will go fast," he assured her.

"Yeah, and I keep reminding myself about the house. Our own little house. It will be like a miracle."

"My proposal might not be accepted, Mike. I could come home without a dime."

"Don't even think that. You'll do it. You've always done what was right." The mechanical voice interrupted again, and Mike shouted over it, "Bye! Save your money and write!"

He hung up the phone and forced himself to walk toward his building, but the call had not cured him. If anything his mood was worse. As he climbed the stairs to the apartment, he thought that he probably should have gone out to dinner with Holly and her gang. He wouldn't have lost any more time than he'd already squandered, and he wouldn't be so gloomy.

Thursday morning Owen made the trip upstate and entered the courthouse like a seasoned pro with a routine to follow. As he walked into the courtroom, he caught smiles from Marilyn, Ray, Sharon and Gil just as though he belonged, and when he sat down in the aisle seat that had been saved for him, Holly and Pat greeted him eagerly and swept him into their whispering over developments.

Lenore arrived. Watching her walk up the aisle followed closely by Volpe and Riley reminded Owen of a wedding.

Only there were no smiles or blushes or shy hesitations. Lenore's stride was even and her back was straight, and though she kept her eyes down, there was defiance in her carriage.

Somewhere in the rows behind him, he could hear women's voices discussing Lenore's hair—wondering if she always kept it twisted up like that, wondering how long it was when down, wondering if the shine was natural or achieved with some beauty product. When they were finished with the hair they launched into an attack on her clothes. Today she wore another sexless, shapeless dress. This time it was dark brown, and it reminded Owen of the dresses some of the Amish women wore in Kansas.

"Rossner thinks he can fool the jury by dressing her like that," he heard an unknown voice say.

"I don't care how many humble dresses he puts on her, she's never going to look innocent," another voice replied.

"People against Lenore Serian!"

The familiar announcement was exhilarating. Just like the "Let's play ball!" at the start of a game or the "Let's move 'em out!" at the beginning of a cattle drive. He watched the lawyers snap to attention in their chairs and thought about how easy it was to understand what drove them. He could almost feel their adrenaline rushes and the thrills they got from each point scored.

The jury was not summoned as usual. Instead, all the attorneys, the defendant, the court reporter and the court clerk huddled at the side of the bench for a long hushed conference with the judge.

"This is a sidebar," Holly whispered. "I'll hear what it was about later and I'll tell you."

"What about the jury?" Owen asked.

"The whole point of a sidebar is to keep the stuff away from the jury."

"But how can the jury be expected to make a fair judgment if things are kept from them?"

"Fair?" Holly repeated the word as though it was amusing. "It's strategy that scores, Owen. Fairness doesn't count at all."

Thirty minutes later the sidebar ended, and the jury was called in. Owen studied their faces and wondered how many had come to those seats believing that their primary duty was fairness.

The first witness of the morning was Deputy Sheriff Kenneth Havlik. He was a young, soft-looking man. If not for the uniform, he might have been the object of bullies. He wiped his palms on his pants legs, swore to tell the truth, and then wiped them again while stating his name, address, and position with the sheriff's department for the record.

The judge leaned over toward him. "Relax, Kenneth. None of us in here are armed." There was a ripple of laughter but Havlik did not relax.

Brown sauntered forward and smiled.

"Deputy Havlik, could you relate your length of employment for us ... that is, the length of time you had been under the employ of Sheriff Bello at the time of the Serian fire."

"Yes, sir."

"How long?"

"Four months."

"Had you had occasion to visit the scene of a murder prior to this incident?"

"Objection, your honor," Rossner called. "There's been no murder established."

Brown rolled his eyes. "Your honor ..." he complained.

"Approach the bench!" the judge barked.

After a heated exchange of whispers, the judge called out, "Objection sustained! Jury will disregard the reference to murder," and Brown returned to the podium with his jaws locked.

Brown consulted his notes. "Would you relate for us what you did that morning, Kenneth."

"Starting where?"

"From where you had occasion to realize that your services might be required at the Serian home."

"I guess that'd be hearing my dogs. I was asleep when all my huntin' dogs started raising a fuss in their pens. I got dressed and went to check on 'em and quiet 'em down. When I got out there, I saw the traffic passin' on the road ... firetrucks and all. Then I saw the flames from over at the Serian place. From the look of things, I figured they could use help so I went over."

"You were the first member of law enforcement to arrive at the scene?"

"Yes, sir."

"And what did you observe to be occurring upon your arrival?"

Havlik gulped down the water handed to him by a court officer. "I pulled into the yard and saw people running around screaming and crying and guys fighting the fire. I went on up to the firefighters and identified myself as a deputy and asked was there anything I could do to help. One of them told me that there might have been a man inside the building and maybe I should check on the wife."

"Did you then proceed to locate Mrs. Serian?"

"Yes, sir."

"Could you please describe your contact with Mrs. Serian for us, officer?"

"She was standing off to the side by herself and she was real dirty with black smudges all over her and she was just watching and I asked if she was Mrs. Serian and she nodded, but she was so calm I didn't know whether to believe her or not. Then I told her who I was and asked if she was sure there had been someone in the barn. She didn't answer so I asked her again and she said yes that her husband had been asleep in there and that he hadn't gotten out. I asked her if she was positive he hadn't gotten out and she said she was positive."

"What was your response then, deputy?"

"I asked her if there was anything I could do for her and she said, 'No. Not unless you can speak to ghosts.'"

"Please continue, Deputy Havlik. What occurred after that?"

"I was kind of spooked and I thought maybe I shouldn't say anything more so I walked away and that's when I saw the paintings against the tree."

"Would you describe for us your discovery of these paintings and the course of action you proceeded with."

"Yes, sir. There was three of them. Not framed or anything. Just leaned against a tree out there. Knowing what I knew . . . that the guy was a famous artist . . . I got worried something might happen to those paintings . . . A firetruck accidentally backing over 'em in the dark or something so I moved them to the house."

"At what point did you determine that it was necessary to summon the sheriff?"

"Right after that. Miz Raven came running up screaming and crying about the greatest artist in the world being burned alive, and I thought I better call Sheriff Bello and let him know what was going on out there."

"Did anything further happen involving Mrs. Serian before the sheriff's arrival?"

"Yes, sir."

Brown sighed impatiently. "Would you relate it, please."

"Sure. Just after I called the sheriff, I saw Mrs. Serian and Miz Raven get into a fight. I didn't hear what the first words were, but Miz Raven was real upset and whatever Mrs. Serian said upset her even worse and she slapped Mrs. Serian and Mrs. Serian kind of flew at her and knocked her down and they were rolling on the ground in the mud."

"What was your reaction to this spectacle?"

"I ran up and some other men ran up and we pulled them apart. Miz Raven was kind of hysterical, but Mrs. Serian was real calm, like it was all just a normal day in the sunshine."

Owen glanced at Holly and she raised her eyebrows as if to confirm that this was good stuff they were hearing.

Rossner stood and Owen realized that Brown had finished with the deputy. Havlik fidgeted and sucked on his lower lip as Rossner approached.

"Deputy Havlik, you said you were asleep on the night in question and your dogs awakened you and you quickly deduced that there was trouble at your neighbors'."

"Yes, sir."

"Are you always so alert and perceptive?"

"I try to be. That's what I was hired to be."

"Then of course you took careful note of the condition Lenore Serian was in when you spoke to her that night."

"Well . . . yeah."

"Could you describe that condition for us?"

"You mean . . . was she dirty and all that?"

"Yes. Just describe her for us. As a law enforcement officer, you must be a trained observer, so just recount for us everything you can remember about her that night."

"Okay . . . like I said before, she was all dirty and sooty. Her face was streaked with it and her arms were black."

"Was the light good where she was standing?"

"No. It was kind of shadowy because she was near the trees."

"So you couldn't see whether she'd been hurt or not?"

"No."

"Could you see her face closely? See whether she was pale or see the pupils of her eyes?"

Havlik had a puzzled expression. "No."

"Does the sheriff's department give any paramedic training?"

"No."

"Then even if you had been able to see her clearly you couldn't possibly have known whether her odd behavior was caused by shock, could you?"

"Objection, your honor," Brown said, pushing up from his chair and knocking several papers off the table.

The judge frowned but sustained.

There was another sidebar. It dragged on and on.

When the action started again, Rossner declared that he was finished with Deputy Havlik and Brown leaped up for re-direct.

"Deputy Havlik," he began, "have you ever had occasion to undergo first-aid training?"

"Well, I did get a short course of it in junior college. They taught us the basics, like how to do that hug for people who are choking and that kind of thing."

"Did you receive instruction in the condition known as shock?"

"Yes, sir. And even if I couldn't see Mrs. Serian so well . . . from what they taught me about shock I wouldn't think a person who gets in a fight is in shock."

"Objection, your honor," Rossner called. He stood and held out his hands. "With all due respect for Deputy Havlik's first-aid course, he is not qualified to give us medical judgments."

There was more haggling between the attorneys, and Havlik's comments were stricken from the record, but of course the jury had already heard them. Owen wondered if Rossner had gained anything.

At lunchtime Owen was swept into a group that included Holly, Pat, Ray, Marilyn the columnist, Sharon the radio reporter and the other television reporter, Gil Flores. Together they walked to the town pizza joint.

"Proves that she's capable of violence," Holly said.

"Yeah," Ray agreed with a chuckle. "Wish I'd have been there to see those two mud wrestling."

"I sure as hell don't buy the bit about her being in shock,"

Marilyn said and there was immediate agreement. Owen suspected that the reporters' attitudes were similar to the jury's.

Over lunch they speculated about the content of the sidebars; then, on the walk back, conversation drifted into media gossip—who was covering for who and which columnist had been writing without actually attending the trial and what married radio reporter was flirting with the judge's law clerk.

As soon as he arrived back at the courthouse, Owen called Bernie's office to check in with her. She was out to lunch so he spoke to Alex, who was eager to hear every detail of the trial. Owen obliged him with a recounting, but found himself giving Alex a condensed version, thinking that Alex couldn't appreciate all the complexities. The trial had come to feel like a separate world that outsiders could not possibly understand.

When court reconvened at 1:30 a uniformed Sheriff Vincent Bello marched to the stand. He was a stocky man in his fifties with a moon face, a large pockmarked nose, and a pompous, authoritative manner.

"Sheriff Bello," Brown began, "will you please recount for us the time of the call and the actions you pursued subsequent to receiving Deputy Havlik's call."

"I received the call at oh-five-hundred and left immediately for the Serian farm."

"And what was the situation upon your arrival there?"

"Pure confusion. All the power to the yard lights had fed from the studio so there was only headlights and flashlights to see with. There were people everywhere . . . neighbors and firefighters and houseguests of the deceased. I located my deputy, Kenneth Havlik; then I found the man in charge of the fire crew . . . Pete Gadding, and I started getting the scene organized."

Brown fumbled with his note cards. "Pete Gadding. Now that would be Fire Chief Peter Gadding?"

"Yes, it would."

"Did Gadding inform you of the nature of the situation?"

"Yes. Pete told me the building went up too fast to save it. He said they were lucky to have kept it from spreading. And he said it looked like we had a man inside."

"At this time did you have any reason to suspect foul play?"

"No. At that time it looked like a routine fire with a casualty. We get 'em all the time, you know."

"What action did you take after talking to Pete Gadding?"

"I walked around, surveying the situation and looking for Mrs. Serian."

"Were you acquainted with Lenore Serian at that time?"

"No . . . I wouldn't say we were acquainted. But I knew her by sight. I'd seen her in town, and she's not the kind of woman I see around often, so I naturally had noticed her."

"Were you successful in locating Mrs. Serian?"

"No, I was walking around, surveying the situation, and this woman comes running up. She's covered in mud and has a wild-eyed look and she's screaming. But it wasn't Mrs. Serian."

"Were you surprised or threatened by this woman's behavior?"

"No. I'm used to upset women at the scene of tragedies. Matter of fact I'd say her behavior was normal."

"What occurred next?"

"A fellow showed up. Acted as though he'd been chasing her and just caught up. He told her that she had to calm down and that she should come back in the house and wait for the doctor."

"Did this man advise you of the identity of the woman?"

"Yes. He apologized and told me the woman was Natalie Raven, the Serians' housekeeper, and that she was hysterical over her employer's death. Now that surprised me because I knew Natalie Raven by sight and I wouldn't have recognized her. Then I asked him who he was and he said his name was"—Bello looked up at the judge— "is it okay if I check my notes . . . I have trouble with names, judge."

Everything came to a halt while Bello's notes were scrutinized and discussed in a hushed conference between the judge and both attorneys. Finally they were handed back to Bello with a nod of approval. Bello squinted down at them and then continued. "Clay Southey was the fellow's name, and he said he was a guest from Manhattan. I asked him if he had seen Mrs. Serian and he directed me to the house."

"Did you then proceed to the house, sheriff?"

"Yes, I did."

"And were you able to speak to Lenore Serian there?"

"No. She was locked in a room and she refused to see me."

"Who else did you note to be inside the house then?"

"Some firefighters were resting there and some guests were there, and as I was leaving to direct the removal of vehicles from the yard, a doctor arrived."

"Had someone summoned this doctor?"

"Yes. Miss Raven had called him."

"You then left the house and were occupied assisting with the removal of the vehicles from the yard . . . is that correct?"

"Yes."

"What time was it when you finished the vehicle removal?"

"We finished about daybreak."

"Was the light . . . that is to say, the sunlight . . . sufficient to allow your seeing the studio well then?"

"You could see what was left of it."

"Did Fire Chief Gadding approach you at this time about going into the studio with him."

"Yes. He said it had cooled down and he wanted me to go in with him and look for the body."

"At this time, you still were not certain whether you would discover a body inside, were you?"

"That's right. You can never tell. Just because the wife thinks the guy was asleep out there doesn't mean he was."

"And what did you observe when you entered the studio?"

"Everything was black and burned. On the south end, where the damage was the worst, and where we had been advised that the subject in question slept, Chief Gadding located the body."

"Was the deceased in a badly burned state?"

"Like a piece of charcoal."

This brought an involuntary groan from the spectator section, and Owen noticed that a few of the jurors looked immediately at Lenore to see what her reaction was. As far as Owen could tell, she had no reaction at all.

Brown cleared his throat. "Did you and Chief Gadding discuss any concerns over the fire at this time?"

"When the victim is famous and rich, there are always questions, but I wouldn't say we were too suspicious yet."

"Was there anything besides the body that you took special note of?"

"There was a metal chunk on the floor a short distance from the body. I picked it up and showed it to Pete Gadding, and we agreed that it looked like the head of an axe, which at that time we thought, or we assumed, that maybe the deceased had been trying to fight the fire himself."

The chunk of metal was dragged out as evidence and identified by Bello.

"What action did you take then?"

"I started out through the door . . . the door was steel and fireproof and it was still hanging there . . . and I saw that there was a key in the lock."

"Could you describe the lock, please?"

"It was one of those deadbolt locks above the knob."

"And could you describe the key?"

"It was a single key, not attached to a ring or other keys, and it was the standard brass type of key."

The key was produced in a plastic bag for Bello to identify.

"Did you then leave the vicinity of the studio?"

"Pete stayed there to wait for John Bagley, the coroner, and I went to the house for coffee and to round up the guests and get names and addresses."

"Did you find everyone to be cooperative?"

"All except Mrs. Serian. She still wouldn't come down out of her room."

"Had the doctor arrived upon the scene yet?"

"Yes, but she wouldn't see him so he gave first aid to whatever blisters and cuts the Nellicliffs hadn't treated, and he took care of Miss Raven, who was in pretty bad shape emotionally."

"Your honor . . ." Rossner stood and thus began another series of whispered conferences.

After twenty minutes, the judge dismissed the jury for the day and excused the witness. Still the whispering continued. Spectators grew bored with it and trickled out. Finally the press gave up and began leaving as well.

"That's it for today," Pat said.

Owen shook his head. "I can't believe how many confidential things go on . . . and how many fifteen-minute breaks there are and how few witnesses they fit in during a day."

"This is a pretty efficient judge." As Holly spoke she turned toward him and her breast touched his arm. Owen tried to ignore it and concentrate on what she was saying. "There are some judges who convene late every morning and adjourn early in the afternoon, with twice as many recesses in between."

The conversation continued as they went downstairs and stepped out into a gentle snow. Owen tilted his head back to let the feathery flakes fall on his face. Never had he seen such snow. It was the stuff of postcards and fairy tales. Floating from the highest reaches of the windless sky, drifting like goosedown through silver light.

"Surely Kansas has snow," Marilyn commented dryly.

"Not like this." He held out his hand to catch the soft flakes. "We get storms in the Flint Hills. Big brawny run-for-cover blizzards. Everybody usually goes to the house to play games and eat till they're over."

"Eating sounds good to me." Holly glanced at her watch. "We're out so early. I could do my spot, ride back to the station with my cameraman and be through in plenty of time for an evening of fun. Anybody up for Chinatown?"

"I'm in." Marilyn looked at Owen. She was a no-nonsense woman with pronounced creases around her eyes and mouth. "Have you been to Chinatown yet?"

"No, I thought I'd—"

Marilyn cut him off. "No better time than now."

When Owen didn't immediately agree, Marilyn frowned sternly. "You do eat, don't you?"

"Yes."

"Well, tonight you're eating Chinese. Good Chinese."

On Friday morning Sheriff Bello was reseated in the witness stand for cross examination. Rossner approached the man tentatively and began taking him through a description of the chain of events leading to Lenore Serian's being charged. The attorney seemed almost intimidated by the sheriff, and Bello's self-importance expanded as the cross progressed.

Around and around they went, over old material. Rossner had Bello backtrack and repeat everything he'd told Brown during his initial testimony, and as he repeated himself Bello began displaying open contempt for Rossner's questions.

"And so, sheriff, let me see if I understand this correctly . . . you say you were out there till daylight getting the vehicles out of the yard?"

"Yes."

"Why was it so difficult to remove all the vehicles?"

Bello sighed impatiently. "It was a sea of mud out there. The ground was wet to start with because it was a rainy week; then there was all that water they poured on the fire. That yard was a swamp ... slick in some places and deep enough to suck your boots off in others. We had our hands full pulling vehicles to dry ground. Even had a fire truck stuck."

"And you also said it was confusing because it was dark and there were people everywhere?"

"That's right."

"How many guests did you say were at the Serian home that night, sheriff?"

Bellow flipped open his notebook and read from it. "Twenty-two guests."

"You have that in your records? The records that were entered into evidence before?"

"That's right."

"And you're sure the number was twenty-two?"

"That's what I said."

"But didn't you say that you waited until daybreak—until after you'd extracted all the vehicles from the mud and found the body and made coffee—to round up the guests and gather information?"

"Yes." Bello shifted in the chair, and there was a subtle shift to his expression as well.

"So someone could have left by then?"

"Yes."

"Did you check with Natalie Raven to see whether you had all the guests' names?"

"Yes. I did. But she said she wasn't sure who all had been out there."

"So someone else ... someone you had no opportunity to question ... someone you know nothing about ... could have been there that night?"

Bello's mouth twisted as though the answer tasted bad. "Anything's possible."

"So it's within the realm of possibility that others were present and had access to Bram Serian's studio that night?"

"Like I said, anything's possible."

"Is that a yes, sheriff?"

"Yes."

Rossner paused and scratched his head. "You did question these twenty-two guests, then?"

"Yes."

"At the scene?"

"Some at the scene."

"And some not till later?"

"Yes. After the autopsy showed the deceased had been hit on the head, then we questioned everyone at length."

"All twenty-two of these guests were questioned at length?"

Bello fidgeted. "All except one who we couldn't find."

"You couldn't find one of the guests? A witness who may have crucial information about what happened that night?"

"Yes. A man called James Collier disappeared before we could question him."

"Disappeared?"

Bello's chin shot out and his neck swelled. "You know he disappeared, Rossner. We haven't been keeping any secrets or playing any dirty tricks."

"Sheriff," the judge cautioned, "confine your answers to the questions."

Rossner cocked his head and assumed an expression of perplexed innocence. "Now about you and Chief Gadding finding the body . . . you said that the two of you had no suspicions about the fire then?"

"I said I had questions because the man was famous, but I was not yet suspicious."

Rossner consulted a note card. "You said before that you and Chief Gadding discussed things, and then you said *we* were not yet suspicious . . . did that *we* refer to you and the chief?"

"I can't speak for Gadding," Bello replied gruffly. "You'll have to get him up here and ask him."

"Is it fair to say, then, that all you can say is *you* yourself had no suspicions. Is that right?"

"Right."

"Okay . . . on to the key." There was an interruption as the key was produced for Bello to hold.

"Could you describe this key for us, sheriff?"

"It's just your average brass key like any hardware store carries."

"Are you referring to the brass key blanks that hardware stores stock to make copies of keys for customers?"

"Yes."

"Is this, then, a key copy made by a hardware store rather than an original key that came with the lock?"

Bello's face turned a deep, unhealthy red. "I don't know," he mumbled.

"I'm sorry. Could you speak up please?"

The sheriff seemed to be diminishing in size. "I don't know if it's a copy or not."

"You didn't check on the key to determine whether it was a copy or an original?"

"No."

"Was the key checked for fingerprints?"

"Yes."

"Were there any identifiable prints on it?"

"Yes. A thumb print was recovered, but it was not of use."

"Whose thumb print was it, sheriff?"

"Mine."

Rossner studied the ceiling for a moment and tapped his finger on his chin. "Sheriff ... were you aware of Bram Serian's identity at the time of the fire?"

"Sure."

"Did his identity affect you in any way during those hours you were at the scene of the fire?"

"I guess I was a little nervous ... and I think everyone else was nervous ... about who we were dealing with. That artist was famous and rich and everybody was wishing we could clean up the mess and get things settled before the press jumped on us."

"So would it be fair to say that you were in a hurry to resolve the situation?"

"Yes."

"Have you ever heard the old saying about how getting in a hurry can cause mistakes ... Have you heard haste makes waste?"

"Yes."

"Do you think there were mistakes made that morning?"

Bello dropped his eyes. "I don't know."

"You've told us about the mud and the firefighting and the number of people present ... With all this, was it possible to check for suspicious footprints or tracks?"

Bello suddenly straightened, clutching at this chance to exonerate himself. "It would have been totally impossible.

The crime scene was already destroyed by the time I arrived."

"Did you at any time later go back and examine the scene?"

"Yes. After the autopsy results, we went back and conducted a search of the area."

"What kind of a search did you do?"

"A thorough search. All my men participated."

"Did you divide the area into quadrants? Was it a grid search?"

"I'm not sure I follow you."

"You do know about the law enforcement technique known as a grid search?"

"Well ... I'm familiar with that term but it's not something ... I don't think ... that's the one with the squares, isn't it?"

"Yes. Was that your method of search?"

"I could not have used that technique. That is when an area is marked out in squares and searched square by square; however, that would not have been possible for the open area surrounding the Serian house."

"Why is that?"

"Because that area is curved, it could not be divided into squares."

Rossner turned back toward the defense table and rubbed his mouth with his hand to cover a smile. Several of the jurors rolled their eyes, and from the back of the spectator section came muffled laughter. Even the judge ducked his head and shielded his face with his hand for a moment.

Rossner turned back to the witness and pushed on. "But you did search the area?"

"Yes."

"The crime scene area that had already been compromised before you arrived on the morning of the fire ... correct?"

"That is correct and I penalized my men for that and I pointed that out to Detective Kilgren."

"That would be Detective Kilgren of the state police who later joined the investigation?"

"Yes."

"What did you expect to find in this search?"

"Any evidence relating to the death."

"What kind of evidence?"

"The usual ... cigarette butts ... tire tracks ... whatever."

"Tire tracks, cigarette butts and the usual ..." Rossner repeated in disbelief. "In an area that had been a muddy mess and swarmed over by fifty or more people with cars and pickups and fire trucks?"

Bello cleared his throat. "It's routine."

"And what was the purpose of this search?"

"As I said, to find evidence relating to the death."

"But you charged Lenore Serian, and surely you weren't out there looking for tire tracks or cigarette butts to use as evidence against her."

"No."

"You already had witnesses who placed her at the scene, so you didn't need any more evidence for that, right?"

"Right. But this was before we charged her and we were not focused in on her yet and we were looking for another perpetrator."

"Does that mean you thought someone else did it?"

"Yes. That was our initial thought."

"But you changed your mind?"

"Yes."

"What made you change your mind, exactly."

"It was a collection of things ... facts surrounding the death and the suspect and her husband that led us to go in that direction."

"Was it Natalie Raven who led you in that direction?"

"I would say her statement added to the facts."

"And were you anxious to find a scapegoat because of all the media pressure?"

"I do not pay attention to the media."

"But you said earlier that you were anxious to prevent their descending, didn't you."

"I do not pay attention to them. That doesn't mean I like them around."

"Is it fair to say that you arrived at Lenore Serian as a suspect only after failing to find any evidence at the compromised death scene, and after Natalie Raven harangued you and after the media put pressure on you ... is that fair to say?"

Bello crossed his arms and glared at Rossner. "There's nothing fair about that at all."

"Sheriff Bello," the judge scolded gently.

"Sorry, your honor."

"Now," Rossner continued, "yes or no? Did you arrive at Lenore Serian as your accused only after failing to find any evidence at the scene and after Natalie Raven harangued you and after the media pressured you?"

Bello clamped his lips and narrowed his eyes. For a moment it seemed as if he might not answer. Then, with a heavy sigh, he said, "Yes."

There was no longer any question that Owen would join Holly and company for lunch. He simply went. Today they ended up at the smoky coffee shop again. He slid in to the booth, sat back and absorbed the firecracker discussion that followed.

Owen was so acclimated now to the people around him and the aggressive no-holds-barred lunchtime talk that he noticed more individual details than before. He noticed how often Ray looked at Holly and how oblivious Holly was to Ray. He noticed that Pat's opinions seemed to command the most respect and that Sharon changed her mind a lot and that Marilyn's sharp sarcasm flashed very close to cruelty at times but that she always pulled back before drawing blood. And he saw that Holly was their star. They all adored her and in return she favored them with her dazzling smiles and endowed whatever they did with an aura of fun.

Everyone was excited by Rossner's cross examination of Sheriff Bello. They had all known that Rossner was aiming for doubt over whether the death had actually been murder rather than accident, but with this cross Rossner had opened up the possibility of murder by an unknown perpetrator. The reporters' opinions on this were strong and varied. Arguments surged in wild directions. Then Marilyn made a comment that made them all stop. "Rossner has shown Bello up as a fool and made his investigation sound like slapstick comedy, but that doesn't mean Lenore Serian is innocent." With that they were all drawn immediately back to an assumption of Lenore's guilt.

After lunch the prosecution called the coroner, John Bagley, who proudly announced that he was also the owner of the Daisy Dew Septic Cleaning Service and proceeded to give a little commercial for his business. Bagley recounted how he had been called out and had overseen the recovery of the body. At the end of Brown's questioning, Owen thought the testimony had been so straightforward and simple that Rossner might forego a cross examination.

But Rossner ambled up and casually led Bagley through a repeat of his actions.

"That must have been a mess, huh, all that debris and the puddles of water?" Rossner asked, suddenly becoming very solemn and sympathetic.

"It was terrible. And I didn't have boots on either."

"Could you tell much about what was around the body?"

"No. Everything was destroyed and what was left got tromped on and stirred around by all of us."

"Could you tell exactly how the body had fallen? Where the head was, for instance?"

"Oh, yeah. Sure."

Paul Jacowitz stood up to hand Rossner a poster-sized diagram of the floor plan to Bram Serian's studio. Rossner carried the poster over, and it was examined by the judge and taken through the formal process of exhibit numbering. Then Rossner held it up so the jury could see and handed the witness a little black cutout that represented the body, curled into a fetal position but with the head clearly identifiable.

"This has stickum on the back, Mr. Bagley. Would you please lean over here and stick this on to show exactly how the body was positioned?"

Bagley carefully put the black cutout on the floor plan. A juror sneezed loudly, and both Rossner and the judge said, "Bless you" in tandem.

Rossner studied the black figure that Bagley had placed on the poster. "Could you please describe for us, Mr. Bagley, where the head is in relation to elements which survived the fire and were identifiable."

"Okay . . ." Bagley studied the diagram a moment. "The head was about a foot from the bricks here."

"The raised brick platform that the stove sat on?"

"Yes."

"Could you see the brick platform and the stove clearly?"

"Yeah. There was some burned beams laying across it, but I could see it just fine."

"Would you describe it for us?"

"It was pretty standard. A big deluxe antique-looking heating stove mounted on a platform that was two bricks tall and about six foot in diameter."

"And Bram Serian was lying with his head here?" Rossner pointed to the diagram.

"Yeah."

"When a body burns like this, is it common for it to curl into the fetal position?"

"Very common."

"So the body could have fallen and been stretched out straight but then curled as the fire burned it?"

"Yeah. That's right."

"And if it was stretched out straight, given Bram Serian's height, where would that put the head?"

Bagley studied the poster, then looked up at Rossner as though something had suddenly dawned on him. "It would put the head right at the edge of the bricks."

"Right near the edge of a brick platform built two bricks high?"

"Yeah."

"A dangerous edge to strike your head on?"

"Sure. Very dangerous."

Rossner paused to let the implications sink in. The jurors were riveted. Owen turned to see if Holly or Pat or Marilyn were as astonished as he was. All of the women were scribbling furiously on their reporting pads.

Immediately, Brown jumped up for a redirect and managed to patch up the hole by leading the coroner into statements that made the head against the bricks theory sound ridiculous. But it still seemed to Owen that Rossner had scored.

Fire Chief Peter Gadding was called next. He was a man of few words, and Brown had to pry out his testimony. His account of the evening was without adjectives or embellishment of any kind. Owen's thoughts wandered. He studied the back of Lenore Serian's head. What did she think about at night when she was away from the trial? Did she sit down to watch television or curl up with a book in front of the fire just like it was another normal evening?

"And so, Chief Gadding," Brown said, "what happened when Sheriff Bello found the metal object that was later identified as an axe head?"

"The sheriff held it up and said, 'I think I found an axe head. Our stiff must have been trying to play fireman.' "

"And what was your response?"

"I said, 'Put it down, Vinnie, you're disturbing evidence.' "

Brown appeared slightly flustered but recovered quickly. "At this time, did you have any suspicions about the fire not being accidental?"

"Yes. That is why I called Kevin Mullin, the fire inspector."

Brown wrapped up his direct and Rossner stepped into position. The defense attorney was respectful of Chief Gadding, without being deferential. He led the witness through some general questions about the fire, then asked, "Did you convey your suspicions about the fire to Sheriff Bello?"

"Yes."

"And what was his response?"

"Exactly or should I paraphrase?"

"As exactly as you can make it."

"Bello said, 'So the artist got himself cooked. He's not one of ours. Let's not stir up any more trouble than we have to.' "

"Were you shocked by this statement from the sheriff?"

"No."

"Why not?"

"I've known him a long time."

Rossner waited for the laughter to subside. "Let's turn our attention back to the axe head. When you warned the sheriff that he was disturbing evidence, what was his reaction?"

"That the death was an accident and evidence was not necessary."

"So, on the morning of the fire, when there still might have been existing evidence that was subsequently lost or destroyed, how would you describe the sheriff's attitude?"

"He was unconcerned."

As soon as Chief Gadding stepped down, court was adjourned until Monday morning.

Holly turned to flash Owen a smile, and he knew that she had some grand plan for the evening, and, without allowing himself to reconsider, he mumbled his excuses and rushed out. Suddenly he had to get away.

He rode the train back to Manhattan, sitting alone, staring out at the winter countryside. Brief views of the river opened at certain points in the train's progress, and he watched for them. The river looked the same. Ice chunks floated in the dull gray water just as they had the first time he made the trip. Had that only been four days ago? It felt like months. Or longer.

He felt a sudden pang of homesickness. Not for the home he had so recently left, but for the home of his childhood when all of his family was intact and safe, and the rest of the world existed only between the covers of books he read. Closing his eyes, he conjured up his brother, broad-shouldered and smiling as he looked down at a younger Owen. And almost as easily he could picture his mother, her arms dusted with flour as she worked at the kitchen table, her smile for him gentle and sad as she said, "You have to learn not to ask so many questions, Owen."

The old pictures were right there for him, but when he tried to erase the old and replace it with the present, he had great difficulty. It was hard to imagine his sisters, his father, or even Michelle Wheeler, the way they were now, even though he had been with them up until a week ago. His family's faces were vague. And Mike, the woman he made love to and made plans with . . . he could barely summon an image of her face.

Why was the past, which he had always tried to avoid, suddenly so much more immediate and powerful than the present?

He flipped open his notepad. *Mike,* he wrote, then smiled because he hadn't written anything to her since his days in college. Back when he still considered her just the neighbor kid.

He tore that out and began again.

Dearest Mike,

I miss you. I miss your calm strength and your smile and the vision you have of our future together. I miss holding you.

He tore the sheet off and crumpled it into a tight ball. Mike would hate a letter like that. She disliked sentiment of any kind. Even poetry. She couldn't stand poetry.

He started again. He described the gentle snow and the windless days and the farmground he'd seen from the plane. He wrote her a little about the city and a little about the trial and about meeting so many reporters. Then he closed with love, saying he hoped to see her soon.

He folded the letter and tucked it into the inside breast pocket of his coat for mailing later. It made him feel better, sitting there close to his heart, like a talisman . . . a link, a tangible connection to his real life. He had to hold on to that. He needed to hold on to that so he didn't lose the way back. Because this was not his life. This trial and this city were a separate dimension. This was rabbit-hole reality. A through-the-looking-glass dream of reality that would soon vanish.

He opened his notepad again.

Dear Ellen and Meggie. He looked at that, then changed it to read, *Dear Ellen, Meggie and Clancy.* He had always called his father by his name but seeing it written there seemed strange. And what about Rusty Campbell? Should he include Rusty? Finally he started another sheet and simply wrote, *Hello to all.* Then, all the way to Grand Central he tried to think of something to say.

6

Owen was disoriented Saturday morning. For a few moments as he drifted up out of his sleep he thought that the trip to New York had been just a long vivid dream.

The clock read 7:55. He had stayed up late, transcribing his notes and working on the bones of his proposal, and had decided to allow himself the luxury of sleeping in. But after years of rising with the sun, 7:55 was the best he could do.

He started coffee and sat down in front of the work he'd abandoned last night. There was something wrong. The proposal had no life, no heart. He propped his elbow on the table next to the typewriter and looked at the newspaper picture of Lenore Serian that he had taped to the wall.

If he was a juror and had to vote that day . . . He tried to imagine himself judging her. Was she innocent or guilty? Or did she fall into some halfway category—innocent by reason of insanity maybe, or innocent due to mitigating circumstances . . . Maybe Serian's head wound really had been an accident and then she panicked and tried to cover it up with the fire. Or maybe she was guilty as hell. Just like Spencer Brown and the district attorney's office and the police thought she was.

He stared at the grainy newsprint image. The sharp lines and shadows, the knife-edged cheekbones and the dark almond-shaped eyes. Looking at her was like looking at a dark river. He could almost feel the turbulence and the undercurrents beneath the surface.

His coffee was ready and he drank it gratefully, thinking about the day that stretched before him. First, he had to get some exercise. A whole week without sweat or exertion had left him feeling caged. He had to run it off. Jump it off. Work it off any way possible. And then he had to make the proposal better. But how?

Maybe he needed to delve deeper into Lenore Serian's

character and understand her . . . empathize with her . . . get more of her as a flesh-and-blood human being rather than the mythological Black Widow that the press so loved. He tried to picture Lenore as someone's mother or sister. Mother didn't work at all and sister was tough, too. She seemed totally removed from such commonplace ties.

Sister.

Reluctantly he picked up the letter that had been in his mailbox when he got home last night. It was from Ellen.

Dear Owen,

I hope you're doing okay and not working too hard, though I'm sure you are (working too hard). How does a murder trial go? Do you have to sit there all day every day? You should take some time and see things because it would be a crime to be in such a famous place and not see the big sights. Wish I was there with you. I'd drag you to the Empire State Building and Ellis Island and the Statue of Liberty and on and on.

Things are not good here with you gone. Don't worry, it's nothing to do with the cattle, it's just me. Meggie makes me feel like I don't have a place here anymore, and I definitely don't have a place as a wife anymore so I don't know where my place is.

With you here all the time to cushion things I wasn't doing much thinking, but now I am. I'm trying to remember what it was that I wanted in high school (besides being head cheerleader and marrying Danny). Do you remember? I think if I could get myself back to that point in my life maybe I could start over. Sometimes I'm scared that I'll end up just like Terry.

Write soon,
(No long distance calls!)
Love, Ellen

The letter worried Owen. End up like Terry? How literally did she intend that reference to their dead brother?

He wished he could write back immediately with something wise and soothing, but he couldn't think of what to say. And he never had known what she wanted in high school. He could remember those years well, but he couldn't say what she had wanted. She had been one of those kids who was active and popular while managing to keep her grades high. Yet she could not stay out of trouble. Her irreverent wisecracks and her attitude toward authority kept her in a state of constant punishment.

Owen had been in awe of her then. She was only three years older, but the gulf between them had seemed huge. He had believed she was destined for greatness, that she would explode out into the world and do something big when she was old enough. But then, when she turned eighteen the summer after graduation, she eloped with Danny Langmore and moved to Texas.

In the beginning she had seemed happy. Danny found high-paying work in the oil fields, and Ellen was thrilled to get a part-time position in a very exclusive department store. She wrote long effusive letters about her wealthy customers and the wardrobe she was building with the store's generous employee discounts. She wrote about dinners out, and dances, and parties where famous country music singers entertained.

The first two Christmases of her marriage she flew home alone and joined in the cookie decorating and the domino and pitch tournaments with her old enthusiasm. The third Christmas she was recovering from a miscarriage and not well enough to travel. After that her long weekly letters dwindled to monthly notes that were subdued and vague. She didn't make it home again until Terry's funeral.

The night before the funeral, Owen went to the airport to pick her up. He watched for her in the stream of exiting passengers, expecting the mischievous energetic sister he had last seen, but the woman who stepped off the plane was a hesitant, nervous, unkempt parody of the girl he remembered. He'd been just twenty then and overwhelmed by loss, and he had accepted that the appalling change in Ellen was due to her grief over their brother.

Her next visit home was for their mother's funeral. She and Danny drove up together. Again it was an occasion of grief, and Ellen's condition was easily attributable to the situation. No one else remarked on it. But this time Owen could not dismiss the changes in his sister or believe that grief was solely responsible. She reminded him of a dog that's been whipped so often it cowers at every sound.

He tried to talk to her. He even coaxed her outside one night in an effort to recreate the long hot nights of their childhood when they had sneaked from their beds and crept out behind the barn to choke on stolen cigarettes and talk until dawn. Nothing worked. She was closed to him. And his concern seemed only to frighten her.

A month later Owen was waiting for his father and Meggie to return from a Fourth of July fireworks display in town when the phone rang. It was Ellen. Her voice was so hoarse he had to strain to understand her. In one long expressionless monologue she told him that Danny had tried to strangle her the night before and the police had been called and Danny had run away and she knew if she stayed he would eventually kill her and the police wouldn't stop him and could she please come home now.

Owen left a note saying only that he'd gone to get Ellen, and then he got in his truck and headed for Texas. He drove fourteen hours straight, arriving at his sister's duplex in Houston just before noon of the following day. Ellen was sitting on her couch staring vacantly at the television set when he walked in through the open door. Dark bruises marked her neck and one of her eyes was swollen purple.

"Are you packed?" Owen asked her. His exhaustion from the all-night drive was immediately replaced by deep, gut-wrenching anger over the marks of violence on his sister.

She shook her head. "I tried to call you back, but there was no answer."

Her face was still, but her hands twisted in her lap as if they had a will of their own. "I shouldn't have dragged you into this. Everything is all my fault. I have to stay here and try to make up with Danny."

"Ellen . . . Danny may be your husband but he has no right to hurt you . . . *ever* . . . not for any reason. It is not your fault and you don't have to stay here."

She looked up at him. Her expression was childlike. Fearful.

"Let's pack your things, Ellen. You can come home and rest awhile. Then you can decide what to do about Danny."

"But what if Danny comes home and catches me packing? He'll be furious. I'm not even allowed to go to the grocery store without his permission."

Owen did not allow his reaction to show. "If Danny comes, I'll talk to him. Don't worry."

Together they filled suitcases and boxes with her belongings. There wasn't a lot. She said that Danny sometimes threw away things of hers as punishment instead of hitting her. The only piece of furniture she wanted was a rocker that had belonged to their grandmother. It had been broken and clumsily glued together. Owen didn't ask what had happened to it.

He was loading the back of the pickup when Danny drove up in a flashy red sports car. Danny Langmore was a handsome man, lean and fit from physical labor, tanned and blond and expensively dressed. He walked up the driveway carrying a bouquet of flowers and a box of candy, looking like the perfect suitor.

"Hey, Owen! What a surprise. Man, I never thought you'd make it down our way."

Owen choked down the violent rage he felt toward Danny, wedged a suitcase into place and turned to face his brother-in-law. "I'm taking Ellen home," he said.

Danny's face fell. "Aw, come on. Just because we had a little fight?"

"How could you do that to her, Danny? How could you hurt her like that?"

"Hell, she's been filling you full of bullshit. I'd never hurt her."

"Where did she get all the bruises then?"

Danny laughed confidently. "You know Ellie ... she's clumsy as a three-legged toad ... always falling or bumping into something."

Owen turned away from Danny and went into the house. "Danny's here," he warned his sister quietly. "Are you finished packing?"

She nodded. Her expression was one of pure terror.

"Go on and lock yourself into whichever room locks. I'll finish loading and we'll get out of here. Okay?"

She disappeared into the bathroom just as Danny rounded the corner.

"Sugar," Danny called to the locked door. "You aren't really leaving, are you? I got you some flowers here and some of that See's chocolate you're so crazy about. Come on, sugar ... come on out. I'm real sorry we had that fight." He glanced over at Owen. "Ellie, you know everything that happened was an accident. You know I'd never hurt you on purpose."

Owen carried the last two boxes out, stuffed them in and hurried back to the house. Danny was trying to kick open the bathroom door but stopped as soon as he saw Owen.

"Goddamn," Danny said sheepishly. "These women sure know how to get a guy mad, don't they?"

"Ellen, we're ready to go," Owen said.

She opened the door a crack, saw Owen and then stepped out into the hall.

"Get in the truck," Owen said. "I've just got these two things left.

Ellen edged past Danny without meeting her husband's furious gaze. Danny waited a beat, then trailed after her. Owen picked up the two remaining items, a leather carryon bag and a small suitcase. Both felt like they'd been filled with rocks. When he came to the end of the hall, he had a straight line of sight through the open front door to where Ellen was climbing into the cab of the truck. Danny was fumbling for something in the coat closet beside the front door. Owen started across the room. Then Danny was out of the closet and standing in the doorway with a rifle and he was raising that rifle and Owen lunged forward and swung the bag at Danny's head and Danny sprawled out onto the cement.

It happened so fast that Owen had trouble accepting that it did actually happen, even though he knew it was true and he sometimes had nightmares about missing Danny's head with the bag and Danny firing that gun. But when he was awake and rational, he refused to believe that the gun was even loaded. Danny had just been trying to scare Ellen. That was all. And Owen sometimes felt remorse over having walloped him so hard with that bag.

Maybe Lenore Serian had been caught in a situation like that. Where no one meant for anyone to get hurt but things went wrong. Maybe she'd been scared like Ellen. Maybe she'd been abused like Ellen? He had read nothing to indicate that Bram Serian was capable of such behavior, but then his experience with Danny Langmore had taught Owen to disregard appearances. Through Danny he had learned that you could be acquainted with a man, work beside him, even know his relatives, yet still have no idea what he was capable of or how he behaved in intimate relationships.

Suddenly Owen jumped out of his chair, pumped with renewed energy. That was what he needed! To understand Bram Serian. To find out more about him. Not about his career or his art or his mysterious house, but him. The man. What kind of a person had Serian been? What had driven him? What had inspired or excited him? Somewhere there were answers. Or at least clues. That was the key to making this proposal live—he had to bring Bram Serian to life.

The huge central research library on Fifth Avenue was another building to marvel at. Owen climbed the massive stone steps and passed through the splendid columned entryway, lifted by the grandeur and tantalized by thoughts of the great wealth of information such a place had to offer. He picked up a brochure and read through the list of collections and special exhibits. Then he took the vaulted marble stairway up three floors to the main reading areas.

He walked through the stately rooms, breathing in the scents of old wood and aging books and intense humanity, filling his eyes with the beauty and scope and promise of the place, and then he began the hunt. Within such a venerable temple of the printed word, he would find Bram Serian, the man behind the artist, and he would see everything more clearly. He would have a focus. And the tragedy would assume a more human dimension.

Hours passed. He labored over catalogs and computer screens. He scratched notes on his steno pads. But he found almost no new information. If anything he found more puzzles.

He went downstairs to the breathtaking current periodicals room, but had no better results there. It didn't seem possible that a celebrity as colorful as Bram Serian had escaped dissection by the press during the course of his career, yet he had. There was piece after piece about his artistic versatility and his angry, tortured paintings, about his house and his influence on other artists, but little about the man himself.

Through the twenty-plus years that Bram Serian's name had been worthy of reportage there had been five different birthdates mentioned and a romantic's choice of birthplaces. A sheep station in the Australian outback, an old-time cattle ranch in Montana, a logging camp in the Northwest, a rodeo stock headquarters in Texas, and a cabin in the wilds of Alaska. Owen thought it probable that Serian himself had fueled the rumors and the erroneous reports about his history, and if so the artist either had been amusing himself with the spinning of a giant practical joke or had been caught up in his own fantasies. Or he had been deliberately hiding the truth. There was no indication that any of the facts were correct. And the various obituaries that had appeared after his death were just a rehash of old information.

Owen pulled off his reading glasses and leaned back in the chair to stretch out the kinks. Lunchtime had come and gone, and that fact was registering in his empty stomach so he went outside into a gloriously mild late-February day to buy a hot dog from a street vendor. Fifth Avenue buzzed with Saturday traffic. He joined the festive crowd seated on the massive stone steps to eat and watch.

His thoughts drifted. He wondered what it would be like to live in such a city and have access to all the libraries and museums and entertainments. To exist within the flow of so much daily human drama. To be charged with the energy and speed and aggressiveness that sizzled in the air constantly.

Then he tried to imagine himself seated beside Bram Serian. What would Serian have to say about living in Manhattan? What would he say about the research Owen was doing? Would he be annoyed or amused by Owen's efforts?

If anyone knew the truth about Bram Serian, it was probably the widow. But even if Lenore Serian wasn't so reclusive, he couldn't approach a woman who was fighting for her life.

Owen went back inside. After studying his options, he headed straight up to the more specialized art section, discouraged but still unwilling to accept that such a vast library did not hold all that he needed to know.

The periodicals in the art collection yielded a list of specific entries on Serian. Owen read and made notes and photocopied. Then, with the aid of a knowledgeable librarian, he waded through general material about the art world of the seventies and eighties, hoping to find mentions of Serian as well as gain an overview of his milieu.

When he was finished, he knew that contemporary art was divided by region as well as theory. He knew that in addition to styles of art, there were styles of showing and selling art. There were even styles of arguing about art. He knew what Serian thought about other artists' work and about the direction of art and about various curators and critics and gallery owners. He had a list of reference books to buy and a list of museums and galleries to visit. He had the names of every person in the art world who had figured in Serian's life. But in spite of all the steno pads he'd filled and the folders he had stuffed with photocopies, his quarry was still eluding him. He had no real grasp of the man Bram Serian had been. The answers were not to be found in print.

Reluctantly, Owen sought out the library's pay phones. He had never liked doing business over the telephone, and he certainly hadn't ever called complete strangers with requests for their time, but he was left with no alternatives. He had to talk with Serian's colleagues and friends. After a search of the phone book, Owen began dialing. The task did not get any easier as he progressed. There were disconnected lines and lines that rang unanswered. He was cursed and hung up on. But when he was finished he had a few solid interview appointments and several maybes. One man surprised him by insisting they meet that same night.

He stepped out of the library. The sun was low in the sky, but the air temperature was still pleasant. He stood at the top of the stone steps, flanked by the huge lions, and he took a deep breath as he looked out over the broad swath of Fifth Avenue and the busy sidewalk below him. He felt the same quiet sense of well-being that sometimes stole over him when he was looking down from a windy hilltop in the Flint Hills. Which made him smile because it seemed almost perverse that two polar opposites should cause the same reaction in him.

An awestruck whisper started deep within him, and as he stood there looking down, the whisper grew. He would be the first to capture Bram Serian in print. This book would not just be about Serian's death—it would unravel the mystery of his life.

He thought of something he'd read and copied down in a notebook years ago. Something from Rilke. "What we call fate does not come to us from the outside: it goes forth from within." And he felt the truth of that, felt that he'd been waiting for this, that there had been an invisible cord pulling him toward this book and this man and that somehow Bram Serian had been waiting for him.

* * *

Owen arrived at his Saturday night interview early and waited on the cold sidewalk for fifteen minutes before going in. The building had a uniformed doorman and a big sign saying, ALL GUESTS MUST BE ANNOUNCED. He gave his name to the doorman and waited. This was the first doorman-attended building he'd ever been in. Worse, it was the first interview he had ever conducted. He hoped that his nervousness and inexperience wouldn't be too obvious, and worried that Hillyer might not cooperate if he realized what an amateur he was dealing with.

Gregory Hillyer had been a mid-level artist in the early sixties and had taught at the legendary Art Students League on Fifty-seventh street in Manhattan. Hillyer had been the closest Bram Serian came to having a mentor.

Finally, the doorman gave him a nod and he boarded a narrow elevator. When the doors slid open Owen saw a very old man peering out from an apartment down the hall. "Mr. Hillyer?" Owen asked. The man acknowledged the greeting with a gruff response.

Gregory Hillyer was the color of old parchment. His eyes were rheumy and his hands were gnarled. He was dressed in yellow flannel pajamas beneath a brown tweed overcoat. But for all his frail appearance his manner was brusque and his voice was firm as he instructed Owen to sit down.

"So you're writing about Bram Serian," Hillyer said.

"Yes."

Gregory Hillyer settled in a chair, picked up a glass of something that looked like scotch whiskey and said, "Get on with it, then. What is it you want to know?"

"Would it be all right if I tape recorded?"

"Go ahead. It's no skin off my nose."

Owen set up his recorder. He had no idea what the proper beginning to an interview was, but he tried to sound confident. "Why don't you tell me about meeting Bram Serian, how you became acquainted . . . whatever you recall about that."

Hillyer cleared his throat with a low rumble and took a sip of the scotch. "Bram Serian stood out from the first, but not because of his talent. His art was crude. Undistinguished. Masturbatory. Not that much art isn't masturbatory. We all do it to a certain degree. But his early tries were beneath acceptability.

"The reason he made such a stir when he first showed up at Art Students League was not his art at all. It was his physical presence. He stood out from the other art students. He was well over six feet and built like an ox, and he dressed like he did his shopping at hillbilly castoff sales. You'd certainly never have guessed he was a Vietnam veteran. He gave a fresh-from-the-hills impression. Like he'd just picked the straw out of his hair.

"But as soon as I worked with him, I knew he had something that so many of my other students were lacking . . . *desire*. Not just the desire to create, because for an artist that desire arises with no conscious effort—like lust. No, his desire was for greatness, for recognition, for . . . significance.

"That's not to say that his art was unimportant to him. No. It was vital. The creating. The making. The building. It was his method of expression, and his own personal means of psychotherapy. A common condition among artists."

Hillyer chuckled dryly.

"God knows how many more deranged killers there might be in the world if not for art.

"But as far as being gifted . . . he wasn't. There were other students, Jonas Watkins, for example, who had true natural genius. Not Serian. His work was marked by struggle and frustration. Of course, he'd not begun to paint seriously yet. The painting and drawing classes he took were of little consequence to him then. His interests lay in molding and shaping and building with his hands . . . forceful, tactile activities . . . and he had no patience for dabbing color on canvas. In fact, I recall him expressing disdain for it."

Hillyer cleared his throat, then was seized by a fit of coughing. When it was over, he took a long drink before continuing.

"Jonas Watkins . . . that's a man you should talk to if you can find him. He was Serian's roommate for a time, and they seemed to be friendly. Until Watkins fell away . . .

"That's what happened to the majority of them. I taught so many over the years, worked with so many . . . I saw so much talent . . . The kind of natural talent that takes your breath away. They'd come to me . . . young and eager and starry-eyed . . . with no inkling of what lay ahead in the world for them . . . or of how hard it was to stay up on that heavenly plane where the only reality is what you gather into your senses to translate in your art.

"Then, the wheels of life ground them down with the burdens of respectability and child rearing and taxes and mortgages and they turned to the anesthesia of television and commercial consumption . . . and they fell. Like angels. They fell down into the cogs of the machine and became landlocked drones with only a memory of that higher plane where they'd once lived.

"That's what I witnessed over and over again through the years. The seduction of my students. Their fall from grace. They couldn't resist temptation like I did . . . like Serian did.

"Look around you, Mr. Byrne. Except for the artwork and the clothes on my back, nothing in this room belongs to me. I am unencumbered. I live with my sister. I never allowed myself to be tempted into marriage or materialism.

"And I could claim that I taught that wisdom to Bram Serian, but I didn't. He already had it. He may have learned to understand it more fully through me, but he already had the raw feel of it in his gut.

"Oh ho . . . I can see it in your eyes. You're thinking that this old man doesn't know about Serian's becoming rich and taking a wife and all that. But I do. I remained Bram Serian's guru, his spiritual aide if you will, right up until the end. That is not to say that I was his personal confessor or confidant. He was not that sort of a man. We spoke only of art. But I spent a great deal of time at Arcadia and I saw how things were.

"To an outsider, he may have appeared to have all the trappings of a fallen one, but that was merely an illusion. The money meant little to him. It was incidental. The big house was not the typical mortgaged bungalow of the suburban animal—it was a work of art in progress. And the marriage . . . it wasn't real."

"I don't understand," Owen said. "Weren't they legally married?"

Hillyer chuckled knowingly. "Who knows or cares? I'm speaking about spiritual matters. The marriage had no hold on him, drained him of nothing, so it didn't interfere with his creativity. I always believed that was because of her Oriental blood. They're very submissive, you know. That's why Oriental women are so popular as mail-order brides. Very submissive—" He grinned suggestively. "Sexually too. I've heard they'll do anything a man wants."

"So you think Serian married Lenore because she was submissive and didn't make demands on his time?"

"No. No. No. I didn't say that was *why* he married her. I

said that was what made being married to her so easy for him." Hillyer frowned in thought. "As I recall, he married her out of a sense of obligation. Some sort of promise during the war."

"You mean he knew Lenore when he was in Vietnam?"

"Obviously, he must have."

"You're sure of that?" Owen asked with excitement. This was the first proof that some of the rumors about Lenore might be true, and he pressed Hillyer for more.

"This is the first I've talked about it." Hillyer sighed heavily. "Since Bram's gone now, what can it hurt for an old man to talk? He's not here anymore to get angry, is he?

"I think the woman must have had some kind of unsavory background. A spy or a prostitute perhaps. Because he was very careful of protecting her identity. And because that's the kind of women he liked."

"Spies and prostitutes?"

"Specifically prostitutes. He had an affinity for soiled women."

Owen probed, gently trying to determine if Gregory Hillyer had any real facts to back up the Vietnam angle, but the old man did not.

"I'm telling you it was not a romantic match," Hillyer insisted. "Bram was repaying her for something that happened in Vietnam. You should find some of his fellow soldiers if you want to know more. All I can tell you is that the marriage itself meant nothing to him. He lived through his art ... and his identity as an artist. He lived for the power and respect his art brought him.

"That was true at the beginning and it was true at the end. And that is why the woman finally killed him. Because he was beyond her reach. Because she couldn't hurt him any other way."

Gregory Hillyer drained his glass, pulled up out of his chair and shuffled over to a cabinet for a refill. It was indeed scotch. He didn't offer Owen anything.

When Hillyer had returned to his chair, Owen asked what else he knew about Lenore.

"Oh, she's an enigma, that one is. There's no actress who could do a better job of being mysterious than Lenore."

"How is she mysterious?"

"That's hard to describe. She never joined in conversations, and if you asked her a question she would usually ask you a question back. If you said, 'Isn't it a nice day, Lenore?' she'd look at you and respond with 'Do you think it's a nice day?' And she never joined in on the laughter of others. She was never spontaneous like that." Hillyer hesitated. "It just occurred to me that she was very much like an art model. Have you ever observed an experienced art model?"

Owen shook his head no.

"When they pose, they are the focus of an entire roomful of people, but they act as though they're not aware of an audience at all. Good ones can create an incredible aura about themselves with their body language, yet they seem not to notice or care about the effect they have on those watching. That's what Lenore was like. She drew attention with her strangeness and her sexual aura, but she was indifferent to that attention."

"How did she relate to Serian?"

"As I said before, she was submissive to him. Respectful. One look from him and she was chastened. She knew her place."

Hillyer took a long pull on his scotch. "My sister doesn't like me to drink," he explained. "When she sees how much is gone from the bottle, I'll tell her that you, my guest, were responsible. If you're still here, please don't contradict me."

Owen glanced nervously at the door.

"Don't worry. We have an hour or so before she descends." Hillyer's eyes were glazing over and his words were losing their crisp edges, but he seemed eager to talk further.

Owen flipped through his notes. "I've found conflicting information on Serian's origins . . . birthdate, birthplace, family . . ."

Hillyer smiled. "Bram was quite sly about that. He wanted his past to stay in the past, and he either avoided discussion of it or lied. One time he told someone that he had sprung forth fully formed from the bowels of the bus that carried him here, and that's probably truer than anything else I heard him say on the subject."

"Did he ever mention his parents?"

"No."

"Did you get the impression that he had a particularly bad childhood or that he was running away from something?"

"In all the years I knew him, I never heard enough clues

to form an impression of his past at all. He dressed like a hillbilly in the beginning, and later he switched to dressing like a cowboy. Both may have been affected. I don't know. His manner of speaking was not eastern, but it was not identifiably Deep South or Texas or Canadian or that bland California style either. For all I know, he grew up in a middle-class suburb somewhere and his whole denial of the past may be rooted in a horror of mediocrity.

"Like so many other creative people, he came to New York and reinvented himself. It's not unusual."

"Can you recall any hint, however small . . . ?"

"Nothing more than what I've already told you."

"Besides Jonas Watkins, did he have any other friends who I might want to talk to?"

"Serian was not one for intimacies. He became quite a leader in the students' art group, but aside from Watkins he formed no special attachments that I was aware of."

"And girls? Did he have girlfriends?"

Hillyer smiled. "Girlfriends. That is such a frivolous term and Bram Serian was never frivolous. He had his share of sexual adventures. As I mentioned before, he was fascinated by prostitutes. And he did have an arrangement for a time with an art model. A tall black woman who was considered quite a prize. They were completely unsuited for one another. I'm sure Watkins will recall her name."

Owen retreated into scanning his notebook though he had no other questions written down.

"You say you continued as his creative advisor. Can you explain to me how his shift from sculpting to painting came about?"

"Ah . . ." Hillyer polished off the remainder of his scotch. "Divine intervention is the only way to explain it.

"He'd never truly enjoyed painting, though he'd done a little of it here and there. I remember one time we were drinking together after classes. There were a dozen or so students and myself and one other teacher crammed into a corner of our favorite dark little bar, and the subject turned to a debate over which was the purest art form, sculpting or painting. The argument raged on and on with the painters accusing the sculptors of being glorified crafters, just one step above knitting and bricklaying, and the sculptors accusing the painters of being effete dabblers relying on color to carry the work. As usual Bram hadn't said a thing. He was leaning against the wall with that amused expression of his that made so many people think he knew the answers to everything already ... but which really was caused by his not caring what the answers were ... and someone insisted that he explain why he didn't like to paint. And Serian said it was because of the flatness. He said he hated flatness ... whether it was a woman, a canvas, or a piece of land.

"We laughed for a long time over that. It was one of those lines that everyone repeated for years. And I never heard him say he'd changed his mind.

"Then one day he called me out to his farm to look at something. I went expecting to see the usual, and instead he had some canvases. That was before the big house ... and he didn't ever take people into the studio or the old farmhouse that was there ... so we just propped those canvases up outside. He left and went back inside the studio for awhile so I could examine them undisturbed, and then he came back out and asked what I thought, and I was nearly speechless. The work was brilliant.

"And the rest ... as they say ... is history. The paintings skyrocketed him to fame. They were never his passion though. He seemed puzzled over their success. Angry too. Frustrated that his other work didn't get the same attention. Later, of course, it did. And now everything he ever did is fawned over. Death does that, you know. The truth is that Serian was just luckier than the rest of us. He even died in a way that added to the mystique instead of fading away into obscurity."

Owen frowned in thought. "If you had to explain what kind of a man Serian was—what kind of a person he was—how would you describe him?"

"He was driven. Absolutely driven. And I believe he could have been quite happy with no intimacy in his life at all. He liked having followers, and helping the young and the struggling, but he was very uncomfortable with closeness. And he didn't like to be touched. He hated it when anyone touched him."

Hillyer gripped the arms of his chair and leaned forward as though he might fall out.

"She'll be home soon and I need to flee to my bed," he declared.

Owen helped Hillyer from the chair and held his arm as the old man negotiated the path to his bedroom. When he was safely perched on the edge of the bed, Owen said, "Thank you for your time."

"Get this coat off me," he ordered, and Owen gently pulled the frail arms free. "You can come again if you must," Hillyer said. "But I warn you . . . I expect a free copy of the book upon publication."

"That will be my pleasure," Owen told him and started for the door.

"Who are you speaking with next?" Hillyer called.

Owen turned back to face him. "Tomorrow I have an appointment with Edie Norton. The woman who—"

Hillyer scowled. "I *know* who Edie Norton is. That vampire bitch."

7

Owen spent the remainder of Saturday night organizing his trial notes, typing a transcript of Gregory Hillyer's interview and laboring over his proposal. He worked till late, but still, when he went to bed, he couldn't sleep. He lay in the dark, listening to the street noises from below.

Originally, Lenore had seemed the bigger mystery to him. He had thought of Bram Serian as a man much like himself and had imagined a character for Serian that he now realized was wrong. Tomorrow he had an appointment with Edie Norton, owner of Norton Galleries and Bram Serian's long-time art dealer. Surely she would have answers to his questions.

His mind raced with anticipation. The lighted dial of the clock recorded the passing hours.

Bram Serian's comment about hating flatness in a woman, a canvas or a piece of land kept rebounding in his thoughts. Serian had to have been from farm country to have said that.

Owen himself had been born on flatland. A quarter section of wheat ground twelve miles outside Maynard, Kansas. One hundred and eighty acres of prime farmland bounded by osage orange trees and broken only by the buildings and the cedar windrow on the north side of the yard.

The hedgerows and windbreaks in that country had been planted by settlers in the distant past, presumably to mark fencelines and slow the ever-present wind, but Owen suspected the early settlers had planted them for other reasons as well. He thought it had been their way of harnessing the land and rendering it harmless, for it could be soul-draining to face the relentless flatland, to look straight to the horizon in every direction without relief, without one interruption of line to lead the eye or the heart upward.

His family's quarter section was called the Hadley place.

The Hadleys were his mother's people; they had owned the land for generations before leaving it to her. There was a wrought-iron gate to the garden with the name HADLEY worked into the design. The flowerbed in front of the house held rambling, old-fashioned roses that had come from the East in a covered wagon with the first Hadleys. At the end of the drive was a mailbox mounted on a milkcan that said HADLEY in brass letters.

Clancy Byrne never changed a thing or put the name BYRNE up. That should have been a warning maybe, but Clancy's lack of possessiveness fit so well with his other carefree attitudes that no one suspected the root of it. Maybe Clancy himself had not been aware of his intentions. Then again, maybe the plan was clear in his mind from the beginning. From the day he met their mother.

Stella Hadley was a lonely nineteen-year-old, reeling from the closely spaced deaths of her parents and brother, when she met Clancy Byrne at a Fourth of July picnic. He was just visiting in the area so there was an instant air of mystery about him. That combined with his charm and his legendary blue eyes had every female at the picnic curious. He ran an impressive second in the men's footrace and won the horseshoe pitching tournament. Then he took the mandolin out of a performer's hands and entertained everyone with a round of Irish folk songs.

Stella Hadley was lost.

That was the story they'd all heard time and again while growing up. The tale of the sad, pining princess being swept off her feet by the charming handsome prince. Even toward the end of her life, when it was clear that the fairy tale had not ended happily, their mother still loved to recount the story of the enchanted meeting.

Stella and Clancy were married within three months of that meeting. The starry-eyed bride converted to Catholicism and signed over the deed to her inherited farmground on her wedding day. None of her aunts or uncles could dissuade her from these drastic acts. Stella was determined to prove how strong her faith in Clancy was. Or maybe she was determined to bind him to her so tightly that he could never escape.

Until Owen was nine, Ellen twelve, Terry sixteen, and Meggie three, they lived on the farm, surrounded by doting great-aunts and a community where their mother's parents and grandparents had been established and liked. There was hard work to be done, but most of it was seasonal—centered around planting and harvest. They grew winter wheat, which meant they planted in the fall, leased grazing rights so that local dairymen could pasture cattle on the tender growth, then watched as the crop miraculously recovered from the grazing and the months of heavy snowcover to shoot upward with the spring sun and develop into the waving sea of gold that blanketed so much of Kansas farm country.

The wheat income combined with the small but steady profit from the oil lease on the back forty provided a decent living for the family in spite of their father being a notably bad farmer. Their ground was fertile so skill was not crucial to production. The black loam of their fields had been enriched for centuries by the silt of overflowing creeks, and their mother's forebears had been careful guardians, feeding the land with manure and periodically resting a field by rotating sorghum or corn with the wheat. In one generation Clancy could not undo all that.

In fairness, Clancy was not so much a bad farmer as he was an apathetic one. Farming bored him. Owen had vivid memories of his father's planting techniques. The season began with Clancy hanging out in the café near the grain elevator, presumably picking up planting tips. Then he would make a major occasion out of dragging the drill from the equipment shed and buying the seed. When the big day came he would take Terry and Ellen and Owen to the field and he would make a little speech about God and the saints being good to them. Then he would hop on the tractor and make that ceremonial first round, creating the outline of a design that Owen now knew could be seen by airline passengers high overhead. As soon as that first exhilarating pass was finished, he put the tractor into idle and ordered one of his children to take over.

They worked in shifts usually, walking back and forth from the house to the fields and waving each other down to take over. During the last thirty minutes of Owen's shift, he had always hallucinated, repeatedly imagining his relief waving the red handkerchief from across the field.

He recalled driving a lumbering, roaring machine in circles around a huge open field as one of the most mind-numbing, spine-jarring activities possible. Even without wind the dust rose up to coat every inch of skin and clothing, and in Kansas there was almost always wind. Other farmers held back on bad days, fearful that their precious topsoil was blowing away, but topsoil was not an important concept to Clancy. Owen remembered bouncing along on that tractor seat at times when the blowing dirt whipped so hard against his face that he was blinded and his furrows staggered out across the earth behind him like agricultural modern art. When that happened Terry always drove a double shift to redo the work.

There were other smaller chores too. They kept a Jersey cow that had to be milked twice a day, and the dogs had to be fed, and there was always a pig or a lamb or a steer being fattened in the pen behind the equipment shed. Fences and equipment had to be maintained, though Clancy's low standards didn't put much pressure in that area. Winter brought lots of snow shoveling, and spring meant that the driveway had to be regraveled. During the summer all of them had to help with their mother's garden and with the canning and jelly making that resulted. But through it all they still managed to have fun. And while their labor was frequently exhausting, there was no bitterness in it. They were happy.

Their father was away often. He was a regular at the café and at all the area domino games. He left for days at a time to go coyote hunting or dog trading or on some vague errand. While his absence was in some ways a relief, they were always glad to have him return. He brought gaiety to the household with his hilarious tales and he made their mother sparkle. They were proud to have a father who was so charming and so much fun.

It was Meggie's birth that changed everything.

Clancy took off on unexplained business that morning. There was snow in the forecast, his pickup was up on blocks awaiting a new fuel pump, and his wife was nine months along, but he drove away, waving out the window of the family car with the promise that he would be back soon.

The predicted snow struck as a full-fledged blizzard. Phone lines fell as they always did during major storms. Electricity went next. They were huddled around the old iron woodstove telling ghost stories when their mother's first contraction hit. Their ordinarily stalwart mother panicked.

Terry put on two layers of long underwear and insulated coveralls and two sets of gloves and a hand-knitted face warmer with only eye holes left open, and he set off on the tractor for help. Owen was a little worried for his mother, but after years of assisting at calving or foaling or lambing, birth seemed a natural occurrence and he did not fully understand the dangers his mother faced.

It was Terry's leaving in the midst of that violent storm that really terrified him. Owen went with his brother out to the equipment shed. The wind was gusting so hard and the snow had already piled so deep that they had difficulty pushing the back door of the house open and negotiating the open space between house and equipment shed. The tractor looked small in the darkness. Even at top speed it was slow. Very very slow. And it was a standard old-fashioned tractor with no cab or heater to protect Terry from the storm.

When his brother finally chugged off into the snow-curtained night Owen had the sudden realization that he could die. Their mother's father and brother had both been killed in a tractor mishap under much less hazardous conditions. He knew that Terry could be blinded by the snow, run off the road and get stuck, and freeze to death before he found help. He knew that the snow on the ground and the poor visibility made it easy for Terry to misjudge the terrain and drive too close to a deep ditch, tilting the tractor so that it fell sideways. So that the driver was crushed beneath it or thrown off to lie helpless in the frozen night. And that was the moment that everything changed for Owen. From that time forward he would never feel the same toward his charming will-o-the-wisp father.

Ellen and Owen sponged their mother's forehead and let her squeeze their hands during contractions, and they said every prayer they had ever learned during their sporadic religious training. He had no idea how much time passed—it felt like forever—before they heard the sound of rescue. The blessed roaring of the road grader. Terry had gone to the one person he knew could get their mother to the hospital, the man responsible for maintaining the county's gravel and dirt roads. He kept the road grader at his farm, and this monstrous piece of equipment had the strength and power of a tank.

They bundled their mother into the heated cab of the grader. A half-frozen Terry had stayed at the man's house to warm up, so it was Ellen who climbed up into the grader to go to the hospital with their mother and cry with her at Meggie's birth.

Clancy didn't show up for days. Not until the evening after their mother came home from the hospital.

She was in bed with the baby when they heard the car and she got up and went out onto the porch. Owen ran out with her, throwing a blanket around her shoulders. And they both stopped in midstride. There staring out from the back of the car were five long grayish faces. Dogs. Greyhound Russian-wolfhound crossbreds. Those big slinking, shaggy, vacant creatures that run like the wind and kill like machines. Clancy Byrne had missed the birth of his child and left his family stranded for a week to go after some hunting dogs.

Stella Byrne sagged against her son for a moment, then drew herself up and set her mouth into the hard line that was so characteristic of her later years. "Tell him I'm resting," she said and disappeared back into the house, leaving Owen to greet Clancy and listen to his long tale of learning about how a farmer had suffocated in his silo and realizing that farmer owned some of the best coyote dogs in the state and tracking down the widow and finally getting them from her for a steal. "I jewed her down," Clancy had said triumphantly. "I jewed her good."

It wasn't until later that they heard how five full-grown hounds had fit into the backseat of their new car—the first brand-new car they had ever owned and the only automobile their mother had ever chosen herself.

When Clancy finally clinched the deal with the widow, she'd said she wanted the dogs gone immediately, so without hesitation Clancy went to a truck stop and had the mechanic rip out the backseat of their showroom-shiny sedan. Then he loaded those flea-infested hounds into the newly created cargo space and hit the highway. He thought it had been a clever solution, and of course he intended to go back and get the seat.

Their mother stayed locked away with the baby for days. Clancy begged and pleaded at the door, promising that the car would be as good as new, promising that he would have it professionally cleaned and have the seat re-installed at a dealership. He went clear over to Hutchinson and bought her a present, an expensive wooden jewelry box that was made like a miniature chest of drawers and was big enough to hold the contents of an entire store display. He made Terry take it in to her across the battle line of their bedroom threshold.

Though she owned no jewelry except her wedding ring

and a brooch her mother had left her, the gift worked its magic and Stella unlatched the door. It didn't seem to bother her that Clancy had obviously bought the first thing he saw without regard to what she might want or need. She treasured that chest, filling the velvet-lined drawers with her most precious keepsakes. Besides the heirloom brooch she kept baby teeth and first haircut curls and the silver dollar her father had given her at her high school graduation, the blue ribbon Terry won for the eighth-grade spelling bee, the bullet that had been cut out of Ellen's thigh after Clancy accidentally shot her while hunting, and years down the road she added Terry's class valedictorian medal and Ellen's head cheerleader pin and the engraved gold pencil that Owen won in the county essay contest.

Clancy did get the car cleaned and de-fleaed. He never managed to put it back together though. Months passed before he went back for the seat, and by then the truckstop mechanic had given up on his return and sold it. Terry wired wooden crates into the hollowed out sedan then tied bed pillows on top of them, and that is what served as the backseat for the remaining two years that they owned the car. Terry and Owen and their mother never spoke of it, but Ellen gave Clancy endless grief, using that ruined car against their father in ways that would have made the devil himself smile.

Flatland. The flatlands were part of Owen's childhood. Part of his well-remembered past. But he could understand Bram Serian's hatred.

He stared up into the darkness of his noisy city room. What would Serian think of the Flint Hills, he wondered. And he smiled to himself. Because he thought he knew. He thought he finally had the key to Bram Serian's character.

Owen had an appointment with Edie Norton for four o'clock at her SoHo gallery. Having done his homework, he knew that there was another Norton Gallery uptown and that the Nortons were very well known in their field.

As was his custom Owen arrived early. He strolled through the spacious rooms. They appeared similar to other galleries he had passed on his way there, with high ceilings and white walls and floors of polished oak. There were two Serian paintings on display. One was a dark angry abstract and the other a quiet but desperate melange of melting bodies.

There was a sullen, haughty young woman in a tight knit dress behind the desk. Owen gave her his name. She disappeared for several minutes, then returned to escort him into the office. As Owen followed her to the back of the building, he wondered how someone with her attitude could keep a job.

When he stepped into the lushly decorated office, he was greeted by a woman who was somewhere past fifty, though so handsomely turned-out that her age was incidental. She extended her hand and said, "Hello, Owen. I'm Edie Norton," while her gaze coolly appraised every inch of him.

"May I offer you tea or coffee?"

Owen declined and she settled behind her ornate desk.

"Beautiful furniture," he commented.

"Antique French. That is my second passion after art."

He nodded. She smiled.

"I had you checked out quite thoroughly, Owen, but still I feel I must warn you . . . if anything we say here is sold to tabloids or used for any purpose other than your book, Norton Galleries will make a great deal of trouble for you."

"Oh?"

"Yes. We've had to be very careful, you know. Everyone who knew Bram has been approached, and since we were so intimate with him . . ." She shrugged delicately.

Owen put this unsettling news aside and concentrated on his purpose. "I understand you're scheduled to testify at the trial," he said.

"Yes. Forced to testify. If my husband, Barry, weren't in Europe on business they would drag him up there too." She frowned, but the skin on her face was so tight that no vertical creases appeared. "Tell me about this book you're researching, Owen."

There was something about the way Edie Norton said his name that made Owen want to back away from her. He tried to avoid eye contact.

"As I explained on the phone, it's essentially a true crime book. I'm concentrating on the trial and the tragedy of Serian's death, but I also want to tell about Serian's life. I want to show who he was. Not just as an artist but as a man."

"Ummm . . ." She folded her hands on the desk and pursed her lips in thought. "Something like—how can the tragic death have meaning without knowing the human side of the creative genius who was destroyed?"

Owen blinked. "Yes. That sounds about right. Can I quote you on that?"

Her laughter was dry and mechanical.

"I'm sure I told you how limited my time is today."

"Yes."

"And you can put that tape recorder away. No tapes."

"Okay." Owen opened his notebook.

"And you are aware of the areas I will not discuss?"

"If I overstep any boundaries, please call it to my attention . . . Mrs. Norton."

"Edie," she insisted.

"Fine," he said, feeling uncomfortable beneath her scrutiny. "Let's start at the beginning. What do you know about Serian's childhood?"

"Not much. He kept his early years to himself."

"Where was he from?"

"Somewhere out there." She waved a jeweled hand disdainfully to indicate the hinterland. "The great beyond. The land where men grow to be men." She smiled. "Like you."

"I . . . ah . . . When you first met him, did he have an accent or speech pattern that might have led you to guess at his origins?"

"No."

"Did he ever say anything about his parents?"

"No. But he always had this thing about orphans. Nothing specific . . . but . . . well, for instance, he was infuriated by those stories in the paper where people abandon their babies. And if there was ever a movie with an orphan or an orphanage in it he couldn't wait to see it. So, I always wondered if one of his parents was an orphan or if he was an orphan himself."

"Did you ever ask him?"

She sighed impatiently. "You must understand about Serian. He *never*, and I mean *never* discussed anything about his past." She frowned thoughtfully. "I'm not certain how much of his past I'd even want to see surfacing at this point. I do have a sizable financial stake in Bram Serian's image, and I wouldn't want that jeopardized."

Owen considered this. "Yes. I understand what you're saying. But how can Bram Serian's artistic image be damaged by restoring his humanity? Whatever his past . . . however complex or mundane . . . revealing it won't alter the respect and fascination people have for his work. If anything the mystery he wove around himself will create more interest."

She regarded Owen in silence.

"Mrs. Norton ... Edie ... People like Serian, the people who follow their visions and rise above the rest of us ... their lives are treasures that should be in the public domain. We can learn from them. Be inspired by them. Be moved to compassion or to understanding some aspect of the human condition that we wouldn't have understood otherwise. Serian's history is important."

Edie Norton's mouth curved into a faint smile. "So you can be eloquent when you speak as well as when you write," she teased. She seemed to drift into memory then, her shrewd gaze losing focus. When she recovered she smiled wistfully at Owen and said, "My, what I could do with you if you were an artist instead of a writer. All that homespun sincerity and those blue eyes and those lovely calloused hands. You remind me of Bram when he was young."

Owen cleared his throat and stared down at his notebook.

She sighed. "Well, I suppose a sensational book about Serian will generate more attention for his work ... and publicity for the gallery." She leaned forward over her pink leather desk blotter and steepled her hands. "Get on with it, then. What is it you want to know?"

Owen launched into his list of prepared questions.

"Was Bram Serian his full name?"

"I doubt it. But that's the only one he ever used."

"Do you know his correct birth date?"

"No. And I doubt that anyone else does either. He changed it frequently."

"How about a birthplace?"

"No idea. But my favorite version was the one about the logging camp."

"Did he ever mention people from his past? Acquaintances, relatives, teachers ..."

She hesitated. "After we made his first big sale, we were drinking champagne together and he said something about wishing he could rub his art teacher's nose in it. I told him I'd be glad to send her some impressive notice and he became very angry. Broke one of my crystal champagne flutes and told me to mind my own business."

"That's a strong reaction."

"Serian was a man of strong reactions."

"Can you think of any clues to his early life?"

She shook her head. "Only ... many assumed that the outdoorsman-cowboy pose was strictly for show. But it always seemed real to me. I'll never believe he grew up in a suburb. He was the strong, deep, quiet type, you know? Like you. Except that Serian had a dark streak. You could feel the possibility of cruelty in him. And he had a lot of trouble relating to people. He either ignored them or he expected too much of them, and he was constantly disappointed or angry or adding a name to his famous blacklist."

Owen waited, giving her time to add more if she chose; then he asked, "How about Vietnam? What's the story there?"

"I think that whatever happened to him over there was bad. I think he carried a lot of pain over that."

"What branch of the service was he in?"

"I have no idea. He was never specific."

"What did he say about the war?"

"Oh, vague things. Life, death, injustice. The government hypocrisy involved. Things like that. But if someone else brought up the subject of Vietnam, Bram would walk away. He didn't want to hear others discuss it."

"What about Lenore? I've been told that Serian met her in Vietnam during the war and that he may have married her as payment of a debt."

"That's absolute nonsense! Lenore Serian didn't come from Vietnam. She just told Bram that to win his sympathy. You've seen her. She could be half-Japanese, half-Korean, half-Filipino ... She could be one of those California mutts that's a little of everything. What proof is there that she's half-Vietnamese? None. And that accent of hers! She's toned it down over the years, but it used to sound like someone from Toledo imitating a bad French movie." Edie Norton rolled her eyes and clicked her tongue in disgust. "Everything about Lenore is fake. She created an entire persona just to trap Bram Serian. And it worked. She fooled him and she's fooled a hell of a lot others too."

Owen tried to swallow his surprise. "If she's an imposter, wouldn't the district attorney bring that out at the trial?"

"Hah! Those thick-headed idiots in that backwater district attorney's office will never uncover anything on a woman as clever as Lenore. And I've begun to wonder if Bram didn't help her ... if he didn't discover the truth about her at some

point and, rather than face the humiliation of it coming out
... if he didn't help her bury her true identity even deeper."

Edie Norton glanced at her watch and frowned as though
wishing their time was up. "Lenore," she said bitterly. "The
subject always comes around to Lenore, doesn't it?"

"You sound as though you resent her."

Edie stood and wandered through the room, trailing her
fingers over her ornate furniture.

"When we met Serian, he was enrolled at the Art Students
League and living in the West Village. He hadn't been in
New York long. His work was minor, but we saw his enormous potential, so we took him on. Tried to guide him. Tried
to help him get in touch with his own brilliance, so to speak.
His sculpting improved and we were finally able to sell
some of it, but ... oh, you know ... he just didn't fit in anywhere. He wasn't a minimalist, he wasn't a realist, he wasn't
a surrealist. There just wasn't a way to market him.

"But we stuck by him. He was increasingly troubled by
his inability to find an audience, and he went through a period where he almost disappeared for a time, buying that
farm and becoming a recluse. Then his genius for painting
was discovered and he became *the* Bram Serian.

"During that entire period, he was linked with some black
art model, but I rarely ever saw her and he never spoke of
her. If it hadn't been for the art world gossip line, I wouldn't
have known she existed. You see, he had absolute tunnel vision then, and he didn't let personal trivia interfere with his
creativity.

"Then he married Lenore and she destroyed his ability to
do that. She wore him down with her manipulations and her
childish, neurotic behavior, and eventually she *destroyed* his
ability to create. When he couldn't create anymore, she *destroyed* him."

Edie Norton covered her face with her perfectly groomed
hands. Owen sat in silence. When she recovered her poise
she was angry.

"Lenore Serian is not the subject I agreed to discuss!"

"I'm sorry," Owen said. He waited to see if she would
throw him out. She didn't. Instead she returned to her chair,
sagging into it as if defeated.

"Do you know the art model's name?"

"No. She wasn't important."

"But it sounds as though Serian was involved with her for a number of years ..."

"She wasn't important!" Edie snapped.

"All right." Owen stared down at his notes, wondering which direction was safe. Finally he asked, "After Serian showed Gregory Hillyer his paintings, did he bring them directly to the gallery?"

Edie Norton laughed disdainfully. "So you've talked to old Hilly, have you? I would not use him as a source of information, Owen."

"Why not?"

"Let's just say that eighty-year-old alcoholics don't have reliable memories."

"He seemed lucid."

Her eyes narrowed. "I could tell you some things about Greg Hillyer ..." Then she stopped herself and smiled stiffly. "But then we're off the subject, aren't we?" She glanced at her watch.

Owen turned back through his notes. "Did you go out to the farm much?"

"Not in the beginning. He didn't want visitors. He was working on the studio and the conditions were primitive."

"Did he remodel the barn alone?"

"Not completely. He hired professionals for the wiring and plumbing and all those skylights in the roof. And then there was Al, too. He helped with the studio."

"Who's Al?"

"Al? Why, he was a fixture out there for years. I don't know where Bram found him. There was a rumor that Al might have been a distant cousin or something, but I doubt there was anything to that. Anyway, Al was a basketcase. Mentally impaired. There was no way the man could have functioned in society. Bram took care of him and let him live in the studio as a kind of general helper and creative assistant."

"What is a creative assistant?"

"Oh, you know ... someone who stretches canvas, maintains the blowtorches, cleans up paint. That sort of thing. A busy artist can keep several assistants going."

"What happened to Al after Bram died?"

"Al was gone long before that." Edie Norton toyed absently with the large emerald ring on her finger, then glanced at her watch again.

Quickly Owen asked, "How did Serian's breakthrough paintings come to your attention? Did Hillyer call you?"

"Hillyer? Certainly not. The old fool had no part in it."

She inhaled deeply and her expression softened. "After Bram started working out at the farm, he became like a hermit. We could hardly coax him into town. Barry and I were so worried. Months would go by without anyone seeing him. And we were all told in no uncertain terms that he didn't want visitors popping in. Then one day Bram called and said he had something to show us and would we like to come out to his place.

"We dropped everything and rushed out. It was our first visit to the farm and we were somewhat shocked. So far out in the middle of nowhere and with that sad little house . . . That was before he'd begun the big building project. But he was very proud of the place and especially of the studio he'd just finished. It was huge. A real barn actually, that he'd remodeled into this ultimate studio with perfect skylighting and everything. Or so he said. He wouldn't let us look inside. No one was allowed inside. Except his assistant, of course.

"He didn't take us in the house either. I think he was embarrassed over it. There was a sagging wooden porch on the front of the house, and he showed us a stack of canvases there and asked us to take a look. Barry glanced at me and we were both thinking, 'Oh no . . . what is this going to be . . .' because Serian had never been interested in painting, and then we started going through the canvases and we were stunned. Stunned! Barry got so excited he lapsed into stuttering."

Edie Norton smiled at the memory. "Those paintings were the turning point. We staged a big show and made Bram a star. From then on he was in constant demand. He divided his time between his loft in Manhattan and the country place, and he did all his socializing in the city, so years went by without anyone going out to his farm. Years, where all we knew was what was happening when he was in Manhattan. Then he started talking about a house he was building, and people were interested and offering help and so Bram's weekend sweat parties began. He'd have groups of people out and everyone would hammer and paint and eat barbecue and get wild.

"In the summer Bram hired a van to pick people up in the

city on Friday evenings and return them Sunday nights so there was a regular schedule of sweat parties. Everyone wanted to go, but Bram was very selective about who he included."

"When did Lenore move in?"

"I don't know. We used to go out every few weeks or so and occasionally we'd catch a glimpse of her. She was very behind the scenes, creeping around before people were up in the morning and that sort of thing and we just assumed she came in as part-time household help. Finally we realized she lived out there, but we still didn't think anything of it. She was kind of a bedraggled creature then and everyone thought he'd gotten one of those illegals from Korea or the Philippines to do the housework. We hardly ever saw her. She kept to herself. Most of the time you forgot that Bram had two other people living out there with him because both Lenore and Al were so good at keeping themselves hidden. Barry always said that they were his idea of the perfect servants—silent and nearly invisible.

"Eventually, we heard she was supposed to be some kind of war refugee. One of those half-Vietnamese orphans.

"As soon as I heard that I became suspicious of what her game was. I knew she was after him. I mean Bram was such a sucker for orphans to begin with, and he had that leftover mental baggage from Vietnam, so she was really playing on all his weaknesses.

"Then he threw a big party one weekend, invited a group of us to the country for an overnight to see a newly finished portion of the house. And while we were there the girl drifted in. Only she wasn't a girl anymore. She had evolved into this dramatic creature. And Barry said, 'I see that you still have your little refugee living here,' and Bram looked around like he didn't know what Barry was talking about for a minute; then he said, 'Oh, yeah, I married her.' "

Edie Norton drew in a deep breath.

"We were all speechless, but Bram just brushed it off as if it was unimportant. In fact, later that afternoon he took us down to a pond to see some exotic ducks he'd bought, and he was far more enthusiastic and forthcoming about the ducks than about the marriage business.

"I never understood why he married her. She's aesthetically interesting, of course. You've seen her. That lush coloring and the bone structure ... For an artist I suppose it was natural to view her as a piece of art. Living art. And I understood how she'd played up to him with the Vietnam orphan angle ... but why marriage?

"She was already out there. She was already available. They probably slept together from the beginning. So why on earth did he marry her?"

Edie aimed the question at Owen as though he had the answer.

"Did they not seem to be in love when they married?" Owen asked carefully.

"Absolutely not! It was the most bizarre thing. No one could explain it. Even other men found it inexplicable. Everyone talked about it endlessly."

"Did you ever ask him about his reasons."

"I wouldn't have dared. By then Bram had developed his legendary bad temper, and even I was a teensy bit afraid of him."

"And Lenore? Did you ever have a personal conversation with her that shed any light on things?"

"No one had conversations with Lenore, personal or otherwise."

"She had no close friends?"

"No friends, period. If you ask me, Lenore Serian was and always has been insane. Why, even after she started—" Edie Norton stopped herself and glared at him. "I will not give personal assessments of Lenore Serian."

"All right ... let's backtrack ... you're saying that Lenore was not involved with Serian until long after he'd returned from Vietnam. So the rumors about his having met her there, about his having been involved with her there or obligated to her for something that happened there are totally without foundation?"

"Yes." Edie shifted in her chair and turned her bracelet watch to read the time. "You have five more minutes," she said.

"Okay. Just talk to me about Serian, then. What was he like when you first met him and how did he change as his career progressed?"

She smiled. "I remember the first time I saw him. At a party. Oh, he was glorious. He had an artistic aura that positively glowed. And he was innocent and kind and incredibly sexy."

She looked around as though afraid someone might be

watching; then she reached down into a desk drawer and pulled out a framed eight-by-ten photograph. "Bram would have killed me if he knew I had this," she said. "But it's meant so much to me."

She handed the photograph to Owen. It was the first good facial shot he had seen of Bram Serian, and he studied it hungrily. The man had thick fair hair, a handlebar mustache, and a face that would have looked perfect in an old tintype sepia from the 1800s. He was looking off as though unaware of the camera. Several women stood around him, all with their eyes on him. One was a younger version of Edie Norton. In the background was the profile of a striking black woman.

"Why was he so set against having his picture taken?" Owen asked.

"He said that he wanted people to concentrate on his art. Not on him." She shrugged. "Whatever his reasons he was adamant about it."

"This is you, right?" Owen asked.

Edie smiled. "Yes. It was taken at one of Bram's early shows. And that's . . ." She pointed at the woman beside her. "Oh, I can't remember her name. Some society type. The slut threw herself at Bram all night, but I did get her to buy a painting."

"And who's this?" Owen asked, indicating the woman in the background.

"That's Geneva," Edie answered; then she stopped herself and glared at Owen.

"Is she the art model that he was involved with?"

"Of course! That's Geneva Johnson."

Edie snatched the picture from him, stared down at it a moment, and then tucked it away with a sigh. "Bram lost the innocence but he stayed sexy. And through the years he remained kind. Heaven knows how many hangers-on he was subsidizing. The retarded assistant out in the studio and other washed-up artists he'd known from Art Students League . . ." She snorted disdainfully. "And that nasty old Greg Hillyer . . . that man must have lived off Bram for years . . . And of course he was always generous to young artists and to art programs and groups. But it was hard for most people to remember his kindness because he became so . . . formidable. Everyone was afraid of his temper."

"Was Lenore afraid of him?"

"Who knows. They certainly never interacted when I was around."

"Even at parties, openings, public events?"

"My dear Owen, Lenore never accompanied him to Manhattan. She was like one of his exotic ducks. She stayed near the pond."

"Why do you think that was?"

"My guess is that she was an *objet d'art* for his grand house, and one doesn't usually carry household decorations around. But that is positively my last comment on Lenore."

"I'd like to hear more about Serian's friendships and—"

"It will have to be another time. I have a very full schedule today."

"Then I can call you again?" Owen asked.

She smiled suggestively. "Maybe we should meet for a drink next time."

Owen stepped out of her office, mulling over what he had and hadn't learned. The young woman with the tight dress and the attitude was waiting to walk him out. She threw him a contemptuous over-the-shoulder look and said, "How was your interview?"

"Fine."

"Did she tell you about fucking him?"

Owen could not conceal his shock.

"Oh yeah. She swallowed a bunch of pills when he married Lenore. Not enough to kill her, though."

"Desiree!" Edie's voice floated out from the back. "Have you made those phone calls yet?"

"Yes, Mother!"

Owen walked east toward his apartment. The sky had turned a flat gray and the temperature was falling. He walked with his hands in his pockets and his eyes on the sidewalk, stretching out his legs in a ground-covering stride, but he couldn't outdistance the heaviness he felt. The truth of people's lives was often so sad or pathetic or tragic. Edie Norton's wanting to die for love and Serian's marrying a woman for inexplicable reasons, and Lenore, possibly unwanted and without a home or possibly so desperate she had to scheme and lie for security. And Serian dead and Lenore accused and Edie with all the hard calloused layers protecting her heart and her daughter caught in the crossfire.

And his own family, tangled and broken in so many ways.

He reached his apartment building in a state of depression. He went through the unlocking rituals, opening the outside door and then the door between the vestibule and the lobby.

"There you are!" a female voice called, and he was surprised to see Holly Danielson sitting at the bottom of the stairs.

"Hi," Owen returned, instantly cheered by her energetic greeting.

"I hope you don't mind me dropping in . . ." She stood up, brushing off the seat of her jeans. Her cheeks were flushed and her eyes were shining. "I've got some material for you and I had to be down this way, so I thought I'd just give it to you but since you don't have a phone I had to take a chance that it was a good time."

"How long have you been waiting?"

"Oh, not long. And as you can see I managed to sneak in here to the lobby so it wasn't bad."

She didn't seem in a hurry to hand over the material and leave so Owen asked, "Do you want to come up? I could make you a cup of coffee."

"Actually . . ." She picked up the white bag and the brown bag on the floor at her feet. "I sort of brought my own feast."

Owen took the white bag from her and started up the stairs. The pungent aroma of Chinese food struck him immediately.

"There's this little place down here that does the best Szechuan," she said as she followed him up the stairs. "I never can resist it. So . . . I thought . . . if you hadn't eaten dinner . . ."

He was enormously relieved at being lifted from his brooding, and he was grateful for the comfort of food promised by the tantalizing smells. "This is great," he said. "I can't believe you did this."

"I've got Chinese beer too," she told him eagerly. "I didn't know if you were into wine or beer, but with Szechuan I figured that I couldn't go wrong with Chinese beer."

"Beer sounds terrific."

They unpacked the food on the apartment's narrow coffee table, then sat down on the couch to eat. She opened a carton and handed it to him.

"Cold noodles with sesame!"

She beamed. "I remembered that you liked those after Marilyn talked you into trying them."

"I never would have believed a cold noodle could be so damn good," he admitted, laughing as he hungrily loaded his plate.

They ate in silence for awhile; then Holly started talking, commenting on the drabness of the apartment and the lower-class nature of the East Village in general. She lamented the boring lack of murder and mayhem in her work Saturday, and related the sordid tale of a producer at her station who couldn't keep his hands off his female subordinates.

"Why don't you report him? Make him stop."

"Yeah, right." Holly snorted sarcastically. "We could probably even get him fired. But whoever opens her mouth will be treated like a leper for the rest of her career in television." She grinned. "Don't look so shocked. That's the way things are. Either you learn to live with it or you find a job where the only males are beneath you."

"Or find a job outside of television," Owen said.

"Hah. It's the same in most fields. You've just never seen it because you've always lived the good country life. When men get power, most of them can't resist taking advantage. It's male nature, I guess." She shrugged ruefully. "Who knows, maybe women would be just as bad statistically if enough of them had the chance. Maybe power is the ultimate temptation."

Owen watched her add more ginger chicken to her plate. His own appetite was gone and his earlier gloom returned.

"I talked to Edie Norton today," he told her.

"Did you get anything good?"

"I suppose so. I'm beginning to wonder if Bram Serian wasn't destined for tragedy from the beginning."

"What makes you say that?"

"I don't know. Nothing specific."

"Well, you'll figure out a way to use it. It's such a good angle. *Destined for tragedy from the beginning.* Sounds like a line that will make your publisher see dollar signs."

Owen wanted to tell her that the East Village was just fine in his opinion and a Saturday night without murder was not something to complain about and tragedy wasn't just an angle to create dollar signs. Instead, he stood suddenly and carried his plate to the sink.

"Is that all you're going to eat?" she asked.

"I had enough," he said, occupying himself with assembling the coffee machine.

"Did I say something, Owen?"

He turned to smile at her, but the effort was half-hearted. "I'm afraid I'm not very good company tonight. Too much on my mind. But thank you for dinner. That was a nice surprise."

She began gathering half-empty cartons of food, insisting on leaving them in his refrigerator. Insisting on scraping plates and tidying up. He wished he hadn't started the coffee because he wanted her to leave.

"Boy, I envy you your growing up in the country," she said. "I always dreamed of that as a kid. All the animals and space and the whole family happily eating apple pie."

He laughed. "And I dreamed about living in a city where I could ride my bike to the library and go to the movies and find other kids with the same ideas that I had."

"I never thought of it like that," she said.

She leaned her elbows on the counter to watch as he got out the cups and the milk and sugar. "If I were describing you for a feature piece, I'd say you have an intellectual outdoorsy look." She tapped her cheek thoughtfully with a finger. "Or maybe it would be better to say that you're the soulful, dark Irish type."

"But you'll never be doing a piece with me in it," he said, both flattered and annoyed by her attention.

"Were you a brain in school?" she asked.

"Fix your coffee," he said, pushing a cup toward her.

She added milk and sugar, studying him playfully as she stirred. "Come on . . . Were you a brain?"

"No." He knew she wanted to hear more, but he had no desire to encourage her.

She carried her coffee to the couch and sat down. "What's your family think about your being here in bad old New York City?"

"They're horrified."

"Ummmm." She smiled and sipped her coffee. "I can imagine. Mine were horrified when I came here, too. And I'm from a city."

He leaned his hip against the kitchen counter and drank his coffee.

"You like it here, though, don't you?" she asked, sounding more serious than before.

"Why do you say that?"

"You just . . . fit in." She set her cup down carefully on the glass table top. "You've got the right attitude."

Owen wearily rubbed his eyes. "Listen, Holly . . . I need to get to work on my proposal, so—"

"But that's why I came," she insisted quickly. "I've got copies of all kinds of things for you." She reached into the oversized purse she'd stashed on the floor beneath the coffee table and pulled out a manila envelope. "Come over and sit down." She patted the cushion beside her. "I'll show you what I've got."

Reluctantly, Owen carried his mug over and sat down next to her. She leaned close to him to go over the material, crushing her breast against his arm as she pointed out key items. The soft press of her flesh caused his skin to heat at the point of contact. He tried to ignore it and concentrate on the contents of the envelope. What she'd brought turned out to be mildly interesting information that she could have given him the next day at the trial. He started to point that out to her, but didn't.

"I appreciate your help," he said.

She slipped off her shoes, curled her legs under her and fingered the fabric of his sleeve. "All your shirts seem new. Do you throw them away and buy new ones instead of doing laundry?"

"Isn't that the way you're supposed to do it?" he asked. He could smell her perfume and see down the front of her blouse. She wasn't wearing a bra. Had it been unbuttoned that low before, or was it just the way she was leaning toward him that revealed so much?

"You're tense," she said sympathetically. "All that pressure over your proposal and everything . . ." Her fingers gently massaged his neck. "Turn around. You're so tight. How can you possibly work like this?"

He turned his back to her, closing his eyes and submitting to the exquisite pressure of her fingertips. They traveled up and down, kneading and rubbing.

"Unbutton your shirt," she said, and he did, without glancing back at her.

She pulled the shirt down to the middle of his back so she had free access to his neck and shoulders. Her hands caressed his skin, melting away the tension but sending it straight to his groin. He shifted position slightly, and she leaned into him, pressing against his back and letting her hands slip from his shoulders down the front of his naked chest. And he realized that the breasts against his back were bare, that she'd unbuttoned her blouse and that the warmth was from her skin. He heard a soft moan of pleasure and realized it was his own.

"Relax," she whispered, and he turned beneath her guiding hands so that he was once again sitting back against the couch.

She was in front of him now. Kneeling between his legs. Her soft white breasts brushed against his thighs. Her fingers reached for his zipper. He closed his eyes, focusing on the sensations, inhaling sharply as the zipper came free. He felt her mouth, feather-light on his belly, kissing and nuzzling, moving down . . . down. And he was afraid to open his eyes or to breathe again, afraid to do anything that might stop that wet, soft mouth from its downward course. He had never been inside a woman's mouth. And he wanted it. God how he wanted it. He clenched his fists to keep from pushing her head down faster.

The kisses stopped. "Oh, Owen," she breathed, "I knew from the moment I met you that we'd be good together. I've thought about you so much since that day."

Her words were like a bucketful of ice water. His erection shriveled, and the fog of lust cleared from his brain, leaving him feeling like the world's biggest jerk. There was no good way to escape. No magical finger snap that could erase the situation. Holly stared up at him with a puzzled, vulnerable expression that made it even worse. Awkwardly, he stood up, abandoning her and the couch altogether as he pulled his shirt back into place.

"I'm sorry, Holly. I'm really sorry. I don't know what got into me."

She blinked hard. "You don't want to make love to me?" she asked in a small voice.

She was still on the floor. Looking up at him with a film of tears glistening in her eyes. He picked up her blouse from the arm of the couch and handed it to her, then averted his eyes, but she did not put it on. She pulled herself up from the floor to the edge of the couch, clutching the blouse to her chest.

"I think it was obvious that I wanted to make love to you.

But it's not right. I told you, Holly ... I've got someone at home and this wouldn't be fair to you or to her."

"Is that what you're worried about?" Some of her confidence returned and she pulled on the blouse, making no effort at modesty. He forced himself to look away.

"Owen, we are two consenting adults who are attracted to each other. Happiness is for those who know how to grab it. Being together would make us both happy. And who's going to know? Who's going to be hurt?"

He considered his words carefully. "I'm flattered that you want me. You're an incredibly attractive woman, and if the circumstances were different ..."

"Maybe things will look different if you really examine them," she said. "Maybe the reason you're attracted to me is that you're not in love with her. You should think about that."

He turned away. "Right now, all I can think about is how I'm supposed to be working tonight and how my proposal is due soon." It came out a little more brusque than he'd intended, compounding his guilt. But he didn't apologize. He wanted her out of the apartment.

"Sure," she said, apparently unaffected. "I know how deadlines are."

He retreated to the kitchen nook and watched as she slipped on her shoes, fluffed her hair, gathered her purse and coat. When she seemed safely ready to go, he went to the door and unlocked it for her.

"Don't worry," she said. "I'm not mad at you. Seeing how true-blue you are just makes you more attractive. Most men are so easy. Doesn't matter if they're engaged or married or whatever. If they think they can get away with it." She shrugged. "That's why I haven't gotten married. You can't trust men. Most of them are slaves to their dicks."

"Maybe you've just been with the wrong men," Owen suggested.

"Yeah ... I think you're right." She smiled ruefully and shouldered her purse strap. "But I'm trying to change that."

He ignored the meaningful look she cast him. "Do you want me to walk you down?" he asked. "Wait while you get a cab or—"

"That's very sweet, but no. I'm a big bad city girl." She rose up on tiptoes to kiss him quickly on the cheek. Then she was out the door and heading for the stairs. "See you tomorrow," she called. "Bye."

"Bye," Owen responded automatically. He started to close his door, then noticed that the elderly man across the hall was peeking out.

"So she finally found ya," the man said.

"What?"

"She waited a long time. Hangin' around and sittin' on the stairs. You aren't sellin' drugs, are ya?"

"No."

"Girls don't like ta wait, ya know."

"I'll remember that."

"Yeah. Tonight wadn't so bad. Wadn't but twenty minutes from the time she banged on your door to the time you showed up. But last night she hung around for three hours. I almost called the cops."

"Sorry she bothered you," Owen said.

He closed his door. Last night she'd been in the building waiting for him too? God. What a fool he'd been. Why hadn't he seen that she was attracted to him?

But then he had to stop himself because he wasn't innocent. He couldn't deny responsibility for what had happened. He had known what she wanted as soon as he sat down on the couch beside her. Maybe even before that. And he had been intrigued by the possibilities. By the unknown. Even by the forbidden nature of it all.

What a mess it would have been if she hadn't spoken and snapped him back to reality. She hadn't been Holly to him at all. She hadn't even been someone he knew. She'd been nothing more than a player in a fantasy. And what a fantasy . . . Even with his rational self in control, his cock still stirred at the memory of it. Wild, unencumbered sex with a creamy blonde in a New York hideaway. Straight out of a teenage wet dream.

The trouble was that it wouldn't be unencumbered. It would start a chain of guilty secrets to keep from Mike. Or it would mean telling Mike the truth and hurting her. And it would eventually mean hurting Holly too, because he could tell that in spite of her sophisticated veneer, she wanted an emotional response from him as well as a physical one. She wanted to be more than the anonymous blonde in his fantasies.

He wished he could call Mike and hear her voice. But that

would mean going out to a pay phone, and besides, he'd promised he wouldn't spend any more money on long distance. He paced awhile, then took a shower, easing the residual sexual pressure in the only way available, then finally settled in to work. Five days was all he had left before the proposal was due. Five days to patch together the promise of a book when he still wasn't sure what he was doing.

To get himself started he began by transcribing the notes of his Edie Norton interview. Then he went back over Gregory Hillyer. And then he flipped through the notes he'd made on everything ever printed about Bram Serian's personal background. Why would someone want to obliterate their past so completely? What had driven Serian? What shaped him into the strange creative force that he became? And what kind of relationship had he had with the woman on trial for his murder?

At two A.M. Owen forced himself to quit and go to bed. Tomorrow the trial resumed. He was anxious to immerse himself in that drama once again even though he had begun to realize that he would get few answers from it. The street sounds lulled him and he drifted into the half-sleep that had always been his most creative time. It was the time when his imagination took over and he could dream what he chose. Now it was filled with Bram Serian.

And with the dreams came an idea. Maybe, just maybe he had a new lead to pursue in the morning.

8

When Owen entered the courthouse Monday morning, he did not go up the stairs to courtroom 6. Instead, in pursuit of his nocturnal idea, he turned into the first-floor office area and went down the hall to the county records office. The clerk there was friendly and talkative. The records showed that Bram Serian had bought his farm from one John Potter. A few minutes of conversation with the clerk revealed that John Potter lived with his daughter just five blocks away.

It was almost time for court but Owen couldn't wait. He walked out of the building and straight to Potter's.

The woman who answered the door was suspicious. It took a lot of explaining before she finally let him in. "You better not be some sneaky salesman," she warned as she led Owen to a room behind the kitchen.

She opened the door. "You got company, Dad. Now behave and don't make any messes."

John Potter was a frail man with cloudy eyes, but he sounded alert. "Course I remember selling my place to that artist fella," he said gruffly. "Worst mistake I ever made."

"How so, Mr. Potter?"

"Cause I ended up here when I could have stayed out there with my livestock and my fishing hole."

"Had you known Serian or his family before the sale?"

"Nope. He didn't have any family around here."

Another dead end. Owen tried to overcome his disappointment.

"Did he talk to you much? Say why he wanted the farm or anything?"

Potter reached for a cold pipe. "He was a pretty close-mouthed fella, but he did say why he wanted my place. He liked my barn and my big pond. Liked all the trees and the way nobody could see the buildings from the road." Potter grinned. "Said he liked it 'cause it was private and it wasn't flat. Nearly caused that old realtor to swallow his teeth 'cause he'd told me when I listed it that the ground was too damn hilly and rough to get much of a price for."

With a shaking hand Potter steered the pipe into his mouth.

"Can I light that for you?" Owen asked, glancing around for matches.

"Daughter doesn't allow me to smoke in here," Potter said.

Owen watched him for a moment, wondering if he should offer to carry the old guy outside and light his pipe for him.

"Go on ... go on," Potter urged. "What else? This is a good test for my memory."

"Did he have a woman with him ... a girlfriend, fiancée, whatever."

"Nope."

Owen thought for a moment. "Did you sell your cows with the place?"

"Nope. The fella didn't want 'em. Wasn't interested in cows at all. Said he was gonna buy some horses."

"Did he mention what kind of horse operation he was planning—race, show, jumping ... ?"

"Didn't say."

"I wonder if he was thinking brood mares or—"

Potter chuckled. "I don't believe the fella had a clue. He didn't know diddlysquat about livestock."

"Really? Did he strike you as city-raised then?"

"Nope. Matter of fact he made a point of lettin' me know he was a farmer." Potter scratched his head and sucked on his pipe. "I'm tryin' to think just what he said exactly. Somethin' about growin' wheat. I told him then that my land wouldn't grow wheat, and he said that was fine because he'd had his fill of wheat."

Wheat! There it was again, that recurring mention of wheat and the aversion to flatlands. Owen was excited for a moment, until he reminded himself how little that really told him.

He checked his watch. "I have to go back over to the courthouse now, Mr. Potter. I appreciate your time and I was wondering if you do any reading? I could send you a few books or ..."

"Time was I did enjoy a good book. Westerns and war

stories especially. But I can't read a word with these old eyes anymore, son. Not a word."

With that he hacked and coughed, then spit a huge glob of phlegm out onto the floor. His raspy chuckle followed Owen all the way out.

Owen walked uphill to the courthouse, thinking about John Potter and his daughter, bound together till death. About Mike at Wheeler Ranch and her father, uncle, and grandmother. About his own family. Each story was different, yet the tangles of love, duty, and need turned out to be remarkably similar in the end. He wondered about Bram Serian. What ties had he severed in his escape to New York? And what dark coalescence had locked him to Lenore for so many years?

Mechanically, Owen passed through security, took the stairs to the second floor and entered Judge Pulaski's courtroom. There was a witness on the stand and Spencer Brown was strutting his stuff. The officer at the door scowled a warning against disturbing the quiet and Owen nodded understanding, but then hesitated. He wasn't sure where he should sit. There was his usual spot up next to Holly, but would Holly want him there after last night? Should he slide in toward the back of the press section? Or would that be an insult to Holly and get him into worse trouble?

Indecision gripped him and the officer's scowl deepened and he knew he had to make a move.

"Your honor!" Rossner called in the front, and he was saved by a sidebar. The jury was excused and people jumped up to leave the courtroom for a quick smoke or a trip to the bathroom.

Holly turned to speak to someone in the row behind her, saw Owen and immediately waved him forward.

"I thought maybe your train had been hijacked," she whispered, smiling as though nothing was changed. Except that there were faint circles beneath her eyes and her gaiety was overdone.

Seeing her sent a wave of guilt through him. He considered apologizing again, then decided it would only make them both uncomfortable, so he forced a smile and asked, "Have I missed much?"

"Fire inspector Kevin Mullin has been on the stand." Holly flipped through her notepad. "Let's see . . . Those of us who've managed to stay awake have been treated to a technical lecture on the nature of fire and accelerants. Then he talked about the pattern of the Serian fire and how the center of the fire was Serian's body. Then we were just to the good part where he discovered the remnants of the oil lamp when this sidebar started."

Owen jotted down notes as she spoke; then, mercifully, the sidebar was ended and they were both able to relax into concentrating on the trial. The jury filed back to their seats and the witness was reseated. Spencer Brown squared his shoulders and strutted back into position. His body language made it clear that he had won the sidebar argument.

"Can you tell us, Mr. Mullin, if these pieces you indicated finding were subsequently sent to an expert for analysis and identification?"

"Yes. And as I had suspected they were the remnants of a glass oil lamp."

Obviously pleased with himself, Brown returned to his seat and Rossner rose for the cross.

"Hello, Mr. Mullin," Rossner began, approaching the fire inspector as though they were in a business meeting. "Do you see many fires involving oil lamps?"

"Some. I wouldn't say they're common, but they're not rare either."

"You told us an impressive amount about this fire and where it started and what the pattern of the burn was, but I was wondering ... are there things that you can't tell us about the fire?"

"Certainly."

"Now, you've said that an accelerant was definitely present in the vicinity of the body ..."

"Yes."

"Can you positively identify that accelerant as lamp oil and not paint thinner or some other chemical that was present in Bram Serian's studio?"

"No. I cannot."

"Can you tell if the oil lamp was lit when the fire broke out?"

"No."

"Can you tell if the lamp was broken prior to the fire or if it was the fire that destroyed the lamp?"

"No."

"Can you tell if the deceased was holding the lamp?"

"No."

"Or if he had fallen and dropped the lamp?"

"No."

"Or accidentally knocked over the lamp?"

"No."

"Or whether lamp oil was poured on him or spilled on him or accidentally splashed on him or whether he was lying on the floor in a puddle of oil from the broken lamp . . . Can you tell whether any of these is true?"

"No."

"Can you tell if a cigarette ignited the blaze?"

"No."

"Is it possible that a cigarette started the whole thing . . . a dropped cigarette or a carelessly handled cigarette?"

"It is possible, given the proper set of circumstances."

"Could you give us an example of a proper set of circumstances?"

"Yes. For instance, if the deceased had a lighted cigarette in his mouth or his hand and he dropped the lamp and then bent down toward it . . . that would be one scenario."

"A scenario that would result in an accidental lighting of the fire, correct?"

"Correct."

Rossner paused to let that sink in; then he smiled politely and said, "Thank you, Mr. Mullin. No more questions."

The judge sent the jury for an early lunch, but the business of the court ground on. Brown reluctantly informed Pulaski that Dr. Gavril, the pathologist, had had a personal emergency and was unable to testify that day as scheduled. Brown assured the judge that the witness scheduled after Gavril could be on the premises by one o'clock so the trial could continue, and that he would keep the court advised as to when Dr. Gavril would become available.

Although Judge Pulaski agreed to this, it was clear that personal emergencies were not a valid excuse in his courtroom. Owen wondered what the judge was like away from his symbols of authority. It was hard to imagine the man having a life outside the courtroom.

Finally, everyone was dismissed. Owen fell in with the media crowd headed for the coffee shop. Holly was pretending nothing had happened, so he decided that he ought to do the same.

The lunch table discussion was as energetic as ever, but Owen was not interested in following it. His thoughts wandered. Bram Serian loomed so large in his imagination now that the trial was not holding his attention as completely as before. The courtroom strategies, the maneuvering, the guessing games and the theories seemed suddenly absurd to him. Bram Serian was dead. Lost to them all. His tragedy and mystery gripped Owen completely.

Brown had Detective Douglas Kilgren of the state police ready as his witness after lunch. Kilgren was tall, straight, and dignified and, though he had on a suit and tic, he somehow reminded Owen of a Canadian Mountie.

Eagerly Brown led Detective Kilgren through his credentials and his impressive police record; then he took the detective step by step through a two-hour rendering of the events that took place from the moment Kilgren arrived on the scene to the moment when Lenore Serian was brought in on murder charges. When everything had been said twice, Brown backtracked to highlight the major points again.

"So you never once had a question occur in your mind that a murder had been committed?" Brown asked.

"Never," Kilgren answered firmly.

"Based on your long experience in law enforcement, was there any question in your mind after the investigation was complete that anyone other than Lenore Serian should have been charged with this murder?"

"Absolutely not."

Brown kept Detective Kilgren going in the same manner for another twenty minutes. Nothing new was conveyed, but the detective's calm assurance smoothed over all the doubts created by Sheriff Bello's performance. Brown had a hard time giving up the witness, but finally did so and sat down.

When Rossner introduced himself to Kilgren and began his cross, Owen detected a subtle wariness in the attorney's demeanor. This was a witness that Rossner was concerned about.

"Detective Kilgren, you oversaw the investigation that followed the autopsy report on Bram Serian. Is that correct?"

"Some aspects I oversaw and on some I functioned as an advisor or observer."

"In your expert opinion, did Sheriff Bello conduct a thorough and competent investigation into Bram Serian's death?"

"To answer that I would first have to have a definition of *thorough and competent* because those words are open. There is no one right way to do things in an investigation, and so there is no scoreboard or grading system to judge an investigation. The important thing here—the thing to remember—is that Sheriff Bello put together a strong case based on many different evidentiary criteria."

"So you are saying that you completely approve of the techniques, or lack of techniques, used in this investigation?"

"I approve of any technique that gets the job done. If more law officers got the job done, we wouldn't have so many criminals threatening decent citizens on the streets."

"Can you say that you believe it is proper procedure to zero in on a suspect and not pursue any other avenues of investigation and not keep an open mind about other possible suspects?"

"In certain circumstances I can say precisely that. In this case specifically, there was a preponderance of evidence pointing directly at the accused so it would have been a waste of time and energy to look for alternate suspects upon nonexistent information just for the sake of appearances."

Abruptly Rossner announced that he was finished with the witness. Owen watched as the attorney returned to his chair and for the first time he saw a betrayal of emotion. Rossner was visibly frustrated.

After Detective Kilgren, the state called a forensic science specialist named Tonnessen. Tonnessen described his education and job experience and then was offered to the court and accepted as an expert.

Tonnessen was an energetic, bearded man who looked more like a logger than a scientist, but as soon as he spoke there was no doubt about his professional passion. Tonnessen gave detailed scientific answers to everything. He told the court more about his job than anyone wanted to know and certainly more about the axe head and the remnants of the oil lamp than anyone had ever wanted to know.

When Rossner got to cross examine him, Tonnessen sadly admitted that the one thing he could not tell from the axe head or the lamp was exactly how Bram Serian had met his death.

* * *

"Owen! Wait!"

Holly caught him just as he was leaving the courthouse.

"Can we talk just a minute?" she asked. "Maybe you could wait till after my spot and go for a cup of coffee with me?"

"I'm sorry, Holly. I have to meet my agent and my editor tonight for dinner so I'm in a hurry. I need to make this next train."

"Okay . . . then . . ." She glanced around. "Well, I was just wanting to say that there shouldn't be all this tension between us. I mean, things happen. We're attracted to each other and there's no crime in that. The thing is, there is no reason we can't be good friends, and I'm worried because I feel like you're uncomfortable with me now. Don't you think men and women can be friends?"

"This is out of my league, Holly. In my town just going to the coffee shop with a member of the opposite sex is about the same as being engaged so I don't have much experience with female friends. The woman I'm engaged to now used to be a friend, but obviously we didn't stay just friends."

Holly laughed. "But you're not in Kansas anymore. Here in the city men and women work together and get to be friends all the time. Sometimes they even sleep together and stay friends."

Owen shook his head. "There's no sense in me trying to figure it out or learn new habits because I'll be back in Cyril before you know it."

"Oh, come on. Lighten up. I've been a good friend to you. I've helped you and introduced you to people and everything."

"You have. And I'm grateful."

"Okay, then . . ." Her smile was teasing as she held out her hand. "Let's shake on it. Friends, right?"

"Friends," Owen agreed quietly.

Later, staring out the train window, he thought about being back in Cyril where he never shook hands with women or made friends with them and where he never saw a person of a different race and where everything was so familiar and unchanging that he could live there blindfolded and get along fine.

He got off the train at Grand Central. The terminal had

lost a little of its glow for him. He now noticed the garish metal cash machines and the ugly fast-food booths and the waterstains on the heavenly ceiling and the panhandlers cruising back and forth like vultures. But curiously he felt even more attached to it than before. The entire island of Manhattan was like this building—grand and inspiring, sizzling with energy and vitality, yet also dirty and crumbling and sometimes dangerous. And he loved it all. He wanted to embrace it, to experience all of it, to absorb it.

He stepped out onto Forty-second Street and took a deep breath. To the east was the art deco elegance of the Chrysler Building and the swift, dark waters of the East River. To the west Forty-second Street stretched out, crossing Fifth Avenue near the central research library and the jewel-like Bryant Park, crossing Broadway near the great theaters and all the bright glitter and sleaze, crossing the netherworld of Eighth and Ninth avenues, and then ending at the gray expanse of the Hudson River.

It was night but the streets were alive with people. The sidewalks overflowed with laughter and conversation. People hurrying. People strolling. People out with other people instead of parked in front of a television set in their living room.

He stood there on the sidewalk, watching, listening, reveling in the electric magic of so much life. And then he set out for his dinner meeting with Bernadette Goodson, smiling as he stepped into the flow of humanity.

On Tuesday morning, Owen was running late. He rushed into the courthouse and up to the security check. The lobby was deserted except for one woman. All three guards were busy pawing through her voluminous bag and questioning her.

"I'm here because I'm a witness," she insisted. "Now give me back my bag and let me through."

Owen studied her. She was tall, only two or three inches below his own six foot three, with wide shoulders and substantial bones, long legs and long expressive hands. Her skin was as dark as roasted coffee beans. She was facing away from him and he couldn't see her face.

"You wait down that hall there," one of the guards ordered. "Go on back around to the bench by the snack ma-

chines and sit. I'll let them know upstairs that you're here."
He consulted a clipboard. "You're Johnson, right?"

She nodded.

Geneva Johnson! Right in front of him was Geneva Johnson. The art model Serian had been involved with during his early years in New York.

Owen had tried every way he knew to locate this woman from Serian's past and now here she was. He watched her pass through the metal detector and turn down the hall. She had a fur coat over her arm and she was wearing a bright orange outfit that wrapped and tied and overlapped and flowed in a complex profusion of fabric. Her hair was plaited into tiny, long braids adorned with beads and then all the braids were gathered into a pony tail high on her head. The angle was such that he couldn't get a full view of her face.

The guards snickered and whispered lewd comments to each other as soon as she was out of sight. Owen clenched his jaw to keep from remarking on their unprofessional behavior. He couldn't afford to make them angry or attract their attention at all because he intended to follow Geneva Johnson and he didn't want to chance their interference. When they were finished pawing through his bag he picked it up, bypassed the stairs and turned down the hall.

Owen found Geneva Johnson seated in an alcove just beyond the vending machines. She was reading an oversized paperback book.

"Excuse me," he said.

She looked up. Her facial features were strong and timeless. Her eyes were a languid brown. Her bearing was regal.

"Are they ready for me so soon?"

"No. My name is Owen Byrne and I—"

"I'm not talking to reporters," she said.

Though he was standing and she was seated, he still had the sensation of being looked down upon.

"I'm not a reporter, I'm a writer."

"Same difference. Go away."

"No. It's not the same. I'm not doing newspaper or magazine stories. I'm researching a book."

Her expression did not change, but she was listening. Owen spoke more rapidly than usual, anxious to explain himself completely before she stopped listening.

"I'm writing about the trial. But I can't make any sense out of Bram Serian's death unless I know more about his life. I'm looking for background information ... trying to piece together his past and see how he became what he was."

Her eyes narrowed. "How do I know you're legitimate?"

"You could check me out," Owen said, flipping open a notebook to write out his name and the names and numbers for both his editor and agent. Below that he added his temporary address in Manhattan and his permanent address and phone in Kansas. "I'm told that I'm easy to check out," he said, unable to resist smiling a little as he tore off the sheet and handed it to her.

She glanced over the list, then eyed him warily.

"I'm not out to exploit anyone," Owen said.

"If that's true, they should stuff you and put you in a museum, mister, cause that makes you a rare cat for your gender."

"All I want is information about Serian's past. You knew him when he first came to New York, didn't you?"

She studied him with a shrewd, measuring stare.

"What astrological sign are you?" she asked.

"I don't know," he admitted.

She folded the paper and dropped it into her huge bag. "I didn't want to testify," she said. "The scumbags are making me testify. You, on the other hand, cannot force me to do anything."

"Of course not. I wouldn't want to. I—"

"Who have you talked to so far?"

"Gregory Hillyer and Edie Norton."

She gave a sarcastic snort. "I can just imagine the trash they were dishing out."

The book on her lap slipped to the floor, and Owen bent to retrieve it. As he handed it to her, he saw the title—*Spells and Ceremonies in Directing Spiritual Energy*.

"Is that about magic?" Owen asked.

Her smile was devoid of warmth. "It's about things you couldn't possibly understand."

He gave up then, figuring that the woman was never going to agree to an interview. The acceptance of defeat relaxed him. "Lady ..." he laughed, "that covers a lot of territory because I don't understand most of what goes on in the world. That's why I write. I'm just trying to make some sense of it all."

"You got your life's work in front of you then."

He laughed again. "I guess you're right about that."

She frowned. "Bram Serian was a creation. A brilliant creation. And you don't wanna be messin' with art."

"I'm not sure I understand . . ."

"There you are, then!" Her smile was more genuine this time. "There's something for you to work on. See if you can figure it out and understand. In the meantime, why don't you go away and let me wait in peace."

"Okay. You've got all the information in case there's anything . . ."

"There won't be. Good-bye."

Owen hurried upstairs to courtroom 6 and slipped into the empty spot on the aisle beside Holly. She shot him a questioning glance then turned her notebook so he could read *Sven Eklund—The Stoveman.* Owen knew immediately that the elderly fellow on the witness stand was the man who had installed the stove in Serian's studio nearly twenty years ago.

Eklund's testimony was dull, and Owen had trouble keeping his mind from wandering. He watched Lenore Serian. He watched the jury. He watched the judge. He thought about Bram Serian.

On and on Brown went with his witness, taking old Sven Eklund through a history of the stove company and a showing of stove pictures and a discussion of the percentage of installations of faux stoves as opposed to real wood-burning stoves. The attorney tried repeatedly to lead Eklund into an examination of the psychological motives of his electric stove customers, but Rossner blocked that angle with numerous objections until finally the judge advised Brown to drop it unless he could show the court that Sven Eklund had a degree in psychology.

A soft snoring started in the back of the room, and the judge halted everything while a court officer woke the offending spectator. During the interruption, Holly leaned over to whisper that she'd seen one of the jurors nodding off, too.

When testimony resumed, Brown tried to lead Eklund into remembering statements Serian had made to him about the stove, but the old man couldn't recall much. On cross examination, Rossner gently coaxed Eklund into admitting that he hadn't even remembered installing the stove for Serian until after the police called him and refreshed his memory. After an entire morning of the stoveman, Owen couldn't see that either side had gained or lost an inch.

As soon as Eklund stepped down from the stand, Judge Pulaski sent the jury to the juryroom and called both the prosecution and the defense up to discuss a note that the judge had received from the jury foreman.

"Where were you?" Holly whispered.

"I was talking to a witness," Owen admitted. "I saw her downstairs and I couldn't resist giving it a try."

Holly chuckled softly. "You're learning," she said. "By the time this thing is over, you might be a real journalist."

"There aren't any rules against talking to witnesses, are there?"

"No. But you have to be careful. You can really step on some toes . . . make some enemies . . . and the last thing any of us needs is to have the district attorney's office mad and uncooperative."

Owen nodded his understanding.

"So . . ." Holly arched an eyebrow in question. "Who was it you were talking to?"

"Geneva Johnson."

"Get anything good?"

"No."

"Don't be discouraged. None of us has come up with anything good on Geneva Johnson."

Pat leaned around Holly to join the conversation. "The Johnson woman is too far in Serian's past. Anything juicy about her is strictly old business."

"I don't see why the prosecution needs her testimony," Holly said, as though personally annoyed.

"According to Marilyn," Pat began, explaining to Owen that Marilyn had a solid pipeline into the district attorney's office so anything she said regarding Brown and Dapolito's strategy was the absolute gospel. "According to Marilyn, Geneva Johnson is the only person they could find who was directly involved with Serian when he was building his studio."

"What's that got to do with anything?" Holly demanded.

"Her testimony will develop their fire theme. That's supposedly all they want her for. Strictly the fire stuff. Even though she is an unfriendly witness."

"Does that make a difference?" Owen asked.

"It can," Pat told him. "If a witness has to be forced to

testify and is declared unfriendly, then the attorney can be more combative in the questioning process without it being considered harassment. You'll be able to tell if Brown decides to—"

Pat broke off and turned her attention forward as court was called back to order. The jury was reseated.

The judge glanced at the clock, gave the jurors his customary advisory about not discussing the case, and then dismissed everyone for lunch.

Owen fell in with the crowd, which today included not just reporters but courthouse employees and even Spencer Brown and Tony Dapolito. The occasion was a benefit lunch put on by the Methodist Auxiliary in the church basement. All told it was a boring affair, with everyone on their best behavior and no one discussing the murder trial that they were all assembled for.

When his group left, Owen was surprised to see Judge Pulaski crossing courthouse square near them. Without his robes the judge was a small man, unremarkable in appearance except for the fact that his suit was exceptionally well cut. The judge was carrying two books. Owen stared, trying to make out the titles. The hardcover was *Capital Games,* the book about the Clarence Thomas Supreme Court nomination. An appropriate choice for a judge, Owen thought. The smaller paperback was a Clive Cussler novel featuring the exploits of Dirk Pitt.

Promptly at two the trial resumed. There was a new level of tension in the room, and the spectator section was jammed. Owen could feel the hunger. They were all tired of technical details and ready for something juicy ... something sensational. And Geneva Johnson was the first witness who might feed that hunger.

When her name was called, Geneva Johnson strode down the aisle like a queen whose virtue had been challenged. She did not even glance at Lenore, though she did sweep a look of contempt across the rest of the room as she lowered herself into the witness chair.

The room was completely quiet. Owen wondered what Lenore was thinking.

Spencer Brown moved into position. He reminded Owen of a rooster all puffed up and ready for a fight, and Owen saw that Brown intended to intimidate Geneva Johnson.

"What is your occupation, Miss Johnson?"

"I have a store."

"Have you had other occupations prior to this?"

"Of course. I didn't just turn sixteen and open my own store."

The sharp retort made Brown hesitate a moment.

"Could you tell us a little about this store."

"What would you like to know, Mr. Attorney. Sales per square foot? Customer profile? Dunn and Bradstreet rating? Employee satisfaction index?"

Brown glared at her. "What category of establishment is it?"

"Designer clothing for women."

"You own and operate this store entirely by yourself?"

"Yes."

"So it would be fair to describe you as a business woman."

"I've been called that."

"And to be successful at this business it is a necessity to have a sharp memory and an awareness of people and what they say and do so that you can entice them to buy from you, is that not so?"

"That is so."

"Moving back into the past, could you relate for us how you came to know Bram Serian?"

"In the biblical sense, or otherwise?"

Brown coughed. "When did you meet him?"

"We met in 1968."

"Did you subsequently become romantically involved with Bram Serian?"

"No. But we started sleeping together."

Brown looked at her with genuine puzzlement. "Are you saying that you did not have a romantic involvement with Bram Serian?"

"Romance is for fools, Mr. Attorney. Neither of us was a fool."

"I see." Brown studied his notes nervously. "Let us move to that period of time in which you were residing with Bram Serian."

"Yes. Let us," she replied sarcastically.

"Where did you reside with Bram Serian?"

"In his Manhattan loft."

"Was this loft used for anything else in addition to functioning as living space?"

"Yes. Serian also worked there."

"And did he advise you of rules for this space where he lived and worked?"

"Yes."

"Could you relate for us what those rules were?"

"I could never have visitors up there unless I had cleared it with him. He kept his work covered with sheets and no one was allowed to look under them."

"Anything else?"

She sighed. "He had lots of rules. No Barry Manilow music, no hats on the bed, no Kahlil Gibran, no mention of Vietnam, nothing colored orange, no animals except birds, no mention of God, no chewing gum ... Want me to go on?"

"Let's narrow it down to specifics," Brown said. "Did Bram Serian have any rules pertaining to fire or flames?"

She had been staring Brown straight in the eye during their exchange but now she dropped her gaze. Signifying what, Owen wondered ... Resignation? Defeat? A painful memory? Or a lie on the way?

"He would not let me burn candles," she said.

"Would you repeat that a little louder for us, please?"

"He would not let me burn my candles."

"Are you saying that twenty years ago, when he was still a young man, Bram Serian would not allow a simple candle flame in his working and living area?"

"Yes."

Brown paused to let that sink in. The attention of everyone in the room was riveted to the prosecutor and his witness.

"Now, Miss Johnson, was your relationship with Bram Serian still an active one and were you still residing in the Manhattan loft with Bram Serian when he bought the farm outside of Stoatsberg?"

"Yes."

"Did you move out to occupy the farm with him?"

"No. I stayed at the loft and Serian went back and forth between the farm and the loft."

"Why did you not change your residence with him?"

"Because he didn't want me to. There was no good place

to stay out there, and he only went out when he was building on that studio."

"He was at that time engaged in remodeling the old barn into an art studio, was he not?"

"Yes. He was engaged all right."

"Did he discuss this building project with you?"

"Sometimes."

"What was his general attitude about it?"

"He was very excited about it."

"Did he discuss his choice of a heating stove with you?"

"Some."

"Could you please relate to us what he said to you regarding his choice of a stove?"

"He showed me a picture of a stove and told me that it looked just like a woodburner but it was a fake. The stove was really an electric space heater with a blower."

"Was this stove expensive?"

"Very."

"Did he say why he chose such a stove instead of installing the customary wood-burning variety that was so readily available around Stoatsberg?"

"He didn't want the fire in his studio."

"Didn't he in fact say that he was terrified of fire?" Brown demanded. "That he had a long-standing fear of fire and—"

"Objection!" Rossner called.

"Contain yourself, Mr. Brown," the judge ordered so quickly that Owen was sure Pulaski had been waiting for a reason to yell at the prosecutor.

Brown's jaw tightened. "Didn't he say, often and within the hearing of others, that he was afraid of fire?"

"He never told me he was terrified or afraid of anything in the world," she shot back.

"Are you telling me that he did not say to you within the hearing of others that he was afraid of a fire in his studio?"

"He talked about the barn being made of old wood and how easily it could burn."

"So he was afraid that his art studio might catch fire?"

"Yes."

With that, Spencer Brown wisely thanked his recalcitrant witness and returned to the safety of his seat.

Rossner approached her with exaggerated politeness, introducing himself and asking her a series of benign questions to begin. Then he zeroed in on the fire issues.

"You say he didn't want you to burn candles. Is that right?"

"Yes."

"Is it possible that he simply didn't like candles in the same way that he didn't like Barry Manilow music?"

"Yes."

"And that he was no more afraid of candle flames starting a fire than he was afraid of Barry Manilow's music causing a riot?"

Soft chuckles came from all over the courtroom.

Either Rossner's attitude or her own resignation had dampened Geneva Johnson's hostility and she answered readily. "He had very strong opinions that he did not always give reasons for."

"Was Bram Serian the sort of person who tolerates messes?"

"No. He was a cleanliness fanatic."

"Candles can be messy, can't they? You've got all that dripping wax, right?"

"Yes."

"And the stove for his studio ... did he ever say that he ordered an electric stove specifically because he was afraid of a fire or was the possibility of fire one of many reasons?"

"It was one of many reasons."

"And the wood stove would have been messy, wouldn't it, and he mentioned that, didn't he?"

"Yes. He was especially worried about how mice and insects like to live in woodpiles, and he didn't want a woodpile around his studio."

Rossner studied the wall a moment, then looked at the witness. "Could you tell us where you were living when Bram Serian brought Lenore to the farm to live with him there."

Geneva Johnson drew in a deep breath, and Owen thought he saw her glance in Lenore's direction.

"I was living in the loft."

"In Bram Serian's Manhattan loft?"

"Yes."

"He had you living in the loft and Lenore living at his farm?"

"Yes."

"Did you know about this at the time?"

"Yes," she answered, appearing increasingly uncomfortable.

"How did you feel about your lover having another woman living in—"

Suddenly Lenore Serian, who had not moved once during a week of testimony, jumped from her seat, ran down the aisle and disappeared through the double doors. There was a moment of stunned silence and then the entire courtroom exploded. Judge Pulaski banged his gavel futilely. Volpe and Riley sprinted out the doors after the escaping defendant. Several radio reporters followed close on their heels to call in the newsflash. Still on the stand, Geneva Johnson buried her face in her hands.

When the court officers finally restored a semblance of order, the judge sent the jury to the jury room, ordered the attorneys into his chambers and instructed the court officers to clear the court for a fifteen-minute recess.

"Wow," Holly breathed as they left their seats to follow the judge's orders.

A knot of reporters gathered in the corridor. Everyone was talking at once in hushed, eager tones. "I've never seen that happen in all my years of trials," Marilyn said, grinning with amazement.

"This is great!" Ray repeated over and over.

"She stopped him," Holly said thoughtfully. "That's why she flew out like that . . . to stop her own attorney. She must have been afraid that he was about to stumble into some ugly, dangerous stuff about the love triangle."

"I'll bet you're right," Marilyn agreed. "She was desperate to shut him up and that was the only way she could think to do it."

"Won't Brown just go after the truth now on re-direct?" Owen asked.

"Are you kidding?" Marilyn's tone was sarcastic. "Brown doesn't want to highlight any animosity between Lenore and Geneva. It's too far in the past to do any damage to Lenore's character, and it will just make the jury wonder if Geneva had a grudge all this time and is out to get Lenore."

Owen shook his head. "It's impossible for the whole story to just be laid out in the open, isn't it?"

Holly gave him an exasperated look.

When they were allowed back into the courtroom, everyone waited expectantly. Volpe and Riley escorted Lenore back into the room and into position beside Charles Rossner. Rossner whispered something to her and she shook her head.

"Mrs. Serian," the judge said sternly. Rossner gripped her elbow and pulled her up with him to a standing position.

"It is my understanding that you were suddenly taken ill. Be that as it may, this is a court of law, and I will not tolerate improper behavior. Any future interruptions will be dealt with harshly. Is that clear?"

Lenore nodded, and Rossner said, "My client understands, your honor."

The remainder of Geneva Johnson's testimony was anticlimactic. Rossner did not resume the line of questioning that he had been following before the interruption. Instead he went back over the candles and woodstove and then quit. Brown had no re-direct.

The witness was dismissed, and the judge launched into a lecture to the jury about their duties.

The whole fire business bothered Owen. Something about fire was nagging at his memory. He leaned over to whisper to Holly, "I think I might have something about Serian and fire. Something from my research . . ."

"Oh? Something you'd want to release to the media?" she asked, teasing but hopeful.

"I don't even remember exactly what it is. But if it would make a difference, I'd give it to the court."

"You mean the judge? You can't do that. You'd have to give it to one side or the other, and if I were you I wouldn't get involved like that."

"If you had crucial information, wouldn't you come forth with it?"

"Crucial?" Holly gave a soft snort of laughter. "I doubt that what you've got is crucial."

"Probably not," he admitted. "But if I've found even a small truth, I have an obligation to step forward."

"What if your little bit of truth could obstruct justice? What if it helped Lenore Serian get free when she was really guilty?"

"What are you talking about, Holly? Just because you're certain of the woman's guilt, do you think evidence to the contrary should be suppressed?"

"I didn't say that. I just think that you should keep sight of the larger picture."

Owen might have pressed her further, but the jury began trooping out. That meant the judge was adjourning for the day and a court officer would open the doors momentarily. Gil Flores, the television reporter, was seated behind Holly and now tapped her on the shoulder. "What are you going to go for as your lead?" he asked.

As both Holly and Pat turned for a whispered huddle with Flores, Owen picked up his things and slipped away.

He kept thinking about the fire testimony on the train ride home. Brown was trying to take it beyond the realm of a man who was cautious about fire. The prosecutor was trying to portray Serian as having a terror of fire. And Owen didn't think that rang true. Bram Serian had not struck him as a man who was afraid of much . . . but it was more than that. Owen was certain that somewhere, in the volumes of material he had collected, Bram Serian had actually spoken about fire.

Instead of stopping for dinner, he went straight to his apartment to dig through his files. He tried to do it calmly, without making a mess, but as he searched he grew increasingly excited. This was a real clue. This was something important.

Finally he found it. In the middle of an obscure and long-defunct art publication was a feature piece entitled "Young Artists in Manhattan." Buried in that piece was a brief interview with Bram Serian when he was still attending Art Students League. The interviewers had gone to one of those nonprofit co-op gallery spaces that cater primarily to students and talked to everyone there who claimed to be an artist. Serian's part was brief:

Q. Can you tell us your name and where you're from?

A. My name is Bram Serian and I'm an American.

Q. Could you be more specific?

A. I thought we were going to talk about my art?

Q. We will, but I'm trying to put you in context.

A. My only context is my work.

Q. Great. But first we'd like to know how coming to New York has affected you . . . and your work.

A. New York is the center of American art. If an artist isn't here he's dead.

Q. You don't feel that the city intrudes on your work, then?

A. No. I'm a truer sculptor here than I've ever been before. The city has given my work a new linear range.

Q. And what are you working on now?

A. I've just finished a metal series I call Heartland.

Q. Is that the one with all the tractor parts?

A. Yeah. Do you know it?

Q. There's a picture on the bulletin board downstairs. It looks very large. Does that cause problems when you want to exhibit?

A. Yeah. But I don't shape my work to fit exhibit spaces.

Q. Well, we hope to see it in a show soon. Have you started anything else yet?

A. I'm planning a piece using elements from burned buildings. I've been following fire trucks and collecting materials for months.

Q. Isn't it a little disturbing—going to all those disaster scenes?

A. Fire is one of nature's basic forces and the only predator with no fear of humans. It is mysterious and cleansing, not disturbing.

That was it. The rest was inconsequential. It was the fire statement that he'd remembered. Bram Serian didn't sound like a person with a longstanding fear of fire. If anything he sounded like he admired fire.

Owen stared at the photocopied pages for several seconds. Then he headed downstairs to a pay phone to call Charles Rossner's office.

9

The Greystone Hotel was just across courthouse square. It was on a corner, a four-story granite building with old double-hung windows and an air of lost grandeur. The brass-trimmed entryway huddled beneath a faded maroon awning.

Owen stepped into the lobby. He took in the threadbare elegance of the furnishings, the caged cockatoos in the corner, the wooden reception desk and the PLEASE RING FOR SERVICE sign, then crossed the room to speak to the man behind the desk.

The man eyed him suspiciously.

"Can I find Mr. Rossner here?" Owen asked.

The man cocked his head and gave Owen a smug look. "Maybe you can, maybe you can't. If you're a reporter, forget it."

"My name is Byrne. Owen Byrne. I have an appointment."

He picked up the phone and had a muffled conversation that included Owen's name. "Second floor," he said, pointing to a stairway. "The executive suite."

Owen had not actually spoken to Rossner yet. On the phone he had talked to Paul Jacowitz, Rossner's assistant, who had been skeptical at first. Then, after hearing Owen's information, Jacowitz had apologized, explaining that they'd been besieged by crank callers and reporters trying to talk their way into the defense's inner sanctum. Jacowitz then set up an early-morning meeting at the Greystone.

Owen turned right at the top of the stairs and was met in the hallway by the two detectives, Volpe and Riley. Riley was Owen's height but with the look of a football player gone to seed. His ruddy skin and watery blue eyes could have been either genetic or the result of years of hard drinking. Volpe was his opposite, short and dark-eyed and as sharp as a fine-honed blade.

"Any weapons? Any hidden recording devices?" Volpe barked.

The experience was so foreign to anything Owen had ever encountered that he stared at the men several seconds before replying, "No."

Riley smiled. "You don't mind if we check that out, do ya, boyo?"

Owen shook his head and was frisked for the first time in his life.

"Nothing personal," Riley assured Owen while his broad hands traveled up and down. Volpe watched as if he expected his partner to find a machine gun in Owen's pocket.

When the body search was over, Riley threw a beefy arm across Owen's shoulders and said, "I know some Byrnes. What's your dad's name, boyo?"

"Clancy. But he's not from New York. He's from Kansas."

"Ah, well. There's something to that, isn't there?" Owen nodded agreement though he had no idea what Riley meant.

Volpe's beady black eyes continued to bore into him, daring trouble, so Owen turned to Riley to say, "I have an appointment with Mr. Rossner."

"Sure you do." Riley grinned. "Now here's the deal. Mr. Rossner does the talking. You do the answering. Got that? And you don't say word one to Mrs. Serian."

"This is business, not a interview," Volpe said, projecting menace from every pore. "And it better not be some wiseass trick."

Mrs. Serian. With those words Owen was suddenly unsteady. She was here. He was going to meet Lenore Serian.

He followed Riley through a door. Jacowitz greeted him. Riley took his coat and nudged him forward, toward a round table next to the room's only window. Rossner was seated there in the morning sunlight.

"Mr. Byrne, is it?" Rossner asked with affable amusement.

"Yes. Owen Byrne."

Riley pointed at a chair and Owen sat down.

"You've met my investigators, Joe Volpe and Frank Riley . . ." Rossner's gesture indicated that this was the official introduction so Owen nodded toward the men. "And this is Paul Jacowitz, my associate." Owen nodded toward Jacowitz.

"So, you've gained admittance to our war room, Mr. Byrne." Rossner smiled and Owen surveyed the surroundings. It was a large irregularly shaped room, full of shadows except for the spill of sun from the single sash-hung window. The predominant color was a faded gray-green. In one corner was a wet bar with a tiny refrigerator and an automatic coffee maker. Besides the table he was seated at, the furnishings consisted of an old chesterfield-style couch, various overstuffed chairs, and scattered end tables and standing lamps. There were no beds. He suspected that any sleeping quarters were behind one of the several doors. There was no sign of Lenore Serian.

Rossner watched with a lazy, knowing expression. "Joe," he said to Volpe finally, "would you ask Lenore to join us?"

Volpe tapped on a door. Owen could not keep from staring as it swung open and Lenore appeared. She stood there, once again the woman in the tabloid photograph: sullen, haughty. Sensual and aloof. Only the anger was missing.

"Please join us, Lenore." Rossner stood and pulled out the chair opposite Owen. "Come sit down and meet the man who wants to help you."

Owen was stricken with a gust of intermingled emotions. Guilt, excitement, curiosity, and something more intense, something that went deeper than curiosity.

Lenore Serian crossed the room, clearly an unwilling participant, and sat down without glancing at Owen or acknowledging his presence at all. She had on a shapeless suit and a white blouse that tied primly beneath her chin. Owen was certain they were not her own. Her hair was pulled back into the usual twisted knot. She wore no jewelry other than a wedding band and no makeup that he could detect. Her skin was flawless. In the light from the window it was a golden shade. Like honey. Or honey and cream.

"Lenore, this is Owen Byrne. He says he has something important to show us."

She turned toward Owen with a cool, wary gaze. His customary politeness failed him and he stared unabashedly. This was the woman who had shared Bram Serian's life, and possibly his death. Owen was suddenly overcome by a need to see past all the poses and surfaces. He wanted to know her. To understand who she was. Her coolness wavered a fraction, and there was a brief flicker of something in her dark eyes, something he felt more than saw. Then her gaze became shuttered, as though she had retreated behind something, and all he could see was the shadow of her watching him.

"All right, Byrne," Rossner said, "let's see this earthshaking information."

At the sound of Rossner's voice, Owen immediately regained control of himself and pulled the photocopies from his bag. Everyone in the room was still while Rossner read. When he was finished, he handed the pages to Jacowitz. "Read this out loud for us, would you, Paul?"

Jacowitz read the pages in a monotone at first, but by the end his voice was charged with suppressed excitement. Lenore stared at the tabletop, emotionless and impassive.

"Tell me exactly how you found this," Rossner demanded, and Owen recounted his search for Bram Serian's past and his hours digging through the musty forgotten journals in the library's art collection.

"This could be quite a coup for us." Rossner stroked his clean-shaven chin thoughtfully.

"Will you be able to use it today?" Owen asked.

"Possibly." Rossner leaned across the table toward Owen, and all semblance of his easy, good-natured demeanor fell away. "Who else have you offered this to, Byrne?"

"No one. I called your office as soon as I was certain."

"And what's your price for exclusivity? For turning this over to us with the promise that it will stay out of the news until we can make use of it."

Owen started to say that there was no price. That he was glad to have helped find the truth. But then he looked over at Lenore Serian and heard himself say, "I'd like a brief interview with Lenore."

Everyone in the room stirred. Lenore's eyes flew up to lock angrily on Owen.

"You scumbag!" Volpe blurted out, and Riley had to restrain him physically to prevent his advancing.

Rossner had a thoughtful measuring expression. "That might be arranged," he said.

Quickly Owen offered assurances. "It won't be about the trial. I've hit a stone wall around Bram Serian's past, and she might be able to fill in some blanks. That's all it will be. Just Serian's past."

Rossner studied him with one eye narrowed. "And this information would be used only for the purposes of your book?"

"Yes. I'll sign an agreement if you want me to."

Rossner turned toward Lenore. "It's up to you," he said. "I see nothing wrong with a little exchange. Mr. Byrne has supplied us with useful material . . . and who knows . . . he may find something else for us, right, Mr. Byrne?"

"I can't guarantee anything," Owen said, "but . . . I'll certainly be watchful."

Lenore Serian looked from her attorney to Owen. There was such alarm in her expression that Owen weakened and was about to withdraw his request when suddenly she said, "Yes. I'll do it."

It was the first time he had heard her voice.

Owen went straight to the downstairs pay phone in the courthouse to place a call to Bernadette Goodson. He couldn't wait to tell her that he had arranged to interview Lenore Serian. It was still early, and Bernie's office wasn't open yet. He left a message on the machine and wished that he could be there to watch Bernie and Alex when they heard the news. He suspected that his proposal would sound a hundred percent better to DeMille with an exclusive Lenore Serian interview included.

Word had spread that Natalie Raven, the housekeeper, would be on the stand that morning, and the courtroom was packed with people wanting to see the show. Raven was something of a celebrity, having been featured in a number of national tabloids and a well-known weekly television program that mixed stories about crime with stories about housewives who sold phone sex in their spare time and other subjects Owen had never cared to watch.

The reporters were all gleefully counting the extra inches or seconds of exposure Natalie Raven would earn them. The courtroom artists were poised for action, ready to sketch Raven from every possible angle. The court officers, the court clerk and court reporter, as well as the attorneys and their minions—all appeared tense. Everything was ready. Everyone was in place. But for the first time since the proceedings began, Judge Martin J. Pulaski was not already seated at the bench.

He came in some minutes later sporting a bright white cast on his left arm and announced that he'd had an accident in his karate class. All around him Owen heard reporters chuckling.

Natalie Raven's name was called, and the entire courtroom swiveled their heads to watch the woman enter. She was of average height and build with medium brown hair in loose curls, and she was dressed in a casual blouse and a denim skirt. If Owen had been asked about her, he would have guessed that she was a suburban mother on her way to a parent-teacher meeting.

The preliminaries were carried out, and Brown took her through a few meaningless warm-up questions to get her comfortable. She did not seem to need it, though. From the moment Natalie Raven settled into the witness box, she appeared completely at ease.

"How long were you in the employ of Bram Serian, Miss Raven?"

"I moved into Arcadia almost exactly four years before the fire."

"How did Bram Serian come to employ you?"

"We met and he found out I was looking for a job and he had me come out for a get-acquainted period. I never left."

"Was Mrs. Serian involved in the decision to employ you?"

"No. Before me Bram subscribed to a service that sent cleaning teams out once a week, and he had a local woman who came in to cook dinner every evening. Lenore was happy with that, and I don't think she had ever considered anything different. But then the woman who cooked died, and he couldn't find a replacement. And he didn't like so many strangers going in and out so he thought having just one person would be better. But I don't think he discussed that with Lenore because she wasn't interested in things like house cleaning or cooking. She just expected it to get done."

"Would you say you started out on unfriendly terms with Mrs. Serian?"

"No. I'd say it was more like neutral. She didn't particularly care."

"Did she ever give you instructions or discuss matters relating to the household with you?"

"No."

"Was it Bram Serian, then, who issued you your instructions and administered the household?"

"At first. But after a while he just expected me to make things run without him having to bother with it."

"And you resided at the Serian home, Arcadia, full-time, did you not?"

"Yes. I had my own room and bath, and I stayed there just like it was my home. It was my home."

"Did your duties eventually extend to more than the cleaning and cooking?"

"Oh yes. Basically the whole place became my responsibility. I bought new sheets and towels when they were needed, and I called repairmen and ordered groceries and made sure the bills were paid and hired extra help when we needed it. Like if we needed any heavy cleaning done, I'd call a cleaning service, or, after Bram's assistant left, if we had extra outside chores I'd call Tommy Kubiak to come over."

"Did the time come when your duties extended to personal services for your employer or his wife?"

"Sure. It got to be like I was the mother sort of. I'd notice Bram was missing a button, and I'd tell him to give me the shirt so I could see that it was fixed. Or I'd notice, when I was putting away his laundry, that he had some socks with holes and I'd throw them away and buy new ones. Things like that."

"And what about Mrs. Serian? Did you function in the same capacity for her?"

"I tried. But she was very particular about things and very hard to please."

Owen listened and jotted down notes as Spencer Brown slowly drew a picture with Natalie Raven's testimony. In this picture, Raven was the tolerant, benevolent mother figure without whom the Serian household would have collapsed. Bram Serian was the distracted artist who was so caught up in the call of his own genius that he seldom noticed the world around him. And Lenore was a self-centered, ungrateful bitch. Bram Serian was an energetic, loving man with lots of friends and worshippers, and Lenore was maladjusted, friendless and spiteful.

Raven talked about how Lenore behaved strangely at times. How Lenore was almost phobic about leaving Arcadia. How Lenore alternated between flaunting herself sexually in front of Serian's guests and rudely ignoring them.

Owen tried to stay focused on what they were saying, but

something about their exchange bothered him. He studied Raven and then Brown. They were too familiar. Raven knew how to decipher Brown's convoluted questions without so much as a pause for thought, and Brown knew just what to ask to lead her in the proper direction. They were as comfortable together as a couple, pleasing and flattering, each of them trusting the other, cuing and accepting cues like partners in a well-rehearsed dance. Even the emotional fluctuations seemed programmed.

Owen leaned toward Holly. "Are they allowed to practice together before the trial?" he whispered.

Holly frowned in annoyance at the interruption. She kept her eyes on the action as she whispered back, "She's his star witness. They probably went over it a lot. That's standard, Owen."

Noon came and went without Judge Pulaski declaring lunch, but no one seemed to mind. Brown was into the questions everyone had been waiting for.

"From your viewpoint as a full-time member of the household, how would you describe Bram and Lenore Serian's behavior toward one another?"

"Lenore was always very cold and distant. Sometimes she would sulk or get angry and throw a tantrum ... say really hateful, ugly things. And Bram ... he was the soul of patience with her. He was always very kind and ... well, he was committed to his artwork so he didn't spend a lot of time just hanging around, but when he was in the house he would always check on her, say hello to her, see what she was doing ... that kind of thing."

"Did there come a time when Bram Serian had a discussion with you regarding the possibility of his divorcing his wife?"

"Yes. About five months before the fire he told me that he had begun to think about divorce. He said he was very worried about discussing it with Lenore, though, because he didn't think she would be able to accept it and he didn't think she could take care of herself without him."

"What was your response to this?"

"I told him that he had to do what was right for him and that Lenore was a beautiful woman and I didn't think she'd have any troubles getting along."

"Did Bram Serian subsequently reveal to you that he had discussed divorce with his wife at any time?"

"Not exactly discussed it outright. At first he said he was bringing up the idea of separation to see how she reacted. Then, later, he said that he had gone ahead and talked about divorce with her."

"Were you a witness to any of Lenore Serian's reactions to her husband's discussing the possibility of a separation or a divorce?"

"Yes. Two different times."

"Would you please tell us when this was and describe for us what you witnessed."

"The first time was about two months before the fire. They were fighting and he said, 'You just want to bleed me dry,' and she said, 'I want it all,' and he said, 'Haven't I given you enough? Without me you would probably be dead,' and she said, 'Maybe I would have preferred death,' and he said, 'Don't you understand . . . our being together was wrong.' "

"Could you please tell us about the second time?"

"The second time was on the night of the fire. Just before Bram went into the studio to go to sleep. They weren't screaming or anything but their voices were very hateful . . . almost like they were beyond shouting. She said, 'How can you do this to someone who's spent so many years with you . . . who's meant so much to you. Has everything been a lie?' He said, 'This is the way it has to be,' and she said, 'I'm warning you, I won't let you do it,' and he said, 'You can't stop me.' "

Natalie Raven used a tissue to wipe her eyes. "That was the last thing I ever heard Bram say. He went into the studio then and . . ." The woman pointed at Lenore. "She killed him."

"Objection, your honor!" Rossner called indignantly.

"Sustained. Strike that last sentence from the record." The judge took off his glasses and put them aside. "Mr. Brown, is it safe to assume that you have quite a bit more ground to cover with this witness?"

"Yes, your honor, that would be a correct assumption."

"In that case I think we ought to let these good people have their lunches. The jury is dismissed until two o'clock."

Owen watched Natalie Raven leave the courtroom, and he saw that Lenore was watching her too. Only after Raven was safely away did Volpe and Riley lead Lenore out.

"This is some great stuff, huh?" Holly said, reviewing her notes as they walked out.

"More to come," Pat reminded her.

As soon as they reached the hallway, Ray announced that it was pizza day and all with a craving should meet at the little Italian joint at the end of Main.

"You're coming, aren't you, Owen?" Pat asked.

"Not today. I've got some phone calls to make, and then I need to check something at the local library."

"Well, have fun," Pat said.

"We'll bring you back a slice," Holly called as he walked away.

Owen went to the pay phones and tried Bernadette Goodson's office again. The receptionist told him Bernie was out to lunch so he asked for Alex.

"Owen!" Alex said as soon as he picked up the phone. "We got your message this morning. You clever dog! How did you get an interview with the Black Widow herself?"

"Just luck, Alex. Basically, I found something that helped her attorney and I guess you'd say this is my reward."

Alex laughed. "You should have seen Bernie. She went wild when she heard."

"So she thinks it's important?"

"Are you kidding!"

"Then I won't turn my proposal in tomorrow, okay? I'll hold onto it another day so I can include something on the interview. Will that be all right?"

"I'm sure it will. How can DeMille complain?" Alex chuckled. "Even Arlene Blunt may get excited about this."

They talked for several minutes, mostly about Natalie Raven's testimony, which Alex wanted to hear word for word.

"Oh, I should have gone up there with you today," Alex said. "Bernie told me I should just admit what a voyeur I am and go."

"You could come tomorrow," Owen told him. "Raven might still be on the stand and then Edie Norton is scheduled. I'm sure she'll be interesting too."

Alex hesitated. "No. I just can't. That would be too frivolous and bad when I have work piled up here." He sighed. "Remember, though . . . if I can help at all—just say so. And my roommate, Cliff, is back again. He's the computer freak

... so if you need any fact checking or whatever, don't hesitate to call. I'll make him give you a bargain price."

Owen thanked him and hung up. Alex's on-again, off-again roommate was a computer hacker who did freelance research in the daytime and bartended at night. The idea intrigued Owen. He had read about people who were magicians with computers, and he wondered if Cliff fit into that category. He also wondered about Alex's arrangement with Cliff. Alex sounded extremely attached to his roommate. Was it possible to know a gay man without being able to tell he was gay? He had always imagined homosexuals to be so different from ordinary people, but maybe that wasn't true at all.

He started calling names on his telephone list, trying to find more interview subjects who were willing to talk about Bram Serian. Every call was a dead end. By the time he was finished it was nearing two, so he skipped the library and bought a plastic-wrapped special from the sandwich cart.

Tomorrow he would talk to Lenore Serian. The promise of that fluttered in his belly like the pregame jitters he'd had in high school basketball. Tomorrow he would actually sit down face to face with her. She would know who he was. He would never be an anonymous face in the courtroom to her again. He threw the untouched sandwich away and headed back upstairs.

When Natalie Raven was reseated on the stand, Brown took her through a long rambling look at the Serian household again, emphasizing Bram Serian's brilliance and kindness while portraying Lenore as sullen, spoiled and possessive. Then he guided her into a discussion of the oil lamp purchase and Serian's fear of fire.

"Did Lenore Serian often ride into town with you when you went on errands?"

"No. Not often. She seldom left Arcadia."

"Did she usually offer to go into stores or do any of the shopping?"

"Rarely. I was surprised when she asked to go. And even more surprised when she asked for my Fugate's Hardware list."

"Did she go into Fugate's Hardware alone?"

"Yes."

"Did you have an opportunity to see what all she purchased?"

"No. By the time I got back to the car—it was a station wagon—George Fugate had packed everything into the back of the wagon and all I could see was the box of canning jars that were on top and the garden hose."

"Canning jars?"

"Yes, we had wild berries on the place and I was going to make jam."

"And this box of canning jars was large enough to obscure whatever was beneath it?"

"There were other boxes of jars too and some things like a garden hose and some other things, and they were all piled up so that they were hiding what was underneath."

"When did you learn the nature of the hidden items that day?"

"When we got home and unloaded the car. Tommy was in the yard—Tommy Kubiak, the teenager who did odd jobs around the place—and he came over and lifted out the canning jars and some other things, and I saw a box with a picture of a clear glass oil lamp on it and then I saw two large jars of colored lamp oil."

"What did you do?"

"I asked Lenore why she had bought them when we have several metal security lanterns in the house."

"What transpired then?"

"She said she had bought the lamp for Bram's studio. And then I told Tommy to leave it in the car because we would have to return it, and I told Lenore that Bram would never use a lamp like that in his studio."

"And how did Mrs. Serian reply?"

"She said that Bram wanted the lamp, which I knew was a lie because—"

"Objection!" Rossner called indignantly. "Is the witness a mind reader?"

The judge sighed. "Sustained. Strike that and please try again, Mr. Brown."

"How did Mrs. Serian reply?" Brown asked again.

"She said Bram wanted the lamp . . . which I wondered about because Bram never wanted fire of any sort in his studio. He had even stopped smoking, he was so paranoid about fire in his studio."

"What happened to the lamp then?"

"I don't know. I assumed Tommy returned it because I told him to. It was lunchtime then, and I didn't want Bram to have to wait for his lunch so I went inside to cook. Last time I saw the lamp and the oil they were still in the back of the car."

"Did you subsequently say anything to Bram Serian regarding the lamp?"

"No. I didn't want to cause trouble between him and Lenore."

"Did you ever see that oil lamp in the house or know of its whereabouts?"

"No, I did not. And I was the person who saw most everything. I mean, I was the one going into the closets and everything."

"Except for Lenore Serian's room, right?"

"Yes. Except for Lenore Serian's room where anything could have been hidden and I wouldn't have known."

"Let's go back a little to talk about Bram Serian. Was there ever an occasion when you discussed with Bram Serian his fears about fire in his studio?"

"I wouldn't say there was ever one big discussion. It was more like a series of mentions. Shortly after I moved in to Arcadia, there was a bad storm and I tried to give him candles and he said no that he didn't want candles and I tried to push him a little ... you know ... tried to convince him to take the candles because I didn't understand why he was saying no and he said he didn't want candles around his work. He said it angrily, like it was a touchy subject. So I asked what was the matter, and he said he didn't want any open flames around his work.

"Then another time he let me look inside the door of his studio—just to show me what it looked like—and he pointed out his heating stove, which he was very proud of. And he told me that he had all the benefits of a woodstove without any of the dangers or problems. And I was being smart ... teasing him a little ... and I said that lots of fires were caused by electrical shorts. And he got very upset at that and had an electrician out that afternoon to check over all his studio wiring."

"Was there anything else regarding fire that came up in your conversations with Bram Serian."

"Yes, there was. About two years ago he came in to breakfast one morning and sat down with me—Lenore was in her room refusing to eat breakfast with us so we were alone—and he said that he had had a nightmare about fire. He described to me how the fire had come at him from all sides and how helpless he felt. He said it was one of the most terrifying nightmares he had ever had. Then he sort of broke down and told me all about how he'd always been scared to death of fire and how he'd always been embarrassed to tell anyone about it."

There it was. The fire angle. Owen kept himself very still, but he was jumping inside with his secret knowledge, and he realized that Rossner must be feeling the same excitement only much more intensely. He thought about how it must feel to sit at that defense table, watching Brown with a witness, cataloging every weakness and thrilling to every slipup, every possible tochold that appeared. Ready to strike.

"Now, let's turn our attention to the night of August sixth and the morning of August seventh. First of all, could you describe for us the party that Serian had organized and the nature of that party?"

"Bram often had weekend parties. They were not so much parties in the way that everyone thinks of that word. What it was was that Bram didn't get to see friends very often because of his being out at Arcadia so much so he just brought his friends to him. This was a way he could socialize and also help out young artists by giving them good food and a free bed for a few days and letting them be with other more established artists. Also this was a way that he could involve other artists in the creation of his house, which he was always building on."

Brown smiled encouragingly. "So what you're saying is that these were not the type of parties where everyone stands around with a drink in their hand?"

"No. People went all directions and did all kinds of things. There was fishing and swimming and rowboating and games, besides all the carpentry work on the house, and then the meals were usually cooked out . . . barbecued."

"So this was not a wild orgy type event where everyone went crazy?"

Natalie Raven chuckled to show how ridiculous that was before answering, "No."

"What were Bram Serian's drinking habits at these parties?"

"During the hot part of the day he would have some beer.

Then with dinner he would have beer or wine. On hot nights he liked to have everyone sit outside and talk about art or just visit and then he would drink socially. But never to the point where he was drunk. Bram Serian was a big man and he could hold his liquor."

"Was he drunk when he went to his studio on the morning of August seventh."

"Absolutely not."

"Where were you when you witnessed the fight between Bram and Lenore Serian subsequent to his going to his studio?"

"I had gone upstairs and was in my bed when I thought I heard their voices through the window. I sleep with it open in the summer. So I got up and went to my window to look out."

"And you had a clear view of them?"

"Yes."

"And you could hear them well?"

"Yes. It was very quiet in the yard area between the house and the studio. I could hear them perfectly."

"Describe for us what happened after their fight."

"He went to his studio and unlocked it and put his keyring back in his pocket, then went inside and slammed the door. Lenore stood in the yard staring at the door for several minutes; then she came into the house."

"Did you see what she was doing in the house?"

"No. It's a very big house."

"And there was enough light outside to see all this clearly?"

"Yes. There are lights mounted in the trees all around there."

"When did you see Bram Serian or Lenore again?"

"Later, at four-twenty, I was awakened by something. I don't even know what, but since I sleep with my window open in the summer, it could have been the smell of smoke. I ran to a hallway where there was a window overlooking the studio, and I saw smoke rolling out of it and some flames, and I saw Lenore standing in the yard facing the studio door and watching."

"Watching?"

"Yes. Just standing there very still and staring at the fire spreading."

"What did you do then?"

"I screamed at her. I don't remember exactly what, but it was something like, 'Where's Bram,' or, 'Is Bram in there,' and that's when she called for help."

"What did you do then?"

"The house has a very elaborate security system, and one of the features is a panic button that sets off a loud alarm so I pushed that to wake people up for help and then I called the fire station."

"Go on . . . please . . ."

"I ran downstairs and grabbed Lenore by the shoulders and shook her and asked if Bram was inside and she nodded, so I tried to enter the studio through the door, but it was impossible. There was too much fire and smoke."

"When you made this effort to enter, was the studio door open or closed?"

"It was open."

"Did you notice this at the time or have any thoughts about it at the time?"

"Yes, I thought it was strange because Bram was really paranoid about that studio door. He *never* left it open, and I had seen him close it earlier."

Owen thought Brown could have finished then, but instead he made Natalie Raven's testimony last another forty minutes, asking her to recount the arrival of the firefighters and the police from her point of view—an exercise which seemed to yield nothing new. Her account of rolling in the mud with Lenore and being ordered to leave was very effective, though, and very damaging to Lenore.

When Natalie Raven's direct was over, Judge Pulaski called a fifteen-minute recess. Most of the spectators stayed put, worried they might lose their places, but the reporters flocked to the hallway. Owen drifted out with them and stood against the wall. The radio people were on the phones in the corner, and everyone else was eagerly dissecting the meaning of what they'd heard, speculating about the prosecution's strategies and anticipating Rossner's cross.

Owen felt very separate now that he'd had the secret meeting with Rossner. He watched them all with the same analytical distance as he watched the witnesses on the stand. And he wondered if he had previously been blind to the pettiness and flashes of ignorance he saw or if he was just viewing them all in a more pessimistic light now.

"It's just too bad that New York doesn't have the death

penalty," he heard Holly say as they filed back in through the double doors.

Rossner leaned casually against the podium. He was exaggerating his perplexed role to the point that he sounded almost slow-witted as he took Natalie Raven back through the events on the night of the fire. Her testimony did not change. In fact, when Owen checked back through his notes, he realized that her phrasing was identical and that most of what she said had to have been memorized. That didn't make it a lie. He knew that. The fire was more than six months in the past, and the woman had been asked the same questions over and over and repeated her answers over and over. Maybe it was bound to come out sounding rehearsed.

Rossner scratched his head and chewed the corner of his lip a moment. Owen was almost sure that this was the turning point and that Rossner was ready to sink some arrows into the saintly housekeeper.

"So, let me see if I have it right . . . Bram Serian hired you on his own without his wife having met you?"

"Yes. He was very good about things like that. Very good about taking charge and getting things done."

"And you lived full-time in the Serian house, and Bram Serian gave you the authority to plan all the meals and generally run the house?"

"Yes."

"And you frequently had breakfast alone with Bram Serian?"

"Yes. Because she was sulking and wouldn't come down."

"And you frequently went through Bram Serian's dresser drawers, and you generally had the run of the house except for Lenore's room?"

"Yes."

"How did you come to be barred from Lenore's room?"

"Oh . . ." Natalie Raven sighed and shrugged. "She just had a fit one day and yelled at me to stay out of her room."

"Had you been in her room? Was that what disturbed her?"

"I had been trying to fulfill my duties in the household."

"Did that include going through Lenore's dresser drawers like you went through her husband's?"

"I don't recall what I was doing exactly."

"But you could have been going through her drawers?"

"I could have been straightening the room, which might have included neatening the dresser."

Rossner turned away from the witness for several beats, then swung back to shake his head in puzzlement. "Did it ever occur to you, Miss Raven, that Lenore might have been a little sullen and out of sorts when you were around because ... without her approval ... her husband brought a strange woman home to live in their house, gave that woman total control of the house, including free access to his personal space. Did it ever occur to you that it was not a normal employer-employee relationship for Bram Serian to frequently breakfast alone with you and to have intimate discussions with you and to confide his nightmares and fears to you, and that Lenore might have been annoyed at this?"

"You are twisting it around!"

"I am? I was just repeating what you've told us today. And I ask you, Miss Raven, if Bram Serian had been your husband, wouldn't you have been a little out of sorts?"

"I don't know."

"But Bram Serian wasn't your husband, was he?"

"That should be obvious."

"Yes, it should be, but was it? Was it obvious to you when you were living under his roof and sharing the breakfast table with him and hearing his intimate thoughts?"

"I don't know what you're getting at."

"I think you do. Isn't it true that you were the one pressing the issue of divorce with Bram Serian?"

"I can't imagine who told you that."

"Why can't you imagine it, because there was no one to sneak around and eavesdrop on your conversations with Serian the way that you crept around the Serian house spying on Bram and Lenore?"

Natalie Raven turned a shade of red so brilliant that she looked like a cartoon character.

"How dare you hint around like that when you have a murderer for a client!"

The judge rapped his gavel sharply. "I'll have to caution you, Miss Raven, against outbursts of that nature."

She mumbled an apology and set her shoulders and her mouth in a hard angry line.

Rossner considered his notes, leaving her to stew in the silence; then he raised his eyes and said, very calmly, "Isn't it

true that you were pregnant by Bram Serian and had an
abortion three months before—"

"Objection!" Spencer Brown shouted. "This is unconscionable, your honor! This is—"

"Both counsel approach the bench!" the judge ordered
sharply, and both men went up to have a fierce whispered
confrontation. When it was over, Rossner and Brown stalked
away and the judge called out, "Sustained as to form. Mr.
Rossner, you'll have to lay a proper foundation if you intend
to pursue this line of inquiry."

But the damage was done. Owen could see the doubt in
the jury's eyes.

Rossner took a few seconds to look over his notes, giving
the jury more time to digest the implications, then said,
"Miss Raven—"

"Wait a minute. Don't I get a chance to defend myself?"
she cried.

"Miss Raven," the judge said gently, "please confine
yourself to answering the questions."

She bowed her head and Rossner went on. "When you
overheard these arguments that you believed were relating to
the divorce, did you happen to overhear every single word
that was spoken?"

"No," she replied softly.

"Is it possible that ... since you didn't hear everything
... that you misunderstood and that the arguments were
about something entirely different?"

"I don't think so."

"But is it possible?"

"I'd say that the subject was divorce," she insisted, but
her voice lacked conviction.

"Is it possible that Bram Serian did not tell you everything that he was thinking or doing or planning on doing?"

"Yes."

"Is it possible that Bram Serian kept things from you?"

"Yes."

"Is it possible that he might have even misled you at
times?"

"I doubt it, but yes, it's possible."

"Is it possible that Bram Serian never discussed divorce
with his wife at all?"

The witness sighed. "I don't ..."

"Is it possible?" Rossner demanded.

"Remotely."

Rossner paused. "All right, let's go back to your meeting Bram Serian. Where did you meet?"

Natalie Raven shifted in the chair as though she'd suddenly felt something sharp beneath her. "We met in Manhattan."

"But Manhattan is a big place ... Specifically, where did you meet?"

"I don't recall."

"Let me try to help you refresh your recollection. Where were you living when you met Bram Serian?"

"I don't recall."

"Where did you move from when you moved to Arcadia?"

"I don't recall."

"You don't recall where you moved from four and a half years ago?"

The witness darted a cornered look around the courtroom. Brown and Dapolito were sitting very straight at their tables, trying not to appear worried. Owen was certain they didn't know where Rossner was headed.

"I was living with some friends in Chelsea," she finally answered.

"The Chelsea section of Manhattan?"

"Yes."

"Do you recall the names of those friends?"

"Sure. Sandy, Doreen, Cindy ... there were a lot of girls sharing this place and we kind of moved in and out."

"And how were you paying your share of the rent?"

"What?"

"What were you doing to support yourself?"

Natalie Raven looked as though she might bolt and run at any minute.

"I was ... you know ... this and that. Self-employment kind of things."

"Everything was completely legal, right ... you did have a social security card and file income taxes and all that?"

"Oh ... yeah ... sure ..."

"But what if I was to tell you that there are no records for a Natalie Raven?"

She looked at the judge. She looked at Brown and Dapolito.

"Wait a minute," Rossner said suddenly. "That must be

because you were not using the name Natalie Raven then, were you?"

"That's right!" she agreed eagerly.

Brown's shoulders sagged several inches.

"Were you using your real name then?"

"Yes."

"And what would that be?" Rossner looked down at an index card as though he had it written right there.

"Norma Bretcher."

"Is that the same Norma Bretcher that was arrested for prostitution and possession of—"

"Objection!" Brown jumped up indignantly. "May we approach the bench, your honor?"

That was the start of a thirty-minute sidebar. Owen went down to the coffee machine. All around him reporters were fighting for pay phones, calling in to alert their editors or producers that they had bombshells for their evening reports.

Marilyn fell in beside Owen as he went back up the stairs. "Well," she said, "they're not snoring in the back rows anymore, are they?"

"No," he agreed. "And Holly is going to have to do some fancy sidestepping to keep from admitting that there's room for doubt now."

Marilyn laughed. "Holly would have made a good hanging judge. Oops, here she comes."

"Can you believe this?" Holly demanded. "Rossner is twisting it around so everybody looks guilty! Who cares if Natalie or Norma or whoever she is didn't come out of a convent? That doesn't make Lenore Serian innocent! It just means Bram had a liberal attitude about who he hired."

Marilyn flashed Owen a smile with her eyes as they hurried back inside.

Excitement was tangible in the room as the jurors filed back in. Owen surveyed the crowd. No one made a sound. Eyes were gleaming, and breaths came shallow and quick. They wanted Lenore Serian to be guilty, and so they should have been rooting for the housekeeper, but the smell of blood was too dizzying. They were eager to see Rossner tear her apart. Owen couldn't help but feel a little bit sorry for her.

First Rossner went after her on the lamp, trying to ridicule all of the woman's sinister implications regarding the purchase of the lamp and the packing of the lamp into the station wagon. Then he attacked on the fire angle, using the article Owen had provided to raise doubts about Serian's alleged fear of fire and emphasizing the fact that only she had heard Serian's purported statements about fire in the studio. Then he tried to get her to admit that Serian had started smoking again. Then he began on the events preceding the fire.

Rossner stopped and tugged at his ear. "Wait a minute . . . I'm confused. You said that you went up to bed, in your room where you always sleep with the window open in summer?"

"Yes."

"And you couldn't help but overhear and see Bram and Lenore Serian's argument in the yard?"

"Yes."

"And then you saw Bram go to the studio and unlock the door and go inside, slamming the door behind him?"

"Yes."

"Then what? You got back in bed?"

"Yes. I had been in bed when I first heard the fight, and I got up to look. So when it was over, I went back to bed."

Rossner paused for a round of head scratching and puzzled expressions. "Then later, you were awakened by the smell of smoke?"

"I think that's what woke me. I'm not sure. When I woke I definitely knew there was smoke somewhere."

"And you knew immediately that the smoke wasn't in the house?"

"Yes. As I've said before the house has an incredible security system and that includes smoke and fire detectors everywhere, and none of those had gone off so I guess I just knew instinctively that it was outside."

"So you ran to . . . ?"

"I ran out in the hallway to a window where I could see—" Natalie Raven stopped and her eyes widened in sudden understanding.

"Go on," Rossner urged. When she didn't respond he said, "That's all right, I have it from before." He flipped through the pages of a yellow legal pad. "You said, 'I ran to a hallway where there was a window overlooking the studio and I saw smoke rolling out of it and some flames and I saw Lenore standing in the yard facing the studio door and watching.' Does that sound right?"

"Yes," she admitted weakly.

"But if your bedroom window had a view of the yard and the studio that allowed you to see the argument and Bram Serian's opening the door with his key on his keyring, why did you have to run to a hall window to see if the studio was on fire?"

"I . . . I don't know . . . I was sleepy. I just got out of bed. I guess I wasn't thinking too clearly."

"That's understandable." Rossner nodded sympathetically. "But which is it, then? Could you see the yard and the studio from your bedroom window, or did you have to go to another part of the house to see it?"

"I . . ."

At that moment, Jacowitz produced a poster-sized diagram showing the outline of the house and the outline of the studio, and it was entered into evidence.

"Can you take this pointer and point out the location of your bedroom for me?" Rossner asked the witness.

Hesitantly, she pointed to an area that could not possibly have a good view of the yard and studio.

Rossner examined the drawing with a perplexed frown. "But then your window couldn't have . . . Maybe what happened before . . . when you heard the argument and got up . . . got out of bed . . ."

"Yes. I was in bed when I heard them."

"Maybe you were sleepy and disoriented."

"Yes. Yes."

"And you went out to the other window in the hall without even realizing it?"

"Yes. Yes, that's what happened."

"And then in this state . . . so sleepy and disoriented that you didn't know if you were in the hall or still at your own bedroom window . . . you witnessed the argument?"

"Yes."

"Yet, even though you didn't know what window you were at, you absorbed a word-for-word recollection of Bram and Lenore Serian's argument?"

"Well, I was awake by then."

"And you saw him put his key in the lock?"

"Yes."

"But didn't the studio door have a protective overhang that would have made it almost impossible to see the lock when you were looking down from above?"

"Well, it was ... I saw him unlock the door, so maybe I was at a downstairs window."

"You mean you were so disoriented that maybe you not only went out into the hall but went all the way downstairs without realizing it?" Rossner asked in an incredulous tone.

"Yes."

"Maybe ..." Rossner thundered. "Maybe you were so disoriented that it was you who went into the studio and killed Bram Serian that morning!"

"Your honor!" Spencer Brown screamed, and Owen watched the expression on Charlie Rossner's face. Rossner didn't care if it was stricken from the record. He had scored big and the jury wouldn't forget.

10

Owen did not rest well Wednesday night. He planned his questions for Lenore Serian, worrying over what he could safely ask her. Worrying over how far he could go. How much she would answer. When he slept he dreamed that there was a key hidden somewhere and that if he found the key he could unlock all her secrets. He spent hours searching for that key, fighting and running and being tortured in pursuit of that key. He woke before dawn, damp with sweat and tangled in his blankets. Then he lay there waiting for the alarm to buzz, watching the hands of the clock move and the light change to gray. Somewhere out there Lenore Serian was also lying in bed. Also alone. What dreams did she dream? What tortures did darkness bring to her each night?

When he arrived at the Greystone Hotel for his interview with her, he was extremely nervous. This time Volpe's greeting was marginally less hostile, and Riley was positively friendly. Inside the suite, the atmosphere was relaxed, with shirt collars open and feet propped up among scattered legal pads and half-filled cups of coffee. Jacowitz joked about the collapse of Spencer Brown's star witness, and Owen joined in the laughter, feeling as though he'd passed a test and had been deemed trustworthy.

"Coffee?" Jacowitz asked. "Or soda perhaps?" Even in a disheveled state, bow tie undone and shirtsleeves rolled up, Paul Jacowitz was the picture of propriety. If he had been elderly and white instead of young and black, he might have been referred to as "dapper." Owen wondered what sort of old-fashioned genteel upbringing had produced a young man of such distinction.

"Coffee's fine," Owen answered, whereupon Rossner patted him on the back and said, "Lenore is waiting so you'd better go on." Another pat, then, "Paul will sit in during the interview."

Owen realized that maybe he wasn't so trusted after all.

Jacowitz handed him coffee, then led him through one of the side doors into a smaller room. This one was all in flat beiges and browns with the requisite hotel grouping of two beds, dresser, desk, and vintage armchairs facing each other near the window. Lenore was seated in one of the chairs. It was rounded and overstuffed, a chair to sink into, but Lenore's back was perfectly straight and she held her chin high. She looked both defensive and untouchable.

In contrast, her appearance seemed more genuine than before. She had on a forest green sweater, a slim wool skirt, and oxblood leather boots. More flattering clothes than any he'd seen her in previously. Her hair was loosely arranged on top of her head, and a faint shade of cinnamon stained her lips and cheeks. Again Owen was struck by how young she looked, and he wondered at her age. Wondered how much of an age difference there'd been between her and Serian.

Jacowitz settled unobtrusively across the room, and Owen took the chair facing Lenore by the window.

He met her eyes, as unrevealing as dark glass, and the nearness of her hammered in his pulse and tightened in the pit of his stomach. Was he looking into the soul of an innocent grieving victim or the cold eyes of a murderer?

"What is it you want from me?" Lenore asked in a clear but faintly accented voice. Almost a French accent, but not quite.

A chill touched the back of his neck. He considered his answer carefully.

"I'm doing a book on the trial, but I can't write it without understanding Bram Serian." And understanding you, he wanted to say, but dared not. "I began researching, and talking to people, and realized what a mystery Serian's past is. Now, I'm trying to unravel that past. And I'm hoping you have some pieces to the puzzle."

She studied him. He could read nothing.

"You want to create a history for Bram?" she asked.

"I don't want to create a history, I want to find a history."

One side of her mouth curved up slightly, like the ghost of a lingering smile. Her eyes reflected an enigmatic amusement.

"Maybe I should say I want to make Serian more human."

She regarded him with a direct, uncompromising gaze.

Her black eyes picked up a touch of green from her sweater, transforming them into the eerie night forest color of childhood terrors. He felt an odd twisting sensation and another rush of uncertainty.

"Bram would have laughed at you," she said. "Then thrown you out and put your name on his blacklist."

"I'm lucky to be talking to you, then, aren't I?"

She looked away from him momentarily, then turned her dark gaze on him once again. "Go ahead. Ask your questions."

He flipped open his notebook and drew a deep breath. "What do you know about Serian's early life?"

"Nothing."

"Okay . . . Did he give any hints as to where he was born and raised?"

"No."

"Ever talk about growing up in farm country?"

"No." The tiniest flicker of interest stirred in her eyes. "Why? Do you believe he grew up on a farm?"

Owen repeated what John Potter had told him and the small hints he'd picked up from Gregory Hillyer and Edie Norton. She brooded over the information awhile, but made no comment.

"Did he ever mention the names of his parents or any other family members?" Owen asked.

"No. No one but Al . . ."

"Al? His assistant?"

"Yes. They were cousins."

"The art assistant who lived out in the studio was definitely his cousin?" Owen asked, excited at this news.

"Yes. A distant cousin."

"Where is he now?"

"I don't know. He left two years ago. Bram always said he would come back . . . but he never did." She stared off at nothing.

"What is Al's full name?"

She shrugged delicately. "Al Serian."

"Did Al ever talk about his family or his childhood?"

"Al didn't talk much at all except when he was having one of his bad spells, and then most of it was rambling."

Owen took a drink of his coffee and considered which direction to go next.

"Al was retarded or mentally impaired, right?"

She hesitated, then shrugged.

"Well, was he or wasn't he?"

"Why? What difference does that make?"

"I thought ... maybe if he'd been treated somewhere for his problems, they might have files on him that would lead me to the Serian family, and to Bram's origins."

"Bram was the only family Al had. That's why he took care of him."

"Where was Al while Bram was away in Vietnam?"

"I don't ... I'm sorry. I don't know much about that."

"What was Bram Serian like when you first met him. What sort of person was he?"

The sun had climbed higher and was pouring through the window, enveloping her in a silvery winter light that turned her skin to antique ivory and her hair to gleaming black silk. He had never known anyone with hair so truly black. Like India ink or obsidian.

She touched her fingertips to her temple in thought, struggling with the memories and the answers to his question. There was vulnerability in the gesture. Her fingers were slender, her nails as neat and plain as a child's and her wrist so thin that he could imagine it snapping. Suddenly he was stricken with remorse. The woman was suffering, and he was taking advantage of her for the sake of a book. He was using her. Feeding off her misfortune. How could he have fallen to such a despicable level?

"That's it," he said, standing quickly and grabbing his bag.

Jacowitz jumped up. "What's wrong, man? What's wrong?"

Owen brushed him aside, snatched his coat off the bed and escaped into the hotel hallway, disgusted with himself and the entire book project.

Rossner caught him at the top of the stairs.

"Hold it, Byrne!"

Reluctantly, Owen stopped and turned. "You've seen the last of me," he said.

"Not so fast. You owe an explanation for this."

"I'll write you a letter."

"No. If you're angry at Lenore, I want to clear it up now."

"I'm not angry," Owen realized that his voice was close to a shout, and that he *was* angry. At himself. He tilted his head back and let out a deep sigh of frustration. "I was wrong, okay? I never should have intruded on her like that."

Something kindled in Rossner's eyes. It could have been warmth, but it appeared closer to triumph.

"You know, Byrne . . . what I said before still goes. You could help Lenore a lot. Who knows what we've missed? Who knows what more you might find?" Rossner paused a beat. "I'd like to have you working on my team."

"What does that mean? Your team?"

"That I'd pay for your research services and you'd concentrate your efforts for us and not reveal anything to the prosecution."

"I don't want your money, Rossner."

The attorney frowned and his eyebrows met over the bridge of his nose. "What's your price, then? What *do* you want?"

"I want to see justice done . . . I want the truth to be found . . . just like everybody else. If I uncover anything more, it's yours. No price. No conditions."

"Ah," Rossner said. He smiled gently, cynically. A smile that was infused with an odd melancholy. "A man of virtue. When we checked you out there were indications of that, but virtue is such a rare quality . . . we didn't believe."

Owen turned away, ashamed of the entire episode and disgusted with the games and the "checking out," knowing that his life had been pried into and scrutinized. As he headed toward the stairs, he glanced back and saw Lenore standing in the doorway, watching. And there was something close to hope lighting her dark eyes.

Tommy Kubiak took the stand first that morning. Witnesses were not allowed to attend the trial, but Owen was sure that Phyllis, the enthusiastic spectator, had attended daily and kept her son informed so that Tommy knew every word that had been said previously from that witness stand. Owen looked across to the spectator section and saw Phyllis sitting in the second row, beaming proudly, just like a mother watching her son come up to bat at his school baseball game.

Spencer Brown took Tommy through a recitation of his duties at the Serian home as though the boy was seven rather than seventeen. Tommy talked about his two years working for the Serians, and he smiled at everyone. He smiled at

Brown and the judge and the jury and at his mom in the audience. Owen would have sworn that Tommy even smiled at Lenore.

"Now, Tommy, let's go to that particular day when you were working out in the yard and Miss Raven and Mrs. Serian drove up in the station wagon and you went over to help unload and—"

"The day the lamp was in the car?" Tommy asked eagerly.

"Yes. Did Miss Raven and Mrs. Serian discuss the lamp within your hearing?"

"They sure did. I started to get it out of the back and Miss Raven said something like, 'Stop, what's that for?' And Mrs. Serian said it was for the art studio and Miss Raven got kind of mad like and said Bram don't want that thing in his studio."

"What was Mrs. Serian's reply?"

"She didn't say anything. She just kind of stood there, and then Miss Raven gave me the keys and told me I could drive to town later to return the lamp, and then she said she had to hurry in and get lunch fixed."

"Did you return the lamp later as you had been instructed to do?"

"No. I went on off to finish the list of stuff Serian had give me to do earlier, and then when I got finished the lamp and the oil was gone, so I just hung the car keys inside the house where they was supposed to go and I went on."

"Did you say anything regarding the lamp to anyone?"

"Nah. The best way to stay out of trouble around there was to never say nothing to nobody unless they spoke up first, so that's what I did and nobody ever come and asked me what happened to the lamp so I just forgot about it."

"Now Tommy . . . was there ever an occasion when Bram Serian lectured you?"

"Lots of occasions."

"Was there ever a time when he specifically lectured you about something to do with fire?"

"You mean what I told you before about the smoking?"

"Yes. Please relate that for us."

"Well, I was taking a break one day and sitting on the ground with my back up against the studio and having a cigarette and Serian comes up and yells at me to put it out. I was kinda surprised 'cause he'd never minded me smoking before and he'd even give me a light sometimes with that high-powered lighter of his, but then he started in telling me how the studio was just an old wood barn and how easy it could burn up and he made me promise I'd never smoke around there again."

"So he was afraid you might accidentally set fire to his studio?"

"You got it. That's what he was afraid of."

Brown smiled indulgently. "Now did there come a time, in the course of your duties at Arcadia, that you had occasion to have a conversation with Mrs. Serian regarding the subject of fire?"

"What?" Tommy asked blankly.

"You said before that one of your duties at Arcadia was disposing of trash, correct?"

"Yeah. Which mostly we burned trash but there was some things I had to haul out and dump."

"Where did you burn trash?"

"Oh, a long ways from the house over near the equipment shed."

"Did Mrs. Serian ever come out to watch you burn trash?"

"Yeah. Lots. And she would always bring things out to add to the pile, and she would stand there with me and watch while it all burned."

"What kind of things did she bring out to add to the fire?"

"Just things . . . I don't know. Things she didn't want to put in with the rest of the trash."

"Did she tell you that?"

"Sort of. She said nothing was private and nothing belonged to her until she watched it burn."

"Nothing was private and nothing belonged to her until she watched it burn?"

"Yeah . . . kind of a weird thing to say, but then she was always saying kind of weird stuff."

"Do you recall some items that you watched her burn?"

"Yeah. I saw her burn a doll. A perfectly good doll. I saw her burn clothes that didn't look like they had nothing wrong with them. I saw her burn pictures."

"Can you describe the pictures for us?"

"They weren't like pictures from a camera. They were drawings. But I never really got a clear look at them cause she'd fold or crumple them up before she threw them on the pile."

"Did she say anything as she watched these various

items—the doll and the clothing and the drawings—did she say anything as she watched them burn?"

"No. She'd just pitch them in the fire and then just stare while they turned black and shriveled up."

"Anything else that you recall watching her burn?"

"Yeah, sometimes she brought out some of those candles of hers—you know after they were burned down to the end or if the glass got broke or something."

"Could you please tell us more about these candles?"

"They were spooky, you know, with voodoo sayings on them."

"Objection!" Rossner called.

"Sustained," the judge responded immediately. "Strike that from the record."

"Tommy, would you please describe the candles for us? Tell us the details of their appearance without trying to characterize them."

Tommy nodded. "They were colors—red ones, blue ones, green ones—and they had sayings printed on them that were like hexes."

"Do you recall one of those sayings?"

"One I remember real good was *Bad Luck to All Enemies.*"

"Did you ever ask her about the candles?"

"Uh-uhh. No sir. Like I said before, the way to get along around that place was not to say nothing, so I kept my mouth shut and pretended I didn't notice those candles."

"Did she ever say anything about the candles?"

"No. Never did."

"Was there anything else she burned that struck you as particularly odd?"

"Yeah, I hadn't been working around there too long when she came to burn some things made out of paper. They were real cute like little models of things . . . cars and animals and furniture . . . all made out of paper."

"And what did she do with these models?"

"She threw them on the fire one at a time, and she told me that you could burn things like that to give people stuff after they were dead."

"Could you repeat that, please, so we understand exactly what you are saying?"

"Sure. She said that if you burned like a little paper car

that you were sending that car to a dead person to use. After they were dead. Like in heaven . . . you know?"

"Yes. Thank you." Brown let this testimony sink in a moment before continuing. "Did you have occasion to speak with Mrs. Serian after her husband's death?"

"Yeah. It was after the funeral but before they . . . you know . . . arrested her or whatever. She called me to come clean up some stuff around the yard where the firefighters and everybody had made such a mess. I went over and was working, and when I went to burn some stuff she came and stood there staring down into the fire real sad like, so I said—I was trying to cheer her up—and I said something about 'Well, anyway all of Bram's most important stuff burned up with him so now he's got it with him, you know . . . in heaven.' I was thinking that because of all the weird stuff she believed that would make her feel better."

"Did Mrs. Serian respond?"

"Yes. She said she should burn up Natalie and the house so he'd have everything."

"Did she say she should burn up models of Natalie and the house?"

"No. She didn't say models."

Rossner approached Tommy Kubiak like a good-natured uncle. He asked the teenager about school and about how he'd gotten the job at Arcadia and about what he did with his spare time. Owen could see what Rossner was attempting, but he didn't know if it was working. The attorney was gently trying to show that Tommy was a very narrow, very inexperienced young man who might easily misunderstand the unfamiliar and who might have misinterpreted much of what he saw at the Serians' because the people there were so different from what he was used to.

Owen watched the jury. He suspected that they were as narrow and inexperienced as Tommy Kubiak and that Rossner's strategy was losing rather than gaining him points.

Rossner led Tommy into admitting that he had never felt threatened by Lenore and that indeed he'd liked Lenore. That if anyone at Arcadia had made him feel threatened it had been Natalie Raven, whom Tommy described as grouchy. Then Rossner brought up the smoking incident and Tommy repeated the story.

"And you say Bram Serian had at times given you a light from his high-powered lighter?"

"Yeah. The fancy silver one that ran on butane or whatever. That thing had a monster flame."

"And this is what Bram Serian used to light his own cigarettes?"

"Yeah. Sometimes we'd kind of take a smoking break together. He kept promising he was quitting but he couldn't."

"Who was he promising that he would quit?"

"Natalie. She was all over him all the time. Said he was going to kill himself."

"How did she say he was going to kill himself?"

Tommy shrugged. "Cancer, I guess. She never really said."

"But she could have been referring to killing himself by burning, by catching himself on fire with the flame from his monster lighter or—"

"Your honor," Brown said with impatient disgust. "Objection. Counsel is on a fishing expedition into imagined thought processes that this witness couldn't possibly have any knowledge of."

"Sustained!"

Rossner backed off then and went in another direction, asking Tommy if he was aware that there were religions in the world where paper possessions were routinely burned for the dead. Of course Tommy was unaware of that. Owen could not tell if Rossner's sociology lesson had any effect on the jury at all. He doubted that it had.

Marilyn and Pat persuaded Owen to join the lunch gang at the coffee shop. There were nine of them and two tables had to be pushed together. Holly was dressed all in red. When Owen looked at her his thoughts divided. On the one hand, she looked beautiful, and it was interesting to consider that she was available to him. On the other hand, he felt completely unmoved by her charms. During the walk back to the courthouse, he kept up an animated conversation with Marilyn and Pat so he wouldn't have to talk to Holly at all.

When court reconvened, it was Edie Norton to the stand. Away from her gallery and her elegant office, she was diminished somewhat. Owen couldn't help but feel sympathy for her, knowing the kind of adversary she faced in Charles Rossner.

Brown moved into position and the machinery ground ruthlessly forward. Edie Norton talked about Bram Serian, glorifying him, and the art world, and her gallery in particular. She gave her expert opinion as to the value of both the art collection in the Serian home, which she said was considerable, and any Serian works that Lenore might inherit—also considerable. She answered carefully. Owen could almost hear her thought processes, could hear her asking herself which slant on the answers would serve her best, which image would be the most profitable for her gallery.

"And so, Mrs. Norton, exactly how long were you acquainted with the deceased?"

"Since 1970 or '71. We discovered Bram Serian and were the first to sell his work."

"And did you continue to represent his work?"

"Yes. We are still representing it."

"And in the process of this long-term business relationship, would you say that you came to know Bram Serian fairly well?"

"Absolutely. For many of our artists we function as advisors, therapists, parental figures and confidants as well as financial support systems."

"And what were you to the deceased?"

"All of them at one time or another."

"So you were intimately acquainted with him?"

She hesitated. "Yes."

"You mentioned before that Bram Serian's career had had its ups and downs. Could you elaborate on this for us?"

"Certainly. It was slow in the beginning. There was little appreciation for his work. Then he made the breakthrough when he took himself in a new direction . . . with the painting . . . and then there was a period when everything he did was greatly appreciated. That peak period was followed by a rather disappointing number of years . . . disappointing for Serian . . . wherein there was interest only in his painting. You see, for Serian, the painting was not as important as the sculpting and it wounded him deeply when the critics focused on the painting and disparaged the rest of his work. During this time he became obsessed with the house building, pouring his creative energies into the house. And, as often happens in the art world, his work . . . painting as well as sculpting . . . fell temporarily out of favor."

Brown looked as though he was concentrating hard to absorb all of Edie Norton's meanings. "During this period, Mrs. Norton, this out-of-favor period when his work was not in demand, was Bram Serian also not in demand?"

"I'd have to say yes. Sad but true. When respect for an artist's work dissipates, then there are no more social invitations or speaking engagements. However, Bram's personality was so strong that he did always maintain a group of followers."

"So during this out-of-favor period, what did Bram Serian do with his time and energy?"

"As I've said before, he became obsessed with the house and he spent most of his time out there in the country tinkering around with it."

"Whereas previously how had he spent most of his time?"

"When he was popular, he spent a lot of time in Manhattan, and he was in demand at all sorts of social occasions and benefits, and he was treated like a celebrity with people grabbing at him and women putting their phone numbers in his pocket—all that nonsense."

"During this period of popularity, when he spent so much time in Manhattan and was socially in demand, did his wife take part in the activities as well?"

"Never. Lenore was almost an agoraphobic. She never went to Manhattan or attended social events with him."

"Did he ever comment on this to you?"

"Only in roundabout ways."

Brown became suddenly agitated.

"Could you please be more specific, Mrs. Norton? Did Bram Serian make statements to you and if so what did he say?"

"He did not make definite statements. No, it was more like he made small comments which could have been partially teasing or jokes in the manner that—"

"Mrs. Norton! Are you changing the statements you previously made?"

"I am saying that . . . before, for the grand jury, I was led to make statements that I have since reflected on and decided were unfair. I was at the time still distraught over Bram's death, and with your encouragement, Mr. Brown, I was interpreting long-ago comments in the least flattering manner for Lenore. I now realize this was wrong, and I am attempting to give a fairer portrayal of what I recall."

Spencer Brown's mouth gaped open. The resulting sidebar

was brief, but allowed time for Holly, Pat and Marilyn to whisper in amazement to each other. Owen was not amazed. He knew exactly what was going on. Edie Norton was well recovered from her grief over Serian. She'd been following the trial in the news and saw that there was a possibility Lenore might be acquitted, and she saw the dollars and sense of ducking over to Lenore's side. No one knew better than Edie how much art Lenore would control if she was found innocent.

Brown was obviously angry when he resumed his direct. "Mrs. Norton, what turn did Bram Serian's career take shortly before his death?"

"One of those inexplicable shifts of the wind happened and interest in his work began to surface."

"Did you and Bram Serian do anything in response to this renewed interest?"

"Yes, we immediately planned a big show. He was very enthusiastic."

"A show?"

"Yes. It was to be an unveiling of significant new paintings."

"So he was optimistic? Hopeful? Excited?"

"Yes. The art world was in love with him again, and he was like a man reborn."

"Did you have occasion to visit him at Arcadia during the planning for this show?"

"Yes."

"And while you were there did you have contact with Lenore Serian?"

"Yes."

"And what was her reaction to all this resurgence of renewed interest in her husband and all the new attention?"

"She was very concerned."

"In what ways was she concerned?"

"She was . . . at the time, and later, after his death, I believed that she was jealous and did not want to lose her husband to the spotlight again. However, when I look back now I can see that Lenore was also concerned because Bram had been so hurt before and the art world—the critics and the collectors and the groupies—everyone can be very fickle, and I think maybe she saw Bram as being set up for another fall."

Brown crossed his arms, stared up at the ceiling and clenched his jaw into a ridged line.

"But at the time, Mrs. Norton, it seemed to you that Lenore Serian was jealous and did not want to lose her husband to the spotlight again. Is that correct?"

"At the time, while planning the show, yes."

"While Bram Serian's work was out of style, he spent most of his time with his wife at Arcadia, did he not?"

"Yes."

"And this would not be true . . . he would not spend most of his time at Arcadia with his wife any longer if he became popular again, would he?"

"Probably not, but that is only a guess on my part. Who can say?"

"Let's turn our attention to the night of August sixth and morning of August seventh. Were you present at the Serian home?"

"Yes. I was. I did not usually attend Bram's weekend parties because they had turned into such workfests with him expecting everyone to sweat over that house of his, but this party was also to be a celebration of the upcoming show and he had promised to let me look at some of the paintings he'd been working on."

"When did you arrive?"

"I drove up with my husband, Barry, on the afternoon of Saturday the sixth."

"Could you describe for us please what was the atmosphere and what transpired that afternoon and evening?"

"Everyone was very lighthearted. Some old faces were there, but many of the people were unknown to me. Bram collected people . . . followers. He was like the Robin Hood of the art world, with his merry band of loyal men, and he was always helping them and giving handouts. When we arrived everyone was working on the house, and then in the afternoon people split off for fishing and other outdoorsy pursuits. I asked Bram then if I could see the paintings, but he said no, not yet. He said they were all locked away in the studio, and he wasn't ready to get them out yet."

"Go on, Mrs. Norton . . ."

"Barry and I were not much for the outdoors, so we joined Natalie Raven in the gazebo for a drink. Miss Raven was not in high spirits like everyone else. She seemed very depressed and so we tried to cheer her up. Then we had dinner. It was a big production, a whole barbecued pig, which I tried to avoid since I am a vegetarian, but Bram kept teasing me and at one point he talked someone into sneaking a disgusting pig's foot onto my plate. I was very annoyed at that and went into the house. Inside the house I came across Lenore. She was sitting at a window, watching the festivities."

"And what did she say to you at that time?"

"She said a number of things. We chatted. Made small talk."

Owen thought about how Edie Norton had told him just last weekend that she *never* talked to Lenore Serian at all.

Brown looked as though he might explode with fury at his unpredictable witness. "Did she not specifically say something to you regarding the upcoming art show?" he demanded.

Edie Norton hesitated a moment, then said, "Yes. I made a comment about fate and about how Bram's turn had come around again, and she said that it was wrong. That the whole thing was wrong, and that it would be Bram's greatest mistake."

"Did you ask her what she meant?"

"No. Lenore was always very cryptic and I knew that she would not explain herself. However, I think that she was showing genuine concern, the concern that anyone would have for a loved one who is opening himself up to pain. Because, you see, when I look back I have to admit that there were no guarantees. The show could have turned out to be a big flop. And the paintings, which were burned and so never viewed, might have been terrible."

Brown breathed an exasperated sigh.

"But didn't you in an earlier statement interpret Lenore Serian's comments as a desire to see her husband fail so that she could hang on to him?"

"That was then and this is now. Now I think I have a more objective viewpoint."

Spencer Brown threw up his hands in disgust. "No more questions, your honor."

Charles Rossner stood and gave a polite bow of the head to Edie Norton. "The defense has no questions for Mrs. Norton at this time, your honor."

Edie Norton batted her eyes at both the judge and Rossner, then marched out of the courtroom. Owen couldn't

help smiling as she passed the seething Brown and the be-
wildered Dapolito.

"I don't understand why you won't relax and unwind a
little," Holly said. They were all standing in the hallway outside the courtroom. The judge had announced that he had
other business to attend to on Friday, so there would be no
trial the next day. Then Pulaski had adjourned early due to
the unexpected brevity of Norton's time on the stand and the
fact that Spencer Brown's next witness was not waiting in
the wings.

Holly's red suit was cut in a vee in front and had a very
tight skirt. Ray had to mop his brow with a handkerchief every time he looked at her.

"Come on, go with us," Marilyn urged. "Our teams won't
be even otherwise."

They were all trying to coax him into dinner and a dart-
throwing tournament at an Irish pub in Manhattan.

"I can't," he said.

"Ahhh, he's just afraid," Ray said. "Doesn't want any of
us to know that Jayhawkers can't throw darts."

"What's a Jayhawker?" Marilyn asked.

"A Kansan," Ray said.

Owen was surrounded by Ray and Holly and Marilyn and
Gil Flores and several others whose names he had forgotten.
They were all in high spirits, happy over the trial's continued entertainment value and the points they were earning at
their respective jobs.

"I wish I could," Owen laughed. "But I have to turn in my
proposal first thing tomorrow. I'm going to be working all
night as it is."

They gave him the address just in case he changed his
mind; then they dispersed to go do their stories. Owen went
straight to the pay phone.

Bernie was on another call, which was fine with Owen because he wanted to speak to Alex anyway.

"So it's all set for me to turn in the proposal tomorrow,
right?" he asked.

"No problem," Alex answered.

An anxious sigh escaped Owen and Alex laughed. "Stay
calm. It will be fine. I've got a good feeling about this one."

"I hope you're right. I just hope I'm doing a good enough
job on the thing. If they turn it down . . . I don't know if I

could just quit and go home. I want to see it through. I really want to do this book."

"Well, I'll be rooting for you."

"Thanks, Alex. Listen, before, when you said your friend could do some computer research for me, is that still possible?"

"Sure. What do you need?"

"I'm not certain how much of this information is available through open channels, but I thought, whatever there is on Serian's stint in the military might help. Especially his time in Vietnam."

"Okay, I'll see what Cliff can do. You'd be amazed—no, horrified—at the information banks he can get into."

"And also there's a cousin, Al Serian, who's got mental problems of some sort. He lived at Arcadia up until two years ago. I don't know if there's anything we can dig up on him or his whereabouts, but it might be worth a try."

"Got it," Alex said. "Check with me again in a few days for a report." There was a mumbling, and Owen could tell that Alex was holding his hand over the receiver and speaking to someone else.

"Hey, Owen. You just had a call come in here. The receptionist took a message. Some woman wants you to phone her as soon as possible."

"Who was it?" Owen asked, immediately worried that there was an emergency at home.

"She wouldn't leave her name. Just the number."

Owen copied down the number, then thanked Alex and hung up. The area code made him suspicious. It was the same as the courthouse. He was afraid that this was a Holly Danielson ploy.

Reluctantly, he dialed.

"Hello," said a female voice. It didn't sound like Holly.

"Yes, my name is Byrne and someone at this number left a message for me to call."

"Yes."

She hesitated and Owen listened to the silence over the phone line and suddenly he knew. Before she said anything else, he knew who it was.

"This is Lenore Serian. Charlie Rossner explained to me why you left so abruptly yesterday."

His pulse was racing. Why would she call him? What

could she possibly want? He tried to keep his tone casual. "I'm sorry if I seemed rude . . ."

"There's no need for an apology. He said that you agreed to help with some further research."

"Yes. But if you're calling to find out whether I've started, I'm afraid I haven't had a chance yet."

"No." Another hesitation. "I'm calling to ask you to come to Arcadia."

"You want me to come to Arcadia?" he repeated in disbelief.

"Yes."

He took a long slow breath.

"When?"

"Tomorrow, if that's possible."

He took another deep breath.

"What time do you want me there?"

11

The gateway to Arcadia was an imposing rock affair spanned by a tall wrought-iron gate. It was out of place on the country road. All the other farms had simple barbed-wire fences with cattle guards across the driveways or at the most an aluminum gate secured with padlock and chain. Owen got out of the car and pressed the buzzer on the intercom beside the gate. Nearly a minute passed before Lenore Serian's voice asked, "Who is it?"

"Owen Byrne."

The gate immediately slid open on a recessed metal track. He barely had time to get back in the rental car and drive through before it began to close. Once he was inside he stopped the car and looked around.

When he had called Bernadette Goodson that morning to tell her the news about his trip to Arcadia, and beg for yet another extension on his proposal deadline, she had been excited but concerned. "What could that woman be planning?" Bernie had said several times during their conversation. And when she said good-bye Bernie had added, only halfjokingly, "Remember, Owen, if you smell kerosene . . . run!"

There was nothing to see but trees. He started forward. Gravel crunched beneath his tires and he drove slowly, trying to see through the heavy woods that crowded the road. Glimpses of sloping grassland showed through in spots. Nothing startling or luxurious. Just the same winter-poor pasture that covered the other farms he'd passed. Then he topped a rise and saw the house.

No description he'd read conveyed the spectacle of Arcadia. It was at once beautiful and ugly, logical and surreal, a shimmering mirage of turrets, terraces, gables, galleries, pinnacles, spires and towers. A gothic cathedral from a sciencefiction vision of the future. Sunlight reflected at so many points that the building seemed to be made of light. His eyes stung from the brilliance, but he couldn't stop looking. It struck him that this view of Arcadia was reminiscent of a fantasy miniature of New York City, and he wondered if Serian had intended it as such.

The effect changed as he drove closer. Details emerged. But not until he pulled into the circular driveway where the shadows of sixty-foot cedars cast the entry in deep shade was the house transformed from ethereal to substantial. He saw then that the walls were made of dark irregular rock interspersed at random with jagged chunks of lucent glasslike stone. Enameled tiles of lapis blue scalloped the roof, and the towers were topped with hammered copper that had weathered to a soft verdigris. Oversized windows appeared at odd intervals, circles and ovals and rectangles of darkly patterned glass. Stained glass, he guessed, though the colors weren't discernible from where he stood.

A gust of wind rattled through the dry leaves on the ground and swept up to the tops of the cedars. He pulled his coat collar up. The swaying trees admitted flashes of sun, and he saw how many reflective surfaces there were to create the mirage of light.

Around to the side he could see a corner of the charred remains that must have once been Serian's studio. The sight chilled him more thoroughly than the cold wind.

Slowly, he walked up the steps to the broad porch, which wasn't really a porch at all but one of a series of stone terraces that embraced the house. The front door was large and heavily carved. It was framed by insets of deeply hued blue-green glass—not transparent machine-tempered glass but the old handblown variety, beautifully dense and imperfect, with streaks of tiny bubbles and flowing gradations of color.

He rang the bell and waited.

The door opened, and he was face-to-face with Lenore Serian, only this was a Lenore Serian that would never be seen in court. This was a lithe woman in an open-necked red silk shirt and trim faded jeans, gleaming black hair falling loose over her shoulders. She leaned against the door a moment, regarding him with an undecipherable look. Then her lips curved into a slow, knowing smile.

"Mr. Byrne," she said, drawing him into an entryway that glowed with undulating deep-water light. Drawing him in as if she were some ancient Atlantean goddess luring him into her deep-sea chambers.

Her eyes burned darkly in the sea light. They held him. Pinned him in place, mute and helpless beneath their enigmatic regard. Then, abruptly, she turned away and led him through dim, twisting hallways. He followed. Watching her long hair sway against her slender back as she moved.

They emerged into the brightness of an enormous high-ceilinged kitchen with a stone fireplace, exposed beams and hanging copper pots.

"Coffee or tea?" she asked, without so much as a glance over her shoulder.

"Whatever is easiest," he answered, moving up to stand across the island counter from her.

She looked up sharply. "Just tell me what you want. Don't make me guess."

"Coffee. With a little milk if you have it."

"Fine. Throw your coat over a chair."

He watched as she made coffee with a glass, European-style press pot. Her movements were studied but graceful. She handed him a mug, then picked up one for herself and disappeared through the far door. Again he followed. This time to a small, square sitting room that was bathed in the jeweled light of an eight-foot stained-glass window.

She put her mug down on the massive, hammered metal coffee table and settled into one of the plump loveseats surrounding it. He followed suit, then turned to stare at the remarkable window. It was a waterfall tumbling into a pond, or the illusion of a waterfall, and down in the corner a tiny sprite with opalescent wings knelt on a boulder to study her reflection in the water.

"I noticed the windows as I drove up, but I couldn't tell much about them from the outside. Are they all this . . . impressive?"

Her mouth softened slightly. "Yes. But this is one of my favorites. It's by Emile Gallé, Tiffany's French contemporary. The style is not Gallé's really. He did it at the request of a friend . . . so that makes it all the more rare."

Owen nodded, not ready to admit that Gallé meant nothing to him and that he had only a vague idea of Tiffany's significance. She studied the window with a wistful expression, losing herself in it as she absently stroked the inside of her wrist with a fingertip. He could see the blue veins beneath the delicate skin on the underside of her wrist. The wedding band she wore at the trial was missing, but she had added slender gold earrings. She appeared tired and her angled features had a brittle sharpness.

"How old is the window?" he asked finally.

"About two hundred years."

"I don't know anything about stained glass. I've always thought of it as something belonging in churches."

She seemed distracted. Distant. "There are many levels of glasswork, just as there are many levels of painting. But art is about light, and with glass an artist can capture the living light."

"Are you an artist?" he asked.

"No."

They drank their coffee. She was not the sort for small talk. Silences fell naturally around her. And as Owen settled into the fact of his being inside Arcadia and in her presence, the silence became comfortable for him as well.

"I'll tell you what I know about Arcadia," she finally said. "Then I'll take you through it. Seeing it might help you know Bram better."

He asked if he could tape record, and she reluctantly agreed. As soon as he turned it on her voice changed to a monotone.

"There are 160 acres here. Originally, the only buildings were a farmhouse, an old barn, and an equipment shed. Bram redid the barn as an art studio with skylights and a living space. Al lived out there all the time, and whenever Bram was engrossed in a project he stayed out there too.

"As soon as the barn was finished, Bram began on the house. He made small changes and repairs at first; then he began having visions of what was possible, and he realized that a building could be the ultimate work of art. Because with a building the art could be experienced with all the senses."

"How much bigger did he plan to make it before he finished?"

"Size wasn't important to him. He considered it organic and growing."

Owen considered that, then asked, "How was the name Arcadia chosen?"

"Bram named it."

He flipped open his notebook. "In the dictionary the definition for *Arcadia* is 'a region of ideal rustic simplicity and contentment.' Was that his theme?" He held the notebook out for her to read, but she waved it away.

"Bram never said how he chose the name." She rose. "Come. I'll take you on a tour."

He stood up. "I can't thank you enough for this."

She inclined her head in a subtle acknowledgment. "The room we are in had no special use. Bram built it to showcase the window."

She led him back to the kitchen.

"This is the meeting point for all of the wings. It was the first addition made to the original farmhouse."

Owen canvassed the room more thoroughly than he had on his first pass through and counted seven doors. The huge room was built on varying levels, each being two steps higher than the last. There was a great deal of intricate stonework and a fireplace with an old iron kettle hanging in it and tiles around the sink that were individual works of art and cabinetry that was a stunning mix of crudely chiseled wood and leaded glass. Skylights were set into the pitched ceiling, and a huge mullioned window filled one wall.

"Bram built the table," she said. She rested her fingertips on the long surface, which appeared to be handhewn from massive logs. "It seats thirty."

Owen touched the wood.

"We'll cover the south side first." She threw a nubby shawl around her shoulders. "Bring your coat. Not all of the areas are heated."

He followed her through a door and into a dizzying maze of hallways and rooms, many of which were unfinished. There were dozens of different staircases leading to rooms or groups of rooms that were not connected in any logical way. There were doors that opened into walls and stairs that led to nothing.

"A person could actually get lost in here," Owen commented.

She didn't answer.

He followed her through bedrooms, some of which had dormitory-style bunkbeds built into the walls, and bathrooms that doubled as jungle sunrooms, and a strangely shelved library. After going up and down numerous times, they ascended five chiseled-rock stairs and entered an enormous room with a glass dome in the ceiling and a trickling rock waterfall in one corner. Centered beneath the dome was a raised bed.

"You could do a great *Frankenstein* here," Owen said. "All you need is a little lightning."

"This is Bram's room." Lenore used the present rather than the past tense, Owen noticed. "He built the dome so it could be opened and the bed would feel like it was floating in the sky."

"Did it work?"

"Yes." The corners of her mouth curved up a fraction. "But it leaked during storms and on summer nights the mosquitoes came in by the thousands."

Suddenly she stopped and held very still, listening.

He looked around, then whispered, "What is it?"

The question seemed to startle her. "Nothing," she said sharply, then tilted her head back to study the dome again. "They finally had to seal it shut, but by then Bram was tired of it anyway."

Owen wandered through the room. There were no personal effects, no small forgotten items.

"What did you do with all of his things?" Owen asked.

She hesitated. "Natalie took them. She cleaned the room out completely. I knew she was doing it and I let her."

Owen continued his wandering, pausing at the waterfall to dip his fingers in the pool, and at the window seat to look out upon the view Serian had chosen for himself. In the curve of the window seat, partly obscured by a pillow, an open book lay face down. He picked it up, always curious about what people were reading, and was surprised to see that it was a philosophy classic. *Fear and Trembling and The Sickness Unto Death* by Søren Kierkegaard.

"Who's interested in philosophy?" he asked.

She jerked the book from his hand, tossed it back down on the cushion and spun on her heel abruptly. "Come on. We're wasting time."

"I'm sorry," Owen said. "I'll ask before I touch anything else."

On and on she led him through the dizzying maze, pointing out pieces of art and stained glass in passing. Owen found himself losing his ability to absorb it all. Then she opened the door to a room that was remarkably austere in comparison to the rest of the house. There was no art or stained glass, no carvings or hammered metal. The walls were off-white, the floor was unfinished wood and the furniture had a Shaker simplicity.

"This is my bedroom," she said. He nodded silently, wondering if she and Serian had not slept together in the same bed when he was alive.

"One more stop," she announced as they left her bedroom, "and that will complete the south side."

"We've only done one side?"

"Yes. The house covers nearly four acres, you know."

"I read that, but I didn't realize . . ."

She threw open double doors, and Owen stared into a pantrylike rectangular room lined with shelves. It was stocked with sunscreens and toothpaste and toothbrushes and Band-Aids and soap and condoms and nail polish remover and a selection of over-the-counter drugs, along with a supply of antibiotics and prescription painkillers.

"This is better than the Cyril Drug and Sundry," Owen said with amazement.

"Everyone called it the store. Stanley still keeps it full even though I hardly use anything."

"Stanley?"

"Stanley Cantor. He comes every week with groceries and refills for the store. He'll bring special orders, too. Videotapes . . . magazines . . . whatever. I couldn't get along without Stanley."

She closed the store and led Owen down a long dark hallway, then through a door. Having lost his bearings completely, he was surprised to find himself back in the room where they had had their coffee. The afternoon sun flooding through the stained glass created a dazzling, almost dizzying effect.

"It's like being inside a piece of jewelry," he said.

She smiled indulgently. "Or inside a piece of art." She gestured toward one of the love seats. "Turn off that tape machine now and sit down. We'll rest awhile before doing the other side."

She left and returned almost immediately with a bowl of fresh strawberries so large that they appeared unreal. "Stanley brought these when he came this morning," she said, placing the bowl on the table. "He always brings me a surprise."

Owen suddenly felt awkward and too large for the room. His legs bumped the table. His hands had no place to rest.

He considered reaching for a strawberry, but was almost afraid to eat. He had skipped lunch on the way up because his stomach was in knots, and it was no better now.

"I use very little of the house," she said as she reached for a strawberry. "But I like to be in here."

Silence.

He watched her slowly pull the green sepals from the berry as if she were doing the question game with daisy petals.

"Sounds like the wind has died," he said, resorting to the most reliable subject in Kansas. "Maybe we won't get that storm they were predicting."

She took a bite of the berry and the juice stained her lips.

He shifted his gaze back to the safety of the window. "I really appreciate your inviting me out here. I know . . . with the trial and everything . . . how you must . . ." The words ran down before he could make them mean anything.

Her cool detachment unnerved him. He ate several strawberries to occupy himself and avoid the bottomless pit of her eyes. But there was no escape. He could feel her watching and measuring him.

She rose and moved to the window as though to look out, but of course there was no view through the glass. He could see the sharp line of her shoulder blades through the silk shirt. See the delicate straps of a camisole beneath the silk. See the narrowness of her waist and the slender mold of her hip.

"You're the one I've been waiting for," she said.

Owen had the urge to turn around and see who she was talking to because it couldn't possibly be him. But he sat very still instead.

She faced him. The window was at her back, surrounding her with brilliant light, painting her shoulders and one side of her face with colors. "I need someone to help me. Someone I can trust."

Owen took longer than usual to answer. "I've already assured Rossner that I'll turn over anything I find," he said carefully.

"I'm not talking about the trial. That has nothing to do with me. It's a battle between the attorneys." She moved away from the window and sat down directly across from Owen. Her eyes had ignited and all trace of detachment was gone.

She leaned toward him. "There are things I have to find out. Things I have to know."

The heat she radiated had its source in something deeply felt—need? Obsession? Madness? He was afraid to guess which.

"I dreamed that I put out offerings," she said. "And in my dream there was a sign that someone would be sent." Her voice lowered almost to a whisper. "The next day . . . you came to the hotel to talk to Rossner."

His breath caught and his throat tightened and he didn't trust his voice to respond.

"Don't you feel it?" she asked. "I didn't know right away. But it's so strong now. Surely you can feel it?"

Owen did a mental retreat, pulling himself warily to safety.

"What do you want from me, Lenore?"

"I want you to help me find out some things."

Owen stared at her.

"You're already digging into Bram's history," she said. "Looking for what you call the puzzle pieces. You could find the answers I need as well."

"If what you're saying," Owen began carefully, "is that you want some serious research done, then I'm not a very good choice. I'm an amateur at uncovering information. I'm learning as I go. You need to hire someone . . . a detective who specializes in this kind of thing. Rossner could recommend an investigator with experience who—"

"No."

"But why do you think that I—"

"We're tied together by Bram's past. You want to unravel his secrets for your reasons. I want to unravel his secrets for my reasons. We can help each other. And I know I can trust you. That wouldn't be true of some detective I hired. Besides"—she lowered her eyes—"I have no money to pay anyone. The estate isn't settled and won't be until my trial is over. My legal and living expenses are paid by the trustees, but beyond that I have nothing."

Owen tried to clear his thoughts. If she really was proposing that they collaborate on a search into Serian's past, then he ought to be ecstatic. He ought to be racing to the phone to give Bernie the big news. Yet he couldn't overcome his apprehensions.

"You can't say no," she told him quietly.

He met her dark gaze. So intense. So fevered by passions he dared not guess at.

"I can't say no," he finally agreed.

An incandescence suffused her features, and she gave Owen a slow, intimate smile that went straight to his groin. He would have been shaken by the sudden sexual stirring had it not been for the deep sense of foreboding that overshadowed all else.

"Let's go outside before it gets any later," she said. "I'll show you where he died."

Silently, Owen picked up his coat and followed.

She led him out the back, through a screened patio and across several flagstone terraces, to the charred ruins of Bram Serian's studio.

"This is it," she said, looking out across the huge blackened pile of debris. "This is all that's left."

Owen walked along the perimeter. "From the news accounts, I expected part of it to still be standing," he remarked.

"The firemen said it was a hazard, and they came out the next day with equipment and trucks to tear it apart and carry it away." She kicked angrily at a burned chunk of wood. "I didn't want them to do it. I told them to go away. But they wouldn't."

Owen kept a careful silence.

"The prosecution said that I arranged the demolition to destroy evidence. But it's not in the trial. They haven't mentioned it. Charlie was all ready to prove they were wrong, but they haven't mentioned it."

With a faintly puzzled frown, she regarded the ruin. "It's strange how things happen and when you look back at them, or when others look back at them, nothing is what you thought it was."

Owen toed the ashes and stared down at the black soot covering his boot tip. He didn't dare raise his eyes and let her see into his thoughts. Because at that moment he was convinced that Lenore Serian was dangerously over the edge.

"It's after four," she said abruptly. "Let's finish the tour before we lose the sun. Some parts of the house have inadequate lighting." She was silent on the way back inside but then resumed her tour-guide monologue.

"The north wing probably has just as much square footage," she explained, "but the rooms are larger and fewer."

The first stop was an enormous living area with a twenty-foot-high spoke-beamed ceiling and a stone fireplace big enough to roast a side of beef in. A series of tall windows fanned out from either side of the fireplace.

"Bram called this his giant room," she said. "Everything in it is oversized. The couches are so long that they won't fit through doorways, so they had to be brought in here before the walls were finished."

Next she led him into a windowless cave room with curved stone walls and seating that appeared to be carved into niches. Thick wall-to-wall carpeting cushioned the floor, and oversized pillows were scattered around for reclining. Instead of hanging art, the walls here had been decorated with cave paintings and intricate graffiti. At one end was a large projection screen and a shelf unit filled with videotapes. He made a comment about it being the largest television he'd ever seen and she told him it wasn't a television. Bram Serian had hated television. It was strictly for watching videos.

They passed through several rooms that were unfinished and one that was partially boarded up. She pointed out another staircase to nowhere, then led him around a corner and up to a long open room flooded with northern light. The floors were bare as were the high banked windows. One end had a mirrored wall and a ballet barre. The other end had a narrow daybed, a low table and a small television monitor and VCR. Running through the center of the room was an enormous multipurpose table constructed of thick, scarred wood supported by metal crossbars. On the table were assorted tools and devices, some of which were shrouded by cloth dustcovers.

"Is this where you spend your time?" he asked.

The question appeared to startle her, and then she smiled. It was a shy, almost childlike smile that surprised him with its sweetness.

"How did you guess?" she asked.

"It was just that . . . a guess," he admitted.

She smiled again, with such brightness and innocence that all of his previous opinions of her were shaken.

The last stop on his Arcadia tour was the basement. The floor was concrete, and the walls were a rough material that must have been sprayed on. Every inch of it was painted and signed by various artists. There were two Ping-Pong tables, a pool table, a western-style bar and scattered couches. To the side louvered folding doors opened to a room filled with appliances: an industrial-size washer and dryer, a commercial presser, and the biggest freezer Owen had ever seen.

Lenore opened the freezer and motioned him forward. "What do you want for dinner?" she asked, gesturing toward shelves crammed with every variety of prepared frozen food. It was after six, he had skipped lunch and was ravenously hungry, and he had a long drive ahead of him. All compelling reasons to accept her dinner invitation. And he knew that every moment spent at Arcadia and in her presence would add to and enrich his book, but still, he considered telling her that he had to leave immediately.

"You have to eat somewhere," she said. "As you can see, I have plenty."

They carried up an eclectic assortment of foods. When Owen had been in the kitchen before, he hadn't taken note of the working end of it, but now the scope of Bram Serian's cooking arrangements struck him. The kitchen was the most elaborate Owen had ever seen. There was a stainless-steel restaurant stove with eight gas burners and an overhead broiler. There were two conventional ovens, a convection oven, a microwave oven and a deluxe toaster oven. On the end was a setup to do charcoal or wood grilling.

"You could feed an army in here," he commented while she opened boxes and set the microwave.

She glanced around as though puzzled. "Bram had a chef pick out everything. Does it seem excessive?"

"It's not the typical American kitchen," Owen said dryly.

"Oh" was her blankfaced reply. "I don't use much but the microwave."

While they ate she asked him questions about his family and the ranch. Questions about Kansas. Questions about the book and about writing in general. He grew increasingly uncomfortable beneath the microscope of her attention, feeling that he was being studied and measured, but he couldn't divert her. She ignored his attempts to change the subject.

He helped her clean up afterward, which amounted to little more than dropping the frozen food trays in the trash, and he reminded himself once again that he was there only as a writer. That he was supposed to be objective and alert without letting his own reactions or emotions intrude. In spite of the reminder, the urge to bolt and run away was growing stronger. Not just away from Serian's surreal house and back to Manhattan, but all the way back to Kansas. Back to his real life.

"Do you want coffee?" she asked.

"No. Thanks."

She froze and cocked her head, listening to something just as she had earlier in Serian's bedroom.

"Anything wrong?" Owen asked reluctantly.

"Did you hear that?" she asked.

"No."

She looked up at the ceiling. "What do you know about ghosts?"

"Nothing," he said. "Anyway . . ." He started inching toward the kitchen door, looking around for his coat but willing to leave without it if he had to. "It's a long drive and I have to return the rental car and get my notes typed. So . . . thanks again for dinner and the tour."

She watched him with flat, cool eyes. "Your coat is on that chair by the door."

He grabbed the coat and headed down the hall, sensing her following. His lungs were tight in his chest. There wasn't enough air. And he wasn't sure how to get to the front door.

"You've turned the wrong way," she said from somewhere behind him.

He stopped. He didn't turn around, but he knew she was moving silently closer.

"I'll show you the way out," she said.

She slid by him in the dim, narrow hallway without touching him at all. Her movements were wraithlike. He watched her with both fascination and dread. And it struck him that he would never have been able to imagine Lenore Serian. She was beyond imagining.

"What time will you come tomorrow?" she asked.

"Tomorrow?" Owen felt a surge of panic. "I have an interview with Serian's old roommate tomorrow morning, so I don't know if . . ."

They were in the entryway now. It was partially dark but filled with shadowy, shifting patterns from the tree-mounted exterior lights shining in through the glass-paneled ceiling. The sight of the front door was reassuring.

"Come when you're finished, then," she said. "There are papers you need to look at."

He had to swallow and clear his throat before he could speak. "What sort of papers?"

"Bram's papers."

"You're going to show me Serian's personal papers?"

"Yes. Come as soon as you can. Time is running out."

12

As soon as Owen was back inside the familiar confines of the apartment, his afternoon at Arcadia assumed the qualities of a bizarre dream, and he thought that he'd been foolish for letting the woman and the house affect him the way they did. It was the pressure, he decided. The worrying about whether his proposal would be accepted, and whether he'd done the right thing by leaving his family and the ranch in a stranger's care. That was all it was ... just pressure.

The next morning he got up early for his interview with Jonas Watkins, the man who had been Serian's roommate during the artist's early days in New York. Watkins lived in Brooklyn and had given Owen instructions to his house by subway, but since Owen had to keep the rental car for another trip to Arcadia, he had decided to drive to Brooklyn.

The day was clear and dry. Owen accomplished the hair-raising merge onto the FDR Drive, made it to the Brooklyn Bridge and then sat idling in the bridge exit lane for ten minutes before he realized that he was going to have to forget courtesy and cut off the stream of cars crowding in front of him or no one would ever let him have a turn. By the time he had crossed the bridge, fought off lane-jumping taxis for a shot at the off-ramp and negotiated the unmarked twists and turns to the Brooklyn-Queens Expressway, he decided that maybe he should have used the subway after all. All his years behind the wheel in Kansas had not prepared him for the honking, screeching, screaming aggression and complete disregard for rules that characterized the New York City driving experience.

Following Watkins's directions Owen headed toward the Verrazano Bridge, then exited the expressway and found himself in a pleasant neighborhood of small brick apartment buildings and old brownstone and limestone rowhouses, converted over the years to hold several families. He parked and rang Jonas Watkins's bell. The door opened almost immediately, and he saw that the long-haired, beret-wearing young sculptor was now a balding, hunch-shouldered man in brown beltless slacks and a tan cardigan sweater.

Watkins ushered Owen inside and led him down a hall to the living room, rattling on nervously about his neighborhood, and how it was almost in Bay Ridge and how the public schools were decent which had been important because he couldn't afford private schools, and how he was still *almost* in Manhattan, and how he owned the brownstone and rented out the top floor for extra income, and how his wife was only a part-time librarian so it was good that he had such a stable job and hadn't tried to support them with something as chancy as art.

Owen sat down and listened to the nonstop monologue, letting the man wind down at his own speed. Eventually he did.

"I appreciate your seeing me," Owen said.

Jonas Watkins zipped and unzipped his sweater several times. "I have to go into the office so the day is shot anyway. Couldn't go to the in-laws with the wife and kids last night. And there's not enough time to get involved in a project."

Owen opened his bag. "Do you mind if I tape?"

"Go ahead. No problem." Jonas Watkins ran his hand over his bald crown as though he found the smoothness of it soothing. "You know . . . after our phone conversation, I thought a lot about Bram Serian. More even than when I heard he'd died." The hand drifted back up to his head. "I was so damn surprised when he died. That guy had everything. I didn't think he'd ever slip up."

"When was the last time you saw Serian?"

"Oh, God, ten years ago. He called me out of the blue and invited me and Carmella out to that place of his. It was very weird. Guess I better tell you about the beginning, though, before I get to the end."

"Okay," Owen agreed. "Tell me how you met him and what he was like . . . the whole story."

Jonas Watkins stroked his head a moment, then fixed his eyes on the tape recorder and began.

"I was twenty-one. Just graduated with a degree in business—that was my dad's doing. He made me promise I would finish college before I tried my hand at art. He was a practical guy, you know . . . raised in the depression and all.

"I rode the bus from Omaha to Manhattan and enrolled in Art Student's League. Damn . . . those were the days. We walked art and talked art and lived art and read art journals while we sat on the toilet. Nothing else mattered.

"There was this core group of about twenty, mostly guys but a few girls too, who stuck together and took all the classes and were active with exhibiting and promotion and the whole nine yards. Almost everybody was from somewhere else, but I'd say Bram and I were the biggest hicks in the bunch. Most of the rest of them had been brought up in the East or were rich and well-traveled or had already been to art school in Europe or whatever. I was embarrassed about my lack of sophistication, but Bram, who was much more of a hayseed than me, flaunted his and used it. He had a beard and wore backwoods clothes and workshoes like he was fresh out of the sticks.

"All of us looked up to him. I guess you'd say he was our spiritual leader. Our flag bearer. Although when I think back I can't figure out what he ever did that warranted such adoration.

"Anyway, I was living in a fleabag hotel and Bram asked me if I wanted to share his loft. Damn! A real loft in SoHo. I couldn't get over my luck.

"I moved in and he laid down all these rules, which didn't bother me because it was his place. Things went fine for a while. We used to sit up till dawn drinking tequila and planning our futures. I'd dream about how someday I was going to have a show of my own, and Bram would dream about how he was going to be world renowned.

"You know, I think about it now and I wonder if the art was ever important to him, or if it was always just a means to an end. Which is pretty damn ironic because the guy turned out to be a fucking genius, didn't he?"

Watkins looked at Owen as though he wanted to be told that he was wrong, that Serian had not been a genius.

"Anyway, after I'd lived with him for six months or so, we started having problems. He was on me all the time. Wanted to tell me when to come and go and what classes to take and which women to go out with. And I realized he was a control freak. One of those people who thinks he has to run the show.

"See, Bram was a pretty shut-tight kind of a guy. I mean, on the one hand he was hanging out with everybody and talking it up, but on the other hand he never let any one person get too close to him. Including girls. He attracted plenty of girls, but he never got involved with any of them. And he never made close friends."

Watkins sighed deeply.

"Except for me. For some reason he picked me to be his friend. Maybe because I reminded him of his brother. He said that once . . . that I reminded him of his brother."

"His brother?" Owen asked in astonishment. "He talked about a brother?"

"Yes. He lost his brother in Vietnam. He was very bitter about the war. Very angry."

Watkins paused a moment in thought.

"Anyway, I lasted a year and a half as his roommate. But it got to where I felt like I was fifteen again and living with my folks. I had to clear everything with him and keep set hours. I had to discuss all my work with him and . . . hell . . . he wanted to chart my whole damn future in art. He didn't approach it in terms of having an idea and executing a piece. He was into making statements.

"Maybe I'm too passive a person because I put up with everything. But then I started getting serious about a girl—my wife now—and I had to sneak around to see her because Bram thought that long-term relationships with women were poison to an artist. He said that marriage was society's method for sucking men dry and grinding them down . . . 'course, we all heard that from Hillyer.

"Eventually, Bram found out what I was doing and he got mad—and we'd been having other disagreements too—and he threw me out and that was it. I moved in with Carmella and she got pregnant and we married and I had to get a job and quit art school, and . . . well, that was that.

"Then, ten years ago, Serian called one day out of the blue and invited me and Carmella out to Arcadia for the weekend. I didn't really want to go, but Carmella was thrilled about it so we left the kids with her mother and went up.

"The studio was finished. I wanted to see inside but he said he couldn't because he had his cousin living in there and the guy was around the bend. Violently paranoid or something. And it really disturbed him to have anyone but Bram enter his space.

"So we toured the house instead. It was an eyeful. I've read that he built much more after I saw it, but even then, it was the kind of thing you never forget.

"His wife, Lenore, was there. A beautiful Asian girl. Bram told us she was older than she looked, but Carmella was suspicious. She thought he was just saying that because he was embarrassed about having married a much younger woman." Watkins sighed. "But then Carmella had a chip on her shoulder and went out there determined not to like him. Not to like either of them actually. But she couldn't resist Lenore. Such a quiet, gentle person . . . of course that was ten years ago. And even then I remember Carmella saying that Lenore had haunted eyes so I guess she was already . . . mentally disturbed, or whatever.

"Carmella was very drawn to her, though. When we were leaving, she whispered to me that we ought to take Lenore with us—get her out of Serian's clutches and save her from that monstrous house." Watkins shook his head. "Little did she imagine that if we had stolen Lenore away it would have been Bram we were saving."

The man studied his neatly groomed hands for a moment.

"When we got home, we found a package in the trunk of our car. It was one of Serian's paintings with a note saying that it was a gift from him to me. Boy, did Carmella feel guilty for all the bad things she'd said about him."

Watkins shrugged and looked guilty himself. "When Serian died and the price of his work shot up, I sold that painting and paid off the mortgage on this house. Paid for a vacation for my whole family to go to California too, and I still have some left in savings.

"That's it. Not much of a story, I guess." Jonas Watkins held up his hands and forced his mouth into an off-key self-deprecatory smile.

"It's a big help," Owen assured him. "There's not much information on Serian out there."

"I'm not surprised." Watkins bounced out of his chair. "I've got some coffee made. Would you like a cup?"

"Please."

The man walked down the hall toward his kitchen, and Owen tried to imagine him as a young artist in a loft in

SoHo, drinking tequila with Bram Serian. It was impossible to picture.

Owen let his gaze wander through the room. The woodwork and floors had all been lovingly stripped and restored. He could imagine Jonas Watkins patiently laboring over it, heedless of the passing years. On a table nearby there was a gallery of framed family photographs. Owen studied the dark-haired woman with the quiet smile and the two feisty-looking kids, a girl and a boy, and wondered how Jonas Watkins felt now. Did he regret the course he had taken? Did he wish he had listened to Bram Serian and put his career first? Or was he contented?

"That's my gang," Watkins said, re-entering the room with two cups of coffee. "The kids are in college now, both of them on scholarships." He grinned and shook his head. "Before you know it, I'll have pictures of grandbabies to put up."

"Just a few questions and I'll let you get back to your Saturday," Owen said.

"No problem. No problem. Don't have to leave for another hour or so."

Owen flipped a page in his steno pad. "Do you know where Bram Serian came from?"

"Not exactly. He was very secretive about that. But I had the feeling, from little things he said, that he was a middle child like me."

"Meaning?"

Watkins shrugged. "Nebraska, Iowa, Oklahoma, Missouri, Kansas, Illinois . . . you know. That big fat middle out there. What do they call it? The nation's breadbasket?"

"Did he say anything else that would give a clue to his background?"

Watkins thought a moment. "No. Not that I can think of."

"This brother, did he ever say anything more about this brother? Anything at all?"

"Not really. And I knew better than to ask any questions."

Owen thought for a moment. "What kind of jobs did Serian have? How did he support himself and pay for the loft?"

"Oh, he didn't work. He had money. I don't mean he was rich or anything, but he just always had enough to live. I don't know where he got it exactly but I always suspected he had a trust fund or something."

"Hmmm . . ." Owen circled the word *money* in his notes and followed it with a big question mark.

"Had he met Geneva Johnson yet when you were living with him?"

Watkins stiffened and looked momentarily abashed. "Actually . . . she was one of our big disagreements. I guess it won't hurt anything to tell you. He moved her into the loft shortly before he kicked me out."

"Was she an Art Students League model?"

"Are you kidding?" Watkins laughed hollowly. "League models were fifty-year-old cleaning women."

"How did he meet her, then. Was she modeling for someone he knew or—"

"Geneva wasn't modeling yet when Bram met her. He's the one who got her started modeling."

Owen might not have pushed for more information about Bram and Geneva, but Watkins's obvious discomfort over Geneva piqued his curiosity.

"Do you know how Bram met her?"

Jonas Watkins frowned and sighed deeply.

"Bram liked to go bar hopping, not to drink so much as to watch the people and pick up women. The seedier the joint, the better he liked it. One night we were in a place over near the meat-packing district, and Geneva was there and he sat and watched her for a long time. He said she looked like she'd do things that nice girls from Kansas wouldn't dream of."

A thrill ran through Owen. "Nice girls from Kansas? Are you sure he said Kansas?"

"I'm sure because I was pretty dense in those days, and I was thinking he meant Dorothy from the Wizard of Oz."

"So that was the start of their relationship?"

Watkins gave a sharp bark of laughter. "I guess you'd call it that. She was going by Gena Rae Johnson then. Bram spoke to her, and the guy she was with pulled a knife, and that place erupted into the damnedest fight you ever saw. Scared me to death. Made me a little scared of Bram too— seeing how ferocious and physically violent he could be. That was the only time, though. The only time I saw him like that."

"She moved in with him shortly after that, then?" Owen asked to keep him talking.

"You could say she moved in that night. Bram took her

home with us to hide her from the guy with the knife. Two weeks later I was history and she was in solid."

Watkins glanced at his watch. "Gee, I hate to rush you, but I just realized it's later than I thought."

"No problem." Owen rose and gathered his things. "Thanks again for your trouble."

"Sure. Sure."

As Owen was putting on his coat, Jonas Watkins said, "So you talked to old Hillyer, huh?"

"Yeah. He's the one who gave me your name."

"I can't believe he remembered me."

"He seemed to remember you well. Said you were one of his more talented students."

"Really? He said that?"

Owen nodded.

"You know I remember him jumping on Bram once, yelling at him, saying Bram needed to put as much passion into his art as he put into being an artist. It took me years before I understood what he'd meant by that. Old Hillyer . . . he was a good guy."

Jonas Watkins led Owen to the front door, then paused with his hand on the knob and shook his head. "There's no justice in the world, you know. Bram Serian shouldn't have been the one who made it. His art had no soul or purity. For Serian art was just a tool. The rest of us were pure. We burned for art. We would have traded our souls for our work."

Watkins's eyes took on a faraway look. "Then again, maybe Bram did trade his soul. Maybe that's what was wrong with him."

From Brooklyn, Owen took the Battery Tunnel to the West Side Highway, then headed upstate. The drive was easier this time. Partly because he knew where he was going and partly because he had overcome his trepidation about returning to Arcadia. He was anxious to get back. Anxious to learn more.

As he drove he fantasized about Bram Serian's papers. He imagined journals, diaries, letters—a window into the internal workings of the artist's mind as well as a source of clues to his past. And he was amazed at the good fortune that had brought him such a treasure.

Excitement built inside him when he pulled through Arcadia's gate. He negotiated the narrow road quickly without pauses for the view. As soon as he stopped the car in the parking area beside the house, the door opened and Lenore appeared. He could tell she'd been waiting for him. She stood silent and watchful as he walked up the steps.

"Hello," Owen said, holding tightly to his cheerful confidence.

Instead of answering, she stepped back into the undersea light of the entryway. He followed, this time pausing to study the room and determine how the sea light effect was achieved. It was all done with glass, he saw. Not only was the dense blue-green glass set in panels around the door, but it had also been used in the large octagonal skylight overhead.

"I thought you'd be here earlier," Lenore said.

Owen ignored the impatience in her voice. "I told you, I had an interview this morning." He continued to look up at the unusual skylight. "This is really extraordinary," he said. "Did Serian design it around the glass, or did he have the glass made after he'd created the design?"

"Bram didn't have anything to do with it," she said shortly. "There was a man, Guy Demaree, who came to restore an eighteenth-century window Bram had found and ended up staying for nearly a year. He's the one who encouraged Bram to find so many old windows and use them to build, and he's the one who made this entryway." Sadness surfaced briefly in her eyes. "He said it was an idea he'd always wanted to try. 'Demaree' means from the sea."

Owen wanted to ask her more about the glass artist, but Lenore wheeled and started down the hall, and all he could do was fall into step behind her.

Today her hair was pulled up into a high ponytail, accenting the angle of her cheekbones. She was dressed in a dark green sweater and black pants. The sweater turned her black eyes the velvety forest color again, and he wondered if someone had given the sweater to her for just that reason. Her husband perhaps? Or Guy Demaree? Maybe the Frenchman had done more than windows. The thought took him by surprise because it carried something close to jealousy with it.

"The house has three towers," she said, glancing back over her shoulder at him. "Did you notice them as you drove up?"

Owen recalled the towers in detail. All were of stone and all had metal caps and spires. One was large and simple with expanses of clear glass so that it resembled the top of a lighthouse. Another was designed so that it could have been the tower on a medieval castle. And the last appeared to be not so much a tower as an ornamentation that mimicked a tower.

She was moving quickly and purposefully, taking him to a destination that she had obviously planned before his arrival. "On the south side," she said, "there's the lookout tower and the castle tower. We can go up to them if you want, though they're both very cold this time of year and the stairs to the lookout tower are accessible only from the roof."

"I'd like to see them," he said.

"Later, then. Right now I want to take you to Bram's private tower."

"The one on the north? It's so narrow . . . I thought it was just for show."

"He built it to be deceptive. He wanted a secret place."

She led Owen past the big living area and the cave video room and the boarded-up room, then stopped at one of the staircases to nowhere. "Can you guess how to get there?" she asked.

He looked around. "The stairs really do go somewhere?"

"Try it."

He went up the fourteen steps and unlocked the door. "Be careful," she cautioned. "It's a long fall."

He opened the door a fraction. Outside was nothing but air and a piece of slanting roof.

"I give up," Owen said.

She motioned him back down, then led him around behind the staircase to a small door. The door opened onto a narrow but deep closet that was stocked with brooms and mops. She stepped inside, beckoning him to follow. There was barely enough room for the two of them. He stood close to her, breathing in the stale closet smell and the heady exotic scent of her hair while his eyes adjusted to the lack of light, and he had a prickling moment of déjà vu. Then she twisted something high up on the wall and a section of wooden paneling swung open.

"Come," she said, and he ducked through the opening behind her.

When he straightened up, he saw that he was in a tall, narrow space, not unlike an oddly formed vertical tunnel. In the center were spiral stairs leading up to a white door. It was a completely enclosed area, yet it was not dark. The curve of rough rock wall was inset at random with translucent stones that filtered in weak natural light.

"The carpeting on the stair risers absorbs sound so people in the rest of the house won't hear anything," she said as she started up the stairs.

He was fascinated by the wall and moved closer to touch the jagged translucent stones. With the sunlight glowing from behind them, they looked semi-precious.

She stopped midway up the staircase to watch him. "You know how the walls of the house sparkle? That's glass. Chunks of glass set in with the stone. What you're looking at is actually an outside wall, and the light comes through wherever a piece of glass was used."

"But it all looks so solid from the outside."

"It is solid. That's a very raw, dense glass, almost like a chunk of quartz. In most respects, it's as strong as the stone."

Slowly, Owen backed away from the wall and followed her up the stairs. Everything about this house was bizarre. Fantastic. Unimaginable. Yet someone had imagined it. Someone had created it. His admiration for Bram Serian increased. The man's genius had had so many facets. No wonder he'd been frustrated by all the attention focused on his paintings. Painting was such a small window into his creativity.

The white door opened into a large oddly shaped room with a semicircular end. The curved end was stone and glass, which was the actual tower that showed from the outside, but the room got its size by extending back beneath a sloping section of roofline. That was how it fooled people. The tower itself looked small and purely decorative because it was.

Owen wandered through the piles of boxes and shrouded shapes to the chair, desk, and narrow daybed that were huddled together toward the circular stone end. The natural light was strong near the wall, and he saw that vertical strips of clear glass had been built in at evenly spaced intervals. They were no wider than a finger, but if he put his eye right up to a strip he could see out over the yard. It reminded him of peering through a keyhole.

"Bram designed it for the light," she said, "and so that he could spy on people outside without their knowing. At night, if there's a lamp on in here, the glass insets are so narrow that it just looks like a lighting effect from the outside."

"No one ever guessed this room was here?" Owen asked incredulously.

"No. Not even the police when they swarmed over everything."

"You didn't show this stuff to the police?"

She shook her head.

"You withheld evidence from the police?"

"I didn't withhold anything. They had a search warrant and they searched the house."

"But they didn't find this room?"

She shook her head again. "I would have showed it to them if they'd asked me. Even if they'd said, 'Is this everything?' or asked whether Bram had an office. But they barely spoke to me. They just threw things around and dumped drawers out." She sat down on the chair and crossed her arms against the cold. "Bram didn't trust the police. He would have hated them pawing through his things."

"How about Rossner? Has he seen all this?"

"No. Nothing here relates to the trial."

Owen stared at her.

"Do you want to look through Bram's papers or not?" she demanded.

He stared at her, tempted to tell her what she could do with the papers, and her manner changed.

"I was afraid Rossner might be required to report me to the police for hiding things," she admitted grudgingly. "And I didn't want Rossner's people going through it. Bram wouldn't have allowed it."

"Would he have allowed me in here?"

"No," she said. She shivered and hugged her arms closer to her chest. "Even I wasn't allowed. The only reason he showed it to me was that he was afraid he might die up here and no one would be able to find the body."

Owen shook his head in disbelief and looked around at the jumble of boxes and unidentifiable shapes. "What is all this stuff?"

"Papers . . . records . . . keepsakes . . . Art." She let her eyes wander around the room. "Bram liked to keep things. But he didn't want them down where other people might snoop through them. Natalie in particular."

"What about the art? His studio was kept locked and off-limits to people, wasn't it? So why would he drag art all the way up here?"

"I don't know."

Wonderment filled him. A secret tower room crammed with treasures. Who was going to believe this? He could hardly believe it himself.

"Where do we start?" he asked finally.

"Wherever you want," she said.

"Well, is there a beginning point? Or any kind of order to the way things are stored?"

She shrugged.

"Haven't you looked at it?"

"Not really." She lifted her chin a notch. "I wasn't ready."

"And you are now?"

"Yes."

The boxes were all uniform, with detachable lids, the kind that could be used to store oversized files, and so Owen expected to see files or something resembling files when he opened the first lid. Instead the box was crammed with a mass of papers. He opened several more boxes and they were all similar.

"This is going to take a lot of time," he said.

She sat on the chair impassively.

"It's freezing up here and there's not any room to spread things out. I suggest we carry the papers to a more comfortable location."

"Bram wouldn't like that," she said.

"Bram wouldn't like anything about this," he reminded her.

She gave in but was edgy as they carried load after load down the stairs, almost as if she expected Serian's ghost to jump out at any moment.

They took the boxes to Bram's giant living room. There were twenty-two in all. Owen settled his long legs into a tolerable floor-sitting position and opened one at random. His first handful of papers yielded a note from Edie Norton, canceled checks, bills for horse feed and groceries, and a clipped article about buying a large-screen video monitor. Lenore sat down on a nearby couch and watched.

It didn't take him long to realize that Bram Serian had saved everything and had used no particular system to do it. Going through it all was going to be a much bigger job than he'd anticipated. Apparently, Lenore thought it was all his problem, though, as she'd settled in like a spectator in the bleachers.

"Do you know what you're looking for?" she asked.

"Sure. Letters, journals, smoking guns, treasure maps, signed confessions . . . the usual."

"Why are you being sarcastic?"

"Because it's annoying to be treated like the hired man and to have you demand that I help you look for *things* from the past without having a clue as to what those *things* are. I know you're using me, but I can't figure out what you're using me for."

"We're using each other."

"Right now it doesn't feel so mutual."

"You'll end up with plenty for your book that you wouldn't have otherwise had."

He took a deep breath. "You're right. I'm sorry. But this avalanche of paper is overwhelming. And I really don't know what you want me to look for."

She sat there for several long moments with her hands folded in her lap and a pensive expression on her face. Then she stood. Her voice was firm and her manner determined as she said, "Come. It's time for a walk."

She took him outside through a silent wooded area. There were scattered evergreens, but most of the trees were deciduous so a thick carpet of leaves covered the frozen ground.

Lenore glanced sideways at him. "This morning Rossner called, and I told him I was working with you. He's angry. He thinks I'll say or do something that could be damaging to me in the trial and that you will leak it to the press."

"And what did you tell him?" Owen asked her.

"I told him I trusted you. And that you'd be a fool to reveal information now because then it would lessen the value of your book."

"What was his reaction to that?"

"He wasn't very happy." Her mouth curved into a brief mocking smile. "He said he'd try to draft an agreement for you to sign."

"That's fine with me," Owen said.

The path they were on was almost wide enough to allow

the passage of a vehicle. Though it was overgrown in places, Owen could tell that it had been cut through the woods with a piece of machinery years ago.

"You're not asking me any questions," she said, sounding suddenly nervous.

"I'm assuming you've got something to tell me." He kept his eyes on the path. "And you'll do it on your own terms."

She stepped off the path to circle the split and blackened hulk of a large tree. "Lightning," she said.

Owen waited.

"To understand what I'm looking for and why, you have to know more about me. You have to know how I came to be here in this country." She fixed him with an intense look. "Do you want to know? Do you want to go further?"

He met her eyes and was seized with a deep hunger. "Yes," he said. Yes. He wanted to go as far as she would allow.

13

Lenore Serian leaned back against the dead tree trunk and stared off into the distance.

"I was eight years old," she said. "It was late afternoon and very warm. I was on a water buffalo . . . leaning across his back so that my cheek was on his neck.

"Suddenly there was the sound of a truck. I had lived most of my life in the city so trucks were not that interesting. Not nearly as interesting as the buffalo. But the truck came right up to the house, and soldiers jumped out and there was shouting and loud gunshots.

"A woman pulled me from the buffalo. She held my hand and we ran. The jungle was forbidden, but it was the only place to hide so we ran there.

"I don't know how long we ran or how far we went. The next thing I knew a man caught me. A big foreign soldier with long hair and dirty hands. The dirt on his hands touched me and I pulled his hair and hit his face but he wouldn't let me go. He wouldn't take his hands away. Another soldier came and together they tied me with ropes.

"They put me into the back of the truck which was like a cave and had more soldiers in it. As they drove away I heard women crying. All I could think about was the buffalo. I hoped the soldiers hadn't hurt the buffalo.

"The truck ride lasted a long time. They gave me candy bars. After it was dark they took me out to urinate by the side of the road. From the truck they carried me to a helicopter.

"I knew about helicopters and was afraid they were taking me to a war prison. Or to a place for children whose fathers were American soldiers. A lot of people hated children like me whose fathers were white soldiers.

"Only three of the men from the truck got into the helicopter. They all seemed big and dirty and hairy to me. Like giants from a nightmare. They gave me some food from a can, then tied me to a seat in the back. The helicopter roared and shook. It lifted into the sky. I vomited up all the food from the can. Then I must have gone to sleep.

"When I woke up again it was dark and I was inside something that was moving. I thought it was another truck. There were loud engine noises and there were crates and metal things tied down around me. After a while one of the men came to look at me. He sat me up and fed me more disgusting things from a can. Then he went away. Some time later light came and I saw round windows with blue sky. I was in an airplane.

"I lost track of things then. I remember dreaming of dying and being sad when I woke up because it had only been a dream. I tried to stay asleep after that. I didn't ever want to wake up.

"I remember suddenly waking up in the backseat of a car. I wasn't tied anymore and I had on different clothes. A beautiful pink dress and shiny white shoes that I could see my face in.

"There were two men in the car. A driver, and a passenger in the front seat. Neither was a soldier. I didn't know if they were new men or if they were some of the original soldiers who had cleaned up and changed clothes.

"The driver turned around to look at me. He was talking and laughing. I didn't know many American words but I could understand a little. Eat. Go. Yes. No.

"He kept smiling and talking to me. Then he pointed out his side window ... pointed and gestured for me to watch ... and suddenly there was a monster staring in the window. I thought the man had called up a demon. It had a big round shiny face and an ugly metal mouth. Sounds came out of the metal mouth and the driver talked to it. I remember thinking how fearless he was. He talked to it; then he drove the car to a building where they gave him bags of food through the window.

"The driver handed back paper-wrapped food to me and then a huge cup. The biggest cup I had ever seen. It was brightly decorated plastic with a lid and a straw. I took a drink. It was cola. I had had cola before, tiny sips from a shared bottle, and I couldn't believe that I had the entire glass of cola to myself.

"I ate the strange-tasting food and drank the coke. And ate

and drank. Until my stomach felt like bursting. But there was still more left, and I'd been taught that it was very very rude not to finish what was given, so I kept eating and drinking. Until I threw up all over my pink-flowered dress.

"The driver yelled at me. He stopped the car and jerked me out by the arm. We were beside a road. I remember that he kept yelling at me and I was so ashamed, so humiliated, that I dropped to my knees in the gravel and bowed my forehead to the ground. Then the other man got out of the car and there was more yelling and the two men got in a fight. I was afraid to watch so I closed my eyes and didn't open them for a long time."

Lenore Serian drew in a deep breath.

"That is how I came to America, Owen. That is the real truth of it."

Owen stared at her, shocked by the story.

"This happened when you were *eight years old?*" he asked incredulously.

"Yes."

"My God, Lenore. I thought you came from Vietnam as an adult."

She smiled ruefully. "Everyone does. Serian loved all those rumors about my being a spy during the war. I suspect he started some of them himself."

"What happened next? Where were you taken?"

Lenore sighed. "After that there is a big blank. And before ... before the soldiers came ... I can't remember that either." She turned to fix Owen with a frustrated, pleading expression. "I've tried and tried, but the memories just aren't there."

"That's not so surprising. My childhood memories are a blur before the age of nine or so. And that's even with having old snapshots to look at and a family to recall the past with."

"Really?"

"Yes. And then if you add in the trauma ... An eight-year-old suddenly being taken away from everything she knew ... I think children frequently just block out things that worry or scare them."

She seemed relieved.

"You think I'm normal, then?" she asked.

He wanted to say that he wouldn't quite go that far, but

instead he told her, "I think it's normal for children to forget easily. Maybe it's one of nature's survival tricks."

That seemed to satisfy her. She motioned Owen back onto the path and they resumed walking.

"So," she said briskly. "What do you know from that story? I've gone over it all endlessly. Tell me what you think."

Owen considered it all for a moment. "It sounds like you were out in the country, but that you were either visiting or you had just moved there from the city. Your father was an American soldier but you didn't seem to know any of the soldiers that came that day. It sounds like, aside from your terror and confusion, you weren't actually mistreated. Is that about right?"

"Yes," she said softly. "That's not much, is it?"

"No, but it's a beginning."

She looked at him with a hopeful expression.

"How about your mother?" he asked. "Where does she fit in?"

"I don't know. I don't know where she was that day or who I was with. The memories I have of her are no help at all." She stopped walking and closed her eyes. "I know what her arms felt like when they were around me. I know what her hair smelled like. I remember sleeping curled against her. Sometimes I'll think of a strange little story or fable and I'll know I heard it from my mother when I was small."

She looked at Owen with an anguished expression in her eyes. "I try so hard to remember everything about her, but I can't picture her face. And I can't remember her name."

"And your father? Do you know anything about him?"

She shook her head. "Nothing. I have no memories of him at all."

"Who were these soldiers who brought you out?"

"I don't know," she admitted quietly.

"If you were afraid of the soldiers because they were foreigners, then that could mean—"

"No!" she said eagerly, as if discovering something new. "I wasn't afraid because they were foreign. I was afraid of them because they were running and shooting, and shouting words I didn't understand. I think foreigners were very . . . familiar to me."

Slowly, they began walking again.

"Okay." Owen mulled this over for a moment. "What about the refugee agency or whatever it was that took responsibility for you after you arrived here? What did they tell you? Surely they had some information about who you were and how you got out."

She hesitated and looked away.

"My first few months are a complete blank. I don't know where I was. Then . . . for a long time I couldn't communicate with anyone because I didn't understand English."

"Wasn't there a translator available?"

She shook her head.

"That's unbelievable. Weren't there other refugees who could help you?"

"No. By the time I was conscious of my surroundings, I was alone with Americans."

"How did you learn English then?"

"Like a baby learns it."

Owen shook his head. "That must have been hell."

"It didn't matter, really, because I couldn't speak for years. I couldn't make a sound. So even if I had known English I wouldn't have said anything. I was more like an animal than a child."

"Was there something wrong with you?"

"Physically, no. I've been told that I had some form of mutism induced by trauma. And even when I did start to speak it was only to certain people."

"So you never found out who brought you out or why or how, or what records there were on you?"

"No."

"How did you live? Were you placed with a foster family?"

She dropped her eyes. "I was taken to a farm. People there took care of me."

"And then you married Bram?"

"Yes."

Suddenly it was all coming together. She had been in a bad foster home and then she had met Bram Serian.

"You were very young when you married him, weren't you?"

"Yes."

"How young, Lenore?"

She didn't answer.

"I can probably guess pretty close," he said. "Knowing

what age you were when you came here and what year you were married and—"

"I was fifteen," she said flatly.

"My God. Fifteen. And neither of you wanted people to know how much younger you were than him so you lied, and he told everyone that you just looked young."

"Yes."

They walked in silence a moment.

"Okay," Owen said, trying to sound more assured than he felt. "Do you remember the names of any places from your early childhood, or anything about the city you lived in?"

"Nothing that helps. I remember a wooden house on stilts and lots of water, but not much else."

"I wonder if Vietnam has records or—"

"Someone checked into that for me years ago. It's a dead end."

"Your name . . . They must have changed it when you got to the States. What was your name before it was Lenore?"

"All I remember is Lenore."

The path emerged from the trees into a clearing that overlooked a good-sized frozen pond. Owen shaded his eyes to look across the water. In the glare he could just barely make out a short wooden dock on the other side.

"Bram built a permanent camp over there," she said. "He liked to take friends for what he called roughouts. No women allowed. Also no radios or anything that used batteries. They stayed for a weekend or a week depending on Bram's mood. Most of the men made it through, in spite of the mosquitoes and snakes and spiders and skunks. The few who abandoned camp and escaped back to the house were never welcome at Arcadia again."

Owen stood beside her and looked out over the pond. He imagined how beautiful it would be with all the trees green and the water teeming with life.

"I'm still not sure what I'm supposed to do, Lenore. What exactly am I helping you look for?"

"Who I am," she said.

"But how can my research into Bram's background tell you that? What has one got to do with the other?"

She continued to stare out across the frozen water. "Bram knew who my father was," she said bitterly. "He knew things that he wouldn't tell me."

Owen shook his head in confusion. "Bram Serian knew who your father was? How can that be? Are you sure?"

"Yes. It began when I was—" She glanced at Owen. "When Bram and I had been married for a few years. I became obsessed with my father . . . dreaming about him . . . cutting pictures out of magazines and pretending they were of him . . . fantasizing about what it would be like to find him and about what he would say to me . . . what he would think of me . . . what he would tell me about my mother.

"Bram got furious when he realized what I was doing. I tried to explain it to him, thinking that he was just hurt because maybe he thought I wanted my father more than him. But nothing calmed him down. He forbid me to think about my father."

She laughed sadly. "Can you imagine anyone believing they had the power to do that?

"But Bram thought he could control everything. And for the most part he was right. He controlled my life. Except for that dream of a father.

"I tried to explain my feelings to him and I pleaded with him to help me. We fought about it. I learned how to fight Bram carrying my father as my torch. I learned how to stand up to him.

"Then, one time after he'd been drinking, I brought up the subject and he started raving about what a fool I was. He said that my father had no use for me as a daughter. That my father had always known my whereabouts and that obviously it had been his choice to keep himself secret.

"I was stunned. I was enraged. To think that Bram, this man I worshipped, had known the secrets of my past all along and had never given them to me. That he had willfully and cruelly deprived me of my identity . . . I can't tell you how much I hated him then.

"I coaxed him into drinking more. Until he fell out of the chair onto the floor. And then I asked him if my father was still alive. If my father had another family. If my father was ashamed of me. He started crying and he said that I was inhuman because I didn't understand about regrets or weakness.

"That was all I could get him to say. He didn't even remember it when he sobered up. But from then on I was vigilant and relentless. I asked him questions about Vietnam, about his friends, about whatever might possibly yield a clue to the connection he had with my father. Most of the time he wouldn't answer, but once in a while I'd get a tiny scrap of information."

"But how on earth could Serian have learned the identity of your father? And why wouldn't he tell you?"

A dark and powerful emotion showed for a moment in her expression.

"He didn't just learn it," she said bitterly. "He knew all along. He found me and he brought me to Arcadia because of who my father was."

"My God," Owen breathed. "Are you certain?"

"He knew all along," she repeated. "I was never important to him for who I was. He never wanted *me*. I was only important because of who my father was. Because he knew my father in the war."

Owen wanted to pull her into his arms and hold her until her pain subsided. He could feel her anguish. She believed that both the men in her life, father and husband, had betrayed her. That neither had wanted her.

Helplessly, he tried to console her with words, saying, "Even if Bram found you because of your father . . . that doesn't mean he didn't fall in love with you afterward."

She glanced up at him. "That makes no difference anymore. All I want is my father. And to know who I am. Bram had no right to cheat me of that!"

"And you think the key to your identity is hidden somewhere in Bram's papers?"

"Yes. You saw how compulsive he was about saving things. There has got to be something in those years' worth of papers that will show his connection to my father."

Owen had no response.

She drew in a deep breath and moved away from him as though suddenly self-conscious. At first she drifted randomly, kicking at piles of leaves. Then she developed a purpose. He watched as she pried a good-sized rock out of the ground, carried it down the steep bank to the pond and heaved it about a foot from the edge. The rock smashed through the ice, creating a dark hole with cracks radiating from it like zigzags of lightning. She picked up a fallen branch and finished the job, punching through the broken ice as far as she could reach until there was a wide stretch of open water.

Owen didn't have to ask what she was doing. He knew all

too well. He had broken ice so the livestock could drink on more winter mornings than he cared to count.

"Are there horses on the place, or cattle?" he asked.

"No. But there are lots of wild animals out here—raccoons and coyotes and woodchucks and birds." She stared down into the frigid water. "To sleep like a fish," she said. "I used to wish I could do that. Burrow down into the cold mud and lapse into senselessness for months at a time."

Owen reached for her hand.

Abruptly she jerked away and started back up the path. He watched her for a moment, a long solitary moment, then followed.

Owen surveyed the line of boxes stacked in Bram Serian's giant living room.

"Okay," he said, trying to sound confident. "It's obvious Serian used the drop-it-in-the-box method of record keeping, so I guess we're going to have to do the organizing. Maybe we should start by sorting things into categories and making piles on the floor. We certainly have enough floor space in here. That is, unless you have another idea."

"You're the researcher," she said. "I wouldn't know where to begin with all this."

"Right. Well, do you want to work separately or maybe one of us sort and the other make the piles or—"

Instead of answering, she started for the door. "While you're getting started, I'll get us something to drink," she said.

She came back some time later with a large pitcher of cold tea and two ice-filled glasses.

"I thought easterners didn't appreciate iced tea," he said.

She poured both glasses full. "Bram liked it."

He took a long drink. "Okay, these are the categories I have going so far." He showed her the piles he'd made while she was gone. "Banking, personal correspondence, bills, art clippings, and miscellaneous clippings. Why don't you arrange them out where there's more room."

He went back to his sorting, not paying any attention as she carried the papers to the center of the room. When he looked up, she was standing over him, watching.

"Listen," Owen said, "it's obvious you're not too enthusiastic about this approach, and maybe you're right."

There was something close to panic in her eyes. "No. Please, go on. Who knows what you'll find or what might be important." She gathered everything he'd laid out and took it away.

They worked for thirty minutes to finish the first box. When it was empty, he stretched his cramped legs, then walked over to admire the stacks of papers stretching across the room. "Now we can start labeling and get some organization."

He bent to straighten some things. "Lenore, why did you put ..." He sifted through the letters. "Wait a minute ... these are all mixed up. And the clippings ... these don't go ..."

"Do it yourself, then! I'm through!"

She wheeled to leave, but Owen caught her arm. "What's wrong?"

"Don't touch me."

"All right. All right." He held his hands in the air. "Do you want me to leave? Do you want to forget this whole project? What do you want?"

"I want you to do this part by yourself."

He tried to control his annoyance. What a spoiled bitch she was. Unwilling to do any work at all. Even for something she badly wanted. "Fine. I can handle it."

She sat on a couch while he worked. A tense silence hung in the room. He tried to keep his attention on Serian's flotsam, but it felt like an exercise in futility. What was important? What was he looking for?

He soon realized that each box represented a year, so he opened all the lids, labeled them, and arranged them chronologically. Twenty-two boxes. Twenty-two years. Now he at least had a goal. He went straight for the oldest one.

His excitement dampened when he found that Serian had been saving the same stuff twenty-two years ago. If anything, he'd been more compulsive then, squirreling away subscription renewal reminders and dry cleaning receipts and parking tickets and endless magazine clippings. Owen inspected each item before assigning it to a pile. When he finished he chose his next box at random again just to vary the tedium.

Several inches down he uncovered a cardboard tube and knew immediately that he'd found something interesting. He peered into it. Something was rolled inside. Gently he dislodged the contents and spread it out. It was a plain white sheet with a rectangle of gray charcoal or pencil, printed over with a white list of names. No. Not printed exactly.

"Lenore, look at this. Does this mean anything to you?"

She bolted off the couch and knelt beside him.

"Do you suppose it's some kind of art?" he asked.

"It looks a little like a rubbing," she said hesitantly. "Bram had friends who did rubbings. You know . . . where you lay a piece of paper over something—a wall or a gravestone or whatever—and rub charcoal on it."

"A rubbing." Owen considered this. He remembered reading something. "This is a rubbing from the Vietnam memorial! Look . . . that's exactly what it is!"

Lenore stared down at it. "From the Vietnam memorial?" She sounded awestruck.

"It might mean nothing but"—Owen tried to keep his excitement in check—"who knows . . ."

"Could you . . ." She clutched her hands together over her mouth as though afraid to ask. "Could you read them to me."

"Sure."

There were three lines with complete names. The rest were partials that faded out at the edges. He read them aloud to her. "Peter Tsosie, Luis Veranza, and Leroy Wilson. Donald Abcock, Luther Bachman, and Rodney Benedict. Oscar Gibney, Mohammed Hamid, and Morris Isaacs."

She shook her head to signify that none were familiar.

"Do you think one of those names is my father, Owen?"

"I don't know. Scriun obviously had a reason for keeping a rubbing of these particular names . . . but remember, he served with lots of men, probably lost a number of friends. And then Jonas Watkins said that he also lost a brother to the war. If his brother had a different last name . . ." Owen shrugged.

She buried her face in her hands and hunched forward. He was afraid it was the start of something terrible, and he felt a wave of helplessness. The breakdown did not come, though. Instead she straightened, wiped her face with her hands and met his eyes.

"I owe you an explanation," she said.

Owen tensed. "You don't owe me anything . . ."

She didn't retreat. She was determined to confess something to him and he wasn't sure he wanted to hear it, but there seemed no escape.

Shame and defiance, trust and fear mingled in her dark eyes. She took a deep breath. "I can't read, Owen. It's not that I don't want to help you, it's—"

His first reaction was relief. He'd been afraid her confession would bare something dark and unforgivable. His next reaction was puzzlement. "You mean you need glasses or you're dyslexic or what?"

"No. I . . . I don't know what the words say."

"You actually . . . don't know how?"

"I know my name. I practiced copying it over and over so that I can write it. I also know my numbers."

"You never learned to read English? Did Serian know this?"

"Of course. He knew everything about me." Her posture became defensive.

Owen was shocked for the second time that afternoon. He rose from the floor and moved around the room, seeing nothing. It was incomprehensible. This intelligent, well-spoken woman did not know how to read?

"This is so strange, Lenore. I mean, it's not that there aren't people who don't know how to read. I know there are. I just . . . I would never have guessed. You hide it so well."

"You think less of me now," she said solemnly.

"No! That's not it at all."

"Bram told me how people would react if they knew. He told me to keep the secret. But it's hard now that I'm alone."

"No one else knows?"

"No one who's around anymore."

"But the attorneys . . . the forms you've had to sign . . ."

"They tell me to read things and I pretend. Then I write my name on the lines they mark."

"But banking . . . bills . . . daily life . . . I don't see how you manage."

"All of my bills are sent to the bank that handles the estate. Stanley comes in his truck and brings me whatever I need and sends the bill to the attorneys. I don't have to do anything."

"I can't even imagine how hard that's been for you. Not reading. My God."

"It's very difficult now. There are things I want and things

I would like to do. And I can't make the arrangements. But I don't dare let anyone know."

"Why not, for Christ sake? You're paying Rossner a bundle and you're trusting him to defend your life. Why can't you trust him to know this?"

"Because then he would be suspicious and he would start asking other questions."

"Like?"

"Like how am I here without taking the citizenship classes and passing the tests? How was such an ignorant person allowed to become a citizen?"

"What do you mean?"

She gave him a calculating sideways look. "I'm not legal, Owen. There was no refugee relief agency, no sponsor program. I was smuggled in for some reason and hidden. If the truth got out, I'd be deported."

"Wait a minute." Owen shook his head. "You're the child of an American soldier and you were married to an American citizen. That has to convey some kind of status. Didn't Serian ever look into it?"

She nodded. "There is no official proof of who my father was. And my being smuggled into the country . . . being an illegal alien . . . marriage couldn't erase that. If you're a criminal then getting married doesn't save you. Bram showed me pictures of the detention camps I should be in. And he read me a story about a woman who was sent back to Vietnam and executed."

"I don't think that's right, Lenore," Owen said carefully. "I think he must have got the wrong information or something."

"He was trying to protect me," she insisted.

Owen raked his fingers back through his hair and wondered what the hell Bram Serian had been up to.

"I've been waiting," she said. "For the lawyers or the judge or one of those news people to find out the truth about me. When they do the trial won't even matter because I'll be sent back and shot. Without ever knowing who I am."

"*No.* Listen to me, Lenore. That is not going to happen. Things don't work that way. We have to get some legal advice on this because—"

She shook her head vehemently.

"But maybe Bram didn't find out all there was to know.

Or maybe the laws have changed. We need to find an expert for you to talk to so that—"

"No! It's too dangerous."

"Okay, okay. Just let me think about this."

Owen regarded her in silence. He understood so much about her now, and it filled him with fury. What had Serian been trying to do to her? And what kind of a hell had her years in hiding been?

"When you were with this family that took you in and hid you . . . didn't anyone care that you weren't learning to read?"

She looked away from him and shrugged. "You forget, Owen, I couldn't utter a sound at first. The people around me thought I was hopelessly disabled. It was years before anyone realized I had a normal intelligence, and then what were they supposed to do? For a child that old with a background in such a different language it would be impossible to learn to read in English without going to school every day. And I couldn't go to school because then people would have found out about me. I had to stay hidden."

"Lenore . . ." he began, but she cut him off.

"When you get beyond a certain age, it becomes too late to learn something that complicated anyway."

A sigh escaped Owen. "Who told you that?" he asked.

"It's true!"

"Who told you?" Owen demanded softly. He could picture her—a damaged child in a neglectful foster home. And not just the average bad situation but an illegal one. Maybe the people had been paid by her phantom father to take her in—only her father had not been able to buy love or real caring for her. God knew what she had suffered through before she escaped into her marriage with Serian. And then the marriage wasn't really an escape. It was just a different kind of hell with Serian playing on her fears, controlling her with fear . . . Yet she was still desperately trying to hang onto her illusions. She didn't want to believe that she had been abused and lied to by everyone in her life.

"Look." He picked up a piece of paper and shoved it close to her face. "See this. It's the letter L. Your name starts with it. There are twenty-six of those letters in the alphabet. I could teach you those letters." She shook her head and slapped the paper from his hand, but Owen kept talking. "Then I could teach you how to put them together into words. There's nothing mysterious about the process. And schools don't hold the monopoly on it."

She backed away. Her eyes had ignited into a low burn. "Why don't you just leave. Go away and forget everything."

"I can't," he admitted.

"Then take them!" She scooped up a handful of Serian's papers and threw them in his face. "Take whatever you want for your book! And get out!"

He stood very still for a moment, considering what to do. Then he walked over to the phone in the corner and dialed the number Bernie had given him for her home.

"What are you doing?" Lenore demanded.

He held up his hand to stop her.

"Hello, Bernie, I'm sorry to bother you at home, but I need to get something to Alex."

"Owen! Tell me everything! How was Arcadia? And what's *she* like?"

"Yes, well, I'm there now."

"You're there now?"

"That's right. And I need information on some names from the Vietnam memorial wall. I was wondering if Alex's roommate could help."

"Ah, yes. Cliff the computer snoop. Give me the names and I'll pass them along. I'll give you Alex's home number too, so you can speak to him directly next time."

He read the names to her and then took down the number.

"I'll dump it on Alex or his machine immediately," Bernie promised. "Meanwhile, hang in there. If you manage an inside scoop, you'll have DeMille on their knees begging you for this book before you even hand in the proposal!"

"Thanks, Bernie. I'll talk to you Monday."

"Who was that?" Lenore asked suspiciously as soon as he'd replaced the receiver.

"My agent. Bernadette Goodson."

He sat down on the floor beside a box and began sorting again.

"The way I see it," he said. "Nothing has changed. Now, you can help or you can sit and watch, but it seems to me that things would go a lot faster if you helped."

It was nearly six o'clock, and Owen had a neck ache and his legs were cramped, but he was pleased with what they'd accomplished so far. Papers had been paper-clipped or stapled together and arranged in folders. He had a file of phone bills, which he thought might prove interesting, a file of personal letters that could be valuable to his book and a coffee table covered with odds and ends that had caught his attention. Within that assortment he had been particularly drawn to a magazine article on locating MIAs in Vietnam, a receipt for a large amount spent at an army-navy surplus store, and a lifetime warranty certificate for a deluxe fireproof safe.

"I think I've about had it," he said, standing and stretching the stiffness out of his body.

"I hate to quit," she said.

"We don't have to quit. I just need a break. I'm willing to work all night if that's what you want."

"Yes."

"Okay. Then let's go to town for dinner. Just to get away from all this for a while."

"No!" She shook her head. "People recognize me in Stoatsberg. Everyone would point and talk."

"Then we'll go somewhere else." He thought about the stories—how reclusive she was, how she'd rarely left Arcadia through the years. Now he knew why. It had been Bram Serian's sickness, not hers. He had been the one twisting her mind and keeping her isolated.

"How about Manhattan?" Owen suggested casually. "I ought to pick up some things from the apartment anyway if I'm going to be staying out here much longer."

"Right now? Go to Manhattan?"

"Why not? You can be perfectly anonymous there."

"But you don't need anything from your apartment. Stanley has the supply closet full, and there are men's clothes that would fit you."

"I was thinking more of my work. All my notes and research materials. I'd like to have them here to refer to as we go."

She stared at him. He saw intense fear in her eyes, but with a tiny undercurrent of excitement.

"I could get caught, Owen. The immigration police could pick me up or—"

"That is *not* going to happen. Trust me, Lenore. Manhattan is a huge place crammed with people. I'll bet a quarter of the population is illegal. The police are busy with real crimes and real criminals . . . not half-Americans who were smuggled in as children."

"But Bram said—"

"Forget Bram! Fuck Bram! Bram is *dead!*"

She blinked, startled by his uncharacteristic outburst.

"Come on. I like to drive. The trip will go fast and we can brainstorm on the way. Besides, this may be my only visit to New York. How can you deny me a dinner out?"

She touched her fingertips to her lips, and he saw that her hand was shaking. "I've never been to Manhattan," she whispered.

"Well, damn it, get your coat!"

She stared at him for a moment longer. Then she went for her coat.

14

Owen had noticed a small Thai restaurant not far from his apartment in the East Village, and that was where he took Lenore Serian.

"What is this?" she asked as he led her to the door.

"It's Thai," he told her. "I don't know where to find Vietnamese food, but I figured since Thailand was a neighboring country, maybe this little place would be fun for you."

She looked nervously up and down the street before entering.

Once inside they sat down at a corner table for two, and Lenore's eyes took on the shuttered look she wore during the trial. Owen wondered if he'd done the right thing by bringing her out.

The tiny, dimly lit restaurant had mismatched tables and plastic flowers. Travel posters of Thailand decorated the walls, and there was a small shrine set up near the door to the kitchen. Four of the eight tables were occupied so there was a buzz of conversation, and in the back two Asian women, one small and gray-haired and the other in her late twenties, were huddled together at the cash register, giggling.

Gradually Lenore began to relax and look around the room.

"Should I try to read this menu to you or just describe what the choices are?" he asked her.

"Read it, please. I want to hear everything on it."

He struggled with the unfamiliar Thai names that preceded each entree description while Lenore listened. When he was about halfway through the listings, the younger of the two women appeared beside the table, smiling. "You need help order?" she asked brightly.

"Well, maybe you could just recommend some things to

us. What would you like, Lenore? Beef . . . chicken . . . sea-food?"

Lenore looked at the woman intently without answering.

"How about if you choose some things for us," Owen said to the waitress. "A selection, maybe."

The older woman came over to the table then. "You have trouble?" she asked.

"No, everything is—" but Owen didn't finish because the younger woman had started a rapid explanation in Thai.

Owen glanced over at Lenore, apologetic at having brought on this attention, and was alarmed at the expression of horrified astonishment she wore.

"What is it?" he asked.

The women stopped talking and peered down at Lenore with interest.

"Do you want to leave, Lenore?"

She rose unsteadily from her chair, staring at the women. They giggled nervously. The younger one rattled off something in Thai to the older.

"Lenore?" Owen stood.

Her expression was almost childlike. She whispered something Owen couldn't understand, and she reached out to touch the younger woman's cheek with her fingertips.

Quickly Owen moved around the table. "Lenore?" She seemed oblivious to him. Her eyes were fixed trancelike on the younger Thai woman.

"Let's get you outside for some fresh air," he said, and he circled her shoulders with an arm and maneuvered her toward the door.

The older woman followed with their coats and insisted on helping Lenore into hers.

"Could you understand what she was saying?" Owen asked the woman.

"Yes. She say, 'Mommy, mommy.' "

"You speak Vietnamese?"

"No. She say, 'Mommy, mommy' in Thai."

"In Thai?"

"Un huh," the woman nodded vigorously.

Lenore started as though awakening and turned to grip Owen's arm. "I understood them," she said in stunned disbelief. "I understood what they were saying."

"I'm sorry," Owen told the Thai woman. "This is a shock

for her. She left home very young ... from Vietnam ... and ..."

"My mother," Lenore whispered. "Suddenly, I thought she was my mother."

"You okay now?" the woman asked. "Come inside. I bring tea."

Lenore held her forehead. "I don't want to go back inside. I don't want to see her again."

The woman peered closely at Lenore, worrying over her customer as though personally responsible for Lenore's upset.

"Could you make our dinner take-out?" Owen asked.

"Okay. Okay." The woman hurried to the door and called in instructions, then returned to smile at Lenore. "You Vietnamese? I live in Vietnam long time. I speak very good." The woman said something in a rapid singsong.

Lenore shook her head and turned searching, troubled eyes to Owen.

"That's Vietnamese," the woman assured them. "Say go home. Be well."

"Could you say something else?" Owen asked. "Anything. Just talk."

The woman talked and Lenore's expression edged into fear.

"Thank you," Owen told the woman. "My car is parked right over there. When the food's ready, could you just wave out the door at me?"

The woman executed a subtle bow of the head over steepled hands. *"Sawadee ka,"* she called as Owen helped Lenore into the car. *"Sawadee ka,"* Lenore whispered in response.

When Owen opened the door to his apartment he saw a note that had been slipped under the door.

Stopped by to see if you were interested in a roaring good time. Hope you're not working too hard. It is Saturday night, you know! Remember what they say about all work and no play. If you want to play you can find us at the Lion's Head for dinner and then the Tenth Street Jazz Club for the rest of the night. (How can you stand not having a phone?)

It was signed by Holly and Marilyn.

"What's that?" Lenore asked, looking at it over his shoulder.

"A note. Some people wanting me to go out with them tonight."

"What people? I thought you didn't know anyone in New York."

"People I've met at the trial. Reporters."

"That blonde you sit next to every day?"

"That's one of 'em," he said, crumpling the note and throwing it in the trash.

They ate. Or at least he ate. Lenore was still so agitated that she didn't do much beyond tasting things.

"What does this mean?" she kept asking. "What do you think it means? How can I understand Thai and not Vietnamese?"

Owen tried to come up with answers. "Maybe you were raised in Thailand? Maybe your mother was actually Thai but lived in Vietnam? I don't know."

On the drive back to Arcadia, she was still asking what it meant and Owen was trying to be patient, trying to help her sort it out.

"Are you sure you don't remember anything about how you lived before you came to the States," he asked.

"I remember that we were near water."

"Anything else? Try . . ."

"A *wat*. I remember a *wat*."

"What's that?"

"A temple. With priests in yellow robes."

"Your house was near a temple?"

Her voice faded to a whisper, "My house."

"You remember your house was near water, and a temple?"

She covered her face with her hands. "I don't know. I don't know. Maybe it's from a dream."

"Take it easy. You're almost home. Think of how exciting it is to learn that you understand a language you didn't know about."

She leaned her head back and stared out into the night. "And that I don't understand a language I assumed I spoke."

The miles passed in silence. Owen reviewed all that he'd learned about Bram Serian, twisting and turning it, trying to make it fit together. But Serian seemed more elusive than ever, and there was not one clue to Lenore's phantom father.

"That safe warranty has got to mean something," Owen said aloud after they'd pulled through the gate to Arcadia.

"I told you before," she sighed, "Bram never mentioned a safe at Arcadia. And the police made a point of searching for a safe without finding one."

"But then the police didn't find his tower room either, did they?"

"True," she admitted.

"I have this gut feeling that the safe is there at Arcadia," he said. "Where else could he have put it? You said it absolutely wasn't at the loft in town."

"No. Rossner said the loft was easy for the police to search because it's nothing more than a huge room, and they went over every inch of it without finding a thing."

"All right. With the warranty certificate we discovered today, we now have more information than the police had. We know the dimensions and the brand and the weight of that safe. We could even call the manufacturer and ask for suggestions. It has to be built into the house and tomorrow we're going to find it."

He glanced over at her. She was watching him. The eye contact brought the shadow of a smile to her mouth and he had to look away. He had to concentrate on the road and the puzzle and the fact that this wasn't his life. This wasn't reality. Reality was Kansas and the farm and Michelle Wheeler, whom he'd known since he was ten years old.

As soon as they were inside the house and had the alarm system reactivated, Lenore led him back to the living room and the waiting stacks of papers. He immersed himself in reading the letters Serian had saved over twenty-plus years. Lenore drifted in and out of the room without speaking. After several hours had passed Owen took a break. He leaned his head back against the top cushion of the couch, closed his bleary eyes and let his thoughts drift. The letters were interesting, yet they hadn't yielded any specific facts that he could use. Thai. Thailand. Vietnam. Bram Serian. How did everything fit together?

The scene at the restaurant replayed itself in his mind, and he thought about the travel posters. One of them had showed a canal. Water. Had Lenore's house been near a canal in

Thailand? But hell, from what he read about Vietnam there was plenty of water there too. Rice paddies and rivers and whatever. That whole part of the world was wet.

Thailand. Suddenly he sat up straight. Where had he seen a mention of Thailand? In a clipping of some kind.

He was sorting through the drift of paper on the oversized coffee table when Lenore came back in.

"I remember seeing something about Thailand," he said. "I don't know if it means anything but . . ." He let his words trail off as he concentrated on his search again.

She moved closer to watch.

He skimmed through a one-page magazine article about an obscure artist, one which was continued but was missing the additional pages, and turned it over on his reject pile. Lenore picked it up, but he paid no attention. Somewhere in that haystack of printed words on the table he had seen Thailand mentioned, and he was determined to find it. His eyelids had turned to sandpaper by the time he picked up the newspaper clipping and saw the word *Thailand* jump out at him from the third paragraph.

"This is it," he said.

It was a standard *New York Times* obituary from seven years ago, and he remembered adding it to the collection in the hope that the deceased was somehow connected to Serian.

"Tell me," Lenore urged.

Owen read it to her. The subject was Howard Newman, a man of advanced years who had died in a Danbury, Connecticut, hospital from complications following a heart operation. He had been a teacher, a merchant, a philosopher and a world-class butterfly collector. He was survived by his wife, the former Françoise Beaujon. In the third paragraph it was reported that "Mr. Newman lived in Thailand for many years and wrote extensively on the area."

"It's not much," Owen admitted. "But maybe there's a connection."

"Or a coincidence," she said, sounding disappointed and frustrated. "Here." She handed Owen the page on the artist that he'd skimmed earlier. "Is this anything?"

"It's nothing—" he began, but she reached across to take it from his hands and flip it over. On the reverse of the artist story was a full-page ad for fireproof safes.

"Isn't that a picture of a safe?" she asked.

"I missed that completely! There's an article about an artist on the other side and I thought . . . Just goes to show that two heads are better than one." He laughed. "This is the brand of safe he bought, all right. And listen to this. 'Installed under a ground floor or in a basement floor or wall this safe is the ultimate in fireproof protection.' That gives us a pretty good idea where to look."

"The police were all over the basement," she remarked wearily.

"It's got to be somewhere." He dropped the safe ad and his reading glasses together on the table. "I'm going to make some coffee. Is that okay with you?"

"Go ahead," she told him, stretching out on a couch.

Owen made his way to the kitchen, the one room he knew he could locate. By the time he had rooted supplies out of the cupboards, made the coffee, and returned, she was sound asleep. He watched her. She was curled on her side with her black hair spread out across her back and shoulder like a shawl. Everything about her looked so fragile. The fine bones of her wrists. The delicate skin of her eyelids with their dark fringe of lashes. The faint rise and fall of her chest. Yet she wasn't fragile. He knew that. She was stronger than sturdy Michelle Wheeler or either one of his country-raised sisters. She had a strength of spirit that the other women lacked.

She moved in her sleep, then cried out.

"Lenore," he said, touching her shoulder.

She sat bolt upright, breathing hard, with a panicky look in her eyes.

"It's okay," he assured her softly.

Her eyes were unfocused and bright with fear. "There was a cobra in the rafters. He was coming down for me and his eyes were so cold and my mother was screaming but I couldn't move."

"You're safe now. No cobras. No rafters even."

She looked at him as though just realizing he was there. His hand was still on her shoulder and she pulled sharply away. "This will make your book more interesting, won't it?" she said as she pulled herself off the couch to stand up. "What stories you'll have to tell . . . Breakdowns in restaurants and strange nightmares . . . in addition to all the other dirt you've already got."

"Lenore, I'm not going to write anything that will hurt you."

She laughed hollowly. "Poor Owen. You really believe that, don't you?"

Owen held out his hands helplessly. "I don't know what . . ." He shook his head. "Did I say or do something? What is this about?"

"Nothing's new. Nothing's different. Maybe you're just seeing it all more clearly."

"You're talking in riddles, Lenore."

After a deep breath she said, "You're tired. I'm tired. Where do you want to sleep?"

Thoughts sprang up that he didn't want to acknowledge or examine. "I . . . ah . . . If you have some blankets, maybe I'll just sleep out in the car."

A burst of laughter escaped her. "Don't be ridiculous. It's freezing out, and you have this enormous house open to you." One side of her mouth curved into a scornful, challenging smile. "You're my guest, Mr. Byrne. What's wrong? Are you afraid of the Black Widow?"

"I'll just use one of these couches," he said. "If that's all right with you."

"That's fine with me." She spun on her heel and left. Ten minutes later she reappeared with an armload of blankets and pillows. "Sleep well," she said, then was gone again.

He did not sleep well.

First, he couldn't go to sleep. Tired as he was, the muscles in his body would not relax. He twisted into every position possible, but could find no comfort. Then, when he did finally slip into blackness, he was plagued by disturbing dreams. His efforts to escape the images brought him to the edge of wakefulness over and over, but then he was dragged back down again. There was a woman with slender legs and elegant breasts whose lips curled back to reveal vampire fangs. There was a masked woman in filmy black lace who opened her legs to him and plunged a knife into his back as he entered her. There was a sinuous woman with sleepy eyes and erect nipples lying in a pool of blood. He was alternately aroused and terrified for hours.

Finally he found himself sitting up, staring at fading afterimages in the darkness with a pounding heart. The sharp details of the dreams were lost immediately, but their essence remained. And even though he knew he was awake, the heightened, chimeric sense of unreality stayed with him. He threw off his blankets, feeling feverish. His blood pulsated with heat. His fingertips and his head and his groin throbbed with heat.

He lay back against his pillow.

Lenore.

His breath caught just at the thought of her.

Lenore.

He closed his eyes and whispered her name.

"Lenore."

He could feel her lying nearby in the silent house. Breathing softly in the silence. Weight of breast and hip against cool sheets. Lenore. Waiting in the darkness. Waiting. Open and waiting.

He threw on his jeans and shirt and stumbled out into the black hallway. Her bedroom wasn't far from the stained-glass sitting room. He could find it. He had to find it. Round and round he fumbled through the darkness. Eventually he came to the open door and stepped into a flood of moonlight. The bed was empty. Untouched.

Suddenly, the fever was gone. He was standing barefooted on a chilly wooden floor in an empty room. Feeling as empty as the room. He crossed to the bed and sat down. It looked virginal in the moonlight. Smooth and tight and cold. He ran his hand over it, then pulled a pillow free and brought it to his face. Her scent wasn't there. She didn't exist. He had imagined her. He dropped the pillow and cradled his head in his hands, afraid for his sanity. Thinking that maybe it was possible to be possessed and that Serian's spirit had possessed him. Or Lenore had possessed him. Or something completely unknown and even more fearsome had taken control of him.

He calmed himself with the thought that he was still under the influence of his dreams. What he needed was to go back to sleep and ride it out till morning when everything would be normal again. He left the bedroom, more cautious and uncertain of the way now that he had returned to his rational self, and he started down the dark halls, silently cursing the house and the crazed mind that had conceived it. He walked into closets where he thought there were connecting hallways. He hit dead ends. Finally, he decided to settle for sleeping in the first warm comfortable spot he encountered, whether it be couch or bed, and worry about where he was in the morning. Then he saw the flickering glow.

Curious, he stepped through the doorway into a small windowless room that was filled with dancing shadows. A couch faced the fireplace with its back to him and an assortment of little tables were scattered about. The glow came from the remains of a wood fire on the hearth and the dozens of burning candles filling the tabletops.

He moved farther in, wondering over the scene, when suddenly a figure that had been lying hidden from view on the couch sprang up like a cat-demon rising to strike. He froze in horror, pulled into nightmare once more. This was the woman from his dreams, naked beneath a cascade of inky hair. Teeth gleaming and eyes wild in the primitive light. A double-barreled shotgun pointed straight at his heart.

In the clarity of an instant he knew that she would kill him. And in the strange netherworld of his half-dream he believed that he deserved it.

They hung there together. Captives of the nightmare. Gradually, the feral panic in her eyes changed to confusion.

"Owen?"

He was afraid to move or speak.

"Owen?"

She lowered the gun and began to tremble.

He eased forward, took the gun from her and laid it aside, then pulled the blankets up around her.

"I don't . . . I thought . . ." She turned shocked eyes toward him. "I could have killed you."

"Do you always sleep with such a dangerous companion?"

She nodded. "Since I've been alone. Yes."

"You have the alarms. Doesn't that make you feel secure?"

"Nothing gives me security."

The remaining log on the fire broke apart in a hiss of sparks.

"Why were you up?" she asked.

"Bad dreams," he said. "And you? Why aren't you in bed?"

"I sleep in different places. Tonight I wanted to be here."

He glanced around the room at all the tiny flames. They weren't like any candles he'd ever seen. Each was inside a tall glass cylinder with writing or pictures on the outside. He started to ask her about them, then realized that he didn't want to know.

She was watching him. Crouched there on the couch with the blankets capelike around her and the candlelight dancing on her face. She was naked beneath the blankets. Watching him.

The vision of her naked body was imprinted on his retinas so that he could close his eyes and see her again with the skein of black hair hanging down across her bare breasts. He backed away from her, nearly upsetting a table full of candles.

"Good night . . . again," he said, then abruptly left the room without waiting for a reply.

A sound awakened him. He opened his eyes and was completely disoriented. Beams like rafters overhead. Strange yellow light. Creak of leather. Smell of coffee.

He swung his feet over the side of the couch and sat up. He was in Bram Serian's fanciful living room. Lenore was seated on the facing couch. There was a coffee service on a table between them. It was morning. Everything was normal.

She was studying him over her coffee mug. Her hair was gathered into a clip at the nape of her neck and she was dressed in an oversized shirt and faded jeans.

Had she been naked in a room full of candles last night pointing a shotgun at him or had he dreamed everything?

"Morning," he said, helping himself to the coffee. The strange sulfuric light was coming in through the windows.

"It might snow," she said.

"Looks that way," he agreed.

By afternoon they had tapped and pried and gone over every inch of the basement without finding the safe. Finally they gave up and wandered to the kitchen for a dispirited lunch. He stared out the window at the dense quiet air as he ate. The moisture was gathering overhead, roiling in the metallic clouds. The light had changed from yellow to silver.

To the left he could see a corner of the rubble that had once been Serian's studio. It would soon be covered with snow. All the ugliness hidden.

"Lenore," he said, staring out as he spoke. "Were you ever inside the studio at all?"

"No. I don't think anyone ever got in there but Al."

"Did the police go over the studio floor ... push around the debris and actually examine the floor during any of their searches?"

She froze and looked at him, a spark catching in her eyes.

They were outside in minutes, digging into the ruins with bare hands. Only after their hands were raw and cold and their clothes were smeared with soot did common sense descend, and they returned to the house to regroup. Lenore found him old jeans and a worn down-filled coat. From the basement they brought up thick work gloves, heavy snow boots, crowbars and shovels and flashlights. Dressed for the Arctic and armed with equipment, they approached the blackened mess again. It seemed to have grown larger and deeper than his first impression of it.

They walked the margins, mapping it out according to the diagrams Rossner had shown the jury. Here had been the door. This end had been the living quarters. Along that wall was the raised brick platform for the stove. They divided it into thirds, digging out gashes to mark the sections.

"Let's do a grid search," she said with a wry smile, surprising him with the humorous reference to Sheriff Bello's inept investigation.

The work was hard. Moving chunks of blackened beams and shoveling piles of rubbish in a repetitive action of scoop and throw that burned deep into Owen's shoulder muscles and raised blisters in spite of the heavy gloves. His face was freezing, but he was sweating inside the coat. Once an area was scraped clear, they pried up the ruined plank flooring to expose the concrete.

He thought about Serian as he worked. How the man had labored over this building, pouring the concrete over the packed dirt floor of the old barn. How he had cut and shaped the wood. Creating the workshop for his dreams, and later his funeral pyre. He thought about where the body had been found and where the sharp brick corner was. He thought about the axe head. But then he stopped himself because he could not face the possibility of her guilt anymore. If she was guilty ... But no. No. He couldn't think about it.

When the first flakes drifted down, they both straightened and looked up into the sky.

"Not much time." Lenore rubbed the back of her gloved

hand across her cheek, leaving a carbon smudge. He could tell that she was afraid he might give up.

"We can keep at it for a while," he said.

She smiled at him. Sweet and grateful. A heartbreaking smile. He bent back to his work with renewed determination, refusing to consider whether the smile had been genuine or not.

The sky darkened and the flakes fell faster and the wind picked up, stinging bitterly against exposed skin. They finished the middle third, crossing the mark that put them into the final section. He shoveled away a charred line of floorboards and there it was. A square steel door, smooth and solid except for a round disc in the center.

They fell on it together, tugging and prying and straining. But the safe had been set down into the concrete and wouldn't budge. He ran his hands along the metal, unable to see how it opened. He tried to pry up the circular centerpiece with a screwdriver but nothing happened. In frustration, he pounded on the smooth metal face with the butt of the screwdriver. One of his blows landed on the circular portion of the disc and it popped open to reveal a keyhole inside.

"Keys," she said and ran for the house. Their mouths were too cold to form sentences.

He huddled in the wind, tucking his face down against his chest and leaning over the exposed safe to keep the snow from gathering there.

Lenore returned with three jammed keyrings. They each took one and alternated trying them. Snow collected on their shoulders and backs. It swirled into drifts around their feet.

The door opened in response to a nondescript brass key, flipping up with a spring action as soon as it was unlocked. Owen was so startled he fell backward. Lenore pulled on his arm to help him regain his balance, and together they stared down into Serian's mystery. Serian's secret.

She had been thinking ahead when she went for the key and had stuffed her pockets with plastic garbage bags. Now she pulled one out, and, fighting to keep the wind from snatching it away, she held it down close so he could stuff the contents of the safe into it. His hands were numb and clumsy with the cold. He was worried about the snow ruining things or about the wind blowing something away.

Some of it was money. He saw that immediately. The rest was a blur.

When the safe was empty they closed it. He forced his stiff arms to cover it again with debris, and then they ran to the house with their treasure.

15

She led him to a cozy room just south of the kitchen. It had a fireplace with logs already laid out, and he lit the fire immediately. They collapsed on the thickly carpeted floor in front of it and sat there, stunned into inertia. Gradually, he peeled off layers of sodden outerwear. Every part of his body either stung or ached. His fingers were bright red with the sudden rush of warmth.

He helped her out of her coat and gloves and clumsily rubbed her hands. She was wooden. Eventually, she forced herself up and left. She returned in a wraparound robe, carrying folded men's clothing. Wordlessly, she handed him the dry clothes and walked out again. By the time she was back with hot tea, he had changed into the old jeans and soft flannel shirt.

They drank the tea side by side in front of the fire.

"Why did you cover the safe back up?" she asked finally. It was the first either of them had spoken since coming inside.

"I don't know," he said. Why had he been compelled to bury it again? Was he simply protecting it from the snow, or did he want to hide it from others? To horde Serian's secrets even before he knew what they were?

They moved the furniture to allow more open space in front of the fire, and then they poured the contents of the bag out onto the floor.

The most obvious thing was the money. Bundles and bundles of it. Twenties. Fifties. Hundreds. Mostly hundreds. Neatly held by rubber bands.

"This is so like him," she said, laughing mirthlessly. "Bram hated banks. And the key . . . He would have insisted on a safe with a key because a combination would have annoyed him."

"There's a lot of money here," Owen said.

She pushed the money aside as though it had no value for her, and she hungrily picked up an old black-and-white snapshot of two women in aprons. On the back was printed *Camille and Celeste*. There was another black-and-white photo, of two grinning little boys holding up catfish they had caught.

"This could be Bram and Al," she said, handing the picture to Owen. There was no writing on the reverse.

She opened a box and uncovered several small wood carvings wrapped in tissue. Another box contained old-fashioned jewelry. Nothing extravagant, but the kind of jewelry ordinary women had worn years ago. And the third box held a delicate, crocheted baby sweater.

There was a leather folder with an old portrait of a woman holding an infant. Her expression was solemn, verging on sadness.

The remainder was papers and letters. Lenore gathered them loosely and handed them to him. "Read everything to me, Owen. Please."

He scanned a sheet. "This is a list of everyone Bram has given gifts to through the years. Do you want me to read you the list?"

"Later," she said impatiently. "What else is there?"

"These sheets describe every piece of art sold. And there are a number of letters here from major artists, nothing very personal, mainly congratulations. And this . . ." Owen unfolded a sheet. "Lenore! Here's a letter from Al."

"Read it," she urged. "Read it!"

Owen held up the soiled piece of sketch paper. There was no salutation, it simply began:

By now I'm gone. I took money but it's just as much mine as yours so I'm not stealing. I've been thinking a lot clearer the last few months and I've been throwing away my pills when you weren't looking. I feel fine without them so that proves I am close to being well.

The bad dreams have stopped. My nights are good and I can sleep in the darkness again. Last night I dreamed I was with Aunt Milly at Arcadia. You and Luke were there too and we were all happy and chasing fireflies like the old days. When I woke up I knew that I had to do something. I can't just keep on the way I have been and hope that everything will someday be good again. I have to take over. And I know you would never agree I am ready so I made the decision myself.

I know you tried hard to make Arcadia for us here and I know how much I owe you. Now that I understand what's going on, I don't like some things much, but I know the burden has been heavy and that you thought you were doing what you had to do so I hold no blame. I'm not leaving out of anger. I am leaving to try to find my own life.

Tell Lenore that I will miss her. As soon as I am strong enough I will come back. That is a promise.

Al

"Damn him! Damn him!" she cried with tears in her eyes. "Bram lied to me! He said Al just disappeared." She took the sheet of paper from Owen and stared down at it as though she could read it. "Why? Why did he lie?"

She clutched the letter to her chest. "I was so worried. I didn't know that Al was better . . . I thought . . . I was afraid he'd gone completely berserk and run away into the countryside to starve to death . . . or to hurt himself . . . or other people. I was . . ." Her voice caught and she drew in a deep breath and blinked hard to fight back the tears. "Why did Bram let me worry like that? He knew how upset I was, thinking about Al out there alone . . . the danger of it and Al's helplessness. I couldn't sleep. I couldn't eat. I even begged Bram to let me go with him when he searched for Al. I . . ."

Her mouth tightened into a hard line, and she fought against the rage, trying to regain control. Owen kept silent, knowing she had to work it out on her own.

When the storm of emotion had abated, she sighed raggedly and handed the letter back to Owen. At her urging, he read it aloud again.

"Maybe Bram was afraid that you would think less of him if you knew what Al's farewell words had been," he suggested.

"He could have kept the details of it from me easily! I couldn't read the words myself. He could have told me a little bit . . . just that Al left on his own terms, sounding sane and able to take care of himself. But no! He lied completely.

He pretended that Al had just vanished. And he pretended to agonize over it with me."

Owen started to say that Serian might have been so hurt and angry over Al's leaving that he hadn't wanted to acknowledge the letter, but he stopped himself. He had lost the desire to defend Bram Serian.

"The safe was my last hope," she said. "We aren't going to find any answers."

"We're finding answers, Lenore. Or clues to answers. What were you expecting? Did you think Serian would have written out a detailed explanation to be revealed after his death like those dramatic scenes in the movies?"

"Yes. I did." She stared into the fire. "I thought . . . out of love or pity or guilt . . . that he would have felt obligated to leave me the truth."

Owen watched her, aching for her, wishing he could confront Bram Serian for her and tear the truth out of the man. She turned to meet his eyes. "My whole life with Bram was a lie. I see that now."

"Sometimes people think they have to lie to protect those they love," Owen said, mouthing that platitude in a futile attempt to ease her pain.

Her mouth twisted into a bitter half-smile. "Oh, if you had said that to me before, I would have been so grateful . . . so eager to cling to that. But if Bram was protecting someone with his lies, it wasn't me.

"I've had a lot of time since he died. Time to think. And I've had my eyes opened through Rossner's investigation and through listening to witnesses . . . and through you, I know the truth now. Bram never loved me. Never. Not as a child or a woman. Whatever reasons he had for wanting me had nothing to do with love."

Owen had the urge to touch her cheek. To cup her face in his hands and draw the pain out of her with his own force of will. Instead he held up the letter. "Let's forget Bram Serian and study this for information. We can beat him, Lenore. We'll dig out the secrets no matter how deeply he's buried them."

She gave a hesitant nod, and her expression of fearful hope and trust crashed through his chest like a fist and lodged in his throat so that he had to force words out.

They puzzled over the letter sentence by sentence. First there was the question about the money. Why would Al have

considered Serian's money as part his? But then Jonas
Watkins had assumed Serian had a trust fund . . . If it was a
family trust fund, then Al may have felt entitled to a portion
of it.

Then there were the references to Al's illness, and pills
and bad dreams and being well.

"I don't understand," Owen said. "I thought Al had some
kind of retardation or brain damage. That's not something a
person recovers from. And this letter . . . it sounds very like
a normal, reasonably educated person wrote it."

Lenore bowed her head. "I let you believe that," she said.
"Because that's the way Bram always wanted it. He didn't
want people to know the truth about Al."

"Which was?"

She hesitated. "Al was fine growing up. Then he went off
to the war in Vietnam and was turned into a . . . I don't know
what the medical term is, but he was very . . . unpredictable.
And he didn't trust people. No one but Bram and me. Everyone else either scared him or made him angry. Sometimes he
imagined he was back in the war and that people were after
him. And he was terrified of the dark.

"The real reason Bram built the studio with no windows
in the walls and with only one door was so that Al would
feel safe in there. It was Al's fortress. And even though
Bram was touchy about his work-in-progress being seen, the
reason he never ever let anyone into the studio was because
that was Al's home, and Al would have been terribly upset
by anyone entering his home whether he was there or not."

Owen considered this new information. "Isn't it strange,"
he said, "how Vietnam keeps popping up. Bram served in
Vietnam just before coming to New York. He told Jonas
Watkins that he lost his brother in Vietnam. He kept a rubbing from the Vietnam memorial wall. His cousin, Al, was
emotionally wounded in Vietnam.

"And then there's you . . . Your father was a soldier in
Vietnam. You're supposed to be from Vietnam . . . only
you're really from Thailand. It feels like everything should
fit together, only I don't know how."

Lenore frowned sadly. "I can't believe Bram never mentioned losing a brother. He never mentioned his family at all.
Even to me."

"I can sympathize with his not wanting to talk about his

brother," Owen admitted quietly. "I lost a brother and I know how hard it is for me to talk about him."

Instantly her expression turned compassionate. "How did your brother die?"

"I'll tell you some other time, but not right now . . . okay?" He turned his attention quickly back to the letter. "It sounds almost as though Al ran away. *Escaped.* Was Bram keeping him from leaving or restricting him here?"

"It didn't seem that way to me then," she said. "It just seemed natural that Bram would watch Al carefully and have rules for him and sometimes even lock him up to keep him from trouble. But now I realize that Al was imprisoned."

"Why did Bram lie about Al's condition? Emotional and psychological war trauma is a well known and pretty well accepted condition. I'm sure people would have been understanding."

She clasped her hands together and held them against her mouth as though afraid to allow herself to speak further. Her dark eyes searched Owen's fearfully. "I should never have told you about Al. You can't write about him in your book. Wherever he is, whatever he's doing . . . writing about him could harm him. It could destroy him."

"Lenore . . . no one is going to ostracize Al because he's—"

"You've got to promise me that he won't be in your book."

Owen had the urge to argue that the vague web of information he had on Al could not possibly do anyone damage, but he saw from her eyes that argument would be dangerous.

"I'll only mention Al in the most general of terms, and I'll clear it with you beforehand. I promise."

She relaxed then, and they went on with their scrutiny of the letter.

"You never heard of an Aunt Milly?" Owen asked.

"Never."

"Well, it sounds like the two cousins had an Aunt Milly in their lives when they were boys. And someone named Luke. Could Luke have been Bram's brother? Damn. There's just so little to go on."

Owen raked his fingers through his hair in frustration and studied the letter again.

"Listen to this, Lenore . . . 'I was with Aunt Milly at Arcadia ... I know you've tried to make Arcadia for us here ...' Doesn't that sound like Arcadia is a real place? Another place. Maybe a place that Bram named this house after."

Lenore's eyes widened. "Another big house somewhere?"

"Or even a town?"

He jumped to his feet, pulling Lenore with him. "Where was that library you showed me?"

Owen thought he'd have to look state by state in the encyclopedias, but instead he found a large North American atlas with the towns and cities listed for each state. California, Florida, Indiana, Kansas, Louisiana, Ohio, Oklahoma and Wisconsin all had Arcadias.

"So," Lenore said, "all we have to do is find a woman named Milly who lives in Arcadia in one of eight states."

"No, we can do better than that. If Aunt Milly lives near the area where Serian was raised then we're looking for flatland. Flat wheat-growing country." He read the list again. "That narrows it down some. And ..." he shook his head. "I have this gut feeling that it's the Kansas Arcadia we want."

"Why?"

"There have been small hints, and ... this may sound strange, but all along I've felt a connection to Bram and I think that's what it is."

"Kansas?" she asked.

"I know it sounds crazy but—"

"Nothing sounds crazy to me."

Owen pulled a couch pillow to the floor, stretched out his legs and basked in the warmth of the fire, letting his mind wander through the new discoveries. Without intending to he fell deeply asleep.

When he woke later the fire was down to a glow and the room was dark. He scrubbed at his face with his hands and tried to force alertness. The room was empty. No Lenore. No letter. No money.

He stumbled upon a bathroom, splashed water on his face and pushed the hair out of his eyes. Then he searched through the silent house, cursing it once again as he took wrong turns, banged his shins in the dark, felt for light switches that weren't there. What if Lenore had gone? What if she'd lied about knowing how to drive and she'd taken the money and disappeared? What if there had been some obscure clue to Al's whereabouts in the letter and she had gone to find him? Or what if she'd decided not to chance a murder conviction and had headed for the border?

He slammed open a door and nearly fell into the kitchen. Lenore was inside, standing there in her robe, feeding trays of frozen food into the microwave. She cast him a coolly amused glance and said, "Maybe you should have slept longer."

Chastened, Owen mumbled a reply and made his way to the long dining table where she had set two places. There were cloth napkins and unlit tapers in pottery candlesticks. She carried the food over, dimmed the overhead lights and lit the candles. A fire roared in the kitchen's stone fireplace, and the windows rattled from the force of the storm outside. She smiled and served. The perfect hostess. As though everything about their circumstances and their surroundings were completely normal. But then what did Lenore Serian know of normal? Very little, he feared.

Normal. Hell, what did he know about normal either? Being raised on a ranch in the middle of nowhere wasn't the average childhood anymore. Who was normal? Holly Danielson maybe. The bright all-American girl from the nice family in the nice neighborhood. It occurred to him that Holly's appeal was very much that promise of wholesomeness, of normalcy.

"Are you thinking of a plan?" Lenore asked.

"Uh . . . no . . ."

She studied him intently. The candlelight bathed her skin with gold and burned in her eyes. He had to look away.

"The clothes fit perfectly," he said.

"They're Al's. He took almost nothing with him."

"There are paint spots on the jeans. Did Al really work as Bram's assistant, or was that just part of the story?"

"I wasn't allowed in to see anything of course, but I got the impression that he helped Bram a lot. Sometimes the supply lists were even written by Al. I remember because Stanley had trouble reading Al's handwriting."

"Supply lists?"

"Just the usual. Canvas and stretcher frames and endless colors of paint. Bram paid Stanley extra to go by a particular store in Manhattan for him every other week."

"You know . . ." Owen's rest had refreshed his mind, and it was running in new directions. "If someone went on a serious search for Al, the art could be a factor in finding him."

"What?"

"The art. If he was a good assistant and enjoyed the work—he might try to get a job somewhere doing something similar."

Lenore frowned.

"Did Bram ever seriously search for Al? By hiring a detective or whatever?"

"No. Why are you asking me in that tone of voice? You sound like you suspect something."

"There's a scrap of paper out there in the two-year-old box that has the name and phone number of a detective agency written on it. And I was just wondering . . ."

"You think Bram hired a detective to search for Al," she said, mulling it over aloud. "Yes. That may be what happened."

"It might be worth looking into. With all that money from the safe, you could hire the same detective and who knows where that might lead."

She frowned thoughtfully. "In terms of finding Al, you mean?"

"More. If Bram was sending a detective after Al, he would have to give the guy information. Places Al might go. People Al might be with."

"But we have to be careful, Owen. If we come close and scare Al, he might disappear forever."

"We'll be careful. I just think we could use Al to pick up a trail back into the past. And who knows . . . if Al is lucid now, he might be able to tell us Bram's entire life history. I don't suppose you have any pictures of Al."

"No," she said regretfully. "Bram never allowed a camera at Arcadia except for the one time he let the art magazine photograph the house."

They ate in silence for several minutes. Owen was conscious of her eyes on him. Her expression was expectant and hopeful.

"We'll think of something," he assured her. "We'll think of something."

What he thought of after dinner was to call Alex. Alex's friend had indeed come through with some information, and Alex was eager to share it.

"You won't believe this," Alex said. "The stuff you wanted about Bram Serian in Vietnam . . . there was no

Bram Serian in Vietnam. No Bram Serian in the service at all during the time frame you specified. No other Serians either in that time period—Cliff checked that in case Bram was a nickname."

Owen sighed and glanced at Lenore. "Somehow, I'm not surprised. I suspected that he might have created the name when he came to New York. Guess that blocks us completely. But thanks, and tell Cliff—"

"Wait! I've got more. You asked about the names from the wall. We weren't sure what you wanted, but they were all reported killed or missing in 1966 and Cliff got you hometowns on them."

"Okay." Owen shifted the phone to his other shoulder so he could write.

"Abcock is from Boise, Idaho. Bachman is from Hutzell, Kansas. Benedict is from Goteen, Mississippi. Gibney is Lafayette, Louisiana. Hamid is Brooklyn, New York, Isaacs is San Francisco, California, Tsosie is Shiprock, New Mexico, Veranza is El Paso, Texas, and Wilson is Brielle, New Jersey. Cliff said he can probably get you more, but he has to know what kind of information you want."

"Thanks, Alex. I'm not sure what else I need. I'll have to get back to you."

"Anything helpful in what I gave you?" Alex asked hopefully.

"Possibly. I don't know yet."

As soon as Owen hung up the phone, he told Lenore that the name Serian was no doubt a fiction.

"What can we do?" she asked, dismayed. "Now we don't even have a name anymore."

"I'm disappointed too," he admitted, "but when you think about it, this could be a break. Now we can stop chasing after a nonexistent family and concentrate on figuring out what Bram's real name was."

Owen considered the new information a moment, then held up the pad he'd written on. "These are the names from the rubbing. Remember one of them was Luther Bachman? Well, guess where he's from ... Hutzell, Kansas. What if Bram's family name was really Bachman? And remember the mention of Luke in Al's letter? What if Luke was short for Luther? And what if Luther Bachman was the brother Bram lost in Vietnam?"

Excitement flared in Lenore's eyes, and she picked up the

phone and thrust it at Owen. "Quick," she said. "Call Arcadia, Kansas, for Bachman and see what happens."

Their excitement faded as they learned that there were no Bachmans listed there at all. Next he asked for Bachmans in or near Hutzell, Kansas. There were no listings in that area either.

Owen refused to give up, but he could not help worrying that Bram's secrets and Lenore's answers were out of his reach. He was also beginning to question the wisdom of finding her father. This was a man who had abandoned the mother and child. Meeting him might be an ugly and destructive experience. In a way Owen thought she might be lucky never to have known the man, and he found himself wondering what it would be like to trade places with her and be fatherless. To wipe all trace of his father away, erasing the indelible imprint of Clancy's character that Owen feared he carried.

Lenore stared down at the phone.

He had to think of something. He couldn't fail her.

"You know . . . there are all those old phone bills Serian saved. We should go over those. The long-distance calls will have the numbers recorded. This Aunt Milly sounds like she was important to them. Maybe there was a call to her sometime through the years. Or other calls to Kansas numbers. It's worth a try."

Lenore rose to go with him to the living room where they had left all of Serian's records, but her enthusiasm was giving way to pessimism. Or perhaps fatalism.

Twenty-two years' worth of Bram Serian's telephone bills were piled on one end of a giant couch. Mechanically, Owen sorted through the years of long-distance calls, approaching the task as if it were a dull but simple assignment. Lenore lit the huge fireplace and watched him. He could feel her eyes, and he wished he could crawl inside her head and see how she saw him. Was he just a means to an end for her?

When he came across the 316 area code in Kansas he allowed himself no expectations. Garland, KS the printed statement read. He opened the atlas but could find no Garland, Kansas. Lenore's eyes were dark and quiet. "What can it hurt?" he said as he picked up the telephone.

"Hello," answered an elderly male voice over the miles.

"Hello, is this the Bachmans'?"

"Huhh? Wrong number."

"Wait, please, is Milly there?"

Silence. Owen was afraid for a moment that he had been disconnected.

"Milly? Now you wouldn't be callin' Milly Corwin at this number, would ya?"

"Yes." His heart began to pound in his ears. "Milly Corwin."

"Shoot ... she's been gone for years. Phone company gave us her number after she moved."

"Are you in Garland?"

"We're kinda between Garland and Arcadia. Same as Milly was."

Owen's gaze flicked up to Lenore's face, but he had to drop it immediately. It was too much. The pounding in his ears and the sudden electric heat in her eyes.

"Do you know how I can reach Milly?"

"Well now," the old man's voice became sly. "Just how do I know you have any business with Milly?"

Owen knew immediately that he had to be careful. This was a man who sounded a lot like Clancy Byrne, and one hint of lying could make the old guy decide that Owen was a car repossessor or a spy for the IRS. Yet the unvarnished truth was far too convoluted and unbelievable to tell.

"This is Owen Byrne," he said. "From over in the Flint Hills."

"Umm. Can't say as I know any Byrnes."

"My mother's people were Hadleys. From over near Maynard. Had a wheat operation there."

"I did know of some Hadleys. Think they were from round Chanute. Any kin to you?"

"Can't say as I knew 'em."

The old man hesitated. "So what's this about Milly, then?" he asked.

Owen gathered himself and took a chance. "Well, actually I was wanting to talk to Milly Corwin about those nephews of hers."

"Oh, yeah ... them boys she was so crazy for. Well, I tell ya what, Mama and Milly was in the same church group and all. Likely as not she knows where Milly got to."

"Could I ask her?"

"Sure can. She's visitin' sick kin tonight, but you just call back here tomorrow and she'll be around."

"Could I give you a number and have her call collect soon as she comes in?"

"Uh uhhh, I ain't havin' no long distance on my phone."

"But ... collect ... no charge to you."

"Nah. You just call here tomorrow. Round eleven would be good. She'll be home cookin' my noon dinner then."

Owen thanked him and hung up. Lenore was very still. He could tell she was holding her breath.

"I think we've struck Aunt Milly's trail," he told her. "Her name is Milly Corwin. I'm supposed to call back tomorrow to get her number. It's an hour earlier there, so it'll be noon our time."

Lenore appeared so stunned that it worried him. "Hey." He reached to touch her arm and discovered that she was trembling. "Are you all right?"

She nodded.

"Let me get you something," he said, though he had no idea what until he was in the kitchen and saw the tea bags in a jar on the counter. He heated water and carried fragrant mugs of tea back toward the living room.

"Thank you," she said.

He turned off the glaring overhead fixtures, and the room was instantly transformed, bathed in the soothing glow of a small shaded lamp and the hypnotic dancing light of the fire. She cupped her hands around the steaming mug, sighed, and settled back with her legs curled beneath her. In spite of their progress she seemed melancholy.

They finished their tea in silence; then she rose and drifted over to one of the long windows flanking the fireplace. Owen couldn't tell if she was staring out at the storm or looking at her own reflection in the expanse of black glass.

"I'm sorry we haven't found any clues to your father yet," he told her. "Maybe Aunt Milly will know something."

She continued to stare at the dark glass. The face reflected there was a gaunt mask with empty holes for eyes. A ghost face.

"Tomorrow the trial starts again, Owen. Time is running out for me."

"I'll keep working on this," he promised. "I won't stop."

She turned her head to look at him over her shoulder. "You won't find him in time."

"In time for what?"

"Before I'm convicted and sent away."

"Lenore . . ." he protested. He started to say she shouldn't think like that, but he realized how meaningless the words were. The woman was on trial for murder. She had every right to pessimism.

He got up to add more wood to the fire. It was a soothing task and he lingered over it, using one of the heavy hand-wrought implements to shift the logs and position the new ones. She moved from the window to stand beside him and watch. Her nearness was unsettling. He hung the poker up as an excuse to move away from her.

Then a shower of sparks exploded, forcing them both back a step and somehow closer together. She turned toward him, just inches away, and he could smell the fragrance in her hair and see down the shadowy wrapped neckline of her robe. Everything stopped. Every cell in his body waited. He could hear the whisper of her breathing and see the faint pulse in her slender neck. Without conscious effort his hand lifted to trace her cheek. It was so fiercely angled, yet so soft and smooth to the touch. Slowly, she raised her hand to his face in return, and the feather-light braille of her finger-tips made his blood burn.

He caught her hand and held it to his lips. Her wrist was so thin. He brushed his mouth against the delicate underside.

"Are you real?" he asked.

"I don't know," she whispered.

He drew her closer, pressing against the length of her. Gently, he kissed her mouth.

"Do you want me, Owen?"

"Yes."

"Then take me. Now. Make me real."

He pulled her robe open. She was naked beneath it. Golden skin and small perfect breasts with dusky nipples. Dark mysterious triangle. He wanted to consume every inch of her, but he was careful. Gentle. Controlled. Careful not to offend sensibilities. Not to play too rough. Not to push too far.

She closed her eyes, seeming to enjoy his soft caresses and his lips on her mouth and neck. Her breathing quickened. He rubbed his palms across her taut nipples and cupped her breasts with his hands. Careful. Gentle. Afraid that any moment he would startle her into running away.

He kissed his way down from her neck, teasing with his

tongue, until the firm bud of her nipple was inside his mouth. Her low moan made him shiver.

Slowly, he fumbled with his shirt buttons and she surprised him by reaching for the zipper on his jeans. Her hand closed around his erection, making him gasp with the pleasure and surprise of it.

When he could stand it no longer, he swung her into his arms and carried her to one of the giant couches, then sat down with her across his lap and kissed her till he was dizzy from the taste of her mouth.

"Lie down," she said, pulling away from him.

He lay back against the soft pillows and looked up at her as she shrugged the open robe from her shoulders. He had never seen such beauty. A wave of reverence filled him, followed by amazement and wonder.

Slowly, she straddled his thighs and touched him. He watched her hand on the thick shaft of his erection. Watched her breasts sway in the firelight. Watched her roll the condom down over the length of him. Then he closed his eyes, and she traced his eyelids and mouth and chest with her tongue.

"Look at me, Owen."

He obeyed and her black eyes took him, sucked him inside and spun him into their darkness. Then she lifted herself and eased forward so that he felt her, wet and hot against his belly.

"Don't close your eyes," she whispered. "Look at me."

She slid downward, swallowing him in her velvet heat. Swallowing him with her black, black eyes. Swallowing him so completely that he would have to be born again or die forever.

She was asleep. Lying close beside him beneath a blanket on the couch. He stayed very still and listened to the even rhythm of her breathing, letting her rest as long as possible. Gray dawn light was filtering in when he finally moved his numb arm and said, "Lenore . . ."

Her eyes flew open.

"It's all right. It's morning."

She relaxed and pushed the hair back from her face. "I was dreaming," she said. "I was small and barefoot, walking with my mother. Holding her hand. I wanted to see her face, but she was so much taller than I was, and every time I tried to look up at her the sun hurt my eyes. So I looked at the sack she was carrying in her other hand. It· moved and bulged.

"We went down to the canal. She knelt and opened the sack and it was full of squirming, wet eels. 'For luck,' she said, and dumped the eels into the water, and I knew that she meant the luck for me and that she was trying to protect me. Then she turned and I was finally going to see her face only the eels became a serpent that lashed out of the water to grab her. And I couldn't hold on to her. I couldn't save her."

Owen hugged her closer to him.

"Do you believe in the power of dreams?" she asked.

"I believe there are powers I know nothing about," he answered carefully.

She nodded. "I've thought about my father almost every day for years. I seldom think of my mother." She paused. "Yet it's only my mother who comes in my dreams."

"Maybe that's because you live in America," he offered, "and so you feel like you're living close to your American father, while your mother, and your mother's country, is a mystery. Dreams are full of mystery."

"Or maybe it's because she's dead."

"What?"

"Maybe she comes in my dreams because she's dead. Because that's the only way she can come to me."

"Well . . ." Owen said. "Maybe." He leaned to the right so he could see out the window. "We're going to have a hard time getting out of here with all that snow."

"Joe Volpe comes for me every morning."

"Will he come in a snowplow? It's a long ways from your front door to the road." Owen was suddenly annoyed. He focused it on the problem of the snow, but it had more to do with the idea of the sharp-eyed, hot-tempered Volpe driving alone with Lenore to court every morning.

"What did Serian do when you were snowed in?" he asked.

"He'd get out his tractor. Snow was another excuse to play with his tractor."

"You mean there's a snow blade for the tractor?"

She shrugged. "It's all down in the equipment shed. No one but Bram ever used it."

"You get ready and do something about breakfast," he announced, enjoying the thought of outdoor work. "I'll go down there and take a look."

He found insulated coveralls and gloves and snow boots in a mud room closet near the back door. They were slightly larger in girth than Al's clothes had been so he suspected that he was wearing something of Bram Serian's. He refused to think about it, blocking it from his thoughts along with the thoughts of Mike Wheeler that had surfaced since waking with Lenore in his arms.

The equipment shed turned out to be a fairly new enclosed building not unlike an oversized garage. Inside was a shiny John Deere tractor, one of the open traditionally styled models. He surveyed the line of implements with amusement. Bram Serian had not scrimped on anything. He had every fancy gadget available to hook to his tractor—gadgets that a true farmer would have considered either luxuries or toys.

Owen started the tractor, hooked up the snow blade in front and went to work. The snow was deep, but Serian had lined the drive with trees and bushes so it was easy to keep on course. When he was nearly to the gate, he looked back and felt a wave of satisfaction at the smooth path he'd carved.

He opened the gate and left it standing open while he pulled out to do a turnaround in the road. Then he decided that, since there was plenty of time, he should plow down the road a ways toward town just to make sure no one got stuck later. He plowed all the way to Deputy Havlik's pens of barking dogs, where he saw that the deputy had already been out with his tractor and the road was clear from his place on.

Owen used Havlik's driveway to turn around in, and as he was maneuvering the tractor around, a car drove past on the road. It was too early for Volpe to be picking up Lenore, and the car didn't look like the one he remembered Volpe driving, but who else could it be? There were no other houses in that direction. He put the tractor into its highest gear and rumbled back to Arcadia.

When he got up to the house, he saw that the car wasn't there. The driver had probably been lost and was now stuck somewhere on the unplowed road beyond Arcadia. He would have to take the tractor up toward the dead end and look for the car, which was probably stuck in a snowbank. But just as Owen was turning the wheel he caught sight of tire tracks going around the equipment shed. Puzzled, he drove closer, climbed down and walked around to the back of the shed. A car was parked back there, out of sight of the house and the drive and even the front of the shed.

Cautiously, Owen approached the car, but it was empty. He thought maybe it was Bram Serian's car, which someone had finally brought home from wherever it had been abandoned by fleeing partygoers so many months ago. But why had it been pulled around the shed?

He tried the door and it was unlocked so he opened it and peered inside. The car was clean except for a paper coffee cup. He opened the glove compartment, but there was nothing in it. Straightening, he saw two small paperback books on the backseat. He reached over the seat for them and read the cover of the top one. *The Confessions of St. Augustine: The Classic Autobiography of the Man Who Journeyed from the Darkness of Worldly Ambition to the Changeless Light of Grace.* Beneath that was the same Kierkegaard he'd seen in Bram Serian's bedroom—*Fear and Trembling and The Sickness Unto Death.*

He carried the books with him to the house, utterly confused, afraid to let his imagination loose. He went around to one of the back doors and stepped inside to shed his plowing garb; then he headed for the kitchen. And as he went down the hall he distinctly heard Lenore's voice call, "Jimmy?"

"Oh," she said, when Owen entered the kitchen.

"Who's here, Lenore? Is that Bram's car behind the shed?"

"Yes, it is Bram's car. I loaned it to someone to use."

"But why is it behind the shed?"

"Here," she said, handing him a plate of toaster waffles. "Eat quickly. You have to leave soon. Before Joe Volpe gets here."

"But who did you loan the car to? Who's here? Whose books are these?" He dropped the paperbacks onto the counter.

Her eyes flicked nervously to the books and then to the doorway behind Owen. She was dressed in a shapeless brown suit with her hair pulled severely into a knot at the nape of her neck, and she seemed almost like a stranger.

"I do have friends, Owen. And they park where they like. Now, you have to hurry."

"What's going on?" Owen demanded. "Are you hiding someone from me?"

She fixed him with a glare of controlled anger. "You can't know everything, Owen."

"You didn't mind me knowing pretty much everything about you last night, did you?"

She laughed contemptuously. "You men are all alike. You think that having sex is the same thing as knowing someone."

The sting of her words was so fierce, he couldn't answer.

"Get out of here," she said, dismissing him.

"No."

She whirled but he caught her arm and spun her back around to face him. Suddenly, she was looking at him from some distant, untouchable place.

"I don't have time for games, Owen."

"Is that what this is to you, a game?"

"No," she said evenly. "This is a murder trial. My murder trial."

He let go of her and dropped his hands to his sides, chastened. "I'm sorry."

"If that's true, then please, hurry."

She waited outside the bathroom door while he changed to a clean set of his own clothes. She had already gathered his things together, so there was nothing more to do but leave.

"Will you still make the phone call to Milly?" she asked as she walked him out to the front door.

"Yes. At noon."

She nodded. "Make it from the hotel. I'll tell them at the desk and leave my key there for you. Then . . . maybe you could just wait in the room and I'll be there as soon as court dismisses for lunch. That way the press won't see us together, and you can tell me what you find out about Milly."

"Right," he said, suppressing the urge to reply with a sarcastic "Yes, boss," at the same time that he was feeling relief because he would get to be with her.

She reached for the door handle, then hesitated. "I'm very grateful, Owen. No one could have tried as hard as you have."

"It's not over," he said. "We'll keep working on it." He wanted to kiss her good-bye but didn't because this wasn't the same woman he'd made love to last night. This was the distant, guarded woman of the courtroom.

He drove away from Arcadia tortured by questions. Who was she hiding? What secrets was she keeping? Why?

16

The drive from Arcadia to the courthouse was just under thirty minutes. It was very early when Owen arrived, so he parked and walked the three blocks to the coffee shop for breakfast.

He felt strange. As though he had emerged from a timeless dark period. Or a long surreal dream. He also felt extremely agitated, angry, and helpless. He got out his notebook and began writing things down. Committing the puzzle to paper, where it was more manageable.

The waitress came by to refill his cup for the third time, saying, "Here ya go, hon. You look like you could use more of this."

He barely glanced up at her, before bending back over his notebook, detailing what he thought had happened, summarizing what he knew and what he hoped to find out. The writing steadied him. Calmed him. When he was satisfied that he had it all down, he straightened to finish his coffee. The notebook was still open. Idly, he turned to a clean page and began making marks. Circles that he filled with question marks. Little lines that evolved into a drawing of Arcadia's gate. Then he printed—

JIMMY?

KIERKEGAARD? CONFESSIONS OF ST. AUGUSTINE?

WHO IS JIMMY?

WHY IS SHE HIDING HIM?

And he was angry once again. Angry and hurt by her secrets and by the way she had so coldly ordered him away.

"Owen! What got you here so early?" It was Holly's voice. He looked up to see Holly and Marilyn. Marilyn waved and continued speaking to the waitress, but Holly crossed to the table and leaned over his shoulder.

"Wha'cha' doing?" she asked brightly. "Got a hot lead?"

He closed his notebook and forced a smile. "Hi, Holly. How's the news business?"

"So-so." She sat down opposite him. "Kind of a dull weekend actually." She played with the sugar dispenser. "Did you find my note Saturday night?"

"I did. Thanks for the invitation, but it didn't work out."

"Mmm." She tore off a corner of a paper napkin and rolled it into a ball. "How's your work going?"

"Fine."

"Must be tough," she said. "Working so hard with no guarantees."

"I try not to think of it that way." He glanced over at Marilyn. "Are you two going to sit down and have breakfast?"

"No. We just came by to pick up the group take-out order. We do it on our way in to the courthouse every morning, and then everyone gathers for coffee and rolls before trial time. If I'd known you were ever going to get here early, I'd have told you about it."

"Next time I'll know," he said.

She continued shredding and rolling the napkin. "Marilyn wants to drive out to a diner by the highway for lunch today. Three people are taking cars. I'll probably ride with Pat and you can come with us or—"

"Not today . . . thanks. I've got phone work to do."

Disappointment registered on her face. "Ohhh . . . are you sure?"

"Yes. I've got some important leads I need to follow up right away."

Marilyn joined them then. "It will be another five minutes," she announced. "Someone drank up all their coffee and they have to make a new pot." She frowned at Owen. "You look like hell. Bad night?"

"He works too much," Holly said.

"Do we know who's on the stand this morning?" Owen asked.

"George Fugate. Owner of the hardware store where she bought the lamp."

Owen tapped his pen absently against his hand for a moment. "The neighbor kid's first name is Tommy, right? Not Jimmy."

"Right," both women answered.

"Has there been a Jimmy connected with the case?"

The two women exchanged glances and Marilyn shrugged. "All I can think of is James Collier. I seem to remember he went by Jimmy at times."

"James Collier?" The name was very familiar to Owen, but he couldn't quite place it.

"He's the vanishing witness," Marilyn explained.

"The vanishing lover," Holly insisted with a smirk.

"No one knows that for sure, Holly. That's what keeps the mystery fun."

"Refresh my memory," Owen said. "What were the details on Collier?"

Marilyn leaned forward, savoring her role as informant. "What we do know is that Collier was at Arcadia the night of the murder, and there were rumors that he was there for a romantic liaison. The police have been hot to talk to him, and the prosecution would give somebody's left nut to get him on the stand ... but the man disappeared. Pouf. No trace of him."

"The weird part about it," Holly added, "is that he was not the type of man you'd expect to be involved in this ... or to disappear either. He was a brother in the Catholic church ... not quite a priest but almost ... and he taught at a very prestigious boys' school."

"A *prominent* citizen," Marilyn stressed. "He wrote articles on morality and served on dozens of committees to put God back into the schools and teach teens abstinence. That kind of thing."

The facts sunk into Owen like acid-tipped arrows. Jimmy ... James. It would be natural for a religious man to read Kierkegaard and St. Augustine.

Holly grinned at the expression on Owen's face. "The plot thickens, huh?"

"You weren't here for the early stuff with the grand jury and the pretrial hearings so you kind of missed out on the excitement over Collier," Marilyn explained. "Everyone wanted to know what a man like Brother James was doing at Arcadia in the first place. The rumor was that he was lovesick and obsessed. A man undone. But no one ever got a chance to ask him because as soon as his name surfaced in the investigation, James Collier vanished."

"I can come up with some theories about what happened to him," Holly announced smugly. "Lenore seduced him into helping her kill Serian; then when the heat came down she killed Collier too. But with the second body she did a better job of disposal."

The waitress called over to let them know that the take-out order was ready. Marilyn went to the cash register and started digging in her purse.

"Coming with us?" Holly asked.

"Not yet," Owen said, attempting to sound normal. "I'll be over in a few minutes."

Holly made no move to join Marilyn, and he could tell that she was going to offer to wait for him so he quickly mumbled something about the bathroom and escaped. He stayed in the little cubicle a long time, alternating between an urge to punch holes in the wall and a draining, abject despair. Lenore was hiding James Collier at Arcadia. The missing lover. Every explanation he could find for that was ugly and sordid. Finally, when he was certain that it was safe, he emerged and returned to the table.

His notebook and pen were still on the tabletop, but the notebook had been opened to the first blank page and on it was a message from Holly. IF WE AREN'T UP NEAR THE COURTROOM YOU CAN FIND US DOWNSTAIRS IN THE HALL NEAR THE VENDING MACHINES. She had signed it H & M . . . Holly and Marilyn.

He tore out the note, crumpled it and dropped it in the ashtray, then left the coffee shop. Snow was piled everywhere, not in natural drifts but in long, dirty berms that had been scraped together by snow plows and individuals wielding shovels. He hunched his shoulders and walked slowly, certain that he must have changed form, that he appeared as brutally foolish as he felt.

The courthouse came into view. He still had a job to do. A book to write. Obligations to be met. Money to earn.

He had to focus on that and pull himself together.

He sat down in the pew beside Holly with just minutes to go before court convened. Both the prosecution and defense were already seated at their tables. He avoided looking in Lenore's direction.

Holly gave him a strangely quiet greeting without any eye contact, but Pat Melville, sitting on her other side, leaned around immediately with "Is it true? You can't sit here without telling."

Owen stared at her and Pat laughed. "Don't look at me like that. I just want to know if you really got to see Arcadia."

"How did you . . . ?" His bewilderment was such that he couldn't finish the question.

"Major mistake, sweetie. You were on a pay phone here in the courthouse and a vigilant reporter overheard part of your conversation. It was the major gossip over coffee this morning."

"That's where you were this weekend, isn't it?" Holly asked accusingly.

"Yes. I did get to see the place."

"Wellll . . ." Pat urged. "Tell us!"

"It's almost indescribable," he said. "Like it was built to be a haunted house."

"What was *she* like?" Holly asked, sounding spiteful.

"I can't figure her out," he said, trying to keep his bitterness in check. "I don't know what she's like."

Holly frowned. "What about the rumors that she and that sharky-looking detective . . . what's his name . . ."

"Volpe," Pat inserted.

"Yeah. That she and Volpe are an item . . . Did you see any evidence of that?"

"He drives her in every morning, but I wouldn't call that evidence of anything."

Pat reached over and patted his hand. "That's okay," she said. "We understand. You can't tell us much because that would blow your book scoop." She nudged Holly. "But nothing says we can't be green with envy . . . right, Holly?"

Holly did not respond. Her manner was uncharacteristically subdued. Owen suspected that her feelings were hurt, both by his disappearing act at the coffee shop and by the discovery that he had kept his trip to Arcadia from her.

"It's showtime," someone behind them said in a loud whisper, and once again the lumbering machinery of the people versus Lenore Serian came to life.

George Fugate was a dour-faced man in a sagging brown suit that had no doubt served for years as his funeral and wedding attire. He had the righteous manner of a soul called to duty.

Spencer Brown took him through a brief history of Fugate Hardware and Dry Goods, establishing the man as a respected member of the community, a good merchant and a shrewd observer of human behavior. Then Brown jumped to the day of the lamp purchase. Fugate's store log from that day was entered into evidence as well as the specific handwritten receipt for Lenore's purchases.

"Now, Mr. Fugate, could you relate for us what happened and what went through your mind . . . what your thoughts were . . . when Mrs. Serian entered your store."

"Certainly. I recall it all well. I heard the bell at the top of the door and knew that someone had entered my establishment so I went up to the front. I was very surprised to see that it was Mrs. Serian."

"Why were you surprised?"

"Because in all her years of living out there she had not come in more than a dozen times. And when she had come in she had always been in the company of her husband."

"What happened then?"

"I greeted her as I greet all customers, usually commenting on the type of weather the day has brought."

"And what was her response?"

"She said hello but she was acting very nervous. Very . . . shifty. Looking back over her shoulder and all around like she was worried about someone seeing her."

"Did she browse through the store then, like a normal shopper?"

"Objection, your honor!" Rossner called without rising from his seat.

"Rephrase that last question, Mr. Brown," the judge instructed.

"What did Mrs. Serian do next?"

"She didn't look around or waste a second. She just handed me two shopping lists."

"Is it standard procedure in your store for customers to use lists even though they are there in person and could simply tell you what they want?"

"Yes. It kind of goes back to the old ways of doing things and I like to keep the old ways. Customers usually come in and look around a little; then they give me a list and we make small talk or they look around some more while I fill the order."

"So it would have been unusual for Mrs. Serian to come in and hand you one list and then tell you out loud that she also wanted a lamp and oil?"

"Yes. That would have been unusual."

"You said there were two pieces of paper, Mr. Fugate. Was one list so long that it filled a page and had to be continued onto another?"

"No, that wasn't the case at all. The first paper had a list of seven items that did not nearly fill the page. It was written by Natalie Raven, who was the usual list writer for the household and who usually brought her list in personally to me, and it was her customary—"

"Objection, your honor," Rossner said, shaking his head in disgust. "Is Mr. Fugate a handwriting expert as well as a storekeeper?"

There was a brief sidebar sparked by this, and then Fugate was back in business, with his statements amended to reflect that he had become familiar with Natalie Raven's lists and the one presented to him that day appeared to be one of her lists.

"Please tell us now, Mr. Fugate, what was on the second piece of paper Mrs. Serian handed you that day?"

"It was a separate list in completely different . . . It was a list that looked to me to be made by a different person than Natalie Raven because Miss Raven always printed her lists very neatly and this was just scribbled out. One glass oil-burning lamp. Two large jars oil. That was all that was on it."

"Would there have been enough room on Natalie Raven's list for the lamp and the oil to have been added at the bottom?"

"Definitely."

"Did you draw any conclusions—strike that." Brown paused and studied his notes. "Could you see any reason for there being two lists?"

"I assumed . . . My common sense told me that the long list was Natalie Raven's list of household needs and the other . . . the lamp and the oil . . . had been requested by someone else and that Natalie Raven had not been asked to add the lamp and oil to her larger list."

"Someone who, for whatever reasons, did not tell Natalie Raven to add the lamp and oil to the big list for the house?"

"Yes."

Brown then led Fugate through a description of tabulating the bill and packing the purchases in the car, dwelling on how Lenore had carried out the lamp and oil and how she had put it in first so that he was forced to pile other things on top of it even though he was concerned about breakage.

Owen could not concentrate. And he could not take notes because his writing hand was clenched into a fist. The implication was that Lenore had written the order for the lamp and oil, and Owen knew that to be impossible. Not only had she not written it, she might not have known what was on it at all. Why had she kept something so vital from Rossner?

Lenore was protecting someone. That was the only logical explanation. How had he missed seeing that before? All of her odd behavior, all the secrets she kept from her own attorney . . . she was shielding someone else. She was willing to sacrifice herself for someone else. James Collier no doubt. A lover who had given up his faith and his calling for her.

Had it been James Collier who wrote the order for the glass oil lamp and two jars of oil? Had it been James Collier who plotted with her to get rid of Serian? Or could James have acted without her knowledge—so desperate to possess her that he had to destroy the man who was in his way . . . yet not so desperate that he didn't try to make it appear an accident.

Or had Lenore used James Collier to kill Bram, just as she was using Owen to find her father? Had she used Collier to plan an accident and then the accident went wrong and now she was hiding Collier because with his testimony the state would have absolute proof of her guilt whereas now all they had was a circumstantial case?

Brown finished with the witness, and Rossner launched into his cross, darting and nipping at George Fugate's testimony, inflicting tiny wounds.

"And so you're saying, Mr. Fugate . . . Is it fair to say, Mr. Fugate . . . Is it true, Mr. Fugate . . ." The attorney ridiculed the man and his version of events and his claim to recognize all his customers' handwriting. In the end, he even managed to elicit a festering resentment from Fugate. The man had been angry for fifteen years over the fact that Serian bought most of what he needed through Stanley Cantor and not through Fugate Hardware and Dry Goods. As far as George Fugate was concerned, the Serians deserved whatever happened.

Fugate left the stand and Owen allowed himself his first look at Lenore. The sight of her straight back and slender neck pierced his chest. Lenore. Lenore. The scent of her body was still on him. What a fool he had been to believe she was his. Or even that there was a chance she could be his. She had been using him. Every word and gesture and touch had been a lie.

Suddenly he was overcome with a wave of something so intense that he could not put a name to it. Longing? Yearning? Desire was too simple and too purely physical. Yet it was physical as well as emotional. A hunger in both body and spirit.

He thought of her. The slender golden body. The blackness of her eyes. The erotic feel of her hair spilling across his chest. Yet, try as he might, he could not recapture the full memory of their joining. It was lost. Leaving an emptiness inside him that could only be satisfied by having her again.

Oh, God . . . was she guilty? Completely guilty? Fractionally guilty? Guilty of murder? Guilty of conspiracy? Guilty of using and betraying him? What proof did he have? Conjecture could not establish guilt. He had to put aside his anger and jealousy . . . yes, jealousy . . . that ugly emotion he'd not believed himself capable of . . . He had to beat it all back and put his rational self in charge again. Not just for his work but for Lenore, too. He could not condemn her on so little. Not when there was a shadow of a doubt left that she might be innocent.

"And so Dr. Oliver . . ." Charlie Rossner was saying, and Owen realized he'd missed Spencer Brown's entire direct on Dr. Samuel Oliver, the psychiatrist that the prosecution had found to offer expert opinions on pyrophobia, or fear of fire.

". . . in your experience with pyrophobics . . . did you, Doctor, ever know of a pyrophobic who voluntarily went to the scene of a fire as Bram Serian did in his search for art materials?"

"No. But there are individual anomalies in every condition."

"And did you ever know of a pyrophobic who used a butane lighter with what has been described as a 'monster flame'?"

"No. But again, there are anomalies to be considered."

"But a person who went voluntarily to fire scenes and used a large-flamed butane lighter to light his cigarettes would not be within your definition"—Rossner waved a medical journal containing one of Oliver's writings—"of a pyrophobic or a person who was afraid of fire, would he?"

"No. He would not."

"And is it not true, Doctor, that you never met Bram Serian and that you have no direct medical knowledge of him?"

"That's true."

"Is it not true that in all the records you looked at and all the accounts you heard there is no indication that Bram Serian ever sought psychiatric help for pyrophobia or any other fear of *anything?*"

"That's true."

The hands of the clock reached twelve. Owen closed his notebook and gathered his coat and bag. Both Holly and Pat eyed him quizzically. "Phone calls," he whispered to Holly. "See you after lunch."

As he slid out of the pew Lenore turned and glanced over her shoulder at him. The sudden eye contact caught him off guard and he missed a beat. Forgot to keep moving. By the time he collected himself and ducked away he was certain that both Holly and Pat had noticed. Probably the whole courtroom had noticed.

Paranoid now about the potential for intrigue, he circled the block, went through an alley and entered the hotel through the delivery door. The desk clerk knew who he was immediately and gave him the key Lenore had left.

The key opened the door to the bedroom where he had had his interview with her. He entered the silent room and sat down beside the phone, then mechanically dialed the number.

"Hello," said a woman's voice after three rings.

"Yes . . . I called last night about Milly Corwin."

The woman chuckled. "Ain't that the strangest thing. We were just talkin' about Milly after church last week and here comes this phone call."

"That's strange," he agreed.

"Milly had this number back when she lived here with

Lois. I'm surprised my husband figured out who you was talkin' about."

"I knew right off, Neddy!" a man yelled in the background.

"Do you know where Milly's living now?" Owen asked.

"I'd say I do. Milly writes to us regular from that place. It's called Golden Age Village. And it's right outside Wichita. She says it's pretty fancy—private apartments and such—but you know there was nobody like Milly for puttin' on airs and if ya ask me a old folks home is a old folks home, and it's about like puttin' a dress on a pig tryin' ta make it into somethin' else."

"Would you have her address or phone number there?"

"Got it right here for ya. Called three ladies in my church group ta make sure I had it right."

She read him the information; then he thanked her and finally convinced her that he had to hang up. He could just imagine the buzzing he'd started. The ladies in the church group would be talking about Milly's caller for weeks.

He called the number in Wichita.

"Milly Corwin speaking," said a precise elderly voice.

"Hello, Miz Corwin? This is Owen Byrne. I was just talking to Neddy in Arcadia. Actually I called the number trying to reach you, and she told me you were living in Wichita now."

"Do I know you, young man?"

"No. You don't. This is hard to explain, but if you'll just bear with me a moment."

"As long as it doesn't cost me," she agreed cautiously.

"I'm not a salesman," Owen assured her. Then he hesitated, wondering how to explain what he was. "What I'm calling about is your nephews."

"And what about my nephews?"

"Bram and Al, right? And ... Luke?"

"Bram and Al and Luke! Is this a hoax?! I'll have the police on you, young man. I may be old but I am neither senile nor confused, so you can just pack your bag of tricks and go try to swindle someone else."

"No! Please. This is no hoax. This is serious and I've had a very hard time tracking you down. They may have changed their names. I realize I might not have the names right."

"They're dead, aren't they?" she said softly. "That's what

you're calling to tell me, isn't it? I knew . . ." She stopped herself abruptly. "Well, say what you've got to say."

"I'm sorry. One of them is dead. I'm very sorry."

"Oh dear. Dear me . . . who?"

"It was Bram."

"Bram? How could that boy have called himself Bram?"

"Serian," Owen added. "Bram Serian."

"Lordy me. My sister must be spinning in her grave." She was silent for a moment, absorbing the news. "But the other one is alive? My other boy is fine?" Her voice rose on a hopeful note.

"No one knows where Al is, but he was alive and well when his sister-in-law last saw him."

"Al . . . I can't believe they both changed their names. Wait, did you say sister-in-law?"

"Yes. Bram was married. I'm calling partly on behalf of his widow. Someone would have contacted you sooner but it wasn't known that you existed. We just recently found a mention of you in an old letter."

"Those boys . . ." she sighed sadly.

"I need to see you . . . to talk to you about your nephews . . . to find out the facts. If I could—"

"Now you hold on there," she said resolutely. "If the boys were keeping secrets, then I ought to respect that and keep my silence."

Frantically, Owen cast about for an argument to sway her. He was so close to Serian's past. He was not about to let it slip away.

"You'd be helping your nephew's widow. All the unanswered questions about her husband are going to weigh on her the rest of her life. And you'd be helping Al, because maybe if we knew more about him then we could find him and make sure he's all right."

"Why wouldn't he be all right?"

"Well . . . the reason he lived with his brother was that he had a lot of problems. Emotional problems. Problems coping with other people."

"You mean he wasn't quite right in the head?"

"Yes. And we don't know if he's doing okay now or not."

She sighed. "I'm the keeper of the family, you know. When I'm gone there won't be a family anymore. It will be buried with me. The boys didn't want anything to do with it.

I thought they'd change with age, but there was too much bitterness."

She sighed again. "If Benjamin's mind isn't right, I guess I'm partly to blame for that."

"Could you help, then? Could you answer some questions?"

"Maybe a few. If it would help find my missing boy."

"Could I come see you tomorrow?"

"Suit yourself."

"I'll get a flight to Wichita as soon as I can . . . tonight or tomorrow morning."

She was crying. Very softly. Trying to disguise it.

"Is there anyone I can call? A friend or neighbor who could come sit with you?"

"Young man, there is nothing that you or anyone else can do for me. Good-bye."

Adrenaline rushed through Owen's veins as he called the airlines and booked a flight to Wichita that night. This was it. In just a matter of hours he would possess the truth. He would unlock the mysteries and capture Bram Serian. His book would make history. Maybe he would even find the answers Lenore so desperately wanted. Maybe he would end up helping her in spite of everything.

He tried not to consider the expense. After he returned the rental car and paid off the bill, the trip to see Milly Corwin would just about finish what was left of his money. After which he had no idea how he would manage to eat and pay his transportation costs. But he couldn't let that stop him. He wouldn't let that stop him. This was it.

There were sounds from out in the hall, and Owen went through the connecting door to the war room as Paul Jacowitz entered, followed by Rossner, then Riley, Lenore and Volpe. Rossner and Jacowitz were deep into a trial discussion and barely acknowledged Owen. Volpe helped Lenore out of her cape. Her eyes were full of questions. Owen refused to meet them or give her any sign as to the success of his call.

"Excuse us," Lenore said to Rossner. "I need to speak with Owen privately for a few minutes."

Rossner waved them away and Owen followed her to the

bedroom. "Did you talk to her?" Lenore demanded as soon as the door was closed.

Owen sat down, telling himself that all he wanted to do was maintain a professional demeanor, but realizing that he also had a desire to torture her.

"About the call?" he asked.

"Of course about the call. Did you get Aunt Milly?"

"Yes. I did. She lives in Kansas. I'm flying to Wichita tonight and meeting with her tomorrow morning."

"You couldn't just ask her everything on the phone?"

Owen started to explain, but he stopped himself. He owed Lenore Serian no explanations.

"No. I couldn't."

She crossed her arms and paced over the small rectangle of floor. "I wish I could go with you. It's close. I can feel it. All of Bram's past is cracking open and my past is right there too."

"Even with all this, you still may not find any of the answers you want, Lenore."

"I will. I will," she said fiercely. "Aunt Milly will know something."

Owen watched her pace. Her suit was so unflattering that it was almost ridiculous. "Are these your own clothes that you wear to court?"

She stopped and stared at him. "I didn't have the right clothing for the trial. Rossner told me to get things with bows and high necks and loose skirts. I ordered them from catalogs."

"Did you purposely choose things that would look . . ." he hesitated.

A faint, mocking smile curled her lips. "You don't like my murderess wardrobe?"

His resolve to be professional fell away, and he jumped out of his chair and came very close to doing what he'd wanted to do since that morning which was ram his fist through a wall. But he caught himself. Stopped himself. Controlled his fury and turned it into words instead, saying, "I know who you're hiding. James Collier."

She drew herself up, never taking her eyes from his, and said, "What will you do about it?"

He had to turn away from her then because the fury evaporated and he was left feeling small and empty.

"Nothing," he said.

"It's not what it seems, Owen."

"Nothing is with you, is it?"

She was silent for a moment. Then in a wary voice, she said, "None of this matters. All that's important is that I continue the search for my father as long as I can."

He turned back around to face her. "Lenore . . ."

Volpe cracked the door open and announced lunch.

"We'll be right there, Joe," Lenore called. "There isn't much time left, Owen. I put some of the money that we found in your suitcase. Use it however you need to."

He was insulted. Indignant. Did she think she could buy him off? "I don't want your money," he said.

"Don't be noble. If you were a detective, you'd be charging me for every move you make. And it's not my money anyway. It's Bram's. Besides . . . if it hadn't been for you finding the safe there would be no money."

They joined the others in the main room of the suite for sandwiches. Tension hung in the air and at first Owen thought he was causing it, but he quickly realized it was unrelated to his presence. It was the trial. The defense was not happy with the current direction of the game.

"I don't suppose you've come up with any more gems of information for us?" Rossner asked Owen with a sardonic smile.

"No," Owen admitted.

"Lenore says you're making some progress digging into Serian's life, though."

"I'm trying," he said.

"Just remember, one untimely leak to the press, one inconvenient piece of information surfacing, and you could do Lenore's case irreparable harm."

"I'm aware of that."

"Good."

"Just keep aware, my boy," Riley said.

Volpe eyed Owen with a hard stare. "Especially around blond news bitches," he said.

"You're out of line," Owen warned the man, whereupon Volpe puffed up like a banty rooster ready to fight.

"Boys, boys . . ." Frank Riley soothed with a jovial smile. "We're on the same team now, aren't we? Let's be saving our tempers for the enemy."

When the time came to return to court, Owen was instructed to stay behind for fifteen minutes to allow the press time to clear away. He held the door for them like a host closing down a party. Lenore went out last, intentionally he was sure, and she paused to grip his wrist with talonlike fingers.

"Call me from Kansas as soon as you know anything," she whispered. "Either here or at home. You have both numbers."

He nodded. She released his wrist and went down the hall to where Volpe held her cape for her. Like an actress preparing to walk on stage, she cloaked herself in the voluminous folds of cloth and assumed the shuttered expression so familiar to courtroom spectators. Then she was gone.

Owen slipped into the courtroom just as Brown's first after-lunch witness was being sworn in. "Dar Quintana," Holly whispered. "One of the party guests at Arcadia that weekend."

Nodding, Owen settled in with his notes. He already knew who Dar Quintana was—a young sculptor from Nevada who had idolized Bram Serian. Quintana and two other party guests were scheduled to testify for the prosecution.

Dar Quintana described Bram Serian as a brilliant artist and the kindest man he had ever known. He described his weekends at Arcadia in the most glowing of terms and estimated that he had spent two and sometimes three weekends a month at Arcadia in the year preceding the fire. He spoke reverently of Natalie Raven and even had a good word for Tommy Kubiak, who had occasionally been around doing yard work.

When asked about Lenore, Quintana's attitude changed and his dislike for her was obvious. He said that he'd had the feeling, and that others had had the feeling that she hated Bram's friends and wished they would vanish. He said that all of them tried to be nice to her and to include her in things that they were doing, but she treated them like dirt. And one time, after having a few beers and feeling pretty loose, Quintana recalled telling her, 'Hey, we're not so bad, ya know. Why don't you join in and have a few laughs with us?' And he claimed he would never forget her answer because it was so weird. She said, 'I haven't been programmed for laughs.'

"That kind of stumped me," Quintana said, "but I still thought I could crack through that shell of hers so I said, 'Ya know, everyone here loves Serian. You oughtta be glad that your husband has so many friends, and stop being so stuck-up and cold and giving everybody a hard time.' "

Dar Quintana glanced over at Lenore, and something flickered briefly in his eyes that made Owen suspect Quintana was far more devious and vengeful than he appeared.

"And Lenore . . . She laughed at me then like I was an idiot, and she said, really sarcastic like, she said, 'Oh . . . so what you're telling me, Dar, is that I should be grateful for the chance to share Bram, day and night, with hordes of mindless leeches.' "

Brown feigned shock over this as if he hadn't already had a statement from this witness and hadn't been expecting such a revelation. "Mr. Quintana, when you were at Arcadia, did you see anything to indicate that Mrs. Serian might want to hurt her husband?"

"You mean when she shot him?" Quintana asked as though eager for Brown to get to a well-rehearsed question.

"You saw her shoot him?" Brown asked, half-heartedly pretending that this was a surprise.

"Yes, I did," Quintana answered. "A bunch of people were in the yard having target practice with BB guns. High-powered air guns, ya know?" Rossner started from his chair as though to object but then sank back down. "And Lenore came slinking out along the edges and someone handed her a gun and told her to take a shot and she turned and fired right into Bram's back. Bruised him good."

There were gasps throughout the courtroom, and Owen saw the jurors' eyes widen.

"What happened after she shot him?" Brown asked.

"Nothing. She left and he pretended like nothing happened. It was Natalie who insisted on raising up his shirt and taking a look and then made him put ice on it."

"On the weekend of the fire, Mr. Quintana, when did you arrive at Arcadia for the party?"

"I went up on Friday night, that would be August fifth, because Bram wanted me to help get things ready. He was really planning a blowout with a whole pig barbecued in the ground and everything."

"Was there anyone else who went up early?"

"Lance Zabel went up with me. We took the train to Stoatsberg and Natalie picked us up."

"Besides you and Mr. Zabel, who all was present on that night of August the fifth at Arcadia?"

"Bram of course, and Natalie and Lenore. That Tommy kid was there for a while helping us, but then he went home around ten or so. Then, just about the time we were getting ready to pack it in for the night, some guy I'd never seen before showed up."

"Did the Serians indicate that they had been expecting him?"

"No. Just the opposite. They were definitely not expecting him. Bram acted very mad and Lenore just acted surprised."

"Was this man who arrived late introduced to you?"

"He was introduced as Jimmy. No last name, just Jimmy."

Owen could feel Marilyn's eyes on him. She had to be wondering how in the hell he could come up with a question about a Jimmy on the exact morning that the name Jimmy was first mentioned in court. Let her wonder, Owen decided, and pretended not to notice her scrutiny.

"What took place, then, after this stranger's arrival?" Brown asked.

"Everybody said good night. Me and Lance started to go on in to bed but it was a hot night and we changed our minds and went for a walk. When we got back to the house, we came up on Bram and Lenore arguing out behind the studio. We tried to detour around them, but we couldn't help hearing a lot because voices carry out in the country on a quiet night."

"And what did you overhear on that night of August the fifth, Mr. Quintana?"

"I heard Bram say, 'How dare you invite him out here?' and then Lenore said, 'He wanted to come. What's wrong, Bram, can't you handle it? Is it too much for you?' and Bram said, 'You're pushing me too far, Lenore,' and she said, 'I haven't even started to push you, Bram.'"

The remainder of Quintana's testimony centered around the fire and how he had joined with the others in a bucket brigade and how they'd waited in the kitchen, hoping and praying that their worst fears would not be realized and how devastated they had all been when Bram's body was discovered and the horrible truth was revealed.

Brown thanked the witness solemnly and sat down.

It was soon clear in the process of Charlie Rossner's cross that the defense attorney had no magic silver bullets to use on Dar Quintana. All he could do was develop one of the themes he'd used with Natalie Raven, which was that it would be natural for a woman to get peevish about her home not being her own and her husband continually having company.

Owen thought he detected resignation in Rossner's posture when the attorney finally released Dar Quintana and returned to sit beside Lenore at the defense table.

The next witness was Lance Zabel, the man who had accompanied Dar Quintana out to Arcadia on Friday, August the fifth. Zabel was a large bearded fellow who announced his occupation as painter. He corroborated all of Quintana's testimony with the exception of the BB gun episode, which he had missed out on. But he made up for that with his own tale.

Zabel had awakened early on Saturday morning and had left the house thinking that everyone else was still in bed. He took a fishing rod and walked down to the pond. There he saw the mystery guest, Jimmy, and Lenore. Lenore was swimming nude in the pond, and Jimmy was sitting on the bank keeping her company.

Owen couldn't stand listening to any more. He quietly gathered his things in preparation for leaving.

"Where are you going?" Holly whispered.

"Airport. Have to go to Kansas for a day or so."

"Trouble at home?"

"Not exactly."

"Safe trip." She smiled teasingly. "Don't worry . . . I won't let anything good happen while you're gone."

He forced a smile and ducked out of the pew and out of the courtroom. A sick emptiness sat in the pit of his stomach, but he refused to acknowledge it. Instead, he thought about how it was probably wise to get an early start to the airport since he still had to return the rental car and pay for his ticket and . . .

His thoughts were interrupted by the sudden realization that one of the photographers stationed just outside the security station in the lobby was aiming a video camera at him.

"What are you doing?" he asked.

"Oh, hey . . . just playin' around, man . . . you know."

"Aren't you Holly Danielson's cameraman?"

"Yeah . . . hey . . . cool. You recognized me, huh?"

"Why were you filming me?"

"Take it easy, man. I'm just ... ya know ... Holly said she'd like to have a little footage of you." He laughed. "Hey, must be nice to have a chick like that stuck on you, huh?"

"No more filming," Owen said. "You got that?"

"Yeah. No problema, amigo. I got it good."

All the way to the airport Owen fumed. About Holly. About Lenore. About the whole damn screwed-up world. The anger was good. It kept the dread at bay and got him safely aboard the flight to Kansas.

17

Upon landing in Wichita, Owen took a shuttle to a hotel near the airport. It was night and the hotel was generic. He had no sense of being back in Kansas. In the morning he rented a car after learning that Milly Corwin's home was far enough outside the city to be inaccessible by taxi or public transportation; then he found 235 and headed north. He was still trying to adjust to the fact that he was well and truly in his home state, when he saw the exit for Golden Age Village, *a premier retirement community* according to the billboard near the gate.

He knocked on Milly's door.

"Promptness is a virtue," she said as she opened the door. "I'm glad to see you have it, Mr. Byrne."

She was a small stooped woman, but her movements were steady and her eyes were sharp behind heavy-framed glasses. Her hair was as silky and white as cottonwood fluff.

"Sit down. That gray chair should be comfortable for a man your size."

He sat where she pointed, careful not to disturb the crocheted doilies that were pinned to each arm. The room was full of handwork. Embroidered table runners and doilies graced every surface, and cross-stitched mottos hung on the walls.

"This is very nice," he said, looking around.

"I'm fortunate to be here in such a deluxe place," she said. "We have everything—medical and dental, food service, beauty shops, a library . . . And the price includes full-time nursing when a person can no longer manage." She let her gaze trail lovingly around the room. "Benjamin got me this apartment. It's mine till I die."

"It's a good place," he agreed, unsure who Benjamin was.

"Yes. It's the perfect place, even though I don't get company and I get a touch of cabin fever now and then; still, it's a darn sight better than I would have in Arcadia if I'd stayed." Without missing a beat she glared at Owen and said, "Would you care for coffee or tea?"

"Whichever you're having, thank you."

Milly Corwin served coffee with arthritic hands, then made small talk about the weather and her old church group in Arcadia. Owen listened to her, forcing himself to be patient.

"Those women back home are jealous of me, you know," she confided. "They always were. It started when I was young. Celeste and Camille Corwin were the most popular girls in town. We were the ones with dresses that looked like magazine pictures and boys following like puppies. We were greatly envied. Even hated sometimes."

She frowned at him and raised a gnarled index finger. "Those deep feelings from our youth don't ever go away, Mr. Byrne. We carry them with us always."

"I know what you mean."

"Maybe you do, maybe you don't. Maybe you're just trying to humor an old woman to get what you want."

Owen couldn't help smiling.

She stiffened. "Next thing you'll be prattling on about how I remind you of your grandmother."

"No. I never knew either of my grandmothers."

"Well, I don't feel a bit sorry for you on that count so you may as well drop it."

With that all the frenzied determination that had carried Owen from New York to Kansas leaked away like helium from a balloon. What was he doing in this old woman's living room trying to coax her secrets from her? Owen felt suddenly weary and disgusted with himself.

"Have I shocked you dumb?" Milly Corwin asked.

"No. Just thinking."

"About the best way to bamboozle me? Well, you can quit thinking so hard because I've made up my mind. The boys' past is nobody's business but their own."

Owen nodded. "I don't know why I rushed out here. I should have told you everything straight out on the phone, then given you time to think about it. I got so involved in my work that I'm afraid I got carried away."

"What do you mean by work? Are you one of those detectives who digs into people's privacy? Is that what you call work?"

Owen's thoughts drifted for a moment.

"You're one of those deep thinkers, aren't you?" Milly asked. "Can't answer a simple question without thinking it to death."

"I'm not a detective," he admitted. "I'm a writer."

"What kind of a writer?"

"A book writer."

She paused to consider this a moment. "That puts a whole different color to it." Owen couldn't tell by her tone whether it was a good color or a bad color.

The room was warm and claustrophobic. Owen glanced at the clock on her wall and saw that it was nearing eleven-thirty. He had hoped to have all the answers and be on his way by twelve-thirty. Now he doubted that he would accomplish much at all.

"Could I interest you in lunch out somewhere?" he asked.

"My . . ." Her arthritic hands fluttered to her hair and then smoothed the front of her dress. "I can't recall the last time I had lunch out. That would be a fine treat, Mr. Byrne."

"Please, call me Owen."

"Very well . . . Owen. But I do think of myself as Miz Corwin. People are entirely too loose with themselves these days, if you ask me."

He helped her into her coat, catching the scent of baby powder and eucalyptus; then he offered his arm. She took it and solemnly accompanied him to the car.

Wichita had never particularly interested Owen. It had always seemed caught somewhere between rural and urban, like a fast-talking politician straddling both sides. So instead of going back south into the jumble of shopping malls and housing tracts, Owen headed north toward Newton, a town he remembered as having some charm.

Milly seemed to be absorbed in the passing scenery. She held a dainty handkerchief in her hand, a perfectly pressed square with pink embroidered flowers and a lacy tatted edge, and Owen wondered if she'd brought it for sneezing or crying, or if she simply considered it a ladylike touch. He wondered if his grandmother Hadley had owned such handkerchiefs.

"I didn't tell you the whole truth about your nephews and the situation in New York," he said.

"I know that," she replied tartly.

"Would you like to hear it now?"

She twisted the handkerchief in her fingers, creasing the tissue-fine linen. "What I'd like is for you never to have told me anything. To put things back in my head the way they were with both boys doing fine and living good lives somewhere. But that's not possible, is it? I can't go back to not knowing anything . . . so I guess I'd just as well learn the rest. Go ahead. Tell me."

Owen told her everything. Every detail. Who Bram Serian was in the art world and how troubled Al had been and about the big house and Bram marrying Lenore. He told her about the trial and about his writing and how he had come to be involved in the story. And then he told her about Lenore, the woman who was accused of murdering Bram Serian, and who was obsessed with finding her long-lost father.

"Oh dear . . . dear, dear, dear."

Milly tortured the handkerchief. "My mother was a teacher before she married. And she never lost her love of books. When Celeste and I were growing up she used to read to us from the classics and talk for hours about what the stories meant. She was considered quite strange and uppity by our neighbors."

She wiped her eyes and adjusted her glasses.

"Those stories my mother read to us always seemed so far away and unreal, but what you've just told me here could have been a tragedy straight out of one of those books. Only my own blood is mixed up in it."

They reached the outskirts of Newton, and Owen let her choose the restaurant. It was a lovely old restored building full of light and plants. She seemed delighted at first, but after ordering she lapsed into thought and compressed her mouth into a tight-lipped frown.

"Why would my Abe go back to the name Bram Serian?" she demanded. "Are you sure you have that right?"

"Absolutely." Owen wanted to know why that upset her, but he would not ask. He could not push. If she wanted to tell him she would. If not . . . then he would try to find answers some other way.

She eyed him shrewdly. "Those boys were like my own children. Circumstance gave me a fiancé who was a coward. Declared himself a conscientious objector rather than go off to fight in the big war like all the decent boys were doing. So I cut it off with him and didn't marry when other girls my age did. Then later I had another suitor, who also proved to be a coward, but of a different stripe. I never married. Never had my own family. I spent my life as a spinster lady and a maiden aunt."

"No one uses those terms anymore," Owen said gently.

"They did when I was young and cared about such things."

The food arrived. She inspected both of their plates with great interest, and Owen offered to share so that she could taste everything. That pleased her and she made a fuss over dividing and exchanging, worrying over whether he had enough to fill him up. Finally she settled down to eat.

She concentrated on her food for some time, then sat back to ask, "Exactly where in Kansas are you from and how did you work up the nerve to go to New York?"

Ordinarily, Owen would have evaded such a question, but he was guilty of stirring up this old woman's secure life and darkening it with tragedy, and so he felt obligated to answer any question she asked.

"I was born near Maynard, one of four children. My family farmed wheat ground. Around the time I was nine, my Dad moved us to the Flint Hills . . . near Cyril . . . onto a cow/calf operation."

"Go on," she prompted.

"My older brother died, and so I ended up leaving college to run the ranch. It's a good life. I like working with animals."

"Mmm . . . What happened to the rest of your family?"

"My mother is dead. My father and my two sisters live on the ranch."

"But it's your ranch now?"

"No. I actually work for my father."

"But you don't get paid, do you?"

"Well . . . no. I don't get a paycheck. But my room and board is free and I get to train horses and dogs on my own, so I make a little money that way. And I am running a place that will be mine someday."

"A third yours," she said shortly. "Divided up with your two sisters, I reckon."

"But with controlling interest to me," he said defensively. "That's the way my father set it up. To make sure the ranch survives and that I continue to run it."

"So neither of your sisters can demand their share in cash and force a sale?"

"Yes. But it's their home too. They wouldn't want to sell."

"So they say now." She sighed. "Oh, I'm all too familiar with what's done in the name of passing on the land. All too familiar."

She studied him with her bright birdlike eyes.

"Now you still haven't explained how you got from tending cows to writing a book in New York," she reminded him.

"I still don't know if I understand it myself," he said. "I'm not a real writer. Oh, I'm working at it. I'm working hard at it. And I have some people fooled. But all I really know is ranching."

"Ummm. What about your family? Do they think you're a real writer?"

He laughed. "They think I'm a real fool."

"Is Owen Byrne your born name, or did you change your name like my boys did?"

Owen had to grin at her bulldog tenacity. "It's my birth name. My father's name is Clancy Terrence Byrne."

"An Irishman?"

"Yes."

"Didn't used to meet many Irish. He isn't Catholic, is he?"

"Yes, he is. Though only in a picturesque way."

"Gus couldn't tolerate Catholics. My, how he used to take on about Catholics and Democrats and Japanese and reservation Indians and farmers with fallow ground. Those were all topics we tried to keep him away from."

"Gus?"

"The boys' father. My sister's husband."

"Wait a minute!" Owen gaped at her. "Bram and Al were *brothers?*"

"Why, of course. They were my sister's boys. What did you think?"

"They presented themselves as cousins."

"No. They were brothers, all right. By law if not by blood. And closer brothers never lived."

Owen stared at her in confusion. "Then who was Luke?"

Milly made a scolding humfph in the back of her throat. "I expect you won't quit, will you?" she asked. "You're going to keep hunting down my nephews' past, aren't you?

You'll just go around me to get what you want some other way."

Owen didn't want to say yes, but he would have been lying if he told her no.

"You will. Don't bother to deny it. And if you back off, then pretty soon someone else will come sniffing around. It's all clear to me. If my nephew was as famous as you say and if his widow is as determined as you say, then it's just a matter of time till someone or other hunts it all down."

"Yes," he admitted. "I'm sorry."

"Well, I'm not excusing you from blame, mind you, but I've been pondering over all this, and it's come to me that I'd just as soon you had the facts first. At least with you, I know there won't be any funny business or twisting things around."

Owen was too surprised to reply.

"And besides, you're a book writer and my mother put great store in books. She thought they could save the world. She was wrong, but that's neither here nor there. The fact is that she believed and I know she'd be proud of me for helping a writer like you."

"I . . . I'm surprised," Owen managed to say.

"You're going to be a lot more surprised when you hear what I've got to tell you."

"Aren't you still worried about Al, though? He's out there somewhere . . . What if he doesn't want this told?"

Her face turned very quiet. She folded her cloth napkin over and over into a neat square, laid it on the table and pressed it flat with her fingers.

"I fear that both boys are lost to me," she said. "There's never been this long a time without a note or a postcard."

The waitress came by with a coffee pot and Milly said, "I'm ready to go home and do the rest of my talking there," so Owen asked for the check.

Owen didn't say much on the ride back to Golden Age Village. The mood was too serious for small talk, and he wanted to give her time to put her thoughts in order.

"Funny thing," she said, when they were about halfway back to her home. "This is not really part of the story at all. Just something I find curious. My mother, bless her soul . . . I haven't gone a day in my life without missing that woman . . . My mother's name was Lenore. The boys had no real memory of her because she died before they were even born, but they always liked to hear me talk about her, and they both loved that name. They told me they'd looked it up at the library and its meaning was 'light' in Greek, or some such."

"Your mother's name was Lenore," Owen parroted dumbly.

"That's quite a coincidence, isn't it? That one of the boys should marry a woman with that same name."

"Yes," Owen agreed, thinking it too much of a coincidence. "You still haven't said who Luke was," he reminded her.

"Oh, he was the boys' good friend when they were high school age. They were the three musketeers for a while, and he joined in and listened to my stories and called me Aunt Milly too."

She didn't speak again until they were inside her apartment and out of their coats.

"Get ready," she warned. "I'm about to get wound up here."

"Do you mind if I record?"

"Not at all. I'd prefer it. I couldn't talk if you were writing . . . I'd be too busy wondering what you'd put down.

"Turn it on," she said, staring at the recorder.

He pressed the button. She didn't hesitate.

"Did I tell you how my mother raised us? Yes, I think I did. She raised us to have proper manners and dress just right and talk like we'd been to school somewhere else. That was all well and good because we were the banker's daughters and lived in a fine house, one of those grand old ones with a wide porch and a round turret room. But as we grew older we could find no boys who we wanted to come courting. They all seemed vulgar and unpromising to us. Other girls married and had babies, but there we were, still waiting for *gentlemen* to appear.

"Then things turned bad for our father, Albert. Ours never was a rich area, not with depending on the strip mines so much, and he had some setbacks at the bank. Then he had a stroke and was confined to bed at home.

"Around that time I met my fiancé, who was in the area on a road survey. Suddenly I had a sweetheart. Celeste, who was two years older than me, cried a lot and carried on about her life being over and how she'd never meet a husband, until finally our mother sent her to Kansas City to stay with an

old schoolteacher friend of my mother's. Before we knew it
Celeste had written home that she'd met a man, a fellow
named Gus Hanselmann.

"That's how it began. Right there. With my sister who
was always too impulsive, and who was desperate to find a
husband. And with Gus who was still unformed and seemed
harmless enough.

"Gus had had a hard childhood. His father was a violent
man and died violently. The mother lost their farm and they
ended up moving in with a bachelor uncle who lived in the
back of a shop he owned. Gus nursed his mother till she
died, then struck out for Kansas City to try his luck.

"When Celeste met Gus in the city, he was free from care
or responsibility for the first time in his life and was looking
to try his wings and explore. And of course that's all Celeste
saw. She was in too much of a hurry to spend the years that
getting to know a person can take, and she became engaged
to Gus at the drop of a hat.

"In the meantime, the uncle sold his store in town and
turned around and sunk his money into a wheat farm. He
wrote to Gus and asked him to come back, promising that if
Gus came home and helped him work the farm, it would be
his one day.

"Gus and Celeste married and went out to live with the
uncle on the farm. Right off Celeste started writing to me
about how different Gus was in the country than he'd been
in the city. Nothing too strong, mind you, because she liked
feeling superior to me, being that my engagement was over
and I was still single, and she always finished by adding that
her lovely home made everything else insignificant.

"The uncle died and Gus inherited the land. Celeste lost
some babies. Couldn't get past her fifth month with them.

"Then our mother died. After the estate was settled, there
was hardly anything left, and there I was, an unmarried lady
without a home or a way to support herself. I did the only
thing a woman could do in those days—I went to live at the
mercy of my sister's husband.

"To get there I took several buses, then was met by Gus,
who drove me the last forty miles without saying anything
more than hello. The place was way out west of Wichita.
The nearest town was Ridley, where the old uncle had had
his shop, and that was a good twenty-minute ride on wash-
board gravel roads.

"Oh, it was an ugly piece of ground . . . flat as a cookie sheet with trashy Osage orange in the fence rows but not another tree on the place. Nothing decorative or pleasing to the eye at all.

"And the house was nothing more than a painted-up shack compared to what I was used to. A poor old shack of a house with not a bush or a flower or a little garden fence or anything to make it homey.

"Celeste was with child again so I took over the house and she kept to her bed on doctor's orders.

"Now, my mother had never coddled us. We always did our share of cleaning and ironing and needlework while we were growing up. But life on that farm was hard. The only water in the house came from the handpump at the kitchen sink. There was electric, one wire strung from a pole at the end of the lane, but it wasn't built into the house. There were no outlets in the walls or light fixtures in the ceilings, just wires tacked around and painted over. And they were still using an outhouse.

"I was dumbstruck at first . . . seeing my sister, Celeste, with all her airs, living in such primitive conditions. But I learned quick to keep my mouth shut. Celeste was real touchy about her circumstances and sorry that I'd finally come out and seen the truth of her grand life, and Gus wouldn't tolerate any female complaining.

"Well, Celeste stayed in bed faithfully and carried that baby to term. He was a big boy, thirteen pounds, and healthy as a horse, but Celeste had trouble delivering him. She ruptured something and the doctor had to take out her female parts. Scooped her out like he was gutting a fish.

"When she finally came home from the hospital with that fine baby boy, Gus was beside himself with happiness. He went out and bought the baby a toy tractor and hired men from town to come build a septic tank and a proper indoor bathroom. They laid pipe to the kitchen sink too so we had a real faucet there with running water instead of that horrible old hand pump.

"Celeste didn't enjoy her new bathroom, though. Just like she didn't enjoy that sweet baby. All she could think about was what she'd lost. About how she wasn't a woman anymore and about how there wouldn't be any more babies for her.

"That was Benjamin's beginning. And he was as much

mine as any babe I might have borne, because his mother was too buried in grief to love him and his father loved only the promise of a big strapping son, not the drooling softness of a baby."

Milly Corwin paused for a deep breath and Owen interrupted her, anxious to know, "Was this Bram Serian?"

"Just hold on," Milly instructed. "You'll see who Bram Serian was and where the name came from in just a bit.

"Benjamin grew. Celeste came out of her convalescence with a toughness that made even Gus take heed. She went head to head with him, arguing about the state of the house and how money was spent. It got to where they fought every time they were together, and gradually Gus found reasons to stay gone. If he wasn't in his own fields, then he was helping at a neighbor's or sitting by the woodstove at the co-op or down talking equipment at the dealership. And that suited Celeste just fine. She started doing things to that house on her own. Putting up wallpaper and gluing down carpet remnants to the floor.

"By the time Benjamin was five or so, he was a miniature of his father. He was big and stocky, built like a blue-ribbon show steer, which made Gus real proud. The sad thing was that the more he looked like Gus and the more Gus bragged on the boy the less interested Celeste was in mothering him. It didn't matter how much that child loved her . . . to her he was Gus's boy.

"When Benjamin was six or seven—I should recall exactly but I don't—Celeste heard about a boy out at the county home.

"A good Lutheran girl from the area had run off to Chicago and gotten herself pregnant and married to the wrong sort of man. The man was killed and the girl came crawling back, but her parents had passed on years before so she had to go into the county poor home with her little boy.

"Come to find out she was dying and she signed a paper saying that she wanted her boy to be adopted by a local family and raised to be a good Lutheran after she was gone.

"Well, Celeste heard about all this at church one Sunday and without telling any of us she drove out and met this woman and her little boy. That night at supper she started talking nice to Gus. Putting him off his guard. She said things about how sad it was that there would never be another boy to help farm and be a brother to Benjamin. I guessed what she was up to pretty fast, but Gus was always kind of slow. He wouldn't have noticed a train hit him till after the caboose passed.

"Then one day all of us were gathered around the table for the noon meal and Celeste said, 'You know, Gus, what you've been talking about . . . how hard you have to work and what a shame it is that you'll never have more than one son to help . . . I've been feeling real bad about that, especially since I'm the one who can't bear you another son. So I've been doing some thinking about how I could make things right.'

"Gus grunted and kept shoveling food into his mouth. I was watching them both, knowing that Celeste was about to make her move. Even little Benjamin was watchful, like he knew a storm was brewing.

"Celeste had made Gus's favorite pie, and she fetched that to the table and set it in front of him. Then she said, 'I reckon that the best way for me to make things right is to make a sacrifice, so I am willing to take in a boy and raise him as my own so that you'll have you another son to help with the work.'

"Gus stopped eating and stared at her like she'd spoken in tongues or announced she was flying to the moon or something. 'What in the samhill are you blabbering about, woman?' Celeste got her back up a little at that but kept her voice real nice. 'I'm talking about adopting a boy Benjamin's age so he can have a brother and you can have more help in the fields.'

"Gus started to cut himself a piece of that gooseberry pie. 'Whatever put such a plumb stupid idea in your head?' he asked.

" 'You did,' she said. 'You've been saying how it wasn't fair for a man to have only one son to help him.'

" 'That may be so,' he admitted, 'but I never said nothing about adopting.'

" 'I know adopting is a hard decision to make, and it's even harder for a woman because it's admitting to the world that she is not a whole woman, but I have learned of an orphan boy who can be adopted without much fuss and could be doing his share of chores for you within the month.'

" 'I'll never have another man's bastard under my roof,' Gus declared, and Celeste bristled up. 'He's not a bastard. He was born legitimate.'

" 'Huh. That's what they all say. I know which boy you're talking about. The one whose mama's been staying out at the poor farm. And I'll lay you dollars to doughnuts that old gal was a slut who never had a husband when that boy was born.'

" 'You're wrong. That boy is as decent as they come and he deserves a good Lutheran home. Fact is he's already more civilized and smarter than this boy you fathered.'

"Gus roared up out of his chair shouting about how Celeste was a no-account spoiled city girl and the worst wife a man could have, and Celeste jumped up and started screaming about how Gus was a big dumb oaf who'd spawned a big oaf child that had torn her womb right out of her, and I grabbed Benjamin's hand and pulled him away and we ran. For hours we hid behind the equipment shed where we couldn't hear anything but the wind and the crows squabbling down in the hedgerows. And he buried his head in my skirts and begged me to tell him a story. That was the beginning of my Arcadia stories. See, I just started telling him about me . . . about what a wonderful life I had growing up in Arcadia in my big beautiful house with my wonderful mother and father . . . Lenore and Albert, or Al as folks called him.

"I remember it clearly. How much he liked that story and made me stretch it on and on. How that sweet face of his took it all in like it was some kind of fairy tale. He cried when I said we had to go back to the house. Asked if we couldn't run away to Arcadia instead.

"When we went inside the back door, everything was dead quiet. I was scared. Thinking they might have killed each other.

"There were broken plates on the kitchen floor and that gooseberry pie was splattered everywhere. I made Benjamin start picking up while I looked through the rest of the house. The bathroom sink was splattered with blood. And there was a little trail of red drops on the linoleum. I followed them out to the living room. Two fist-sized holes had been punched out of the wall. Below them Celeste was propped up on the couch, with her left arm at a funny angle. Her face was pure white . . . except for the parts that were red or purple.

"I've never been one for hysterics, and I don't think I did much except stand there and stare.

" 'Help me, Sissy,' she said. 'I need you to drive me to the hospital.'

" 'I'm calling the law first, Celeste. So they can see all this with their own eyes.'

" 'No, Milly! I promised not to tell the sheriff or anyone at church in exchange for Gus signing my paper.'

"I bent closer to see what she was holding with her good hand, and I saw it was the adoption papers and Gus had signed them all right. He'd signed right above her name. Right through the little specks of blood.

"I went out and got the car from the shed and pulled it up to the house. Then I had Benjamin bring a blanket and pillow and I helped her into the backseat and we headed for the hospital, which was a good drive from there. Who was I to argue? She had what she wanted, and she didn't seem to think the price was too high. Course looking back I see it all differently. I see that I should have taken Benjamin right then and gone somewhere far away. But that's looking back. And I can't say it ever crossed my mind at the time.

"At the hospital we told the doctor some cockamamy story about how she'd tripped and fallen down over the rocks into the creek. I don't think that doctor believed us, but he kept his doubts to himself. Benjamin watched the whole thing. They stitched up her eye and stuck that rod up her nostril and popped her nose back into place. Then they put a cast on her arm. And Benjamin sat real still and never said a word. Would he have been seven then? I just can't be sure. He wasn't in school yet . . . but then that was back before they had a kindergarten in Ridley so kids didn't start going till late.

"Things were pretty calm after that. We patched over the holes in the wall and scrubbed the blood out of the couch. I drove Celeste in to take the papers to the lawyer's office and then out to speak to the mother and boy. Celeste told Benjamin he was getting a brother and she let him pick out bunkbeds and cowboy bedspreads from the Sears catalog.

"Up to then, Benjamin and I had shared a room with an old double bed that Celeste bought at a garage sale in town. But with the new boy coming she decided to do the room up special for the children and move me to the attic.

"Gus was pretty agreeable for the first few weeks after the fight, and he helped fix up the attic without one complaint, laying pine board for a floor and nailing up sheetrock on the walls and ceiling. There was a rectangular cutout at one end, covered with heavy screen. Houses used to be built like that, you know, so they could breathe. Well, Gus went in and had a window made to fit that hole—without me even asking. Celeste, she was all for just boarding it over but no . . . Gus reached right into his pocket and paid to have a window made. That was the nicest thing he ever did for me. Or anyone else that I know of.

"We couldn't get the old double bed up the attic stairs, so I got to order a new bed from Sears too. And when it was finished, I loved my room with the slanted ceiling and the tiny little window. It didn't matter that Gus never finished off the sheetrock or sealed over the cracks. It didn't matter that Celeste forgot about her promise to buy me wallpaper. It didn't matter that it was freezing in winter and blistering hot in summer. For the first time in years, I had a door to shut and a place that was mine.

"But I'm getting ahead of myself.

"We went for the boy the day after his mother died. Celeste just swept him up, talking to him a mile a minute about how happy he was going to be and what a good mother she would make him. And he watched us all with those eyes of his.

"Celeste let Benjamin show him the room and the new bunk beds; then we stowed what few belongings he had and Celeste sat us all down in the living room. 'As of now,' she said, 'your name is Hanselmann. You are never to use Bram Serian again.'

"Benjamin asked, what about his first name? And Celeste said, since his given name was Abram that he could be called Abe. That would suit Gus and still let the boy keep something familiar.

"So that was it. Bram Serian was gone and Abe Hanselmann came into the family. A brother for Benjamin. A son for Celeste. And a whipping boy for Gus."

Milly Corwin sagged back into her chair as though drained by the tale she had told.

"Can I get you something?" Owen asked.

"That would be nice. There's tea made in the refrigerator. Pour yourself a glass, too."

When Owen returned with the tea, she seemed to have revived somewhat. She pushed herself up out of her chair, crossed the living room and went to the hall closet. "Give me a hand here," she said, and Owen retrieved two boxes from the top of the closet for her. One was an old flowered hatbox that was fairly light. The other was a sturdy container that had originally held size thirteen work boots and was heavy enough that Owen wondered how she had ever gotten it up into the closet.

She took the hatbox to her chair. Owen carried the weighty boot box in and set it on the coffee table between them. He guessed it might contain pictures, and he could barely keep his excitement in check.

"Go ahead," she said, nodding toward the boot box. "Open it."

The box was crammed with loose pictures and photo folders and old leather albums. Owen was elated. He held up a sepia-toned portrait of a young couple for her to identify.

"My parents," she said. "Albert and Lenore Corwin. As fine a pair as ever walked the earth. Gentle and learned and tolerant. I only wish I would have appreciated them more while they were living."

He carefully pulled out another old print, a shot of two little girls in old-fashioned clothes sitting side saddle on ponies.

Milly pointed. "That's Celeste and that's me."

She let Owen sift through them in silence for a few minutes, then said, "You can use whatever you'd like for your book."

He thanked her, nearly overwhelmed by the avalanche of material and the thrill of knowing that his book was taking on new dimensions.

"Tell you what," she said. "I'll let you take the whole box for now. You show them to the widow and pick out some for the book. Then you worry about returning them later. I'm not much for enjoying old pictures these days. They make me too sad."

"Before we stop, would you mind if I found some pictures of your nephews? There are almost no photographs of them as adults and . . ."

She bent over the box and tugged on an exposed cardboard corner. "There," she said. "Get that one out."

He pulled it free. It was a deluxe cardboard photo holder, wood grained with a faux gold edging. Carefully, he opened

it. There were two five by seven portraits inside, facing each
other from oval cutouts.

"They're the last pictures I have of the boys," she said.
"Taken at the high school just before . . . before everything
changed."

Owen studied the portraits. The boy on the right had a
rounded face, wavy sandy blond hair and an engaging smile
that crinkled the corners of his eyes. This was a younger,
clean-shaven version of the face that Owen had seen in the
photograph at Edie Norton's office. A teenaged Bram
Serian. The adopted child.

The boy staring out from the left was unsmiling. He had
medium brown hair that hung carelessly across his forehead,
a sensitive mouth, sharply planed cheeks, and solemn eyes.
This had to be Al, the Vietnam-damaged brother whom
Bram Serian had imprisoned to protect. Al, the unfortunate
biological son.

The differences between the boys were so definite. So
clear. Owen could see why no one had ever suspected that
they might be more than distant cousins. But then, of course,
they weren't actually related by blood.

Owen glanced up at Milly. "In this picture, Benjamin already looks . . . sad. Even haunted. It's easy to understand
why Vietnam had such a destructive effect on him."

Milly Corwin screwed her face up into a frown. "What
are you talking about?" She snatched the folder from
Owen's hand, and looked at it as though checking her own
sanity.

Owen leaned over and tapped the cardboard next to the
picture of the solemn-eyed boy. "You don't think he looks a
little sad?"

She laughed. "You've mixed them up. That's not Benjamin. That's the adopted boy." She pointed to the smiling
face. "That's my Benjamin."

Owen took the folder back from her and stared at the two
young men. "Milly . . . Miss Corwin . . ." he began gently.
"The man who called himself Bram Serian. The man who
became famous and married Lenore and died last August is
the one who is smiling here. And this"—he indicated the
somber, darker-headed boy—"this is the man who was
called Al and whose whereabouts are unknown."

"But . . ." Milly shook her head. "I don't understand."

"Your nephew Benjamin was the one who was using the

name Bram Serian. And your other nephew . . . your adopted nephew, called himself Al."

She put a shaking hand to her forehead. "My Benjamin took his adopted brother's birth name?"

"I'm afraid so. And Abe, the adopted boy, took the name Al."

"Then it was my Benjamin who died in August." She clutched her hands to her bosom as though trying to control the pain. "I knew in my heart something bad had happened to that boy, as soon as the mail stopped. But I still hoped . . ."

Several moments passed before she spoke again. Then she said, "Yes. It makes sense that Benjamin would be the one to make something of himself.

"Benjamin was always the one who wanted things. The one who had ambitions. And it makes sense that he tried to take care of his brother. He was protective of his brother from the very first, and his brother always needed it."

"Why do you think Benjamin would have changed his name to Bram Serian?" Owen asked. "Why would he have discarded his own family name and wanted to be known by his adopted brother's birth name? Can you make any sense of that?"

Milly sighed. "I suppose I can, if I want to face up to the truth of his life. I suppose I can. Sit back and I'll tell you the rest of the story."

18

___

Milly Corwin was very still for a moment, as though considering where to begin.

"Celeste had been worried that there might be jealousy or fighting between the boys, since they were thrown together so sudden without even a chance to get acquainted first. But from the very start those boys were close, like they'd been halves waiting to join up and make a whole. It was something to see. Almost spooky at times. One of them would look across the room at the other one, and you'd get this goosebumpy feeling that they'd just talked something over and made a decision without so much as saying a word.

"When they started school together, they were quite a sight. Benjamin all healthy and sunny-looking and Abe, bone-thin with that straight brown hair that never would stay combed and those eyes that soaked up everything. Celeste always said he had the gift of sight, that he saw more sharply than the rest of us.

"The fact of Abe's being adopted out of the county home was common knowledge, and though the adults flapped their jaws about it being a Godly act to take in such a child, they saw Abe as inferior and they passed that opinion down to their children. At school the other kids bullied Abe, and Benjamin had a time trying to protect his new brother. Celeste and I spent weeks patching those boys up and soaking spots of blood out of their shirts every single day after school. Then the fights stopped. But the boys dragged home everyday looking miserable anyway and begging not to have to go back to school. What I learned later, upon running into the schoolteacher at the hardware in Ridley, was that Benjamin and Abe had both become total outcasts. Like little lepers.

"Now this didn't bother Celeste or Gus. Parents didn't fret about their children having friends or enjoying themselves back then. As a matter of fact, Gus and a lot of men like him didn't believe in fun for children at all. They thought a child's character had to be shaped by hard work and strong discipline. But it bothered me to think of those two little boys huddled together in a schoolyard full of enemies, so I always tried to be a special friend to them to make up for it.

"We went along like that for years. Gus had his farming. Celeste and I cleaned and cooked and canned and worked on the house. We sewed all the clothes except for denim—jeans and overalls and such. We made tea towels out of flour sacks and quilts out of extra cloth and rag rugs out of scraps. Eventually, I talked her into planting iris and lilac bushes, though I understood her reasons for not having prettied up the outside before. She hated that house with a passion, and she was determined not to make it look homey from the outside, because that would have reflected well on Gus. Men are always judged by the outside and women by the inside, and she didn't want anyone thinking Gus had provided a nice home.

"As for the boys, they got pulled in both directions. Gus wanted to keep Benjamin with him most of the time, and Celeste wanted to keep Abe with her. Trouble was the boys wanted to stay together. So sometimes they'd go with Gus, making Celeste sulk and carry on about how nobody appreciated her, and sometimes they'd stick with Celeste and me, making Gus say all sorts of mean things about how they were sissys and mama's boys and babies.

"Celeste and Gus had small standoffs and battles during this time but nothing memorable. Not until the summer the boys were nine.

"Nine is a good age for a child, you know. A nine-year-old can do things. He can follow instructions and hold a flashlight steady and hand over the right tools when asked. He can bait his own hook. He knows a joke when he hears one, and he knows how to behave around other adults if you should want to take him to town. So as soon as the boys got out of school that summer, their ninth summer, the wars started. Celeste wanted Abe. Gus wanted Benjamin. And neither one liked it that the boys wanted to stay together.

"Celeste was angry at Benjamin all the time, telling him he was a troublemaker, telling him he should let his brother be and just stick with his father, who was his own kind. And Gus got meaner and meaner to Abe, telling him to keep his sissy ass in the house and let his brother go work with the men. Both of the adults blamed the child they didn't like for depriving them of the company of the child they wanted. And the boys were miserable, caught in the middle, but more miserable when they were separated. I think those boys knew all along that the adults were their enemies and their only hope was to hang on to each other.

"Now don't get the idea that these boys didn't have work to do. They did a load of chores. But during the summer there's time for chores and fun too.

"Celeste started offering more trips to town with ice cream cones from the Dairy Queen and comics from the drugstore as incentives to make herself the more attractive parent. And Gus came up with fishing. If they'd go with him, he'd take them fishing down at the river for flatheads and bull cats just as soon as all the farm work was done.

"The boys liked going to town with Celeste and they liked going fishing with Gus in about equal measure so neither adult won out. And I thought the point would come when Celeste and Gus would call it a draw and quit trying so hard. But neither one would back down.

"Celeste softened on Benjamin and stopped being so nasty to him. I think she could see that Abe depended on Benjamin being near, and she gave in because she wanted what was best for Abe more than anything else. But Gus never softened on anything in his life. And he sure didn't soften on Abe. He was determined to hold a grudge against his adopted boy, and he found fault with Abe just about any way he could.

"When I was living there, right in the middle, I didn't see what a cruel childhood those boys were having. I was a meek sort of woman then, and I was fearful of Gus and fearful of losing my place in his home. But when I think back on it now, my blood boils at the way those boys were treated. Celeste was no kind of mother to them. She bribed them for attention and she cried and sulked and made them feel terrible guilt when she didn't get what she wanted. She never disciplined them or reminded them of their chores; then, when they forgot a job or did something wrong, she sat back and waited for Gus to blow up at them. She liked it when that happened because she liked being the one who comforted them after they'd been in trouble.

"And Gus . . . he'd walk around town or sit around at

church suppers with that quiet, calm way about him, listening to his neighbor chat about the weather and the price of wheat and such but hardly ever saying much himself, and everybody thought he was such a princely fellow. Such a modest, humble, Godly man. Such a smart farmer and a good husband and a fine father. But at home he had a true mean streak. Anger boiled up in him at the slightest thing, and he treated those boys like they were dogs . . . to be petted, whipped, starved or cursed according to his moods.

"Course, if he was whipping or cursing it was always Abe who got the worst of it. Abe automatically got more whacks with a stick or more lashes with a belt or more ugly and profane cursing. Gus called him a papist bastard and a devil-spawned greaseball on account of it being rumored that Abe's natural father was from Portugal. He called him other things too, which I will not repeat. And it wasn't just Abe's being adopted and unwanted that fired such hate in Gus. Abe had this way about him that made Gus turn into a raving maniac, this way of looking straight up at Gus without the least bit of cowering or guilt. And he didn't cry even a little when Gus whipped him. He'd get this blankness to his face, like his spirit was hiding someplace deep down.

"Well, the usual state of affairs was bad enough, but toward the end of the summer something more started. Celeste and I noticed it about the same time, how the boys were getting quieter and less playful whenever we had them with us, and how Abe was turning skittish, jumping at little noises like a half-broke colt. We tried to question the boys, but they just looked at each other and shrugged it off. We watched them with Gus, automatically suspecting that he was the cause, but strangely enough Gus appeared to have lightened up on the boys.

"Then one day we were doing the laundry and Celeste said something about how the boys' undershorts seemed to be disappearing. There weren't as many as there used to be. I laughed about that, but when we got the folding done it was clear the underwear stack wasn't as big as it should have been.

"We agreed that was curious. We had just ordered a big supply of underwear for them from the Sears catalog, all the same because, in spite of the fact that Benjamin was thicker built than Abe, they were equal in height and wore the same sizes. So we couldn't tell who was losing his shorts.

" 'You think one of the boys has maybe had the runs and dirtied his pants and been ashamed to let us see them?' I asked.

"Celeste didn't speak her mind, but she went through that stack piece by piece, peering at the inside panels.

" 'There's some little stains in a few of these all right,' she said. 'But it's blood not diarrhea.' Her eyes narrowed up the way they always did when she was ready to explode. 'That cussed man has been beating on these boys too hard again. Damn his soul!'

"After supper that night, Gus went outside to sit and whittle and listen to the radio like he usually did. The boys started to follow but Celeste told them to stay put. Once Gus was out of hearing range she ordered both boys to her bedroom.

" 'One of you have a sore bottom?' she asked. 'Or is it both of you?'

"Those boys looked at each other like a ghost had just walked on their graves.

" 'I'm fine,' Benjamin said.

" 'And you, Abe?'

" 'I guess I hurt myself some way,' he admitted.

"Celeste pushed Benjamin back out of the way and ordered Abe to drop his pants and lay face down on her bed. 'Get some gauze and peroxide and iodine, Milly. Maybe a little salve too.'

"I rushed to the bathroom and back. Abe's pants were around his ankles and he was laying down when I got back. He was moving real slow like something hurt. His undershorts were still on.

"Soon as he got in position Celeste pulled down his underwear for him. I expected to see bad gashes or belt marks on his poor baby buttocks, but there wasn't anything like that. The cheeks of his butt were just as smooth and clean as could be.

"His bottom was fine. It was his anus that was all chewed up. Red and scabby and sore-looking.

" 'Lord in heaven, Abe, why didn't you tell me about this?' Celeste said.

" 'What is it?' I asked. 'Some kind of ringworm or infection?'

" 'I don't know,' Celeste said, but I could tell something was going through her mind because she got real white-faced and tight-lipped, and that scared me because I thought Abe might have some serious disease I didn't know about. Maybe something from skinnydipping in that dirty creek. Celeste was constantly lecturing on germs and cleanliness, but the boys didn't always listen.

" 'Think we should try to call a doctor right away?' I asked her.

" 'No,' she said. 'I think we can take care of it ourselves.'

"We cleaned him up gently as we could and put on a thick layer of salve and sent the boys out. And I whispered, 'What is it, Celeste? Are you sure we shouldn't take him to the doctor?'

"And my sister looked at me in a way that raised goose bumps all over my body. Her eyes were mad and terrible, but her lips were smiling. 'We can handle it, Milly. Don't worry. Everything's going to be just fine, now.'

"But she wouldn't tell me anything more.

"She set it up so the boys would go out with Gus for sure on Thursday. And over breakfast Thursday morning she started stirring Gus up. Nagging at him over little things and bragging on how smart Abe was and saying smart boys didn't grow up to be farmers. Gus was tight-jawed and muttering, and the boys were hunched up like scared rabbits by the time they all pulled out of the yard.

"We knew what their plan was. Gus was headed to a neighbor's place to help repair some machinery. They'd eat noon dinner at the neighbor's; then they were going to the gas station in town to pick up the patched truck tire. Then they were going down to Nowa Creek to fish.

"Celeste insisted that we both dress in pants. Then she prowled around the house like a caged tiger all morning. She called the neighbors to check on whether Gus and the boys had finished eating and left yet, saying she wanted to catch Gus and have him bring something for her from town. The neighbor said they'd been gone thirty minutes. Then she called the gas station with the same excuse. The station man said she'd missed them by five minutes.

"She turned into a wild woman then, grabbing her purse and hustling me into the car. We went straight to Nowa Creek with Celeste driving so fast I had to close my eyes most of the way. Gus's pickup was parked off to the side of the little bridge like we knew it would be.

"She pulled in behind it real quietly and put her finger to

her lips to warn me to be quiet. Then she did the strangest thing. She pulled her camera out of her purse. It was the one she used for family snapshots, a real simple thing with a hole on top for attaching a flash cube, and there was a fresh flash cube on it all ready to go. She handed me the camera. Next she leaned way over the backseat and lifted a blanket she'd put on the floor and pulled out one of Gus's shotguns.

"I started stuttering and stammering, but she told me to hush up and follow her.

"Nowa Creek runs in a deep cut. We had to slip and slide down the bank to get to the creek bed. It was pleasant and cool down there, and private . . . shut off from the comings and goings above. Unlike the rest of the land, native trees grew down there. Cottonwoods and willow and black walnut. I wanted to just stop and sit down and enjoy the peace, but Celeste grabbed my arm hard and gave me a look that kept my feet moving and my mouth shut.

"The creek varied in depth, being only two feet or so for stretches and then pooling up deeper in spots. We walked along the edge on stones and little patches of sandy silt. I was wondering if we'd gone the right way when we rounded a clump of brush and spotted Benjamin's blond head. He was sitting on a pile of rock with his line in the water, but he didn't look like a boy fishing for fun at all. His face was all screwed up like he was trying not to cry.

"When he saw us, he dropped his pole and came toward us like a banshee spook, white-eyed with his arms flying. 'You can't go down there, Mama! Abe's in trouble and Papa's punishing him and Papa said if I went down there—'

"Celeste had the shotgun cradled in one arm, and she reached out with the other and grabbed Benjamin's neck and pulled him close so his face was buried in her clothes. 'Shush, Benjamin. I'm going to fix this once and for all. Now, where did he take your brother? Did they go on down the creek?'

"Benjamin nodded.

" 'Okay boy, now you just sit on those rocks and wait for me.'

"We crept on, hunched over and quiet, though the natural noise of the water and the wind rattling the cottonwoods covered up any sounds we were making. I was scared to death.

" 'The camera is all set,' Celeste whispered to me. 'When

we get there, you snap a bunch of pictures. Just keep winding and snapping.'

"We heard something and Celeste eased up next to a willow that trailed into the water. Then Gus's voice boomed out loud saying, 'This is God's punishment for sneaky little lying papist bastards. Say it, boy, say *Thank you God!*'

"Celeste pulled aside the willow branches so we could look through and we saw them. They were in a cutout where a chunk of creekbank had washed away to make a little protected spot. In that spot some illegal dumpers had dropped a washing machine. It was sitting there upright and it hadn't gone to rust yet at all. It was still shiny white. And sideways across the top of it lay my adopted nephew Abe, on his stomach, with his head and arms hanging down one side and his butt perched on the edge and his legs dangling down the other side. He had on his shirt, but his pants and underwear were laying over a bush.

"One part of my brain said that the boy was like that so Gus could whip him. Gus had always been one for whipping on bare skin. But Gus's own pants were down partway and what was going on wasn't whipping at all. I saw it clear as day and I have a picture of it frozen in my mind that comes to me in nightmares still, but right then I couldn't understand what I was seeing.

" 'The pictures,' Celeste hissed at me. 'Take the pictures!' And I put that little camera to my eye and snapped away. Everything was small-looking through that camera, and it wasn't nearly as ugly. It didn't even look real.

"The flash went off twice before Gus noticed it. Through that camera I saw him stop and turn, exposing the full evil of his doings. I saw him drag his pants on and charge toward us like a murder-bent bull.

" 'I'll fix you, Celeste!' he screamed.

"I stopped taking pictures then and got set to run, but Celeste stepped right up. Ducked through that willow with the shotgun pointed straight at his belly and brought him to a dead stop.

" 'You wouldn't shoot me,' he said but his voice didn't sound so sure, and he didn't give it a chance by moving.

" 'Abe,' she called, 'can you get down and get your pants on by yourself?'

"Abe didn't answer but he eased on down, real painful like, and started into his pants.

" 'See that camera Milly's got?' Celeste said to Gus. 'How many pictures did you get, Milly?'

"My hand was shaking, but I held the camera up close and read the number. 'Nine,' I said, surprised because I didn't remember winding and clicking that many times at all.

" 'You know what happens to a man who does what you did, Gus?'

" 'I'm the head of this family, and I'll punish my boys the way I see fit.'

" 'That's not punishment. That's a crime! Before God and before the law!'

" 'God don't watch over that bastard child you crammed down my throat, woman.'

" 'You wouldn't know, Gus Hanselmann, because you have lost God. And now you've just lost a whole lot more.' She smiled that real terrible smile again. 'These pictures are the proof of what you are, and if you don't do exactly as I say I'll march that film right down to the sheriff's office and put you away in prison where you belong.

" 'Abe, you go way around him. Don't get near the filth. And you go on and collect your brother and you two get in the car. It's parked at the bridge.'

" 'What are you fixin' to do?' Gus asked and it was the first time I'd ever heard him fearful.

" 'You're gonna march ahead of me and get into your pickup and follow us to the lawyer's office. Then we'll go in together all nice like with that film tucked away in Milly's purse, and you'll tell the lawyer that you've decided to change your will so that Abe inherits the farm equally with Benjamin. And you'll tell him you want that in some sort of trust or something that can't ever be changed. That you decided it wasn't fair for one boy to be left out in the cold with nothing.'

"Gus's face went dark red and his breathing turned funny so that I thought he might keel over and die right there.

" 'Then that film is going into safekeeping,' Celeste went on. 'I'll put it in an envelope with a letter about what to do with it should anything suspicious ever happen to me or should you try to break the will. And I'll say in the letter that Milly or Abe can have that film to use against you if I should die and you start misbehaving.

" 'You always said I was smart, Gus. And I've thought

this out real carefully. Do you hear what I'm saying? Do you understand that this little roll of film here puts your privates in a vice grip, and I can crush them to pulp if you don't mind me from now on. You owe Abe and you owe me, and it's time you started paying up.'

"Gus was a different man by the time we'd marched him back to his truck. He appeared ten years older and a darn sight tamer than he had before.

"That was the ugliest most evil thing I'd ever seen in my life, and later, after all Celeste's business was attended to and we were safely back home with Gus left sitting in his pickup in town, I just wanted to gather those boys to my bosom and cry and cry. But Celeste wouldn't have it.

" 'No time for breakdowns,' she said. She let Abe take a bath and lie down, but she put Benjamin and me to work. We moved Gus out of the master bedroom lock-stock-and-barrel. Carried all his things up to the attic. And we moved me out of the attic and down to sleep with Celeste.

" 'That man will never share my bed again,' she said, and I knew she meant it.

"Things went pretty smooth for a few months after that. The boys started back to school. Gus kept to himself, staying outside or in the attic or just plain gone most of the time. At meals he sat like a stone while Celeste talked about gossip and crops and daily doings. The boys and I never said a word except for please pass the potatoes and such.

"That was when Celeste started getting so carried away about germs. It didn't seem so odd in the beginning. She'd always been one to take those magazine articles to heart, the ones about cleanliness and bacteria and infection and all that, and when she started scrubbing with toothbrushes and vacuuming more often and cleaning the sinks and toilet and tub with bleach every day no one thought much of it. But then she started on herself, washing her hands every fifteen minutes and taking two or three baths every day and spraying Lysol on her skin afterward like you'd spray on cologne. She harped on the boys constantly about their grooming and she was full of stories for them about the disgusting germs lurking in the crevices of their bodies.

"We were forbidden to wear shoes in the house and we got to be like those Japanese families where the shoes stay lined up by the door and everyone pads around in socks inside.

"Now through all this Gus stomped around, muttering to himself. Pushing her in little ways. Not taking off his shoes for one thing. Purposely tracking in mud and manure, or leaving dirty handprints around. As time went on he got bolder and found new ways to get back at her. He never laid a hand on either boy again, but he said the ugliest things to Abe whenever Celeste was out of earshot. And he turned sour to Benjamin too, barking at him all the time about how clumsy and stupid he was.

"About that time Fred Kunstler came into my life. I'd known the man for years, him being a regular member of our congregation and all, but I'd never said more than the usual that passes between one churchgoer and another when one of those folks is a single female and the other a married man.

"Fred's wife had been real sick for a time and she'd finally gone on to her final rest. He kept to himself for six months or so after she went, showing up at church services but not taking part in any socials or potluck suppers, and refusing all offers of help. But we all knew he was being looked after, because he had married children scattered around and they showed up pretty regularly to visit him.

"Then one day, out of the blue, Celeste and I were scrubbing out the refrigerator and up drives Fred Kunstler. Celeste waved to him out the window and yelled for him to come in.

" 'Gus isn't here,' she said as soon as Fred came into the kitchen.

"Fred didn't say anything. He watched us going at that refrigerator a minute, then said, 'You wouldn't have a glass of tea for a thirsty fellow, would ya?'

"I got him the tea and he sat down at the table and visited about this and that till we were done with our chore and joined him at the table.

"He started talking about how long it had been since he'd seen a movie and Celeste told him that Gus thought movies were a waste of time and Fred said an interesting movie was better than hitting the whiskey bottle and she agreed on that. All the while Celeste kept glancing at me and we were wondering what in the world had gotten into Fred Kunstler, who hadn't been inside the house more than twice in all the years Celeste had lived there.

" 'How bout you, Miz Milly?' he asked. 'What do you think of movies?'

" 'I like a good movie,' I said. 'Though I can't remember when I last saw one.'

" 'Would you care to see one tonight in my company?'

"My mouth fell open and I could have been knocked off my chair with a feather.

" 'My stars,' Celeste said. 'Are you asking Milly to go out on a date with you, Fred Kunstler?'

" 'I guess I am, Celeste.'

"I could tell Celeste was about to put her foot and both elbows in her mouth, so I said, 'Mr. Kunstler, I would be happy to go out to a movie with you tonight.'

"Looking back I realize that was the beginning of my second chance at a real life. Fred and I started keeping company once a week. Celeste made fun of it and told me I was a fool if I let him take any liberties with me. Gus got furious over the whole thing. Ranted and raved about how the whole town was gossiping and about how I was too old for such carryings on. But he never let Fred hear a word of it.

"By that time Gus's room was finished. Celeste had gotten fed up with him tracking filth through her house and up and down the attic stairs so she'd used her secret savings to hire carpenters and have an addition built. It connected on the back with one door opening to the outside and the other opening into the kitchen. She had it built extra big so she could put Gus's recliner in there, and his cabinet full of important papers, and an end table and lamp, and a gun rack for all his guns. When she was finished, there wasn't a trace of Gus in the rest of the house.

"Gus seemed pleased with the new room. And I got to move back up to my private attic so I was happy. And we all breathed easier with Gus out there separate from the rest of us. Fred thought that Celeste was wrong to stick her husband out there like that. He still thought highly of Gus, just as the rest of the community did. Thought of Gus as a topnotch farmer and a good family man and a solid member of the church.

"I can still remember the stunned look on Fred's face when he had his first peek at the real Gus. It was a Saturday evening. Fred came for me after supper as usual. We were headed out for a slice of pie at a cafe two towns over and a comedy movie that we were both excited about seeing.

"I kissed the boys good-bye and Fred fussed over them a little. Then we went out through the back and Fred held his car door open for me. Suddenly, like a madman, Gus came flying out of his door cussing at us and shaking his fist.

" 'I know what you two are doin'!' he screamed. 'I know what dirty things you been up to!'

"Fred hustled me on into the car and we drove away without saying a word to each other. Finally I said, 'Now you see why Celeste built him a separate room of his own.'

"Fred nodded but we didn't discuss it further.

"Oh . . . I was quite taken with Fred. He didn't make me all starry-eyed like my fiancé did when I was younger, but he was a steady sort. His company was pleasant, and he was kind to his animals and his children. And he could give me what I'd never had before . . . a life of my own. Even if it was another woman's leftovers, as Celeste always reminded me. I knew that Fred would eventually propose if given enough time, and I was worried sick that Gus might drive him away and ruin my chance.

"I started thinking real sneaky. Arranging to meet Fred at the end of the lane or having Celeste drive me somewhere to meet him. Anything to keep him away from Gus.

"But Gus knew what I was doing. He made nasty comments about the new ways I was fixing my hair and the new dresses I'd made to wear with Fred. And the times he'd catch me sneaking out he'd grab me and rub his dirty hands on my face and my dress, or he'd tear the pins out of my hair . . . anything to make me look bad for my date with Fred.

"I insisted that Fred drop me at the end of our drive when we returned at night. He'd kiss me real proper like at the mailbox, then watch me walk up to the door before he drove off. The front door was sealed shut to keep people from tracking up the living room, so I always had to go around to the back and in through the kitchen. I'd go in as quietly as possible, but Gus took to listening for me and the minute he'd hear a floorboard creak he'd barge out of that room of his.

"That man said terrible things to me. And he said them loud so I know Celeste and the boys heard, though no one ever spoke of it. He accused me of being a whore and of seducing Fred into sin. By the time I'd escape and get upstairs to my room, I'd be shaking like a leaf. I'd crawl beneath the covers and pray with all my heart that Fred Kunstler proposed soon. And then I'd soothe myself with imagining how it would feel to be mistress of my own house.

"Fred got close to asking. My, but he got close. He'd circled the question for weeks, and I knew it was just ahead. I got so excited I could hardly eat.

" 'What's the matter, Milly?' Celeste asked at the supper table. 'Can't eat? Got the lovesick jitters?'

"I hated her for saying that in front of Gus, and I kicked her hard under the table, but instead of shutting up she said, 'Oowww, real touchy, huh? He must be close to popping the question.'

"Gus didn't say anything, but he left without finishing his food.

"That night when I tiptoed in I was high as a kite. Fred had asked me if I would come to his home in two weeks for a big dinner. All of his children and their families were driving in. I knew what that meant. Fred was gathering his family for an announcement.

"I made it through the kitchen without Gus bursting out of his door, and I was sailing along on a cloud as I went up my narrow stairs. The realization that Gus was behind me and the pressure of his arm on my neck came so close to each other that I didn't have time to do a thing. He lifted me up and that arm squeezed in on my throat and I couldn't breathe and everything went spinning.

"The next thing I knew I was on my bed with my dress flipped up and he was tugging at my underpants. I was still dizzy but I tried to sit up. He shoved me down and smashed a pillow on my face. I managed to turn my head sideways so I could breathe and then ... Well, I'm not about to tell the rest. I had been pure to that point in my life, but I was pure no more.

"After he was gone, I lay still for a long time. Then I went downstairs and vomited. I can remember kneeling in front of the toilet for a long time, till I finally started wondering what I was doing there. Then I remembered, and I was sick again.

"I got real scared, knowing there was only a wall between me and him and thinking that he could come out after me again. My knees were stiff from pressing into that tile floor, and when I stood up and tried to walk I was sore in my privates.

"I went into Celeste's room and sat down on her bed and

started to cry. She reached to turn on the light and I told her not to. I couldn't have her look at me. She listened to what Gus had done; then she told me to lay down beside her and she started patting me like you do with an upset child.

" 'We'll give you a hot bath,' she said. 'With bleach in it. And you can use my douche to clean inside. Then we'll strip the sheets off your bed and boil them.'

" 'But what should I do?' I asked her. 'Should I call the police?'

" 'If you do,' she said, 'chances are no one will believe you. At least they won't believe it was Gus. And there'll be a scandal. And Fred Kunstler will never marry you.'

"I started crying again.

" 'Hush now,' Celeste said. 'It's over. You've paid your dues just like the rest of us, but it's over. We'll get you clean. And you'll marry Fred and have a house of your own.'

"I took my bath and I slept there the rest of the night, safe and clean beside my sister.

"Gus didn't act any different the next day, and somehow I got through it. Then another day went by. Then another. And that horrible night gradually got far away and dreamlike in my mind.

"Word got around town that Fred's family was all coming in. On Thursday a woman called to ask Celeste if Fred and I were going to make a big announcement over the weekend. And someone must have told Gus.

"Because when he came up to my bedroom late that night he said he was going to fix me where Fred wouldn't want to show me to his family on Saturday. He had his way with me; then afterward he hit my face real hard. I stayed up there till I was sure he'd gone back to his room, then went downstairs and straight to the phone. I dialed Fred and I cried and begged him to come get me. To take me away from Gus forever.

"Celeste heard me on the phone, and she came out in her robe about the time I hung up.

" 'What have you done?' she asked.

" 'What have *I* done?' I got kind of hysterical then and started screaming about how I hadn't done anything. And the boys came peeking out of their room.

" 'You're a fool,' Celeste said; then she turned and yelled for the boys to shut their door and get back to bed. Through all this noise Gus never came out. He stayed there in his room. Safe and comfortable.

"Fred got there quick with his shirt buttoned crooked and his hair sticking up. He ran right in without knocking. When he saw me he stopped dead in his tracks. I hadn't looked in a mirror yet so I didn't know how bad I looked.

" 'Please, Fred,' I begged. 'Please take me to your house. I'll do anything for you. I'll make you the best wife any man ever had, but please take me away now.'

"Fred's Adam's apple worked itself up and down a few times, and then he said, 'What were you and Gus fightin' about?'

" 'We weren't fighting! He attacked me, Fred. He came up to my bed while I was asleep and he . . . he attacked me. You've got to get me away from here. If you care for me at all . . .'

" 'Did he . . .' Fred put his hand over his mouth like he was trying to keep the words in. Then he took his hand away and said, 'Did you and Gus have relations?'

"That question cooled my hysterics fast and made me suddenly very ashamed. I couldn't look at Fred anymore. 'I wouldn't call it relations,' I said; then I started saying how I loved Fred and wanted to make him a good wife.

"And he said—I'll never forget what he said—Fred Kuntsler looked at me and said, 'I thought this was a good family, with strong, God-fearing people. I thought you were a fine woman, but now, heck, this bears some thinking, Milly,' and he walked right out of that house.

"Next day Celeste heard that Fred suddenly closed up his place and went for a long visit with one of his children.

"Gus didn't bother me again. But then I didn't give him much chance either. With the boys' help I put a hasp and padlock on the inside of my door. Celeste complained that if there was a fire they'd never be able to get me out but that didn't worry me. I started sleeping with a butcher knife under my pillow, too.

"Shortly after, in my monthly correspondence with my old church group in Arcadia, I learned that a crippled woman in the group, Lois, had become widowed and was in need of a home companion. I wrote to her and was gone from Gus Hanselmann's house in short order. I swore I'd never set foot in it again.

"The boys were heartbroken about my going, and I was

every bit as torn up about having to leave them behind. But I had to go. Even for them I couldn't stay on. They were thirteen by then and I think they understood.

"They wrote me faithfully. Every week there was a letter. They told me all about school and about their latest interests. Sometimes they mentioned their mother, but they never ever wrote a word about their father. A couple times, during summer vacations, they came on the bus to visit me.

"Celeste wrote me too, though not as faithfully. Then about the time the boys were sixteen she wrote to say she had a big lump in her bosom and that the doctor guessed she was too far gone to save.

"I went back then. What Gus had put me through and what I'd learned while caring for my crippled friend had changed me mightily and I wasn't afraid to go back there. I was ready to stand up to Gus Hanselmann and put a bullet in him if that's what it came to. So I made arrangements to have my friend taken care of and rode the bus to my sister's side. Nursed her for the two months it took her to die.

"I asked her why she'd let that lump get so big, and she said she hadn't known it was there. That she certainly wasn't the sort of person who touched herself without a washcloth in her hand. Her suffering made me question a lot of things . . . my faith for one. How could it be right that a woman like Celeste was being punished so horribly while Gus Hanselmann was healthy as a horse?

"The boys were glad to see me. They'd grown to be big strapping fellows, and my heart nearly burst when I saw them. Benjamin was big as an ox but still had that sweet round face. Abe was tall as his brother but built more like a racehorse, and he'd developed the kind of face that interested the girls.

"Through that time, I never spoke to Gus Hanselmann or looked at him. He ate the food I cooked, but he took it to his own room to do so, and he never came into the house past the kitchen. I think he behaved himself because he knew that he'd be in a pickle if I packed my bags and left Celeste to him. His being proper couldn't have been forced by the boys because they were still cowed by him. Big as Benjamin was, the boy quaked in his boots when his father hollered.

"It goes without saying that those two months were hell. But there was a good side to it. The boys and I had a chance to get real close again. In the evenings after I had Celeste medicated and settled into sleep, we'd sit together in the living room. Celeste had put a wood stove in after I left, and it made the room real cozy on winter nights.

"We'd sit and visit for hours watching the stove pop, and I got to where I could see the men those boys were coming to be. Benjamin and Abe. My poor little boys.

"Benjamin was quiet and strong. Strong in his opinions and strong in his loyalties. He could be short-tempered and quick to take offense, but he was the soul of kindness to his brother and me.

"Abe was too gentle for his own good. And he'd grown too darn handsome for his own good. He'd gone from being an outcast to having all the girls after him, and he didn't know what to make of it. He was easily confused and had no confidence in himself, so he looked to his brother for guidance in just about everything.

"As to the art business . . . Both boys made things then. Little carvings and such. It was Benjamin who talked it up, though. He was always telling Abe about some country boy who made good as an artist. Abe would follow Benjamin's lead, carving if Benjamin told him to carve, but he wasn't driven by anything the way Benjamin was. Funny thing, though, Benjamin would work and sweat over something, some crazy welded statue or some such, and then Abe would wander over and make a better one in half the time. Used to drive Benjamin wild.

"And of course it was all a big secret. Farm boys had to be careful about being interested in such a thing as art unless they wanted to be laughed out of the county. Cutting designs into leather was fine and welding up a fancy gate was fine and making a nice pencil drawing of your neighbor's mule was fine . . . but art . . . big city art . . . that was for sissys and weirdos. I was the only one they shared the secret with.

"We buried Celeste in the Ridley town cemetery. There was a nice service at the church, another at the gravesite and then a buffet supper in the church basement. Fred Kunstler didn't come. Judging from the fine turnout and all the sympathies expressed to Gus, Fred had never told anyone what he knew about Gus. Either that or folks decided Gus was a prince anyway. The whole thing made me sick, watching how everyone fussed over Gus like he was the poor grieving widower, when the only thing he was going to miss about my sister was hot meals and clean laundry.

"I left the day after the funeral. The boys took me to the bus station.

"We went back to writing letters and things went along okay for the boys. Or at least that's the way it sounded from what they wrote.

"Abe turned eighteen and Benjamin was due to turn. I sent Abe his card and a little gift. And I had Benjamin's ready to go, and I'd even done my shopping for their high school graduation, which was a few months off. I'd decided on suitcases. Nice ones with their initials on the handles. And I was planning to put a note in each about how I hoped they used them to see more of the world than I ever did.

"When out of the blue one day, Abe drove up. He was in that old car of Celeste's, and he was real pale but all spotted and stained.

" 'Is that blood? Have you hurt yourself, son?' I asked.

" 'It's Benjamin. I think Gus might'a killed him, Aunt Milly.'

"Well, I sat him down and pried the whole story out of him, and this is what he told me. He said Gus got real spooked after Celeste's death, wondering what would become of that roll of film and the letter that lawyer had. Finally, he went in and asked that lawyer some questions, and when he came back he was all puffed up and bragging about how he knew things now that Celeste never knew and about how he had a way to get rid of that film for good and change his will back to favor Benjamin and disinherit Abe.

"Abe didn't know what the big plan was, but it was something that needed Benjamin's cooperation to work. And Benjamin wasn't cooperating. Benjamin kept saying that Abe was his brother and by God he deserved half that farm.

"Gus got to where changing the will was all he could talk about. Not harping on Abe being a bastard so much as he was making it sound like he was in some kind of war with Celeste that he was determined to win in the end.

"It all blew up when they went out early in the morning together in Gus's pickup, heading to the back forty to check the electric fence because the neighbor's cattle had been through in the night. Abe started walking the fence and Gus lit in on nagging at Benjamin, telling him how everything was going to be his someday if he had the gumption to do what was right and help Gus set the will straight.

"Benjamin ignored his father and just opened the back of

the pickup and got out the toolbox, and Gus got madder and started yelling. And suddenly Benjamin yelled back at him. Just stuck out his chin and said, 'Who says I even want your goddamn farm!'

"And Gus exploded. Gus jumped on Benjamin. He beat him with his fists and kicked him and slammed Benjamin's head into the tailgate. And Benjamin never even fought back. Just tried to protect himself. And while he was being beaten, Benjamin hollered, 'Run, Abe!' and Abe ran. He ran all the way back to the house and called the law. Told them to come quick because Benjamin Hanselmann was being killed.

"Then he grabbed a shotgun from the house and jumped in the old car and drove back near as he could to where they were. He could see them. Benjamin on the ground and Gus standing over him like a statue. He took the gun and ran across the field. Benjamin was in a heap. Covered with blood and not moving.

"Abe dropped the gun and knelt beside Benjamin, who was breathing real raspy and not conscious at all, and Abe held his brother's head and he screamed at Gus to get away before he shot him. Then old man Vern arrived. He was the law.

" 'Call an ambulance!' Abe yelled and Vern said an ambulance was on the way and Vern asked what happened here, and Gus pointed down at Abe and said, 'That sorry bastard tried to kill my true son. Lock him up, Vern. He's madder'n a rabid dog.'

"And Abe jumped up and ran to Celeste's car. And he drove all the way to me in Arcadia without stopping for anything but gas.

"I calmed him down as best I could. Then I picked up the phone and called long-distance to the hospital, where I figured they would have taken Benjamin. The woman I talked to in the emergency room said they had a Benjamin Hanselmann in surgery.

"I gave this news to Abe, and he put his head down on my table and cried like a baby. I got him a blanket to wrap up in, and my crippled ladyfriend wheeled her chair out to sit with him while I washed his clothes and packed a few things.

" 'You better stay here,' I told him, 'while I go see to your brother and straighten old Vern out on who did what to who.'

"I called for one of the church ladies to come take over my chores and I climbed into Celeste's car and headed up to 54 west. It was the first time I'd ever driven so far on my own, but I figured there was no great trick to it.

"Took me five hours. But the time went fast with all the worrying and hoping I had to do. I kept thinking that if I'd been Celeste I'd have killed Gus Hanselmann soon as the doctor gave me the news that I was dying of cancer.

"It was around eight in the evening when I arrived at the hospital. I found Benjamin's room. It said no visitors but I went in anyway. He was all patched up and casted and his head was wound round like a mummy with tubes stuck here and there.

"I took his hand, which was the only part of him that didn't appear to be hurt, and he stirred a little so I leaned down close and whispered it was me and that Abe was at my house and had told me the story. I said Abe would come see him soon as I set old Vern straight. That made him sort of sob and he gripped my hand real weak like and I could tell he wanted to say something so I put my ear right by his mouth but I couldn't hear anything.

" 'I can't hear you, son,' I said. 'Why don't you rest and I'll sit here with you. I'll stay all night if you like.'

"But he seemed upset, moving his head a little like he was shaking it, so I put my ear close again and told him to try speaking real slow. And he said, 'Keep ... Abe ... away. Safe.'

"And I asked did he not want Abe to come home? Was he afraid of what Gus might do to Abe? And he squeezed my hand.

"I talked to a nurse. Found out Benjamin had a cracked skull and a broken jaw and a broken arm and a busted spleen ... plus a lot of stitches. She said it looked bad at first, but that the doctors were satisfied that he was going to make it.

"I called home and told Abe everything. Told him Benjamin wanted him to stay there where he was safe from Gus. Told him his brother was going to be a long time healing.

"I sat there with Benjamin every day for a week. Gus came by once a day. When he did, I left the room without speaking to him. I talked to old Vern. He didn't believe me about it being Gus who was guilty. Princely Gus. Said he'd have to wait until Benjamin could tell the story.

"Letters came from Abe. They were mostly for me to read to Benjamin. But I didn't read them to him because I was worried they might upset Benjamin too much. Whenever the nurse brought one in, I hid it, or I skimmed through and only read certain parts. Because they were full of confusion. Abe felt terrible guilt over not having saved his brother from Gus, and he felt guilt at not being there at Benjamin's bedside. I wrote back and tried to soothe him, but I don't think it helped much.

"Finally, after about two weeks when Benjamin was feeling much better, there came a letter saying that Abe had joined the service. Said he figured it was best for all if he went away for a time, and he thought maybe the army would give him some courage. Said he'd write again soon.

"Benjamin was torn up about his brother going off like that, but he was relieved too, knowing Gus couldn't get at him. He told me that he and Abe had talked about running off to the army before. Just like their friend Luke had done. And it didn't surprise me to hear that it had been Benjamin's idea in the first place because I don't think Abe would have done something that his brother hadn't thought of first.

"Benjamin healed pretty fast considering what he'd been through. When old Vern came by to talk to him he was real thoughtful. He asked old Vern if he could count on Gus going to prison if he pressed charges for assault. Old Vern said that seeing as how it was a first offense and it happened during a domestic quarrel and Gus Hanselmann was a fine upstanding member of the community, probably nothing much would happen to Gus.

"Benjamin considered that and said he didn't see that a family fight should be blown up too big. And that he'd tripped and hit his own head on the tailgate. And that the fight had probably been his fault in the first place. Old Vern nodded and said that was okay by him and the whole thing was dropped.

"I was mad as a hornet but I knew why Benjamin did it even before he explained himself. If he could have put Gus clean away, that would have been one thing, but speaking out against Gus and having him still walking around free would have been stupid and dangerous.

"Benjamin went home from the hospital with his jaw

wired shut and a cast on his arm and a lot of new scars.
Soon as I saw that he could manage for himself I left him.
But first I marched up to Gus Hanselmann and I told him
that I didn't care what that lawyer had led him to believe. I
still knew what was in Celeste's envelope. I knew what I'd
seen and I knew what I could prove he was. And if he laid
another hand on Benjamin, I was going to tell both Old Vern
and the pastor the whole story and give them that film.

"After I left Benjamin wrote me letters that made it sound
like Gus was treating him better than ever. Course Gus had
lots of reasons to be happy. He'd finally gotten rid of Abe
and he'd beaten Benjamin into submission.

"Benjamin said that, in spite of everything, Gus managed
to change the will, but Benjamin said not to worry because
as soon as he inherited he would give Abe half anyway. The
high school let Benjamin graduate and I sent him his suitcase. Abe wrote to say the army had fixed it so he'd gotten
his diploma, so I sent along his suitcase. There was no joy
for me in the giving, though, just worry for both those boys.

"Abe wrote how great life in the army was. Said it wasn't
as much work as living with Gus and not near as much
abuse. He was real excited about meeting up with Luke and
anxious to be shipped to Vietnam, because Luke's letters had
made Vietnam sound so exotic, you know. And I could tell
Abe's excitement was having an effect on Benjamin because
Benjamin started writing to me about how he was going to
join his brother in the army as soon as he healed up completely.

"But then Abe went to Vietnam and his tune changed.
Said Benjamin should stay out of the army if he could. That
he ought to find out about farming deferments or whatever
because Vietnam was bad. He said Luke had not been writing home the truth. Then he sent word that he couldn't write
letters to us anymore or receive them either, because he had
been chosen for some top-secret assignments and he would
be undercover.

"I didn't know what would happen next. Seemed all my
time was spent worrying about one boy getting shot way off
on the other side of the world and the other boy being at the
mercy of a lunatic right there at home.

"Then, one day . . . just a regular day with no warnings or
sudden chill bumps or anything to signal such a change, the
phone rang. I was ironing tea towels and I just picked it up

casual like, expecting it to be a neighbor. It was Benjamin. He was calling from the hospital where Gus Hanselmann had just been pronounced dead. Just like that, we were all free. Or so it seemed at the time.

"Near as anyone could figure, Gus had been out by the equipment shed, dragging something on a chain behind the tractor. The chain broke and snapped up, whipping Gus off the seat. Then the runaway tractor pinned him up against the shed wall. He was dead from internal injuries by the time Benjamin found him.

"I took the bus out and I stayed by Benjamin's side through all the carrying on. Together we chose the coffin and made all the arrangements.

"He needed me beside him to get through it all because I was the only person who understood that he wasn't mourning his father's passing. That there was no grief.

"Course as soon as we could we called the army so that Abe could be notified. We were even hoping Abe might get to come home for the funeral. The army said they'd get back to us. We went ahead with the funeral. Two days later we found out that Abe couldn't be told about his father's death because Abe was missing.

"Benjamin broke down then. Got down on his knees and started praying. Asking God to forgive him and not take out his sins on Abe. Begging that Abe be all right.

"And then he confessed the truth.

"The accident happened like he said. Only he was driving up into the yard in his pickup and he saw it happen. He saw Gus get pinned. And he ran to help, and Gus, smashed up against that wall as he was, yelled, 'Get your ass over here, boy!'

"And Benjamin said that just stopped him. He turned his back and got in his pickup and thought of an errand and went and did it. Two hours later, when he drove back into the yard, his father was dead.

"And he was afraid that God had taken Abe to punish him.

"What could I say to that? Maybe Gus would have died in any case, even if he'd been hauled straight to the hospital. But I didn't believe that then. I believed it was murder. And I knew that Benjamin believed it was murder.

" 'You have a stain on your soul that will never go away,' I said. 'This whole family has been tainted. Your father's heart was black as pitch and his sins corrupted us all. Fouled us all. Your mother spent her life trying to scrub it away, but she couldn't. And God took her and now He may have taken Abe too.'

"You see I was so deep wallowing in my own guilt and misery that I didn't see what my words were doing to Benjamin. I should have been more careful of him. I should have protected him instead of rubbing salt on the wounds.

"I heard him up all night prowling around the house, but I didn't go out to him. I figured I had time. I figured the next day we'd start the healing together.

"When I got up in the morning, he was gone with the pickup. I made breakfast, thinking he'd be back anytime. Then I made noon dinner thinking he'd surely be home for that. Along about two o'clock I got a call from the banker in town. Said he had a letter for me from Benjamin and also he wanted to explain some things to me.

"I took Celeste's car in. The banker told me Benjamin had been in most of the day meeting with him and the attorney about the estate. Benjamin had fixed it so as soon as the estate was settled I'd have some money to do with as I pleased. The banker gave me his card with his name and number. Then he gave me Benjamin's letter.

"The first part told me more details about what I'd already heard from the banker. Benjamin was selling the farm, the whole kit and caboodle. Except for the pickup, which he was keeping, and the car, which was to be mine. As for the household goods, he said for me to help myself, and he asked if I'd please take a few things to keep for Abe ... whatever I thought he'd like to have. He said not to be shy about it because the leftovers would be auctioned and this was my only chance; then he went on to explain how I could ship it or store it if I had the mind to.

"I memorized the second part of his letter. Read it over so many times that I could recite it like a grade-school poem.

" 'I thought all night about what you said, Aunt Milly. I guess it's true that God now looks on me as a murderer. I am worse than Gus ever was since now I have the mark of blood forever on my soul. All I can see are two choices which are to put a gun to my head or to quit being who I am and go on to being someone else. Since Abe might still be out there somewhere I am going on and trusting that I will be reunited with him. Whatever happens I will always remember you with love, even though you now see me as the same evil that my father was. I will always make sure you are taken care of and you can be sure that if Abe is alive I will find him and take care of him too.

    'Good-bye.

    'Your loving nephew,

    'Benjamin.' "

19

Milly Corwin closed her eyes and was so still for a moment that Owen worried she might have fainted.

"Just rest," he said, feeling emotionally wrung-out himself.

"No," she said firmly. "I don't want to stop till I'm completely finished. I want to get it all done."

She cleared her throat and roused herself to continue.

"The farm and all the machinery sold for a pretty penny. And it turned out that Gus had a savings account stashed away too. Even with taxes and such Benjamin was well fixed, and he had a good start in that new life he wanted.

"I got money orders from him every month. Wrapped in plain paper and never with a return address. All I knew was that they were always postmarked from New York City. A lot of years passed like that. Then finally I got a letter from Benjamin saying that Abe was home safe. Unlike poor Luke who never came back. He said Abe and him had new lives that would probably make my mouth drop open, and that he hoped I could spare a kind thought for him now and then. If I could have just written back to him, I would have told him how sorry I was and how much I missed him. But he never gave me a chance.

"The money orders kept arriving like clockwork. Then out of the blue I got a phone call. It was Abe. He was crying and not making too much sense. Saying things like "Why, Aunt Milly?" over and over, and telling me how sorry he was. I tried to get him to tell me where he was at but he said he didn't know. Then he called me again about a week later and sounded perfectly fine. Told me he'd missed me and wished he could talk Benjamin into all of us having a visit. Told me he was painting lots of pictures. But he said he couldn't give me his address or phone because Benjamin would be real mad if he did. I begged him to ask Benjamin to call me.

"The third time he called he was crying again and told me he'd done terrible things. Told me he'd seen things that made Gus Hanselmann look like a saint. But at the last he calmed down and sounded almost happy. Said he had a surprise for me.

"And that was it for the calls. I never got another from him after those three. Then one of my money orders came with a note from Benjamin, apologizing for his brother's calls. Said he hoped Abe hadn't upset me. Said Abe wasn't himself all the time, but not to worry because Benjamin was taking good care of him.

"Years passed. Along about 1985 my crippled lady died and I was out of a home and a job. I took a room in a boarding house and was getting by. Then one day papers came telling me Benjamin Hanselmann had bought a share in Golden Age Village for me. Starting whenever I wanted. I moved here and shortly after I got a letter from Benjamin saying he hoped I liked Golden Age.

"He said they had a good and happy life. And that he had put the past behind him so well that he couldn't remember a lot of things anymore. But that he'd always remember me. He signed it with love, and it made me ache with missing him. I got so filled up with regrets and guilt from the past that I couldn't leave my bed for days.

"From then on he wrote something every month when he sent me the money order. Sometimes it was just *Hello Aunt Milly* or some such, and other times it was a note. One time he told me all about how he hated banks and how the banks worked with the government to get you. He said he hoped I wasn't keeping my money in a bank. That worried me because it sounded so like his father.

"There were other things that put me in mind of his father too ... things like ... well, one time he warned me against doctors and dentists. Said they were all greedy crooks and that they invented most of the ills people had just so they'd have a reason to cut on you. Specially if they knew you had some money. Then I also recall him saying that he had come to realize that most people were out to get him, but he knew how to deal with people and he knew how to protect himself. That kind of talk made me shake my head and worry that he had turned into a man like his father. But then there was his kindness ... That never wavered. And I figured that as long as he had that kindness in his heart, he'd never become Gus Hanselmann.

"The kindness could take strange turns, though. Like one time he wrote that he was glad to hear my wrist wasn't broken. Now that gave me chill bumps for days. Because I'd never been able to write a word to that boy, and how did he know I'd hurt my wrist, much less that it was sprained instead of broke? I started asking questions and sure enough Benjamin had been calling the doctors and the Golden Age manager and checking up on me ever since I'd moved in. I was madder'n a hornet over that."

Aunt Milly paused, lost in thought a moment.

"A year or so ago I suddenly got a letter from Abe. It was just as fine as you please, neat and with all the proper punctuation and spelling and such. He said that he had temporarily separated from his brother but that he was doing fine and starting life over, and that he intended to make amends to everyone, which included me. And that he promised to see me soon and to reunite all of us. The postmark was from Canada.

"That letter filled me with such hope, but the months passed without anything happening. Then the money orders from Benjamin stopped. Just dead stopped. And there were no more calls to Golden Age to check up on me. And I said to myself, Milly Corwin, something terrible has happened."

Camille Corwin sighed heavily and took a long drink of her tea. "I guess I knew in my heart right then that they were dead. And that's the end of the story."

The clock on the wall ticked loudly. Outside the windows a relentless Kansas wind rattled in the Golden Age trees.

Owen inhaled deeply. "We don't know about Al—I mean Abe . . . the adopted one," he reminded her. "He could be doing fine somewhere, just like his last letter said."

"That's hard for me to hang on to," she said sadly. "I don't think that boy could handle things on his own. Without his brother he was helpless."

"But we don't know," Owen insisted. "You could hear from him any day."

"I'd like to believe that." Her expression changed and the pain was visible in her eyes. "If you find Abe with all this research . . . you will tell me, won't you?"

"Absolutely. Right away. And if I can't get Abe to come to you, I'll find a way to get you to him. I promise."

She reached over to pat Owen's hand. Then cleared her throat and recovered her primness.

"Well, go ahead, young man. Do your job. Ask me questions."

Owen tried to collect his thoughts. "Let's see ... Okay, when you got the call from one of them ... you said it was Abe ... and he was talking about painting. Did you mean to say it was Benjamin who'd called you?"

"No. It was Abe. And now, from what you've told me, I realize that it was just Abe pretending to do what his brother did. Pretending he was painting pictures."

"This friend of theirs named Luke who went off to the service. That wouldn't be Luther Bachman, would it?"

Her face registered surprise. "It sure would. How did you know that."

"I found his name in some of Bram's ... Benjamin's things."

"Go ahead. You can call him Bram. Sounds like that's the way he wanted it."

"Could you tell me more about Luke Bachman?"

"Oh, he was a sad case. A real Dutchey from over at Hutzell. A Mennonite gone bad. You don't find many of them. He was working at a neighbor's and the boys got acquainted with him. Those three got on so well together that the boys begged Gus to let Luke move in with them. You can imagine Gus's reaction to that. Well, those three boys were thick as thieves till the neighbor accused Luke— wrongly, it turned out—of stealing. Before he could be cleared, Luke ran off and joined the service. He wrote to those boys every week faithfully, and they wrote to him. But he was killed in Vietnam, just after Abe went off and joined. The boys were real torn up over his death."

"Did you ever see any of Luke's letters?"

"No. Don't know what happened to them."

Owen's thoughts were racing. Luke Bachman was Lenore's father. He was certain of it. In seeking out Lenore, Bram had no doubt been fulfilling a promise to Luke, or maybe he'd just decided to find her and take care of her in honor of his dead friend. And Lenore ... the name "Lenore" ... Luke had named the baby after his friends' grandmother—the kind and gentle woman of the Arcadia tales Milly Corwin had spun. That was it. That had to be the answer.

Owen wanted to jump up and call Lenore immediately, but it was three central time, so it would be four in New York. Lenore would still be in court.

"I guess Benjamin hated his father so much that he took his adopted brother's name for spite," Owen said.

"Yes," Milly agreed sadly. "Abram Serian . . . That was the name that poor orphaned child came to us with."

Owen shook his head. "So Benjamin, or Bram . . . canceled out his father's name . . . canceled out the entire Hanselmann bloodline with the name of someone his father considered a 'Papist bastard.' That had to have been an act of extreme hatred."

Milly nodded. "But there may have been something more than hatred working. That boy may have always wished that he had been the adopted one—the one his mother loved and the one without Gus Hanselmann's blood running in his veins. He may have always wanted to be Bram Serian."

"But Abe. Why would he have changed his name too? Why wouldn't he have kept calling himself Abe?"

"I don't know," Milly said. "But the name he chose to use was my father's name . . . Al or Albert was my father's name. Maybe he changed his name so that he could always live in my fairy tales. So he could forget his growing up. It's almost too much to grab ahold of at once, isn't it?"

Owen shook his head and let his thoughts drift for a moment. He knew that there were questions he was forgetting to ask about Bram-Benjamin or Al-Abe, but he couldn't think of what they might be. Instead, something else was bothering him.

"Milly . . . I'm sorry, I mean Miz Corwin . . . why did you tell me so much? I mean, exactly why?"

She eyed him with her sharp, birdlike stare. "That's my business, isn't it? Point is you got your story."

"You wouldn't be trying to get back at your nephews, would you? Trying to punish them for deserting you by telling all the secrets they'd guarded so closely?"

"I would never hurt those boys! Never! I want the truth known on all this, and the truth is that those boys were innocent victims. Just like Celeste and I were victims. Victims of one evil man. And even when Benjamin turned his back on his dying father, it was his father's own evil that caused it."

She frowned at Owen. Then she dropped her gaze and studied the gnarled hands folded in her lap. "There's mostly women in this place. At least the ones who are well enough to socialize are women. And we get together a lot. We talk a lot. And I've heard woman after woman tell of how she was treated when she was younger. One used to eat her dinner off the kitchen floor like a dog anytime her husband didn't think the house was clean enough. Another has little cigarette burns on her arm from when her husband thought she was flirting in church. I've heard about rapes and beatings and I've heard about pregnant bellies being kicked. I've heard about abuse from fathers and brothers, and kitchen table abortions to get rid of the evidence. And that's from the women who talk. God knows what all the silent ones like me are keeping inside.

"And it's occurred to me through these many years, that men aren't naturally bad any more than women are naturally bad. But it's like in all those old king and queen stories my mother used to read. When a person has too much power over other people, there's always trouble.

"You take a man like Gus Hanselmann and put him out there in the country as the head of a family, and he becomes the ruler of his own little kingdom. His own little world where he steps out onto his own fields every day and settles in his own home at night . . . and he's in a position to take out every unhappiness and frustration he's ever known on those below him—his wife and children. And the law and the pastor and even the closest neighbors figure that what goes on in his kingdom is his business.

"I'm different now. I see things different. I've had all these women here open my eyes, and I know that what happened with us was maybe more ugly than most, but it wasn't so rare at all. There's a word for it, for having too much power and misusing it . . . *tyranny.* You know what that means."

He nodded.

"Well, I hear a lot of things these days on the television about rights and such. About how much better women are doing now. I don't know how much is true because I also see shows about how women are still getting black eyes at home and how children are still having unspeakable things done to them."

She shrugged, suddenly hesitant and self-deprecating. "Listen to me, will you. A rambling old lady."

"I think I understand what you're trying to say, Miz Corwin. You want the ugly truths brought out for people to face."

"Yes," she said gratefully. "I want folks to know that it happens in a lot of families that appear to be fine from the outside. And maybe . . . maybe if enough stories like this are told folks will learn for the future."

Her eyes took on a faraway look. "My mother was a great lover of history. She said that the only thing that made humans so smart was the ability to learn from the past and plan a better future. Well, I think it's time folks started realizing that history is more than wars and politics and flying into outer space. History is also Gus and Abe and Benjamin and Celeste and me. And all this talk about living in a free country doesn't mean anything if you live with tyranny in your own home."

Milly crossed her arms and set her mouth self-consciously. She toed the flowered hatbox on the floor at her feet. "You take this with you. It's got the letters from the boys in it. And you take that box of pictures. And you use whatever you need.

"You take it all and write a book that will make people understand. That will teach people."

Owen didn't know what to say.

"You were meant to do this, son. You're the right person to do this. You know that, don't you?"

He hesitated a moment, then nodded. The silence stretched out between them.

"Well, go on," she said. "Take it all and get to work."

"These things are probably valuable," he warned her.

She shrugged. "By rights maybe they should belong to this widow woman you keep talking about."

"Lenore?"

"That's right."

"Yes. They should be hers."

"Before you go . . . tell me something about this Lenore."

"Oh . . . she's . . . she seems very sophisticated and aloof, but after you're around her for a time you realize how insecure she is. How troubled. And alone."

"Go on. Tell me more. What's she look like?"

"She's younger than your nephew was. And she's . . . striking. Exotic, I guess you could say. Half-Asian."

"By Asian you mean Oriental?" Milly asked in surprise.

"Yes. Some refer to her as Amerasian or Eurasian . . . Whatever . . . she had an Anglo-American father and an Asian mother."

"Oh, my." Milly chuckled softly. "Gus Hanselmann must have turned over in his grave . . . to have his son marry a foreigner outside his race. I wonder if that wasn't part of her attraction."

"There might be something more than that to Bram's marrying her," Owen told her. "From everything I've learned . . . I believe Lenore's father was Luther Bachman."

Milly's mouth opened in an astonished O.

"I think that is exactly why Bram married her. Because she was his dead friend's daughter."

As soon as Owen left Golden Age Village, he stopped at a convenience store pay phone. First he called Alex's number, hoping to reach Cliff for more computer work. Failing to do so, he left a message on the answering machine explaining where he was and why the proposal still hadn't been turned in. Then he asked if Cliff could check into the basic facts of military service for Abe or Abram Hanselmann and for Benjamin Hanselmann, both of Ridley, Kansas. Then, with a quickening inside him at the thought of hearing her voice, he called the Greystone Hotel in Stoatsberg. The line in Lenore's room rang unanswered. Disappointed, he called the desk and identified himself. The clerk told him that Rossner's party had not been back since lunch.

Owen was anxious for Lenore to know. But he did not want to leave such momentous news in a message. So he asked the clerk just to tell her that Owen Byrne had called and would try to call again later.

He tried Bernie's office and started to speak to the machine, but Bernie picked up as soon as he identified himself.

"I'm still here, Owen. Just hiding behind my machine. Where are you?"

"Kansas."

"You're kidding?"

"No." He explained about the trip to see Milly Corwin.

"Well, this is almost an eerie coincidence, but you had an emergency call from your sister Ellen just a few hours ago."

Owen's heart rate accelerated instantly.

"What did she say?"

"Just to call home immediately. I'm sorry. I wasn't in and it was the receptionist who took the message."

"Okay, I'd better hang up then and—"

"Wait! When are you coming back?"

"There's a flight tonight I think I can get on. If not, then early tomorrow."

"Will you *promise* me that you'll throw something together so that we can get this proposal to DeMille as soon as possible!"

"I promise."

"Good. Well, call your sister then. And take care."

Owen disconnected with Bernie and quickly dialed his home. The phone rang and rang. He waited in his rental car for fifteen minutes and then got out to try again. Still no answer. How could there be no one home? Ellen was always home this time of day.

He imagined Clancy having another stroke. Or Meggie in a car accident. Or Rusty Campbell killed in a fall from the filly. Ellen had made the call so it couldn't be Ellen. He dialed again and listened to the hollow ringing.

The last thing he wanted to do was talk to Michelle Wheeler, but desperation led him to try her number.

"Owen! You aren't supposed to be spending money on long distance, remember?"

The sound of her voice made him wince with guilt.

"Mike, I got an emergency message to call home, but now nobody answers the phone. You don't know what's going on at my place, do you?"

"No . . . haven't heard a peep from your way. Want me to run over there?"

"No. If they're not answering, then they're not there. I just thought maybe you might know."

"Sorry. Hey, I—"

"I've got to go, Mike. I'm . . . I'm very worried and I can't talk now."

"Sure . . . okay . . . bye."

He hung up the phone, closed his eyes and cradled his forehead in his hand. He felt like a heel, a louse, a jerk. He felt like . . . But then he drew in an angry breath and pushed down the fomenting guilt because what was important now was his family. There was trouble and they needed him. He tried the phone one more time; then he got into the rental car and headed north on 135. Away from Wichita and the airport. Toward highway 50 and the Flint Hills. Toward home.

Owen remembered his first sight of the Flint Hills, when he was ten years old. Terry had been driving the car with their mother up front as a passenger. Owen had been riding in the back with Meggie, who was just four then and stretched out asleep across the seat. It was a new car. The one that had lost its backseat during the dog deal had been traded in on the purchase.

They were following their father and Ellen, who were several lengths ahead in the pickup. The pickup itself was obscured from their view by the huge slat-sided goose-necked cattle trailer that was hooked on behind it. The cattle trailer held all their household goods. What hadn't fit hadn't made the trip.

Each of them had been nursing a grudge as they made that drive, remembering which of their possessions had been left behind sitting in the yard of the old house. Owen's was a bookcase full of books and his bed. Ellen's was a mirrored dressing table. Terry's was five years' worth of aviation magazines and his bed. Meggie's was a rocking horse. Clancy had promised to go back and get it all, but they knew he never would.

Nothing of the leftovers in the yard had been special to their mother because Clancy had loaded her things first. Yet she was leaving the most behind. She had been born and raised on that farm. Her family had built the buildings and planted the gardens with their own hands.

Owen had heard her up crying the night before, but her eyes stayed dry on that drive to their new home. She just sat there staring out the window, quiet and stoic. He remembered her best that way—quiet and stoic. Not quite sad but with an undercurrent of sadness that was never far from the surface.

The country around the Flint Hills was completely different from what they had always known. So different that their first sight of it that day was shocking.

The farm ground they had come from was anchored to civilization. Its rectangles of flatland were bisected with manmade windbreaks, hedgerows, and gridworks of roads, and never was the eye far from farmhouses and outbuildings. The soil was a rich coffee-colored loam. The fields were intensely green or pale gold at harvest time. Houses were white or buttercup yellow, and barns were white or that red-brown that the paint companies called barn-red. The occasional towering silo was either a dull metallic gray or a deep gleaming blue. The lines of machinery were bright primary colors of green or blue or red. And everything fit together. Everything complemented every other thing and added to the pleasing, picture-book whole of it. It was a domesticated land. A civilized land.

But what Owen saw with his mother and brother when they reached the Flint Hills, a region they had heard of but never experienced, was an empty expanse of rolling waves, an endless sea of undulating grassy hills that stretched to the horizon and beyond. With not a tree or a building in sight. Nothing to show that civilization had ever existed there.

None of them said a word. They just followed that bouncing stock trailer into Clancy Byrne's fantasy.

Clancy Terrence Byrne had been born to an Irish family that immigrated to Dodge City, Kansas, so Clancy's father could become a cattle baron. The closest the man ever came to the cattle business was the job he held in a meat-processing plant, but he infected his youngest son, Clancy, with his cowboy yearnings.

When Clancy met and married Stella Hadley, he transformed himself overnight from itinerant worker to landowner. Had the elder Byrnes still been alive they surely would have been ecstatic over their son's good fortune. To step off a boat and in one generation be the owner of a mortgage-free farm was the fulfillment of the American dream. Or it should have been. But it was not Clancy Byrne's dream. He hated being referred to as a farmer, saying that the farmers were those big German and Swede fellows without enough brains to do anything but dig.

Clancy's favorite part of the Hadley farm was the small oil well. That, combined with the parade of animals he dragged in and out, gave him the license to refer to himself as an oil- and stockman. And indeed his farming was so sporadic and ill-advised that there were years when the trickle of income from the oil lease paid most of the bills, and the animals they kept out back provided most of the food. They should have been forewarned, but none of them, least of all their mother, saw what was coming.

One day after he'd been gone on an unexplained weeklong jaunt, Clancy sauntered into the house all puffed up and full of himself. "Guess what!" he announced.

Owen and Terry were just in from a long day in the fields, doing a job that their father had apparently forgotten was needed. Ellen had spent the entire afternoon shoving the push mower over the grassy parts of the yard because Clancy had inexplicably traded off the mower blade that hooked on to the tractor. Their mother had just come in from chasing a renegade goat that Clancy had dragged in some weeks before with the announcement that it was a purebred Toggenburg buck and that maybe he would go into the milk-goat stud business. There wasn't a pen on the place that would hold the goat, and every time it got loose another of their mother's cherished flowerbeds or bushes was devoured. So the entire family was hot, dirty and mad when Clancy appeared, and no one responded to his "Guess what!"

Finally, sweet little Meggie said, "What, Daddy?"

"I made the deal of my life." He looked around, oblivious to Terry's exasperation, his wife's glare and Ellen's rolling eyes. "How 'bout a glass of tea for your old dad," he said to no one in particular. Grudgingly, their mother poured one for him, leaving out the ice to show her annoyance.

Clancy drank deeply, saying how thirsty and tired he was. Everyone but Meggie exchanged exasperated looks.

"I'm now a true stockman," he announced. "I traded this farm for a real live cattle ranch over in the Flint Hills. Traded straight across. For nearly three times as much land and some cows ta boot. What do ya think of that?"

He rocked back in his chair, beaming with self-satisfaction, and everyone stared at him in dumb silence.

"You did what?" their mother finally asked.

Owen headed along highway 50 with the lowering sun at his back. South of the highway the Cottonwood River ran. The river he had fished with Terry so many times. He passed a mileage sign for Strong City. Soon he would turn off the highway and away from the river, northwest toward Hymer and Diamond Springs; then he would cut east toward Cyril, into the blue-and-purple shadows mottling the hills, and into Clancy Byrne's kingdom.

He tried not to think about what might be wrong. There was no use letting his imagination get carried away. Instead, he let his thoughts go in other directions.

He tried to untangle his father and Gus Hanselmann, who had somehow become twined up together in his mind. Which was wrong and unfair because Clancy Byrne had never been evil or violent like Gus Hanselmann. Never even close. But he had been a tyrant. And a spoiler and a destroyer. He had certainly been all those. And his rule over the family had always been absolute.

It was dark when Owen passed Cyril. Billowing cumulus scudded across the sky, nearly blotting out the moon and stars. Everything seemed different to him. As though he had been gone for a very long time. He passed the little store near the road that he'd loved when he was younger. The shelves there held food and fishing line and motor oil and shampoo and pipe wrenches and bovine-sized hypodermic needles.

He could remember the pleasure of accompanying his brother there. The long process of selecting supplies, followed by a stop at the old horizontal Coke cooler with its taped-over nickel slot on the end. Customers paid at the counter, then opened the heavy lid and reached in for a bottle of soda beneath the icy water. No soft drink since had ever matched the taste of those, guzzled down so burning cold as he and Terry sat on the store's warped wooden porch.

He could picture Terry on that porch, his legs dangling over the edge, rundown cowboy boots swinging back and forth slightly, as he said, "Did you know, Owen, that you can dissolve a tooth in a glass of Coke?" Then he'd winked and grinned. "What d'ya say, little brother? Think it would dissolve dentures too? Or elk teeth? Or walrus tusks? Or piano keys?"

Owen bumped over the cattleguard and through the entryway Terry had built as a surprise for their father, two thick creosote poles stretching twenty feet high and capped with an ornate welded crosspiece saying BYRNE RANCH in a design of shamrocks. Clancy had registered his brand as a shamrock at first, but there were too many hot spots, areas where the edges of the brand design were close enough together that they heated more hide than was intended, and instead of a nice clover outline he had cows with festering bald patches.

He went back to register a B brand instead, either a rocking B or a circle B, but the woman taking the papers convinced him that the closed sections of the B could also be problematic and so he came home with a C brand. Simple and open. Actually, it was a C lying on its back, which was called a lazy C and which Owen thought was so appropriate that he wondered if the woman helping him had known Clancy personally.

The ranch buildings came into sight. The yard lamps cast cones of white from overhead, and the windows of the house glowed yellow. It was like an island of light there in the dark hills.

Meggie's car was gone. He pulled up between his father's pickup and an unfamiliar one he assumed was Rusty Campbell's. He shut off the engine, killing the radio at the same time, and the eerie moaning of the wind surrounded him. Kansas had been named for the Kansa Sioux—the People of the South Wind. Terry had told him that a lifetime ago.

He rushed into the house. It was empty. In spite of the number of lights burning, it was completely deserted. There was no sign of an evening meal and no clue to anyone's whereabouts. He went to the bunkhouse and found that to be empty, too.

Frantically, he got back in the car and headed to Wheeler Ranch, thinking Mike might have found out something since he spoke to her earlier.

Mike came running out of the house as soon as he pushed open the car door.

"Owen! Quick!" she called breathlessly, "let's drive somewhere, before Daddy makes it outside and starts hollering."

He drove just a short ways from the house.

"This is such a surprise, Owen! Were you just fooling me on the phone before? Making me think you were still in New York. How did you—"

"Mike, I'm worried about my family. Have you found out anything. It's suppertime and no one is there."

"No. You told me not to go over there so I didn't."

"Okay ... well, I'd better go back."

"Owen! I haven't seen you for weeks!" She threw her arms around his neck and hugged him tightly.

He didn't pull away from the hug, but he didn't return it either.

"What's wrong?" she asked immediately.

"Mike . . . I . . . this isn't the right time."

Her smile faded and fear dawned in her eyes. Owen hated himself. Loathed himself. Would have gladly taken the pain from her and driven it into his own head if he could.

"The right time for what?"

"For . . . a serious discussion."

"So what are you going to do? Drop that on me and then just drive away?"

He took a deep breath. "We need time to talk, Mike. I just can't—"

"Tell me, Owen. What do we need to talk about? It will be worse if you don't tell me now because I'll imagine all sorts of terrible things."

"I can't marry you, Mike. I'm sorry."

"You . . . can't . . . marry . . . me?"

"I'm sorry."

"If it's the money, Owen . . . if it's because you're not hired to write the book . . . that doesn't matter to me."

"Money has nothing to do with it." He hesitated. Not sure how much to say. Wanting to be honest and yet wanting to spare her all he could. "Being away . . . working and living somewhere else . . . has made me realize that I don't know myself as well as I thought I did. I don't really know what I want. Or what's important to me."

"You don't love me anymore, do you?"

"I'll always love you, Mike. And I'll probably end up regretting this."

"That's bullshit! New York has screwed up your head! There's loving somebody or not loving somebody. Either you love me or you don't love me. And if you do still love me, then you should still want to get married."

"I'm sorry."

"Oh, shut up! I don't want to hear another word from you until you've regained your senses!" She slammed out of the car and stalked down the drive toward her house.

Owen watched her for a moment, wondering whether he should try to get her back in the car and drive her home. But it wasn't much of a walk, and she had her heavy coat on. He decided it was best to let her go.

* * *

He made the short trip home even shorter, but his own house was still empty when he returned. He paced back and forth in the kitchen. There were three possible hospitals—none of them close. He called one and spoke to the emergency room nurse. He was just calling another when his family came pouring in the back door.

"It's Owen!" Meggie squealed, and they all started talking at once about how surprised they'd been to see a strange car in their yard and how they couldn't imagine who would be visiting.

Meggie, Rusty and even Clancy appeared to be in a festive mood, but Ellen seemed to be in an angry sulk. There had never been physical displays of affection in his family, so there was no hugging or kissing, but Rusty Campbell enthusiastically shook his hand.

"Where have you been!" Owen asked. "God, I was worried sick. I get an emergency call and then I come home to an empty house! Last time this house was empty at suppertime was when we had to rush to the hospital."

Meggie's laughter was as giddy as a teenager's, and Owen suddenly noticed that her cheeks were unnaturally flushed and that she had her arm linked with Rusty's.

"Rusty took us all out for dinner," Ellen said, with her eyes shifting back and forth between Meggie and Owen. She didn't mention her long-distance call to New York.

"Ah hell, just get on with it and tell him," Clancy blustered.

"We announced our engagement," Meggie blurted out, beaming as she held up her left hand to display a ring.

Owen dropped into a chair with a sigh of frustrated relief. "That's what all this was about?" He looked at Ellen, who averted her eyes.

"Well, that's great, you two. Congratulations! I wish I had a bottle of wine or something for a toast."

"Just as well you don't," Clancy said, pushing past them to head for his chair in the living room. "Then we'd have to drink it, and all them fancy wines taste like cow piss to me."

They lit the fireplace in the living room and all sat down. Owen studied Rusty Campbell. He knew the man was younger than thirty, but his weathered skin and quiet manner made him seem older. He was medium height and build with slightly bowed legs and an old-fashioned handlebar mustache. Every inch of him looked like the true cowboy Clancy had always wanted to be.

Owen waited for someone to ask a question about New York or about the book. Ellen was staring into the fire. Meggie was staring at Rusty. Rusty was staring at the toes of his boots.

"I'm just home for one night," Owen said. "I had to go to Wichita, and then I got this message from Ellen ..." He glanced at Ellen, who was still not meeting his eyes. "So I drove on up, but I'll have to leave tomorrow morning."

No one commented. Only Ellen looked as though she was listening.

"Traded one of them pups you was trainin' on, Owen," Clancy said suddenly. "Yeah, it was some trade. I pulled up to the truck stop for coffee and I saw this ole boy with the cutest little pony saddle in the back of his pickup ... like a miniature roper with the ropin' horn and all ... so I just kinda strolled up to him and started talkin'. Tellin' him about the fine cow dogs I had at home. Got him all stirred up. Time I was done I had the saddle and he followed me home to get the dog."

Owen bit back his anger. Those were his dogs. But Clancy never did see things that way. Clancy had always believed he was entitled to anything he wanted. Owen remembered coming home from school when he was twelve to find that his show heifer was gone. He had been working with the heifer for months—haltering her and breaking her to lead, trimming and brushing and bathing her every day—and Clancy, with the state fair and the judging just weeks away—had sold the heifer. The boy whose father bought her won the blue ribbon that should have been Owen's. Clancy never did understand what was wrong, since he'd gotten a "damn good price" for the animal.

"You don't have any ponies to use that saddle on," Owen pointed out. "And that dog was worth a lot of money."

"Ahhhh," Clancy waved his hand as if to dismiss Owen's words. "What do you know? What does a damn story writer know about anything?"

"We got some new heifers," Meggie said quickly in an effort to head off unpleasantness.

"Where did the money come from to buy them?" Owen asked.

Meggie glanced at Rusty. "Well, we didn't exactly buy

them yet. Rusty got them from his family, and we'll just pay for them when we can."

"They're nice ones," Rusty said. "Good leg under 'em. Good motherin' stock. They'll raise some choice calves."

"That's very generous of your family, Rusty," Owen remarked. "Do they know how long it could take us to pay them back?"

"They ain't frettin' on it," Rusty said.

"Hey, did ya hear about ole Waldo Skiddy?" Clancy asked. "Got hit by lightnin'. He was talkin' on the phone with one hand leanin' on the 'frigerator, and the electric shock come through the phone and went all the way through him into the 'frigerator. He showed me the black hand print where it went outta his hand into the metal."

Everyone expressed amazement.

"Bet New York City hasn't made you any better at dominoes," Clancy said to Owen. "Bet you still can't beat your old man!"

"Not now . . ." Owen began, but Clancy was already pulling the old wooden cigar box out of the cupboard. "Move your chair around," he ordered. "Meggie, push that coffee table over here between us."

"Let's play with three," Owen suggested. "Somebody else get in here with us."

No one made a move.

Clancy dumped the dominoes out of the box. They were handsome once-white tiles with etched black markings. Time and frequent handling had given them the patina of antique ivory. Owen picked one up and rubbed the smooth back with his thumb. The color reminded him of Lenore Serian's skin.

"Come on! Quit your lollygagging, boy, and draw up."

Owen chose his tiles and went meekly to the slaughter, knowing he hadn't a chance of winning. Knowing that Clancy had everything memorized, every possible number combination, every possible strategy. As the play progressed, Clancy would remember what had been used and he would know what remained in the pile.

The room was quiet. No talking allowed while Clancy Byrne whipped the pants off someone at dominoes. He beat Owen quickly, then tried to insist that they play to a hundred. Owen refused.

"Come on, Daddy," Meggie pleaded. "Owen wants to visit."

"What're you, a quitter?" Clancy demanded. "Gonna quit after one loss?"

"You win, okay?" Owen told him. "I'm only here for one night. I don't want to waste it playing dominoes."

That made Clancy mad. He slammed the pieces into the box and stalked to the cupboard with it. Owen pushed the furniture back into place, wondering what Rusty thought of his prospective in-laws.

"I'm starting to work full-time," Meggie said. "So I can build up a little nest egg for me and Rusty."

"In my day a wife didn't work unless she was married to a no-account," Clancy grumbled. "In my day a woman was home to put a good noon dinner on the table."

"Not too long ago," Rusty said quietly, "a fella could sell twenty calves and earn the price of a pickup truck. Today it costs forty-five calves to pay for that same truck. And God only knows how many calves it would cost to go to the hospital and have a baby. Times have changed a lot, Clancy. That day a yours you keep talkin' about is long gone."

Owen was amazed that Clancy let Rusty talk to him like that. And not only was he allowing it—he actually seemed to be listening. Clancy and Rusty discussed ranching for several minutes; then the conversation wound down, and everyone watched the fire.

"So . . . Rusty, Meggie . . . what are your plans?" Owen asked.

Glances were exchanged.

"Why do I get the feeling that I've been left out of something?" Owen said.

"Well . . . we're set to marry right away," Meggie said. "Next month." She licked her bottom lip nervously and glanced at Clancy. "We didn't know you'd be here like this. We were saving everything for when you came back for good, you know . . . It's probably not something we want to get into while you're just here for a one-night visit."

"Oh hell," Clancy said. "Let's quit beatin' round the bush and get it said."

"I'm not listening to this shit!" Ellen announced and stalked out of the room.

"I changed my will," Clancy said. "Soon as Rusty and

Meggie get hitched they get control of the ranch. You and Ellen will still have third shares, but it'll be their show."

Owen was too stunned to speak.

"Hell, son, you never cared nothin' about bein' a cowman. You never could fill Terry's boots. Your head's always been off in some cloud or another. Rusty's got cowboyin' in his blood. He'll put this ranch back on top again for all of us."

"Nobody's telling you to leave, Owen," Meggie assured him. "That bunkhouse out there is yours till the day you die. Make no mistake about that."

Owen stood up. He stared down at his father. Seeing the man so sharply that the aging flesh and colorless hair and faded eyes seemed magnified. He waited to feel something massive—a blast of uncontrollable anger or white-hot hatred—but instead he felt nothing. Absolutely nothing.

"Guess that's how it is then," he said. "Where should I sleep tonight?"

"You should have the bunkhouse. Definitely," Meggie insisted. "So you can sleep in your familiar bed. Rusty can have my room and I'll take the extra bed in Ellen's room."

Owen left them and went to the back of the house into Ellen's room. She was sitting on her bed, and he could tell by her eyes that she had been crying.

"Hey," he said, settling on the bed across from her. "Are you okay?"

"I can't believe they've done this to you, Owen. I only found out about it this morning, and I tried to call you right away."

"Don't worry about me, Ellen. I'll be fine."

"It's so unfair. So sneaky and underhanded and rotten! Daddy would have lost everything a hundred times if it hadn't been for you. This place wouldn't even exist if it hadn't been for you! And all that shit about you not being a cowman ... What is Daddy talking about? I think he's gone haywire. And Meggie ... that conniving little bitch!"

"What is wrong with this family, Owen? You've put your heart and soul into this place. You *are* this ranch. How can they do this?"

"But the bunkhouse is mine till the day I die," Owen said, teasing her with gentle sarcasm. "I can become the eccentric old guy in the bunkhouse just like Uncle Kaye if I want to."

"Oh God ... that sounds like what they said to me. They

said the spare bedroom was always mine . . . no matter how many kids they had." Tears leaked out of her eyes and she laughed soundlessly.

"What are you going to do?" he asked.

"I'm going to school, dammit. I'm not going to stick around here and play Auntie Ellen and cook and clean for everybody the rest of my life. Shoot, I'm a terrible cook anyway.

"I think I'd like to become something worthwhile . . . work with kids some way. I don't know . . . teach or go into social work."

"Good. That sounds good, Ellen. You know I'll help you any way I can."

"I know," she said and buried her face in her hands to sob.

Later, when Owen came out of Ellen's room, the living room was empty. Snoring came from Clancy's bedroom. Meggie's room was dark. He suspected that all the talk about Meggie sleeping in Ellen's room had been for Clancy's benefit, and that she and Rusty slept together every night.

The fire had burned down to embers. He leaned against the rough limestone fireplace, the same handcut native stone that the whole house had been constructed of, and he thought about all the years he had thought of the house as his home. Even when he moved to the bunkhouse. This had always been his home. And he'd believed that he belonged here and that someday he would raise his own family in this house.

He heard a noise and looked up to see Meggie watching him in a long white flannel nightgown with a faded quilt around her shoulders. She was ghostly in the half-light.

"You aren't gonna cause trouble over all this, are you?" she asked defensively.

"Now when have I ever been a troublemaker, Meggie? This is Clancy's ranch. It's always been Clancy's ranch. He's got a right to do whatever he wants with it."

"Well, I'm glad you're bein' so reasonable about it. I told Rusty you were always reasonable. And that you'd want what was best for everyone."

The CB radio in the corner crackled to life. "Got one down, Meggie. You better come on out."

Meggie picked up the microphone. "Gotcha, Rusty. Where are you?"

"I'm clear up past the north waterin' hole. I've got my lights on. You'll see me."

Owen didn't need to ask what was going on. Rusty had gone out to check cows, probably worried that some of those brand-new first-calf heifers from his family were close to calving, and he'd run into trouble out there.

"Call the vet," Owen said. "I'll go out."

"Doc Miller crashed up his truck last week. He's in traction."

Owen sighed heavily. "Guess we'll do without him, then."

He went into the porch and zipped himself into old insulated coveralls, then added a knitted wool cap and an old coat. The coat pockets were filled with warm gloves and handkerchiefs and a pocket knife. Owen slipped on the gloves. He went out the door and Meggie came running out behind him.

"Why don't you stay here?" he said, but she was already climbing into the passenger side of his truck. He didn't ask her why she had never come out to help him in the middle of the night.

The wind was vicious with a below-zero chill factor, and the sky was completely blanketed by a dense layer of clouds that rendered the night moonless and starless. After the city, it was breathtaking to see how black a Flint Hills night could be. "Blacker'n Satan's heart," Clancy used to say. They bounced across the pastures for what seemed like forever before they saw Rusty's truck lights.

The cow was on her side, breathing heavily.

"I got a hell of a mess here," Rusty said. He was smeared with blood and wet manure, and his voice sounded close to exhaustion.

Owen squatted down beside the heifer, patting the red shaggy winter hair, crooning, "That's a good mama," in the singsong way that came automatically.

"Found her already down," Rusty told them. "Finally got my arm up inside her, but the calf's legs are tucked under him."

"Oh no . . ." Meggie wailed. "What will we tell your father, Rusty, if we lose one of these heifers?"

Rusty ignored her and squatted down beside Owen. "I'm

afraid there's more wrong than just the calf's position," he said. "She's been bleedin' a lot."

"Got any more gloves?" Owen asked. "If we take turns at it maybe we can get those feet straight."

Owen pulled on a plastic glove that covered him almost up to his armpit, and he knelt close to the cow and worked his hand up inside her. She fought him with the powerful muscles of her vagina, squeezing his arm and trying to expel it as she would have expelled the calf if she had the chance. He felt the baby's nose in the birth canal and worked his way on past it to feel for the legs. They should have both been straight forward, presenting with the nose, for a normal delivery.

"There . . . I've got one."

Meggie and Rusty both leaned against the cow just in case she decided to move, and Owen worked the leg up and forward, inch by frustrating inch. Sweat popped out on his forehead in spite of the cold. He was half lying, half sitting behind her, pressed against her rump, straining for leverage and fighting those mercilessly contracting muscles. When he finally got the tiny cloven hoof worked all the way up to lie beside the calf's nose, he pulled out and fell back to lie on the ground. His arm was shaking uncontrollably.

Rusty immediately went in for the other leg. Owen pulled himself up and peeled off his soiled glove, then moved to wedge himself up against the cow's back, even though he could tell that she wasn't going to try escape. She had given up. Owen had seen that look before in an animal's eyes.

He watched Rusty. The man had already been tired and freezing and had had his arm in the cow before they arrived. Now he looked as though he was using his last reserves. "I'm . . . almost . . . there . . ." He panted. "Meg . . . get . . . the . . . chain."

Meggie raced to the pickup cab for the chain. It was a common birthing tool for cattlemen. Looped around the calf's hocks, just above the hooves, the narrow linked chain could be used to pull the baby on out when the cow couldn't do the final pushing herself.

Suddenly, the labored breathing stopped. The bloated sides went still, and the wide pink nostrils sank in with a final sigh.

Owen jumped up and pounded her chest with his fist in a futile attempt at bovine CPR.

"No! No! No!" Meggie screamed. She turned and threw the chain into the pickup bed, where it clattered resoundingly.

Rusty pulled his arm out with a dazed expression.

Owen didn't stop to think. He reached into his pocket, flipped open the blade of the knife and sank it into the dead cow's belly. Rusty leaped up to help, and in moments they had the calf cut free. He was breathing. They cleaned out his nose and rubbed him with feed sacks like his mama would have done with her tongue if she'd been able, and for their efforts they got a weak little bleat from him.

Meggie got in on the passenger side of Rusty's pickup, started the engine and the heater, and they handed the calf in to her. She cradled the calf in her lap as best she could, gangly legs sticking every which way, and Owen saw that she was crying.

"Thank God you saved the calf," she said. "Nobody knows it yet, but all these bred heifers are to be our wedding present from Rusty's folks. To start our own herd with."

Owen closed the door and turned to Rusty.

"How'd you have the nerve to try that trick?" Rusty asked.

"Saw a vet cut a calf out of a cow once. Same circumstances." Owen shrugged. "I figured it couldn't hurt to try."

Rusty shook his head and flashed Owen a grin.

"Want to take him up to the house now?" Owen asked.

"Can't, pardner. It's a bad night. Got another one just over the hill. She was straining hard when I left."

"Lead the way," Owen told him. "I'm right behind you."

They left the poor butchered heifer there on the ground and went on to the next cow. Thankfully, she was in better shape. As they drove up, she clambered awkwardly to her feet and walked away from the headlights. Two little hooves were visible poking out from under her tail. They got a rope around her neck and snubbed her tight to a bar Owen had welded onto the side of his pickup.

Without discussion they looped the chain around the calf's hocks and took turns pulling. This was nothing compared to what they'd just been through, but it was hard work nonetheless. The calf wasn't coming easily, and it was difficult to pull with so little leverage.

Finally the calf slid forward and plopped out onto the ground in a wet rush of birth fluids and amniotic sac. The heifer let out a long groan that shook her sides. She rolled her eyes and swung back and forth, straining against the rope. Now that her difficulties were over she was indignant and irritated.

"How's this?" Rusty said. "We'll let her clean the baby up and get to know it a minute; then we'll put the baby in the back of the truck and snub her up tight and lead her on in to the barn. That way we can try putting the lil' orphan to suck on her too."

"Yeah ..." Owen hesitated. His philosophy had always been to try to make use of and respect the natural order of things. "Why don't we get the orphan out of the truck and rub him around in the afterbirth. Maybe he'll smell so familiar that she'll believe she had twins."

Rusty grinned and fetched the calf. They kept the mama's head tight to the truck so she couldn't get to her baby or even watch it, and they rolled the orphan in the muck till he matched his brand-new cousin, who was still wet and curled up on the ground. Then they put the calves close together and loosened the rope so that the heifer could get to them.

She was highly agitated by now, jerking hard against the rope, squealing and bellowing. When she realized she had some slack, she pulled sharply back then wheeled to nose the calves. Her huge tongue went to work on the newest calf, her own natural baby, and they all waited.

"Come on, mama," Rusty whispered.

If the cow wouldn't take the baby, he would be difficult to save. Orphaned newborns who didn't get that first nursed colostrum frequently died in spite of the most diligent care and bottle feeding. Of course there was still Rusty's plan to fall back on. If she wouldn't accept the calf here, they could take all three of them to the barn and try to force him on her. But getting a first-calf range heifer to take an orphaned calf was seldom successful, and if she wouldn't take him here, smelling of her own birth fluids, then Owen knew she wouldn't take him at the barn.

Roughly she tongued her baby clean. Then she nudged the orphan. Her wide nostrils flared. She nudged him harder. It was common for a cow to seriously injure or kill an unwanted orphan in her efforts to drive him away, so Owen was on edge as he watched, ready to leap in should the calf be endangered. Then out came that incredible tongue, rasping across the impostor's wet fur, and they breathed a collective sigh of relief and exchanged grins.

"Twins," Rusty told the cow as he slipped the rope from her neck. "You're gonna have your hands full, mama."

In answer she dropped her head and lunged, sending him diving for the refuge of the pickup cab. Owen laughed until Meggie called, "Heads up!" and he too was diving for safety.

Later, after they had returned to the house, cleaned up, and wolfed down sandwiches, Rusty walked Owen partway up to the bunkhouse.

"I just wanted to say thank you, again, pardner." Rusty pumped his hand. "I'll be proud to call you brother-in-law."

Owen nodded and turned to go.

"Ya know . . ." Rusty admitted. "You're not like Meggie and Clancy described you. I was expectin' a completely different feller than you turned out to be."

Owen shrugged and smiled. He bore no grudge against Rusty Campbell.

"I sure do hope you see fit to stay on. We could make a helluva team."

"Let's just give it some time," Owen told him. "We'll see what happens."

He went on inside the bunkhouse. Ellen had come up and lit the stove and a lantern while he was out so the room was warm and welcoming. A cozy place for the hired hand to go at the end of the day, he thought bitterly.

No one knew what year the last real ranchhands had been fired. When the ranch came into Clancy Byrne's possession, the bunkbeds had already been torn out and the building was in use for storage. Owen looked around at the firelit room. Those oldtime ranchhands had loomed large in his childhood. He had wanted to be just like them. A chuckle of irony escaped him. What was the saying? *Be careful what you wish for* . . . Well, he certainly had achieved his childhood wish.

But then he had also wanted to be a fireman. And a veterinarian. And an undersea explorer. And a doctor who found cures for terrible diseases. And after he saw the Blue Angels fly over the state fair, he'd wanted to be a precision jet pilot. He smiled regretfully. Not just at the memory of

wanting to be all those things but at the memory of a time
when he thought he could be anything.

He wondered what he would have become if things had
been different and he'd stayed in college. Considering this,
he found he had no idea of the answer. It was hard to connect the classes he had taken with the end result of an occupation. At the time, he supposed that college had seemed an
end in itself.

He sat down in a chair to pull his boots off, and a picture
came to him of his mother, carrying that chair up the hill,
calling gleefully, "Look what I found for you!"

His mother was everywhere in the room. When he had
moved back to the ranch after Terry's funeral, it had been his
mother who understood why he didn't want his old bedroom
back in the house, and it had been she who helped him turn
the bunkhouse into his own private living quarters. While he
repaired the roof and the windows, she worked on the interior, patching and painting the scarred walls so well that it
was impossible to tell where the old bunkbeds had been attached. She sewed the burlap curtains that still hung at the
windows. She cleaned the old stove till it shone like new.
She searched far and wide for furniture, haunting auctions
and estate sales.

He recalled how pleased he'd been with his private space,
but he couldn't remember what else he'd been thinking. How had he imagined his life would proceed from
there? When he was twenty years old and lying beneath the
quilts on that iron bed, staring up at the ceiling after a long
day's work, had he ever once questioned the wisdom of his
actions? Had he regretted leaving school? Had he envisioned
himself twelve years later in the same bed? He could not remember. He did recall, though, that beneath the grief for his
brother and the deep sense of obligation he'd felt toward his
family, he had been shamefully eager to step into Terry's
place as the favored son.

What would have happened if he had realized then that he
could never replace his brother? That he would always be a
poor substitute in his father's eyes. Would his life have progressed any differently?

Owen climbed into the bed. Stared up at the ceiling. No
longer able to imagine much about his twenty-year-old self,
but all too aware of himself as a thirty-two-year-old man. He
knew that if he got the DeMille contract he would not return

to the ranch. Those two calves tonight would be the last he delivered. This night would be his last in the iron bed, staring up at the familiar ceiling. He knew these things in his heart and his gut. They were not the result of a conscious thought process.

Tomorrow, he would get up early and ride the filly out across the hills. Then he would pack. Sort through some things so that it would be easy for Ellen to ship the remainder of his belongings to New York if he needed her to. Then he would board the one P.M. flight and be gone.

And in just hours he would see Lenore. It had been too late to telephone her after he finished with the calving. Though he had been tempted. He had wanted to hear her low sleepy voice and know that she was warm and naked beneath the blankets as they spoke. But he didn't want to frighten or startle her with a late night call. So he resisted.

He thought he understood now. She had only pushed him away out of fear. Fear that he was becoming too possessive, too demanding. Fear that she was slipping into something harmful.

It no longer seemed important to him that she was hiding James Collier and protecting him. Hiding Collier didn't make her guilty. And it no longer seemed important what her relationship was to James Collier. Lenore was all that mattered.

Lenore.

Just the thought of her sent a wave of heat through his body and he had to close his eyes. He wanted to get through the night. Get through the hours. Until he could see her again.

20

It was after nine o'clock when Owen pulled up to the wrought-iron gate. He never had reached Lenore by phone, but he'd left several messages saying that he would be back that night. Now, having driven straight from the airport, he was going to surprise her. He had kept a key when he cleared the drive of snow, so he could bypass the intercom. Just a twist of the key and the gate slid open. He drove through the groves of trees and the rolling fields, then saw the towers and spires of Arcadia shimmering in full moonlight. It should have been an awesome sight. But Bram Serian had lost his mystery for Owen, and now Serian's grand creation stirred pity rather than awe.

Lenore opened the front door as he pulled up. She had the shotgun cradled in her arm. He got out of the car quickly to reassure her.

"It's Owen!" he called, reaching into the backseat for the tapes of Milly's interview. Two sets, since he had duplicated them—making copies for Lenore to keep. "You can put away the weapons."

She didn't move.

"Lenore?" He started forward. "Lenore, what is it?"

"Stay there," she ordered, moving the muzzle of the gun for punctuation. It wasn't actually pointed at him, but it was definitely there as a threat.

"Lenore, I don't—"

"Don't pretend with me, Owen. Don't lie. They came for Jimmy today, and you were the only one who knew he was out here."

"Came for Collier? But . . . who?"

"Don't play dumb, please. You're insulting us both."

"Lenore, I didn't tell anyone about him being here. I swear I—"

"I trusted you!" Her voice broke and the barrel of the gun drooped downward slightly.

His eyes followed the gun. Would she shoot? Was she capable of murder after all?

She recovered the gun and her composure together. "Leave," she said coldly. "Get away from me."

Slowly, he held up a set of tapes. "I'll go," he said, too stunned to argue. "But here are the tapes of my interview with Camille Corwin. You need to hear them . . . regardless of what you think of me. They have your answers, Lenore. They have your father."

She used the muzzle of the gun to indicate a place at the edge of the stone terrace. "Put them there," she said. "Then get in your car and don't come here again."

Owen drove erratically. Faster than he should. Slower than he should. He missed highway exits and had to double back.

It was all a mistake. James Collier. Damn James Collier. He had to make Lenore see. Make her understand. He had to set things right.

He stopped at the apartment to unload, then returned the rental car in uptown Manhattan and got on the subway to go back downtown. It was after midnight. Tomorrow he would go to the trial. See Lenore. Tomorrow she would be calmer. Would have listened to the tapes. Tomorrow she would know that he'd found the answer for her. He had found her father.

He looked up suddenly and realized he had missed his stop. Quickly he jumped off the train. Not knowing where he was. What did it matter? He could walk. How far could it be? He never got enough exercise here anyway. Not like he was used to. No more chopping wood or wrestling recalcitrant animals around or riding horses or building fence. Oh, God. He sank down on a cement stoop. It was cold through his jeans. Where in the hell was he? What was he doing?

Street people crept past him, whispered things. A skinny woman with a baby on her hip offered him a blow job for ten dollars.

He got up and started walking. One street became another. Nothing looked familiar, but he no longer cared. He wanted to lose himself so completely that nothing would ever be familiar again. When the sky began to lighten, he stopped walking. He gave up. Because the island of Manhattan wasn't big enough for what he needed to lose.

Somehow he got himself back to the apartment and cleaned up in time to make his usual morning train. It was Thursday. Day twelve of the trial. He knew that because he had kept careful records. Number of days. Number of witnesses. Number of pieces of evidence. But it didn't seem like only twelve days. It seemed like he had spent years in courtroom 6 at Lenore Serian's trial.

He arrived at the courthouse early and went in search of Holly and Marilyn's morning coffee klatch, so hungry for news that he didn't mind seeing Holly. He found the group downstairs by the vending machines, but Holly wasn't among them. No one knew where she was. Marilyn, Pat and Ray gladly recounted the events of Tuesday and Wednesday for Owen. Clay Southey, another one of Serian's party guests, had testified, claiming to have heard the exact same late-night argument between Bram and Lenore that Natalie Raven had already elaborated on. This was the guest who had helped break up the fight between the two women and who had assisted in trying to comfort Natalie Raven that night.

Owen could barely write fast enough to keep up as the three reporters consulted their notes and talked at once, quoting testimony, and adding dashes of supposition and gossip. After Southey, there had been a lawyer from the firm handling Bram Serian's estate. Brown had used him to show how much Lenore would have lost in a divorce and how much she would have gained if her husband's death had been determined accidental.

Then on Wednesday, Dr. Gavril, the pathologist who autopsied Serian's body, finally overcame his personal problems and was brought to the stand. Gavril flung out technical terms about the degree of heat necessary to produce the amount of damage Serian's body sustained. He announced with authority that accelerant had been present on the trunk area but not the limbs. He explained at length about the lung tissue and how he had determined that smoke was not inhaled and thus death had occurred before the fire. Then he spoke of the injury to the skull and how it was consistent with the shape and size of the axe blade.

Ray gleefully recounted the gory details of Gavril's testimony and the reactions of the jury when pictures of the incinerated body were distributed. With relish, Ray described the melted remains of Serian's watch, rings and heavy Indian silver bracelet that were entered into evidence. Then he ridiculed Rossner's cross questions, saying that the defense attorney had been too dense to even understand most of what Gavril was saying.

"Don't speak too soon," Marilyn cautioned. "The remainder of defense's cross is today."

"And then there's the big witness . . ." Pat said. "You do know about the *big* witness?"

"What big witness?" Owen asked, but he already knew the answer.

"James Collier!" they all responded at once.

"Oh my God! Don't you know about Holly's major scoop?" Pat cried.

"Don't you read the paper?" Ray demanded.

"He's been in Kansas," Marilyn said dryly, as though Kansas were equal to the outer reaches of the Himalayas.

"Our girl Holly scored big," Ray told him proudly.

"She had a source that gave her a tip about the D.A. finding the missing witness," Pat explained. "And somehow she convinced the D.A.'s office to cooperate with her and she got her crew all the way out to Arcadia in time to film Collier being picked up. It was a major coup for her. She's probably off collecting some kind of award or promotion this morning."

"Do we know yet whether they're bringing any charges against Collier?" Ray asked. "I heard he might even be charged as an accomplice."

"No." Marilyn shook her head. "The prosecution has dropped that angle. I don't know if there'll be charges for the hiding or not."

"He's going to be an unfriendly witness, isn't he?" Pat asked, and both Marilyn and Ray laughed and assured her that he was as unfriendly as a witness could get.

"I heard that Rossner's been trying every trick in the book to keep him from testifying," Ray said.

Marilyn lowered her voice conspiratorially. "None of the tricks worked. Rossner has also tried for a delay. He's been screaming about this sudden surprise witness and needing time to prepare, etc., etc.—which is a real crock because Rossner knew all along that if they found Collier they were slapping him immediately on the stand. So far old Pulaski hasn't budged an inch. I think his honor is anxious to get this thing over with and get his courtroom back to normal."

"What's been going on?" Owen asked. "What have they done to Collier?"

"Nonstop questioning." Marilyn shrugged. "Depositions up the ying yang. What else? My sources tell me that Brown isn't quite sure how to handle him on the stand. It's touchy. The jury is going to see a religious man swear on the Bible to tell the truth, and, unless Brown can catch him in a blatant lie, the jury will probably believe that Collier is telling the truth, regardless of how despicable Brown can make him look. So Brown is going to have to be careful what questions he asks."

"Will Collier tell the truth?" Owen asked.

"Who knows?" Marilyn flashed them a little catlike smile. "But you can judge for yourself soon because, unless Rossner comes up with a magic button, James Collier will be on the stand either today or tomorrow. Right after Gavril. And then the prosecution will rest its case."

Owen had to get away. He thanked them, mumbled a meaningless excuse and went upstairs to a bench at the opposite end of the building from Judge Pulaski's courtroom.

Anger churned in his gut and squeezed the air from his lungs. Holly. Holly had turned in James Collier.

Holly had leaned over his shoulder in the coffee shop while his notebook was open, and she had seen something. Then, while he was in the bathroom hiding from her, she opened his notebook, writing him a message to give herself an excuse . . . and she read the page that said, WHO IS JIMMY? WHY IS SHE HIDING HIM?, and whatever else Owen had so foolishly committed to paper. And the ever-alert reporter in Holly knew immediately that she had stumbled upon a gold mine.

He wondered if her conscience had bothered her at all as she made her big "scoop" deal with the district attorney's office. He wondered if she'd felt anything but avaricious glee when she reported from Arcadia on the apprehension of James Collier.

Oh, God. He cradled his forehead in his hand. Just weeks ago, if someone had presented this to him as a hypothetical situation, a remote moral question, he would have said yes, absolutely, turning in James Collier was the right thing to do. But now ... Holly's actions struck him as a greater crime than Collier's hiding from the law.

At ten minutes till nine, he went back down the hall to the courtroom. Lenore and her two escorts came around the corner from the opposite direction as he approached the doors. He wanted to speak to her. But he could find no words, and all he could do was stand there in guilty silence.

She swept past him as if he were invisible. Volpe leveled a murderous glare at him, and Riley glanced at him with something akin to sympathy. He waited several minutes, then went through the double doors. Holly was in her usual seat up front with the spot beside her awaiting him. He slid into a pew three rows back next to some reporters whose names he had forgotten.

Lenore was sitting rigidly forward, not even bending toward Rossner when the attorney spoke to her. There was a disheveled, almost frantic air about Rossner this morning, and Owen could tell it was genuine. What did that mean? Rossner wasn't losing, was he?

Gavril entered and took the stand. He was a slightly pudgy man, soft-looking in spite of his sharply tailored suit. His bearing suggested great confidence, and as soon as he sat down he crossed his legs and leaned back, smiling a superior, professional smile.

Rossner stepped forward. "Dr. Gavril, I know what a busy man you are, and I will try not to keep you from your important duties too much longer."

Gavril inclined his head slightly.

"Now, where we left off yesterday, Doctor, was with you explaining again how you knew that accelerant had been present on the trunk of the body but not the limbs. And you very patiently took us through tissue analysis and all that, and it is amazing how much you could tell us ... so could you please tell us whether Bram Serian was cut anywhere from all that broken glass?"

"No. I had no way of determining that. Even had it not been for the extreme level of destruction to the tissues, high temperatures cause the skin to burst open in numerous locations, and these lesions would be indistinguishable from cuts after a fire."

Rossner feigned a rapt, slightly mystified expression. "It sounds like the fire itself causes wounds to the body—is that right?"

"Definitely. Fire is extremely destructive." Gavril smiled complacently. "That is why cremation exists. At a high-enough temperature, everything is reduced to ash."

"So fire can even harm bones?"

"Certainly. The various fractures present in the deceased resulted from the fire."

Rossner stared at the witness in total perplexity. "Various fractures? You mean that Bram Serian had other broken bones besides his skull?"

"They weren't 'broken' in the same sense that his skull was damaged, but yes, there were fractures. This is common in bones that have been subjected to high temperatures."

"Could you tell if any of these injuries were prefire?"

"No. However, it would be highly unlikely."

"Why is that?"

"Because, as I've already stated, these fractures are common in high temperatures."

"So, on Bram Serian's body, could you tell the order the injuries happened in?"

"No. As I've said, the only certainty is that he was not breathing when the fire started."

"That's the only certainty?"

"Yes."

"So you can't tell us much about the skull fracture, then, can you?"

"On the contrary, I can tell you quite a bit about the skull fracture."

"Do you see skulls with that kind of damage often ... where there are broken pieces that have pressed inward?"

"Yes. That is consistent with any number of circumstances."

"What are some of the ways that a person could get that kind of an injury?"

"Various traumas to the head. Being hit with an object that has a sharp edge or point." He shrugged. "Being underneath falling rubble at a building collapse."

"Does this sort of skull injury always result in death?"

"I wouldn't characterize it as one hundred percent fatal but the chances of a victim surviving such an injury are slight."

"Car wrecks? Could you hurt your head like this in a car wreck?"

"Certainly. If you were thrown around and your head struck the right surface."

"Accidents in the home ... could this injury happen in your own home?"

Gavril sighed impatiently. "Yes. A fall down the stairs ... a fall in the shower ... slipping on a wet kitchen floor."

"But you couldn't just hit your head on the floor?"

"No. You would have to strike your head on an appropriate edge or object. The corner of a counter, the corner of a wooden step ..."

"A brick corner, maybe?"

"Yes. That sort of thing."

"So Bram Serian's skull injury could have been caused by a fall where he struck his head against the edge of the brick hearth in his studio?"

"That is not my conclusion."

"But didn't you say that this injury could have been caused by such a fall?"

"Yes."

"And didn't you say earlier, to Mr. Brown, that there was no way to positively determine that the axe head was involved because there were no traces of metal recovered from the area of the injury?"

"Yes. But—"

"And didn't you tell us that there wasn't even a way to tell if the fractures were caused by the fire or happened before or after his death?"

"I was referring to hairline fractures in other bones."

"So there *was* a way to determine that Bram Serian's skull fracture happened before his death?"

"No. However, there are logical conclusions to be reached. Something killed him."

"Oh. *Something* killed him? You mean something as in some unknown thing? Like choking on an ice cube and then wondering what the cause of death was because the ice melts and then what do you have?"

"I, as a trained pathologist, studied all the physical indicators, and determined that the most likely cause of death was the depressed skull fracture."

"Most likely, huh?"

"Yes. Medicine is often a combination of art and science."

"Does that mean you don't know, absolutely and positively, without a single doubt, whether Bram Serian struck his head and died or fell dead and struck his head on the way down?"

"I can—"

"Doctor, are you absolutely certain, one way or the other?"

"No."

"Can you say absolutely, positively, without a single doubt, exactly what object or surface or edge caused Bram Serian's skull fracture?"

"No."

"It could possibly have been the brick edge, then, couldn't it?"

Gavril sighed distastefully. "Yes."

"Striking his head against the brick edge in the course of a fall, right?"

"Yes."

"You mentioned slipping on a wet floor before as a cause of a fall . . . so he could have broken the lamp, then slipped on a puddle of lamp oil and struck his head on the bricks . . . does that sound possible?"

"Remotely possible."

"But possible, correct?"

"Correct."

Owen slipped out just before the judge announced lunch and quickly left the courthouse. He headed back downtown toward the train station to a bar he'd passed several times. It seemed like a safe place to eat without encountering anyone he knew.

The hamburger was greasy, and the atmosphere was depressing. He sat alone at the end of the bar, considering what had happened and his role in it. He had betrayed Lenore. With carelessness if nothing else. He'd been so busy wallowing in his own emotional turmoil that he hadn't protected the secrets well enough.

There was a pay phone in a booth at the back. He called Bernie. She was out for lunch so he gave Alex the summary of the trip to Milly Corwin's. And he promised that the proposal would be in Bernie's hands the next day, that he would drop it through her office door's mail slot in the morning before he got on the train.

Alex raved about what a dynamite book Owen was going

to have, then commented on how down he sounded. Owen said he was just tired.

"Must be jet lag," Alex laughed. "I've heard those flights to Kansas can be murder."

"Right." Owen forced an agreeable laugh.

"Oh ... Cliff got the message you left on our machine Tuesday, and he's already on it. He's having a problem getting army info on Abe Hanselmann. I don't know why exactly. He was calling around to some hacker friends trying to solve it. But as for the other name—Benjamin Hanselmann of Ridley, Kansas—he said to tell you that the guy never served. Not in any branch of the military. And there's no record of him working in Vietnam in a sanctioned civilian support capacity or medical capacity either."

"Thanks," Owen said, wondering what this news meant. Was Bram Serian's Vietnam war experience a total fiction?

He walked back uphill toward the courthouse. His emotions and his thoughts were in such a state of disorder that he didn't trust himself. He didn't know what to expect. He could not predict what he might do or say next.

Frantically, he tried to think of a way to redeem himself quickly with Lenore. If only he hadn't left the tape with her. He could have used that to lure her into a meeting. What did she need from him now? Nothing. He had to come up with new information for her.

It occurred to him that there was a fairly simple lead that he hadn't pursued—the obituary he had found in Serian's papers. The deceased had spent most of his time in Thailand, and Owen had to believe that Thailand was the connection Serian had with the man. If the widow still lived in Connecticut, maybe he could track her down. Maybe she would have information. It was a slim possibility, but worth a try. Anything was worth a try. Anything.

"The people call James Collier!"

James Collier came to the witness stand in a plain dark suit, looking like a pallbearer at a funeral. His rugged, faintly pocked skin was sallow, and his eyes were puffy and shadowed. No doubt due to the grillings he'd been subjected to since the moment of his capture. When he lifted his hand to swear on the Bible, it trembled so badly that Owen was aware of it from ten rows back.

"Mr. Collier," Brown said, making a show of sarcastic antagonism, "or is it Brother Collier?"

"Actually, I'm addressed as Brother James."

"Ah. Very good. Brother James, then . . ."

Brown asked the man about his life as a Catholic brother and his work teaching children, discrediting him at every opportunity through innuendo, facial expressions, and constant sarcasm.

"Tell us, Brother James, how did you come to be acquainted with Lenore Serian?"

"I met her through her husband, Bram Serian."

"How and when did you meet Bram Serian?"

"He came to a charity fund-raiser for my school eight months prior to his death."

"Was Lenore Serian in attendance with him?"

"No."

"When you met Bram Serian, did you immediately feel a kinship with him or have something in common?"

"Yes."

"And how did you progress from this meeting at a public function to a more personal level of acquaintance?"

"He invited me out for a drink and we discussed art. I was concerned about the art program at my school not being adequate."

"And then what?"

"Time passed. He bought me dinner."

"So the man was extending his friendship to you?"

Collier hesitated. "Yes."

"When did you become acquainted with your new friend's wife?"

"Bram took me out to dinner several more times, and he came to the school to give a talk to our student body. I had known him for four months when he invited me out to see Arcadia the first time."

"Was this to one of his parties?"

"No. It was a quiet day with just him and Natalie Raven and his wife."

"How long were you on the premises?"

"I went up on Friday morning by train, spent the night, and then returned to Manhattan after . . . after the fire."

"Was Lenore Serian friendly to you?"

"Yes."

"Did you spend any time solely in her company?"

"There was a period during which Bram went into his studio and Natalie was busy, and during that time Lenore took me for a walk to see the pond."

"Whose idea was that?"

"Actually, it was Bram's idea."

"What did you find to talk about with this woman you had just met?"

"Good and evil. Lenore was very interested in my personal views on that, and she also wanted to know about the views of the church."

"Ahhh." Brown nodded knowingly. "And how long did this walk and this philosophical discussion last?"

"Several hours."

"I see. And when was the next occasion that you had contact with Lenore Serian?"

"The next time I was invited to Arcadia. Two weeks later."

"Whose invitation were you responding to?"

"Bram's."

"Did you again have occasion to be alone with Lenore Serian?"

"Yes."

"For how long?"

"Two to three hours."

"And what did you discuss when you were alone with Lenore Serian this time?"

"We talked about Bram and his art."

"Did you enjoy this woman's company?"

"Yes."

"How many more visits were there to Arcadia prior to Bram Serian's death?"

"Five. Including the weekend when ... the weekend of the fire."

"Did each of these visits include several hours alone with Lenore Serian?"

"Yes."

"Did you not find that uncomfortable?"

"No. Lenore was very kind to me."

"Did you ever have contact with Lenore Serian away from Arcadia?"

"No."

"Did you ever speak to her without her husband's knowledge?"

James Collier drew in a resigned breath. "Yes. On the phone."

"How often?"

"It varied."

"In the last two weeks before her husband's death, how often did you speak to Lenore Serian?"

"Every day."

"Who was it who initiated these calls, you or her?"

"Mostly me. I usually called her."

"What did the two of you discuss in these phone conversations that her husband was not aware of?"

"We talked about Bram and about when I would be coming out to Arcadia again."

"Did she talk about what your lives would be like if she was free of her husband?"

"She did not!"

Brown turned away from the witness for a moment in a show of disgust. Then, reluctantly, he turned back.

"Who invited you to the party on the weekend of August fifth through seventh?"

"Lenore."

"Did you ask her to invite you?"

"I told her I wanted to go."

"Why did you not call your friend Bram Serian and ask him for an invitation?"

Collier lowered his eyes. "He didn't want me to come."

"Oh? Did he give you a reason for not wanting your company?"

"He didn't think it was proper for someone from the church to be at one of his parties."

"What was your response to that concern of his?"

"I told him that I was confused about the church. That I was becoming uncertain about the totality of my commitment to the church."

"And what was Bram Serian's reaction to this confession of yours?"

"He warned me to be sure before I took any drastic steps."

Brown paused to shuffle through his notes and then shifted his attention to the weekend of the fire. He took Collier through a recitation of Friday night's events: his arrival at Arcadia and Bram Serian's anger over his appearance.

"What did you attribute that anger to, Brother James?"

"To my disobeying his wishes and coming to the party."

"Did he say anything to you to indicate that he was upset over your intimate relationship with his wife?"

"No. He did not."

"What happened then?"

"Natalie Raven showed me to a room, and everyone went to bed."

"Did you have any other contact with Mrs. Serian that night?"

"No."

"But you saw her first thing the next morning, didn't you?"

"Yes."

"Tell us, please, how you came to be with Mrs. Serian the next morning."

"I did not sleep well, and as soon as it was light out, I got up to take a walk. It was very hot. Even in the morning. I walked to the pond and sat down along the edge, thinking I was alone. Then I saw that Lenore was also there. Swimming."

"Swimming in this pond at dawn?"

"It is not so much a pond as a miniature lake, springfed I was told, and so the water is very clear and pleasant. Everyone swims in it. And as to the time . . . I don't think it's that unusual for people to be up and about at seven-thirty in the morning."

"Did you then call out to Mrs. Serian . . . let her know of your presence?"

"Yes. I did and as I called out to her I realized she was swimming nude and I was worried that she might be embarrassed so I immediately told her that I was leaving."

"And what was her response to that?"

"She called back and told me not to leave. That I was fine there. And then she swam out of my sight and five or ten minutes later she came walking through the trees, fully dressed and with a towel around her hair."

"And what happened then?"

"She sat down and we talked."

"About the usual, I suppose," Brown said sarcastically.

"Yes. Plus, she told me that she liked to swim early on party weekends so she could have the lake to herself."

"So this was a habit of hers? This swimming nude in the early morning?"

"Yes."

"And you could have heard about this habit . . . known she was out there beforehand, couldn't you?"

"I could, but I didn't."

Nearly two hours passed with Brown dragging James Collier through every move he had made on Saturday during the party. He managed to goad Collier into admitting that he shouldn't have been there, and that Bram continued to be annoyed with him, and that he did not fit in with the other guests or with the activities. But no matter how he approached it, he could not get Collier to admit a physical relationship with Lenore.

To Owen, James Collier evolved into an object of pity. The man had been troubled about his religious commitment, miserable and uncomfortable at the party, upset by Bram Serian's annoyance, and apparently involved in a frustrating, unconsummated romance with Lenore.

"Now, Brother James, where were you on the morning of August seventh, just shortly before the evening's festivities disbanded?"

"Everyone was gathered outside drinking and generally enjoying themselves to excess, and I was seated off to the side a little ways."

"Enjoying themselves to excess?"

"Drinking heavily and engaging in various drugs."

"Oh. But you were not?"

"No."

"Were any others abstaining from this behavior?"

"I believe Lenore was the only other person completely abstaining."

"Could you tell us what happened?"

"There were several minor arguments and someone turned on a radio, which Bram didn't like, but there was so much noise . . . and a few people got up and started doing wild dances . . . and so Bram's annoyance over the radio was not noticed. But I was sober and I had been watching him, trying to get a moment when I could have a word with him in private, so I saw him get up. At first I thought he was going toward the radio to turn it off, but then he veered off and went over into the darkness, back to where the food tables were left from dinner. I waited a moment and then followed. It was hard to see back there after being in the lantern light, so I came nearly up to him before I realized he wasn't alone."

"What did you do then?"

"As soon as I saw that he was talking to someone, I turned around and started back . . . and then I saw Lenore in the trees . . . watching him."

"Did she appear to be spying on him?"

For the first time, James Collier showed a spark of anger. "I don't think so. I think she had probably followed him . . . probably wanted to see him in private . . . just as I had, and was waiting for the other man to leave so she could approach."

"Then what did you do?"

"I returned to the group."

"And did you see Mrs. Serian return as well?"

"No."

"When did you see Bram Serian again?"

"In about twenty minutes he came back, out of breath, like he had been running, and he announced to everyone that he was going to bed. And he told them they should too. Then he headed off in the direction of the studio."

"Was Mrs. Serian anywhere in sight at this time?"

"I started after Bram once again, hoping to have a word with him, and I saw Mrs. Serian come out of the trees and follow him to the studio."

"Did you overhear any conversation that passed between Bram and Lenore Serian?"

A look of profound regret passed over James Collier's features. "Yes, I heard her call ahead to him. She said, 'I won't let you, Bram. I swear I'll stop you.' "

21

Friday morning there was a crush of people trying to get past courthouse security. Holly's continued news flashes had rekindled a frenzy of excitement, and once again there were long lines of eager spectators.

Owen waited his turn through the metal detectors and followed the flow of people up the stairs. He was eager too, but for quite different reasons. He had spoken with the widow of the man from the obituary the night before, chasing after the Thai connection.

It had been so simple. All he had done was call information for the Ridgefield, Connecticut, area, and within seconds he had been given a listing for Françoise Newman. Then he dialed the number, plugged in the coins, and listened to a telephone ringing somewhere in Connecticut.

"Hello." It was a female voice with a strong French accent.

"Is this Mrs. Françoise Newman?"

"This is she."

"My name is Owen Byrne. I'm looking for information about people who had a connection to Thailand some years ago."

"Oh? Tell me your name again so I can copy it down." He spelled his name for her.

"What kind of information were you seeking, Mr. Byrne? My husband has passed on, and I'm afraid he was the expert on Thailand."

"I don't need an expert on Thailand," Owen assured her. "I'm in search of people. Did you know of a Luther Bachman—a young American serviceman?"

"Sorry, no."

There it was. A dead end. He had thought the call was too easy.

"How about an Abe Hanselmann?"

"No."

"Any Hanselmanns at all?"

"No."

"How about young men with the last name of Serian?"

"No. I'm afraid not."

"Did you know any American soldiers?"

She hesitated. "Why do you ask that?"

"I should have explained myself better. I'm trying to get information on a young man who fathered a child during the war, Mrs. Newman. I believe the man's name was Luther Bachman, and about all we know of him is that he went to Vietnam and never came back, and he had a child who seems to have lived in Thailand. She is here in the States now and is trying to learn about her father."

"Why are you asking me? Why not ask the army?"

"It's a long story . . . But in my search I came across a mention of your husband, his obituary actually. And I was hoping there was a connection through Thailand."

"I cannot imagine why."

"Well, I realize I'm chasing shadows here. But I have to try everything."

"I'm sorry I can't help. There are many tragedies still haunting us all from that war."

Something about her tone bothered Owen. "Can't help or *won't* help?" he asked her.

She was silent for a long, uncertain moment.

"Why are you calling me?" she demanded. "Who do you really represent? I've told you, my husband is dead! What could you possibly want from me?"

"Mrs. Newman . . . I don't know what is upsetting you so much, but there is a woman who has been suffering for a very long time, desperate to know who her parents are. Who she is. And if you could tell her anything, you would be doing a great kindness."

Françoise Newman sighed heavily. "We knew many American soldiers during the Vietnam tragedy. We knew them through my husband's antiwar activities. And, sad to say, there were probably a number of them who left Thai women with babies. But none of your names are known to me, Mr. Byrne. I swear that is true."

"Can you give me any suggestions . . . other people I might talk to?"

"How about the mother? What do you know about the mother?"

"She can't remember any facts about her mother."

"So sad." Françoise Newman sighed again. "But I really can't help you."

"Well, thank you for your time. Can I leave my number in case you think of something . . . anything?"

"Certainly." Françoise Newman took Bernie's agency number and read it back to him, then as a kindly afterthought said, "Perhaps if she remembered some Thai names. I still have many native friends there. The Thais are a lovely, warm people and perhaps you should try seeking help from the Thai side."

"Unfortunately, she doesn't even have a Thai name for herself. She thinks she was called 'Lenore' from birth, though no one is—"

"What!"

"Excuse me?"

"Did you say 'Lenore'?"

"Yes. Her name is Lenore. Why? Does that mean something to you?"

Françoise Newman didn't speak for some moments.

"Her last name isn't Corwin, is it?" she finally asked.

Owen felt the intense rush of relief and elation that accompanies great achievement. This was it. Full circle. Not only had Luther Bachman named his daughter in honor of his friends' grandmother—the fairy-tale grandma of Milly Corwin's Arcadia stories—he had also transformed himself into a Corwin.

"This all fits," he said. "His using the name Corwin fits with a pattern. You know exactly who she is, don't you?"

More silence. Then in a voice thickened by emotion, Françoise Newman said, "Lenore was born in my house. My house in Thailand."

Owen had to cover the mouthpiece and clench his jaw together to keep from shouting.

"Could I come out and talk to you? Please?"

"Yes. And I want to see her, to see Lenore. Will she come?"

"I think so. But it will have to be this weekend. Tomorrow or Sunday."

"Good. Come as soon as possible. I'll be waiting."

* * *

Now all he had to do was get this news to Lenore. At the door to courtroom 6, he asked the officer if the defense had arrived yet, and was told no. He stood there uncertainly for a moment, then decided that with the renewed circus atmosphere, his best chance for a word with Lenore would be outside the courthouse. Urgently, he fought his way downstairs against the upward moving crowd and hurried across to the hotel.

The desk clerk nodded a greeting when he entered, but he knew better than to have himself formally announced. Lenore would no doubt send down Riley and Volpe to throw him out if she knew he was there. So he sat down in the corner and waited.

Charlie Rossner and Paul Jacowitz came down first. They were engrossed in conversation and did not see him. He let them pass without calling attention to himself. Several minutes later, he heard footsteps on the stairs. He stood and moved toward the center of the room.

Riley was first down the stairs, saw Owen and frowned. Lenore and Volpe spotted him at the same time. Fury ignited in Lenore's eyes and Volpe erupted, lunging forward, yelling, "You're dead, scumbag!" and nearly landing a fist in Owen's face except that Riley caught him from behind, circling Volpe's chest in a tight bearhug that left the smaller man flailing wildly. Lenore bolted for the door with her cape billowing out around her, and Riley ordered Owen to get away. But he ran after Lenore instead.

"Wait! Lenore! It's about Thailand! Your father—" was all he got out before Volpe wrenched loose and tackled him from behind.

Owen had always been disgusted by men who solved their problems with fights, but suddenly all the anger, frustration, guilt, and jealousy were channeled directly into his fists, and he countered Volpe's attack with mindless savagery. Only gradually did he return to his senses. He became aware of Lenore screaming and the desk clerk shouting, then of Riley's hands trying to pry him off the prone Volpe.

Then he realized that both his face and his knuckles hurt.

Stunned, he held his hands out and stared down at them, seeing them as foreign—no longer a part of him. He straightened, staggered backward and leaned against a pillar while Riley pulled Volpe to his feet.

"Ahhh, look at you now, boys," Riley scolded. "Upstairs

with you, Joseph," he ordered Volpe. "And I hope you've a clean shirt on hand."

Volpe shot Owen a murderous look.

With a firm grip on Volpe's shoulder, Riley said, "I'll handle things here now, Joseph. The trouble's over. Just make yourself decent so we can get the lady to court the way we're bein' paid to do."

Volpe jerked free of his partner's grip, straightened his sport coat and stalked away up the stairs.

Owen watched him go. He touched the corner of his mouth and there was blood on his fingertips. He looked down at his shirtfront and saw spatters of red.

Riley shook his head. "You have a bathroom this gentleman can use?" he called over to the desk clerk.

"I guess so," the clerk agreed grudgingly and produced a key with an oversized tag attached to it.

"Wait, Owen."

It was Lenore. Lenore had spoken his name.

She crossed to stand in front of him, her face pale within the hooded cape and her eyes like black holes, pulling him toward the edge, sucking him down into the void.

"What about my father and Thailand?" she asked in a low, menacing tone.

Owen glanced over at Riley, wondering how much he knew and how much should be said in front of him.

"Frank, could you give us some privacy?" she said.

"I'll just wait over by the stairs," Riley told her. "But I can't let you outta my sight, ya know."

As soon as they were out of Riley's hearing, Owen told her about his call to Françoise Newman. Lenore was very quiet for a moment. Her fingers gripped the front of the cape together so tightly that they grew white and bloodless from the pressure.

"You have listened to the Milly Corwin tapes, haven't you?" Owen asked her.

"Yes."

"Then you know about Luther Bachman. I think he was using the name Corwin when Françoise Newman knew him. When you were born."

"I want to go with you," she said.

"When can you go?"

"Tomorrow morning. As early as possible."

Owen felt a wave of shame. "You could bring someone

along . . ." He looked down at his swollen hands. "If you don't want to be alone with me."

"There is no one I can bring," she threw back at him. "No one but you knows about this."

"You haven't told Rossner about anything we've learned?"

"Of course not!"

"But he might be able to use some of that in your defense, Lenore."

"That is *not* your business."

Volpe came down the stairs wearing a fresh shirt and a different sport coat. "C'mon!" he barked at Lenore. "We're late!"

Owen watched out the window as she hurried toward the courthouse, her cape sweeping out like the wings of a great dark bird. Then the photographers closed around her and she disappeared.

James Collier looked even worse than he had the day before. He could have been seriously ill and not looked as bad.

Rossner was very gentle with him, exuding concern, and the jury seemed pleased with this. The prosecution's fears had been well founded—the jury was sympathetic to this man of the cloth, regardless of the indications that he may have fallen from grace.

Rossner took James Collier through a history of his servitude to the church, emphasizing every good word, thought, and deed ever associated with Brother James and transforming him from sinner back to saint. Then he zeroed in on Collier's relationship with Bram Serian.

"In the eight months you knew Bram Serian, how many times did he take you to dinner in Manhattan?"

"Oh, numerous times. Twelve maybe."

"Even after the invitations to Arcadia began . . . the dinners in town continued?"

"Yes."

"So Bram Serian obviously found something meaningful in your friendship?"

"I'd like to believe so."

"Was he a troubled man?"

"Yes. Very troubled."

"Did he confess sins to you?"

Brown bounded from his chair. "Objection, your honor! Priest penitent privilege."

"Sustained," Pulaski replied immediately.

"My apologies," Rossner said. "What did you discuss, Brother James?"

"Our discussions were abstract. As a brother I don't hear confessions."

"Generally speaking, what were some of the things he discussed with you?"

"He was concerned about eternal damnation and about the sins of one unrepentant soul being transferred to another."

"Did he ever discuss Lenore with you?"

"I wouldn't call it a discussion, but he did mention her at times."

"In what way did he mention her?"

"He was . . . he said things to indicate that he was mystified by her."

"Did he ever give you any reason to believe he didn't love her?"

"None at all."

"Or that he was ready to divorce her?"

"Absolutely not. There was a connection between them. Something very strong. You could feel it whenever they were together."

"How did Natalie Raven treat her employer on the occasions when you visited Arcadia?"

"I'd say she doted over him."

"Doted?"

"Fussed. She was always straightening his collar or brushing something from his sleeve or bringing him a cold drink. That sort of thing."

"How did Bram Serian react to this fussing?"

"He seemed oblivious to it."

"And how did Natalie Raven behave toward Lenore?"

"She was overly friendly to Lenore, while at the same time doing everything she could to make Lenore look bad. Pointing out mistakes Lenore had made or things Lenore had forgotten."

"Did you enjoy Lenore Serian's company?"

"Yes. She was very kind to me. Very understanding. I didn't feel like I had to be wise when I was talking to her."

"Did you ever meet her for dinner alone the way you often met her husband?"

"No."

"Did you ever have sexual relations with her?"

"No!"

"Do you have other women friends?"

"Yes. I have a number of women friends. Women who work with me on certain charities. Mothers of some of my students."

"Do you call them on the telephone?"

"Sometimes. Yes."

"Have you ever broken your vows with a woman?"

"No. I have not."

Rossner stared up at the ceiling and rocked on his heels a moment.

"All right, let's go to the party. Bram Serian was annoyed at you for coming, right? And annoyed at his wife for inviting you?"

"Yes. He thought I was compromising myself by being seen at one of his parties. But I wanted to go and so I asked Lenore and she said, of course, that Bram certainly had no right to dictate my behavior."

"So Bram Serian's annoyance with you had nothing to do with your friendship with Lenore?"

"Nothing whatsoever."

Rossner turned away and mulled this over a moment. He had note cards in his hand but had yet to consult them.

"Would you say . . ." Rossner began carefully, "that Bram Serian was afraid of something in those last weeks of his life?"

"Not afraid. But worried. Very worried."

"Do you think he was being threatened in some way?"

"I tried to ask him about that, but he waved it off. He told me that he had all his enemies under control."

"Enemies? He used that exact word?"

"Yes."

"In the final two weeks of his life, he was deeply worried and talking about controlling enemies?"

"Yes."

"Did he ever name any of these enemies?"

"No."

Rossner paused to absorb this news, which was in reality a pause for the jury to absorb it. Then he asked, "When you followed Bram Serian away from the gathering, and you saw him in conversation in the darkness by the tables . . . could you tell who he was with?"

"No."

"Man or woman?"

"Definitely a man."

"But no one you recognized?"

"I . . . it was very dark and my attention was mostly on Bram. All I can tell you is that it was a man."

"Young or old?"

"Not old. Middle-aged maybe."

"Dark- or light-skinned?"

"I don't know."

"Short or tall?"

"About the same as Bram. Tall, I guess."

"Could you hear what they were saying?"

"I couldn't hear any specific words, but the conversation sounded . . . heated."

"When you saw Lenore watching him . . . could you tell if she appeared to be concerned for him?"

"She did look very concerned, yes."

"When you returned to the group, did you notice who was gone . . . who might possibly be out in the dark having a heated conversation with Bram Serian just hours before his death?"

James Collier's face looked as though something momentous had just dawned on him.

"I didn't notice anything. What I mean to say is that there were a lot of people and so it would have been hard to notice if everyone was still right where they'd been before. But the man with Bram didn't strike me as being the least bit familiar, which . . . by that time . . . I'd met everyone . . ."

"So you think this big man having a heated conversation in the dark with Bram Serian was not someone who had been at the party?"

"That's right."

"Then Bram Serian returned to tell people that he was going to bed?"

"Yes."

"But the unknown man, the man from the dark, did not come back with him?"

"No. There was no sign of him."

"And Bram Serian left then, headed for his studio?"

"Yes."

"What was his appearance as he left? Did he seem sleepy, alert, what . . . ?"

"He seemed . . . a little drunk. He was swaying and slurring his words slightly."

"And Lenore followed him then?"

"Yes."

"How did she follow him? Was she sneaky?"

"No. Not really. If she had wanted to be sneaky, she could have cut through the trees and caught him at the studio."

Rossner pondered this a moment, then said, solemnly, "Thank you, Brother James."

Brown shot out of his seat and attacked in a blaze of redirect questioning, but he couldn't reclaim the high moral ground he'd held before. After a while he gave up and let Collier go.

Spencer Brown remained standing as James Collier left the room; then he announced in an authoritative tone, "The people rest, your honor."

A buzzing started in the pews, and Judge Pulaski rapped his gavel sharply. "We will adjourn for the day, and Mr. Rossner can begin presenting his case on Monday morning. The defense will be ready on Monday morning, will it not, Mr. Rossner?"

"Yes, your honor."

Pulaski's mouth stretched into a tight smile. "Then we all have something to rejoice about because we are at least half-finished."

Owen left with the crowd to avoid contact with Joe Volpe. Holly was nowhere in sight, and he guessed that she had run somewhere to film another news flash, so he dropped his guard and walked at a leisurely pace.

It seemed so strange that the entire subject of Collier's hiding out at Arcadia had been absent from the questioning. Some legal point or another had no doubt rendered it a taboo subject. So if the jurors had been following orders and avoiding contact with any news sources, they had had no idea of the level of drama behind James Collier's testimony.

Outside the courthouse doors, he paused to take in the day. The afternoon sky was a bright turquoise blue, and the temperature had climbed to the fifties. Every trace of snow was gone. Winter itself seemed to have retreated. He started down the granite steps.

"Owen?"

He froze. Without turning, he knew that it was Holly and that she had been waiting in ambush for him behind the evergreens that flanked the building.

"I've been waiting for you." She moved tentatively toward him. "Please, won't you talk to me?"

He looked at her. The gray-blue of her coat brought out the blue of her eyes. The sunlight turned her hair to spun gold.

"We have nothing to say to each other, Holly."

Her full bottom lip quivered slightly, and she blinked several times against impending tears. And he realized that his anger was gone. The warm friendliness she'd stirred in him was gone. Even the general goodwill he felt toward complete strangers was absent when he looked at Holly Danielson. And he realized that the opposite of friendship was not hate. It was total disregard.

"What happened to your lip?" She lifted her hand toward him, but he jerked back out of her reach.

"We could go someplace quiet and have lunch," she suggested.

"No. I'm headed home."

"You're really, really mad at me, aren't you?"

"I was."

Her face brightened. "You're not anymore?"

"No. I'm just disgusted with myself for my bad judgment."

Holly lowered her eyes and sighed. "I shouldn't have left you the note. I realized that later. Once you saw that I'd opened your notebook, you were bound to figure out that I'd looked at the stuff you wrote in there."

He started to ask her if leaving the note was all she was sorry about, but he didn't care enough about her to find out.

"I never thought you'd get so mad at me," she said sadly. "I mean the James Collier stuff wasn't really connected to your book or anything. But I guess she blamed you for Collier being caught and now you probably won't get to go back to Arcadia or get any more personal interviews with her."

Owen studied her, wondering . . .

"I can understand how you'd be mad about that. Having all that hot information cut off. But your editor said that you already had enough to make your book great so—"

"You talked to my editor?"

"Well, I just ... Yeah. I'm a reporter, remember? And I just called and asked if the rumor was true that DeMille had a book in the works on this case."

"Holly ..."

"See! I was trying to protect you. I made sure that your editor thought you had enough before I tipped the D.A. about Collier."

"This was more than a sleazy career move for you, wasn't it, Holly? You wanted to destroy my connection to Lenore Serian."

She looked up at him with teary, frightened eyes. "I was worried about you," she said.

"Oh. You did it with my best interests at heart? Is that right?"

"I could see it happening! I could see that evil bitch getting her hooks into you and using you! You weren't going to save yourself, so I had to do it."

Owen stared at her with detached amazement.

"You wanted me that night at your apartment, Owen. And you would have kept on wanting me. Eventually, we would have gotten together ... if she hadn't twisted you around."

"It wasn't you I wanted. I wanted the sex. The same as I would have wanted it with any attractive, willing female who offered her body to me in the privacy of my apartment. It was very tempting." He shook his head. "But it wasn't you I wanted, Holly. It was the blow job."

Her face contorted into something ugly. "And I'll bet she's good at sucking your cock, isn't she? Someone with all her experience ..."

Owen turned and walked away.

"She was using you, Owen!" Holly called after him. "You're nothing to her!"

Owen walked to the train station with a fast, ground-covering stride, walking away his anger. Erasing Holly Danielson and all her vicious words. He was determined to go to the apartment and catch up on his work. There were Milly's tapes to transcribe and his notes from the trial to write out. And then there was his promise to Bernie. He had to turn in the proposal tomorrow morning no matter what.

He walked into the station house and nearly bumped into a man in a long trench coat. "Excuse me," he muttered, glancing at the man's face as he did so, and realizing, in a sudden time-stopping flash, that it was James Collier.

"Hello," Collier said.

"Hello," Owen replied tentatively.

"I took the chance that I might catch you here," Collier admitted. "I know you take the train."

"Me?" Owen asked. "You must have me confused with someone else."

"No. You're Owen Byrne, aren't you?"

"Yes."

"I came here so those vultures around the courthouse wouldn't spy me talking to you and write that we were planning to rob a bank or something."

Owen nodded his understanding. "But aren't you supposed to be in custody or something?"

"No. They're finished with me." Collier moved away from the door to stare out the window that overlooked the tracks. Owen followed, led by curiosity. "I've come to talk to you about Lenore," Collier said.

"Oh?"

"Yes. After that morning when I so clumsily arrived and she sent you off so roughly . . . she told me all about you."

"How cozy," Owen said. "I hope she didn't get any of the details wrong."

"It wasn't like that. Lenore and I . . . I am not your competition. Lenore and I are not lovers. We have never been lovers. The only thing we had in common was Bram."

"Then why all the secrecy? Why all the hiding? Why was she protecting you?"

Collier's face betrayed an intense emotional struggle, and Owen thought he wouldn't answer, but finally he said, "I was weak and I was afraid and she offered help. What better place to hide than Arcadia? Who would ever look for me there?

"I wanted to keep my life the way it was, and I fooled myself into believing that if I hid, everything would blow over, and then I could come back out with my reputation intact. A very foolish pipe dream of course because even though I wasn't found and the truth wasn't known, the papers printed horrible things about me. I was ruined in absentia.

"I kept hiding, then, out of shame. And she encouraged me to continue hiding. If I had thought that I could help her case by speaking out, it would have been different. But she said I would only hurt her case. She didn't want me on the stand. She didn't want me to testify."

"Wait a minute," Owen said. "If there was nothing between you, if you weren't in love or in lust, why did your reputation need protection?"

Again the struggle showed in his face. "Oh, but I was in love," he said softly. "I was in love with Bram."

Owen was too stunned to speak for a moment. When he did he blurted out, "Bram Serian was a homosexual?"

"No. He wasn't. And he didn't return my feelings." Collier chuckled bitterly. "You see, my much-discussed fall from grace never happened. I lusted in my heart as they say, but not in the flesh."

"I don't know what to say," Owen admitted, feeling deep compassion for the man.

"There is nothing to say. But I owed this to Lenore. She helped me survive—while Bram was alive, and after he was dead. Now she needs help. She wanted so badly to believe in you. She needs to believe in someone."

Collier's words struck Owen deeply. "I didn't betray her confidence. I wasn't the one who turned you in. I know who did now, and I know I was guilty of carelessness—but not betrayal."

"You must convince her of that, Owen Byrne. You must show her that there is good left, that she was right to trust you. She thought I was good in the beginning, but I failed her. Everyone in her life has failed her. Now, she's so close to being lost. A lost soul."

The train came roaring into the station then and squealed to a stop. "You have to go," Collier said.

"I could stay longer," Owen offered, not wanting to sever this connection to Lenore.

"No. I've said what I wanted to say. Come. I'll walk with you."

They went out of the building onto the platform and joined the small knot of passengers waiting to board the Manhattan-bound train.

Owen gripped Collier's hand. "Thank you," he said. "Thank you." And he rushed aboard the train, buoyant with renewed hope, renewed determination.

22

Only after turning into Arcadia's long drive the next morning did Owen allow himself to consider what he would say to Lenore. Though it was unintentional, the blame for the leak did rest with him, and he could not claim complete innocence. In a way he had betrayed her—through his carelessness and through his blindness with Holly.

The house came into sight, and he had the sensation of slipping away from himself. He was overhead somewhere, looking down on himself, a frantic desperate man, curious about what the man would find to say.

Lenore came out the front door as soon as he pulled up. She was wearing a leather coat over a black skirt and red sweater. Her hair was pulled high into a braided ponytail, and the style sharpened the bones and angles of her face, giving her a fiercely exotic appearance.

His chest ached at the sight of her. He wanted to throw himself at her feet and beg for her forgiveness, but instead he heard himself saying, "Thanks for leaving your gun in the house."

She shot him a disdainful glance, then settled into the passenger seat of the rental, and he shifted the car into gear and started down the drive.

"Françoise Newman is this woman's name, and she says you were born in her house in Thailand." The words spilled out of him. He related his entire phone call to Connecticut, without being able to stop. There was safety in discussing Françoise Newman. He was afraid of a confrontation.

Lenore listened carefully, then settled into silence. Tension gathered, filling the small car like a suffocating, poisonous gas.

"We're going to be together for hours, Lenore. Couldn't we strike a truce?"

She glanced sideways at him. It was a tough, hard look,

but there was an undercurrent of pain that sliced completely through him.

He pulled the car over and turned toward her in the seat.

"Lenore, I was foolish and I was blind and I didn't protect you the way I should have. I'm sorry. I am so sorry. If I could go back and do it over differently, I would."

"What did the district attorney's office give you for turning in Jimmy?"

He shook his head. "I didn't turn him in."

Her gaze was penetrating and cold. "Joe Volpe said you had to be the one who did it. And then you called in the tip to your blond girlfriend so she could get her news scoop. Joe said you must have traded the D.A. for an exclusive interview after the trial is over."

Owen slammed the flat of his hand against the steering wheel. "Volpe *would* think that. But he's wrong. The blonde, who is *not* my girlfriend and now not any kind of friend, sneaked a look at some of my notes. She saw a mention of the name Jimmy and Arcadia, and she put the two together. I didn't know a thing about it until after I got back from Kansas and—"

"You were with her outside the courthouse today at lunch. I could see you from the hotel window."

"Yeah. She was explaining to me that she'd done it all for my own good, and I told her I didn't want her kind of friendship."

Lenore frowned. The smooth wings of her black eyebrows drew almost together over the bridge of her nose. "How was turning Jimmy in supposed to be good for Owen Byrne?"

"Because it severed my connection to you. She wanted it to seem like I'd betrayed your confidence so you'd react just as you did."

Understanding dawned in Lenore's eyes.

He watched, afraid to hope for too much. "Holly thinks of herself as having seized the opportunity to further her career while doing a good deed—saving me from you."

Lenore stared at him. Through him. Into him.

"Does Rossner think Collier's testimony did any damage?" he asked.

"Damage? You should ask Jimmy that question."

"Lenore . . . your friend Jimmy is not on trial for murder. His indiscretions are his own responsibility, and he should never have put you in this position."

"He was helping me by keeping silent."

"He was helping himself. What I don't understand is why you encouraged him. Why were you so afraid of his testimony?"

Her mouth tightened, and she turned her head to stare angrily out the window.

"All right. I don't blame you for keeping secrets anymore. I'm sorry I asked. But you should know that Collier followed me to the train station yesterday and told me why he was hiding."

"Jimmy told you about . . . Bram?"

"Yes."

"Bram used him," she said. "Bram played with him."

Owen pulled back onto the road. After an uncomfortable ten minutes of further silence, he said, "Milly Corwin's box of pictures is on the backseat. I didn't get a chance to show them to you the other night, so I thought you might want to take a look today."

She was engrossed in the pictures for the rest of the trip, and they were nearing Ridgefield before he worked up the courage to speak to her again.

"What did you think of the Milly Corwin tapes?" he asked.

"My thoughts are private," she said.

"Fine. Okay. That's just fine."

Owen tapped out a rhythm on the steering wheel with his fingers.

"Are we in Connecticut yet?" she asked.

"Yes. We're just coming up on Ridgefield."

"I've never been to Connecticut before. I expected it to look different from New York."

"Ridgefield is just across the state border," he said. "How different could it be?"

"Yes. I am stupid, aren't I?"

"I didn't say you were stupid! You are not stupid."

She fingered the sleeve of her coat in nervous silence; then in a voice so low it was close to a whisper she said, "Please don't tell Mrs. Newman that I can't read. Or that I'm illegal. Or that I'm on trial for murder."

"You don't have to ask that. I would never . . ." but he couldn't finish because he had been going to say that he would never betray her confidence.

She looked at him as if she knew what he was thinking.

He studied the road ahead for a while, then said, "There are more pictures in my bag. I sorted some out that we might want Mrs. Newman to look at."

She nodded. Nervousness radiated from her in waves.

Ridgefield was a picturesque area, and the house they pulled up to was a charming cottage set back from the road amid a lavish sweep of garden. He got out, pulling the over stuffed carryon with him. Lenore didn't move. He walked around and opened the door for her. Still no movement. He could tell that she was terrified.

"There's nothing to be afraid of," he told her gently. "You are finally going to have all the answers."

"That's what I'm afraid of," she said, forcing herself to get out of the car.

Owen rang the bell, and it echoed inside. Around them the day had turned warm, warmer even than the day before, and he could almost feel the garden stirring. "It will be spring soon," he said. "You can feel it today, can't you?"

She responded with a faint nod.

"You don't have to go in, Lenore. You could stay in the car and I'll tape it for you."

She shook her head no.

The door swung open, and they were greeted by a heavy-set woman in a gray uniform dress. Without even asking their names, she nodded and smiled. "Please to follow," she said, sounding cheerfully Russian.

Mrs. Françoise Newman was in the sun room, a glorified glassed-in porch that extended from the back of the house. She was an athletically built woman in her sixties, giving the appearance of sturdiness and health, and a lifetime in the sun, except that she was seated in a wheelchair with a blanket covering her legs.

As soon as they entered, her eyes fastened on Lenore. For a moment, Owen thought there would be tears, but she regained control quickly. "Ah yes, I can see both your father and your mother in you."

Lenore sank down into one of the large wicker chairs as though her legs could no longer support her.

"I'm sorry," said Mrs. Newman. Her French accent seemed more pronounced than it had on the phone. "I'm forgetting my manners. Please sit down, Mr. Byrne." She smiled. "How does tea sound to everyone?"

Lenore did not appear able to speak so Owen accepted for

both of them. Without being asked, the uniformed woman left to see to it. They went through the polite formalities, agreeing to call each other by first names. The tea arrived. There was a silver pot and china cups and an elaborate assortment of little pastries and breakfast rolls.

Françoise Newman tore her attention from Lenore to smile at Owen. "Thank you for bringing her." Then she turned back to Lenore. "My dear, have you been ill? You look so drawn."

Lenore flashed Owen a panicky look.

"She's been under a lot of stress," Owen said. "She was widowed in August."

Françoise clucked sympathetically.

"What first name was my father using?" Lenore blurted out impatiently.

"Your father went by Kit. Kit Corwin. Or sometimes his friends called him K. C. It was a nickname. I was told it referred to Kit Carson, a famous early American, and that it was because of your father's considerable talents as a tracker and a marksman. I never heard his real name."

"Could you," Lenore began weakly, "could you tell me." She cleared her throat. "About my mother?"

Françoise nodded. "Do you remember much of your life there?"

"Almost nothing," Lenore said. "Sometimes I have strange dreams that I know are out of my childhood, and sometimes I'll suddenly have a picture in my head, like a flash of memory, but if I force the pictures it all goes black."

"Have you tried studying about Thailand?" Françoise asked. "I'm sure reading would help jog your memories."

Lenore glanced at Owen fearfully.

"This may sound odd," he said. "But since she's been in the States Lenore was led to believe that she was raised in Vietnam. It was only recently and by accident that she learned she had lived in Thailand."

A puzzled frown spread across Françoise's face.

"Why don't you go ahead with your story, Françoise," Owen suggested.

"Yes," she said. "That is better than skipping around with all these questions." She pointed at a bookshelf just inside the adjoining living room. "Lenore, there is a big red book in there on Thailand. Why don't you get it and flip through the pages as I talk. The pictures might mean something to you."

Reluctantly, Lenore went for the book. Owen hoped there were no other big red ones on the shelf to confuse her.

He asked Françoise if he could tape, but she ignored him. Her attention was riveted on Lenore, who had returned to sit down with the book on her lap. It was one of those oversized glossy photographic books, and Lenore relaxed with it as soon as she realized that it had very little text.

Françoise still hadn't responded to Owen's taping request, and he was afraid she was going to refuse, but finally, after watching Lenore's instant absorption with the book, she sighed and said, "You may tape, I suppose. So many years have passed . . . and with my husband gone . . . I don't see how any of this could cause trouble now."

Quickly he set up the recorder.

"Owen . . ."

Lenore's voice sounded odd, and when he looked up she had an expression of rapturous amazement on her face.

"Owen," she said again, her tone reverent and full of wonder, "I can read this book. I know most of these words."

"Why yes," Françoise said. "I taught you to read in French. Don't you remember the book about the little dog? We must have read that together a thousand times."

Lenore looked at him. And he knew that, at that moment, the intensity of her feelings was close to overwhelming.

"Please, Françoise," he said, "tell us everything. From the beginning."

"I met my husband in France, after the Second World War. He took me to California, where he finished his education and then became a professor at the University of Southern California. I was happy there, but he was a wanderer at heart and he had different ideas of how people should live. He became interested in the import-export business. We lived in London for a year and then South Africa. Neither place held his interest. He knew of Jim Thompson, the silk man, through a mutual friend, and he was fascinated with the idea of living in the Far East, so he contacted Thompson and off we went to Bangkok.

"Thailand captured Howard's heart immediately, but I must confess that I myself did not fall under the spell for quite a long time. I was too used to modern conveniences and time clocks and efficiency.

"Our house, which was quite nice in comparison with many others, had an unreliable electrical system, no window screens and only occasional hot water. And it had no kitchen. At least not what I considered a proper kitchen. Behind the house next to the servants' quarters was a squat little building with a water spigot and buckets and a built-in charcoal cooker, and that was supposed to be the kitchen. Needless to say I was appalled. I didn't want to cook in that kitchen but I didn't like the idea of hiring servants either, especially for a couple with no children. As it turned out there was a staff of four who came with the house, and since I couldn't bear to fire them and kick them out of their quarters the question was settled. We had a cook and a gardener and a laundress and a number one whether we wanted servants or not.

"Everything upset me. The way the servants nodded and smiled without paying any attention to my wishes. The exotic foods. The lack of punctuality. My makeup melting off my face in the heat. The unpronounceable names of things . . . *Benchamabopit* and *Rajapardit* and *Yaowaraj* and *Chitralada.* The unsanitary conditions.

"Why, the first time I took a boat ride on a *klong* . . . those are the canals. Bangkok is called the Venice of the East because there are so many canals. They wind through the city like roads, and the houses are built along them so that you can pull your boat right up to someone's porch.

"Canals. Very nice in pictures, but the reality of it was disgusting. On that first boat ride I saw sewage thrown into the water and dogs being bathed in it and women washing dishes in it and children dipping their toothbrushes in it. All in the same water! It didn't matter to me that I wasn't expected to live under such conditions or that the educated Thais didn't live that way. Just the fact that this existed right under my nose was horrifying.

"And the etiquette! Rudeness is close to a mortal sin over there, you see. So I had to get it all straight because I couldn't stand the feeling that I was some kind of insensitive, ugly *farang*—foreigner—who didn't care about their feelings. I had to learn to tuck my legs in just so when visiting Thais because the feet are offensive and mustn't ever be pointed at another. I had to remember never to touch anyone's head or hair, or stand over anyone's head even if they're seated, because the head is sacred.

"And then there were all the *wai* rules . . . Do you remember how to *wai*, Lenore? You put your palms together with your fingers almost touching your nose, like this, and that's the greeting for everyone. Only, just when I thought I'd mastered the gesture, I learned that there were different levels of the *wai*. Fingers almost touching the nose was for equals and higher was for authority figures and lower for those beneath you, including the young. Oh, it was so very complicated. And that was before I started with the language and all the subtleties of spoken politeness. The Thai never refuse or disagree with anything, so it becomes an art to know what people really mean when they answer you. They always say yes, but you have to determine which yes it is . . . absolutely yes or maybe yes or not-at-all yes.

"And I had to get used to all the Buddhist notions, karma and merit and rebirth and all that. And all this business of live and let live . . . rats in the kitchen, snakes on the roof . . . birds flying in and out of the windows . . . none of it bothered those people. So I read up on Buddhism, learned it right out of a book and felt pretty smug, only to find that the Buddhism in Bangkok has this jumble of other things mixed in. Gods from the old days or from other cultures. Ceremonies and rituals left over from who knows where.

"True Buddhism did not recognize the shrines in the backyard for the household spirits or the giant phallic symbols or the four-headed gold thing by the hotel that is supposed to bring good luck. Heavens, there were days a person couldn't drive down Rama I Road because of the singing and dancing and feasting around that four-headed statue. And how was an outsider supposed to learn all that? It wasn't in any book.

"Do you remember, Lenore, how Chit used to take you with her to pray for fertility? On special days she took you by bus to a garden with a huge shrine for Shiva. I went with you once and I couldn't believe it . . . this beautiful lush garden was filled with hundreds of carved penises. Long, short, big, small . . . All quite stiff of course. A jungle of penises to pray to for a baby. Mind you . . . as a young wife of the nineteen fifties I found this shocking.

"And the superstitions . . . the stories I could tell about that! Astrology and fortunes and oracles and amulets. Heav-

ens . . . I never knew that intelligent, grown people could believe in ghosts the way the Thais do.

"I'm telling you those first years in Bangkok were a
nightmare for me. Howard had business colleagues and
friends and an air-conditioned office and respect as a
teacher—he was part-time at Chulalongkorn University
then—and I had nothing at all. I felt like I would never be
at home there or find friends or understand the culture. I was
homesick for France and for America . . . and for that feeling
of fitting in with people. I begged Howard to leave but he
wouldn't. And gradually, over the years, I settled in.

"I learned the language and I absorbed the attitudes and I
began to be charmed by it all. When new foreigners arrived,
I found myself patiently enduring their complaints and
shrugging and saying *mai pen rai,* never mind, to them like
a true Thai. I forgot about girdles and makeup and my upbringing, and I became flexible. I learned to appreciate the
pursuit of fun—*sanuk* as they say in Thailand—and I
learned the meaning of kindness. True kindness.

"My Thai friends became more important than my foreign
friends, and the servants became like my family. There was
Busaba, the cook, whose name meant flower. She was old
with wrinkles and warts and bad teeth, but when she smiled
you could see how she'd been a flower once. And there was
Vichet, the garden boy who couldn't decide whether he
wanted to become a monk or an American rock singer.
There was Chit, the wash *amah,* who was nineteen and giggled behind her fingers constantly. And Chinda, the number
one . . . so tiny and elegant with a Chinese-looking face and
a stern posture. She oversaw the house like she'd been born
to royalty.

"They were your family too, Lenore. You called them all
Auntie and Uncle. And they called you Dang. Red. And they
loved you very much.

"But I'm getting ahead of myself. I'm losing the thread of
how everything happened.

"We had been there three years when one day a young girl
appeared looking for a household position. She was fresh
from the hills and quite lovely. Very pure Siamese-looking
with jet black hair and large dark eyes and the slender,
graceful body of a palace dancer. We didn't need any more
help, and even if we had, I would have thought this girl too
beautiful to be a good worker.

"Chinda took her to the servants' quarters to give her some food before she continued on, but the next day I noticed that she was out in the yard helping Chit hang the laundry. It was not unusual for the servants to have guests. Actually, we never knew who all was living out there and we never minded. That was their house, after all, even though it was inside our compound.

"But after a week of seeing the girl help the others with various tasks, I asked Chinda, 'Is the girl still looking for work every day?'

" 'Yes. Yes. Not to worry,' Chinda assured me, and so I thought that the girl was continuing to go out each day in search of employment.

"After the third week of seeing her hang laundry in back of my house, I marched out and demanded to know whether the girl was ever going to find work. And Chinda very patiently explained to me, 'Not to worry, Madame, she find much work. Today hang wash. Tomorrow polish silver. Each day she look, she find.'

"At that the girl raised her head and gave me such a dazzling smile that all I could do was say never mind and go back in the house.

"When I told Howard about it, he said to leave it to him, and he called Chinda in after dinner one evening. Very firmly he explained to her that we did not need or want another servant and that the girl could not stay. Chinda agreed completely with him. She then proceeded to tell how the girl was an orphan who had lived for years in her uncle's house. Since she was past puberty and had no marriage prospects, the uncle, who was poor, had decided that she would have to be sold the next time a child-buyer from the city came. The girl, who Chinda stressed had never been treated well by the uncle's family and therefore owed no loyalty to them, ran away to Bangkok. Being very young and inexperienced with no papers or references, not one household had wanted her.

"Howard and I were aghast at the barbarism this girl had escaped from. We knew about the practice of selling children. When the poor rural families had too many children and not enough food, they did what families in that part of the world have been doing for ages—they sold off the extras. But never had we encountered such a thing first-hand.

"I was so naive that I wanted to report it to the authorities, until a friend of Howard's explained how ridiculous that would be. The authorities had no control or interest in matters like that. Why, even today, as we sit here, children are still being sold to the brothels in Bangkok. My friends in Thailand write that the practice is increasing, and the children are younger and younger, eight- and nine-year-olds, because the wealthy businessmen who come there from other countries for sex are afraid of AIDS and pay premiums for little ones who look clean.

"Chinda finished her story by telling us that the girl spoke no English and had no education or hopes of being hired anywhere and how she would have to go back to the uncle or just go straight to a brothel in Bangkok. Then Chinda shrugged and told us the girl had bad karma, but maybe she would gather merit for the next life.

"I'll never forget that moment. Chinda left the house, saying she would immediately tell the girl to go. Howard and I looked at each other and then rushed out after her. The girl could stay, we said, but only for a while. Just to give her a start and provide references, and then she would have to move on to another position.

"That is how your mother came to us, Lenore. Her name was Kamsai, which means bright. And she became the sunshine of our household.

"It was a happy exciting time. I made many friends and had wonderful adventures. When my baby was delivered prematurely and died, I put the grief quickly behind me, certain that the tiny girl had not been meant to live, but that there would be others to take her place later. Howard prospered and was greatly respected by highly placed Thais. Then the killing started.

"Do you know how close Bangkok is to Saigon? About the same distance as from San Francisco to Los Angeles. The whole monstrous Vietnam war happened right at our back door.

"You have to understand ... you have to put yourself back in that time. Things were different then. So much innocent blood was spilled. And there we were, close enough to know the truth of what was happening before the American public knew.

"My husband had served his country in World War Two. He lost an eye in battle, yet he never expressed one bitter thought about it or was anything but a patriot. Vietnam was different, though. There was no just cause, no underlying goodness to it.

"Howard joined an antiwar group started by some Frenchmen. At first it was just letters and petitions and items for the press, but one thing led to another, and they were caught up in this tidal wave that was going faster and faster. Who knows what all they became involved in. It was a frightening time and we wives were not supposed to know anything at all ... Though I'll tell you it was hard to ignore cases of medical supplies in your living room or men with guns going into your husband's study or Vietnamese refugees suddenly appearing at your door in the middle of the night.

"Bangkok turned into a wild town as the war escalated. It was flooded with soldiers on leave and con-men after the soldiers' money. New brothels opened every night. Chinda, Kamsai, Busaba, Chit and I stayed closer to the compound than before. Everyone was worried because there were rumors that bands of drunken soldiers molested women on the street.

"Howard's group was part of an underground railroad network by then. They hid political refugees and then smuggled them on to other countries. There were nights when we had refugees hidden in our laundry room or sleeping beneath the table. And sometimes we had American soldiers. Just boys, most of them. Homesick and confused boys.

"We—the wives—were told that these were boys who had been discharged but were so disturbed over the war that they could not go home. I think this was true for some of them. And I know that there are still ex-soldier Americans living around Lampang and Chiang Mai and Nakhon Ratchasima, so some never went home. However, I came to realize that most of the American soldier boys who passed through our household were not just looking for a comforting hand, they were hiding. Some were deserters. Some were men who were waging their own personal wars against the entire war machine.

"One day Howard brought in a young man in camouflage clothing and told me that he was going to be sleeping on the study floor for a few weeks. He was a handsome young man, tall and aesthetic, but when I looked into his face, I knew that he had seen hell. His eyes were so haunted that they might have been frightening, except that he had such a gentleness about him.

" 'What will we call you?' I asked him. Full names were never revealed, but since this man was to be in my home for several weeks I needed some way to address him.

" 'Call me Kit,' he said. And that is how I met your father.

"Kit stayed longer than a few weeks. I asked Howard about it and was told that Kit had decided to work with their group on some special projects.

"We all grew accustomed to having Kit in the household. He was funny in those days. We spoke a mixture of French and Thai with American slang thrown in, and he made us all laugh with his attempts to join in and his garbled pronunciation. And when he was home, he was very considerate and quick to help everyone. When my two-week-old baby died, Kit was the one who sat with me and held my hand through the bad times. Howard was so busy, you see, and the way he coped with the grief was to make himself even busier.

"I don't know when it was that Kamsai and Kit fell in love. Suddenly it was just there, in their eyes. And it grew and grew until they were totally absorbed in it. I thought it was beautiful that such a love could happen right in the middle of all that ugliness and killing. Old Busaba insisted that the two had been lovers in another life and that the love was an old one. Fated to be.

"Kamsai became pregnant with Lenore, and we had the wedding at our house. Chinda arranged it all. A lucky day was chosen with the aid of an astrologer, then Vichet overhauled the garden. Two monks came to chant before the ceremony. Howard made certain there were plenty of gifts for the monks ... that was tradition ... the families of the couple were supposed to give the monks offerings to gain good fortune for the marriage, and we considered ourselves the family. We thought it would be a small affair, but the neighbors came and a few members of Howard's group came and Chit's husband and sister-in-law and both Busaba's and Chinda's extended families and Vichet's sisters and it turned into a crowd.

"Chinda had insisted that both Kit and Kamsai wear white, which all the American men teased Kit about, and Kamsai had jasmine blossom garlands in her hair. We took pictures. I know we did. But I simply don't know what became of them. I haven't found any of our pictures from Thailand.

"The Thai wedding isn't actually a religious ceremony. Many couples simply march down and file the official papers and that's that. But we wanted to give Kamsai and Kit a sense of family and the most auspicious start together, so we had a lovely old-fashioned traditional ceremony. The bridal couple knelt and Chinda's father traced good fortune marks on their foreheads. Then they held out their hands over a gold tub, and each of us took turns pouring lustral water from a conch shell over their joined hands. Then we had a feast.

"Everyone who could contributed to send the couple to the Erawan Hotel for their wedding night. I was worried about them, about their future, but I convinced myself that all would turn out well.

"Kit was gone a lot during the last months of Kamsai's pregnancy. We all worried about him. I assumed he was doing work for Howard's group, but when I complained to Howard that Kit should not be sent out when his wife was expecting, Howard surprised me by saying that Kit was not being used by them. That is when I realized that Kit had other activities. Secret activities.

"And whatever Kit was doing was earning him money because he suddenly told Kamsai that he could buy her a small house of her own. Kamsai begged to stay with us in the servants' quarters, though. She didn't want to be alone with the baby coming, and he couldn't promise to stay home with her. No one asked him what he was doing to get the money. I suppose we were afraid to know.

"Your birth was a joyous time for the household, Lenore. Everyone showered you with love. I was a little sad because I had no baby of my own to hold, but that soon passed and I poured all of my mothering into you. What a sweet, beautiful baby you were. Never crying. Why should you? There was always someone anxious to hold you and rock you and sing to you.

"Kit named you Lenore because he said that name had a very good meaning for him and was important to people who he cared about. Kamsai had a hard time pronouncing it because the Thais can't do *r* sounds well, and so you were eventually nicknamed Dang. Red. Because you loved red things.

"As you grew out of that little infant muddle and your features became distinct, Busaba and Chit and your mother used to study you, amazed at the way you were like them and yet not like them. In spite of their flexibility, Thais are quite conformist when it comes to appearance, and Kamsai began to worry that you would not be accepted by other children.

"In spite of my not wanting to lose you or your parents, I decided that there was only one solution. Kit should go back to the States and take his little family with him. I told Kit this and he became very angry at me. I appealed to Howard, certain that my husband would agree and help convince Kit. That was when Howard confessed to me that Kit had many problems and was considered a criminal by the army.

"I entered a personally difficult time then. I desperately wanted to try for another child, but I did not want it to be born in Thailand. I wanted to go to France or to the States, where my baby would have every modern medical advantage, but Howard said he was not ready to leave Thailand yet. I fell into a depression, and the only bright spot was you, Lenore.

"I ignored what was happening with your father. I told Kamsai not to worry about his long silences and the bad dreams he had at night, because I was too full of my own despair to see someone else's.

"Oh, but you were a constant joy to all of us, Lenore. Your first steps . . . your first words . . . your laughter . . . made each day special. And then we had Chit's wedding and the promise of more babies. And Chinda became a grandmother.

"I'll never forget the night—what must you have been? Three or four perhaps? You spoke both Thai and French passably. I'll never forget . . . We took you down to the water, not to a *klong* but to the Chao Phya River, to the Festival of Floating Lights, and Vichet had made you your own little *krathong* out of bamboo and colored paper. And we all knelt down and let you light the candle and the incense yourself. Then I helped you launch your honor to the river spirits, and we all sat on the bank watching it drift out to mingle with the other floating lights on the water, and you looked up at me with those lights filling your eyes and you said— completely serious, you said—'Mama Fanny, this is the best night ever.'

"Kit's behavior became increasingly erratic. One day he might rave about sending his daughter to school in Paris, and then the next day he would have forgotten that and would be raving about what a good place Thailand was to raise a child.

"Then Kit left and was gone for a very long time. So long that we were all sick with worry. I begged Howard to do something, to go through channels, to collect favors, anything to find word of Kit. Howard agreed that he would try. But he said that he knew Kit Corwin was not even the man's real name.

"Howard never revealed what he learned. Suddenly, one day, Kit came home. Howard immediately called him into the study, even before Kit had said hello to his wife and child. When the meeting was over, Kit came out and announced that he was moving Kamsai to her own house.

"This hurt me, of course, as Kamsai had never been a servant to me and I didn't want her or Lenore to be too far. I begged Howard to intercede and change Kit's mind, but Howard was very cool and said that the separation was for the best.

"We all cried when he took you and your mother away. He'd found a two-room house on stilts along one of the less crowded *klongs*. It was the standard *klong* house of teak with a corrugated tin roof, but it was set off in its own little curtain of foliage and there was a lush peacefulness to it.

"Kamsai had very mixed emotions about the move. She was proud to have a house of her own but so sad about leaving the compound and about taking Lenore away from all of us. When they first moved, Kit stayed home for a few months, but after that he was away as much as ever. Howard said that Kit was a person to stay away from, but he didn't elaborate, and I didn't press him for details. I could tell that he and Kit had had a falling out.

"Chinda taught Kamsai how to travel by bus, and as soon as Kit was gone she would bring Lenore and come straight to us. She would spend the day, then make that long trip back to her house for sleeping because Kit wanted his wife and child in their own beds at night. Kit was adamant about it. The one time he learned that Kamsai and Lenore had slept in the compound he was furious.

"The tension between Howard and Kit increased until Howard refused to speak of Kit anymore and he barred Kit from our house. It was terrible. Kit retaliated by forbidding Kamsai to visit, which Howard said was fine because he didn't want any of them around. The ban didn't last two weeks before we broke it. You can't imagine what we all went through, sneaking around, hiding from both Howard and Kit.

"You turned five, Lenore, and you were very, very smart. You knew never to mention the compound visits to your daddy even without us explaining it to you. You learned so fast . . . like a little sponge. I started teaching you to read in French, and your mother, who couldn't read herself, was becoming excited about having an educated daughter.

"Then I learned that I was pregnant again. That was all I could think about, having a healthy baby, and I told Howard that I was going away to have it whether he approved or not. His sister in Connecticut offered her home to me, and I told him I would go there and he could stay on in Thailand if he wanted.

"I was very hurt when he accepted the arrangement and sent me to Connecticut alone, but I put that aside quickly. The baby was the important thing.

"Howard insisted that I stay on in Thailand with him as long as possible, so I was starting my seventh month when I finally got my plane ticket for the States. Kamsai, who was herself pregnant again, defied Kit and brought Lenore to my farewell party. The household was full of tears, and you, Lenore, kept clinging to me and staring into my face as if you were trying to memorize every line, but I promised that I would be back as soon as the baby was big and healthy and the trip seemed safe.

"The pain began about four hours from New York. At first I tried to pretend that it was nothing, but my previous delivery had been premature and after an hour of regular contractions I had to face what was happening. I told the flight attendant and everyone was very kind. They cleared an area in the back, and a doctor, an eye specialist from Ohio, came back to stay with me.

I delivered easily. A seven-month baby is very tiny, you know. The doctor was wonderful through it all, and the flight attendant kept coming back to tell me news: first, that the plane had been cleared for an immediate landing, and again to say that an ambulance and a doctor were waiting to rush right out to the plane as soon as it touched down. I held my tiny son close to me while we landed. He was struggling for breath and there was nothing the poor eye doctor could do.

"I was still conscious when he died. Then I slipped away. I faintly recall an ambulance siren. When I woke I was tucked safely into a hospital bed with Howard's sister crying by my side. Everyone said the usual about how there would be other babies and how lucky I was to have made it through myself.

"From there it's a fog for me. Clinical depression is the term. Two years of it. My dear sister-in-law saw to everything and made sure I got the proper care. Howard flew to Connecticut once or twice, but I barely remember his presence.

"When I was finally well and strong again, Howard came to see me and he told me the news of Kamsai. He had been keeping it from me for fear of the damage it would do.

"He said that he had also been keeping the truth about Kit from me. When I had asked him to use his connections to find Kit Corwin, he had learned some terrible things about the man. Kit had been passing himself off as a deserter, but in truth Kit Corwin had been on assignment all along. He belonged to some kind of special branch of highly trained men who did secret things ... assassination and sabotage mostly ... and his assignment had been to infiltrate Howard's group and spy on them.

"Howard admitted that he didn't think Kit had done them harm and that indeed there was evidence to indicate that Kit had protected them in some ways, but to Howard, Kit's spying was unforgivable. Howard told his group about Kit. Undoubtedly those men told others. And suddenly Kit had enemies everywhere. All of his various undercover assignments were destroyed.

"I learned all of this from Howard. But as to the remainder of the story ... I won't relate Howard's version because I later learned it was not completely true. Howard was too ashamed to tell me the truth. So the rest of this is Chinda's version, which I learned much later.

"Chinda said that Kit came to the house in a frantic state. He said he was in danger and that his superiors had ordered him back to their headquarters immediately, but he could not take Kamsai and Lenore with him. He begged Howard to allow his wife and child to come stay in the compound for safety until he could arrange for their passage out of the country. He begged Howard to protect them. But Howard refused. Howard told Kit that he should have thought of the consequences before he engaged in such dirty dealings.

"Chinda heard everything and she was very worried. After Kit left, she asked Howard if she could go get Kamsai and Lenore herself. Howard said that if Kit hadn't made arrangements for them to leave in a week, he would allow Chinda to take them in. But he told her he considered it unnecessary because no one would hold a grudge against an innocent woman and child. It was only Kit who was in danger.

"Three days later Chinda could wait no longer and took the bus to Kamsai's house. She walked in and found Lenore in the middle of the floor, cradling her mother's head. There was blood on the walls and the floor. Mother and child were both covered with blood and the flies were crawling everywhere. Lenore didn't move, and even though she was sitting up, the child was so still that Chinda at first feared both of them were dead.

"But when Lenore was bathed there was not a mark or a wound on her. The wounds were all hidden. She stared as though sightless and would not speak at all. The police said that Kamsai had been beaten to death sometime in the night, and from the evidence it appeared that Kamsai had heard the intruders coming in time to hide Lenore. There was no way to know if the child was in a position to see anything, but it was certain that she had listened to her mother's torture and murder.

"Chinda took the child home to the compound and arranged the funeral for Kamsai. Kit came but Chinda said that he was too distraught to think clearly about anything. He disappeared without making any arrangements for his daughter's care. Chinda and Chit kept you in the compound, Lenore, and tried to heal your spirit with their love.

"Out of guilt, Howard hired doctors to help you, but none were successful. Your father visited you. Chinda said they were always brief surprises in the night and that they must have seemed no more than dreams to you. Kit had completely broken down over Kamsai's death, blaming himself for it and alternating between rage and stuporous silence. He was desperately afraid for your safety, Lenore, but completely irrational as to providing for it. With the passage of months he became increasingly unpredictable and disturbing so that Chinda and Chit were afraid of him and afraid to leave you alone with him. Then he stopped coming.

"Chit and her husband had planned to move to the country to live with relatives, and it was decided that the country might offer you some peace, Lenore, so they took you with them. Your father had left an address in Saigon to be used in case of emergency. Chinda sent a message to that address telling him where his daughter was going. There was never a response.

"Then, Saigon fell and the American army tucked its tail between its legs and went home, and Howard heard that Kit had been killed."

Françoise Newman leaned toward Lenore and held out her hands.

"Oh Lenore, I cannot tell you how I felt when I learned all of this. Losing Kamsai in such a senseless brutal way was bad enough ... but to think that I had failed you so. You needed me and I wasn't there for you. Instead I was lying in a bed in Connecticut nursing my own foolish grief.

"Immediately, I booked a flight and sent a message to Howard that I was joining him in Bangkok. I knew he would be delighted and I let him have his delight—I didn't tell him that you, Lenore, were the only reason for my return. I was determined to find you and adopt you for my daughter.

"Five days after my arrival in Bangkok, Chinda and I traveled out to the rice paddies where Chit and her husband had taken you. But you were gone! American soldiers had come to take you, they said. Chit tried to run away into the jungle with you, but the soldiers chased her and caught her. One of them hit her in the head with his gun and would have kept hitting her, but Chit said you turned into a tiger, biting and scratching him to save Chit.

"Together, Chinda and I searched and questioned every-one and followed leads trying to find you. We talked to hundreds of people in military and civilian organizations. We haunted refugee facilities. No one knew anything and the army denied involvement. But I kept searching. For years and years.

"Howard decided to retire early and pursue his butterfly studies since he had the means to do it. We closed up the compound in Bangkok. Vichet became a monk and Chinda went to live with her daughter. I convinced Howard to buy this house in Ridgefield because I had liked it here.

"And that is the end of my tale ... or so it seemed until I got the call from Owen and he said the name 'Lenore.' "

23

The sun was still shining. They were still in Connecticut, and it was still Saturday. Françoise Newman's abrupt ending brought Owen back to the present with a thud.

He looked over at Lenore. She was staring blankly, either deeply entranced or in a complete state of shock.

"That is as much as I know," Françoise said, sighing as though she'd just been relieved of a heavy burden.

Owen waited for Lenore's reaction. What could she be thinking? After all the years of anguished uncertainty, how would she cope with this terrible truth?

A single tear fell from the corner of her eye. "Why don't I remember, Françoise? Why do I have all this blackness inside?"

"Did anything at all come back to you?" Françoise asked. "Did anything I said strike a chord?"

"Yes. Names. Mama Fanny. Auntie Chit. Auntie Chinda. And little things . . . fragments. The lights on the water. Flowers on a four-headed gold shrine. Being safe beside someone on a crowded bus. But I can't make any solid pictures."

"And the book . . . did the photographs mean anything?"

"Some . . . yes." Lenore opened the book. "This picture of the vendors in the little boats selling food door to door along a canal. I remember being excited . . . running down the stairs to the water so I could pick out something sweet." She flipped the pages to a magnificent and marvelously ornate temple. "This one of the Moon God in the Temple of the Dawn. I know him. I went to him often with someone, and we laughed on the way and brought him offerings." She closed the book. "And there are dreams, Françoise. Strange dreams that have frightened me because I couldn't understand them. I've always had a few, but since my husband died, my sleep is crowded with them."

"Tell me," Françoise urged.

"They usually include something mystical—carved god-faces that speak and fortune tellers who can see all the way through me. And ghosts. Lots of ghosts."

"You're a true Thai, Lenore." Françoise smiled gently.

"Yes. I see that now. And the people in the dreams are my aunts or my mamas. I always know who they are, but I can never see their faces well. Either I'm too small in the dream, or the person is standing in shadows."

"I've read a lot about childhood trauma over the years," Françoise said. "I believe it's common to block out memories that are threatening or disturbing. It's a protective mechanism for children." She studied Lenore sadly. "I've worried so over what happened to you and how you got along and whether you ever spoke again, and I suppose I kept reading to try to convince myself that things could have turned out well for you."

Lenore glanced over at Owen.

"Would you like me to leave?" he asked, leaning forward to shut off the recorder. "I certainly don't mind going out for a walk if you two would like to talk privately."

Françoise watched Lenore. Owen waited. Lenore stared down at the book. Finally she looked up at Owen and said, "No. Stay."

"We could meet another time," Françoise suggested. "This has been a strain . . . hearing it all at once. And heaven knows I've got time for visiting. All I'm doing these days is waiting for my knee surgery to heal."

Owen's face must have shown surprise because she laughed. "Did you think I was handicapped? Not me. I'll be up and jogging before you know it. I plan to enjoy my widowhood to the fullest." She stopped and bit her lip. "I'm sorry, Lenore. That was insensitive. I forgot for a moment . . ."

"It doesn't matter, Françoise. It doesn't matter." Lenore closed her eyes. Every line of her body seemed to sag, and for a moment Owen was afraid she might faint.

"Are you all right?" Françoise asked; then she turned her head to call, "Vera! Vera!"

The woman appeared almost instantly.

"Some more tea, Lenore? Or coffee or soda? Or something alcoholic perhaps?" She leaned forward to take

Lenore's hand. "You look half-dead. Are you hungry? How about a banana? Potassium and natural sugar might help."

Vera hurried off and returned juggling a basket of fruit, a plate of oatmeal cookies, three bottles of natural soda and straws.

"Thank you . . . everyone," Lenore said. She smiled weakly. "I'm not used to being fussed over like this."

Vera snapped open the top of a banana, peeled it halfway and handed it to Lenore. Françoise opened a soda, inserted the straw and put that on the table in front of Lenore.

Lenore laughed. But there were tears in her eyes, and the corners of her mouth stayed down. She ate a few bites and drank a little, more to please them than to help herself; then she tensed and took a deep breath.

"All I remember is that I was on the water buffalo. With people around.

"American soldiers came and they chased me and there was screaming and I was sure something bad would happen to me, but it didn't, really. I was simply taken to America."

Françoise shook her head. "Who were these soldiers?"

"I don't know really. But I think now . . . It's confusing because I have to discard what I was taught to believe. I've always been told that I was in danger from the war and I was rescued but that wasn't true, was it? I was completely safe and well taken care of. It sounds more like I was kidnapped."

"But who would have done this thing?" Françoise said. "Your father was already dead and you were no threat to anyone."

Lenore glanced at Owen, and he caught a shadow of anger in her eyes. "I think I can guess now who was behind my kidnapping . . . But that's no longer important, is it?" Lenore's hands were clasped together so tightly that her knuckles were white. "All I care about are my father and mother. I want to remember them. I want to remember all these people who loved me! Why can't I remember?"

"Would you look at some pictures for us?" Owen asked, hoping to ease the tension. "We have a lot of pictures, but we don't know if Lenore's father is in any of them."

"Certainly." Françoise felt in the pocket of her dress and came out with a stylish pair of reading glasses.

Owen showed her all the possible pictures he had found in the box, shots showing groups of men working in the field.

A snapshot of young men at a picnic. Individual pictures of unidentified men. There weren't that many. Aunt Milly had said that she doubted there was a picture of Luther Bachman in the box, and she had been right.

Then Owen handed her the folder with Bram and Al's senior portraits. "I was wondering if either of these two men ever came looking for Kit Corwin, or if you saw them at any time with Kit."

Françoise opened the folder, and suddenly there was a surprised widening of her eyes.

"Why, he's here. Kit Corwin is right here."

Lenore bolted from her seat to look over Françoise's shoulder and Owen leaned in closer.

"This is your father, Lenore. Right here."

She was pointing directly at Abe Hanselmann ... Al ... the adopted one. The troubled cousin/brother. The man who had lived like a hermit in Bram Serian's studio.

"No!" Lenore screamed. Owen reached for her arm, but she jerked away and ran.

She was fast and had the element of surprise in her favor. Finally, crossing the wide lawn, he caught her. She struck out blindly with her fists, and he pulled her into a tight hug until she stopped struggling.

"Should I let you go?" he asked hesitantly.

"Yes," she hissed. "But I can't see her again. Not now. Not yet."

"It's all right. Françoise will understand. Get in the car and I'll go in to get our things and say good bye."

Françoise was just inside the front door, trapped in her chair, completely distraught. Vera stood behind wringing her hands and muttering in Russian.

"What have I done, Owen? What have I done?"

"Don't blame yourself, Françoise. This was something she wanted to know, and she would have found it out eventually one way or another. It's just a shock. I ... The story is very long and involved and it's not mine to tell. It's Lenore's, and I'm sure she'll want to tell you in time. Just give her time."

"She knew who that was, didn't she? Is Kit alive?"

"Yes. Presumably. And she did know him but without suspecting he was her father. I think ... I think the worst part of this is that she had always imagined her father as someone perfect and wonderful who would save her if she could only find him. And the man in that picture is not capable of saving anyone."

Françoise reached out to grip his hand. "I don't want to lose her again, Owen. Do you think I have any chance? Can she accept me as a friend?"

"Françoise, her life is very complicated right now."

"Yes. I know."

"There's more going on. More than just being widowed. It's not within her control."

"Yes, Owen," she said firmly. "I know."

He peered down at her.

"I know," she insisted. "I realized who she was. The newspaper photograph. The name Lenore. And you asked me if I knew any Serians. As soon as I saw her it all fit into place."

"She didn't want to tell you. She's so worried about what you'll think of her."

Françoise sighed. "She's still Kamsai's baby to me."

"I'm sure she'll want to see you again soon. She's very much alone."

"So am I," Françoise said. "Please, please, tell her for me— She's like my child. I'll always love her . . . no matter what."

Owen drove around Ridgefield aimlessly, stopped for gas and then drove some more. A gathering bank of clouds signaled early darkness. He kept waiting for a sign from Lenore, but she was frozen into a distant silence. Finally he pulled up to a charming old inn.

"We're having dinner," he announced.

She stirred slightly. "I'm not hungry. You go in. I'll stay here."

"It's dinnertime. Both of us need to eat, and the only other option is driving all the way back to Arcadia and hitting the frozen food."

"I'm really not hungry." She sounded so definite that he almost caved in, but then she moved her arm and he caught sight of her thin wrist.

"I don't care if you're hungry. Damn it, Lenore! What are you trying to do, starve yourself to death? You think that will help anything?"

"I eat," she said stiffly.

"Obviously not enough. You look like a skeleton."

She sat up and glared at him. At least it was proof that she had some spirit left.

He kept at her. "It's rude to expect someone to drive all the way from Manhattan and pick you up and take you to Connecticut and then reverse the trip without a decent meal all day."

The glare intensified. "I am not rude."

"Maybe not. Maybe you just think I'm beneath consideration."

She threw open the door and got out of the car. It struck him how graceful she was. Even in the midst of anger every movement of her body had a fluid grace.

The restaurant was as pleasant on the inside as the exterior promised. They were seated and Lenore accepted her menu with an icy reserve. The host bowed and fumbled, clearly intimidated by her.

She studied the menu as though she could read it.

"I'll be a chauvinist and order for you," Owen said, plucking the menu from her hands.

"I don't want anything, thank you."

"They don't allow that in places like this. You can't occupy a table without ordering food."

She frowned slightly, and her eyes darted about the room.

"No one can tell, Lenore. No one here would ever guess that you can't read the menu."

She regarded him with slightly narrowed eyes.

"So you're a mind reader now? Maybe a fortune teller too?"

He shook his head and laughed.

After he ordered, she stared out the window at the darkening clouds.

"Rain," he said.

She nodded absently. "It's so hard to accept. He was never a father to me. Never. When I was younger, I was terrified of him. And later, then I felt more pity than affection for him."

"I never would have guessed," Owen said. "Bram was his brother . . . adopted, yes, but still. How could he . . . marry you?"

She lowered her eyes. "I overheard an argument between Al and Bram. At one point Bram started yelling about all he'd done for Al . . . all he'd sacrificed for Al. I couldn't hear Al's response, but then Bram said, 'Everything is always Lenore. I am so sick of hearing about precious Lenore.'

"I heard that and my heart stopped. Why was my name in their argument? What did I have to do with Al? But deep inside, I was afraid I knew."

"You were hoping I would prove otherwise, weren't you?" Owen asked.

She hesitated. "Yes. I refused to believe. What I overheard could have meant something else, so I was determined that it did mean something else. I was determined to find the father I wanted."

"And you wanted it to be Luther Bachman."

"Or anyone but Al! How could I want it to be that pathetic shell of a man? And that was when I still thought he was only Bram's cousin. That was bad enough. Then, after I learned they were brothers . . ."

"Adopted," Owen added quickly. "There was no blood relationship."

"But despicable all the same. You said it yourself just moments ago . . . how could Bram marry me?"

"And why, exactly?" Owen asked. "Why would he do it?"

Lenore stiffened. "I don't want to talk about it anymore right now."

"Okay. Fine. But you're going to have to face it at some point. Maybe you should talk to a therapist."

"You think I'm insane?"

"No. I just think this is a lot to handle on your own. It would be for anyone. I think my brother would still be here if he had gone to someone for help."

"Your brother? Why? Did he . . ."

"He hung himself. From the only tree for miles that would hold his body."

She was quiet then, but her eyes were full of compassion.

"I don't usually tell people that. I'm sorry if I depressed you with it."

"I'm glad you told me. I'm glad you wanted to tell me."

"I want to tell you anything about me that you want to know, Lenore."

"Are you making fun of me?" she asked.

"No. Do I seem to be?"

She tilted her head, amused, quizzical, mysterious, with the tiniest hint of a smile playing on her lips. The look caused something inside him. Not a jolt exactly . . . more like a dropping sensation . . . a falling open. He crossed his arms over his chest and swallowed hard.

"Have I ever told you," she said, "that I like the way you talk?"

He could think of no response.

The salad arrived then, and he thanked the waiter with such heartfelt gratitude that the man backed away a step.

They were careful with each other for the remainder of dinner, treading lightly through various verbal minefields, avoiding the past and the trial and the future, picking their way through impersonal comments on the food and the surroundings. And on the rain when it began to fall.

As he was paying the bill, Owen couldn't resist telling her his news. "Lenore, I talked to my agent last night. I've got the DeMille contract. They want my book. In fact, they're negotiating on the price. My agent thinks it's worth a lot more now."

"Now that you have so many ugly revelations to put in?"

"I wouldn't put everything in. You know that."

"Do I?"

She regarded him sharply for a moment, then averted her eyes and said, "I'm glad they're publishing your book. I'm sure your family will be excited, too. Have you told them?"

"Not yet."

"What does this mean, then? When will you go back to Kansas?" she asked casually.

"I don't know. I'll have to see how my work progresses," he replied carefully.

They ran together from the restaurant to the car. The drizzle became a downpour as they turned onto the highway, sealing them together in the warm womb of the car. In the darkness, he blurted out the question that wouldn't go away. "Did you love him?"

"Who?"

"Your husband."

"Why do you ask that?"

"Lenore, I know you were only fifteen years old when you married him. How can I not wonder what you felt?"

"What difference does it make how I loved him or when I loved him or whether I loved him at all. He's dead now. He's a ghost."

"But you're alive. I want to know what he was to you. I want to know what his death meant."

She was quiet for so long that he thought she wouldn't answer. Then her voice came out of the darkness, cool yet intense. "What you really want to know is whether I killed him."

"No," he said earnestly. "I couldn't ask you that." But it was true. That question too had been torturing him. Because the more Owen learned, the more reasons he saw for her to have killed Bram Serian. "No, Lenore. Just tell me, did you marry him for security or did you actually love him?"

"I loved him," she said. "But not in any way you would understand."

Owen couldn't stop himself. He pushed on though he knew it was unwise. "You've never explained. How did you meet him? Where were you living? How did he approach you?"

"Why? Why does it matter? It's over and he's dead and here I am with you. Isn't that enough for you?"

"Yes," he answered. But it wasn't.

On the drive to Arcadia, she said nothing. Owen's thoughts fragmented in a silent cacophony, and through the static he heard a voice whispering that maybe he should turn north and keep on driving until he had Lenore Serian safely across the border with him in Canada. But he turned down the country road as he was supposed to, and then he went through Arcadia's gate and negotiated the twisting dark drive up to the house. He pulled directly up to the door to let her out, assuming that he wouldn't be invited in. There were a few outside lights that had snapped on automatically at dusk, but the house itself showed black empty windows.

She sat in the car, looking out through the rain with what he took to be reluctance.

He shut the engine off. "I'll come in with you, if you'd like. Help you turn on a few lights . . ."

She gave him a shadowed, sideways look. "Do you want to come in?"

He stared at her, knowing exactly what she was asking.

"Yes," he said quietly.

Neither of them moved. The rain poured over the windows, and the car rocked slightly with a gust of wind.

Hungrily, he pulled her into his arms and kissed her mouth. His fingers circled her slender neck, so fragile and unprotected; then he kissed the hollow at the base of her throat and slid his hands into the warmth beneath her coat. He explored by touch, watching her face in the darkness as he found the curve of her breasts and her hard nipples. Her back arched and he could feel the pounding of her heart.

"Owen . . ." she breathed, "Owen . . ." and the sound of his name on her lips shook him profoundly.

They ran through the rain, holding each other, afraid to lose contact. He fumbled with the door while she managed the alarm. They rid themselves of wet shoes in the entryway and dropped their coats to the floor in the hall, kissing and touching as they progressed.

Suddenly, he was aware of himself as two beings, the sane, rational Owen he had always been and a new, wild and ungovernable Owen. The new Owen tore Lenore Serian's blouse open and sucked the nipples beneath the lace of her bra. She moaned and twined her fingers in his hair and leaned back against the wall, and the new Owen slid his hands up her thighs, so silky warm and bare, up to feel the dampness through her panties and hear her moan again.

The new Owen tongued her mouth and neck while he slipped his fingers beneath those panties, caressing and exploring the wet heat of her until her breathing was fast and her mouth was as greedy as his. And the new Owen pushed her panties down and unzipped his jeans and lifted her to wrap her legs around him. And he shoved his hard cock into her right there, standing up, with her back against the wall, thinking *mine mine mine* and wishing he could push far enough into her darkness to touch her heart.

Later, when the old Owen took control again, he was astonished and discomfited. He felt as though his civilized surface had been ripped open temporarily, exposing a primal core he hadn't known existed. And he wavered between exhilaration, fear, and embarrassment.

"My God," he said. He was lying with her on a couch that he couldn't remember moving to. He sat up. "I'm sorry."

She propped herself on her elbow to look at him.

"Was I too rough? I . . ." He raised his hand to his forehead. "I don't know what to say."

"Stop," she said, touching a finger to his lips. "It was perfect." Her mouth curved into a slow sensual smile. "Come. Come with me."

Holding his hand she led him through the house, pausing

to turn on the barest minimum of lights. They bypassed the living room and wound through the maze to climb the stairs to her glass-and-mirror sanctuary. The room was black. He could see nothing, but he remembered it perfectly—the mirrored wall, the long table, the narrow bed.

Rain beat against the glass and wind rattled the panes. She dropped his hand and moved away from him. He heard the hiss of a striking match, then saw her outline in the dim glow of its flame. She was bending over a table full of candles in tall glass cylinders, but she lit only three.

She turned to face him. The candlelight reflected in the dark windows and danced in her dark hair and caught in her dark eyes. Slowly she undressed. Watching his face as he watched her.

"I've never let myself be touched in this room," she said. "Here I belong only to you."

He woke with her warm back pressed against his chest. They were curved together beneath the quilts on her narrow bed. It was Sunday morning. Outside the windows, rain fell gently through a dense fog.

In the gray light he could see her collection of candles clearly. They were all the same size and all in tall cylinders of glass, but each one had something different painted on the glass. There were zodiac signs, and dollar signs, and crosses, and pyramids with eyes, and hearts dripping blood, and unfamiliar symbols he dared not guess at. There were phrases too. *Fast Luck, Death Unto Enemy, Dream, Magic Spirit, Good Fortune, Jinx Remover.* If they weren't so unsettling, some of them would have actually been amusing.

He moved slightly and she awakened, sitting up with a start. She peered around the room as though searching for an intruder.

"Morning," he said, touching her hair. She brushed him away, threw the quilts off and ran to the closed door to press her ear against it and listen.

"What is it, Lenore?"

She shook her head; then she hugged herself and shivered.

His eyes were drawn to the candles again. "Which ones did you burn last night?"

The look she gave him raised the hair on the back of his neck.

She opened a closet and pulled out two terrycloth robes. "You're cold," she said, handing him one.

Her distance was disorienting. It made the night before seem dreamlike, unreal. She took him to a bathroom with skylights and a huge glassed-in shower complete with two showerheads and a built-in bench. As soon as the water was on the cubicle filled with steam, she stepped inside, motioning for him to follow and his groin stirred even before her soapy hand found him.

The hot water coursed over him, and he leaned back against the cool tiles, rocked by waves of sensation. When he was close to the edge, he pulled away and reached for her, hungry for the taste and feel of her, wanting to bring her to the same edge so they could fall together.

"No!" She twisted away from him, her skin slippery with water. "Don't touch me," she ordered, and he was hurt and perplexed, but her soapslick hand found him again, rendering him helpless, trapping him in his own weakness.

When it was over and the water was turned off, he sat on the wet bench and watched her. Somehow she had used his desire to separate herself from him. To create a greater distance between them. He watched her bend to towel her long black hair, and he realized that she was a stranger to him. He would never know her.

She straightened and looked at him. And he wanted to crawl behind her eyes. Those dark, unreadable eyes. He wanted to tear her open and find the truth, then imprint himself on her brain and her heart and the hot, dark center of her, so that she could never untangle herself, never distance herself, never be completely separate from him again.

"You should go now," she said, tying her robe and heading out toward the hall.

"Why?"

"Because you have to."

He caught her arm and spun her around to face him. "Why are you trying to push me away?"

She raised an eyebrow coldly. "Why are you trying to stay when you're not wanted?"

"Lenore . . . I know you feel something for me. Last night, when we made love—"

She jerked her arm free of his grip. "Fucking means nothing," she hissed. "Do you know how many men I've been with? How many cocks I've had inside me? How many times I've pretended to come?" As she spoke, watching his face, seeing the damage her words were doing, a gleam came to her eyes and a triumphant smile played at her lips. "Do you want me to name them all? Do you want to hear what they begged for or what they cried out when they came inside me?"

He hit her. Slapped her face with a sudden sharp motion that snapped her head back and stunned him. Shook him. Shattered the last of what he'd been and what he'd believed. He looked at his hand. The hand that was still sore from slamming into a man's face just days ago. And he was sickened. Shamed beyond words.

She turned and left.

He stood there for a long time. Too lost to move. Then he went out to the hall and found his way back to her room. The narrow bed had been made so that there was no sign of what had happened there. He picked his clothes up off the floor and dressed. While he was buttoning his shirt, he noticed that several of her candles had small spluttering flames. The thought that she had left him after the scene in the bathroom and come up here to light candles made him seethe with anger, and he wanted to knock them to the floor and smash them all. He moved closer. The candles that were burning were decorated with various picture symbols and labeled *Good Fortune, Strong Wisdom,* and *Love Inseparable by Death.*

He stared at them, moved almost to tears by emotions he could not identify or explain. Then he set out to find her.

She was dressed in old jeans and an oversized sweater, standing at the stove making pancakes. "I put frozen blueberries in them," she said, without looking up.

The scene was so normal it made him question his sanity.

"You do like blueberries, don't you?" she asked.

"Yes," he answered.

He sat down wearily and folded his arms on the table and leaned forward to rest his forehead on his arms. When she brought the pancakes to the table, he sat up.

"What do the candles mean?" he asked.

"Each one means something different."

"Did you light the *Love Inseparable by Death* for Serian?"

"My candles are private," she said. "Now eat the pancakes and tell me what you think."

Mechanically, he began to eat.

"Are they good?" she asked.

"Yes."

She smiled. "Geneva taught me to make them," she said. "They're the only thing I really know how to cook."

"Geneva?" The name cut through his numb, exhausted state. "Geneva Johnson . . . Serian's lover . . . taught *you* to make pancakes?"

Instantly, Lenore's eyes became shuttered, and she picked up the plates and carried them to the sink.

"Were you and Geneva Johnson friendly at some point? I don't . . . The pieces of this don't match, Lenore."

She stayed at the sink with her back to him. "No more questions," she said. "Our business is finished. You got what you wanted and I got my past. We're even now."

"What is that supposed to mean?"

She turned around to glare at him. "It means good-bye. I don't want you here anymore. You can find your own way to the door."

He left.

Owen drove with a fury, taking curves too fast, muttering and swerving around slower drivers. Geneva Johnson. The art model turned store owner. Bram Serian's live-in love until he married Lenore.

How did it all fit together? What had Geneva and Lenore's relationship been?

He had to find Geneva Johnson. He had to make her talk to him.

24

Owen spotted Geneva Johnson immediately in the cafe. She was brightly clothed again, but this time she looked like a gypsy.

"Hello," he said, slipping into the seat opposite her at the small corner table.

"You don't have one of those hidden tape recording things taped to your balls or somewhere, do you?" she asked without preamble.

"No. I . . ." He bent to open the carryon bag and showed her the recorder inside. "This is all I have, and, as you can see, it's not on."

"Don't turn it on," she ordered, and he shoved the recorder back down into the bag to demonstrate compliance.

It was still hard for him to believe that she had agreed to meet him. She hadn't even seemed surprised by his call.

"How did you get my unlisted number?" she asked.

"A computer hacker got it for me within five minutes."

She appeared angry for a moment but then shrugged. "I was going to call you anyway."

"You were?"

"Yes." She fixed him with a hostile and very determined look. "Because of Lenore."

Owen stared at her and waited. Part of him wanted to get up and run because he was afraid this woman was going to tell him something awful, that she was going to confirm Lenore's being a murderer, among other things. Another part of him was riveted, waiting, thinking that finally he would know everything.

"You've got your stories, writer-man. You've got plenty. Now, you leave her alone. Understand me? Leave her alone."

Owen was dumbfounded.

Geneva straightened and lifted her chin. "I've come to

make you a deal, Byrne. You leave Lenore alone, I'll tell you some about Serian's early years in New York."

"Who the hell do you think you are?" he demanded. "My seeing Lenore is none of your business."

Her eyes narrowed and her mouth slid into a nasty smile. "If it's none of my business, then why did Lenore call me as soon as you left Arcadia this morning? Why do I know every single word you've said to her?"

Owen dropped back into his chair. Again dumbstruck.

Geneva nodded. "Just as soon as you drove away she was on the phone to me."

"I don't understand," he said.

"Exactly!" A little gleam of triumph flared in Geneva's eyes. "That's what I'm trying to get through that thick male skull of yours . . . you don't understand. You don't know what you're doing."

"Lenore and I are both adults . . ."

"There's where you're dead wrong, Byrne."

"What are you trying to say?"

"I think it's pretty clear. Leave Lenore alone and I'll give you Bram's early years."

"Yes. I understand that part. But who are you to Lenore?"

"I am her friend. I am . . . Lenore is like my little sister."

"That's hard for me to believe," he said. And in fact if Lenore hadn't made the comment about Geneva teaching her to make pancakes, Owen would have laughed at the woman's claim.

"Believe it, Mister."

"Let's say for now that I do. Why do you think I'm so bad for Lenore?"

She laughed in a short, harsh bark. "Let's be real here. We both know what you wanted out of Lenore . . . all those juicy secrets . . . and a little personal erotic pleasure to spice up your research. Well, I didn't find out about it in time to stop you so you got everything you wanted. Now, I'm telling you to back off. Stop fucking with her mind. She can't take any more men using her and screwing her over."

"I'm not trying to hurt her."

Geneva laughed again. "Yeah. That's what they all say. Only your idea of not hurting her is probably that you're using safe sex and you're not going to knock her teeth out, and her idea of being hurt is: Will he leave me? Is he lying to me? Does he mean everything he's saying? See the difference?"

Owen stared at her. Her proud face and knowing eyes were so hard, it struck Owen that the woman's remarkable beauty must have brought her nothing but pain.

"I don't know what Lenore told you, and I don't know what kind of a relationship you two have. But you've got me wrong. And you've got me wondering if this isn't some kind of a sick revenge ploy for you. That maybe you want to drive me away to punish her because she was the one Serian married instead of you."

Geneva stared down into the coffee cup in front of her for a moment, then lifted her eyes to meet Owen's. "I never wanted to punish Lenore. Her whole life with that man was a punishment. It was him who needed to be punished. And somebody beat me to it on that."

Owen stared at her in puzzlement. "I can't promise to leave Lenore alone," he admitted quietly. "That is not a promise I could make . . . or would want to make . . . not for any reason."

"Okay . . ." Geneva sighed heavily. "Maybe you're not such a bad guy. Lenore has sure been wanting to believe you're not a bad guy. I keep warning her, but she's . . ." The woman shook her head sadly. "I'm going to tell you a few things. A little about Bram and me. A little about Lenore. So that you'll see what's going on here. This is off, off, off the record, though, Byrne, and most of it's unprovable and I'll deny I ever said a word of it. You understand?"

"Yes."

"There was this black girl. She was a fool. She left her mama and her nice little town, and she set off to be a star in New York City. A model. That's what she wanted to be. She'd always been too big and too black and too bony, and everybody had made fun of her while she was growing up, so she was going to show them all. She was going to make it big.

"She was full of ideas. Donyale Luna had just made it into a national fashion magazine, and she thought, hey . . . the color barrier is down and the timing is perfect. Wrong. Oh, she was tall enough and bony enough, but all the agencies told her she was way too black.

"Well, she didn't have even a high school diploma, and

she couldn't find a job that would keep her alive, and she was too ashamed to go crawling back home. And she got more and more desperate, and before you know it she met a bad man. Only he was so sweet-talking and smooth that she didn't know he was bad. 'Smokey's gonna take care of you,' the man said, and she was so young and stupid she believed him.

"Smokey promised to get her all kinds of modeling jobs. And he did too. Oh, she modeled her little buns off. Every day she posed naked in a filthy room so that slack-jawed perverts could come in and take pictures. 'Turn that way, girlie. Put your hand there. Show me a little more of that.'

"And sometimes one of the perverts would get so worked up over her poses that he'd pay extra and she'd have to do more than just pose. She hid some money and ran away, but Smokey caught her and made little designs on her with a lit cigarette to teach her never to try running again.

"Then one night she was with Smokey in a bar. He was talking to her about the future and about the plans he had for her to star in shows. Private shows where men would pay to watch her doing things with other men and with women and with any creature on God's earth that would hold still. Things she'd never even heard of before.

"She didn't like Smokey's plans, and she was upset so Smokey cuffed her around a little to shut her up . . . like he always did. Only this time a guy . . . a total stranger . . . walked up and said to Smokey, 'You shouldn't treat a woman that way.'

"Smokey thought that was real funny. That this big white guy would walk up just like John Wayne and say such a thing to a bad dude like Smokey. He tried to make a joke out of it. But the white guy was dead serious. And Smokey grabbed my arm and said, 'I'll show you how to treat a bitch. Watch this!' and he smashed his lit cigarette into my skin and I screamed.

"You would have thought a bomb went off or something. The white guy, who was bigger than Smokey, grabbed him up off that bar stool and threw him . . . actually threw him into some tables just like in the movies. Smokey pulled his knife, but the bartender already had his baseball bat out, so Smokey just had to watch while this John Wayne asked me, 'You want to stay with him?' and I said, 'No.' And he waltzed me right out of there and into a cab with him and his friend, ignoring Smokey, who was yelling about how he was gonna catch him and kill him, and then kill me, and ignoring his friend who was saying, 'You're crazy, Bram. You gotta get rid of this woman. You're crazy.'

"That was how Bram Serian and Gena Ray Johnson met.

"He took me home with him to his loft and he gave me a place to sleep. The next day he bought me some clothes and fed me. And he started talking about how maybe he could get me some work as an art model.

"Sure, I thought. I'd heard that line before. Except this guy seemed so different. He hadn't touched me yet. He hadn't asked for anything.

"His roommate bitched and complained about me being there, but Bram ignored him. Weeks went by. He did find me a little job. All I did was sit for a few days while some guy drew pictures of my face. And I got paid for it.

"I was so grateful to Bram. And I was . . . I guess you'd say I had a terrible crush on him. It was pretty funny when you think about it because I finally had a guy I wanted to make love to and he acted like my body was invisible or something.

"I thought all kinds of things. That maybe he didn't want me because I was black or maybe he didn't want me because he knew about all the terrible things I'd done with other guys. I got to feeling real low, real sick of myself, and he found me crying and I ended up having one of those spill your guts kind of talks with him. It turned out that he was pretty naive and didn't suspect I'd been a whore at all. He just thought Smokey had been a rotten boyfriend.

"After that everything changed. Suddenly he was so hot for me that he could barely keep his pants on. He wanted to hear stories about things I'd done before . . . things I'd been forced to do . . . and those stories really turned him on.

" 'Pretend,' he'd say, 'pretend I'm a john and you're mad at me. You're punishing me while we do it.'

"Anyway . . . you get the picture.

"The roommate got shown the door and I was in to stay. Bram lined up more modeling work for me, and pretty soon I started getting work on my own.

"We were together for a long time. I tried hard to be respectable and the more respectable I got the less he was interested in me. But he was always good to me, always generous. Like he had an obligation to take care of me even after he'd lost all his desire.

"He always messed around with other women. He wasn't the faithful type. Didn't even pretend to be. Most of the time it was whores, or women like that art dealer bitch, Edie Norton, who were whores at heart. But I never felt threatened. The only thing I was ever jealous of was his art.

"Then suddenly he got real strange and secretive, and he went off and bought that farm. Sprang that on me as a complete surprise by just mentioning one day that he was going to be spending a lot of time at his farm.

" 'What farm?' I asked him.

" 'The place I bought upstate,' he said. 'I'm making the barn into a studio. Got my cousin out there helping me.'

"You could have knocked me over because Bram had never even mentioned liking the country. And he'd never said a thing about his family or about having a cousin. After that he was gone a lot, and he never invited me to go along, and I started getting real jealous of the farm and the cousin too.

"Then he got famous. Bingo. Everything changed. I don't know if he had this stuff festering inside him all along and getting famous released it, or if the getting famous caused the changes in him. But he definitely changed. His little quirky paranoid streak turned monstrous, and he started having suspicions about everybody and everything. He thought the phone was bugged and he thought complete strangers were whispering about him. He thought he was being followed all the time. He imagined he saw FBI agents lurking around corners.

"Whenever he was forced to see a doctor or a dentist, he would make up a name to use, and he wouldn't go back to the same one more than a few times. And the paranoia wasn't all. He became very manipulative. It was like a game for him.

"We had this big blowout of an argument, and I told him I was onto his games so he better not try messing with my mind, and he laughed. He told me that it was fascinating to him to try to control people or manipulate their behavior . . . without them realizing what was happening . . . because the results were like art. Because when he worked on people's minds the results were as unpredictable and creative and satisfying as art. He told me then that I had been one of his first projects.

"That was about it for me. I was getting pretty disgusted with him and ready to cut the cord. Then suddenly he said he needed my help.

"Talk about a shock. Bram Serian never needed anybody's help. He said I was the only woman he could trust. Which was even more of a shock . . . that he would trust me. And I was very touched and also I owed him a lot so I said that of course I would help him.

"He was very mysterious about it but told me to pack for a few days because he was taking me out to his farm.

"Sweet Jesus . . . I still remember stepping out of the car and seeing this skinny little thing peeking at me from under the wooden porch like she was an outdoor dog or something. I screamed when I saw her and she ran away and Bram got mad at me.

" 'What kind of a mother are you gonna make?' he said, and I told him I didn't intend to be any kind of a mother unless it was my own baby.

"Then he sat me down and told me that he had been talked into taking in an orphan from the Vietnam War. A dead soldier's kid. And he'd had her out there trying to take care of her, but nothing was going right and he needed a woman's touch.

"I was mad. I was furious! I felt like he'd conned me and I didn't want any part of mothering a stray and I told him so. But I was stuck there so I settled in to enjoy a few days in the country. Later on I was sitting out on the porch and I saw the kid come creeping back up to the house, and Bram ran out and caught her. That's what he had to do . . . chase her down and catch her like one of those airheaded dogs that streaks out every time the door opens. She didn't kick or fight or anything, and he didn't use any more force than it took to keep hold of her. It wasn't like she was violent . . . she was just out of control.

"He carried her up and plunked her down in front of me, and it was disgusting. Her hair was matted and she was filthy and her clothes were practically rags. I couldn't believe it! She was like something you'd see in an ad for the poor children from India or Mexico or somewhere.

" 'You can't keep a child like this!' I told him, but he said she wouldn't take care of herself and he'd felt wrong trying to force a little girl into stripping and taking a bath.

"Well, I couldn't just sit there so I agreed that I'd try to clean her up and get her on the right track ... but only for a few days. Then I wanted to go back to Manhattan. Bram agreed. The kid just watched us. She didn't speak. There was no telling how much she understood or whether she was maybe retarded or backward. He said she never had said a word but that he'd seen her get real mad and he knew she could make noise.

"The first thing I did was carry her in to the bathroom and put her in the tub. I washed her hair. The knots were so bad I had to cut it off short. She didn't fight me, but I could tell she didn't like what I was doing. I showed her how everything worked and tried to make her understand that she should bathe herself. She gave me no sign that things were sinking in.

"There were no decent clothes for her so I put her into a T-shirt of mine. A white T-shirt with a design painted on the front. It was big enough to be a dress on her, and she looked kind of cute, standing there and staring down at herself like she thought she had on a ballgown. I led her to the mirror on the back of the bathroom door for a look. That occupied her for a good fifteen minutes. She studied herself and her short hair and she ran her hand back and forth over the painted design on that shirt.

"I told Bram I was taking her into town to buy her clothes and he just about panicked. First, he was afraid she might run away in town. Then he told me Stoatsberg was a small town and people there were nosy and that she wasn't in the country legally and we had to be real careful or the authorities would take her away and deport her back to Vietnam, where she'd be tortured and executed.

"By that time, nothing could shock me so I just told him okay. That I would do my best to measure her and then go in and buy some things on my own.

"Well, he was still nervous. He said I'd stick out like a sore thumb in that little town and everybody would see me driving his car and connect me to him and then they'd see me buying children's clothes and there would be questions and he just didn't want to chance it. I ended up having to drive clear to White Plains to shop for her, and even with that Bram kept warning me to make sure I wasn't followed on the way back.

"I fixed up her bedroom for her and put the clothes into the dresser. I wanted to show them to her, but she refused to look, and when I tried to get my T-shirt off of her she ran and hid. I thought, fine, and I went on about my business washing her sheets. That night I found her asleep on a pile of towels back in the laundry room and I carried her in and put her to bed. She woke up and was terrified and I had to hold her down in the bed. Eventually, she calmed down and I sat there on the edge of her bed for a few minutes and an old lullaby popped into my head so I sang it to her and what do you know . . . she went back to sleep.

"It turned out that Bram had had that kid out there for six months! He'd bought clothes for her when she first got there and then he'd just expected her to mind her own business and take care of herself like a miniature adult. He couldn't understand why she hadn't.

"I paid a lot of attention to her the next morning, but that only seemed to make her worse. She'd look away from me when I talked, and as soon as my back was turned she'd run off. So I ignored her. I'd peel an orange and set it down and walk away . . . things like that. When I was cleaning I'd pretend I didn't notice if she was watching. That night I had to carry her to bed and hold her down again. I sang to her again too, thinking it couldn't hurt.

"On the third morning I was getting ready to leave and I was determined to get my shirt off of her and get her into some play clothes. After my breakfast, and after she'd eaten the toast and apple I put out, I took her in the bedroom and forcibly took back my shirt. You'd have thought I'd killed her favorite pet or something. She curled up in the corner holding her stomach and wailing. It was the first noise I'd heard her make.

"So I got mad and I threw the shirt at her. Told her she could have the damn thing but she couldn't wear it every day. She had to wear the other clothes too. To my surprise she grabbed up that T-shirt, holding it real close like it was precious, and then she got up off the floor and came over and let me dress her. She knew what I was saying! She understood.

"After that she treated my T-shirt like it was a stuffed animal or a security blanket, carrying it around and petting it, sleeping with it next to her pillow.

"I felt a little guilty when I left that day, but I sure as hell wasn't going to let Bram con me into living out in that dump and playing nursemaid for him.

"From then on I went back and forth a lot, spending several days a week there. I met the weird cousin, and I started to think that maybe Bram's growing strangeness was genetic. Bram was really into building the studio then, and he and Al worked night and day on it.

"Bram and I were totally finished as a couple by then. I still lived in the loft, but I was more like his housesitter than an old lover. I started seeing men. And I fell for a guy. But I kept going out to see Lenore. I just couldn't turn my back on her.

"I got real sneaky. Bram left town for a week, and while he was gone, I took Lenore away from the farm to see a doctor and have her teeth worked on. I told her she couldn't ever let Bram know, but there wasn't much danger of that because she still wasn't talking. She communicated with her hands and with expressions, but she wouldn't talk. The doctor I took her to said there wasn't a physical problem and that she should see a child psychiatrist . . . But of course that was out of the question. Bram would never allow it.

"That's not to say that he didn't care about her. He did in a funny way. He was very interested in the idea of her . . . amazed by her almost.

"We went on like that for a long time. The studio was finished, and Bram started tinkering with the house. Of course Lenore couldn't go to school because then people would find out about her, so I tried to teach her things. I taught her to sew and to dance. And I brought her videos. Nature shows and history and Disney movies. Bram hated television, but he had one of those setups with a VCR hooked up to a monitor. It was an expensive toy back then, but Bram loved toys.

"I know now I should have taught her to read too, but at the time it didn't seem important. I mean, the poor kid couldn't even talk. I didn't think of her as ever being normal. And, I have to admit . . . I didn't do much reading myself.

"My love affair got really hot, and I went into my own little fantasy world for a while, thinking I was going to march down the aisle in a white dress and do the whole bit. My visits to the farm got further and further between. Lenore was getting big. We figured she was close to twelve or so. I had convinced myself that she didn't need me so much anymore because she was older and because she had gotten so attached to Bram. She just worshipped him. It didn't matter how much he ignored her, she would just stare at him like a little puppy. Then one day the phone rang and it was Bram and he said, 'I think the kid misses you. She just dragged me to the phone and did a little charade to get me to call you. Want to say a few words to her?'

"I said sure, feeling pretty guilty for not having been out to see her for so long, and I listened to the fumbling while he gave her the phone, waiting to start talking till I knew she was on. Then suddenly this funny accented little voice said, 'Geneva, come see me.'

"From then on she talked. Not very well at first. But she tried. And I helped her practice her pronunciation. She practiced like her life depended on it, and when I wasn't there, she called me at the loft to practice on the phone with me. She didn't get to hear people talk very often. Bram never had much to say to her, and the loonybird cousin didn't talk to anybody, and since she was a big secret Bram kept her hidden anytime he had people out. He had her real spooked, telling her all the time how the bad men were going to come get her if anyone found out she was there. By then he'd made this little sealed-off area for her with a room and a bath so she could lock herself away and hide when the cleaning service was there or when he had guests.

"I thought it was all pretty extreme, but I was in no position to do anything about it.

"A year or so later, just after Lenore had started her period and I'd had to explain the facts of life to her, I got pregnant. I thought long and hard and decided that if I wanted a baby ever in my life then I should probably declare myself and accept this one. Soon as I did, my Mister Wonderful packed his bags and took a hike. He said I wasn't the kind of woman he wanted to settle down with.

"Well, that knocked me right out of fantasyland, and I realized that I was never going to wear the white dress, but I decided that by God, I was going to have my child and make myself a family. And I was going to raise that child up in the most normal healthy way possible.

"I told Bram I was moving out of the loft and heading for the suburbs somewhere and I told him why. He asked me how I thought I was going to support my little normal family and I admitted that I wasn't sure.

"Within days he had my life all worked out for me. He even had legal papers drawn up. I was to get a house and a check from him every month for the rest of my life if I agreed to keep seeing Lenore periodically and to never discuss him or my relationship to him or any of his secrets with anyone at any time.

"I took the deal.

"While my daughter was still a baby, I took her out with me when I visited Arcadia. Lenore was crazy about her. But then when she got bigger, I stopped taking her because I didn't want her to have any memory of that part of my life. I wanted her to grow up thinking I was just an ordinary mom who had always lived in the suburbs.

"Lenore missed her, but I had to make a choice. I had to put my own child's welfare ahead of Lenore. By this time Lenore was fifteen and she understood everything. She had this way of looking straight at people and seeing through all the bullshit.

"Bram had decided to let her stay out of her room when people came and he was enjoying making up wild stories about who she was. Lenore was confused about it all. She was so curious about others, but she didn't know how to act around people. That didn't matter to Bram because he was getting a kick out of her effect on his friends.

"She was fifteen going on sixteen when she called me one night and said that Bram had taken her for a very long drive and they had gotten married. She said it like it was the most normal thing in the world, and I practically had a heart attack. I dropped everything and raced out to Arcadia.

"When I got there and tore into Bram, he treated me like I was crazy. He kept saying that I was overreacting. He was angry at Lenore for having told me and he sent her to her room for punishment.

" 'What can you be thinking, Bram?' I screamed at him. 'You haven't touched her, have you? I'll kill you if you've touched her!'

" 'Get your mind out of the gutter, Geneva. Of course I haven't *touched* her. The idea is completely repulsive to me.'

" 'Then why, why have you done this?'

" 'If you can control your hysterics I'll tell you. It's very simple. I needed a legal connection with Lenore. A way to explain her being with me. I couldn't very well adopt her so I hit on this idea of marriage. It's perfect really, because it will protect her from men too. She's already getting furtive looks from men, you know.'

"I tried to tell him how wrong it was and how damaging it could be for Lenore. He brushed off everything I said. Told me that it was all going to work perfectly, and that one day, when Lenore was older and could take care of herself, they would divorce and he would give her a big settlement and she would be set for life.

"He made me leave without seeing Lenore. To punish her. What could I do? I went home to my own life and my own daughter, and I thanked God that my child had no ties to Bram Serian. And I lit my candles and prayed that somehow Lenore would survive.

"After that Lenore slowly drew away from me. I'm sure part of it was just from her being a teenager. But there was a lot more going on ... things I didn't understand then, but that I've come to understand since. Lenore was maturing into a young woman and her emotions were all mixed up. Here was this man she'd adored for years, and now suddenly she was supposed to be married to him. He introduced her to people as his wife.

"Jesus save all of us females, cause we need it. And Lenore was no exception. I'd brought her videos and her head was full of Sleeping Beauty and Cinderella and other fairy-tale crap just like the heads of more worldly girls. And in her confusion she transformed Bram from her father figure to her Prince Charming.

"God, what a mess. She became very jealous and possessive and she saw me as threatening because I disapproved of the arrangement so much. And she was frustrated because she wanted Bram to start treating her like she was his girlfriend and he wanted no part of that.

"She got older and even more attractive to men. And Bram suddenly realized that he had a real live woman on his hands, and he called me in a panic because it had just occurred to him that she might develop crushes on men he brought around and that she might start having sex. He was frantic.

"I told him he should have thought ahead to this before. And I suggested that he do his tricky divorce now and send

Lenore to live with me. He said he'd think about it. But months passed and I didn't hear anything.

"I tried to get Lenore to talk to me on the phone, but she was very cool to me, and I could not tell what was going on there. I went for a visit and didn't learn anything that way either.

"Bram called me and told me that I was upsetting Lenore and that he thought it was time for us to wean ourselves from each other. I was very hurt, but I agreed that I would keep away. Some months later when I couldn't stand it any longer I tried to call Lenore and learned that the number had been changed and was unlisted.

"So I turned my back. I thanked God for my normal life and my wonderful daughter and I shut away Bram Serian and my ugly past. And Lenore too. I shut away my guilt and my cowardice, but I always remembered Lenore when I lit my candles or when I said my prayers.

"And then one day I picked up a paper and read about Bram's death and about Lenore being charged with murder. And I drove out to Arcadia determined to sit at the gate till I saw her.

"And now I'm trying to make up for deserting her. I'm trying to make sure she doesn't get hurt any more.

"The things she's told me about those years with him . . . and even worse . . . the things she hasn't been able to talk about, make me sorry that I didn't kill that man myself.

"And now here you are, Mr. Book Writer. And she knows better than to trust you and she knows better than to believe in you but you keep getting under her skin. And she can't take any more hurt. She's not strong enough to go through what you're going to put her through. So I am begging you. If you truly are as decent as you seem to be . . . then leave her alone."

Owen slammed around the apartment, throwing things into boxes. Gathering up everything that was his. Geneva Johnson's story had answered the questions that Lenore would not answer for him. Now he knew just how low Bram Serian had fallen, and now he understood the devils and ghosts that governed Lenore's sudden shifts of character.

He packed everything into the rental car, filling the trunk and the backseat with his accumulated paper and books as well as his personal items. Then he drove out of Manhattan.

It was dark when he pulled up to the gate at Arcadia. Lenore had made him surrender the key so he couldn't just drive in, but he was determined to push that intercom button until she talked to him.

"Who is it?" she asked.

"It's Owen. I've got everything I own in the car, and I'd like to stay. If you don't want me any other way, then take me as a friend. I need to be with you, Lenore. And I need to know that you're not alone out here every night during the trial."

There was no answer over the intercom. For some moments, he thought that she was just going to ignore him. Then, slowly, the gate slid open.

25

Monday. Day 14 of *The People vs. Lenore Serian.* Lenore requested that Owen stay with the defense team in the hotel and then sit with Jacowitz, Volpe, and Riley in the pew directly behind the defense table. Rossner's dislike for the idea was clear but he consented.

"No touching her, though," Rossner warned Owen. "No whispering to her. No attention at all when we're in public, and be a goddamn sphinx while we're in the courtroom. Act like one of the team. The last thing we need is for the jury to think she's got a boyfriend cheering her on."

So Owen tried to appear very stern and professional as he sat there, waiting for the jury to be called. He caught a glimpse of Holly's face, and thought to himself, with a sense of dark irony, that her expression was murderous. That she was more deserving of punishment than Lenore.

He wanted to stand up and tell the jury the entire unvarnished truth so they would understand what Lenore's life had been, and they would have mercy on her, have compassion for her. So they would absolve her and give her a second chance. A first chance really, for she'd not yet had one.

In the hotel that morning, he had taken Rossner aside and told him that there was much more to the story than anyone knew. That Serian had married her when she was only fifteen and the legality of the union was in doubt. And that Serian had never intended to be a real husband to her.

Rossner had held up his hand immediately, halting Owen before he could blurt out any more.

"What are you telling me this kind of stuff for?" Rossner had asked him incredulously. "Do you realize how much more guilty that makes her sound? How much stronger a motive that gives her?"

The court clerk called the room to order. "The people

against Lenore Serian!" boomed out once more, and Owen's stomach clenched into a knot.

With a solemn air of certitude, Rossner stepped up to the bench and presented the judge with blue-jacketed papers. A motion to dismiss. The judge reviewed the motion, then initiated a discussion which included both Brown and Rossner. Owen was surprised that it was conducted openly and not in a sidebar.

The discussion rapidly deteriorated into an argument with Rossner indignant and Brown repeating statements that managed to be demanding and pleading at the same time.

"The people have clearly demonstrated a legally sufficient case, your honor. There have been demonstrations of motive, opportunity—"

"Yes, Mr. Brown. Thank you." The judge sucked in his cheeks and removed his reading glasses. His cast was tucked out of sight in the folds of his robe. "Motion denied. The people have presented a legally sufficient case."

Owen sank back against the wooden pew. Jacowitz had said the motion probably wouldn't work, but still . . . Owen had hoped.

"Jury entering!" called a court clerk. This was it. The start of Rossner's defense.

The first witness seemed so frustratingly trivial that Owen wanted to shout, *Get on with it! Show them something big.* But he sat there looking professional, taking notes as he listened to Charlie Rossner ask a lock company employee about the subtle differences between factory-made keys and hardware store copies. Then he had the man give a long dull report on how he had inspected every key on the rings hanging by the Serians' back door, and there were at least seven copies of the key to Serian's studio hanging right beside the back door for anyone to use.

Brown waived cross and Rossner called his next witness, a shriveled little man named Frangos who ran one of those corner everything stores in Manhattan near Serian's loft.

Mr. Frangos reported that Bram Serian had been a good customer for nearly twenty years and that one of the things he routinely did was have copies of his keys made. Frangos said that Serian was always losing his keys or afraid of losing his keys. He also related how Serian had told him that it was dangerous to have keys made in the small town near Arcadia because he was always being watched there and because the hardware man there might make extra copies for Bram's enemies. Brown tried a cross on this witness but didn't accomplish anything.

Next Rossner called an accelerant expert to discuss how dangerous it was to smoke around spilled lamp oil or paint thinner. Brown did a perfunctory cross, and then Judge Pulaski announced lunch.

"It's a beautiful day out," he told the jury, "I'd suggest you go out for a stroll in the sunshine after you finish eating." The jurors all nodded and smiled, and Owen wanted to yell that this wasn't a picnic. This wasn't a game. A woman's life was at stake.

A pizza was delivered to the hotel for their lunch. The mood was tense but fairly upbeat. Lenore was quiet. After they were finished eating, Rossner took Lenore into the bedroom for a private conference. Owen paced nervously, wondering what the conference was about. Wondering why Rossner wasn't doing more. Why his witnesses were so dull.

Riley was napping on a couch. Volpe was playing solitaire in the corner. Only Jacowitz, who was deep into a stack of typed pages, looked like he was doing anything productive.

"You better save yourself," Paul Jacowitz warned him. "We've got several days of trial left and then an eternity of jury deliberations to get through."

Owen stopped pacing and stared at him. "Several days?"

Jacowitz pushed his wire-rimmed glasses higher up the bridge of his nose and shrugged. "Give or take a little ... yes."

"My God, Paul, you mean that's all Rossner's got, a few days' worth of witnesses? Brown spent twelve days making her look guilty, and now Rossner is only going to put in a few days defending her?"

"Calm down, man. This is all standard procedure in a case like this. Most of the defense work has already been done in the cross examination of the prosecution's witnesses. All we're doing now is a little reinforcement of what's already been established."

Owen dropped into the chair next to Paul. "'Isn't there something more we can do? Something big and definitive?"

Jacowitz regarded Owen with an expression that blended sympathy and regret. "This isn't Perry Mason, Owen. Nobody is going to break down on the witness stand and confess. Nobody is going to jump out from the spectators' section and scream, *The housekeeper did it!* This is the real world and the real legal system, and the most we can hope for is to sow so many doubts in the jurors' minds that they can't bring themselves to convict.

"Here," Jacowitz handed him a stack of pages. "Help me look through this transcript for statements about Lenore's behavior on the night of the fire. Underline everything you find with that green highlighter. And listen . . . the best thing you can do for Lenore right now is stay calm. She's got enough shit coming down on her without having to worry about you falling apart."

Twenty minutes passed and finally Rossner came out of the bedroom looking agitated. "I'm done with her," he told Owen. "Go on in if you want."

"What happened? What's wrong?" Owen asked immediately.

"Nothing new is wrong," Rossner said. "She's just being as stubborn and hardheaded as she was at the start. That's all."

"How?"

"I want to put her on the stand and she refuses. But that's her prerogative. The law says the accused doesn't have to testify. I think she ought to do it. She says no." Rossner held up his hands and grimaced in resignation. "She's been uncooperative from the start. Then she pulled that stunt to keep me from grilling the Johnson woman on the stand . . . without ever explaining. But hey, she's the boss."

Owen went into the bedroom and found Lenore curled up on the bed. He sat down on the edge and stroked her hair. "Did Rossner give you a hard time?" he asked gently.

She nodded.

"He's just trying to win this thing for you. He's trying to set you free. I understand why you wouldn't let him tear into Geneva, but this is different. Rossner thinks you should go on the stand, and who could you hurt by testifying?"

She pulled herself up into a sitting position so her eyes were level with his. "Don't, Owen. I have my reasons. Please don't question me."

"This is insane, Lenore. You have to listen to Rossner and level with him. My God, if you'd just tell him you can't read or write . . . He could immediately shoot down the lamp on the shopping list! And if you'd tell him—"

"Owen . . . This is *my* life. My trial. Please . . ."

He gathered her in his arms and held her against his chest, resting his chin on her hair, and he prayed to whatever gods watched over her: the gods and ghosts of Thailand, the god of the strange candles, and the God that Brother James Collier had lost out there at Arcadia. He prayed that she would be saved.

After lunch Rossner called Stanley Cantor to the stand. Stanley the delivery man who kept Arcadia stocked with everything from strawberries to toilet bowl cleaner to condoms.

Stanley was a short compact man with sparse hair combed across a shiny scalp. He had the bright eyes and quickness of someone born to energetic optimism.

Rossner had him explain exactly what his business was, and Stanley described himself as a supplier extraordinaire, a purveyor of the unique, a man whose business motto was "Let Stanley worry about it."

"How long did you deliver to Arcadia, Mr. Cantor?"

"I started twelve years ago, and I'm still delivering the goods."

"How many times a week did you visit Arcadia while Bram Serian was alive?"

"Always once, sometimes two or three times depending on whether they had a lot of company or not."

"During twelve years of these frequent visits, did you come to know Bram and Lenore Serian?"

"Sure. I'm a friendly guy. I like to get to know my customers. That's good business too because then I can anticipate what they might want and bring them out surprises."

"What was your opinion of Bram and Lenore Serian?"

"He was your basic tough cookie. A stickler for detail and very particular. Now she has always been just the opposite. She won't ever tell me if I brought something wrong because she doesn't want to cause me trouble or hurt my feelings. I'm always telling her she should speak up if I get something wrong. But she won't do it."

"Has Lenore Serian ever been inconsiderate to you or unfriendly?"

"Are you kidding? Never. She's a real quiet type person, you know. Not too chatty. But she was the one always insisting that I have a hot drink on a cold day or a cold drink on a hot day. And she was the one who'd ask about my family. Bram never could be bothered with the little things like that. And that Natalie the housekeeper . . . she wasn't nice to anybody when I was around unless it was someone she wanted to flirt with."

"Objection, your honor," Brown called in a contemptuous, whining tone.

"Overruled. Proceed, Mr. Rossner."

Rossner cleared his throat and smiled at Stanley Cantor. "Besides the household goods and food and sundries, you bring people personal items too, don't you?"

"Sure. You need it, Stanley brings it."

"Did you ever take her out a doll?"

"Yes, I did. She ordered a special black doll. Wanted it for the child of a friend."

"Did you ever ask her whether the friend's child liked the doll?"

"I did. And she said that something had happened and she couldn't give the doll to the girl. I asked her then if she wanted me to take it back because it was an expensive one. She said no, that she'd already done something with it."

"Did she tell you she burned it?"

"No! She burned that expensive doll?"

The judge suppressed a smile. "Please let counsel ask the questions, Mr. Cantor."

"Sure, your honor . . . judge."

"Did she say anything else at all to you about the doll?"

"Now that you mention it she got a little upset when I asked her about it. And she kept saying that she hadn't been thinking and that she was really sorry she hadn't given the doll to me for one of my daughters."

"Was there anything unusual that Lenore had you bring out for her?"

Stanley Cantor chuckled. "I could tell you about unusual! I took a baby zebra to a person once. Another time somebody asked me if I could get him some of General Patton's underwear. And another time—"

"Thank you, Mr. Cantor, for those revelations," the judge said, allowing himself a small smile. "But we do need to move on."

"Sure. Sure. Judge . . . your honor."

"Were any of Lenore's requests unusual?"

"No. None stand out in my mind as unusual."

"What about candles? Didn't you bring Lenore Serian voodoo candles?"

There was a collective gasp in the courtroom, and Spencer Brown's eyes widened. It seemed that Rossner was defaming his own client.

"Voodoo candles?" Stanley asked, with a disbelieving grin.

"Candles in glass jars that have sayings on them like *Luck to All Friends?*"

"Oh, those candles . . . Sure, I brought them to her all the time."

"You didn't consider them voodoo candles?"

"Hell—I mean heck, no. Those things are harmless. Lots of people like them. They're made right out in Brooklyn in a little family-run factory, and I go right out there to pick them up. It's the same place that makes the shabboth candles I take to my wife." He turned to the judge. "That's for the Jewish sabbath, your honor."

The judge nodded and raised an eyebrow, but his eyes reflected continued amusement with Stanley Cantor.

"Did Lenore ever tell you why she liked the candles or why they were important to her."

"She said a couple of things. One time she said she'd gotten started on them by a friend whose mother was originally from the Caribbean. I think they're popular down there. Another time, when we were discussing what sayings were available, she said that the candles made her feel like she was focusing all her thoughts and her good energies in the right directions. Her eyes are bad, though, you know, and I guess she's too embarrassed to wear her glasses around, because I always have to read the sayings to her when I bring them."

In front of him, Owen saw Lenore drop her eyes and saw the flush of shame creep into her cheeks. He had to force himself to sit still and not try to comfort her.

"Did you ever consider those candles evil or harmful, Mr. Cantor."

"Are you kidding? They're no more evil than a horseshoe over a door or a rabbit's foot on a key chain or one of those calendars that tells you a thought for the day."

Rossner thanked Stanley Cantor and returned to the defense table. Brown moved into position with a skeptical expression on his face.

"Mr. Cantor, are you saying that you believe voodoo is harmless?"

Stanley Cantor tugged on his ear in thought. "I'll tell you, sir, I really don't know anything about voodoo."

"Don't you have an opinion based on popular perception?"

"Well, I like to watch horror movies. Are zombies and werewolves voodoo, or is voodoo just the stuff where they stick pins in little figures?"

"I believe the sticking pins is voodoo and possibly the zombies are voodoo and I believe killing chickens figures prominently ..." Brown said with complete seriousness. "And are you saying that you find nothing offensive or objectionable about that?"

"I like it in movies."

"We're not discussing movies here, Mr. Cantor."

"What are we discussing, exactly?"

"I am calling your attention to Mrs. Serian's candles and whether you can honestly tell this court that you do not find them bizarre, offensive and objectionable."

"I do not. And I'm a religious man. I'd say so if I thought they were wrong. I'd probably still bring them, but I'd damn sure speak up about it."

Brown knew when he was outflanked. He dropped the candles completely and asked questions about Lenore, trying to get something negative. But Stanley either was too smart for him or honestly adored Lenore Serian. Finally, Brown gave up and sat down. And a smiling Stanley Cantor hustled out of the courtroom.

Next was Dr. Bertram Aldrich, the physician who had treated Lenore's burns after the fire. He gave his medical credentials, explained that he was a gynecologist and that he had gone out to Arcadia once a year to examine Lenore and had been doing so for eight years. He said that Lenore had called him at eight o'clock on the morning of the fire and asked him to come out.

"What did you find, Doctor, when you saw Lenore Serian?"

"I found that she was in both physical and emotional distress."

"Could you describe this for us, Doctor?"

"She was extremely distraught. She had a second-degree burn on the underside of her right arm and second-degree burns on the finger pads and palm of her left hand. She also had lesser burns to her arms and hands."

"How serious is a second-degree burn?"

"It requires treatment though does not completely destroy the layers of tissue as a third-degree burn does. And unlike a third-degree burn, where the tissue has been destroyed and has no sensation, the second-degree burn is very painful."

"Is this the kind of burn we get from accidentally touching a hot pan handle?"

"I believe what you are referring to is a first-degree burn, which is the type of common burn that people treat themselves in the home."

"The kind of thing my grandmother used to put butter on?"

The doctor smiled. "Not a good remedy, but yes. That's it."

"So Lenore's burns were more serious than that?"

"Yes. She did have both first- and second-degree burns."

"Judging from the location of her burns, can you tell us, with a reasonable degree of medical certainty, what position her hands and arms might have been in?"

"I think I can." The doctor raised his right arm and bent it, palm out so that his forearm was shielding his face. He then extended his left arm as though to touch something. Rossner had him describe the positions for the record.

"Can burns of this type cause shock, Doctor?"

"Definitely. It's very dangerous. There is even a phrase for it . . . burn shock."

"Are there different levels of shock?"

"Certainly. With the worst being fatal."

"What are the symptoms of shock?"

"Pallor, sweating, thirst, nausea, restlessness, confusion, stupor, disorientation, weakness, unconsciousness."

"A person can have some or all of these?"

"Yes. As the shock deepens the symptoms change."

"Was Lenore in shock when you saw her?"

"Let me correct a misconception. The *term* shock takes in numerous symptoms and conditions due to inadequate circulation of the blood. Primary shock is as simple as fainting. Internal hemorrhage or plasma loss from severe burns can create a situation where the heart fails to pump sufficient blood through the body and if not reversed this condition is fatal.

"Now in medicine we refer to a patient as *shocky* anytime there is pallor and a suspicious behavior pattern such as confusion. This doesn't necessarily indicate that the person is technically 'in shock' at that moment but that if there are any symptoms we treat immediately to prevent shock."

"Okay, so what you're saying is that a person can have symptoms and have the threat of shock but not necessarily be 'in shock' yet?"

"Essentially. Yes."

"So, what was Lenore Serian's condition?"

"She was dangerously shocky, and I transported her to the hospital to restore fluids intravenously and prevent shock."

"Would you have had to take her to the hospital to treat her burns if shock were not a factor?"

"No. I knew that she had burns and I had brought supplies to treat them."

"Could her behavior have been affected by her being what you termed shocky?"

"Definitely."

"And how long can this condition of being shocky last before actual deep shock sets in?"

"For hours."

"Could Lenore have been shocky with the resulting confusion and disorientation shortly after her burns occurred?"

"Certainly."

"In this condition could she have still continued to function on some levels, communicating with people and seeming almost normal?"

"Definitely. One of the more dangerous aspects of shock is that it can creep up without being noticed by others and certainly not by the patient."

"At the time when you treated Lenore and she was in this weakened state, did she say anything to you about how she burned herself?"

"She said she had tried to go into the studio because her husband was inside burning."

"Did you have any reason to disbelieve her?"

"None at all."

"Thank you, Doctor."

Rossner bowed out and Spencer Brown stalked into position. The first thing he did was take the doctor back through his credentials.

"Dr. Aldrich . . . correct me if I am wrong but doesn't the

specialty of gynecology confine itself to the treatment of the female reproductive system?"

"In the strictest sense, that is the definition; however, a gynecologist undergoes general medical training in addition to his specialty training and it is common today for a woman to utilize her gynecologist as her primary caregiver."

"You mean a woman would seek your services for a sore throat?"

"Some of my patients do just that."

"Would a woman go to you to treat a broken arm?"

"Not usually, because with a fracture the person has either recognized it as a fracture and gone straight to an orthopedist or gone to the emergency room."

"So why would Mrs. Serian, who must have been aware that her problem was a burn, call you instead of going to the emergency room?"

"Because she didn't know what treatment her condition required and because she knew me."

"Ahhh. She knew that you could be trusted?"

"I would certainly hope so."

"She knew that you would have her interests foremost in your mind?"

"I would hope that was true also."

"Why did you not call some other more qualified doctor onto the case once you had her in the hospital?"

"I considered myself qualified to take care of her."

"Even when surrounded by specialists?"

"Yes. Her burns were such that I felt qualified to treat them."

"And to treat this shocky condition which can become life threatening?"

"Certainly. Shock can be brought on by many things. Even childbirth. Every doctor must train in preventing and treating shock."

"So you were the only doctor allowed to treat her or get close to her or speak with her during this period in the hospital."

"I was her attending physician."

"Given your explanations of the medical treatment required, the first doctor who was called out to Arcadia could have cared for her burns, could he not?"

"I assume so."

"And if she was in some kind of preshock condition he

could have diagnosed that and attended to it . . . transported
her to the hospital if he deemed that necessary."

"I would hope so . . . if he is at all medically qualified."

"Then why . . . if she was in so much pain and distress,
would she refuse the services of this doctor who was already
on the scene and call you and wait for your arrival?"

"Because, as I've said before, she knew me."

"She knew you would be sympathetic to her." Brown infused the word *sympathetic* with an ugly undertone.

"I am sympathetic to all my patients."

"She knew you could be trusted." Brown made the word
trusted sound like something evil.

"Yes," the doctor answered, clearly flustered by the hostility and the suggestion of dishonorable conduct.

Owen wanted to leap at Spencer Brown and grab him by
the throat for the way he insinuated and twisted things. And
he was angry at both Rossner and the judge for letting him
get away with it. Couldn't they see what Brown was doing?

After a few more jabs, the cross was over and the doctor
was released.

"Ladies and gentlemen," the judge told the jury, "you are
dismissed for the day. Enjoy your time at home and begin
making your preparations for the deliberations, when you
will be sequestered. Thank you and good day."

Owen drove Lenore home that night, much to Volpe's and
Rossner's displeasure. "All we need," Rossner had cautioned them, "is for one media person to see you two snug-
gling in a car. Because don't kid yourself. If something juicy
gets splashed across the tabloids, some of those jurors are
going to see it or hear about it."

So they behaved like characters in a spy movie. Volpe
drove Lenore away as always but then met Owen outside of
town so that she could get in with him. In the morning they
planned to do the reverse.

"I feel so helpless," Owen told her as they drove. "I'm
just standing by and watching all this happen."

"What could you do?" she asked.

"I could tear that unprincipled, lowlife prosecutor's
tongue out for starters."

She laughed. "Don't do that. Paul says that Spencer
Brown's tongue is doing the prosecution more damage than
Rossner is."

26

Hello, Bernie . . . it's Owen."

"Good morning. But why aren't you at the trial?"

"I am." Owen glanced around to make certain that there was no one within hearing range of the pay phone. He had chosen a downstairs phone, but still he was cautious. "I'm in the courthouse. There's been a delay. One of the jurors had car trouble this morning, and they're waiting for her to arrive."

"I had hoped I would have news for you this morning, Owen, but there's still no word from DeMille. I'm going to call over there within the hour. This is ridiculous that they've committed to buying the book but still haven't agreed on an advance figure. This is not the way it usually proceeds." She laughed. "But then this whole deal has been topsy-turvy from the beginning, hasn't it."

"Why are they be stalling, Bernie? What more do they want from me?"

"Well, it's not your editor, I can tell you that. Arlene is anxious to finalize. The delay is coming from higher up. My guess is that this has gone on so long that now they're waiting to see how the trial goes. If they could stall until a verdict, they could argue for paying you less of an advance."

"Why?"

"Because if Lenore Serian is found innocent, the book will have less value. You would be left with an unresolved crime, a possible fading of public interest and, more important, the sticky legal difficulties of what you can and can't say about an innocent person. Convicted criminals are fair game, but not so for the acquitted. Let's just hope it's a guilty verdict."

"You want them to find her guilty?" Owen asked incredulously. "*DeMille* wants them to find her guilty? So the book will be easier to publish? If that's the way it is, Bernie, then you tell DeMille to take their contract and shove it up their collective ass!"

Owen slammed the receiver down. He leaned his forehead against the wall and took several deep breaths, then he hurried back upstairs to courtroom 6.

An early witness was recalled. Deputy Sheriff Kenneth Havlik came to the stand, no less nervous than he had been for his first testimony. *What could Rossner want from Havlik,* Owen wondered.

"Deputy Havlik . . ." Rossner smiled. "You stated that you were awakened by your dogs the night . . . excuse me . . . the morning of the fire."

"Yes, sir."

Rossner held up a sheet so that he could read from it. "What did you mean when you said that your dogs started raising a fuss *again?*"

"That wasn't the first time my dogs had been set off that night."

"How many other times had they been disturbed?"

"Early on in the evening, they were real fidgety and howly for about an hour."

"Could you determine the cause?"

"Yes, sir. That was when several carloads of people passed by going toward the Serian place. My dogs are penned real close to the road and traffic stirs them up."

"They must be stirred up a lot then."

"No. Our road barely gets any traffic. Specially at night. Beyond my place there's just Arcadia and then there's a dead end."

"So your dogs were agitated during the hour or so that the late-coming party guests were arriving?"

"Yes, sir. It was three different cars."

"You're certain of that?"

"Yes, sir. I don't have any trees between my house and the road. Even if I don't see the traffic, I can hear it. Unless I'm in the shower or something."

"So the dogs reacted when the three cars went in to the party early on. And they were very disturbed by the passing of all the firefighters and trucks that began at about four-thirty-five A.M."

"Yes, sir."

"Did anything else bother them in the night?"

"Yes, sir. They woke me twice more."

"Could you tell the cause?"

"I thought I heard a car on the road both times."

"And what time was this?"

"The first time was two something. Two-ten maybe. The second time, I was mad because it seemed like I'd just got back to sleep, and so I looked straight at the clock and it was three-fifty-seven."

"Could you tell whether the car was going to the Serians' or coming from there?"

"No, sir."

"But there was a car on the road at about two-ten that morning and another car at three-fifty-seven that morning?"

"Yes sir."

Brown jumped up even before Rossner was back to his seat. "Now Kenneth ... Deputy Havlik ... did you actually see a vehicle on the road at three-fifty-seven the morning of August seventh?"

"No."

"Did you definitely hear a car on the road?"

"No. But I heard my dogs and—"

"These are hunting dogs, aren't they?"

"They are."

"Trail dogs ... tracking dogs, right?"

"Some are, some aren't. I've got a mixture."

"What would these dogs do if say a raccoon came up along the road near their pens?"

"They'd raise cain all right. Probably tear the pen down."

"Is it not correct that these dogs make noise for other reasons than just the passage of vehicles on your road and that they could have been responding to other possible stimulus on the morning in question?"

Havlik frowned and scratched his neck.

"It's possible, I guess."

Rossner brought an emergency room nurse to the stand to verify Lenore's condition when Dr. Aldrich brought her to the hospital for treatment. Under Brown's cross the nurse admitted that she hadn't spent much time with Lenore and that Doctor Aldrich had hovered over and been very protective of his patient. Brown made this sound terribly suspicious—that a doctor would be so attentive and solicitous.

Owen had trouble concentrating on the testimony. He

watched people, seeing their movements and facial tics and nervous gestures in minute detail, but the words they spoke were so meaningless to him that he might as well have been deaf. It occurred to him that he knew the backs of all these heads by heart. Spencer Brown had a fresh haircut. Dapolito's dandruff was less noticeable. Rossner had developed a red spot on the back of one ear.

The nurse disappeared, and Dr. Wallace Telner, a psychiatrist and phobia specialist, took her place on the stand. He ridiculed everything the prosecution's psychiatrist had said about Bram Serian being a pyrophobic. Brown counterpunched by implying that Dr. Telner had less experience with pyrophobics than the previous witness.

Brown sat down after his cross. The witness left. Rossner stood. "The defense rests, your honor."

That was it. The end. The trial had simply wound down and stopped like an old key-driven clock.

"Ladies and gentlemen," Judge Pulaski said, swiveling his chair toward the jury box, "Mr. Brown and Mr. Rossner need to organize now in preparation for their closing arguments, and I need to meet with both of them.

"Soon you will begin your deliberations, and, as I cautioned before, you must make your personal arrangements. You must make preparations for pets, family members, houseplants, and so on based on your being gone for a number of days." The judge smiled paternally.

"Once the deliberation begins you will remain together. You will deliberate in the jury room, and you will be taken to a hotel each evening where you will have dinner at the state's expense and where you will be housed two persons to a room, also at the state's expense. A court officer will be on duty all night long. In the morning, you will breakfast at the hotel and then be transported by court officers back to the jury room.

"Tomorrow you will hear summations. After that will come my instructions to you, and then your deliberations will begin.

"I must caution you . . . do not allow yourself to be exposed to the news or to anyone else's opinion.

"Court is dismissed until two-thirty."

They ordered deli sandwiches for lunch and ate separately, scattered about the room. Rossner sat at the table poring over legal pads full of notes as he ate. Volpe and Riley had pulled two chairs up to an end table and were quietly playing poker. Lenore was curled up in a chair, staring out the window, watching courthouse square while her sandwich lay untouched. Owen moved restlessly about, unable to sit in one spot for long. His lunch was gone but he couldn't recall eating it.

"Come on," Jacowitz said, motioning toward the door. "Get your coat and you can help me lay in supplies."

They walked a block and a half to a small grocery store. "So what happens now?" Owen asked him.

"The judge is doing the charge discussion after lunch. Do you know anything about that?"

Owen shook his head.

"Basically the jury instructions or jury charge is a set of guidelines or rules for deliberation. Tomorrow the judge and the two sides will start wrangling over exactly what goes into the charge and how it's worded. Then, after the closing arguments, the judge will read the charge to the jury, a performance which is about as exciting as watching grass grow."

Owen opened the door to the little store and held it for Jacowitz to enter.

"If you think you're eating your insides now, you ain't seen nothing yet," Jacowitz warned him as he stepped through the door. "Just wait till we're all sitting around wondering what that jury is doing. It could take days, you know. It could take a whole week for those twelve people to agree on a verdict."

The atmosphere after lunch was entirely different than the evidentiary portion of the trial Owen had become accustomed to. There were only five people in the spectators section, and Jacowitz said he could identify all of them as lawyers or legal interns. The press section held only Holly, Marilyn and Pat. And of course the jury box stood empty.

Rossner submitted his written proposal for the jury instructions, passing a copy to the defense as well as to the judge. And Brown followed suit, handing his proposal to the judge with a copy to Rossner. The men were informal with each other, and there was bantering back and forth and a general air of camaraderie so that it seemed to Owen that the proceedings had turned into some kind of club meeting. Pulaski discussed his upcoming vacation plans with Brown and Dapolito, and Rossner offered traveling tips.

The principals then settled in to read. Tabletops and benches were littered with open law books, papers and glasses of water. The court officers lounged, half-asleep, in chairs along the sides. There was no sound except the shuffling of paper and the occasional cough or clearing of the throat.

After thirty minutes of reading the proposals, it was agreed that there would be another thirty minutes allotted to read and review the cases cited in each proposal. The minutes felt like hours.

Finally, the judge announced that they would begin by going over Mr. Brown's proposal point by point, and the verbal arguments began. They were delivered with good humor but so jargon-ridden that Owen could barely follow them.

Lenore appeared frozen into place. Owen tried to imagine what was going on in her mind. Did she allow herself fear? Did she have any regrets? Was she frustrated or angry over being turned into a passive object, forced to watch in silence while her personal life was dissected and her fate was tossed back and forth—the prize in this glib jousting?

They went on and on, arguing over what the judge should tell the jury about specifics like Natalie Raven's deal for immunity and the broader questions: the two elements of intent to kill and killing, the burden of proof, circumstantial evidence and inference and inference charts and the presumption of innocence.

Judge Pulaski paused to drink a large glass of water, then said, "Now, gentlemen, we come to the terrible problem of moral certainty. I have always viewed moral certainty and reasonable doubt as two different standards. But now CJI tells us that the two are the same. I don't agree."

"Neither do I, Judge," said Spencer Brown. "And the trouble with using moral certainty in the jury charge is that, as lay people, they simply can't understand how these two concepts of moral and certain come together. In their own limited way, they will think they know what the term *moral* means, and they will think they know what *certainty* means, but . . ."

Owen leaned toward Jacowitz to whisper, "What's CJI?"

"Criminal Jury Instructions. It's the bible," Jacowitz whispered back.

Rossner entered the fray then. "The moral certainty language comes from a case that's still good law and is still being used. It is certainly no less a contradiction than reasonable doubt, which is itself a contradiction of sorts, your honor."

"But I have always been comfortable with reasonable doubt as a doubt one can cite a reason for," the judge countered. "Whereas moral certainty implies absolute certainty, and how many things in this world are ever absolutely certain? *Moral* is a vague and easily misconstrued word, while *reasonable* has a direct meaning of rational."

"It's your decision, Judge," Spencer Brown said eagerly, obviously assured that Pulaski was leaning in the direction Brown wanted him to go. "However, we do feel the moral certainty language is difficult for juries to understand, and if you did go with moral certainty that language would not be a fair way to present the charge to the jury."

The judge appeared to be ruminating for a moment. "Gentlemen, this is the single most important legal question in this case. It is the heart so to speak. And CJI leaves it both ways for the trial judge. If moral certainty is not required, then the prosecution is entitled to have it removed."

"Your honor, we have the Court of Appeals using moral certainty for their own standard," Rossner said.

"Yes, and I'm aware that the Court of Appeals could say, 'What's wrong with this judge . . . he knew we used the moral certainty language recently.' But a judge has to base decisions not only on what has been done in the past but on what the appellate courts will do in the future. This leaves much to consider."

"Given the circumstantial nature of this case, your honor," Rossner argued, "moral certainty provides a path to lead through the inferences. Moral certainty keeps the level of inferential thought focused on the case."

"Inference upon inference, what about that?" the judge threw out at them. "What about CJI?" It was clear that Pulaski had heard enough about moral certainty to make his decision though it was not clear what that decision would be.

"Each inference must be based on evidence and fact. Certain inferences can be drawn from the evidence but you cannot use conjecture," Brown insisted. "Nearly all reasoning is based on facts deduced from other facts."

"Let's cross out this third sentence in the second paragraph of Mr. Brown's first page, then, shall we," the judge suggested and Owen realized that they might as well have been speaking a foreign language because he had no idea what had been decided or whose side it favored. And he stopped trying to follow them at all.

"Did Rossner say how he thought the charge discussion was going? Is he making any points?" Owen asked Lenore when they were enroute to Arcadia that evening.

"I don't want to talk about the trial, Owen."

"How can you not talk about it? How can you talk about anything else?"

She turned her head away from him to stare out the window.

"All right," he sighed. After several minutes of silence he said, "Let's not go straight back to Arcadia. Let's have dinner out."

"I'm too tired for the trip to Manhattan."

"I wasn't thinking of Manhattan. The court clerk was telling Rossner about a little French restaurant out in the country. Dimly lit and very discrete, he said. So even celebrities go."

"Where is it?"

"I'm not sure exactly but I know the name of the town it's near. We can drive there and ask directions at a station."

She smiled sadly. "I've always been so afraid to leave Arcadia. Bram had me terrified . . . convinced that the immigration officials were going to swoop down on me if I showed my face anywhere.

"It's hard to get used to being free. In a way, I feel like I'm just breaking out of the prison Bram made for me. And headed right into another sort of prison."

"Don't talk like that!"

"I'm being realistic. I know I don't look innocent to those people on the jury."

"Even if that were true, Lenore, it's not important. All that hassling today was about legal concepts that make their personal opinion of you irrelevant."

She slid her hand over to touch his thigh. "I'm glad I have you with me," she said.

Her touch sent a wave of heat through his body, but it was
followed immediately by pain at the thought that indeed he
might lose her.

They arrived at Arcadia just after eight. Owen had spent
the whole evening in a state of arousal. It began with a dizzying kiss in the restaurant parking lot, then carried through
dinner with the pressure of her leg against his beneath the table and the sultry, teasing glances she cast with her dark
eyes in the candlelight.

As soon as they were safely home and locked into the
house, she twined her arms around his neck and pulled his
mouth to hers. His body responded immediately but he held
himself back.

"Wait," he said. "Where are your clothes? Your real
clothes—not these trial things."

She led him to the plain bedroom, which turned out to
have a huge walk-in closet, dressing area and bath concealed
behind a small door. He switched on a light and surveyed the
hanging racks. She had hardly any dresses and certainly no
party or cocktail dresses.

"What's this?" he asked, tugging at a swath of peach-
colored fabric that was just barely visible. He pulled it out.

"That's a nightgown," she said. "I don't think I've ever
worn it."

The gown was made of a fluid, silk satin and had a bare
neck and tiny straps.

"This will work," he said.

"What are you doing . . . ?"

"Shhh." He put a finger to her lips. "Just stand still and
don't ask questions."

He held her hands and told her to step out of her shoes.
Then he took the shapeless suit jacket and skirt off of her.
Unbuttoned the prim blouse and dropped it to the floor. He
slid his hands up beneath her slip and knelt to roll down her
panty hose. Laughing, she rested her hand on his shoulder
for balance.

He pulled the pins from her hair and combed it loose with
his fingers.

"My turn," she said, reaching for the buttons on his shirt.

"No. Please. Stand still."

He took off the remaining slip and bra, fighting the temptation to succumb to her beautiful lithe body, and dropped

the fluid length of silk over her head. She smiled shyly as he adjusted the delicate straps.

"Now come on," he said, taking her hand. "Lead me to music."

She took him to a room where he picked out CDs and adjusted the lighting down low. All the while she watched him with a quizzical smile. The music started.

"This is your first party," he said. "Your sweet sixteen. Or maybe your junior prom. And I am the boy who's been staring at you for months. The boy with such a crush on you." He held out his hand. "Would you dance with me, Lenore?"

Later, after they had danced and then spent hours exploring every inch of each other, she led him to bed, but neither one of them could sleep.

"Owen," she said in the darkness, "when I told you that about being with other men . . . it was to make you leave . . . but it was partly true. I was with men when I was younger. Different men. Men I didn't care about at all."

"Was that Serian's idea?" he asked, biting back his anger at the dead man.

"How did you know?"

"I guessed. From things I've learned about him."

"He never wanted me . . . physically . . . as a wife . . . which I understand now . . . but when I was eighteen years old and supposedly a married woman and I hadn't even been kissed yet I didn't understand anything."

"You are a miracle, Lenore. How you survived is beyond me."

Her voice was mechanical in the darkness. "He picked them out. The men. And then he set it up. Choreographed it. Told me what to do. I found out after a while that he had fixed it so that he could secretly watch.

"For two years it went on. Each time it happened I felt sicker and emptier. But I kept doing it to please him. To make him love me. Then a man came to work on the glass."

"Guy Demaree?" Owen asked.

"Yes. We became friends. And he stayed long enough that he figured out what was happening. In fact, Bram even offered me to him. Guy was so angry and disgusted with Bram, and he made me see . . . he gave me the courage to stand up to Bram and say no. That was eight years ago. I was twenty then.

"All the lovers I've had since have been in my fantasies. Until you."

"Lenore . . ." he whispered, drawing her close. In the darkness the tears sliding from his eyes were hidden.

At midnight the phone rang. Owen could hear it but he couldn't find it. Lenore reached it first and answered. He listened to her end of the conversation.

"Hi, Paul."

"No, we haven't watched any television."

"What?"

"No!"

Lenore's seething anger was apparent as she listened to the rest of what Paul Jacowitz had to say.

"Fine," she said shortly. "I'll ride in with Joe in the morning, then."

"What?" Owen demanded as soon as she hung up.

"That was Paul. Holly Danielson did an exclusive tonight on my seducing a man from right out of the courtroom. There was tape of us kissing in the restaurant parking lot before dinner. Paul says to expect ugly headlines in the morning."

Owen slammed his fist down on the bed. "That fucking bitch. There's nothing too low for her."

27

The tabloids the next morning were brutal. Rossner and Jacowitz had bought copies of every publication on the Manhattan newsstands and brought them to the hotel. Two of them had front-page spreads with screaming headlines. **BLACK WIDOW SPINS WEB IN COURTROOM** and **WIDOW SEDUCES WHILE JURY DEDUCES.**

All the articles were takeoffs on Holly's story, which, from Jacowitz's detailed description, sounded long on suggestion and short on facts. But Holly did have a tape of the couple embracing in the parking lot of the French restaurant, and she had combined that with a clip of Owen in the courthouse lobby and a clip of Lenore leaving the courthouse in her black hooded cape so that the piece managed to seem very credible. Holly must have then sold still shots to the tabloids so that each of them could have a grainy black-and-white photo of the parking lot embrace to use, along with a candid headshot of Owen that also had to be Holly's doing. These were mixed in with cape shots of Lenore and of course the original emerging-from-the-car-shot of Lenore when she was first dubbed the Black Widow.

Owen exploded. "How can they do this? How can they get away with it!"

Rossner laughed. His tightly harnessed anger was laced with sarcasm. "The writer doesn't like to see his name in print, huh? Feel like you're being violated . . . exploited maybe? That's the name of the game, Byrne. And don't forget, you're playing too. Or isn't your book going to have real people in it?"

Owen voluntarily separated himself from the defense, letting them go ahead to the courthouse and then creeping out the hotel's back service door for his own dash to the courthouse. When he reached the steps, the camera jockeys spotted him and swarmed forward. He raced through them to lobby security, wishing he had a disguise to hide behind. Or maybe his own version of the black cape.

Halfway up the stairs a female voice called his name, and he increased his pace. He could hear his pursuer on the stairs behind him, so he bolted the rest of the way and turned quickly down the hall.

"Owen! It's Bernie!"

He stopped and turned, then waited for a winded Bernadette Goodson to catch up.

"Sorry, Bernie. I just had to fight my way through the camera gauntlet at the door and I'm a little jumpy."

She leaned one hand against the wall and rested the other on her chest while she caught her breath. "I'm so out of shape," she said. "It's embarrassing."

Owen waited. Suffering from embarrassment himself. His last contact with Bernie had been when he slammed the phone down in her ear the day before.

"This morning I stopped to buy a paper on my way to the office and there it all was. I went straight to the train and came up here." She sighed. "Is there any truth to this?"

Owen glanced around to make sure there were no eavesdroppers near, but the hallway was deserted. No doubt the action in courtroom 6 had already started.

"Owen, *are* you involved with the woman?"

"Yes. And I'm staying at Arcadia with her now."

Bernie stared at him in disbelief for a moment, then shook it off and laughed. "I guess I needn't have worried about you finding a place to stay in New York."

Owen attempted a smile.

"This has all been very difficult, hasn't it?" Bernie asked sympathetically.

"You don't know the half of it, Bernie."

"Now I understand why our phone conversation yesterday upset you so much. Of course you don't want to hear this woman's fate discussed in such callous terms."

"You shouldn't have come all the way up here, Bernie. I know how busy you are."

"I couldn't find you any other way, and I wanted to put things right. I know you don't really want to lose this contract. I know the book is important to you. And I did not convey your message to DeMille. As far as they're concerned you're still the eager author, waiting to hear the results of the negotiations."

She paused and searched his face. "You do still want this deal, don't you, Owen?"

He tilted his head back and closed his eyes for an instant, then set his jaw and met her questioning gaze. "Yes," he admitted. "You have no idea how much I want to do this book. Only it's going to be much different now than I originally envisioned it."

"Under the circumstances, I think that's to be expected."

"Are you staying? Do you want to come in to the trial with me?"

"Yes. I planned to go back at lunchtime. I have to admit that the idea of seeing a real murder trial is exciting."

Owen winced at her words.

"I'm sorry," she said quickly.

"No." He shook his head. "Don't apologize. What you're saying is only normal. I thought the same thing myself when I first arrived."

She nodded and pulled out a folded paper. "This is from Alex."

Owen scanned it.

Cliff had learned that Abe Hanselmann's military records were sealed and there were indications that Abe had been in one of the covert units. He was able to find out, however, that Abe had gone missing in the early seventies and was presumed to have deserted.

Owen folded the note and put it away. Abe Hanselmann was a deserter. The man hadn't just been disturbed. He'd been posing as Bram Serian's cousin Al and hiding in that studio at Arcadia for very good reasons.

Maybe that was what Bram was afraid of all along . . . that his brother would be caught. And maybe that was part of the reason he kept Lenore isolated and fearful. Maybe he'd thought that she would somehow bring down the authorities on his fugitive brother.

They started down the hall together.

"I got DeMille to promise that we'll conclude the haggling by the end of the afternoon," she told him.

"How'd you do that?"

"Threats. I hinted that another publisher was interested."

"Is that true?"

She grinned. "Let's say there's an element of truth to it.

The fact is, Owen"—she hesitated and glanced at him with a measure of apprehension—"this exposé business, painful and perverse as it is, has probably doubled your value overnight."

Owen managed to slip Bernie into the tenth row of the press section with him. Heads swiveled but no one dared bother him because the judge was speaking to the jury, telling them that after the summations he would give them the jury instructions and talk to them about the highly disciplined process that a jury must use to reach a verdict.

Judge Pulaski swiveled his chair to the front then and swept the courtroom with a scowl. "We now begin closing arguments. The door shall be locked and any disturbances shall result in immediate expulsion.

"Mr. Rossner, are you ready to begin your summation?"

Rossner rose and the entire courtroom held its breath expectantly.

"Ladies and gentlemen of the jury, this is my last opportunity to speak with you on Lenore Serian's behalf. I hope that my final words will do this woman justice . . . will result in justice being done. That is why I am here. To secure justice for her."

Rossner moved easily before the jury. He was relaxed and friendly, forthright and sincere.

"If she could speak for herself, she would. But she isn't qualified to represent herself before you, just like she isn't qualified to do heart surgery or design a bridge. Our legal system has become too complex for an untrained person to be able to step up and defend himself.

"Don't misunderstand me! I am not criticizing our legal system, I am simply stating the facts. Our legal system is the greatest in the world. The greatest! And you know what the heart of our system is . . . *the presumption of innocence*. Lenore Serian is presumed innocent unless Mr. Brown can prove otherwise.

"In this great United States of America, every single one of us is presumed innocent unless proven guilty. Not *until* but *unless*. See the difference there. *Until* makes it sound like all of us are walking around with a time limit ticking away and that we only have so much time left before someone declares us guilty of something. *Unless,* the word *unless* . . . gives that great phrase its true and legal meaning. Presumed innocent *unless* proven guilty. Which guarantees that each and every one of us is innocent under the law from the day we're born till the day we die *unless* somebody puts together a solid case that proves to a jury that we are guilty beyond any reasonable doubt. That is the cornerstone our system was built on. That is the right each one of us is born to in this great nation.

"Presumed innocent unless proven guilty. Proven guilty by who?" Rossner turned and gave a polite nod toward Brown and Dapolito's table. "The prosecutors. Mr. Brown over there and Mr. Dapolito. That's their job. That's what they get up every morning and go to work to do. To try to prove people guilty of things. To try to prove Lenore Serian guilty of killing her husband. But because Lenore, and each of us, has a basic presumption of innocence, the prosecutors in our system have what is called the burden of proof.

"The *burden of proof.*

"Simply put, all that means is that Lenore Serian doesn't have to raise a finger to defend herself. The law says that she *is* innocent *unless* Mr. Brown and Mr. Dapolito can prove beyond a reasonable doubt that she's guilty."

Rossner spun to glare at Brown and Dapolito.

"But the prosecution has tried to twist things around in this trial. They've got such a circumstantial case, such a preposterous, illogical, full-of-holes case, that they've had to shift things around. They're saying that Lenore bought a lamp which might possibly have played a role in Bram Serian's death, and she was at Arcadia when Bram Serian died, and she was overheard quarreling with him several times during the course of their thirteen-year marriage, so . . . unless *she* can prove that she didn't kill him, then she has to be guilty."

He threw up his hands.

"Whoa, there! Wait a minute. That's not the way it works in our country, folks. The defendant doesn't have the burden of proof. It's the prosecution who has the burden of proof. They can't just accuse people of crimes and then say, 'Okay . . . now you try and prove that you're innocent,' the way the authorities can in other countries. They can't just trample on a person's rights in our system. If they level a charge against a citizen, then they have the burden of proving that charge. And they can't just suggest guilt. They must prove to you that Lenore is guilty *beyond a reasonable doubt.*"

He stopped as though considering the phrase.

"Now there's another legal jewel of ours. *Reasonable doubt.* Judge Pulaski spoke to you a little about reasonable doubt in the beginning of this trial, and he'll speak to you about it again later. It is a crucial concept. Particularly in a circumstantial case like this one. To find Lenore guilty, you, the jury, must be so totally convinced by the prosecution's case that you have no reasonable doubt left in your mind. No *reasonable doubt.* Not one single doubt that you can turn around and discuss with another jury member. Because, you see, in this great country of ours, we give the defendant . . . we give each and every citizen . . . the benefit of the doubt."

Rossner went to the podium for a sip of water; then he tugged at his ear a moment as though considering things.

"Let's look at the circumstances in this case and see how all these fine legal concepts apply. First, we've got the lamp. There is no question that Lenore Serian walked into Mr. Fugate's hardware store and handed him shopping lists, one of which included a glass oil lamp and a supply of lamp oil to go with it. That is a fact. The prosecution did its duty, assumed the burden of proof and proved that fact . . . which we never disputed.

"But did the prosecution prove anything beyond that? No. George Fugate thinks he remembers that the list with the lamp on it was not in Natalie Raven's handwriting. Since that list doesn't exist anymore and since no one but George Fugate saw it, we'll never know how good he is at identifying a shopper's handwriting or how good his memory is. Maybe he's no good at all. But let's assume, just for the sake of getting on with things, that George Fugate is a real whiz at handwriting analysis and has a fourteen-karat memory . . . what has been proved?

"What if Lenore did write that list? Does putting a lamp on a shopping list and going to the hardware store prove that she wanted to kill her husband? Absolutely not! To suggest so is ludicrous.

"What proof were we given that the shopping list was not in Bram Serian's handwriting? Didn't George Fugate say that Serian usually did his shopping in person without using a list? And that Serian never paid by check or had occasion to write Mr. Fugate a note or letter. It would follow, then, that even Mr. Fugate's great store of handwriting knowledge did not include a familiarity with Bram Serian's handwriting. So if this list existed and if indeed it was not in Natalie Raven's handwriting, did the prosecution prove that list was not written by Bram Serian himself? No! They couldn't even prove that! They couldn't prove that Bram Serian didn't come out and hand his wife a list and say, 'Pick that up for me while you're in town, honey.'

"And all these sinister implications . . ." Rossner grimaced in disgusted disbelief. "All these manufactured bits of nonsense that Natalie Raven spun out . . . Let's take a hard look at it all. Natalie Raven wanted us to believe that there was something wrong with Lenore purchasing that lamp. She wanted us to believe that there was something sneaky about it. And how did she justify her interpretation of the lamp purchase? Why, the fact that she knew Bram Serian better than his own wife did. *Wait a minute!*

"What did the prosecution prove with Natalie Raven's testimony about the lamp purchase? Nothing! Except maybe that Natalie Raven was possessive of Bram Serian and jealous of Lenore. Ah! you say . . . sounds like Natalie Raven might have had a motive for murder." He raised an eyebrow thoughtfully and let the suggestion sink in.

"So the lamp has made it home and is in the station wagon and Natalie Raven orders Tommy Kubiak to return it but then it just kind of vanishes. Where did it go? Did anyone see Lenore with it? No. Did Natalie Raven see Lenore bring it in the house? No. Could Bram Serian have taken it into his studio? Absolutely.

"And here again, ladies and gentlemen, here again we are in a situation where we can say . . . okay . . . so what? Lenore didn't unload the lamp from the car, but even if she had, so what? An oil lamp is not a dangerous weapon. An oil lamp is not a gun or a switchblade knife or a bomb! As a matter of fact, an oil lamp is a commonly owned thing in the country, and there were already a number of oil lamps on the premises at Arcadia. Natalie Raven herself admitted to buying some of them. Has any of this lamp purchase testimony proven an iota of guilt? No! Absolutely not!"

Rossner threw up his hands as though helpless in the face of such absurdity.

"How do we know that Bram Serian didn't have a whole collection of oil lamps out in that studio of his? We don't, because no one ever saw inside that studio. We have only Natalie Raven's testimony asserting that she *knew* everything Bram Serian would and wouldn't do, and therefore if she says he wouldn't have an oil lamp out there then all of us are supposed to take that as the gospel. Well, I'd go look out the window to double-check if Natalie Raven so much as told me the sun was shining."

Rossner was on a roll and the entire courtroom was riveted. He went from Natalie Raven and the lamp into Tommy Kubiak's testimony about Lenore burning things. He pointed out how easy it would be for a young inexperienced person like Tommy to misinterpret the actions of another. Then he reminded the jury that Stanley Cantor had showed up the voodoo and burning stories for what they were—pure ignorant nonsense.

Then Rossner gave the jury a mini-lesson in Eastern religion and talked about the tradition of burning possessions after a person dies and how that tradition has been modified so that people now burn paper representations of those possessions. And he talked about how Lenore undoubtedly recalled seeing these traditions in her childhood, and how everyone reenacts the rituals of their childhood at times out of nostalgia.

Next Rossner tackled Natalie Raven's claims about Bram wanting a divorce. He portrayed Raven as a frustrated, unhappy woman who wanted Bram Serian to herself and could not accept that the artist loved his wife. Rossner talked about the arguments the woman claimed to have heard, emphasizing that only one of those claims was corroborated. Then he examined the arguments word by word, showing how they could be interpreted differently. Showing that Bram and Lenore could have been arguing about any number of subjects.

He suggested that even if Bram Serian had been badgered into a divorce discussion with Natalie Raven, that did not mean the artist was actually contemplating divorce or that he ever intended to divorce his wife. And he made it clear that not one other witness could corroborate Natalie Raven's claim that Bram Serian wanted a divorce.

Owen tried to block out everything he knew and hear only what the jury was hearing. What were those twelve people thinking? Were they following Rossner? Did they agree with him? The twelve faces were absolutely impassive, and all Owen could tell for certain was that they were listening intently.

Rossner went on about how various people had tried to imply that Lenore was strange or even antisocial, and then he gave an impassioned plea for understanding among the diverse peoples of the earth. Lenore Serian was raised in a different culture, he said, raised with a different set of social rules, so of course she would seem different to people who had the good fortune to be raised in the United States, but surely, he said, surely folks with any common sense and sensitivity at all would have realized the source of her insecurities and social difficulties. And people like Stanley Cantor who had taken the trouble to see through her differences and her inbred reserve had found her to be a warm and caring person.

"And there's just one more thing I'd like to lay to rest," Rossner said, "before you good and patient people keel over from lack of lunch, and that is this James Collier business.

"I find it shocking. I find it unconscionable that the prosecution has made so many unseemly suggestions about Lenore Serian's conduct with this man of the cloth."

Rossner then expounded on the platonic nature of Lenore's relationship with Collier. He reminded the jurors that this godly man had placed his hand on the Bible and sworn that he was telling the truth, sworn that he did not have physical relations with Lenore.

Then Rossner sadly hung his head and admitted that it did indeed appear that Brother James Collier was a man who had been seduced. But not by Lenore Serian.

Owen held his breath, wondering how Rossner had learned the truth.

After a dramatic pause the attorney said, "Brother James Collier was a man who had devoted himself to a life of religion and teaching, a quiet contemplative life. So when Brother James met Bram Serian he was meeting not just a man but a glamorous and exciting new world. And it was this world that seduced Brother James. It was Bram Serian's world."

Rossner turned toward the judge and nodded. It was 12:45. Judge Pulaski called an hour lunch recess, and the room erupted into a buzzing, shifting mass of people.

"Wellll . . ." Bernie breathed. "He's certainly very good." She frowned, as though exasperated. "All that fuss over the candles is really absurd. My receptionist likes those same candles and she's certainly not evil."

Owen smiled. "Thanks for coming, Bernie." He looked around. Dozens of faces were staring at him. "It's probably best if you just get up and leave by yourself. I may have to dodge some questions. Do you know how to get back to the train station?"

She nodded and gave his hand a quick squeeze. "Sorry I have to desert you . . . Good luck . . . To both of you. And call in every day. That's an order."

Owen made it into the hotel after an elaborate series of maneuvers to shake off reporters. He knocked on the door of the main room and was admitted by Riley, who advised him to keep his voice down. Rossner and Jacowitz were in the bedroom reviewing the remainder of the summation.

Owen sat down with Lenore in the corner and ate his lunch.

"Do you think the jury believes him?" she asked.

He took her hand. "Yes," he said, willing confidence into his voice.

After lunch Rossner went straight to Bram Serian's death. He set up scenarios, backed by quotations from various witnesses, in which Serian's death could have been purely accidental. Stumbling drunk with a cigarette in his hand, knocking over the lamp, then slipping on the spilled oil and striking his head on the bricks while the burning cigarette dropped into and ignited the oil. Falling, again with a cigarette, and knocking the lamp over as he fell. Trying to work—again drunk and with a cigarette—spilling some volatile chemical and accidentally igniting it with the cigarette, then chopping at the fire with the axe, slipping and striking his head.

Or, Rossner said, the axe could have nothing at all to do with the death. It could have been lying there near the fireplace for any number of reasons. Given Serian's habit of including objects in his sculptures, the axe may have been on hand to use in some piece of art. Or it could have been a prop, placed there near the faux wood stove to give the illusion that wood had been chopped.

"Since Sheriff Bello picked up the axe head," Rossner told the jury, "and carried it around, waved it around, saying 'Looks like the guy was trying to fight the fire himself' . . . since the good sheriff disturbed the scene without adhering to any formal evidence-gathering procedures, we have no way of knowing where that axe head actually *was* in the building.

"Just like we have no way of knowing who was at the scene when the sheriff arrived because no one made a list or even tried to count."

Rossner stopped himself. "Okay," he said, using his hands to signal concession. "For the sake of continuing, let's assume that Bram Serian's death was not accidental. There's no proof of that, but let's just pretend and go on from there. Let's look at what was done to catch the murderer.

"Sheriff Bello did not suspect a crime so he did not make a record of the license plates of the vehicles that were pulled out of the mud. He didn't take note of who all piled into Bram Serian's car and drove it to the train station to go back to Manhattan. He didn't even know it was Bram Serian's car. And later he didn't once think to ask what had happened to Bram Serian's car.

"What *did* the sheriff do? What did his murder investigation consist of? Days later he went out and kicked around looking for tire tracks and cigarette butts. Tire tracks and cigarette butts! In an area that had been driven over by fire trucks, police vehicles, and curious neighbors ... An area that was turned into a sea of mud after Serian's death from the water poured onto the fire.

"The sheriff's own deputy heard traffic on the road at two-ten and three-fifty-seven, but that was never investigated. That was never even considered.

"He sent a team of men out to search Arcadia and gather evidence against Lenore, but no one looked at the rings of keys hanging in plain sight by the back door. No one examined those rings to see if a key to the studio was missing from one of those rings and if so could that ring yield some fingerprints.

"And what about that key to the studio? The one Sheriff Bello pulled out of the door the morning of the fire. The one with Sheriff Bello's big fat thumbprint on it. Did he ever try to figure out where that key came from, and why it was separate when Bram Serian kept all his keys in sets, and whether it was a copy from a hardware store or an original key to the lock? Did he ever try to learn anything about the origin of that key at all? No!

"And why is it that Vincent Bello conducted such a

shoddy investigation? Is he incompetent? Possibly. The sheriff did not realize he had a questionable death on his hands. Then, when he did realize what a mistake he'd made, he took the easy way out. He looked for the easiest possible suspect.

"He didn't want all the bad publicity of having an unsolved celebrity death and questions about the quality of his policework. And there was the housekeeper, Natalie Raven, screaming that the widow did it. Calling his office every day to scream that the widow did it. And there was the widow, a pretty darn good choice of suspect because she had no important family or friends to get mad if she was charged, and she was different . . . she was an outsider . . . she was the perfect scapegoat.

"And the press loved it! Sheriff Bello was the media's hero for charging Lenore with her husband's death."

Rossner paused.

"Now let's look at what the sheriff would have seen if he'd opened his eyes and truly investigated this thing. Let's look at the party that night. We've got Natalie Raven, who was jealous and possessive of her employer, having to watch him happily in the company of people who were far more important to him than she was. We've got Brother James Collier, who was no doubt humiliated by his own behavior and possibly blaming Serian for it. And we've got various characters like Lance Zabel, who liked to follow Lenore Serian around and spy on her, and Dar Quintana, who wanted to be Bram Serian's special friend. Then we've got an unknown man talking to Bram Serian in the dark, outside the circle of the party, just a short time before Serian was killed.

"Ladies and gentlemen, I ask you. Even one who is untrained in law enforcement can see the possibilities there. And that does not even take into account the cars that Deputy Havlik's dogs responded to on the road at two-ten and at three-fifty-seven. Which opens up the question of whether the killer might be someone who did not even show himself at the party. Or a party guest who left immediately after the murder but whose absence was not even discovered due to the lack of alertness on the sheriff's part."

Rossner detoured for a drink of water and then came back to talk about the paintings found outside and how that could point to the killer having been a thief who was attempting to steal art and was caught in the act by Serian. He talked about Lenore's burns and how they were completely consistent with her having tried to go in the door to aid her husband.

Charles Rossner paused and lowered his voice to a solemn tone to address the jury about the duty before them. Once again he spoke of the burden of proof and the presumption of innocence. But his emphasis now was on reasonable doubt, and he outlined again all the reasonable doubts that the case presented.

"Bram Serian is dead," he said in conclusion. "Nothing is going to bring him back. Certainly not the punishment of an innocent woman.

"We ... and I mean all of us ... have to be able to step back and say: We don't know what happened. Maybe then Bram Serian's death will be reopened and the real answers will be found.

"The task ahead of you is not an easy one, ladies and gentlemen. It is one of the hardest you may ever face. But remember, as you are deliberating, you are part of a great justice system. And in this system there is no winner or loser. This isn't a contest of the prosecution against the defense. When justice prevails we are all winners.

"Thank you."

Owen and Lenore sat up all night staring into a blazing fire on the hearth in one of the sitting rooms. Neither spoke. Fear sat with them.

To discuss Rossner's summation, they would have had to acknowledge the inconsistencies and untruths it contained. And to do so felt like an invitation to disaster. So they held on to each other, silently, desperately, and waited for morning.

Spencer Brown strode confidently into position at the podium the next morning with a handful of typed pages. He arranged the pages and greeted the jury, thanking them for their time and patience.

He told them how much he respected their sacrifice in order to serve on jury duty, and he talked about how trial by jury was the most important legal concept in the history of the nation.

"What you have before you to consider, ladies and gentle-

men, is a body of evidence that together forms a picture of
a murder. As a jury, you will weigh this body of evidence.
You will consider only the evidence that has issued from testimony in that witness chair and only the official exhibits
that have been entered into evidence. You will analyze all
this through use of a systematic process, examining the ways
in which one bit of evidence compliments another and leads
toward the final conclusion. And how will you reach that final conclusion? Through your common sense, ladies and
gentlemen. There's no mystery about arriving at a verdict.
All that's needed is common sense."

Brown then presented the case, rebutting Rossner's points
as he went. In spite of Spencer Brown's convoluted sentences, the picture he painted was simple and logical.

Bram Serian wanted a divorce. Lenore Serian was a clinging, antisocial agoraphobic who could not face being cast
out of her comfortable nest to fend for herself.

She bought the lamp and the oil weeks ahead of the party,
certain that she could talk her husband into putting it in his
studio so that then she would have a sure way to start a fire
and make it appear accidental. Fire was a natural medium
for her as she had always been fascinated by fire and by
burning things.

She chose the night of the party precisely because it was
chaotic and there was less chance of anyone questioning
what had happened. Also, she had probably counted on her
husband's overindulgence in alcohol during the course of the
party, knowing he would be easier to surprise and strike over
the head while in such a state. The party was her camouflage
and the only occasion when she knew that Natalie Raven's
attention would be diverted.

She struck her husband on the head with the axe, intending only to render him unconscious so that the fire could kill
him; then she broke the lamp beside him to make it appear
accidental. She probably intended to carry out more than the
three pictures found against the tree, but the speed and force
of the oil-driven fire overpowered her. She burned herself
and was stunned by her own handiwork. It was at this point
that Natalie Raven spotted her and spread the alarm, inter-
rupting Lenore Serian's plan.

Mrs. Serian did not have time then to close the door and
remove the key. Or to hide the paintings. So she simply
stood there and tried to appear innocent.

Brown talked about how easy it was for a glib defense attorney to pick apart a witness's testimony, but cautioned the jury not to be fooled by these tactics. He talked about how easy it was to ridicule the facts of the case if you separated them and examined them individually, but he explained that in this sort of a case the facts were not meant to be taken separately. They were meant to be examined as a body.

He told the jury that a circumstantial case was just as strong if not stronger than a case resting entirely on direct testimony. He then went through a step-by-step rendering of how the events on the night and morning of Serian's death proceeded, and he defended the law enforcement involved, saying they were looking at the evidence and at the circumstances and they were using their God-given common sense. He ridiculed Rossner's many versions of events.

At 1:45, when everyone in the room was growing restless, Brown said, "You have a clear body of evidence to consider, ladies and gentlemen. Use your common sense. Don't be swayed by distractions and sleight of hand and glib talk. The defendant has shown no remorse and no contrition. Don't let her walk away from this deed unpunished. On behalf of the people of the State of New York, I ask you to return the only fair and logical verdict possible . . . I ask you to find the defendant guilty as charged."

After a short lunch break, everyone was back in place, though the spectator section had thinned considerably now that the dramatics of the summations were over.

Judge Pulaski called for the jury to enter.

"Ladies and gentlemen," he told them, "you are playing a part in a great and honorable legal tradition. I congratulate you all. I respect and admire you for your patient, conscientious service and your hard work. Because serving on a jury is hard work. It requires dedication, perseverance and the most agonizing attention to detail and to procedure.

"Now you retire to the jury room for the ultimate test of your mettle—to decide this defendant's fate. Think of the task before you! Think what it means! You twelve, strangers before sitting down together in that box, now go to grapple with the ultimate questions.

"I shall now give you the jury charge . . . your instructions . . ." whereupon Pulaski turned to the pages in front of him that were the result of the interminable jury

charge discussion from days before, and he began to read in
the driest imaginable monotone. "A jury must go through a
highly disciplined process . . ."

On and on he droned. Now and then a sentence or two
struck Owen: Each of you must take your own path. You
don't have to agree to everything, but you have to agree on
the material facts. Employ your common sense. Every decision made must be arrived at through logical reasoning
though you may take different inferential paths. You may
not consider that which has been stricken from the record or
not admitted to evidence.

Owen watched the jury straining to understand, straining
to keep their attention focused, and finally, after an hour,
straining to keep their eyes open.

Finally, the judge read to them about reasonable doubt.
"In order to arrive at your verdict, you must employ the concept of reasonable doubt. A reasonable doubt is a doubt
which you can cite a reason for both to yourself and to your
fellow jurors. To find the defendant guilty, each of you must
be convinced of her guilt beyond a reasonable doubt. In
other words, you must have no reasonable doubt left in your
mind."

Reasonable doubt. Rossner had apparently lost in his bid
for moral certainty. Owen watched the jurors' faces and
prayed that they understood the concept. Prayed that they
were riddled with doubts.

Then the jury filed out to begin deliberations and the
courtroom relaxed. The remaining spectators trickled away.
Spencer Brown leaned on the wooden railing and told Holly
Danielson something that made her laugh. Owen clenched
his jaw and tried to ignore them.

Up in the front a court clerk stepped up to the judge and
handed him a folded slip of paper. Everyone came to attention.

"I have a note from the jury," the judge announced. "They
are requesting a written copy of the jury instructions, or a rereading of certain portions of the instructions."

Rossner responded immediately, saying, "I think we
should provide them with the document, your honor."

Brown stood up to disagree, and an obtuse argument began. Owen tried to imagine the jury sitting around the table
in the cramped deliberation room, expecting an immediate

answer. Little did they know what haggling their simple request had spawned.

Jacowitz had been right, the waiting was the worst part. Everyone drifted aimlessly. The reporters went in and out of the room, running downstairs to gossip and drink coffee near the vending machines, then running back up to check on things. Both Rossner and Brown relaxed. The judge wished one of the court officers happy birthday, then began discussing his vacation plans again. Only Lenore stayed quietly in her seat.

Two more notes came out from the jury. They wanted to see the diagrams of the studio floor plan. The poster was sent in to them with a written note from the judge explaining that any exhibits they requested would have to be returned to the custody of the court each night when they adjourned. The judge read the note aloud before sending it in to them.

Owen was hunched over, deep in his own distress, when he sensed visitors. He looked up to see that Marilyn and Pat had moved into the pew in back of him and were leaning forward to speak.

"We're really sorry . . ." Pat began. "We had no idea Holly was going to pull that."

"It was a shock to us too," Marilyn confirmed. "We just wanted you to know that we had nothing to do with it."

"I knew she was ambitious." Pat shook her head. "But I never dreamed . . ."

"It wasn't just ambition," Marilyn said, with a knowing expression. "Owen probably understands better than any of us what a person can find themselves doing, right, Owen? Anyway, we just wanted to let you know . . . we're not the enemy."

"Thanks," Owen told them.

Marilyn grinned devilishly. "You wouldn't have a statement you'd like to make to the press, would you?"

28

The second day of deliberation dragged on even slower than the first. Occasionally, the jury asked for a particular bit of testimony to be read back to them, and there was a flurry of activity as they were escorted back into the jury box and the court reporter read to them in his own unique singsong. The question of the written instructions had finally been resolved and a copy had been sent in to them. Owen wondered if it was helping or hurting Lenore's chances.

Jacowitz told Lenore that she was allowed to wait in the hotel room if she chose, but she refused and remained in her seat at the defense table. Owen alternated between periods when he had to keep moving and periods when he was almost somnolent. There was no true relief. He could not concentrate well enough to read a book, and he was not interested in newspapers. Riley gave him a crossword puzzle, but he could not make himself care what the two-letter word for beast of burden was. Finally, Jacowitz handed him a stack of typed-out trial transcripts.

"Here," he told Owen. "Read this. Make some notes for your book or something."

Owen took it as a joke but found himself quickly engrossed. In reading the testimony, it was possible to notice little things he had missed while it was happening. He finished the section on James Collier and found that his thoughts were once again on the mystery, rather than on Lenore's plight. It was possible that he would never know the whole truth, that there would never be a resolution, and the realization of that festered inside him.

Had Bram Serian died by accident? No. Owen could not accept that a man as powerful and charismatic and cruel as Bram Serian—a man who was loved and hated to such extremes—could die such a simple, almost foolish death.

His inner voice was certain Bram Serian had been murdered. But by whom? Could it have been the man Bram Serian was talking to back in the dark by the food tables? Was it the killer James Collier saw Bram with that night?

A chill spread down Owen's spine. If that was true, then Lenore had also seen him, because Lenore had been out there in the dark that night too, watching Bram from the trees. Suddenly Owen sat bolt upright.

Lenore! God, he had been so blind. Lenore *had* been protecting someone! He had felt that before but discounted it when he learned the truth about Collier. Now he knew it was true. Lenore had watched Bram meet with his killer. She might have even seen him again when she followed Bram to the studio. And Lenore had been shielding that killer from all of them.

That night, safely inside the privacy of Arcadia, Owen asked her, "Who wrote the shopping order for the lamp, Lenore?" She hesitated a moment. "Bram gave it to me. He wrote it and asked me to get it for him because he said he didn't want to ask Natalie."

Owen considered the information. "Do you ever think about who killed Bram? About what happened in the studio that night?"

"No," she answered sharply.

"Why not? Are you so convinced it was an accident?"

"I don't want to talk about it, Owen."

"Well, I do, Lenore. I think I've finally got this thing figured out."

She jumped up and started out of the room, but he caught her arm. "Talk to me, Lenore. Who was it that you saw Bram with that night? Who was out there in the dark waiting for him?"

Her face was still, devoid of expression, but tears welled up in her eyes and fell down her cheeks. It pierced his heart to see her cry, this woman who never allowed herself tears. Who never allowed herself weakness.

"Lenore . . . who could be so important to you? Who are you protecting?"

But then he knew. And the last of the puzzle slipped gently into place.

"It was Al, wasn't it? Al came back that night. And what you told me about overhearing an argument between Bram and Al that made you suspect Al was your father . . . that

was when you overheard it. Right? You didn't hear them
talking about you before Al left. You didn't suspect Al was
your father then. You didn't suspect it until that night. That
very night.

"I'm right, aren't I?"

Her nod was almost imperceptible.

"Did you confront Bram when you caught up with him on
the way to the studio? Is that the argument people heard?"

"No. I didn't confront him because I knew he wouldn't
tell me the truth. I was going to wait and ask Al."

"What were you arguing about, then?"

"Bram admitted to me that he had been in contact with Al
for months and was trying to lure him back. His plan was to
lock Al in the studio again and give him his medicine by
force. He wanted me to help. I told him no. And I told him
I wouldn't let him keep Al a prisoner again."

"What happened then?"

"Al was supposed to meet Bram at the studio, but he
didn't. Bram said I had probably scared him away. That he
was out there in the trees somewhere watching and that I
should go in the house and I could see Al the next day, after
everybody was gone.

"I thought then about screaming. Running out through the
trees and shouting for Al to get away, so that Bram wouldn't
catch him. But I was afraid if I did that Al would run away
again and disappear, and I'd never get to ask if he was my
father."

"Did you see Al go into the studio?"

"No. To coax Al out of the trees Bram went into the studio and turned off all the yard lights, making it impossible
to see the studio door from the house. I was in the kitchen,
waiting. I had told Bram I would go to bed but I didn't. I
was determined to go there as soon as I was sure Al was inside. I waited a long time without seeing anything. Then I
must have dozed off for a while because suddenly I sat up
and I could see that the studio door was standing open.
There was a brightness coming from inside it.

"I ran out. And that's when I found the fire."

"And Al was already gone?"

She nodded.

Owen inhaled deeply and searched her eyes. "So there
was more to your not being able to accept the idea of Al as
your father ... more than the fact that he was a troubled

man who had never shown any love to you in the years you knew him at Arcadia. There was more to your denial ... wasn't there? You were desperate to believe someone else was your father because if it was Al that meant he had abandoned you all over again by leaving you to stand trial in his place for murder."

She folded then and would have sunk to the floor if Owen hadn't caught her. He held her tightly against him, wanting to shut out everything. The need to protect her was so strong that it filled him with a primal ferocity.

"Why? Why did you keep silent? How could he be worth destroying your life?"

"I couldn't turn him in," she whispered. "Not when there was even a remote chance ... And now that I know for sure ... how can I destroy the man my mother loved?"

Owen hugged even harder. "If you're convicted, I won't keep silent," he warned her. "I can't keep silent. I'll tell them the truth."

Saturday was the third day of deliberations. The atmosphere managed to be both lazy and tense. Both attorneys socialized widely, discussing the case and telling entertaining tales from previous cases. The judge worked at a laptop computer on the bench. All over the courthouse, people lounged around, reading, playing cards, knitting, drawing, writing letters. Anything to pass the time. Owen confined himself to the second floor, both to be close to Lenore, who still insisted on sitting at the defense table, and to avoid Holly, who was holding court near the vending machines downstairs.

At 11:20, the jury sent out note number 17, asking to hear Sheriff Bello's testimony again.

Dapolito groaned loudly. "What's wrong, Tony?" Spencer Brown asked him.

"I was hoping for a verdict before lunch recess. I'm sick of eating pizza."

Lunch breaks had been so short that everyone had been ordering pizzas. At noon the entire courthouse would smell like an Italian restaurant.

The jury came out for the readback of Bello's testimony. A few energetic reporters rushed up to study them while they listened to the readback, trying to tell from jurors' expressions which direction they were leaning.

At 11:48 another note was sent out and Dapolito groaned again. "What now?" several people asked, laughing.

"Now they're going to ask for a long readback that will delay my pizza," Dapolito complained.

The judge read the note, straightened and folded his laptop away. Instantly, everyone in the courtroom tensed. Something was happening.

"We have a verdict," Judge Pulaski said formally.

The principles hurried to their appropriate places. Owen hesitated, wondering where his place was, then moved to the front beside Jacowitz and behind Lenore. He touched her shoulder, and she turned to look at him. There was fear in her eyes.

Within five minutes, everyone in the entire courthouse, including county employees on their lunch breaks, had crowded into courtroom 6 to see the finale. The jury filed out and took their seats, glancing around nervously.

Rossner and Lenore stood as the jury was entering, so there was no need for the judge to ask the defendant to rise. Owen saw Rossner lock his hand under her elbow. "Remember," Rossner whispered, "if the worst happens . . . there are appeals . . . there are things we can do."

The court clerk made an official record, noting that all the jury members were present.

"Have you reached a verdict?" Judge Pulaski asked solemnly.

The jury foreman, a thin elderly man, rose and said, "We have, your honor." As he spoke he leaned forward to grip the railing around the jury box as if afraid he might fall out.

"How do you find the defendant?"

"Your honor, we find the defendant Not Guilty."

For a heartbeat there was absolute silence. Then a wall of sound descended. Lenore stood like a statue. Rossner hugged her. Jacowitz leaned across the rail and hugged her. Volpe and Riley hugged her.

"Am I free?" she asked in a stunned whisper, and everyone laughed. Only Owen understood.

Later—after the judge and both attorneys had given thank-you speeches to the jury, after Lenore had refused to participate in the press conference that Brown, Rossner, and all the jurors were going to speak at, after they had run the gauntlet of reporters to escape the building, stopping only long enough for Owen to favor Marilyn and Pat with a statement on Lenore's behalf, "This has been a nightmare, but the truth won out," and after Lenore had told Joe Volpe he could throw away the cape for good—they drove straight to Arcadia. That night there was to be a celebration dinner in Manhattan with Rossner and his wife, Jacowitz, Volpe, Riley and Riley's wife.

Carefully, Owen brought up the idea of staying in Manhattan after the dinner. Lenore frowned at him as though the suggestion was irresponsible.

"Why not, Lenore? What's keeping you at Arcadia now? Why don't we throw my work and a few of your clothes into the car and stay in Manhattan as long as we like? Think of it as a vacation."

She continued to stare at him, but he could see the idea catching hold in her mind. "Do you think I should?"

"Damn right I do. We'll eat great food and see some sights. And you can get a taste of being an independent city woman."

She laughed but he could tell she was apprehensive. "You know, Owen, Bram never took me to Manhattan. No one did. That night with you is the only time I've been."

"Hey, you think I'm a native? If I can handle the city, anyone can."

"But staying . . ." She put her hand to her mouth and regarded him nervously. "I've never spent a night away from Arcadia. Not since I was taken there."

"That settles it. The apartment in Manhattan is not Arcadia's city equivalent, but that is where you're sleeping with me tonight. Discussion closed."

Lenore called Geneva Johnson, Françoise Newman, and James Collier to give them the news in case they hadn't heard. The next day Geneva Johnson came knocking at the apartment door.

Lenore was asleep, so Owen admitted Geneva and they spoke in whispers. "I came to take her out to lunch. To celebrate," Geneva explained.

"We celebrated all night," Owen admitted. "That's why she's still asleep."

Geneva took a seat at the table. "Just what do you think you're doing, Owen? How do you imagine this is going to work out?"

He looked over at Lenore. She was on her side with her hair snaking out behind her in a long braid. Her face was peaceful. Sleeping beauty. How perfectly that fit her. Locked away in a gloomy castle until now.

"Geneva, she loves you. And I know you love her. I'm not trying to belittle that at all. But you may not know what's right for her."

Geneva's nostrils flared in anger. "That girl has been so fucked up . . . She needs a team of therapists and ten years of living in the real world before she could possibly be strong enough for a relationship with a man. Can't you see that?"

"She doesn't have to be strong with me. I can protect her, guide her, help her learn. Who else can do that for her? Who else can she trust as completely as she can trust me?"

"That's just the problem. You're going to become everything to her. Teacher, friend, lover. Then what happens when you want out? You think she'll be a modern gal by then and shrug it off? No! Talk about wreckage. You'll completely destroy her. And the only way to prevent that is to cut her free now before you pull her any deeper."

"What about how deep *I* am? What do I do about that?"

That afternoon Owen was alone in the apartment. Geneva had taken Lenore out for lunch and for what Geneva called "a female look at the city." Owen buried himself in his work, organizing the huge volume of material he had and trying to see how he could shape it into a book. The hours passed. It was Sunday so he wouldn't be calling Bernie. But he felt the urge to call someone.

He went downstairs to the corner pay phone. First he called Milly Corwin and told her about the verdict. Then he called his home.

Ellen answered.

"Hello, sis. How are things?"

"Okay. Everybody went up to see Rusty's parents, so I've got the house to myself."

"Have you seen anything on the news about the verdict?"

"What verdict?"

"In the murder trial I've been working on."

"Oh . . . no. Why, is it over?"

"Yesterday. They found her innocent."

"Oh. Is that good or bad for your book?"

"It's good for her and that's all I care about."

"Ummm. Say, why didn't you tell me you broke up with Mike? I can't believe you never said a word. She's a real mess over it."

"I'm sorry to hear that."

"I knew you would be. Knowing you you'll go soft and make up with her as soon as you come home."

He stared at the battered face of the pay phone. "I'm not coming home, Ellen. At least not for a while. And when I do it will only be to visit."

She was silent for a moment. "Well, I hope you know what you're doing, Owen."

"I think I do."

She began to cry. "Stop that," he said gently. "You're going to leave and make a life for yourself too, remember?"

"I know. It's just so sad. Things will never be the same. We'll never be a family again."

"I think we stopped being a family when Mom died, Ellen. She was what made us a family."

"Do you want me to tell Daddy you're not coming back?"

"Sure. Go ahead. I doubt he'll say much."

"He was wrong to do what he did to you, Owen."

"Maybe. But I'm beginning to think he did me a hell of a favor. I've been saved, Ellen. I'll never turn into Clancy. Or Gus. I'll never be the king, and I'm damn glad of it."

"What?"

"Never mind. It's not important. I've got some things in boxes in the bunkhouse. Would you mind sending them when I get settled?"

"Course not."

"When my book money comes in, I'll have tuition money for you, Ellen. And a plane ticket to New York."

"What!"

"You're coming to visit me. You've got a great big city to meet. And a person to meet too."

"What?"

"That's all I'm saying for now. I love you, sis. Hang in there."

He went back upstairs to work and became so absorbed that he didn't realize the hour. Outside the window there was a brief twilight and then the half-darkness of the city settled in. He stretched the kinks from his back, heated cold coffee and wandered about the room.

He picked up the pillow that Lenore had slept on. It smelled faintly of jasmine. He buried his face in it and breathed deeply.

He had read that the brain and possibly even the chromosomes changed with each skill mastered. That brain tissue after learning language was physiologically different from tissue before language, and that the same was true for crawling and walking and reading and bicycle riding. Every new step engraved forever inside us. Was the same true for love?

He squatted down to open Lenore's suitcase. Again there was the subtle fragrance of jasmine and something else more exotic. He recognized some of the clothes as things she had worn at Arcadia and wondered if they were favorites of hers. There were so many things he didn't know about her. So many details to fill in. He closed the case and opened her smaller bag. It held shampoo and lotion, hairbrush and toothbrush. The jasmine scent was heady. He sat there on the floor, drinking his stale coffee and touching her things and inhaling the jasmine.

Where would she lead him now, he wondered. Would they search for her lost father? Would she ever be able to put it all behind her?

"What are you doing?" Geneva asked when she came through the door. She was carrying a large shopping bag.

"Where's Lenore?" he asked, jumping to his feet.

"Just cool it. She has a surprise for you. Are you ready?"

"Sure."

Geneva stepped away from the door, held out her hand and said, "Ta-da!" and Lenore walked in, self-conscious but with an excited smile. Her obsidian hair was cut to chin length.

Owen's mouth fell open. "Your hair! How could you do that?"

Lenore's face crumpled and she ran for the bathroom. Geneva slammed the front door shut and whacked Owen in the chest.

"That was brilliant," she said. "A great start in your healing program."

"Damn it," Owen whispered, "it was a shock. I thought her hair was important to her."

"No, it wasn't. Serian just never allowed her to cut it. He

liked for her to look like a 'native.' Cutting it was her big statement of independence."

"Oh, God . . ."

There was an explosion of breaking glass and Owen raced to the bathroom with Geneva behind him. The knob lock didn't work well, and the door crashed open with one good shoulder strike.

"Lenore!"

She was kneeling on the floor sweeping up shards of broken mirror with her bare hands. Blood spotted the white tile and dripped from her fingers. "I'm sorry," she said, dropping a handful of glass in the wastebasket, oblivious to the damage she was doing to herself.

Owen pulled her up and Geneva turned on the cold water at the sink and he held both her hands under it.

Owen dried her hands as gently as he could and wrapped clean towels around them. Geneva left to buy bandages and disinfectant, and Owen walked Lenore to the couch, holding her tightly against him for fear of something else happening. But she was docile and settled quietly with her toweled hands in her lap.

"I need to go home," she said.

"Home?"

Her head snapped around and her eyes narrowed to slits. "Yes. I do still have a home."

"Lenore," he said, gathering her into his arms, ignoring her stiffness. He pressed his cheek against her temple. "Lenore . . . we have so much to learn about each other and we're both going to make mistakes. I didn't mean to hurt you. You can shave your head if you want. It was just a surprise, that's all."

Gradually, he felt the tension drain from her body.

"I didn't mean to break your mirror," she said. "I just saw my face in it and I couldn't stand to look at myself, and the next thing I knew . . . it was smashed."

"Why? Why couldn't you stand to look at yourself?"

"Because . . . my face still has ghosts in it. Being here with you . . . being free in Manhattan . . . cutting off Serian's hair . . . nothing takes the ghosts away."

29

For three days after the incident with the mirror, Lenore did not want to see other people, so they stayed in the apartment, ordering food in and making love. Owen had an awareness of her that was almost painful in its intensity. He never tired of watching her, feeling almost as if he could see through her skin, see into her heart and her bones and the racing rivers of her blood. Yet for all that, she was ever a mystery to him. Ever a wonder.

Sometimes he felt her watching him in return. Studying him. Once he heard her breathing stop, then start, then stop again. "What is it?" he asked, and she frowned a little. "I'm trying to breathe with you."

After three days, he told her that he had to get out, and he coaxed her downstairs into glorious spring weather. They walked for hours, from the East Village to the West Village and then up to the Twenties for a Caribbean lunch at Vernon's Jerk Paradise. Food was never so good. Weather was never so beautiful. The purple and yellow of crocuses were never so miraculous.

They rode the subway up to Fifty-ninth and Fifth, where the Plaza Hotel was in its glory with the fountain restored and the flags flying. Horse-drawn carriages lined the drive into Central Park, and street performers played to knots of tourists in the sunshine. Lenore took it all in, asking questions, soaking in the city as though thirsty for every detail of it.

They walked across to Grand Army Plaza and she stared up at the gilded statue. Owen read the sculptor's name for her.

"Saint-Gaudens," she whispered reverently. "I've seen pictures of his work in Bram's art books. I'd like to find out more about him."

"As soon as you've mastered reading, you might want to

take some classes," Owen suggested. "I've read that they have wonderful classes at the museums. Or you could take some courses at one of the colleges around here."

"Can I do that without a birth certificate?"

"I'm sure you can. But these legal questions have to be settled once and for all, Lenore. You have to speak to the attorneys about your concerns. With the number of years you've been here and the fact that you were legally married to an American, I'm certain that it will be a simple matter to establish your citizenship."

She hesitated. "These lawyers ... they worked for Bram and now they work for the estate. I don't think they like me."

"It's not their business to like you."

"No. I mean ... I think Bram set it up so that they're working against me. His will assumed that Al would be around to inherit, you know."

"Lenore, I don't know a thing about how estate law works. But I do know this. You need someone on your side. Call Charlie Rossner and ask him to refer you to someone you can trust."

"I still have plenty of cash from that money in the safe."

"Yes," Owen said, "and there's some left from the stack you gave to me."

"I don't need it back."

"That's not the point. It's yours, not mine."

"All that cash ... shouldn't that be enough money for me? Why do I need more from the estate?"

"I'm not following you."

"Why do I have to go through all of it with the lawyers and accountants? Why can't I just tell them I don't want anything and to leave me alone."

"Lenore ... I don't want to get involved in this, but just promise me that you won't do anything ... anything ... until you've found your own attorney and listened to his or her advice. Promise?"

"I promise. But I don't want Arcadia and I don't want Bram's things."

"Fine. So donate it all to an art foundation."

"Can I do something like that?"

"I really don't know. The answer is to get a lawyer and find out."

The question of Lenore's finances disturbed Owen because he knew she wasn't equipped to deal with the system herself, but he was determined not to get involved. He wanted Lenore's business to be completely her own.

They headed into the park, wandered past the boathouse and stopped to watch children climb on the Alice in Wonderland bronze. Lenore took his arm and pressed her cheek against his shoulder, and a wave of emotion swept him. He felt both tender and savage, weak and strong, protector and ravager—both more and less than he had ever been.

They reached the Poets' Walk, and he realized they had spent nearly an hour in silence. Suddenly, he was anxious over her thoughts.

"Are you worried about meeting Bernie and Alex?" he asked. Earlier he had persuaded her to let him accept a dinner invitation from Bernie for later that evening.

"Yes," she admitted. "But that's not what I'm thinking about."

"What are you thinking?" he asked.

She had been studying the poets' busts, and she turned to look at him. Her hair swung around her face like black liquid silk, hanging slightly over one eye from a side part. And as she turned she smiled, taking his breath away.

"Do you tell me all your thoughts?" she asked lightly.

"Well . . ."

"Thoughts don't matter," she said. "Only what we do is important."

"Schoolyard wisdom?" he teased gently.

Her smile turned faintly sad. "You forget, I've never been in a schoolyard. No, this is a lesson I learned from Bram Serian. You see he had very kind thoughts. Very decent thoughts. He was devoted to his brother and he was determined to give me a proper life and he loved Geneva, and all he really wanted was to be left alone to do his art and create his Arcadia. But he hurt us all over and over again. It didn't matter what his intentions were. It didn't matter what his thoughts were."

"Maybe his thoughts weren't so kind," Owen remarked.

She raised the dark wing of an eyebrow in question.

"I'm not sure his intentions were that good," Owen insisted. "I think he kept Al imprisoned partly because he couldn't stand the thought of his brother leaving him. I think he married you to hold on to you and thereby control his brother. I think he was kind to Geneva only to control her.

And I think he befriended James Collier and led him on as a test of the man's faith . . . a game."

She was very quiet.

"I'm sorry. I didn't mean to get so depressing."

She took his hand. "Let's talk about something else."

"Okay . . . let's get back to discussing bad thoughts," he teased suggestively.

"Do you have bad thoughts?" she asked.

"Ummmm, I feel one coming on right now."

Her lips curved into a lazy sensual smile. "Good," she said. "Let's go home."

The next morning, Owen awoke with a need to get back to work. During their dinner the night before, Bernie had been full of enthusiasm about the book, and she had infected him with it. DeMille had finally agreed to a big advance figure and had accepted his vision of the book as the mystery and tragedy of Bram Serian's life rather than just the sensational end he met.

Owen fidgeted through breakfast trying to come up with a tactful way to explain it to Lenore.

"What's wrong?" she finally asked. "Are you tired of being with me?"

"No! Absolutely not. I just have to get back to work."

She sighed and rested her chin on her palm. "I wish I had something that meant as much to me as your writing does to you."

"Oh, Lenore, you have so much ahead of you. You're going to be on fire with it. All the new things to do and see . . . all the books you haven't read and the places you haven't been . . . God, what a fantastic adventure you've got before you. I just hope you don't leave me behind."

She laughed.

"Okay," he said. "This is what we'll do. I'll work till noon. You go down and explore a little on your own. No, don't look so horror-stricken. You can do it. Just learn a block at a time. Then I'll break and we'll have lunch and we'll head out for a bookstore with a good children's section. Because you are going to start learning to read. In fact, our goal is that by the time I've finished the book, you will be able to read it and help me edit it."

A shadow smile curved the corners of her mouth. "Yes,"

she said thoughtfully. "Cutting my hair didn't work, but maybe learning to read will."

Owen didn't have to ask what she meant. He knew. She was still trying to drive away Bram Serian's ghost. Even here in this strange apartment she listened for Serian's voice and his footsteps, and at times swore she heard them.

They settled into a routine in which Owen made breakfast and they ate together; then he worked on his book while she spent the morning with earphones, tapes, and a workbook, laboring over the alphabet and the combined letter sounds. She furnished lunch by going down for take-out food. Then, in the afternoon, Owen again hunched over his work, and Lenore, at Owen's insistence, went off to explore on her own, stretching her confidence by blocks each day.

At five, no matter how engrossed he was, he put his work aside. Each night was an adventure. They explored restaurants. They strolled across the Brooklyn Bridge. They went to a play. They went to bookstores so she could show off and read him titles. They saw movies and went to jazz clubs. And then they went back to the apartment to explore each other.

There were still moments when she turned suddenly cool or said something enigmatic or drifted into one of her mysterious inward trances and the tiny darts of uncertainty would strike Owen. But he kept them to himself.

A month passed. Charlie Rossner gave Lenore a referral to an attorney, and Owen finally convinced her to go for a meeting. When she returned in the afternoon, she seemed restless but happy.

"How did it go?" Owen asked her.

She flashed him a mischievous look. "The lawyer told me I shouldn't be so trusting of you and I should have a written agreement with you about what you're allowed to use in your book."

"Great. Did you tell him I was the one who insisted you hire him?"

"Her," she said. "My new attorney is a her. Claudia Lai."

"An Asian woman?"

"Yes. And *very* smart."

Owen smiled, thinking that Charlie Rossner was indeed a genius. He had known exactly what Lenore needed—a strong role model. "She may be very smart about everything else," he said, "but she doesn't know a thing about me."

Lenore smiled one of her mysterious smiles, turned away from him and began putting things in the suitcase.

"What are you doing," he asked, with his heart suddenly in his throat.

"Don't worry. Claudia wants me to go out to Arcadia for a few days and make an inventory for our side. I'm supposed to buy one of those instant cameras and a case of film, and photograph the rooms and the art." She crossed to the closet to gather more of her things. "I don't want you to stop working. Claudia gave me the number of a car service that will take me out."

She was taking too much. Far more than she needed for a few days. Especially considering that she was going back to her own home which was still filled with her possessions.

"No problem," he said, reaching for the phone. "My work is portable. We'll rent a car and go up together."

He couldn't see her face because she was turned away, but he saw the hesitation, saw her go very still for a moment.

"The change of scene will do me good," he said quickly. "And what better place is there than Arcadia to write about Bram Serian?"

The rental agency answered and he began making the arrangements. She turned her head to look at him and he could not read her expression at all, but nevertheless it chilled him.

It was late by the time they arrived at Arcadia. She helped him set up a work space in a pleasant room with both a window and a small fireplace, and he spent the balance of the evening arranging his books and boxes of files. When he was finished, he wandered through the house and found her in the central living room. She was staring into a roaring fire.

"Fireplace season is almost over," he said from the doorway.

She jumped. "Oh, Owen . . . I didn't hear you coming."

"Sorry." He crossed the large open space and sat down beside her. Near her feet he saw the butt of the shotgun sticking out from beneath the sofa. "Kind of jumpy tonight, huh?"

"There's been someone here while I was gone," she said flatly.

"How can that be?" he said in his most soothing, reasonable tone. "This place has a more elaborate alarm system than the White House. Nobody could get in here undetected."

She hugged herself and concentrated on the fire.

"Okay ... maybe it was Bram's attorneys. Or someone from the alarm company."

She shook her head no. "I called. No one's been out."

He looked around the room. "Is there something missing?"

"It's hard to explain, but you know how when you've been living alone you have an exact sense of things. How you put the dishes away and how you left the window blinds and how big the bar of soap was beside the sink. Well ... things are different."

He put his arm around her shoulders. "You were just coming out of a terrible ordeal when you were last here. And I was with you. I could have changed things without you noticing, and now that you're back and relaxed you're seeing things differently."

She sighed and leaned her head against him. "I have to do more than just take photographs here. Claudia found out a lot for me. Everything is tangled and she says that with the assets involved and with Al missing, it could drag on and on. Bram's will had Al as the primary heir.

"I told Claudia that I couldn't live out here anymore, so she's making arrangements for me to move into Bram's loft for a while. I've never been inside a loft, have you?" She tilted her head to look up at him.

"No. I've never been in a loft." There was a growing weight of fear in his belly, and he wanted to ask what it all meant. Was moving into the loft her way of leaving him? But he couldn't ask. He was afraid of the answers. And afraid that putting his fears into words would make them come true.

"So," she said, "I also have to sort through things and decide what to take with me and what to leave behind."

"I'll help," he offered immediately.

"No. You have to work. And I have to do this on my own."

"Okay. Then I'll stay in my little room and you go on ahead with whatever you need to do. Unless ... do you want me to leave? Am I smothering you?"

She gripped his shirt, twisting the cloth in her hand. "I didn't want you to come," she said. "I wanted to do this alone. To prove to myself that I could. But now that you're here, I'm glad."

He held her tightly, kissed her neck and her ear and her closed eyelids, and felt the stirring response in her body. But abruptly she pulled back.

"No," she whispered. "Not here." And led him to a narrow windowless bedroom in the south wing.

"This was built for a very famous artist with a bad cocaine problem," she explained. "The drug made him paranoid so Bram fixed this up for him with a steel door and a bolt lock."

Owen looked into the attached bathroom and saw that it too lacked windows.

"Bram called it the fraidy cave because he said it reminded him of a tornado shelter."

Owen laughed and told her about the fraidy cave of his own experience, but he was more than a little disconcerted by her fear of being watched. She slid the bolt into place on the door.

"I guess we're in here for the night," he said.

"I'll make it so you never want to leave," she promised, unbuttoning her blouse with a slow smile.

There was no clock in the room so he didn't know what time it was when Lenore screamed. He bolted upright in the pitch darkness, reaching for her with his heart slamming into his ribs.

She was trembling and confused.

"Did you hear it? Did you hear him trying to get through the door? Oh no . . . no . . . I left the gun. I don't have the gun."

"It was just a bad dream," Owen whispered, pulling her down to lie in his arms.

He stroked her back lightly and listened to her breathing slow until finally he thought she had fallen back to sleep.

Suddenly she whispered in the darkness, "It's Bram's ghost. He knows I'm packing to leave."

"It was nothing," Owen said firmly. "You were having a nightmare. Now, I'm here and you're safe and not even a ghost can get through that door, so try to go back to sleep."

The next morning she seemed fine. They cooked breakfast together, and Owen retired to his work space. Around one-thirty he got hungry and went out to find that she had taken down paintings from all over the house and propped them up in lines against the wall.

"Are you trying to photograph them in groups?" he asked.

"No. I was . . ." She turned back toward the lineup. "Look at these and tell me what you see."

He studied the canvases. "They're Serians. Representative of several styles."

"Yes." She smiled. "You're learning. Claudia told me to photograph them individually and then to put them in groups according to value. But I don't know the value. And I started wondering what photographs you might want for your book. Should I be taking pictures for you, too?"

"I don't think Polaroids can be used for reproduction," he told her. "But if you made a set for me I could use it later in the selection process."

She was pleased at the thought of helping him, and she seemed very lighthearted over lunch. The ghosts were in abeyance.

They headed out the front door for a walk in the chilly March sunshine. There were already buds on the trees and tiny green shoots poking up through the dense carpet of dead leaves.

"Spring is so beautiful here," Lenore said. "The woods are full of dogwood and around the house there's forsythia and iris and daffodils. Bram let me order all I wanted from the garden catalogs every year."

"Won't you miss it?"

"Yes."

"I guess, in many ways, leaving here will be like breaking the cord to your childhood home."

She nodded. "Over there is where I buried my dog. Just beyond is the playhouse Al built for me. This open space is a baseball diamond when it's mowed. And that big tree by the corner of the house is where my swing used to be."

She asked about Owen's childhood, and he told her about the farm and about the move to the Flint Hills.

"Look at this," she said, stopping suddenly to stare down at a fresh pile of dirt. "Someone has been digging here."

"Or some animal. Dogs or coyotes maybe." He knelt to examine the shallow depression that had been created.

"Whatever it was, it was pretty determined. This ground is still partly frozen."

She hugged herself tightly and peered into the woods.

"Where are we in relation to the house?" he asked, still too much a Kansas boy to retain his sense of direction in the presence of so many trees.

"We're directly in back of the studio, or where the studio used to be, and if it weren't for that stand of cedars we'd be able to see the ruins and on across to the house."

"Would you like to mark the spot so we can check it again in a few days?"

"I don't have to mark it," she said. "Look around. It's a natural clearing. Easy to remember."

Suddenly she turned and ran for the house.

"Lenore!" he called, then gave up and ran after her.

She didn't stop until they were both inside the waterlit foyer.

"What is going on?"

She put her finger to her lips. "Speak softly," she said.

"What?"

"Can't you feel it? We're being watched. We're being listened to."

"I need to get you out of this place. How much is left to photograph?"

"I'll show you what I've done so far," she said and took his hand.

Her boxes of photographs were on the long kitchen table. Owen scanned the collection but could get no sense of how much remained to be done.

"I'll help. Let's finish this up as quickly as possible."

She nodded. Her eyes were darting back and forth, checking the various doorways.

"Come on. Let's go to work."

She picked up the camera and started around the table, then stopped, and turned back. "What did you do with our pictures?"

"Hummm?" he said, picking up the bag of unused film.

"The pictures we took of each other when we first got here."

"I don't have them," he said.

She bent to look under the table. She scanned the rest of the kitchen floor area and the countertops. She picked up each of the boxes and looked beneath them. She rifled

through the boxes of prints, her movements growing more
frantic as she progressed. When she was finished, she
straightened and said, very loudly, "Oh, they probably got
mixed in with some of these others."

Owen looked up at the ceiling as though he might see
whoever she imagined was listening.

"Get the film," she said, even though he was already holding it. "We'll go finish off the north side."

She led him into a short hallway and whispered, "We can
talk here."

"You think the pictures are really gone?" he asked, trying
to keep the disbelief out of his voice.

"I left them sitting right on the end of that table."

"At least you know it's not a ghost," he said lamely, uncertain as to how to defuse her fears. "Ghosts don't steal
photographs and dig holes."

"How do you know what ghosts do?" she demanded.

"Lenore . . ." He tried to put his arms around her but she
stepped back. Her face was drawn into a mask with burning
holes for eyes. "You can't protect me from things you don't
understand, Owen."

"Let's just get this inventory done and get the hell out of
here," he said. "Please."

They worked without saying much to each other, moving
from room to room. Click, flash, whirr and another picture
popped out. Pictures of entire rooms. Pictures of small art
objects. Pictures of stained-glass windows. The stack grew
and they left a trail of empty film boxes behind.

At dinnertime, he didn't want to stop, but she insisted, so
they zapped frozen food in the microwave. She got out candles, linen placemats and matching napkins, setting up the
end of the dining table as though for a formal occasion.

"This could be my last meal here," she said.

It was difficult for him to relax but he tried. Ghosts were
of no concern to Owen, but her mental state was.

"What would you say to packing it in for the night and
driving back to Manhattan. Then we could come back tomorrow and finish in the daylight."

"So you're afraid, too?"

"I'm afraid for you."

She pushed her food around, deep in thought over something. "You never told me how your brother died," she said.

"Terry? Yes, I told you. He was a suicide."

"I know that. But exactly how did he do it?"

Owen stopped eating. "I told you that, too. He drove to this one lone tree way out in the pasture. And he hung himself."

"But, what I want to know is, *how* did he do it. Did he leave a note?"

"No."

"Did you have any warning? When you look back can you see anything that should have warned you?"

"I've asked myself that same thing a hundred times. I was away in college then . . . just finishing my second year. Ellen was married and living in Texas. So neither of us had seen him for a while.

"I was living in an apartment with three other guys, and one day I got a delivery. Two cases of toilet paper. Huge boxes that had to be wheeled in on a dolly. I thought there was some mistake but the delivery man showed me his sheet and they were to me from Terry. One of my roommates reminded me that we'd run out of toilet paper while Terry was visiting and we'd gotten into an argument about who should have to go out and buy it. I'd forgotten completely.

"The whole thing was so funny and odd that I called Ellen to ask what she thought about it, and she said she'd gotten a gift from Terry too. A case of plastic trash bags. We laughed about it and we agreed that, since I had no funds for toll calls, she would phone home that night to find out what the gift occasion was. Then she would call me to let me know.

"When she finally got an answer at the house that night, his body had already been found."

Lenore rested her chin on her palm and regarded him with an expression of intense compassion. "You couldn't have known," she said.

"That's what I try to tell myself."

"Your mother's death must have hit him hard."

"It hit us all hard."

"But he was the one left behind, wasn't he?"

"Yes."

"He wasn't mad at you, though."

"You mean . . . that because he sent us presents you think that shows he wasn't angry?"

"No. Because he hasn't haunted you. That's when it happens, you know. When they die angry."

Owen slammed his fists down on the table, rattling everything on it. "This is total ignorant bullshit!"

She stood, her movements detached and mechanical, and began cleaning the table.

"Okay," he said desperately, "if Serian wanted to terrorize you . . . why has he waited so long to begin? Why didn't he start right away?"

"He was waiting to see what happened with the trial."

"Are you kidding? Ghosts don't care about mortal justice, they have their own code of revenge. And where was he all that time? You think souls can just float in and out of ghosthood?"

She fixed him with a direct, thoughtful frown, and Owen rattled on, tapping his fiction writer's imagination for his arguments.

"What kind of person was Serian, anyway? Controlling, forceful, and very creative, right? Do you think a soul like that would fool around with hiding photographs and opening window blinds and digging holes in the ground? Hell no. If he was out to scare you, he'd shake this whole house with his anger and he'd use plenty of special effects."

She didn't respond for a moment; then she said, "If it's not Serian's ghost, whose ghost is it?"

"It's not a ghost. It's a prowler or kids playing a prank or more lousy reporters after a story. Hell, maybe it's someone you know—some unbalanced artist from Serian's pack of leeches. Or . . . maybe it's nothing. Maybe we're both on edge and imagining things."

She accepted everything till the last line. Then she stiffened. "I'm not imagining things. The blinds were changed. The pictures did disappear. And that hole, what about that hole? You saw that too."

"All right, damnit. Let's go back out and look at that hole again."

"Now? It's been dark for hours."

"We've got flashlights, don't we? We're going out and take another look at that hole. I'll bet, if we check closer, we'll see scratch marks from an animal's claws. Animals do crazy things when spring fever sets in."

Lenore was reluctant, but Owen hustled her into a coat and out through one of the back doors. The terrace work had never been completed in that direction and there was a cracked cement block in lieu of a step and then an expanse of raw dirt that had been marked for construction.

A ripe moon hung low in the sky, and they made their way without turning on the flashlights, keeping a wide margin between themselves and the black rectangle of the studio ruins. The treeline loomed ahead, forbidding and dense in the moonlight, and it occurred to Owen that if spirits existed they most surely lived there. Where he'd been raised, on open ground, night was almost as straightforward as day, and he had never known the eerie power that came with darkness in the woods. It was a primal thing. Primal. Primitive. Primeval. Evil. The associations were there in his thoughts, though he wouldn't have admitted that to Lenore.

They turned on the flashlights and she pointed him into the trees. Dead leaves crackled underfoot and a breeze rattled the branches overhead. He had the sudden urge to creep stealthily from tree to tree, but kept the cone of light steadily in front of him and strode confidently in, holding Lenore's hand so that she trailed in his wake. Even in the darkness, he recognized the clearing when they came to it.

"Now," he said, "we'll just take a better look at this and I'll bet we'll find evidence that it was made by animals or at the very least that it's months old. And then we can both—"

He stopped so abruptly that Lenore bumped into him and dropped her flashlight. Reflexively, she bent to pick it up, but she froze halfway, staring ahead.

There in the beam of Owen's light was the hole. Only it was not a vague effort any longer. It was now nearly three feet in depth with a rough gravelike shape, and there was a pick, a shovel and a post-hole digger lying beside it. He jerked the flashlight up, aiming it in an arc around them; then his common sense prevailed and he clicked off the light altogether.

"What are you doing?" Lenore asked.

"Shhh. If he's still out here, I don't want him to be able to see us."

She retrieved her flashlight from the ground, snapping it off as she lifted it, and they both stood still for a moment while their eyes adjusted.

"We're going back to the house and call the police," he whispered.

She ignored him and inched forward into the clearing. Half-blind, he stumbled after her. "Lenore . . . don't . . ."

She knelt at the edge of the hole and leaned down into it. "There's something buried here," she said. "It's metal . . . like the top of a box."

He clamped his hand around her arm and yanked her up. Instinctively, he crouched, his skin prickling in anticipation of whatever lurked in the shadows, and he pulled her with him through the trees and around the studio ruins and across the open space, gaining speed as they neared the house. He threw open the door, then slammed and locked it behind him.

"We've got to call the police. Jesus! Where's that shotgun! Lenore . . . come on!"

Her expression changed from fear to puzzlement to the dawning of wonder.

"Lenore!"

"It's Al," she said. "Don't you feel it, Owen? My father has come back!"

She unlocked the back door, opened it and stared out into the night. "Do you think he's still out there or do you think he's back in the house?" Without waiting for an answer, she turned and headed down the hall. Owen followed helplessly. There was logic to what she said. Who else would know the alarm sequences and have keys. Who else would know the place so well that he could stay completely hidden. Who else would have buried something here.

She stopped in the kitchen. "If he doesn't want to be seen, I doubt that we'll be able to find him," she said.

"We've got to get out of here, Lenore. He could be dangerous. He's already killed once."

"He's not dangerous! He hurt Bram only to protect himself, and I know he didn't mean to kill. He was just trying to get away."

"Lenore . . ."

"No! My father has come back. I'm not going to miss my chance with him again." She was suddenly decisive. Determined. "It's you he's hiding from, Owen. You're a stranger to him. You have to go."

"I'm not leaving you here alone!"

"Yes, you are. This is my house and I want to be with my father. You must go. It's the only way."

She took both his hands in hers, squeezed them tightly,

then tilted her head to give him a gentle, loving smile. "Please," she said. "There are so many things I need to ask him. This is my father, Owen. I'm not in danger. Please don't make me get angry with you. Don't make me drive you away . . . because I will if I have to. I can't lose my father again."

He didn't move, but she must have read the warring thoughts in his eyes.

"I promise you, I'm not in danger from Al. If it makes you feel better, I'll keep the gun with me all evening."

She went to the narrow closet beside the refrigerator and reached inside for the shotgun. Then she turned toward Owen with the gun cradled in her arm. Her eyes hardened.

"What are you afraid of? That I'll love him more than I love you? That I won't need you anymore?"

He could see that it was useless to argue. "I'll go out the front," he said reluctantly.

She walked with him, the gun hanging limply at her side. At the door he stopped to pull his coat on. She looked at him then, and her eyes lit with a fierce incandescence that made him ache inside.

"You love me, don't you?" she asked.

"I've always loved you," he said. "Always."

She rested one hand lightly on his shoulder and rose to kiss his mouth. Then she stepped back and he forced himself to walk out. He made it to the car, slid in and keyed the engine without allowing himself to think. Then he scrubbed his face with his hands and agonized over what to do next.

The car took a minute to warm up, and he raced the engine mercilessly during the process. He wanted there to be no doubt in anyone's mind that he was leaving. All the way down the endless gravel drive, he turned it over in his mind. Al was her father. But Al was insane. Al had been dangerous in Vietnam. Al had killed Bram.

The gate was already open when he reached it. He pulled through, tripping the electronic switch. He gunned the car across the road and into the ditch, stomped on the brake, jerked the key out and ran, making it back through just before the gate slid shut.

He walked at a fast pace. If anyone checked the gate light, they would be assured that he had driven through. That much he had thought out. But no further. He didn't know what he would do when he got back up to the house.

Ahead of him, the graveled drive snaked like a silver ribbon through the dark pastures and darker trees. He kept his eyes just slightly ahead of his feet and concentrated on walking. It should have taken no more than twenty minutes to cover the distance, but it felt like hours before he topped the rise and looked down on Bram Serian's Arcadia. Nothing appeared to be different. The same lights were on in the house as when he'd pulled away. He walked to the edge of the yard, then crept behind a line of cedars and watched. There was nothing to see, but nonetheless he watched. The moon moved across the sky and his feet went numb from the chill, and still he watched.

What was he doing there? Lurking outside the woman's house when she'd ordered him out?

He took a deep breath and crossed the open yard to the shadow of Arcadia's walls. What next? Peeking into the windows? Creeping around to that unlocked back door and then inside to spy on her?

He sank down to sit on his heels with his back against the rough stone, and he asked himself again, what next? Ring the doorbell? Ask if he could please meet her father now? Oh, God . . . what? Maybe what he should have done was wait up by the gate for a while and then call on the intercom and talk to her. Maybe she wouldn't be too angry, and maybe she'd let him drive back up to the house.

The plan shaped itself in his mind, and he pushed up off the wall to stand. The intercom was the best idea. He was achieving nothing crouched by the wall. He stomped his cold feet lightly, soundlessly, to get the blood running. Only it wasn't soundless, there was a boom, and for a moment it seemed that his feet had caused it. Then he ran. Before the thought had time to form, he ran. The boom had been a shotgun blast.

He ran through the unlocked back door and into the kitchen. The house was deathly quiet. "Lenore?" he called softly, silently praying . . . please, please, please . . .

He ran down the hallway and to the giant living room. There was a fire burning. Green logs popped and the firelight reflected on the walls. "Lenore?" he called softly. "It's Owen."

She was sitting near the fire, staring into it. On the floor near her lay the shotgun. Several feet beyond that a man's bloody body was sprawled across a Navajo rug.

"Lenore?"

Time stopped and he was moving without moving. He was watching himself go to her.

"Lenore?"

Slowly, as though she'd turned to glass, she raised her eyes to his. He knelt in front of her. Blood was splattered on her smooth face and her long graceful hands and her white silk shirt.

Her expression was blank at first, then faintly puzzled, then suddenly she said, "You do love me, don't you?"

Owen nodded and her face swam out of focus until he blinked enough to bring it back.

"I told him you loved me but he laughed."

Owen forced himself to walk to the Navajo rug. He squatted down, averting his eyes, and pressed his fingers into the neck to check for a pulse. There was no pulse. No life left in the ruined body. Owen fought back the nausea and revulsion that threatened. He pushed himself up, thinking that he should get a blanket to cover that dead sightless face, and only then did it register on his numbed mind.

"Lenore . . ." He wheeled toward her in shocked disbelief, then turned back to stare at the dead man. Even without the trademark mustache and beard, he knew that this was Bram Serian lying dead on the floor.

She spoke then, in a hollow, distant tone.

"All the time, I thought I was free, but I wasn't. Now . . . I'm free."

Owen sat at the window of his apartment, staring out into the walled postage-stamp garden. He had put up a feeder when the cold weather hit so the place was always busy with birds and squirrels. Whenever the feeder was empty he refilled it with a rueful amusement, thinking of it as his livestock chore.

The sun rose high enough to slant down between the buildings and strike the snow-covered garden, making him squint against the brightness. Another day. He finished the coffee in his cup and considered rising to make more. But he was in no hurry. There were hours stretching ahead of him. Limitless hours. And he did not want to hurry them. He wanted to stretch them out as far as possible and delay the onset of night. Because the nights were the hardest.

The nights were when he missed Lenore the most. When he ached for the warmth of her next to him in bed, for the scent of her hair and the soft rhythm of her breathing.

Lenore.

Just her name, silently whispered in his thoughts, stirred such a profound longing in him that he was caught by it, trapped by it, momentarily doubled over with it.

His sleep was filled with dreams of her, but even in his dreams he knew she was lost to him, so his nights were bittersweet at best. And at the worst . . . At the worst his nights brought horrible heart-pounding visions. He awakened more often than not just before dawn, shaken and sweating and desperately blinking away the afterimages that hung in the dark, clawing his way up out of Serian nightmares.

This morning he had had the one where Lenore was screaming and he was trapped beneath Bram Serian's corpse, suffocating in the bleeding carnage of those terrible wounds. He had yanked himself upright and stared at the lighted dial of his clock to escape the panicky grip of that vision. It had been four A.M. but he got up and dressed anyway. After one of the nightmares he seldom could return to sleep, so he had quit trying.

He glanced at his watch. Though he had been staring out into the garden for nearly five hours, it was still early. Too early for Bernie or his editor to be in the office. Too early for the phone to ring. Eventually a call would come and he'd hear something exciting about his book. *Bram Serian: Legend and Myth* had just been released, and every day Arlene or Bernie called him with a glowing review or a request for his attendance at something. The book was his lifeline. It had kept him going . . . pulled him through.

He should have started to work on something new by now, but he hadn't been able to. On the strength of his success, Bernie had sold his old manuscripts and he had rationalized, telling himself that he was too busy with contract negotiations and revisions to think of anything new. The truth behind all the rationalizing was that he hadn't been able to put the Serian book behind him. It still filled his thoughts. Sucked away his energies. So that nothing new could take root and grow.

The Serian tragedy . . . the Serian mystery . . . the Serian ghosts . . . they were all still with him, festering inside his brain. And he could not try to purge himself with writing them out because all that was left to tell were the parts that he could not and would not ever tell. That he did not dare commit to paper.

A bright red cardinal appeared to snatch seeds from the feeder. Behind him came his mate, a less brilliant red but still beautiful against the snow. Like blood against the snow.

Blood. He leaned back in the chair and closed his eyes. And it was there, ready to unfold for the thousandth time. Lenore's staring eyes like black holes in her too pale face and Bram Serian's bloody, lifeless body.

He would forever remember the weight of that body as he dragged it from the house in the Navajo rug. The deadness of it. The way the arms flopped out to catch on the furniture. And the smell of it. That sharp retched gagging mix of blood, and ruined intestines, and feces.

He had tied the rug then, trying to package up the contents and neutralize them. So that it wasn't a corpse when he dragged it into the woods with the tractor. So that it wasn't a corpse when he shoved it down into the hole that he and Lenore had pried the big metal trunk out of.

It wasn't a corpse, but he had had to turn from it anyway. He had walked away into the trees to rest for a minute. To get away from the thing that wasn't a corpse. To rest just for a minute before picking up the shovel and throwing the dirt back into the hole. The hole that Bram Serian himself had been digging just hours before.

When he turned back, he saw fire through the trees and he ran to Lenore who was standing over the grave. A burning stench choked him as flames ate at the rug, burning away the patterned wool so that a face showed through. Serian's face. The ghost face.

"What are you doing?" he screamed at her.

She had already dropped the can of lighter fluid and the box of matches and was staring. Watching the fire.

"This is what he did to my father," she said.

That was when Owen knew for certain that it was Al who died in the studio. Bram Serian had killed his brother and set the fire to cover up. Bram Serian had run away and left Lenore to face the murder charge. Lenore had not been guilty of anything.

Until she pulled the trigger of the shotgun and killed her ghost. Her betrayer. Her tormenter.

Owen shoveled the dirt on top of the fire and the rug and the melting face. He covered it all. Burying the truth for her. Covering it with dirt and leaves and twigs so that there was nothing left to mark the spot. So that Bram Serian was gone again, for good this time. And Lenore was safe from Sheriff Bello and Spencer Brown and Holly Danielson and Natalie Raven and all the others who would have come after her again and destroyed her.

Lenore was safe. And that was right. That had more rightness and morality to it than all the laws and courtroom justice he had seen.

Owen pushed up out of his chair abruptly, startling the brilliant red birds away, pushing the memories away. And he went to his kitchen to make more coffee. It was a beautiful kitchen. A tiny little jewel of a kitchen. They had chosen everything and organized it together. Learned to cook in it together.

Memories of her lingered in that kitchen. Memories of her

were everywhere. Serian's ghost waited for him to fall asleep, but Lenore was always with him.

Sometimes it seemed to Owen that he was as haunted now as she had ever been. And he saw a dark humor in it when he considered how he would appear to others, living with his ghosts, stopping at times to listen, certain he heard her footsteps outside his door. Or what about the candles he lit? The *Love Inseparable by Death* candle and the *Safe Heart* candle, Guaranteed to Keep a Loved One Safe Over Any Distance. He had found a little bodega that sold them, and he bought new ones each week to burn for her.

With his coffee cup full, he returned to sit by the window. A little plump bird with a pale yellow breast and a black crested head flew down to the feeder. One of these days he would go to a bookstore and buy a bird guide. One of these days when he cared enough to do it.

Lenore. Lenore. Lenore.

She had loved the garden and the birds. When they first moved in she had wanted to eat breakfast outside every morning.

She had still been listless and silent then, back when he found the apartment and moved her into it with him. Then the listlessness turned into brooding and eventually the silence was broken. It was in the garden that she finally told him about shooting Bram.

How she had gone through the house calling for Al to come out. How she had waited then, built a fire and waited for her father in the living room. How she had been staring into that fire, thinking about all the things she would finally get to say. All the things she would finally get to ask.

She heard a noise and turned. But it was not her father standing there at all. It was Bram Serian.

"Are you alive?" she asked.

He laughed. The ghost laughed.

"Nothing can kill me, Lenore. That was Al in the studio."

"Al? Oh, God . . . Oh my God . . . You killed Al? You killed your brother? You killed my father?"

Bram sighed. "I didn't mean to. I was trying to make him understand how things had to be. How he had to stay with me and start painting again."

"Painting?"

"He helped me paint, Lenore. He assisted me."

"Assisted you or painted?"

"Same difference. It was *me* people wanted. I gave life to Al's work. I guided and taught him. I *made* him!

"I rescued him from his purgatory over in that chink hell-hole and I saved his little brat of a child and I put him back together and gave him dignity. And how did he repay me? By running away! By trying to steal the talent that I'd developed in him.

"It took nearly two years for my detective to track him down and then it took me months to make him see that he had to come back. He promised to come home. He promised to bring new paintings with him.

"But then, when he showed up that night, he had it all wrong. He thought he could suddenly take the credit. That the art could be his. He didn't understand. The paintings were only important to people as long as they were mine."

Lenore shook her head in disbelief. "Everything was a lie? *Everything* I believed in was a lie?"

"Still searching for the truth, huh, Lenore? Well, it's a relative concept, you know. One that can be molded and shaped. Like a piece of art."

"No, Bram. Not anymore. I've discovered all your secrets. I know the real truth. I know what you did to your father. I know you stole me away from my life in Thailand. I know how you warped and deprived and twisted me. And now I know how you cheated and used your brother. And how you killed him."

"I see. That changes things some. But not a lot. Because you're weak, Lenore. Just like Al. Without me you're nothing. Without me your life is small and inconsequential. But I'm back now and I'll take care of you.

"I've got plans to resurrect myself. See, when it happened I panicked. I thought I was ruined. Al was dead and people would be going into the studio to investigate and they'd see that there was no art there ready for a big show. I had nothing in there. Not even sculpture or carving. Ever since Al left I'd been blocked. Nothing came out of my hands. Al brought a few paintings with him to show me, but that wasn't enough for a show."

"The paintings that Al brought . . . were they the ones left out against the tree?"

"Yes! Very good, Lenore. I meant to take them with me. I took them out and put them next to Al's car, but then when I left I was in such a hurry that I forgot them.

"See, I started the fire to cover up. I had to destroy the studio so no one would discover it was empty. And I was so panicky that I thought I had to disappear. Before anyone could humiliate me or ask me any questions. I put my jewelry on Al and poured all that oil on his face, hoping people would think it was me. And it worked!"

"You took the car Al came in and you ran away."

"That should be obvious, Lenore. The problem was I didn't plan ahead. Sure, I got rid of myself, but now who am I supposed to be? It's just not coming out right.

"So, I've come up with a plan. I've got plenty of money tucked away . . . I'll have some surgery done on my face, dye my hair brown and then I'll come home to Arcadia as Al. Who's going to know? There aren't any pictures of him around, and he's been gone for more than two years. Who will remember exactly what he looked like?

"And I'll have you to vouch for my identity, won't I? It will be perfect. As Al I'll inherit Arcadia. As Al I'll develop a talent for art."

He smiled and held out his hands to show how simple it all was.

"I'll get rid of that guy you've dragged home, and then we'll have the place to ourselves again."

"Leave Owen out of this!"

"Oh, please, Lenore . . . don't tell me you think you're in love."

"Stop it!"

"And don't tell me that you think he loves you. You are not lovable, Lenore. You're a witch. The only thing he wants is *my* money and *my* house."

"I hate you, Bram. I despise you. I will never, never live with you again. I will never lie for you again, or be a part of your lies."

"You'll change your mind. We're family, Lenore. I'm all you have."

"I'm going away with Owen. I hope you rot in this house. Better yet, I hope you burn in it."

"Going away with Owen? That's a joke. You think I'll let you walk out of here?" He laughed again. "And with all that your lover knows . . . you think I can let him go free to tell tales?

"No, Lenore. You're smarter than that. You know what I have to do. What *we* have to do. You'll lure your lover back here and we'll take care of the problem. We can use that nice hole I've been digging to make him disappear permanently."

Bram smiled and started toward her. And she raised the gun beside her on the couch. She raised it. And he smiled as though she was being foolish. And he reached out, smiling, so absolutely sure of himself and of her . . . he reached out to take the gun from her. And she fired.

Owen checked his watch again—9 A.M. in New York meant 8 P.M. in Thailand. What was Lenore doing? Who was she with? Did she think of him, want him in her bed, miss his smile or his arms around her? Or was he already part of the past to her, someone she recalled with only distant fondness?

He had heard from her just once in the three months since she'd been gone. Not by telephone so that he would have had a chance to argue or plead with her, or even to tell her that he loved her, but through a letter which she had painstakingly written out in her childish script.

My dear Owen,

I am sorry that my leaving upset you so much. I knew it would and that is why I waited until the last minute to tell you I had to go. I wanted our remaining time together to be happy.

Thailand is like stepping into a dream for me. Everywhere I go there are smells and sights and sounds that bring a feeling of déjà vu, but I know that they are simply remembered by some deeper part of me. I have found Chinda and she is helping me look for Chit. Chinda has been able to tell me so much about my mother. So many small things that bring Kamsai to life for me. And she has a picture of my mother so at last I have a face to treasure.

She says that my mother's people were Chao Bon, which is a very old tribe, and they lived around Chaiyahum. (I am relating this to you because I know how you like to look things up in your books.) Though my mother was orphaned young and my chances of finding any direct family are probably slim, I am still planning to travel to Chaiyahum and spend some time there.

I know that you didn't understand my leaving, or my refusal to let you come with me, but I am hoping that you understand it better now after having this time without me to reflect. We are two separate people, Owen. Being together does not release us from our pasts or erase them.

This journey is mine. You can't be included and you can't help me or protect me. I don't know what I'll find or who I'll find. And you were right to suspect that I might not come back to you. I didn't want to admit that to myself or to you while I was looking into your eyes, but it is true.

If I don't return it will be for the best. You must believe that. It will mean that I failed and that I have nothing to bring back and give you. In that case you must forget about me completely.

But that is not the outcome I desire. I hope to put my ghosts to rest and to find peace. Chinda says I am looking for the child self that I left behind here. Maybe that's true. I don't know. But if I can find quiet, if I can find rest, if I can find some part of myself that is worth giving, then I will return and give it to you. Yours is the deepest and truest love I have ever known. I will carry you forever in my heart.

Lenore

And so he waited. He listened for her footsteps, the sound of her key in the lock. He watched his tiny garden, drank his coffee, lit his candles and thought about the unchangeable past. About his life. And he waited.

But in looking back, he saw that he had always been waiting for her. Waiting to be enfolded. To be swallowed by the darkness in her eyes.

She brought the fevered fall, the burning rush that scoured away all that he had been and left him tasting ash. But he knew now, looking back, that he had wanted it.

That he had always been waiting.

Acknowledgments

My gratitude and thanks to:

Charles Fiore, defense attorney extraordinare, for his legal advice and insights, and Gail Fiore for her patience,

Bryna Taubman, journalist, for her generous assistance,

Frances and Jim Bagley, Jack Bradley, Darwin and Carolyn Gidel, Lance and Arlene Gidel, Robert Tine and Karen Day, Judy Wall, and Abby and Don Westlake for support and encouragement during the tough times,

All the New York City media people—Carol, Ellen, Lisa, John, Amy, Sharon, Chris and the others—who answered questions and allowed me in, and David Lewis of Lewis and Fiore whose legal war stories were an inspiration,

My agent, Aaron Priest, who is always there when I need him,

And a deep heartfelt thank-you to Audrey LaFehr, my talented editor and friend.

OFFICIAL **MUSIC TO YOUR EARS** COUPON

Enclosed please find _____ proof-of-purchase coupons from my
Penguin USA purchase.

I would like to apply these coupons towards the purchase of the
following Mercury artist(s): (Please write in artist selection and title)

_____   _____

_____   _____

_____   _____

I understand that my coupons will be applied towards my
purchase at these discounted prices. *

Two book coupons	CD $13.99	CT $8.99
Four book coupons	CD $12.99	CT $7.99
Six book coupons	CD $11.99	CT $6.99

(* Once coupons are sent, there is no limit to the titles ordered at this reduced rate)

Please check one:

___Enclosed is my check/money order made out to: **Sound Delivery**

___Please charge my purchases to:

Amex#	_____	exp. date_____
MC#	_____	exp. date_____
Visa#	_____	exp. date_____
Discover#	_____	exp. date_____
Diners#	_____	exp. date_____

Please send coupons to: **Sound Delivery**
                               P.O. Box 2213
                               Davis, CA 95617-2213

NAME_____

ADDRESS_____

CITY_____STATE_____ZIP_____

All orders shipped 2-Day UPS mail from time of receipt.
Offer expires December 31, 1994 • Printed in the USA

And everyone who redeems a coupon is automatically entered
into the **MUSIC TO YOUR EARS SWEEPSTAKES**! The Grand Prize
Winner will win a trip to see a Mercury Records artist in concert
anywhere in the continental United States.